Ernest Bramah

Kai Lung Boxed Set: The Wallet of Kai Lung, Kai Lung's Golden Hours & Kai Lung Unrolls His Mat

e-artnow 2020

Ernest Bramah

Kai Lung Boxed Set: The Wallet of Kai Lung, Kai Lung's Golden Hours & Kai Lung Unrolls His Mat

e-artnow, 2020
Contact: info@e-artnow.org

ISBN 978-80-273-3591-6

Contents

THE WALLET OF KAI LUNG	13
The Transmutation of Ling	15
The Story of Yung Chang	56
The Probation of Sen Heng	62
The Experiment of the Mandarin Chan Hung	72
The Confession of Kai Lung	81
The Vengeance of Tung Fel	89
The Career of the Charitable Quen-Ki-Tong	100
The Vision of Yin, the Son of Yat Huang	110
The Ill-Regulated Destiny of Kin Yen, the Picture-Maker	117
KAI LUNG'S GOLDEN HOURS	125
The Encountering of Six Within a Wood	126
The Inexorable Justice of the Mandarin Shan Tien	130
The Degraded Persistence of the Effete Ming-Shu	141
The Inopportune Behaviour of the Covetous Li-Loe	154
The Timely Intervention of the Mandarin Shan Tien's Lucky Day	159
The High-Minded Strategy of the Amiable Hwa-Mei	169
Not Concerned With Any Particular Attribute of Those Who Are Involved	178
The Timely Disputation Among Those of an Inner Chamber of Yu-Ping	188
The Propitious Dissension Between Two Whose General Attributes Have Already Been Sufficiently Described	202
The Incredible Obtuseness of Those Who Had Opposed the Virtuous Kai Lung	215
Of Which It Is Written: "in Shallow Water Dragons Become the Laughing-Stock of Shrimps"	230
The Out-Passing Into a State of Assured Felicity of the Much-Enduring Two With Whom These Printed Leaves Have Chiefly Been Concerned	233
KAI LUNG UNROLLS HIS MAT	249
Part I. The Protecting Ancestors	251
The Malignity of the Depraved Ming-Shu Rears Its Offensive Head	252
The Difficult Progression of the Virtuous Kai Lung Assumes a Concrete Form	256
The Further Continuance of Kai Lung's Quest and His Opportune Encounter With an Outcast Band, All Ignorant of the Classical Examples of the Past	273
At the Extremity of His Resource, the Continent Kai Lung Encounters One Who Leads the Unaffected Life	291
The Meeting by the Way With the Warrior of Chi-U and What Emerged Therefrom	306
The Ambiguous Face Upon the One Found in a Wood and the Effete Ming-Shu's Dilemma	325

The Concave-Witted Li-Loe's Insatiable Craving Serves a Meritorious End and Two (Who Shall Be Nameless) Are Led Toward a Snare	328
In Which the Position of the Estimable Kai Lung Is Such That He Must Either Go Up or Down	333
Wherein the Footsteps of the Two Who Have Induced These Printed Leaves Assume a Homeward Bend	338
Part II. The Great Sky Lantern	353
How Kai Lung Sought to Discourage One Who Did Not Gain His Approbation	354
Part III. The Bringer of Good News	367
Whereby the Angle at Which Events Present Themselves May Be Varied	368

THE WALLET OF KAI LUNG

"Ho, illustrious passers-by!" says Kai Lung as he spreads out his embroidered mat under the mulberry-tree. "It is indeed unlikely that you could condescend to stop and listen to the foolish words of such an insignificant and altogether deformed person as myself. Nevertheless, if you will but retard your elegant footsteps for a few moments, this exceedingly unprepossessing individual will endeavour to entertain you." This is a collection of Kai Lung's entertaining tales, told professionally in the market places as he travelled about; told sometimes to occupy and divert the minds of his enemies when they were intent on torturing him.

The Transmutation of Ling

I. Introduction

The sun had dipped behind the western mountains before Kai Lung, with twenty li or more still between him and the city of Knei Yang, entered the camphor-laurel forest which stretched almost to his destination. No person of consequence ever made the journey unattended; but Kai Lung professed to have no fear, remarking with extempore wisdom, when warned at the previous village, that a worthless garment covered one with better protection than that afforded by an army of bowmen. Nevertheless, when within the gloomy aisles, Kai Lung more than once wished himself back at the village, or safely behind the mud walls of Knei Yang; and, making many vows concerning the amount of prayer-paper which he would assuredly burn when he was actually through the gates, he stepped out more quickly, until suddenly, at a turn in the glade, he stopped altogether, while the watchful expression into which he had unguardedly dropped at once changed into a mask of impassiveness and extreme unconcern. From behind the next tree projected a long straight rod, not unlike a slender bamboo at a distance, but, to Kai Lung's all-seeing eye, in reality the barrel of a matchlock, which would come into line with his breast if he took another step. Being a prudent man, more accustomed to guile and subservience to destiny than to force, he therefore waited, spreading out his hands in proof of his peaceful acquiescence, and smiling cheerfully until it should please the owner of the weapon to step forth. This the unseen did a moment later, still keeping his gun in an easy and convenient attitude, revealing a stout body and a scarred face, which in conjunction made it plain to Kai Lung that he was in the power of Lin Yi, a noted brigand of whom he had heard much in the villages.

"O illustrious person," said Kai Lung very earnestly, "this is evidently an unfortunate mistake. Doubtless you were expecting some exalted Mandarin to come and render you homage, and were preparing to overwhelm him with gratified confusion by escorting him yourself to your well-appointed abode. Indeed, I passed such a one on the road, very richly apparelled, who inquired of me the way to the mansion of the dignified and upright Lin Yi. By this time he is perhaps two or three li towards the east."

"However distinguished a Mandarin may be, it is fitting that I should first attend to one whose manners and accomplishments betray him to be of the Royal House," replied Lin Yi, with extreme affability. "Precede me, therefore, to my mean and uninviting hovel, while I gain more honour than I can reasonably bear by following closely in your elegant footsteps, and guarding your Imperial person with this inadequate but heavily-loaded weapon."

Seeing no chance of immediate escape, Kai Lung led the way, instructed by the brigand, along a very difficult and bewildering path, until they reached a cave hidden among the crags. Here Lin Yi called out some words in the Miaotze tongue, whereupon a follower appeared, and opened a gate in the stockade of prickly mimosa which guarded the mouth of the den. Within the enclosure a fire burned, and food was being prepared. At a word from the chief, the unfortunate Kai Lung found his hands seized and tied behind his back, while a second later a rough hemp rope was fixed round his neck, and the other end tied to an overhanging tree.

Lin Yi smiled pleasantly and critically upon these preparations, and when they were complete dismissed his follower.

"Now we can converse at our ease and without restraint," he remarked to Kai Lung. "It will be a distinguished privilege for a person occupying the important public position which you undoubtedly do; for myself, my instincts are so degraded and low-minded that nothing gives me more gratification than to dispense with ceremony."

To this Kai Lung made no reply, chiefly because at that moment the wind swayed the tree, and compelled him to stand on his toes in order to escape suffocation.

"It would be useless to try to conceal from a person of your inspired intelligence that I am indeed Lin Yi," continued the robber. "It is a dignified position to occupy, and one for which I am quite incompetent. In the sixth month of the third year ago, it chanced that this unworthy person, at that time engaged in commercial affairs at Knei Yang, became inextricably immersed in the insidious delights of quail-fighting. Having been entrusted with a large number of taels with which to purchase elephants' teeth, it suddenly occurred to him that if he doubled the number of taels by staking them upon an exceedingly powerful and agile quail, he would be able to purchase twice the number of teeth, and so benefit his patron to a large extent. This matter was clearly forced upon his notice by a dream, in which he perceived one whom he then understood to be the benevolent spirit of an ancestor in the act of stroking a particular quail, upon whose chances he accordingly placed all he possessed. Doubtless evil spirits had been employed in the matter; for, to this person's great astonishment, the quail in question failed in a very discreditable manner at the encounter. Unfortunately, this person had risked not only the money which had been entrusted to him, but all that he had himself become possessed of by some years of honourable toil and assiduous courtesy as a professional witness in law cases. Not doubting that his patron would see that he was himself greatly to blame in confiding so large a sum of money to a comparatively young man of whom he knew little, this person placed the matter before him, at the same time showing him that he would suffer in the eyes of the virtuous if he did not restore this person's savings, which but for the presence of the larger sum, and a generous desire to benefit his patron, he would never have risked in so uncertain a venture as that of quail-fighting. Although the facts were laid in the form of a dignified request instead of a demand by legal means, and the reasoning carefully drawn up in columns of fine parchment by a very illustrious writer, the reply which this person received showed him plainly that a wrong view had been taken of the matter, and that the time had arrived when it became necessary for him to make a suitable rejoinder by leaving the city without delay."

"It was a high-minded and disinterested course to take," said Kai Lung with great conviction, as Lin Yi paused. "Without doubt evil will shortly overtake the avaricious-souled person at Knei Yang."

"It has already done so," replied Lin Yi. "While passing through this forest in the season of Many White Vapours, the spirits of his bad deeds appeared to him in misleading and symmetrical shapes, and drew him out of the path and away from his bowmen. After suffering many torments, he found his way here, where, in spite of our continual care, he perished miserably and in great bodily pain.... But I cannot conceal from myself, in spite of your distinguished politeness, that I am becoming intolerably tiresome with my commonplace talk."

"On the contrary," replied Kai Lung, "while listening to your voice I seemed to hear the beating of many gongs of the finest and most polished brass. I floated in the Middle Air, and for the time I even became unconscious of the fact that this honourable appendage, though fashioned, as I perceive, out of the most delicate silk, makes it exceedingly difficult for me to breathe."

"Such a thing cannot be permitted," exclaimed Lin Yi, with some indignation, as with his own hands he slackened the rope and, taking it from Kai Lung's neck, fastened it around his ankle. "Now, in return for my uninviting confidences, shall not my senses be gladdened by a recital of the titles and honours borne by your distinguished family? Doubtless, at this moment many Mandarins of the highest degree are anxiously awaiting your arrival at Knei Yang, perhaps passing the time by outdoing one another in protesting the number of taels each would give rather than permit you to be tormented by fire-brands, or even to lose a single ear."

"Alas!" replied Kai Lung, "never was there a truer proverb than that which says, 'It is a mark of insincerity of purpose to spend one's time in looking for the sacred Emperor in the low-class tea-shops.' Do Mandarins or the friends of Mandarins travel in mean garments and unattended? Indeed, the person who is now before you is none other than the outcast Kai Lung, the story-teller, one of degraded habits and no very distinguished or reputable ancestors. His friends are few, and mostly of the criminal class; his wealth is not more than some six or eight cash, concealed in his left sandal; and his entire stock-in-trade consists of a few unendurable and badly told stories, to which, however, it is his presumptuous intention shortly to add a dignified narrative of the high-born Lin Yi, setting out his domestic virtues and the honour which he has reflected upon his house, his valour in war, the destruction of his enemies, and, above all, his great benevolence and the protection which he extends to the poor and those engaged in the distinguished arts."

"The absence of friends is unfortunate," said Lin Yi thoughtfully, after he had possessed himself of the coins indicated by Kai Lung, and also of a much larger amount concealed elsewhere among the story-teller's clothing. "My followers are mostly outlawed Miaotze, who have been driven from their own tribes in Yun Nan for man-eating and disregarding the sacred laws of hospitality. They are somewhat rapacious, and in this way it has become a custom that they should have as their own, for the purpose of exchanging for money, persons such as yourself, whose insatiable curiosity has led them to this place."

"The wise and all-knowing Emperor Fohy instituted three degrees of attainment: Being poor, to obtain justice; being rich, to escape flattery; and being human, to avoid the passions," replied Kai Lung. "To these the practical and enlightened Kang added yet another, the greatest: Being lean, to yield fatness."

"In such cases," observed the brigand, "the Miaotze keep an honoured and very venerable rite, which chiefly consists in suspending the offender by a pigtail from a low tree, and placing burning twigs of hemp-palm between his toes. To this person it seems a foolish and meaningless habit; but it would not be well to interfere with their religious observances, however trivial they may appear."

"Such a course must inevitably end in great loss," suggested Kai Lung; "for undoubtedly there are many poor yet honourable persons who would leave with them a bond for a large number of taels and save the money with which to redeem it, rather than take part in a ceremony which is not according to one's own Book of Rites."

"They have already suffered in that way on one or two occasions," replied Lin Yi; "so that such a proposal, no matter how nobly intended, would not gladden their faces. Yet they are simple and docile persons, and would, without doubt, be moved to any feeling you should desire by the recital of one of your illustrious stories."

"An intelligent and discriminating assemblage is more to a story-teller than much reward of cash from hands that conceal open mouths," replied Kai Lung with great feeling. "Nothing would confer more pleasurable agitation upon this unworthy person than an opportunity of narrating his entire stock to them. If also the accomplished Lin Yi would bestow renown upon the occasion by his presence, no omen of good would be wanting."

"The pleasures of the city lie far behind me," said Lin Yi, after some thought, "and I would cheerfully submit myself to an intellectual accomplishment such as you are undoubtedly capable of. But as we have necessity to leave this spot before the hour when the oak-leaves change into night-moths, one of your amiable stories will be the utmost we can strengthen our intellects with. Select which you will. In the meantime, food will be brought to refresh you after your benevolent exertions in conversing with a person of my vapid understanding. When you have partaken, or thrown it away as utterly unendurable, the time will have arrived, and this person, together with all his accomplices, will put themselves in a position to be subjected to all the most dignified emotions."

II

"The story which I have selected for this gratifying occasion," said Kai Lung, when, an hour or so later, still pinioned, but released from the halter, he sat surrounded by the brigands, "is entitled 'Good and Evil,' and it is concerned with the adventures of one Ling, who bore the honourable name of Ho. The first, and indeed the greater, part of the narrative, as related by the venerable and accomplished writer of history Chow-Tan, is taken up by showing how Ling was assuredly descended from an enlightened Emperor of the race of Tsin; but as the no less omniscient Ta-lin-hi proves beyond doubt that the person in question was in no way connected with any but a line of hereditary ape-worshippers, who entered China from an unknown country many centuries ago, it would ill become this illiterate person to express an opinion on either side, and he will in consequence omit the first seventeen books of the story, and only deal with the three which refer to the illustrious Ling himself."

The Story of Ling Narrated by
Kai Lung When a Prisoner in the Camp of Lin Yi

Ling was the youngest of three sons, and from his youth upwards proved to be of a mild and studious disposition. Most of his time was spent in reading the sacred books, and at an early age he found the worship of apes to be repulsive to his gentle nature, and resolved to break through the venerable traditions of his family by devoting his time to literary pursuits, and presenting himself for the public examinations at Canton. In this his resolution was strengthened by a rumour that an army of bowmen was shortly to be raised from the Province in which he lived, so that if he remained he would inevitably be forced into an occupation which was even more distasteful to him than the one he was leaving.

Having arrived at Canton, Ling's first care was to obtain particulars of the examinations, which he clearly perceived, from the unusual activity displayed on all sides, to be near at hand. On inquiring from passers-by, he received very conflicting information; for the persons to whom he spoke were themselves entered for the competition, and therefore naturally misled him in order to increase their own chances of success. Perceiving this, Ling determined to apply at once, although the light was past, to a Mandarin who was concerned in the examinations, lest by delay he should lose his chance for the year.

"It is an unfortunate event that so distinguished a person should have selected this day and hour on which to overwhelm us with his affable politeness!" exclaimed the porter at the gate of the Yamen, when Ling had explained his reason for going. "On such a day, in the reign of the virtuous Emperor Hoo Chow, a very benevolent and unassuming ancestor of my good lord the Mandarin was destroyed by treachery, and ever since his family has observed the occasion by fasting and no music. This person would certainly be punished with death if he entered the inner room from any cause."

At these words, Ling, who had been simply brought up, and chiefly in the society of apes, was going away with many expressions of self-reproach at selecting such a time, when the gate-keeper called him back.

"I am overwhelmed with confusion at the position in which I find myself," he remarked, after he had examined his mind for a short time. "I may meet with an ungraceful and objectionable death if I carry out your estimable instructions, but I shall certainly merit and receive a similar fate if I permit so renowned and versatile a person to leave without a fitting reception. In such matters a person can only trust to the intervention of good spirits; if, therefore, you will permit this unworthy individual to wear, while making the venture, the ring which he perceives upon your finger, and which he recognizes as a very powerful charm against evil, misunderstandings, and extortion, he will go without fear."

Overjoyed at the amiable porter's efforts on his behalf, Ling did as he was desired, and the other retired. Presently the door of the Yamen was opened by an attendant of the house, and Ling bidden to enter. He was covered with astonishment to find that this person was entirely unacquainted with his name or purpose.

"Alas!" said the attendant, when Ling had explained his object, "well said the renowned and inspired Ting Fo, 'When struck by a thunderbolt it is unnecessary to consult the Book of Dates as to the precise meaning of the omen.' At this moment my noble-minded master is engaged in conversation with all the most honourable and refined persons in Canton, while singers and dancers of a very expert and nimble order have been sent for. The entertainment will undoubtedly last far into the night, and to present myself even with the excuse of your graceful and delicate inquiry would certainly result in very objectionable consequences to this person."

"It is indeed a day of unprepossessing circumstances," replied Ling, and after many honourable remarks concerning his own intellect and appearance, and those of the person to whom he was speaking, he had turned to leave when the other continued:

"Ever since your dignified presence illumined this very ordinary chamber, this person has been endeavouring to bring to his mind an incident which occurred to him last night while he slept. Now it has come back to him with a diamond clearness, and he is satisfied that it was as follows: While he floated in the Middle Air a benevolent spirit in the form of an elderly and toothless vampire appeared, leading by the hand a young man, of elegant personality. Smiling encouragingly upon this person, the spirit said, 'O Fou, recipient of many favours from Mandarins and of innumerable taels from gratified persons whom you have obliged, I am, even at this moment, guiding this exceptional young man towards your presence; when he arrives do not hesitate, but do as he desires, no matter how great the danger seems or how inadequately you may appear to be rewarded on earth.' The vision then melted, but I now clearly perceive that with the exception of the embroidered cloak which you wear, you are the person thus indicated to me. Remove your cloak, therefore, in order to give the amiable spirit no opportunity of denying the fact, and I will advance your wishes; for, as the Book of Verses indicates, 'The person who patiently awaits a sign from the clouds for many years, and yet fails to notice the earthquake at his feet, is devoid of intellect.'"

Convinced that he was assuredly under the especial protection of the Deities, and that the end of his search was in view, Ling gave his rich cloak to the attendant, and was immediately shown into another room, where he was left alone.

After a considerable space of time the door opened and there entered a person whom Ling at first supposed to be the Mandarin. Indeed, he was addressing him by his titles when the other interrupted him. "Do not distress your incomparable mind by searching for honourable names to apply to so inferior a person as myself," he said agreeably. "The mistake is, nevertheless, very natural; for, however miraculous it may appear, this unseemly individual, who is in reality merely a writer of spoken words, is admitted to be exceedingly like the dignified Mandarin himself, though somewhat stouter, clad in better garments, and, it is said, less obtuse of intellect. This last matter he very much doubts, for he now finds himself unable to recognize by name one who is undoubtedly entitled to wear the Royal Yellow."

With this encouragement Ling once more explained his position, narrating the events which had enabled him to reach the second chamber of the Yamen. When he had finished the secretary was overpowered with a high-minded indignation.

"Assuredly those depraved and rapacious persons who have both misled and robbed you shall suffer bow-stringing when the whole matter is brought to light," he exclaimed. "The noble Mandarin neither fasts nor receives guests, for, indeed, he has slept since the sun went down. This person would unhesitatingly break his slumber for so commendable a purpose were it not for a circumstance of intolerable unavoidableness. It must not even be told in a low breath beyond the walls of the Yamen, but my benevolent and high-born lord is in reality a person of very miserly instinct, and nothing will call him from his natural sleep but the sound of taels shaken beside his bed. In an unexpected manner it comes about that this person is quite unsupplied with anything but thin printed papers of a thousand taels each, and these are quite useless for the purpose."

"It is unendurable that so obliging a person should be put to such inconvenience on behalf of one who will certainly become a public laughing-stock at the examinations," said Ling, with deep feeling; and taking from a concealed spot in his garments a few taels, he placed them before the secretary for the use he had indicated.

Ling was again left alone for upwards of two strokes of the gong, and was on the point of sleep when the secretary returned with an expression of dignified satisfaction upon his countenance. Concluding that he had been successful in the manner of awakening the Mandarin, Ling was opening his mouth for a polite speech, which should contain a delicate allusion to the taels, when the secretary warned him, by affecting a sudden look of terror, that silence was exceedingly desirable, and at the same time opened another door and indicated to Ling that he should pass through.

In the next room Ling was overjoyed to find himself in the presence of the Mandarin, who received him graciously, and paid many estimable compliments to the name he bore and the country from which he came. When at length Ling tore himself from this enchanting conversation, and explained the reason of his presence, the Mandarin at once became a prey to the whitest and most melancholy emotions, even plucking two hairs from his pigtail to prove the extent and conscientiousness of his grief.

"Behold," he cried at length, "I am resolved that the extortionate and many-handed persons at Peking who have control of the examination rites and customs shall no longer grow round-bodied without remark. This person will unhesitatingly proclaim the true facts of the case without regarding the danger that the versatile Chancellor or even the sublime Emperor himself may, while he speaks, be concealed in some part of this unassuming room to hear his words; for, as it is wisely said, 'When marked out by destiny, a person will assuredly be drowned, even though he passes the whole of his existence among the highest branches of a date tree.'"

"I am overwhelmed that I should be the cause of such an engaging display of polished agitation," said Ling, as the Mandarin paused. "If it would make your own stomach less heavy, this person will willingly follow your estimable example, either with or without knowing the reason."

"The matter is altogether on your account, O most unobtrusive young man," replied the Mandarin, when a voice without passion was restored to him. "It tears me internally with hooks to reflect that you, whose refined ancestors I might reasonably have known had I passed my youth in another Province, should be victim to the cupidity of the ones in authority at Peking. A very short time before you arrived there came a messenger in haste from those persons, clearly indicating that a legal toll of sixteen taels was to be made on each printed paper setting forth the time and manner of the examinations, although, as you may see, the paper is undoubtedly marked, 'Persons are given notice that they are defrauded of any sum which they may be induced to exchange for this matter.' Furthermore, there is a legal toll of nine taels on all persons who have previously been examined —"

"I am happily escaped from that," exclaimed Ling with some satisfaction as the Mandarin paused.

"—and twelve taels on all who present themselves for the first time. This is to be delivered over when the paper is purchased, so that you, by reason of this unworthy proceeding at Peking, are required to forward to that place, through this person, no less than thirty-two taels."

"It is a circumstance of considerable regret," replied Ling; "for had I only reached Canton a day earlier, I should, it appears, have avoided this evil."

"Undoubtedly it would have been so," replied the Mandarin, who had become engrossed in exalted meditation. "However," he continued a moment later, as he bowed to Ling with an accomplished smile, "it would certainly be a more pleasant thought for a person of your refined intelligence that had you delayed until to-morrow the insatiable persons at Peking might be demanding twice the amount."

Pondering the deep wisdom of this remark, Ling took his departure; but in spite of the most assiduous watchfulness he was unable to discern any of the three obliging persons to whose efforts his success had been due.

III

It was very late when Ling again reached the small room which he had selected as soon as he reached Canton, but without waiting for food or sleep he made himself fully acquainted with the times of the forthcoming examinations and the details of the circumstances connected with them. With much satisfaction he found that he had still a week in which to revive his intellect on the most difficult subjects. Having become relieved on these points, Ling retired for a few hours' sleep, but rose again very early, and gave the whole day with great steadfastness to contemplation of the sacred classics Y-King, with the exception of a short period spent in purchasing ink, brushes and writing-leaves. The following day, having become mentally depressed through witnessing unaccountable hordes of candidates thronging the streets of Canton, Ling put aside his books, and passed the time in visiting all the most celebrated tombs in the neighbourhood of the city. Lightened in mind by this charitable and agreeable occupation, he returned to his studies with a fixed resolution, nor did he again falter in his purpose. On the evening of the examination, when he was sitting alone, reading by the aid of a single light, as his custom was, a person arrived to see him, at the same time manifesting a considerable appearance of secrecy and reserve. Inwardly sighing at the interruption, Ling nevertheless received him with distinguished consideration and respect, setting tea before him, and performing towards it many honourable actions with his own hands. Not until some hours had sped in conversation relating to the health of the Emperor, the unexpected appearance of a fiery dragon outside the city, and the insupportable price of opium, did the visitor allude to the object of his presence.

"It has been observed," he remarked, "that the accomplished Ling, who aspires to a satisfactory rank at the examinations, has never before made the attempt. Doubtless in this case a preternatural wisdom will avail much, and its fortunate possessor will not go unrewarded. Yet it is as precious stones among ashes for one to triumph in such circumstances."

"The fact is known to this person," replied Ling sadly, "and the thought of the years he may have to wait before he shall have passed even the first degree weighs down his soul with bitterness from time to time."

"It is no infrequent thing for men of accomplished perseverance, but merely ordinary intellects, to grow venerable within the four walls of the examination cell," continued the other. "Some, again, become afflicted with various malignant evils, while not a few, chiefly those who are presenting themselves for the first time, are so overcome on perceiving the examination paper, and understanding the inadequate nature of their own accomplishments, that they become an easy prey to the malicious spirits which are ever on the watch in those places; and, after covering their leaves with unpresentable remarks and drawings of men and women of distinguished rank, have at length to be forcibly carried away by the attendants and secured with heavy chains."

"Such things undoubtedly exist," agreed Ling; "yet by a due regard paid to spirits, both good and bad, a proper esteem for one's ancestors, and a sufficiency of charms about the head and body, it is possible to be closeted with all manner of demons and yet to suffer no evil."

"It is undoubtedly possible to do so, according to the Immortal Principles," admitted the stranger; "but it is not an undertaking in which a refined person would take intelligent pleasure; as the proverb says, 'He is a wise and enlightened suppliant who seeks to discover an honourable Mandarin, but he is a fool who cries out, "I have found one."' However, it is obvious that the reason of my visit is understood, and that your distinguished confidence in yourself is merely a graceful endeavour to obtain my services for a less amount of taels than I should otherwise have demanded. For half the usual sum, therefore, this person will take your place in the examination cell, and enable your versatile name to appear in the winning lists, while you pass your moments in irreproachable pleasures elsewhere."

Such a course had never presented itself to Ling. As the person who narrates this story has already marked, he had passed his life beyond the influence of the ways and manners of towns, and at the same time he had naturally been endowed with an unobtrusive highmindedness. It appeared to him, in consequence, that by accepting this engaging offer he would be placing those who were competing with him at a disadvantage. This person clearly sees that it is a difficult matter for him to explain how this could be, as Ling would undoubtedly reward the services of the one who took his place, nor would the number of the competitors be in any way increased; yet in such a way the thing took shape before his eyes. Knowing, however, that few persons would be able to understand this action, and being desirous of not injuring the estimable emotions of the obliging person who had come to him, Ling made a number of polished excuses in declining, hiding the true reason within himself. In this way he earned the powerful malignity of the person in question, who would not depart until he had effected a number of very disagreeable prophecies connected with unpropitious omens and internal torments, all of which undoubtedly had a great influence on Ling's life beyond that time.

Each day of the examination found Ling alternately elated or depressed, according to the length and style of the essay which he had written while enclosed in his solitary examination cell. The trials each lasted a complete day, and long before the fifteen days which composed the full examination were passed, Ling found himself half regretting that he had not accepted his visitor's offer, or even reviling the day on which he had abandoned the hereditary calling of his ancestors. However, when, after all was over, he came to deliberate with himself on his chances of attaining a degree, he could not disguise from his own mind that he had well-formed hopes; he was not conscious of any undignified errors, and, in reply to several questions, he had been able to introduce curious knowledge which he possessed by means of his exceptional circumstances-knowledge which it was unlikely that any other candidate would have been able to make himself master of.

At length the day arrived on which the results were to be made public; and Ling, together with all the other competitors and many distinguished persons, attended at the great Hall of Intellectual Coloured Lights to hear the reading of the lists. Eight thousand candidates had been examined, and from this number less than two hundred were to be selected for appointments. Amid a most distinguished silence the winning names were read out. Waves of most undignified but inevitable emotion passed over those assembled as the list neared its end, and the chances of success became less at each spoken word; and then, finding that his was not among them, together with the greater part of those present, he became a prey to very inelegant thoughts, which were not lessened by the refined cries of triumph of the successful persons. Among this confusion the one who had read the lists was observed to be endeavouring to make his voice known, whereupon, in the expectation that he had omitted a name, the tumult was quickly subdued by those who again had pleasurable visions.

"There was among the candidates one of the name of Ling," said he, when no-noise had been obtained. "The written leaves produced by this person are of a most versatile and conflicting order, so that, indeed, the accomplished examiners themselves are unable to decide whether they are very good or very bad. In this matter, therefore, it is clearly impossible to place the expert and inimitable Ling among the foremost, as his very uncertain success may have been brought about with the assistance of evil spirits; nor would it be safe to pass over his efforts without reward, as he may be under the protection of powerful but exceedingly ill-advised deities. The estimable Ling is told to appear again at this place after the gong has been struck three times, when the matter will have been looked at from all round."

At this announcement there arose another great tumult, several crying out that assuredly their written leaves were either very good or very bad; but no further proclamation was made, and very soon the hall was cleared by force.

At the time stated Ling again presented himself at the Hall, and was honourably received.

"The unusual circumstances of the matter have already been put forth," said an elderly Mandarin of engaging appearance, "so that nothing remains to be made known except the end of our despicable efforts to come to an agreeable conclusion. In this we have been made successful, and now desire to notify the result. A very desirable and not unremunerative office, rarely bestowed in this manner, is lately vacant, and taking into our minds the circumstances of the event, and the fact that Ling comes from a Province very esteemed for the warlike instincts of its inhabitants, we have decided to appoint him commander of the valiant and blood-thirsty band of archers now stationed at Si-chow, in the Province of Hu-Nan. We have spoken. Let three guns go off in honour of the noble and invincible Ling, now and henceforth a commander in the ever-victorious Army of the Sublime Emperor, brother of the Sun and Moon, and Upholder of the Four Corners of the World."

IV

Many hours passed before Ling, now more downcast in mind than the most unsuccessful student in Canton, returned to his room and sought his couch of dried rushes. All his efforts to have his distinguished appointment set aside had been without avail, and he had been ordered to reach Si-chow within a week. As he passed through the streets, elegant processions in honour of the winners met him at every corner, and drove him into the outskirts for the object of quietness. There he remained until the beating of paper drums and the sound of exulting voices could be heard no more; but even when he returned lanterns shone in many dwellings, for two hundred persons were composing verses, setting forth their renown and undoubted accomplishments, ready to affix to their doors and send to friends on the next day. Not giving any portion of his mind to this desirable act of behaviour, Ling flung himself upon the floor, and, finding sleep unattainable, plunged himself into profound meditation of a very uninviting order. "Without doubt," he exclaimed, "evil can only arise from evil, and as this person has always endeavoured to lead a life in which his devotions have been equally divided between the sacred Emperor, his illustrious parents, and his venerable ancestors, the fault cannot lie with him. Of the excellence of his parents he has full knowledge; regarding the Emperor, it might not be safe to conjecture. It is therefore probable that some of his ancestors were persons of abandoned manner and inelegant habits, to worship whom results in evil rather than good. Otherwise, how could it be that one whose chief delight lies in the passive contemplation of the Four Books and the Five Classics, should be selected by destiny to fill a position calling for great personal courage and an aggressive nature? Assuredly it can only end in a mean and insignificant death, perhaps not even followed by burial."

In this manner of thought he fell asleep, and after certain very base and impressive dreams, from which good omens were altogether absent, he awoke, and rose to begin his preparations for leaving the city. After two days spent chiefly in obtaining certain safeguards against treachery and the bullets of foemen, purchasing opium and other gifts with which to propitiate the soldiers under his charge, and in consulting well-disposed witches and readers of the future, he set out, and by travelling in extreme discomfort, reached Si-chow within five days. During his journey he learned that the entire Province was engaged in secret rebellion, several towns, indeed, having declared against the Imperial army without reserve. Those persons to whom Ling spoke described the rebels, with respectful admiration, as fierce and unnaturally skilful in all methods of fighting, revengeful and merciless towards their enemies, very numerous and above the ordinary height of human beings, and endowed with qualities which made their skin capable of turning aside every kind of weapon. Furthermore, he was assured that a large band of the most abandoned and best trained was at that moment in the immediate neighbourhood of Si-chow.

Ling was not destined long to remain in any doubt concerning the truth of these matters, for as he made his way through a dark cypress wood, a few li from the houses of Si-chow, the sounds of a confused outcry reached his ears, and on stepping aside to a hidden glade some distance from the path, he beheld a young and elegant maiden of incomparable beauty being carried away by two persons of most repulsive and undignified appearance, whose dress and manner clearly betrayed them to be rebels of the lowest and worst-paid type. At this sight Ling became possessed of feelings of a savage yet agreeable order, which until that time he had not conjectured to have any place within his mind, and without even pausing to consider whether the planets were in favourable positions for the enterprise to be undertaken at that time, he drew his sword, and ran forward with loud cries. Unsettled in their intentions at this unexpected action, the two persons turned and advanced upon Ling with whirling daggers, discussing among themselves whether it would be better to kill him at the first blow or to take him alive, and, when the day had become sufficiently cool for the full enjoyment of the spectacle, submit him to various objectionable tortures of so degraded a nature that they were rarely used in the army of the Emperor except upon the persons of barbarians. Observing that the maiden was not bound, Ling cried out to her to escape and seek protection within the town, adding, with a magnanimous absence of vanity:

"Should this person chance to fall, the repose which the presence of so lovely and graceful a being would undoubtedly bring to his departing spirit would be out-balanced by the unendurable thought that his commonplace efforts had not been sufficient to save her from the two evilly-disposed individuals who are, as he perceives, at this moment, neglecting no means within their power to accomplish his destruction." Accepting the discernment of these words, the maiden fled, first bestowing a look upon Ling which clearly indicated an honourable regard for himself, a high-minded desire that the affair might end profitably on his account, and an amiable hope that they should meet again, when these subjects could be expressed more clearly between them.

In the meantime Ling had become at a disadvantage, for the time occupied in speaking and in making the necessary number of bows in reply to her entrancing glance had given the other persons an opportunity of arranging their charms and sacred written sentences to greater advantage, and of occupying the most favourable ground for the encounter. Nevertheless, so great was the force of the new emotion which had entered into Ling's nature that, without waiting to consider the dangers or the best method of attack, he rushed upon them, waving his sword with such force that he appeared as though surrounded by a circle of very brilliant fire. In this way he reached the rebels, who both fell unexpectedly at one blow, they, indeed, being under the impression that the encounter had not commenced in reality, and that Ling was merely menacing them in order to inspire their minds with terror and raise his own spirits. However much he regretted this act of the incident which he had been compelled to take, Ling could not avoid being filled with intellectual joy at finding that his own charms and omens were more distinguished than those possessed by the rebels, none of whom, as he now plainly understood, he need fear.

Examining these things within his mind, and reflecting on the events of the past few days, by which he had been thrown into a class of circumstances greatly differing from anything which he had ever sought, Ling continued his journey, and soon found himself before the southern gate of Si-chow. Entering the town, he at once formed the resolution of going before the Mandarin for Warlike Deeds and Arrangements, so that he might present, without delay, the papers and seals which he had brought with him from Canton.

"The noble Mandarin Li Keen?" replied the first person to whom Ling addressed himself. "It would indeed be a difficult and hazardous conjecture to make concerning his sacred person. By chance he is in the strongest and best-concealed cellar in Si-chow, unless the sumptuous attractions of the deepest dry well have induced him to make a short journey"; and, with a look of great unfriendliness at Ling's dress and weapons, this person passed on.

"Doubtless he is fighting single-handed against the armed men by whom the place is surrounded," said another; "or perhaps he is constructing an underground road from the Yamen to Peking, so that we may all escape when the town is taken. All that can be said with certainty is that the Heaven-sent and valorous Mandarin has not been seen outside the walls of his well-fortified residence since the trouble arose; but, as you carry a sword of conspicuous excellence, you will doubtless be welcome."

Upon making a third attempt Ling was more successful, for he inquired of an aged woman, who had neither a reputation for keen and polished sentences to maintain, nor any interest in the acts of the Mandarin or of the rebels. From her he learned how to reach the Yamen, and accordingly turned his footsteps in that direction. When at length he arrived at the gate, Ling desired his tablets to be carried to the Mandarin with many expressions of an impressive and engaging nature, nor did he neglect to reward the porter. It was therefore with the expression of a misunderstanding mind that he received a reply setting forth that Li Keen was unable to receive him. In great doubt he prevailed upon the porter, by means of a still larger reward, again to carry in his message, and on this occasion an answer in this detail was placed before him.

"Li Keen," he was informed, "is indeed awaiting the arrival of one Ling, a noble and valiant Commander of Bowmen. He is given to understand, it is true, that a certain person claiming the same honoured name is standing in somewhat undignified attitudes at the gate, but he is unable in any way to make these two individuals meet within his intellect. He would further remind all persons that the refined observances laid down by the wise and exalted Board of Rites and Ceremonies have a marked and irreproachable significance when the country is in a state of disorder, the town surrounded by rebels, and every breathing-space of time of more than ordinary value."

Overpowered with becoming shame at having been connected with so unseemly a breach of civility, for which his great haste had in reality been accountable, Ling hastened back into the town, and spent many hours endeavouring to obtain a chair of the requisite colour in which to visit the Mandarin. In this he was unsuccessful, until it was at length suggested to him that an ordinary chair, such as stood for hire in the streets of Si-chow, would be acceptable if covered with blue paper. Still in some doubt as to what the nature of his reception would be, Ling had no choice but to take this course, and accordingly he again reached the Yamen in such a manner, carried by two persons whom he had obtained for the purpose. While yet hardly at the residence a salute was suddenly fired; all the gates and doors were, without delay, thrown open with embarrassing and hospitable profusion, and the Mandarin himself passed out, and would have assisted Ling to step down from his chair had not that person, clearly perceiving that such a course would be too great an honour, evaded him by an unobtrusive display of versatile dexterity. So numerous and profound were the graceful remarks which each made concerning the habits and accomplishments of the other that more than the space of an hour was passed in traversing the small enclosed ground which led up to the principal door of the Yamen. There an almost greater time was agreeably spent, both Ling and the Mandarin having determined that the other should enter first. Undoubtedly Ling, who was the more powerful of the two, would have conferred this courteous distinction upon Li Keen had not that person summoned to his side certain attendants who succeeded in frustrating Ling in his high-minded intentions, and in forcing him through the doorway in spite of his conscientious protests against the unsurmountable obligation under which the circumstance placed him.

Conversing in this intellectual and dignified manner, the strokes of the gong passed unheeded; tea had been brought into their presence many times, and night had fallen before the Mandarin allowed Ling to refer to the matter which had brought him to the place, and to present his written papers and seals.

"It is a valuable privilege to have so intelligent a person as the illustrious Ling occupying this position," remarked the Mandarin, as he returned the papers; "and not less so on account of the one who preceded him proving himself to be a person of feeble attainments and an unendurable deficiency of resource."

"To one with the all-knowing Li Keen's mental acquisitions, such a person must indeed have become excessively offensive," replied Ling delicately; "for, as it is truly said, 'Although there exist many thousand subjects for elegant conversation, there are persons who cannot meet a cripple without talking about feet.'"

"He to whom I have referred was such a one," said Li Keen, appreciating with an expression of countenance the fitness of Ling's proverb. "He was totally inadequate to the requirements of his position; for he possessed no military knowledge, and was placed in command by those at Peking as a result of his taking a high place at one of the examinations. But more than this, although his three years of service were almost completed, I was quite unsuccessful in convincing him that an unseemly degradation probably awaited him unless he could furnish me with the means with which to propitiate the persons in authority at Peking. This he neglected to do with obstinate pertinacity, which compelled this person to inquire within himself whether one of so little discernment could be trusted with an important and arduous office. After much deliberation, this person came to the decision that the Commander in question was not a fit person, and he therefore reported him to the Imperial Board of Punishment at Peking as one subject to frequent and periodical eccentricities, and possessed of less than ordinary intellect.

In consequence of this act of justice, the Commander was degraded to the rank of common bowman, and compelled to pay a heavy fine in addition."

"It was a just and enlightened conclusion of the affair," said Ling, in spite of a deep feeling of no enthusiasm, "and one which surprisingly bore out your own prophecy in the matter."

"It was an inspired warning to persons who should chance to be in a like position at any time," replied Li Keen. "So grasping and corrupt are those who control affairs in Peking that I have no doubt they would scarcely hesitate in debasing even one so immaculate as the exceptional Ling, and placing him in some laborious and ill-paid civil department should he not accede to their extortionate demands."

This suggestion did not carry with it the unpleasurable emotions which the Mandarin anticipated it would. The fierce instincts which had been aroused within Ling by the incident in the cypress wood had died out, while his lamentable ignorance of military affairs was ever before his mind. These circumstances, together with his naturally gentle habits, made him regard such a degradation rather favourably than otherwise. He was meditating within himself whether he could arrange such a course without delay when the Mandarin continued:

"That, however, is a possibility which is remote to the extent of at least two or three years; do not, therefore, let so unpleasing a thought cast darkness upon your brows or remove the unparalleled splendour of so refined an occasion...Doubtless the accomplished Ling is a master of the art of chess-play, for many of our most thoughtful philosophers have declared war to be nothing but such a game; let this slow-witted and cumbersome person have an opportunity, therefore, of polishing his declining facilities by a pleasant and dignified encounter."

V

On the next day, having completed his business at the Yamen, Ling left the town, and without desiring any ceremony quietly betook himself to his new residence within the camp, which was situated among the millet fields some distance from Si-chow. As soon as his presence became known all those who occupied positions of command, and whose years of service would shortly come to an end, hastened to present themselves before him, bringing with them offerings according to the rank they held, they themselves requiring a similar service from those beneath them. First among these, and next in command to Ling himself, was the Chief of Bowmen, a person whom Ling observed with extreme satisfaction to be very powerful in body and possessing a strong and dignified countenance which showed unquestionable resolution and shone with a tiger-like tenaciousness of purpose.

"Undoubtedly," thought Ling, as he observed this noble and prepossessing person, "here is one who will be able to assist me in whatever perplexities may arise. Never was there an individual who seemed more worthy to command and lead; assuredly to him the most intricate and prolonged military positions will be an enjoyment; the most crafty stratagems of the enemy as the full moon rising from behind a screen of rushes. Without making any pretence of knowledge, this person will explain the facts of the case to him and place himself without limit in his hands."

For this purpose he therefore detained the Chief of Bowmen when the others departed, and complimented him, with many expressive phrases, on the excellence of his appearance, as the thought occurred to him that by this means, without disclosing the full measure of his ignorance, the person in question might be encouraged to speak unrestrainedly of the nature of his exploits, and perchance thereby explain the use of the appliances employed and the meaning of the various words of order, in all of which details the Commander was as yet most disagreeably imperfect. In this, however, he was disappointed, for the Chief of Bowmen, greatly to Ling's surprise, received all his polished sentences with somewhat foolish smiles of great self-satisfaction, merely replying from time to time as he displayed his pigtail to greater advantage or rearranged his gold-embroidered cloak:

"This person must really pray you to desist; the honour is indeed too great."

Disappointed in his hope, and not desiring after this circumstance to expose his shortcomings to one who was obviously not of a highly-refined understanding, no matter how great his valour in war or his knowledge of military affairs might be, Ling endeavoured to lead him to converse of the bowmen under his charge. In this matter he was more successful, for the Chief spoke at great length and with evilly-inspired contempt of their inelegance, their undiscriminating and excessive appetites, and the frequent use which they made of low words and gestures. Desiring to become acquainted rather with their methods of warfare than with their domestic details, Ling inquired of him what formation they relied upon when receiving the foemen.

"It is a matter which has not engaged the attention of this one," replied the Chief, with an excessive absence of interest. "There are so many affairs of intelligent dignity which cannot be put aside, and which occupy one from beginning to end. As an example, this person may describe how the accomplished Li-Lu, generally depicted as the Blue-eyed Dove of Virtuous and Serpent-like Attitudes, has been scattering glory upon the Si-chow Hall of Celestial Harmony for many days past. It is an enlightened display which the high-souled Ling should certainly endeavour to dignify with his presence, especially at the portion where the amiable Li-Lu becomes revealed in the appearance of a Peking sedan-chair bearer and describes the manner and likenesses of certain persons-chiefly high-priests of Buddha, excessively round-bodied merchants who feign to be detained within Peking on affairs of commerce, maidens who attend at the tables of tea-houses, and those of both sexes who are within the city for the first time to behold its temples and open spaces-who are conveyed from place to place in the chair."

"And the bowmen?" suggested Ling, with difficulty restraining an undignified emotion.

"Really, the elegant Ling will discover them to be persons of deficient manners, and quite unworthy of occupying his well-bred conversation," replied the Chief. "As regards their methods-if the renowned Ling insists-they fight by means of their bows, with which they discharge arrows at the foemen, they themselves hiding behind trees and rocks. Should the enemy be undisconcerted by the cloud of arrows, and advance, the bowmen are instructed to make a last endeavour to frighten them back by uttering loud shouts and feigning the voices of savage beasts of the forest and deadly snakes."

"And beyond that?" inquired Ling.

"Beyond that there are no instructions," replied the Chief. "The bowmen would then naturally take to flight, or, if such a course became impossible, run to meet the enemy, protesting that they were convinced of the justice of their cause, and were determined to fight on their side in the future."

"Would it not be of advantage to arm them with cutting weapons also?" inquired Ling; "so that when all their arrows were discharged they would still be able to take part in the fight, and not be lost to us?"

"They would not be lost to us, of course," replied the Chief, "as we would still be with them. But such a course as the one you suggest could not fail to end in dismay. Being as well armed as ourselves, they would then turn upon us, and, having destroyed us, proceed to establish leaders of their own."

As Ling and the Chief of Bowmen conversed in this enlightened manner, there arose a great outcry from among the tents, and presently there entered to them a spy who had discovered a strong force of the enemy not more than ten or twelve li away, who showed every indication of marching shortly in the direction of Si-chow. In numbers alone, he continued, they were greatly superior to the bowmen, and all were well armed. The spreading of this news threw the entire camp into great confusion, many protesting that the day was not a favourable one on which to fight, others crying that it was their duty to fall back on Si-chow and protect the women and children. In the midst of this tumult the Chief of Bowmen returned to Ling, bearing in his hand a written paper which he regarded in uncontrollable anguish.

"Oh, illustrious Ling," he cried, restraining his grief with difficulty, and leaning for support upon the shoulders of two bowmen, "how prosperous indeed are you! What greater misfortune can engulf a person who is both an ambitious soldier and an affectionate son, than to lose such a chance of glory and promotion as only occurs once within the lifetime, and an affectionate and venerable father upon the same day? Behold this mandate to attend, without a moment's delay, at the funeral obsequies of one whom I left, only last week, in the fullness of health and power. The occasion being an unsuitable one, I will not call upon the courteous Ling to join me in sorrow; but his own devout filial piety is so well known that I can conscientiously rely upon an application for absence to be only a matter of official ceremony."

"The application will certainly be regarded as merely official ceremony," replied Ling, without resorting to any delicate pretence of meaning, "and the refined scruples of the person who is addressing me will be fully met by the official date of his venerated father's death being fixed for a more convenient season. In the meantime, the unobtrusive Chief of Bowmen may take the opportunity of requesting that the family tomb be kept unsealed until he is heard from again."

Ling turned away, as he finished this remark, with a dignified feeling of not inelegant resentment. In this way he chanced to observe a large body of soldiers which was leaving the camp accompanied by their lesser captains, all crowned with garlands of flowers and creeping plants. In spite of his very inadequate attainments regarding words of order, the Commander made it understood by means of an exceedingly short sentence that he was desirous of the men returning without delay.

"Doubtless the accomplished Commander, being but newly arrived in this neighbourhood, is unacquainted with the significance of this display," said one of the lesser captains pleasantly. "Know then, O wise and custom-respecting Ling, that on a similar day many years ago this valiant band of bowmen was engaged in a very honourable affair with certain of the enemy. Since then it has been the practice to commemorate the matter with music and other forms of delight within the large square at Si-chow."

"Such customs are excellent," said Ling affably. "On this occasion, however, the public square will be so insufferably thronged with the number of timorous and credulous villagers who have pressed into the town that insufficient justice would be paid to your entrancing display. In consequence of this, we will select for the purpose some convenient spot in the neighbourhood. The proceedings will be commenced by a display of arrow-shooting at moving objects, followed by racing and dancing, in which this person will lead. I have spoken."

At these words many of the more courageous among the bowmen became destructively inspired, and raised shouts of defiance against the enemy, enumerating at great length the indignities which they would heap upon their prisoners. Cries of distinction were also given on behalf of Ling, even the more terrified exclaiming:

"The noble Commander Ling will lead us! He has promised, and assuredly he will not depart from his word. Shielded by his broad and sacred body, from which the bullets glance aside harmlessly, we will advance upon the enemy in the stealthy manner affected by ducks when crossing the swamp. How altogether superior a person our Commander is when likened unto the leaders of the foemen-they who go into battle completely surrounded by their archers!"

Upon this, perceiving the clear direction in which matters were turning, the Chief of Bowmen again approached Ling.

"Doubtless the highly-favoured person whom I am now addressing has been endowed with exceptional authority direct from Peking," he remarked with insidious politeness. "Otherwise this narrow-minded individual would suggest that such a decision does not come within the judgment of a Commander."

In his ignorance of military matters it had not entered the mind of Ling that his authority did not give him the power to commence an attack without consulting other and more distinguished persons. At the suggestion, which he accepted as being composed of truth, he paused, the enlightened zeal with which he had been inspired dying out as he plainly understood the difficulties by which he was enclosed. There seemed a single expedient path for him in the matter; so, directing a person of exceptional trustworthiness to prepare himself for a journey, he inscribed a communication to the Mandarin Li Keen, in which he narrated the facts and asked for speedy directions, and then despatched it with great urgency to Si-chow.

VI

When these matters were arranged, Ling returned to his tent, a victim to feelings of a deep and confused doubt, for all courses seemed to be surrounded by extreme danger, with the strong possibility of final disaster. While he was considering these things attentively, the spy who had brought word of the presence of the enemy again sought him. As he entered, Ling perceived that his face was the colour of a bleached linen garment, while there came with him the odour of sickness.

"There are certain matters which this person has not made known," he said, having first expressed a request that he might not be compelled to stand while he conversed. "The bowmen are as an inferior kind of jackal, and they who lead them are pigs, but this person has observed that the Heaven-sent Commander has internal organs like steel hardened in a white fire and polished by running water. For this reason he will narrate to him the things he has seen-things at which the lesser ones would undoubtedly perish in terror without offering to strike a blow."

"Speak," said Ling, "without fear and without concealment."

"In numbers the rebels are as three to one with the bowmen, and are, in addition, armed with matchlocks and other weapons; this much I have already told," said the spy. "Yesterday they entered the village of Ki without resistance, as the dwellers there were all peaceable persons, who gain a living from the fields, and who neither understood nor troubled about the matters between the rebels and the army. Relying on the promises made by the rebel chiefs, the villagers even welcomed them, as they had been assured that they came as buyers of their corn and rice. To-day not a house stands in the street of Ki, not a person lives. The men they slew quickly, or held for torture, as they desired at the moment; the boys they hung from the trees as marks for their arrows. Of the women and children this person, who has since been subject to several attacks of fainting and vomiting, desires not to speak. The wells of Ki are filled with the bodies of such as had the good fortune to be warned in time to slay themselves. The cattle drag themselves from place to place on their forefeet; the fish in the Heng-Kiang are dying, for they cannot live on water thickened into blood. All these things this person has seen."

When he had finished speaking, Ling remained in deep and funereal thought for some time. In spite of his mild nature, the words which he had heard filled him with an inextinguishable desire to slay in hand-to-hand fighting. He regretted that he had placed the decision of the matter before Li Keen.

"If only this person had a mere handful of brave and expert warriors, he would not hesitate to fall upon those savage and barbarous characters, and either destroy them to the last one, or let his band suffer a like fate," he murmured to himself.

The return of the messenger found him engaged in reviewing the bowmen, and still in this mood, so that it was with a commendable feeling of satisfaction, no less than virtuous contempt, that he learned of the Mandarin's journey to Peking as soon as he understood that the rebels were certainly in the neighbourhood.

"The wise and ornamental Li Keen is undoubtedly consistent in all matters," said Ling, with some refined bitterness. "The only information regarding his duties to which this person obtained from him chanced to be a likening of war to skilful chess-play, and to this end the accomplished person in question has merely availed himself of a common expedient which places him at the remote side of the divine Emperor. Yet this act is not unwelcome, for the responsibility of deciding what course is to be adopted now clearly rests with this person. He is, as those who are standing by may perceive, of under the usual height, and of no particular mental or bodily attainments. But he has eaten the rice of the Emperor, and wears the Imperial sign embroidered upon his arm. Before him are encamped the enemies of his master and of his land, and in no way will he turn his back upon them. Against brave and skilful men, such as those whom this person commands, rebels of a low and degraded order are powerless, and are, moreover, openly forbidden to succeed by the Forty-second Mandate in the Sacred Book of Arguments. Should it have happened that into this assembly any person of a perfidious or uncourageous nature has gained entrance by guile, and has not been detected and driven forth by his outraged companions (as would certainly occur if such a person were discovered), I, Ling, Commander of Bowmen, make an especial and well-considered request that he shall be struck by a molten thunderbolt if he turns to flight or holds thoughts of treachery."

Having thus addressed and encouraged the soldiers, Ling instructed them that each one should cut and fashion for himself a graceful but weighty club from among the branches of the trees around, and then return to the tents for the purpose of receiving food and rice spirit.

When noon was passed, allowing such time as would enable him to reach the camp of the enemy an hour before darkness, Ling arranged the bowmen in companies of convenient numbers, and commenced the march, sending forward spies, who were to work silently and bring back tidings from every point. In this way he penetrated to within a single li of the ruins of Ki, being informed by the spies that no outposts of the enemy were between him and that place. Here the first rest was made to enable the more accurate and bold spies to reach them with trustworthy information regarding the position and movements of the camp. With little delay there returned the one who had brought the earliest tidings, bruised and torn with his successful haste through the forest, but wearing a complacent and well-satisfied expression of countenance. Without hesitation or waiting to demand money before he would reveal his knowledge, he at once disclosed that the greater part of the enemy were rejoicing among the ruins of Ki, they having discovered there a quantity of opium and a variety of liquids, while only a small guard remained in the camp with their weapons ready. At these words Ling sprang from the ground in gladness, so great was his certainty of destroying the invaders utterly. It was, however, with less pleasurable emotions that he considered how he should effect the matter, for it was in no way advisable to divide his numbers into two bands. Without any feeling of unendurable conceit, he understood that no one but himself could hold the bowmen before an assault, however weak. In a similar manner, he determined that it would be more advisable to attack those in the village first. These he might have reasonable hopes of cutting down without warning the camp, or, in any event, before those from the camp arrived. To assail the camp first would assuredly, by the firing, draw upon them those from the village, and in whatever evil state these might arrive, they would, by their numbers, terrify the bowmen, who without doubt would have suffered some loss from the matchlocks.

Waiting for the last light of day, Ling led on the men again, and sending forward some of the most reliable, surrounded the place of the village silently and without detection. In the open space, among broken casks and other inconsiderable matters, plainly shown by the large fires at which burned the last remains of the houses of Ki, many men moved or lay, some already dull or in heavy sleep. As the darkness dropped suddenly, the signal of a peacock's shriek, three times uttered, rang forth, and immediately a cloud of arrows, directed from all sides, poured in among those who feasted. Seeing their foemen defenceless before them, the archers neglected the orders they had received, and throwing away their bows they rushed in with uplifted clubs, uttering loud shouts of triumph. The next moment a shot was fired in the wood, drums beat, and in an unbelievably short space of time a small but well-armed band of the enemy was among them. Now that all need of caution was at an end, Ling rushed forward with raised sword, calling to his men that victory was certainly theirs, and dealing discriminating and inspiriting blows whenever he met a foeman. Three times he formed the bowmen into a figure emblematic of triumph, and led them against the line of matchlocks. Twice they fell back, leaving mingled dead under the feet of the enemy. The third time they stood firm, and Ling threw himself against the waving rank in a noble and inspired endeavour to lead the way through. At that moment, when a very distinguished victory seemed within his hand, his elegant and well-constructed sword broke upon an iron shield, leaving him defenceless and surrounded by the enemy.

"Chief among the sublime virtues enjoined by the divine Confucius," began Ling, folding his arms and speaking in an unmoved voice, "is an intelligent submission —" but at that word he fell beneath a rain of heavy and unquestionably well-aimed blows.

VII

Between Si-chow and the village of Ki, in a house completely hidden from travellers by the tall and black trees which surrounded it, lived an aged and very wise person whose ways and manner of living had become so distasteful to his neighbours that they at length agreed to regard him as a powerful and ill-disposed magician. In this way it became a custom that all very unseemly deeds committed by those who, in the ordinary course, would not be guilty of such behaviour, should be attributed to his influence, so that justice might be effected without persons of assured respectability being put to any inconvenience. Apart from the feeling which resulted from this just decision, the uncongenial person in question had become exceedingly unpopular on account of certain definite actions of his own, as that of causing the greater part of Si-chow to be burned down by secretly breathing upon the seven sacred water-jugs to which the town owed its prosperity and freedom from fire. Furthermore, although possessed of many taels, and able to afford such food as is to be found upon the tables of Mandarins, he selected from choice dishes of an objectionable nature; he had been observed to eat eggs of unbecoming freshness, and the Si-chow Official Printed Leaf made it public that he had, on an excessively hot occasion, openly partaken of cow's milk. It is not a matter for wonder, therefore, that when unnaturally loud thunder was heard in the neighbourhood of Si-chow the more ignorant and credulous persons refused to continue in any description of work until certain ceremonies connected with rice spirit, and the adherence to a reclining position for some hours, had been conscientiously observed as a protection against evil.

Not even the most venerable person in Si-chow could remember the time when the magician had not lived there, and as there existed no written record narrating the incident, it was with well-founded probability that he was said to be incapable of death. Contrary to the most general practice, although quite unmarried, he had adopted no son to found a line which would worship his memory in future years, but had instead brought up and caused to be educated in the most difficult varieties of embroidery a young girl, to whom he referred, for want of a more suitable description, as the daughter of his sister, although he would admit without hesitation, when closely questioned, that he had never possessed a sister, at the same time, however, alluding with some pride to many illustrious brothers, who had all obtained distinction in various employments.

Few persons of any high position penetrated into the house of the magician, and most of these retired with inelegant haste on perceiving that no domestic altar embellished the great hall. Indeed, not to make concealment of the fact, the magician was a person who had entirely neglected the higher virtues in an avaricious pursuit of wealth. In that way all his time and a very large number of taels had been expended, testing results by means of the four elements, and putting together things which had been inadequately arrived at by others. It was confidently asserted in Si-chow that he possessed every manner of printed leaf which had been composed in whatsoever language, and all the most precious charms, including many snake-skins of more than ordinary rarity, and the fang of a black wolf which had been stung by seven scorpions.

On the death of his father the magician had become possessed of great wealth, yet he contributed little to the funeral obsequies nor did any suggestion of a durable and expensive nature conveying his enlightened name and virtues down to future times cause his face to become gladdened. In order to preserve greater secrecy about the enchantments which he certainly performed, he employed only two persons within the house, one of whom was blind and the other deaf. In this ingenious manner he hoped to receive attention and yet be unobserved, the blind one being unable to see the nature of the incantations which he undertook, and the deaf one being unable to hear the words. In this, however, he was unsuccessful, as the two persons always contrived to be present together, and to explain to one another the nature of the various matters afterwards; but as they were of somewhat deficient understanding, the circumstance was unimportant.

It was with more uneasiness that the magician perceived one day that the maiden whom he had adopted was no longer a child. As he desired secrecy above all things until he should have completed the one important matter for which he had laboured all his life, he decided with extreme unwillingness to put into operation a powerful charm towards her, which would have the effect of diminishing all her attributes until such time as he might release her again. Owing to his reluctance in the matter, however, the magic did not act fully, but only in such a way that her feet became naturally and without binding the most perfect and beautiful in the entire province of Hu Nan, so that ever afterwards she was called Pan Fei Mian, in delicate reference to that Empress whose feet were so symmetrical that a golden lily sprang up wherever she trod. Afterwards the magician made no further essay in the matter, chiefly because he was ever convinced that the accomplishment of his desire was within his grasp.

The rumours of armed men in the neighbourhood of Si-chow threw the magician into an unendurable condition of despair. To lose all, as would most assuredly happen if he had to leave his arranged rooms and secret preparations and take to flight, was the more bitter because he felt surer than ever that success was even standing by his side. The very subtle liquid, which would mix itself into the component parts of the living creature which drank it, and by an insidious and harmless process so work that, when the spirit departed, the flesh would become resolved into a figure of pure and solid gold of the finest quality, had engaged the refined minds of many of the most expert individuals of remote ages. With most of these inspired persons, however, the search had been undertaken in pure-minded benevolence, their chief aim being an honourable desire to discover a method by which one's ancestors might be permanently and effectively preserved in a fit and becoming manner to receive the worship and veneration of posterity. Yet, in spite of these amiable motives, and of the fact that the magician merely desired the possession of the secret to enable him to become excessively wealthy, the affair had been so arranged that it should come into his possession.

The matter which concerned Mian in the dark wood, when she was only saved by the appearance of the person who is already known as Ling, entirely removed all pleasurable emotions from the magician's mind, and on many occasions he stated in a definite and systematic manner that he would shortly end an ignoble career which seemed to be destined only to gloom and disappointment. In this way an important misunderstanding arose, for when, two days later, during the sound of matchlock firing, the magician suddenly approached the presence of Mian with an uncontrollable haste and an entire absence of dignified demeanour, and fell dead at her feet without expressing himself on any subject whatever, she deliberately judged that in this manner he had carried his remark into effect, nor did the closed vessel of yellow liquid which he held in his hand seem to lead away from this decision. In reality, the magician had fallen owing to the heavy and conflicting emotions which success had engendered in an intellect already greatly weakened by his continual disregard of the higher virtues; for the bottle, indeed, contained the perfection of his entire life's study, the very expensive and three-times purified gold liquid.

On perceiving the magician's condition, Mian at once called for the two attendants, and directed them to bring from an inner chamber all the most effective curing substances, whether in the form of powder or liquid. When these proved useless, no matter in what way they were applied, it became evident that there could be very little hope of restoring the magician, yet so courageous and grateful for the benefits which she had received from the person in question was Mian, that, in spite of the uninviting dangers of the enterprise, she determined to journey to Ki to invoke the assistance of a certain person who was known to be very successful in casting out malicious demons from the bodies of animals, and from casks and barrels, in which they frequently took refuge, to the great detriment of the quality of the liquid placed therein.

Not without many hidden fears, Mian set out on her journey, greatly desiring not to be subjected to an encounter of a nature similar to the one already recorded; for in such a case she could hardly again hope for the inspired arrival of the one whom she now often thought of in secret as the well-formed and symmetrical young sword-user. Nevertheless, an event of equal significance was destined to prove the wisdom of the well-known remark concerning thoughts which are occupying one's intellect and the unexpected appearance of a very formidable evil spirit; for as she passed along, quickly yet with so dignified a motion that the moss received no impression beneath her footsteps, she became aware of a circumstance which caused her to stop by imparting to her mind two definite and greatly dissimilar emotions.

In a grassy and open space, on the verge of which she stood, lay the dead bodies of seventeen rebels, all disposed in very degraded attitudes, which contrasted strongly with the easy and becoming position adopted by the eighteenth-one who bore the unmistakable emblems of the Imperial army. In this brave and noble-looking personage Mian at once saw her preserver, and not doubting that an inopportune and treacherous death had overtaken him, she ran forward and raised him in her arms, being well assured that however indiscreet such an action might appear in the case of an ordinary person, the most select maiden need not hesitate to perform so honourable a service in regard to one whose virtues had by that time undoubtedly placed him among the Three Thousand Pure Ones. Being disturbed in this providential manner, Ling opened his eyes, and faintly murmuring, "Oh, sainted and adorable Koon Yam, Goddess of Charity, intercede for me with Buddha!" he again lost possession of himself in the Middle Air. At this remark, which plainly proved Ling to be still alive, in spite of the fact that both the maiden and the person himself had thoughts to the contrary, Mian found herself surrounded by a variety of embarrassing circumstances, among which occurred a remembrance of the dead magician and the wise person at Ki whom she had set out to summon; but on considering the various natural and sublime laws which bore directly on the alternative before her, she discovered that her plain destiny was to endeavour to restore the breath in the person who was still alive rather than engage on the very unsatisfactory chance of attempting to call it back to the body from which it had so long been absent.

Having been inspired to this conclusion-which, when she later examined her mind, she found not to be repulsive to her own inner feelings-Mian returned to the house with dexterous speed, and calling together the two attendants, she endeavoured by means of signs and drawings to explain to them what she desired to accomplish. Succeeding in this after some delay (for the persons in question, being very illiterate and narrow-minded, were unable at first to understand the existence of any recumbent male person other than the dead magician, whom they thereupon commenced to bury in the garden with expressions of great satisfaction at their own intelligence in comprehending Mian's meaning so readily) they all journeyed to the wood, and bearing Ling between them, they carried him to the house without further adventure.

VIII

It was in the month of Hot Dragon Breaths, many weeks after the fight in the woods of Ki, that Ling again opened his eyes to find himself in an unknown chamber, and to recognize in the one who visited him from time to time the incomparable maiden whose life he had saved in the cypress glade. Not a day had passed in the meanwhile on which Mian had neglected to offer sacrifices to Chang-Chung, the deity interested in drugs and healing substances, nor had she wavered in her firm resolve to bring Ling back to an ordinary existence even when the attendants had protested that the person in question might without impropriety be sent to the Restoring Establishment of the Last Chance, so little did his hope of recovering rest upon the efforts of living beings.

After he had beheld Mian's face and understood the circumstances of his escape and recovery, Ling quickly shook off the evil vapours which had held him down so long, and presently he was able to walk slowly in the courtyard and in the shady paths of the wood beyond, leaning upon Mian for the support he still required.

"Oh, graceful one," he said on such an occasion, when little stood between him and the full powers which he had known before the battle, "there is a matter which has been pressing upon this person's mind for some time past. It is as dark after light to let the thoughts dwell around it, yet the thing itself must inevitably soon be regarded, for in this life one's actions are for ever regulated by conditions which are neither of one's own seeking nor within one's power of controlling."

At these words all brightness left Mian's manner, for she at once understood that Ling referred to his departure, of which she herself had lately come to think with unrestrained agitation.

"Oh, Ling," she exclaimed at length, "most expert of sword-users and most noble of men, surely never was a maiden more inelegantly placed than the one who is now by your side. To you she owes her life, yet it is unseemly for her even to speak of the incident; to you she must look for protection, yet she cannot ask you to stay by her side. She is indeed alone. The magician is dead, Ki has fallen, Ling is going, and Mian is undoubtedly the most unhappy and solitary person between the Wall and the Nan Hai."

"Beloved Mian," exclaimed Ling, with inspiring vehemence, "and is not the utterly unworthy person before you indebted to you in a double measure that life is still within him? Is not the strength which now promotes him to such exceptional audacity as to aspire to your lovely hand, of your own creating? Only encourage Ling to entertain a well-founded hope that on his return he shall not find you partaking of the wedding feast of some wealthy and exceptionally round-bodied Mandarin, and this person will accomplish the journey to Canton and back as it were in four strides."

"Oh, Ling, reflexion of my ideal, holder of my soul, it would indeed be very disagreeable to my own feelings to make any reply save one," replied Mian, scarcely above a breath-voice. "Gratitude alone would direct me, were it not that the great love which fills me leaves no resting-place for any other emotion than itself. Go if you must, but return quickly, for your absence will weigh upon Mian like a dragon-dream."

"Violet light of my eyes," exclaimed Ling, "even in surroundings which with the exception of the matter before us are uninspiring in the extreme, your virtuous and retiring encouragement yet raises me to such a commanding eminence of demonstrative happiness that I fear I shall become intolerably self-opinionated towards my fellow-men in consequence."

"Such a thing is impossible with my Ling," said Mian, with conviction. "But must you indeed journey to Canton?"

"Alas!" replied Ling, "gladly would this person decide against such a course did the matter rest with him, for as the Verses say, 'It is needless to apply the ram's head to the unlocked door.' But Ki is demolished, the unassuming Mandarin Li Keen has retired to Peking, and of the fortunes of his bowmen this person is entirely ignorant."

"Such as survived returned to their homes," replied Mian, "and Si-chow is safe, for the scattered and broken rebels fled to the mountains again; so much this person has learned."

"In that case Si-chow is undoubtedly safe for the time, and can be left with prudence," said Ling. "It is an unfortunate circumstance that there is no Mandarin of authority between here and Canton who can receive from this person a statement of past facts and give him instructions for the future."

"And what will be the nature of such instructions as will be given at Canton?" demanded Mian.

"By chance they may take the form of raising another company of bowmen," said Ling, with a sigh, "but, indeed, if this person can obtain any weight by means of his past service, they will tend towards a pleasant and unambitious civil appointment."

"Oh, my artless and noble-minded lover!" exclaimed Mian, "assuredly a veil has been before your eyes during your residence in Canton, and your naturally benevolent mind has turned all things into good, or you would not thus hopefully refer to your brilliant exploits in the past. Of what commercial benefit have they been to the sordid and miserly persons in authority, or in what way have they diverted a stream of taels into their insatiable pockets? Far greater is the chance that had Si-chow fallen many of its household goods would have found their way into the Yamens of Canton. Assuredly in Li Keen you will have a friend who will make many delicate allusions to your ancestors when you meet, and yet one who will float many barbed whispers to follow you when you have passed; for you have planted shame before him in the eyes of those who would otherwise neither have eyes to see nor tongues to discuss the matter. It is for such a reason that this person distrusts all things connected with the journey, except your constancy, oh, my true and strong one."

"Such faithfulness would alone be sufficient to assure my safe return if the matter were properly represented to the supreme Deities," said Ling. "Let not the thin curtain of bitter water stand before your lustrous eyes any longer, then, the events which have followed one another in the past few days in a fashion that can only be likened to thunder following lightning are indeed sufficient to distress one with so refined and swan-like an organization, but they are now assuredly at an end."

"It is a hope of daily recurrence to this person," replied Mian, honourably endeavouring to restrain the emotion which openly exhibited itself in her eyes; "for what maiden would not rather make successful offerings to the Great Mother Kum-Fa than have the most imposing and verbose Triumphal Arch erected to commemorate an empty and unsatisfying constancy?"

In this amiable manner the matter was arranged between Ling and Mian, as they sat together in the magician's garden drinking peach-tea, which the two attendants-not without discriminating and significant expressions between themselves-brought to them from time to time. Here Ling made clear the whole manner of his life from his earliest memory to the time when he fell in dignified combat, nor did Mian withhold anything, explaining in particular such charms and spells of the magician as she had knowledge of, and in this graceful manner materially assisting her lover in the many disagreeable encounters and conflicts which he was shortly to experience.

It was with even more objectionable feelings than before that Ling now contemplated his journey to Canton, involving as it did the separation from one who had become as the shadow of his existence, and by whose side he had an undoubted claim to stand. Yet the necessity of the undertaking was no less than before, and the full possession of all his natural powers took away his only excuse for delaying in the matter. Without any pleasurable anticipations, therefore, he consulted the Sacred Flat and Round Sticks, and learning that the following day would be propitious for the journey, he arranged to set out in accordance with the omen.

When the final moment arrived at which the invisible threads of constantly passing emotions from one to the other must be broken, and when Mian perceived that her lover's horse was restrained at the door by the two attendants, who with unsuspected delicacy of feeling had taken this opportunity of withdrawing, the noble endurance which had hitherto upheld her melted away, and she became involved in very melancholy and obscure meditations until she observed that Ling also was quickly becoming affected by a similar gloom.

"Alas!" she exclaimed, "how unworthy a person I am thus to impose upon my lord a greater burden than that which already weighs him down! Rather ought this one to dwell upon the happiness of that day, when, after successfully evading or overthrowing the numerous bands of assassins which infest the road from here to Canton, and after escaping or recovering from the many deadly pestilences which invariably reduce that city at this season of the year, he shall triumphantly return. Assuredly there is a highly-polished surface united to every action in life, no matter how funereal it may at first appear. Indeed, there are many incidents compared with which death itself is welcome, and to this end Mian has reserved a farewell gift."

Speaking in this manner the devoted and magnanimous maiden placed in Ling's hands the transparent vessel of liquid which the magician had grasped when he fell. "This person," she continued, speaking with difficulty, "places her lover's welfare incomparably before her own happiness, and should he ever find himself in a situation which is unendurably oppressive, and from which death is the only escape-such as inevitable tortures, the infliction of violent madness, or the subjection by magic to the will of some designing woman-she begs him to accept this means of freeing himself without regarding her anguish beyond expressing a clearly defined last wish that the two persons in question may be in the end happily reunited in another existence."

Assured by this last evidence of affection, Ling felt that he had no longer any reason for internal heaviness; his spirits were immeasurably raised by the fragrant incense of Mian's great devotion, and under its influence he was even able to breathe towards her a few words of similar comfort as he left the spot and began his journey.

IX

On entering Canton, which he successfully accomplished without any unpleasant adventure, the marked absence of any dignified ostentation which had been accountable for many of Ling's misfortunes in the past, impelled him again to reside in the same insignificant apartment that he had occupied when he first visited the city as an unknown and unimportant candidate. In consequence of this, when Ling was communicating to any person the signs by which messengers might find him, he was compelled to add, "the neighbourhood in which this contemptible person resides is that officially known as 'the mean quarter favoured by the lower class of those who murder by treachery,'" and for this reason he was not always treated with the regard to which his attainments entitled him, or which he would have unquestionably received had he been able to describe himself as of "the partly-drained and uninfected area reserved to Mandarins and their friends."

It was with an ignoble feeling of mental distress that Ling exhibited himself at the Chief Office of Warlike Deeds and Arrangements on the following day; for the many disadvantageous incidents of his past life had repeated themselves before his eyes while he slept, and the not unhopeful emotions which he had felt when in the inspiring presence of Mian were now altogether absent. In spite of the fact that he reached the office during the early gong strokes of the morning, it was not until the withdrawal of light that he reached any person who was in a position to speak with him on the matter, so numerous were the lesser ones through whose chambers he had to pass in the process. At length he found himself in the presence of an upper one who had the appearance of being acquainted with the circumstances, and who received him with dignity, though not with any embarrassing exhibition of respect or servility.

"'The hero of the illustrious encounter beyond the walls of Si-chow,'" exclaimed that official, reading the words from the tablet of introduction which Ling had caused to be carried into him, and at the same time examining the person in question closely. "Indeed, no such one is known to those within this office, unless the words chance to point to the courteous and unassuming Mandarin Li Keen, who, however, is at this moment recovering his health at Peking, as set forth in the amiable and impartial report which we have lately received from him."

At these words Ling plainly understood that there was little hope of the last events becoming profitable on his account.

"Did not the report to which allusion has been made bear reference to one Ling, Commander of the Archers, who thrice led on the fighting men, and who was finally successful in causing the rebels to disperse towards the mountains?" he asked, in a voice which somewhat trembled.

"There is certainly reference to one of the name you mention," said the other; "but regarding the terms-perhaps this person would better protect his own estimable time by displaying the report within your sight."

With these words the upper one struck a gong several times, and after receiving from an inner chamber the parchment in question, he placed it before Ling, at the same time directing a lesser one to interpose between it and the one who read it a large sheet of transparent substance, so that destruction might not come to it, no matter in what way its contents affected the reader. Thereon Ling perceived the following facts, very skilfully inscribed with the evident purpose of inducing persons to believe, without question, that words so elegantly traced must of necessity be truthful also.

"A Benevolent Example of the Intelligent Arrangement by which the most Worthy Persons outlive those who are Incapable.

"The circumstances connected with the office of the valuable and accomplished Mandarin of Warlike Deeds and Arrangements at Si-chow have, in recent times, been of anything but a prepossessing order. Owing to the very inadequate methods adopted by those who earn a livelihood by conveying necessities from the more enlightened portions of the Empire to that place, it so came about that for a period of five days the Yamen was entirely unsupplied with the fins of sharks or even with goats' eyes. To add to the polished Mandarin's distress of mind the barbarous and slow-witted rebels who infest those parts took this opportunity to destroy the town and most of its inhabitants, the matter coming about as follows:

"The feeble and commonplace person named Ling who commands the bowmen had but recently been elevated to that distinguished position from a menial and degraded occupation (for which, indeed, his stunted intellect more aptly fitted him); and being in consequence very greatly puffed out in self-gratification, he became an easy prey to the cunning of the rebels, and allowed himself to be beguiled into a trap, paying for this contemptible stupidity with his life. The town of Si-chow was then attacked, and being in this manner left defenceless through the weakness-or treachery-of the person Ling, who had contrived to encompass the entire destruction of his unyielding company, it fell after a determined and irreproachable resistance; the Mandarin Li Keen being told, as, covered with the blood of the foemen, he was dragged away from the thickest part of the unequal conflict by his followers, that he was the last person to leave the town. On his way to Peking with news of this valiant defence, the Mandarin was joined by the Chief of Bowmen, who had understood and avoided the very obvious snare into which the stagnant-minded Commander had led his followers, in spite of disinterested advice to the contrary. For this intelligent perception, and for general nobility of conduct when in battle, the versatile Chief of Bowmen is by this written paper strongly recommended to the dignity of receiving the small metal Embellishment of Valour.

"It has been suggested to the Mandarin Li Keen that the bestowal of the Crystal Button would only be a fit and graceful reward for his indefatigable efforts to uphold the dignity of the sublime Emperor; but to all such persons the Mandarin has sternly replied that such a proposal would more fitly originate from the renowned and valuable Office of Warlike Deeds and Arrangements, he well knowing that the wise and engaging persons who conduct that indispensable and well-regulated department are gracefully voracious in their efforts to reward merit, even when it is displayed, as in the case in question, by one who from his position will inevitably soon be urgently petitioning in a like manner on their behalf."

When Ling had finished reading this elegantly arranged but exceedingly misleading parchment, he looked up with eyes from which he vainly endeavoured to restrain the signs of undignified emotion, and said to the upper one:

"It is difficult employment for a person to refrain from unendurable thoughts when his unassuming and really conscientious efforts are represented in a spirit of no satisfaction, yet in this matter the very expert Li Keen appears to have gone beyond himself; the Commander Ling, who is herein represented as being slain by the enemy, is, indeed, the person who is standing before you, and all the other statements are in a like exactness."

"The short-sighted individual who for some hidden desire of his own is endeavouring to present himself as the corrupt and degraded creature Ling, has overlooked one important circumstance," said the upper one, smiling in a very intolerable manner, at the same time causing his head to move slightly from side to side in the fashion of one who rebukes with assumed geniality; and, turning over the written paper, he displayed upon the under side the Imperial vermilion Sign. "Perhaps," he continued, "the omniscient person will still continue in his remarks, even with the evidence of the Emperor's unerring pencil to refute him."

At these words and the undoubted testimony of the red mark, which plainly declared the whole of the written matter to be composed of truth, no matter what might afterwards transpire, Ling understood that very little prosperity remained with him.

"But the town of Si-chow," he suggested, after examining his mind; "if any person in authority visited the place, he would inevitably find it standing and its inhabitants in agreeable health."

"The persistent person who is so assiduously occupying my intellectual moments with empty words seems to be unaccountably deficient in his knowledge of the customs of refined society and of the meaning of the Imperial Signet," said the other, with an entire absence of benevolent consideration. "That Si-chow has fallen and that Ling is dead are two utterly uncontroversial matters truthfully recorded. If a person visited Si-chow, he might find it rebuilt or even inhabited by those from the neighbouring villages or by evil spirits taking the forms of the ones who formerly lived there; as in a like manner, Ling might be restored to existence by magic, or his body might be found and possessed by an outcast demon who desired to revisit the earth for a period. Such circumstances do not in any way disturb the announcement that Si-chow has without question fallen, and that Ling has officially ceased to live, of which events notifications have been sent to all who are concerned in the matters."

As the upper one ceased speaking, four strokes sounded upon the gong, and Ling immediately found himself carried into the street by the current of both lesser and upper ones who poured forth at the signal. The termination of this conversation left Ling in a more unenviable state of dejection than any of the many preceding misfortunes had done, for with enlarged inducements to possess himself of a competent appointment he seemed to be even further removed from this attainment than he had been at any time in his life. He might, indeed, present himself again for the public examinations; but in order to do even that it would be necessary for him to wait almost a year, nor could he assure himself that his efforts would again be likely to result in an equal success. Doubts also arose within his mind of the course which he should follow in such a case; whether to adopt a new name, involving as it would certain humiliation and perhaps disgrace if detection overtook his footsteps, or still to possess the title of one who was in a measure dead, and hazard the likelihood of having any prosperity which he might obtain reduced to nothing if the fact should become public.

As Ling reflected upon such details he found himself without intention before the house of a wise person who had become very wealthy by advising others on all matters, but chiefly on those connected with strange occurrences and such events as could not be settled definitely either one way or the other until a remote period had been reached. Becoming assailed by a curious desire to know what manner of evils particularly attached themselves to such as were officially dead but who nevertheless had an ordinary existence, Ling placed himself before this person, and after arranging the manner of reward related to him so many of the circumstances as were necessary to enable a full understanding to be reached, but at the same time in no way betraying his own interest in the matter.

"Such inflictions are to no degree frequent," said the wise person after he had consulted a polished sphere of the finest red jade for some time; "and this is in a measure to be regretted, as the hair of these persons-provided they die a violent death, which is invariably the case-constitutes a certain protection against being struck by falling stars, or becoming involved in unsuccessful law cases. The persons in question can be recognized with certainty in the public ways by the unnatural pallor of their faces and by the general repulsiveness of their appearance, but as they soon take refuge in suicide, unless they have the fortune to be removed previously by accident, it is an infrequent matter that one is gratified by the sight. During their existence they are subject to many disorders from which the generality of human beings are benevolently preserved; they possess no rights of any kind, and if by any chance they are detected in an act of a seemingly depraved nature, they are liable to judgment at the hands of the passers-by without any form whatever, and to punishment of a more severe order than that administered to commonplace criminals. There are many other disadvantages affecting such persons when they reach the Middle Air, of which the chief—"

"This person is immeasurably indebted for such a clear explanation of the position," interrupted Ling, who had a feeling of not desiring to penetrate further into the detail; "but as he perceives a line of anxious ones eagerly waiting at the door to obtain advice and consolation from so expert and amiable a wizard, he will not make himself uncongenial any longer with his very feeble topics of conversation."

By this time Ling plainly comprehended that he had been marked out from the beginning-perhaps for all the knowledge which he had to the opposite effect, from a period in the life of a far-removed ancestor-to be an object of marked derision and the victim of all manner of malevolent demons in whatever actions he undertook. In this condition of understanding his mind turned gratefully to the parting gift of Mian whom he had now no hope of possessing; for the intolerable thought of uniting her to so objectionable a being as himself would have been dismissed as utterly inelegant even had he been in a manner of living to provide for her adequately, which itself seemed clearly impossible. Disregarding all similar emotions, therefore, he walked without pausing to his abode, and stretching his body upon the rushes, drank the entire liquid unhesitatingly, and prepared to pass beyond with a tranquil mind entirely given up to thoughts and images of Mian.

X

Upon a certain occasion, the particulars of which have already been recorded, Ling had judged himself to have passed into the form of a spirit on beholding the ethereal form of Mian bending over him. After swallowing the entire liquid, which had cost the dead magician so much to distil and make perfect, it was with a well-assured determination of never again awakening that he lost the outward senses and floated in the Middle Air, so that when his eyes next opened upon what seemed to be the bare walls of his own chamber, his first thought was a natural conviction that the matter had been so arranged either out of a charitable desire that he should not be overcome by a too sudden transition to unparalleled splendour, or that such a reception was the outcome of some dignified jest on the part of certain lesser and more cheerful spirits. After waiting in one position for several hours, however, and receiving no summons or manifestation of a celestial nature, he began to doubt the qualities of the liquid, and applying certain tests, he soon ascertained that he was still in the lower world and unharmed. Nevertheless, this circumstance did not tend in any way to depress his mind, for, doubtless owing to some hidden virtue of the fluid, he felt an enjoyable emotion that he still lived; all his attributes appeared to be purified, and he experienced an inspired certainty of feeling that an illustrious and highly-remunerative future lay before one who still had an ordinary existence after being both officially killed and self-poisoned.

In this intelligent disposition thoughts of Mian recurred to him with unreproved persistence, and in order to convey to her an account of the various matters which had engaged him since his arrival at the city, and a well-considered declaration of the unchanged state of his own feelings towards her, he composed and despatched with impetuous haste the following delicate verses:

Constancy

    About the walls and gates of Canton
    Are many pleasing and entertaining maidens;
    Indeed, in the eyes of their friends and of the passers-by
    Some of them are exceptionally adorable.
    The person who is inscribing these lines, however,
    Sees before him, as it were, an assemblage of deformed and un-prepossessing hags,
    Venerable in age and inconsiderable in appearance;
    For the dignified and majestic image of Mian is ever before him,
    Making all others very inferior.
        Within the houses and streets of Canton
    Hang many bright lanterns.
    The ordinary person who has occasion to walk by night
    Professes to find them highly lustrous.
    But there is one who thinks contrary facts,

    And when he goes forth he carries two long curved poles
    To prevent him from stumbling among the dark and hidden places;
    For he has gazed into the brilliant and pellucid orbs of Mian,
    And all other lights are dull and practically opaque.
       In various parts of the literary quarter of Canton
    Reside such as spend their time in inward contemplation.
    In spite of their generally uninviting exteriors
    Their reflexions are often of a very profound order.
    Yet the unpopular and persistently-abused Ling
    Would unhesitatingly prefer his own thoughts to theirs,
    For what makes this person's thoughts far more pleasing
    Is that they are invariably connected with the virtuous and ornamental Mian.

Becoming very amiably disposed after this agreeable occupation, Ling surveyed himself at the disc of polished metal, and observed with surprise and shame the rough and uninviting condition of his person. He had, indeed, although it was not until some time later that he became aware of the circumstance, slept for five days without interruption, and it need not therefore be a matter of wonder or of reproach to him that his smooth surfaces had become covered with short hair. Reviling himself bitterly for the appearance which he conceived he must have exhibited when he conducted his business, and to which he now in part attributed his ill-success, Ling went forth without delay, and quickly discovering one of those who remove hair publicly for a very small sum, he placed himself in the chair, and directed that his face, arms, and legs should be denuded after the manner affected by the ones who make a practice of observing the most recent customs.

    "Did the illustrious individual who is now conferring distinction on this really worn-out chair by occupying it express himself in favour of having the face entirely denuded?" demanded the one who conducted the operation; for these persons have become famous for their elegant and persistent ability to discourse, and frequently assume ignorance in order that they themselves may make reply, and not for the purpose of gaining knowledge. "Now, in the objectionable opinion of this unintelligent person, who has a presumptuous habit of offering his very undesirable advice, a slight covering on the upper lip, delicately arranged and somewhat fiercely pointed at the extremities, would bestow an appearance of-how shall this illiterate person explain himself? —dignity? —matured reflexion? —doubtless the accomplished nobleman before me will understand what is intended with a more knife-like accuracy than this person can describe it-but confer that highly desirable effect upon the face of which at present it is entirely destitute... 'Entirely denuded?' Then without fail it shall certainly be so, O incomparable personage... Does the versatile Mandarin now present profess any concern as to the condition of the rice plants?... Indeed, the remark is an inspired one; the subject is totally devoid of interest to a person of intelligence... A remarkable and gravity-removing event transpired within the notice of this unassuming person recently. A discriminating individual had purchased from him a portion of his justly renowned Thrice-extracted Essence of Celestial Herb Oil—a preparation which in this experienced person's opinion, indeed, would greatly relieve the undoubted afflictions from which the one before him is evidently suffering-when after once anointing himself—"

    A lengthy period containing no words caused Ling, who had in the meantime closed his eyes and lost Canton and all else in delicate thoughts of Mian, to look up. That which met his attention on doing so filled him with an intelligent wonder, for the person before him held in his hand what had the appearance of a tuft of bright yellow hair, which shone in the light of the sun with a most engaging splendour, but which he nevertheless regarded with a most undignified expression of confusion and awe.

    "Illustrious demon," he cried at length, kow-towing very respectfully, "have the extreme amiableness to be of a benevolent disposition, and do not take an unworthy and entirely unremunerative revenge upon this very unimportant person for failing to detect and honour you from the beginning."

"Such words indicate nothing beyond an excess of hemp spirit," answered Ling, with signs of displeasure. "To gain my explicit esteem, make me smooth without delay, and do not exhibit before me the lock of hair which, from its colour and appearance, has evidently adorned the head of one of those maidens whose duty it is to quench the thirst of travellers in the long narrow rooms of this city."

"Majestic and anonymous spirit," said the other, with extreme reverence, and an entire absence of the appearance of one who had gazed into too many vessels, "if such be your plainly-expressed desire, this superficial person will at once proceed to make smooth your peach-like skin, and with a carefulness inspired by the certainty that the most unimportant wound would give forth liquid fire, in which he would undoubtedly perish. Nevertheless, he desires to make it evident that this hair is from the head of no maiden, being, indeed, the uneven termination of your own sacred pigtail, which this excessively self-confident slave took the inexcusable liberty of removing, and which changed in this manner within his hand in order to administer a fit reproof for his intolerable presumption."

Impressed by the mien and unquestionable earnestness of the remover of hair, Ling took the matter which had occasioned these various emotions in his hand and examined it. His amazement was still greater when he perceived that-in spite of the fact that it presented every appearance of having been cut from his own person-none of the qualities of hair remained in it; it was hard and wire-like, possessing, indeed, both the nature and the appearance of a metal.

As he gazed fixedly and with astonishment, there came back into the remembrance of Ling certain obscure and little-understood facts connected with the limitless wealth possessed by the Yellow Emperor-of which the great gold life-like image in the Temple of Internal Symmetry at Peking alone bears witness now-and of his lost secret. Many very forcible prophecies and omens in his own earlier life, of which the rendering and accomplishment had hitherto seemed to be dark and incomplete, passed before him, and various matters which Mian had related to him concerning the habits and speech of the magician took definite form within his mind. Deeply impressed by the exact manner in which all these circumstances fitted together, one into another, Ling rewarded the person before him greatly beyond his expectation, and hurried without delay to his own chamber.

XI

For many hours Ling remained in his room, examining in his mind all passages, either in his own life or in the lives of others, which might by any chance have influence on the event before him. In this thorough way he became assured that the competition and its results, his journey to Si-chow with the encounter in the cypress wood, the flight of the incapable and treacherous Mandarin, and the battle of Ki, were all, down to the matter of the smallest detail, parts of a symmetrical and complete scheme, tending to his present condition. Cheered and upheld by this proof of the fact that very able deities were at work on his behalf, he turned his intellect from the entrancing subject to a contemplation of the manner in which his condition would enable him to frustrate the uninventive villainies of the obstinate person Li Keen, and to provide a suitable house and mode of living to which he would be justified in introducing Mian, after adequate marriage ceremonies had been observed between them. In this endeavour he was less successful than he had imagined would be the case, for when he had first fully understood that his body was of such a substance that nothing was wanting to transmute it into fine gold but the absence of the living spirit, he had naturally, and without deeply examining the detail, assumed that so much gold might be considered to be in his possession. Now, however, a very definite thought arose within him that his own wishes and interests would have been better secured had the benevolent spirits who undertook the matter placed the secret within his knowledge in such a way as to enable him to administer the fluid to some very heavy and inexpensive animal, so that the issue which seemed inevitable before the enjoyment of the riches could be entered upon should not have touched his own comfort so closely. To a person of Ling's refined imagination it could not fail to be a subject of internal reproach that while he would become the most precious dead body in the world, his value in life might not be very honourably placed even by the most complimentary one who should require his services. Then came the thought, which, however degraded, he found himself unable to put quite beyond him, that if in the meantime he were able to gain a sufficiency for Mian and himself, even her pure and delicate love might not be able to bear so offensive a test as that of seeing him grow old and remain intolerably healthy-perhaps with advancing years actually becoming lighter day by day, and thereby lessening in value before her eyes-when the natural infirmities of age and the presence of an ever-increasing posterity would make even a moderate amount of taels of inestimable value.

No doubt remained in Ling's mind that the process of frequently making smooth his surfaces would yield an amount of gold enough to suffice for his own needs, but a brief consideration of the matter convinced him that this source would be inadequate to maintain an entire household even if he continually denuded himself to an almost ignominious extent. As he fully weighed these varying chances the certainty became more clear to him with every thought that for the virtuous enjoyment of Mian's society one great sacrifice was required of him. This act, it seemed to be intimated, would without delay provide for an affluent and lengthy future, and at the same time would influence all the spirits-even those who had been hitherto evilly-disposed towards him-in such a manner that his enemies would be removed from his path by a process which would expose them to public ridicule, and he would be assured in founding an illustrious and enduring line. To accomplish this successfully necessitated the loss of at least the greater part of one entire member, and for some time the disadvantages of going through an existence with only a single leg or arm seemed more than a sufficient price to pay even for the definite advantages which would be made over to him in return. This unworthy thought, however, could not long withstand the memory of Mian's steadfast and high-minded affection, and the certainty of her enlightened gladness at his return even in the imperfect condition which he anticipated. Nor was there absent from his mind a dimly-understood hope that the matter did not finally rest with him, but that everything which he might be inspired to do was in reality only a portion of the complete and arranged system into which he had been drawn, and in which his part had been assigned to him from the beginning without power for him to deviate, no matter how much to the contrary the thing should appear.

As no advantage would be gained by making any delay, Ling at once sought the most favourable means of putting his resolution into practice, and after many skilful and insidious inquiries he learnt of an accomplished person who made a consistent habit of cutting off limbs which had become troublesome to their possessors either through accident or disease. Furthermore, he was said to be of a sincere and charitable disposition, and many persons declared that on no occasion had he been known to make use of the helpless condition of those who visited him in order to extort money from them.

Coming to the ill-considered conclusion that he would be able to conceal within his own breast the true reason for the operation, Ling placed himself before the person in question, and exhibited the matter to him so that it would appear as though his desires were promoted by the presence of a small but persistent sprite which had taken its abode within his left thigh, and there resisted every effort of the most experienced wise persons to induce it to come forth again. Satisfied with this explanation of the necessity of the deed, the one who undertook the matter proceeded, with Ling's assistance, to sharpen his cutting instruments and to heat the hardening irons; but no sooner had he made a shallow mark to indicate the lines which his knife should take, than his subtle observation at once showed him that the facts had been represented to him in a wrong sense, and that his visitor, indeed, was composed of no common substance. Being of a gentle and forbearing disposition, he did not manifest any indication of rage at the discovery, but amiably and unassumingly pointed out that such a course was not respectful towards himself, and that, moreover, Ling might incur certain well-defined and highly undesirable maladies as a punishment for the deception.

Overcome with remorse at deceiving so courteous and noble-minded a person, Ling fully explained the circumstances to him, not even concealing from him certain facts which related to the actions of remote ancestors, but which, nevertheless, appeared to have influenced the succession of events. When he had made an end of the narrative, the other said:

"Behold now, it is truly remarked that every Mandarin has three hands and every soldier a like number of feet, yet it is a saying which is rather to be regarded as manifesting the deep wisdom and discrimination of the speaker than as an actual fact which can be taken advantage of when one is so minded-least of all by so valiant a Commander as the one before me, who has clearly proved that in time of battle he has exactly reversed the position."

"The loss would undoubtedly be of considerable inconvenience occasionally," admitted Ling, "yet none the less the sage remark of Huai Mei-shan, 'When actually in the embrace of a voracious and powerful wild animal, the desirability of leaving a limb is not a matter to be subjected to lengthy consideration,' is undoubtedly a valuable guide for general conduct. This person has endured many misfortunes and suffered many injustices; he has known the wolf-gnawings of great hopes, which have withered and daily grown less when the difficulties of maintaining an honourable and illustrious career have unfolded themselves within his sight. Before him still lie the attractions of a moderate competency to be shared with the one whose absence would make even the Upper Region unendurable, and after having this entrancing future once shattered by the tiger-like cupidity of a depraved and incapable Mandarin, he is determined to welcome even the sacrifice which you condemn rather than let the opportunity vanish through indecision."

"It is not an unworthy or abandoned decision," said the one whose aid Ling had invoked, "nor a matter in which this person would refrain from taking part, were there no other and more agreeable means by which the same results may be attained. A circumstance has occurred within this superficial person's mind, however: A brother of the one who is addressing you is by profession one of those who purchase large undertakings for which they have not the money to pay, and who thereupon by various expedients gain the ear of the thrifty, enticing them by fair offers of return to entrust their savings for the purpose of paying off the debt. These persons are ever on the watch for transactions by which they inevitably prosper without incurring any obligation, and doubtless my brother will be able to gather a just share of the value of your highly-remunerative body without submitting you to the insufferable annoyance of losing a great part of it prematurely."

Without clearly understanding how so inviting an arrangement could be effected, the manner of speaking was exceedingly alluring to Ling's mind, perplexed as he had become through weighing and considering the various attitudes of the entire matter. To receive a certain and sufficient sum of money without his person being in any way mutilated would be a satisfactory, but as far as he had been able to observe an unapproachable, solution to the difficulty. In the mind of the amiable person with whom he was conversing, however, the accomplishment did not appear to be surrounded by unnatural obstacles, so that Ling was content to leave the entire design in his hands, after stating that he would again present himself on a certain occasion when it was asserted that the brother in question would be present.

So internally lightened did Ling feel after this inspiring conversation, and so confident of a speedy success had the obliging person's words made him become, that for the first time since his return to Canton he was able to take an intellectual interest in the pleasures of the city. Becoming aware that the celebrated play entitled "The Precious Lamp of Spotted Butterfly Temple" was in process of being shown at the Tea Garden of Rainbow Lights and Voices, he purchased an entrance, and after passing several hours in this conscientious enjoyment, returned to his chamber, and passed a night untroubled by any manifestations of an unpleasant nature.

XII

Chang-ch'un, the brother of the one to whom Ling had applied in his determination, was confidently stated to be one of the richest persons in Canton. So great was the number of enterprises in which he had possessions, that he himself was unable to keep an account of them, and it was asserted that upon occasions he had run through the streets, crying aloud that such an undertaking had been the subject of most inferior and uninviting dreams and omens (a custom observed by those who wish a venture ill), whereas upon returning and consulting his written parchments, it became plain to him that he had indulged in a very objectionable exhibition, as he himself was the person most interested in the success of the matter. Far from discouraging him, however, such incidents tended to his advantage, as he could consistently point to them in proof of his unquestionable commercial honourableness, and in this way many persons of all classes, not only in Canton, or in the Province, but all over the Empire, would unhesitatingly entrust money to be placed in undertakings which he had purchased and was willing to describe as "of much good." A certain class of printed leaves-those in which Chang-ch'un did not insert purchased mentions of his forthcoming ventures or verses recording his virtues (in return for buying many examples of the printed leaf containing them) —took frequent occasion of reminding persons that Chang-ch'un owed the beginning of his prosperity to finding a written parchment connected with a Mandarin of exalted rank and a low caste attendant at the Ti-i tea-house among the paper heaps, which it was at that time his occupation to assort into various departments according to their quality and commercial value. Such printed leaves freely and unhesitatingly predicted that the day on which he would publicly lose face was incomparably nearer than that on which the Imperial army would receive its back pay, and in a quaint and gravity-removing manner advised him to protect himself against an obscure but inevitable poverty by learning the accomplishment of chair-carrying —an occupation for which his talents and achievements fitted him in a high degree, they remarked.

In spite of these evilly intentioned remarks, and of illustrations representing him as being bowstrung for treacherous killing, being seized in the action of secretly conveying money from passers-by to himself and other similar annoying references to his private life, Chang-ch'un did not fail to prosper, and his undertakings succeeded to such an extent that without inquiry into the detail many persons were content to describe as "gold-lined" anything to which he affixed his sign, and to hazard their savings for staking upon the ventures. In all other departments of life Chang was equally successful; his chief wife was the daughter of one who stood high in the Emperor's favour; his repast table was never unsupplied with sea-snails, rats' tongues, or delicacies of an equally expensive nature, and it was confidently maintained that there was no official in Canton, not even putting aside the Taotai, who dare neglect to fondle Chang's hand if he publicly offered it to him for that purpose.

It was at the most illustrious point of his existence-at the time, indeed, when after purchasing without money the renowned and proficient charm-water Ho-Ko for a million taels, he had sold it again for ten-that Chang was informed by his brother of the circumstances connected with Ling. After becoming specially assured that the matter was indeed such as it was represented to be, Chang at once discerned that the venture was of too certain and profitable a nature to be put before those who entrusted their money to him in ordinary and doubtful cases. He accordingly called together certain persons whom he was desirous of obliging, and informing them privately and apart from business terms that the opportunity was one of exceptional attractiveness, he placed the facts before them. After displaying a number of diagrams bearing upon the mater, he proposed that they should form an enterprise to be called "The Ling (After Death) Without Much Risk Assembly." The manner of conducting this undertaking he explained to be as follows: The body of Ling, whenever the spirit left it, should become as theirs to be used for profit. For this benefit they would pay Ling fifty thousand taels when the understanding was definitely arrived at, five thousand taels each year until the matter ended, and when that period arrived another fifty thousand taels to persons depending upon him during his life. Having stated the figure business, Chang-ch'un put down his written papers, and causing his face to assume the look of irrepressible but dignified satisfaction which it was his custom to wear on most occasions, and especially when he had what appeared at first sight to be evil news to communicate to public assemblages of those who had entrusted money to his ventures, he proceeded to disclose the advantages of such a system. At the extreme, he said, the amount which they would be required to pay would be two hundred and fifty thousand taels; but this was in reality a very misleading view of the circumstance, as he would endeavour to show them. For one detail, he had allotted to Ling thirty years of existence, which was the extreme amount according to the calculations of those skilled in such prophecies; but, as they were all undoubtedly aware, persons of very expert intellects were known to enjoy a much shorter period of life than the gross and ordinary, and as Ling was clearly one of the former, by the fact of his contriving so ingenious a method of enriching himself, they might with reasonable foresight rely upon his departing when half the period had been attained; in that way seventy-five thousand taels would be restored to them, for every year represented a saving of five thousand. Another agreeable contemplation was that of the last sum, for by such a time they would have arrived at the most pleasurable part of the enterprise: a million taels' worth of pure gold would be displayed before them, and the question of the final fifty thousand could be disposed of by cutting off an arm or half a leg. Whether they adopted that course, or decided to increase their fortunes by exposing so exceptional and symmetrical a wonder to the public gaze in all the principal cities of the Empire, was a circumstance which would have to be examined within their minds when the time approached. In such a way the detail of purchase stood revealed as only fifty thousand taels in reality, a sum so despicably insignificant that he had internal pains at mentioning it to so wealthy a group of Mandarins, and he had not yet made clear to them that each year they would receive gold to the amount of almost a thousand taels. This would be the result of Ling making smooth his surfaces, and it would enable them to know that the person in question actually existed, and to keep the circumstances before their intellects.

When Chang-Ch'un had made the various facts clear to this extent, those who were assembled expressed their feelings as favourably turned towards the project, provided the tests to which Ling was to be put should prove encouraging, and a secure and intelligent understanding of things to be done and not to be done could be arrived at between them. To this end Ling was brought into the chamber, and fixing his thoughts steadfastly upon Mian, he permitted portions to be cut from various parts of his body without betraying any signs of ignoble agitation. No sooner had the pieces been separated and the virtue of Ling's existence passed from them than they changed colour and hardened, nor could the most delicate and searching trials to which they were exposed by a skilful worker in metals, who was obtained for the purpose, disclose any particular, however minute, in which they differed from the finest gold. The hair, the nails, and the teeth were similarly affected, and even Ling's blood dried into a fine gold powder. This detail of the trial being successfully completed, Ling subjected himself to intricate questioning on all matters connected with his religion and manner of conducting himself, both in public and privately, the history and behaviour of his ancestors, the various omens and remarkable sayings which had reference to his life and destiny, and the intentions which he then possessed regarding his future movements and habits of living. All the wise sayings and written and printed leaves which made any allusion to the existence of and possibility of discovery of the wonderful gold fluid were closely examined, and found to be in agreement, whereupon those present made no further delay in admitting that the facts were indeed as they had been described, and indulged in a dignified stroking of each other's faces as an expression of pleasure and in proof of their satisfaction at taking part in so entrancing and remunerative an affair. At Chang's command many rare and expensive wines were then brought in, and partaken of without restraint by all persons, the repast being lightened by numerous well-considered and gravity-removing jests having reference to Ling and the unusual composition of his person. So amiably were the hours occupied that it was past the time of no light when Chang rose and read at full length the statement of things to be done and things not to be done, which was to be sealed by Ling for his part and the other persons who were present for theirs. It so happened, however, that at that period Ling's mind was filled with brilliant and versatile thoughts and images of Mian, and many-hued visions of the manner in which they would spend the entrancing future which was now before them, and in this way it chanced that he did not give any portion of his intellect to the reading, mistaking it, indeed, for a delicate and very ably-composed set of verses which Chang-ch'un was reciting as a formal blessing on parting. Nor was it until he was desired to affix his sign that Ling discovered his mistake, and being of too respectful and unobtrusive a disposition to require the matter to be repeated then, he carried out the obligation without in any particular understanding the written words to which he was agreeing.

As Ling walked through the streets to his chamber after leaving the house and company of Chang-Ch'un, holding firmly among his garments the thin printed papers to the amount of fifty thousand taels which he had received, and repeatedly speaking to himself in terms of general and specific encouragement at the fortunate events of the past few days, he became aware that a person of mean and rapacious appearance, whom he had some memory of having observed within the residence he had but just left, was continually by his side. Not at first doubting that the circumstance resulted from a benevolent desire on the part of Chang-ch'un that he should be protected on his passage through the city, Ling affected not to observe the incident; but upon reaching his own door the person in question persistently endeavoured to pass in also. Forming a fresh judgment about the matter, Ling, who was very powerfully constructed, and whose natural instincts were enhanced in every degree by the potent fluid of which he had lately partaken, repeatedly threw him across the street until he became weary of the diversion. At length, however, the thought arose that one who patiently submitted to continually striking the opposite houses with his head must have something of importance to communicate, whereupon he courteously invited him to enter the apartment and unweigh his mind.

"The facts of the case appear to have been somewhat inadequately represented," said the stranger, bowing obsequiously, "for this unornamental person was assured by the benignant Chang-ch'un that the one whose shadow he was to become was of a mild and forbearing nature."

"Such words are as the conversation of birds to me," replied Ling, not conjecturing how the matter had fallen about. "This person has just left the presence of the elegant and successful Chang-ch'un, and no word that he spoke gave indication of such a follower or such a service."

"Then it is indeed certain that the various transactions have not been fully understood," exclaimed the other, "for the exact communication to this unseemly one was, 'The valuable and enlightened Ling has heard and agreed to the different things to be done and not to be done, one phrase of which arranges for your continual presence, so that he will anticipate your attentions.'"

At these words the truth became as daylight before Ling's eyes, and he perceived that the written paper to which he had affixed his sign contained the detail of such an office as that of the person before him. When too late, more than ever did he regret that he had not formed some pretext for causing the document to be read a second time, as in view of his immediate intentions such an arrangement as the one to which he had agreed had every appearance of becoming of an irksome and perplexing nature. Desiring to know the length of the attendant's commands, Ling asked him for a clear statement of his duties, feigning that he had missed that portion of the reading through a momentary attack of the giddy sickness. To this request the stranger, who explained that his name was Wang, instantly replied that his written and spoken orders were: never to permit more than an arm's length of space to separate them; to prevent, by whatever force was necessary for the purpose, all attempts at evading the things to be done and not to be done, and to ignore as of no interest all other circumstances. It seemed to Ling, in consequence, that little seclusion would be enjoyed unless an arrangement could be effected between Wang and himself; so to this end, after noticing the evident poverty and covetousness of the person in question, he made him an honourable offer of frequent rewards, provided a greater distance was allowed to come between them as soon as Si-chow was reached. On his side, Ling undertook not to break through the wording of the things to be done and not to be done, and to notify to Wang any movements upon which he meditated. In this reputable manner the obstacle was ingeniously removed, and the intelligent nature of the device was clearly proved by the fact that not only Ling but Wang also had in the future a much greater liberty of action than would have been possible if it had been necessary to observe the short-sighted and evidently hastily-thought-of condition which Chang-ch'un had endeavoured to impose.

XIII

In spite of his natural desire to return to Mian as quickly as possible, Ling judged it expedient to give several days to the occupation of purchasing apparel of the richest kinds, weapons and armour in large quantities, jewels and ornaments of worked metals and other objects to indicate his changed position. Nor did he neglect actions of a pious and charitable nature, for almost his first care was to arrange with the chief ones at the Temple of Benevolent Intentions that each year, on the day corresponding to that on which he drank the gold fluid, a sumptuous and well-constructed coffin should be presented to the most deserving poor and aged person within that quarter of the city in which he had resided. When these preparations were completed, Ling set out with an extensive train of attendants; but riding on before, accompanied only by Wang, he quickly reached Si-chow without adventure.

The meeting between Ling and Mian was affecting to such an extent that the blind and deaf attendants wept openly without reproach, notwithstanding the fact that neither could become possessed of more than a half of the occurrence. Eagerly the two reunited ones examined each other's features to discover whether the separation had brought about any change in the beloved and well-remembered lines. Ling discovered upon Mian the shadow of an anxious care at his absence, while the disappointments and trials which Ling had experienced in Canton had left traces which were plainly visible to Mian's penetrating gaze. In such an entrancing occupation the time was to them without hours until a feeling of hunger recalled them to lesser matters, when a variety of very select foods and liquids was placed before them without delay. After this elegant repast had been partaken of, Mian, supporting herself upon Ling's shoulder, made a request that he would disclose to her all the matters which had come under his observation both within the city and during his journey to and from that place. Upon this encouragement, Ling proceeded to unfold his mind, not withholding anything which appeared to be of interest, no matter how slight. When he had reached Canton without any perilous adventure, Mian breathed more freely; as he recorded the interview at the Office of Warlike Deeds and Arrangements, she trembled at the insidious malignity of the evil person Li Keen. The conversation with the wise reader of the future concerning the various states of such as be officially dead almost threw her into the rigid sickness, from which, however, the wonderful circumstance of the discovered properties of the gold fluid quickly recalled her. But to Ling's great astonishment no sooner had he made plain the exceptional advantages which he had derived from the circumstances, and the nature of the undertaking at which he had arrived with Chang-ch'un, than she became a prey to the most intolerable and unrestrained anguish.

"Oh, my devoted but excessively ill-advised lover," she exclaimed wildly, and in tones which clearly indicated that she was inspired by every variety of affectionate emotion, "has the unendurable position in which you and all your household will be placed by the degrading commercial schemes and instincts of the mercenary-souled person Chang-ch'un occupied no place in your generally well-regulated intellect? Inevitably will those who drink our almond tea, in order to have an opportunity of judging the value of the appointments of the house, pass the jesting remark that while the Lings assuredly have 'a dead person's bones in the secret chamber,' at the present they will not have one in the family graveyard by reason of the death of Ling himself. Better to lose a thousand limbs during life than the entire person after death; nor would your adoring Mian hesitate to clasp proudly to her organ of affection the veriest trunk that had parted with all its attributes in a noble and sacrificing endeavour to preserve at least some dignified proportions to embellish the Ancestral Temple and to receive the worship of posterity."

"Alas!" replied Ling, with extravagant humiliation, "it is indeed true; and this person is degraded beyond the common lot of those who break images and commit thefts from sacred places. The side of the transaction which is at present engaging our attention never occurred to this superficial individual until now."

"Wise and incomparable one," said Mian, in no degree able to restrain the fountains of bitter water which clouded her delicate and expressive eyes, "in spite of this person's biting and ungracious words do not, she makes a formal petition, doubt the deathless strength of her affection. Cheerfully, in order to avert the matter in question, or even to save her lover the anguish of unavailing and soul-eating remorse, would she consign herself to a badly-constructed and slow-consuming fire or expose her body to various undignified tortures. Happy are those even to whom is left a little ash to be placed in a precious urn and diligently guarded, for it, in any event, truly represents all that is left of the once living person, whereas after an honourable and spotless existence my illustrious but unthinking lord will be blended with a variety of baser substances and passed from hand to hand, his immaculate organs serving to reward murderers for their deeds and to tempt the weak and vicious to all manner of unmentionable crimes."

So overcome was Ling by the distressing nature of the oversight he had permitted that he could find no words with which to comfort Mian, who, after some moments, continued:

"There are even worse visions of degradation which occur to this person. By chance, that which was once the noble-minded Ling may be disposed of, not to the Imperial Treasury for converting into pieces of exchange, but to some undiscriminating worker in metals who will fashion out of his beautiful and symmetrical stomach an elegant food-dish, so that from the ultimate developments of the circumstance may arise the fact that his own descendants, instead of worshipping him, use his internal organs for this doubtful if not absolutely unclean purpose, and thereby suffer numerous well-merited afflictions, to the end that the finally-despised Ling and this discredited person, instead of founding a vigorous and prolific generation, become the parents of a line of feeble-minded and physically-depressed lepers."

"Oh, my peacock-eyed one!" exclaimed Ling, in immeasurable distress, "so proficient an exhibition of virtuous grief crushes this misguided person completely to the ground. Rather would he uncomplainingly lose his pigtail than—"

"Such a course," said a discordant voice, as the unpresentable person Wang stepped forth from behind a hanging curtain, where, indeed, he had stood concealed during the entire conversation, "is especially forbidden by the twenty-third detail of the things to be done and not to be done."

"What new adversity is this?" cried Mian, pressing to Ling with a still closer embrace. "Having disposed of your incomparable body after death, surely an adequate amount of liberty and seclusion remains to us during life."

"Nevertheless," interposed the dog-like Wang, "the refined person in question must not attempt to lose or to dispose of his striking and invaluable pigtail; for by such an action he would be breaking through his spoken and written word whereby he undertook to be ruled by the things to be done and not to be done; and he would also be robbing the ingenious-minded Chang-ch'un."

"Alas!" lamented the unhappy Ling, "that which appeared to be the end of all this person's troubles is obviously simply the commencement of a new and more extensive variety. Understand, O conscientious but exceedingly inopportune Wang, that the words which passed from this person's mouth did not indicate a fixed determination, but merely served to show the unfeigned depth of his emotion. Be content that he has no intention of evading the definite principles of the things to be done and not to be done, and in the meantime honour this commonplace establishment by retiring to the hot and ill-ventilated chamber, and there partaking of a suitable repast which shall be prepared without delay."

When Wang had departed, which he did with somewhat unseemly haste, Ling made an end of recording his narrative, which Mian's grief had interrupted. In this way he explained to her the reason of Wang's presence, and assured her that by reason of the arrangement he had made with that person, his near existence would not be so unsupportable to them as might at first appear to be the case.

While they were still conversing together, and endeavouring to divert their minds from the objectionable facts which had recently come within their notice, an attendant entered and disclosed that the train of servants and merchandise which Ling had preceded on the journey was arriving. At this fresh example of her lover's consistent thought for her, Mian almost forgot her recent agitation, and eagerly lending herself to the entrancing occupation of unfolding and displaying the various objects, her brow finally lost the last trace of sadness. Greatly beyond the imaginings of anticipation were the expensive articles with which Ling proudly surrounded her; and in examining and learning the cost of the set jewels and worked metals, the ornamental garments for both persons, the wood and paper appointments for the house-even incenses, perfumes, spices and rare viands had not been forgotten-the day was quickly and profitably spent.

When the hour of sunset arrived, Ling, having learned that certain preparations which he had commanded were fully carried out, took Mian by the hand and led her into the chief apartment of the house, where were assembled all the followers and attendants, even down to the illiterate and superfluous Wang. In the centre of the room upon a table of the finest ebony stood a vessel of burning incense, some dishes of the most highly-esteemed fruit, and an abundance of old and very sweet wine. Before these emblems Ling and Mian placed themselves in an attitude of deep humiliation, and formally expressed their gratitude to the Chief Deity for having called them into existence, to the cultivated earth for supplying them with the means of sustaining life, to the Emperor for providing the numerous safeguards by which their persons were protected at all times, and to their parents for educating them. This adequate ceremony being completed, Ling explicitly desired all those present to observe the fact that the two persons in question were, by that fact and from that time, made as one being, and the bond between them, incapable of severance.

When the ruling night-lantern came out from among the clouds, Ling and Mian became possessed of a great desire to go forth with pressed hands and look again on the forest paths and glades in which they had spent many hours of exceptional happiness before Ling's journey to Canton. Leaving the attendants to continue the feasting and drum-beating in a completely unrestrained manner, they therefore passed out unperceived, and wandering among the trees, presently stood on the banks of the Heng-Kiang.

"Oh, my beloved!" exclaimed Mian, gazing at the brilliant and unruffled water, "greatly would this person esteem a short river journey, such as we often enjoyed together in the days when you were recovering."

Ling, to whom the expressed desires of Mian were as the word of the Emperor, instantly prepared the small and ornamental junk which was fastened near for this purpose, and was about to step in, when a presumptuous and highly objectionable hand restrained him.

"Behold," remarked a voice which Ling had some difficulty in ascribing to any known person, so greatly had it changed from its usual tone, "behold how the immature and altogether too-inferior Ling observes his spoken and written assertions!"

At this low-conditioned speech, Ling drew his well-tempered sword without further thought, in spite of the restraining arms of Mian, but at the sight of the utterly incapable person Wang, who stood near smiling meaninglessly and waving his arms with a continuous and backward motion, he again replaced it.

"Such remarks can be left to fall unheeded from the lips of one who bears every indication of being steeped in rice spirit," he said with unprovoked dignity.

"It will be the plain duty of this expert and uncorruptible person to furnish the unnecessary, but, nevertheless, very severe and self-opinionated Chang-ch'un with a written account of how the traitorous and deceptive Ling has endeavoured to break through the thirty-fourth vessel of the liquids to be consumed and not to be consumed," continued Wang with increased deliberation and an entire absence of attention to Ling's action and speech, "and how by this refined person's unfailing civility and resourceful strategy he has been frustrated."

"Perchance," said Ling, after examining his thoughts for a short space, and reflecting that the list of things to be done and not to be done was to him as a blank leaf, "there may even be some small portion of that which is accurate in his statement. In what manner," he continued, addressing the really unendurable person, who was by this time preparing to pass the night in the cool swamp by the river's edge, "does this one endanger any detail of the written and sealed parchment by such an action?"

"Inasmuch," replied Wang, pausing in the process of removing his outer garments, "as the seventy-ninth —the intricate name given to it escapes this person's tongue at the moment-but the ninety-seventh —experLingknowswhamean-provides that any person, with or without, attempting or not avoiding to travel by sea, lake, or river, or to place himself in such a position as he may reasonably and intelligently be drowned in salt water, fresh water, or-or honourable rice spirit, shall be guilty of, and suffer-complete loss of memory." With these words the immoderate and contemptible person sank down in a very profound slumber.

"Alas!" said Ling, turning to Mian, who stood near, unable to retire even had she desired, by reason of the extreme agitation into which the incident had thrown her delicate mind and body, "how intensely aggravating a circumstance that we are compelled to entertain so dissolute a one by reason of this person's preoccupation when the matter was read. Nevertheless, it is not unlikely that the detail he spoke of was such as he insisted, to the extent of making it a thing not to be done to journey in any manner by water. It shall be an early endeavour of this person to get these restraining details equitably amended; but in the meantime we will retrace our footsteps through the wood, and the enraptured Ling will make a well-thought-out attempt to lighten the passage by a recital of his recently-composed verses on the subject of 'Exile from the Loved One; or, Farewell and Return.'"

XIV

"My beloved lord!" said Mian sadly, on a morning after many days had passed since the return of Ling, "have you not every possession for which the heart of a wise person searches? Yet the dark mark is scarcely ever absent from your symmetrical brow. If she who stands before you, and is henceforth an integral part of your organization, has failed you in any particular, no matter how unimportant, explain the matter to her, and the amendment will be a speedy and a joyful task."

It was indeed true that Ling's mind was troubled, but the fault did not lie with Mian, as the person in question was fully aware, for before her eyes as before those of Ling the unevadable compact which had been entered into with Chang-ch'un was ever present, insidiously planting bitterness within even the most select and accomplished delights. Nor with increasing time did the obstinate and intrusive person Wang become more dignified in his behaviour; on the contrary, he freely made use of his position to indulge in every variety of abandonment, and almost each day he prevented, by reason of his knowledge of the things to be done and not to be done, some refined and permissible entertainment upon which Ling and Mian had determined. Ling had despatched many communications upon this subject to Chang-ch'un, praying also that some expert way out of the annoyance of the lesser and more unimportant things not to be done should be arrived at, but the time when he might reasonably expect an answer to these written papers had not yet arrived.

It was about this period that intelligence was brought to Ling from the villages on the road to Peking, how Li Keen, having secretly ascertained that his Yamen was standing and his goods uninjured, had determined to return, and was indeed at that hour within a hundred li of Si-chow. Furthermore, he had repeatedly been understood to pronounce clearly that he considered Ling to be the head and beginning of all his inconveniences, and to declare that the first act of justice which he should accomplish on his return would be to submit the person in question to the most unbearable tortures, and then cause him to lose his head publicly as an outrager of the settled state of things and an enemy of those who loved tranquillity. Not doubting that Li Keen would endeavour to gain an advantage by treachery if the chance presented itself, Ling determined to go forth to meet him, and without delay settle the entire disturbance in one well-chosen and fatally-destructive encounter. To this end, rather than disturb the placid mind of Mian, to whom the thought of the engagement would be weighted with many disquieting fears, he gave out that he was going upon an expedition to surprise and capture certain fish of a very delicate flavour, and attended by only two persons, he set forth in the early part of the day.

Some hours later, owing to an ill-considered remark on the part of the deaf attendant, to whom the matter had been explained in an imperfect light, Mian became possessed of the true facts of the case, and immediately all the pleasure of existence went from her. She despaired of ever again beholding Ling in an ordinary state, and mournfully reproached herself for the bitter words which had risen to her lips when the circumstance of his condition and the arrangement with Chang-ch'un first became known to her. After spending an interval in a polished lament at the manner in which things were inevitably tending, the thought occurred to Mian whether by any means in her power she could influence the course and settled method of affairs. In this situation the memory of the person Wang, and the fact that on several occasions he had made himself objectionable when Ling had proposed to place himself in such a position that he incurred some very remote chance of death by drowning or by fire, recurred to her. Subduing the natural and pure-minded repulsion which she invariably experienced at the mere thought of so debased an individual, she sought for him, and discovering him in the act of constructing cardboard figures of men and animals, which it was his custom to dispose skilfully in little-frequented paths for the purpose of enjoying the sudden terror of those who passed by, she quickly put the matter before him, urging him, by some means, to prevent the encounter, which must assuredly cost the life of the one whom he had so often previously obstructed from incurring the slightest risk.

"By no means," exclaimed Wang, when he at length understood the full meaning of the project; "it would be a most unpresentable action for this commonplace person to interfere in so honourable an undertaking. Had the priceless body of the intrepid Ling been in any danger of disappearing, as, for example, by drowning or being consumed in fire, the nature of the circumstance would have been different. As the matter exists, however, there is every appearance that the far-seeing Chang-ch'un will soon reap the deserved reward of his somewhat speculative enterprise, and to that end this person will immediately procure a wooden barrier and the services of four robust carriers, and proceed to the scene of the conflict."

Deprived of even this hope of preventing the encounter, Mian betook herself in extreme dejection to the secret room of the magician, which had been unopened since the day when the two attendants had searched for substances to apply to their master, and there she diligently examined every object in the remote chance of discovering something which might prove of value in averting the matter in question.

Not anticipating that the true reason of his journey would become known to Mian, Ling continued on his way without haste, and passing through Si-chow before the sun had risen, entered upon the great road to Peking. At a convenient distance from the town he came to a favourable piece of ground where he decided to await the arrival of Li Keen, spending the time profitably in polishing his already brilliant sword, and making observations upon the nature of the spot and the condition of the surrounding omens, on which the success of his expedition would largely depend.

As the sun reached the highest point in the open sky the sound of an approaching company could be plainly heard; but at the moment when the chair of the Mandarin appeared within the sight of those who waited, the great luminary, upon which all portents depend directly or indirectly, changed to the colour of new-drawn blood and began to sink towards the earth. Without any misgivings, therefore, Ling disposed his two attendants in the wood, with instructions to step forth and aid him if he should be attacked by overwhelming numbers, while he himself remained in the way. As the chair approached, the Mandarin observed a person standing alone, and thinking that it was one who, hearing of his return, had come out of the town to honour him, he commanded the bearers to pause. Thereupon, stepping up to the opening, Ling struck the deceptive and incapable Li Keen on the cheek, at the same time crying in a full voice, "Come forth, O traitorous and two-stomached Mandarin! for this person is very desirous of assisting you in the fulfilment of your boastful words. Here is a most irreproachable sword which will serve excellently to cut off this person's undignified head; here is a waistcord which can be tightened around his breast, thereby producing excruciating pains over the entire body."

At the knowledge of who the one before him was, and when he heard the words which unhesitatingly announced Ling's fixed purpose, Li Keen first urged the carriers to fall upon Ling and slay him, and then, perceiving that such a course was exceedingly distasteful to their natural tendencies, to take up the chair and save him by flight. But Ling in the meantime engaged their attention, and fully explained to them the treacherous and unworthy conduct of Li Keen, showing them how his death would be a just retribution for his ill-spent life, and promising them each a considerable reward in addition to their arranged payment when the matter in question had been accomplished. Becoming convinced of the justice of Ling's cause, they turned upon Li Keen, insisting that he should at once attempt to carry out the ill-judged threats against Ling, of which they were consistent witnesses, and announcing that, if he failed to do so, they would certainly bear him themselves to a not far distant well of stagnant water, and there gain the approbation of the good spirits by freeing the land of so unnatural a monster.

Seeing only a dishonourable death on either side, Li Keen drew his sword, and made use of every artifice of which he had knowledge in order to disarm Ling or to take him at a disadvantage. In this he was unsuccessful, for Ling, who was by nature a very expert sword-user, struck him repeatedly, until he at length fell in an expiring condition, remarking with his last words that he had indeed been a narrow-minded and extortionate person during his life, and that his death was an enlightened act of celestial accuracy.

Directing Wang and his four hired persons, who had in the meantime arrived, to give the body of the Mandarin an honourable burial in the deep of the wood, Ling rewarded and dismissed the chairbearers, and without delay proceeded to Si-chow, where he charitably distributed the goods and possessions of Li Keen among the poor of the town. Having in this able and conscientious manner completely proved the misleading nature of the disgraceful statements which the Mandarin had spread abroad concerning him, Ling turned his footsteps towards Mian, whose entrancing joy at his safe return was judged by both persons to be a sufficient reward for the mental distress with which their separation had been accompanied.

XV

After the departure of Ling from Canton, the commercial affairs of Chang-ch'un began, from a secret and undetectable cause, to assume an ill-regulated condition. No venture which he undertook maintained a profitable attitude, so that many persons who in former times had been content to display the printed papers setting forth his name and virtues in an easily-seen position in their receiving-rooms, now placed themselves daily before his house in order to accuse him of using their taels in ways which they themselves had not sufficiently understood, and for the purpose of warning passers-by against his inducements. It was in vain that Chang proposed new undertakings, each of an infallibly more prosperous nature than those before; the persons who had hitherto supported him were all entrusting their money to one named Pung Soo, who required millions where Chang had been content with thousands, and who persistently insisted on greeting the sacred Emperor as an equal.

In this unenviable state Chang's mind continually returned to thoughts of Ling, whose lifeless body would so opportunely serve to dispel the embarrassing perplexities of existence which were settling thickly about him. Urged forward by a variety of circumstances which placed him in an entirely different spirit from the honourable bearing which he had formerly maintained, he now closely examined all the papers connected with the matter, to discover whether he might not be able to effect his purpose with an outward exhibition of law forms. While engaged in this degrading occupation, a detail came to his notice which caused him to become very amiably disposed and confident of success. Proceeding with the matter, he caused a well-supported report to be spread about that Ling was suffering from a wasting sickness, which, without in any measure shortening his life, would cause him to return to the size and weight of a newly-born child, and being by these means enabled to secure the entire matter of "The Ling (After Death)

Without Much Risk Assembly" at a very small outlay, he did so, and then, calling together a company of those who hire themselves out for purposes of violence, journeyed to Si-chow.

Ling and Mian were seated together at a table in the great room, examining a vessel of some clear liquid, when Chang-ch'un entered with his armed ones, in direct opposition to the general laws of ordinary conduct and the rulings of hospitality. At the sight, which plainly indicated a threatened display of violence, Ling seized his renowned sword, which was never far distant from him, and prepared to carry out his spoken vow, that any person overstepping a certain mark on the floor would assuredly fall.

"Put away your undoubtedly competent weapon, O Ling," said Chang, who was desirous that the matter should be arranged if possible without any loss to himself, "for such a course can be honourably adopted when it is taken into consideration that we are as twenty to one, and have, moreover, the appearance of being inspired by law forms."

"There are certain matters of allowed justice which over-rule all other law forms," replied Ling, taking a surer hold of his sword-grasp. "Explain, for your part, O obviously double-dealing Chang-ch'un, from whom this person only recently parted on terms of equality and courtesy, why you come not with an agreeable face and a peaceful following, but with a countenance which indicates both violence and terror, and accompanied by many whom this person recognizes as the most outcast and degraded from the narrow and evil-smelling ways of Canton?"

"In spite of your blustering words," said Chang, with some attempt at an exhibition of dignity, "this person is endowed by every right, and comes only for the obtaining, by the help of this expert and proficient gathering, should such a length become necessary, of his just claims. Understand that in the time since the venture was arranged this person has become possessed of all the property of 'The Ling (After Death) Without Much Risk Assembly,' and thereby he is competent to act fully in the matter. It has now come within his attention that the one Ling to whom the particulars refer is officially dead, and as the written and sealed document clearly undertook that the person's body was to be delivered up for whatever use the Assembly decided whenever death should possess it, this person has now come for the honourable carrying out of the undertaking."

At these words the true nature of the hidden contrivance into which he had fallen descended upon Ling like a heavy and unavoidable thunderbolt. Nevertheless, being by nature and by reason of his late exploits fearless of death, except for the sake of the loved one by his side, he betrayed no sign of discreditable emotion at the discovery.

"In such a case," he replied, with an appearance of entirely disregarding the danger of the position, "the complete parchment must be of necessity overthrown; for if this person is now officially dead, he was equally so at the time of sealing, and arrangements entered into by dead persons have no actual existence."

"That is a matter which has never been efficiently decided," admitted Chang-ch'un, with no appearance of being thrown into a state of confusion at the suggestion, "and doubtless the case in question can by various means be brought in the end before the Court of Final Settlement at Peking, where it may indeed be judged in the manner you assert. But as such a process must infallibly consume the wealth of a province and the years of an ordinary lifetime, and as it is this person's unmoved intention to carry out his own view of the undertaking without delay, such speculations are not matters of profound interest."

Upon this Chang gave certain instructions to his followers, who thereupon prepared to advance. Perceiving that the last detail of the affair had been arrived at, Ling threw back his hanging garment, and was on the point of rushing forward to meet them, when Mian, who had maintained a possessed and reliant attitude throughout, pushed towards him the vessel of pure and sparkling liquid with which they had been engaged when so presumptuously broken in upon, at the same time speaking to him certain words in an outside language. A new and Heaven-sent confidence immediately took possession of Ling, and striking his sword against the wall with such irresistible force that the entire chamber trembled and the feeble-minded assassins shrank back in unrestrained terror, he leapt upon the table, grasping in one hand the open vessel.

"Behold the end, O most uninventive and slow-witted Chang-ch'un!" he cried in a dreadful and awe-compelling voice. "As a reward for your faithless and traitorous behaviour, learn how such avaricious-minded incompetence turns and fastens itself upon the vitals of those who beget it. In spite of many things which were not of a graceful nature towards him, this person has unassumingly maintained his part of the undertaking, and would have followed such a course conscientiously to the last. As it is, when he has made an end of speaking, the body which you are already covetously estimating in taels will in no way be distinguishable from that of the meanest and most ordinary maker of commercial ventures in Canton. For, behold! the fluid which he holds in his hand, and which it is his fixed intention to drain to the last drop, is in truth nothing but a secret and exceedingly powerful counteractor against the virtues of the gold drug; and though but a single particle passed his lips, and the swords of your brilliant and versatile murderers met the next moment in his breast, the body which fell at your feet would be meet for worms rather than for the melting-pot."

It was indeed such a substance as Ling represented it to be, Mian having discovered it during her very systematic examination of the dead magician's inner room. Its composition and distillation had involved that self-opinionated person in many years of arduous toil, for with a somewhat unintelligent lack of foresight he had obstinately determined to perfect the antidote before he turned his attention to the drug itself. Had the matter been more ingeniously arranged, he would undoubtedly have enjoyed an earlier triumph and an affluent and respected old age.

At Ling's earnest words and prepared attitude an instant conviction of the truth of his assertions took possession of Chang. Therefore, seeing nothing but immediate and unevadable ruin at the next step, he called out in a loud and imploring voice that he should desist, and no harm would come upon him. To this Ling consented, first insisting that the followers should be dismissed without delay, and Chang alone remain to have conversation on the matter. By this just act the lower parts of Canton were greatly purified, for the persons in question being driven forth into the woods, mostly perished by encounters with wild animals, or at the hands of the enraged villagers, to whom Ling had by this time become greatly endeared.

When the usual state had been restored, Ling made clear to Chang the altered nature of the conditions to which he would alone agree. "It is a noble-minded and magnanimous proposal on your part, and one to which this misguided person had no claim," admitted Chang, as he affixed his seal to the written undertaking and committed the former parchment to be consumed by fire. By this arrangement it was agreed that Ling should receive only one-half of the yearly payment which had formerly been promised, and that no sum of taels should become due to those depending on him at his death. In return for these valuable allowances, there were to exist no details of things to be done and not to be done, Ling merely giving an honourable promise to observe the matter in a just spirit, while—most esteemed of all—only a portion of his body was to pass to Chang when the end arrived, the upper part remaining to embellish the family altar and receive the veneration of posterity.

* * *

As the great sky-lantern rose above the trees and the time of no-noise fell upon the woods, a flower-laden pleasure-junk moved away from its restraining cords, and, without any sense of motion, gently bore Ling and Mian between the sweet-smelling banks of the Heng-Kiang. Presently Mian drew from beneath her flowing garment an instrument of stringed wood, and touching it with a quick but delicate stroke, like the flight and pausing of a butterfly, told in well-balanced words a refined narrative of two illustrious and noble-looking persons, and how, after many disagreeable evils and unendurable separations, they entered upon a destined state of earthly prosperity and celestial favour. When she made an end of the verses, Ling turned the junk's head by one well-directed stroke of the paddle, and prepared by using similar means to return to the place of mooring.

"Indeed," he remarked, ceasing for a moment to continue this skilful occupation, "the words which you have just spoken might, without injustice, be applied to the two persons who are now conversing together. For after suffering misfortunes and wrongs beyond an appropriate portion, they have now reached that period of existence when a tranquil and contemplative future is assured to them. In this manner is the sage and matured utterance of the inspired philosopher Nien-tsu again proved: that the life of every person is largely composed of two varieties of circumstances which together build up his existence-the Good and the Evil."

The End of the Story of Ling

XVI

When Kai Lung, the story-teller, made an end of speaking, he was immediately greeted with a variety of delicate and pleasing remarks, all persons who had witnessed the matter, down even to the lowest type of Miaotze, who by reason of their obscure circumstances had been unable to understand the meaning of a word that had been spoken, maintaining that Kai Lung's accomplishment of continuing for upwards of three hours without a pause had afforded an entertainment of a very high and refined order. While these polished sayings were being composed, together with many others of a similar nature, Lin Yi suddenly leapt to his feet with a variety of highly objectionable remarks concerning the ancestors of all those who were present, and declaring that the story of Ling was merely a well-considered stratagem to cause them to forget the expedition which they had determined upon, for by that time it should have been completely carried out. It was undoubtedly a fact that the hour spoken of for the undertaking had long passed, Lin Yi having completely overlooked the speed of time in his benevolent anxiety that the polite and valorous Ling should in the end attain to a high and remunerative destiny.

In spite of Kai Lung's consistent denials of any treachery, he could not but be aware that the incident tended greatly to his disadvantage in the eyes of those whom he had fixed a desire to conciliate, nor did his well-intentioned offer that he would without hesitation repeat the display for a like number of hours effect his amiable purpose. How the complication would finally have been determined without interruption is a matter merely of imagination, for at that moment an outpost, who had been engaged in guarding the secrecy of the expedition, threw himself into the enclosure in a torn and breathless condition, having run through the forest many li in a winding direction for the explicit purpose of warning Lin Yi that his intentions had become known, and that he and his followers would undoubtedly be surprised and overcome if they left the camp.

At this intimation of the eminent service which Kai Lung had rendered them, the nature of their faces towards him at once changed completely, those who only a moment before had been demanding his death particularly hailing him as their inspired and unobtrusive protector, and in all probability, indeed, a virtuous and benignant spirit in disguise.

Bending under the weight of offerings which Lin Yi and his followers pressed upon him, together with many clearly set out desires for his future prosperity, and assured of their unalterable protection on all future occasions, Kai Lung again turned his face towards the lanterns of Knei Yang. Far down the side of the mountain they followed his footsteps, now by a rolling stone, now by a snapping branch of yellow pine. Once again they heard his voice, cheerfully repeating to himself; "Among the highest virtues of a pure existence —" But beyond that point the gentle forest breath bore him away.

The Story of Yung Chang

Narrated by Kai Lung, in the Open Space of the Tea-Shop of the Celestial Principles, at Wu-Whei

"Ho, illustrious passers-by!" said Kai Lung, the story-teller, as he spread out his embroidered mat under the mulberry-tree. "It is indeed unlikely that you would condescend to stop and listen to the foolish words of such an insignificant and altogether deformed person as myself. Nevertheless, if you will but retard your elegant footsteps for a few moments, this exceedingly unprepossessing individual will endeavour to entertain you with the recital of the adventures of the noble Yung Chang, as recorded by the celebrated Pe-ku-hi."

Thus adjured, the more leisurely-minded drew near to hear the history of Yung Chang. There was Sing You the fruit-seller, and Li Ton-ti the wood-carver; Hi Seng left his clients to cry in vain for water; and Wang Yu, the idle pipe-maker, closed his shop of "The Fountain of Beauty," and hung on the shutter the gilt dragon to keep away customers in his absence. These, together with a few more shopkeepers and a dozen or so loafers, constituted a respectable audience by the time Kai Lung was ready.

"It would be more seemly if this ill-conditioned person who is now addressing such a distinguished assembly were to reward his fine and noble-looking hearers for their trouble," apologized the story-teller. "But, as the Book of Verses says, 'The meaner the slave, the greater the lord'; and it is, therefore, not unlikely that this majestic concourse will reward the despicable efforts of their servant by handfuls of coins till the air appears as though filled with swarms of locusts in the season of much heat. In particular, there is among this august crowd of Mandarins one Wang Yu, who has departed on three previous occasions without bestowing the reward of a single cash. If the feeble and covetous-minded Wang Yu will place within this very ordinary bowl the price of one of his exceedingly ill-made pipes, this unworthy person will proceed."

"Vast chasms can be filled, but the heart of man never," quoted the pipe-maker in retort. "Oh, most incapable of story-tellers, have you not on two separate occasions slept beneath my utterly inadequate roof without payment?"

But he, nevertheless, deposited three cash in the bowl, and drew nearer among the front row of the listeners.

"It was during the reign of the enlightened Emperor Tsing Nung," began Kai Lung, without further introduction, "that there lived at a village near Honan a wealthy and avaricious maker of idols, named Ti Hung. So skilful had he become in the making of clay idols that his fame had spread for many li round, and idol-sellers from all the neighbouring villages, and even from the towns, came to him for their stock. No other idol-maker between Honan and Nanking employed so many clay-gatherers or so many modellers; yet, with all his riches, his avarice increased till at length he employed men whom he called 'agents' and 'travellers,' who went from house to house selling his idols and extolling his virtues in verses composed by the most illustrious poets of the day. He did this in order that he might turn into his own pocket the full price of the idols, grudging those who would otherwise have sold them the few cash which they would make. Owing to this he had many enemies, and his army of travellers made him still more; for they were more rapacious than the scorpion, and more obstinate than the ox. Indeed, there is still the proverb, 'With honey it is possible to soften the heart of the he-goat; but a blow from an iron cleaver is taken as a mark of welcome by an agent of Ti Hung.' So that people barred the doors at their approach, and even hung out signs of death and mourning.

"Now, among all his travellers there was none more successful, more abandoned, and more valuable to Ti Hung than Li Ting. So depraved was Li Ting that he was never known to visit the tombs of his ancestors; indeed, it was said that he had been heard to mock their venerable memories, and that he had jestingly offered to sell them to anyone who should chance to be without ancestors of his own. This objectionable person would call at the houses of the most illustrious Mandarins, and would command the slaves to carry to their masters his tablets, on which were inscribed his name and his virtues. Reaching their presence, he would salute them with the greeting of an equal, 'How is your stomach?' and then proceed to exhibit samples of his wares, greatly overrating their value. 'Behold!' he would exclaim, 'is not this elegantly-moulded idol worthy of the place of honour in this sumptuous mansion which my presence defiles to such an extent that twelve basins of rose-water will not remove the stain? Are not its eyes more delicate than the most select of almonds? and is not its stomach rounder than the cupolas upon the high temple at Peking? Yet, in spite of its perfections, it is not worthy of the acceptance of so distinguished a Mandarin, and therefore I will accept in return the quarter-tael, which, indeed, is less than my illustrious master gives for the clay alone.'

"In this manner Li Ting disposed of many idols at high rates, and thereby endeared himself so much to the avaricious heart of Ti Hung that he promised him his beautiful daughter Ning in marriage.

"Ning was indeed very lovely. Her eyelashes were like the finest willow twigs that grow in the marshes by the Yang-tse-Kiang; her cheeks were fairer than poppies; and when she bathed in the Hoang Ho, her body seemed transparent. Her brow was finer than the most polished jade; while she seemed to walk, like a winged bird, without weight, her hair floating in a cloud. Indeed, she was the most beautiful creature that has ever existed."

"Now may you grow thin and shrivel up like a fallen lemon; but it is false!" cried Wang Yu, starting up suddenly and unexpectedly. "At Chee Chou, at the shop of 'The Heaven-sent Sugar-cane,' there lives a beautiful and virtuous girl who is more than all that. Her eyes are like the inside circles on the peacock's feathers; her teeth are finer than the scales on the Sacred Dragon; her —"

"If it is the wish of this illustriously-endowed gathering that this exceedingly illiterate paper tiger should occupy their august moments with a description of the deformities of the very ordinary young person at Chee Chou," said Kai Lung imperturbably, "then the remainder of the history of the noble-minded Yung Chang can remain until an evil fate has overtaken Wang Yu, as it assuredly will shortly."

"A fair wind raises no storm," said Wang Yu sulkily; and Kai Lung continued:

"Such loveliness could not escape the evil eye of Li Ting, and accordingly, as he grew in favour with Ti Hung, he obtained his consent to the drawing up of the marriage contracts. More than this, he had already sent to Ning two bracelets of the finest gold, tied together with a scarlet thread, as a betrothal present. But, as the proverb says, 'The good bee will not touch the faded flower,' and Ning, although compelled by the second of the Five Great Principles to respect her father, was unable to regard the marriage with anything but abhorrence. Perhaps this was not altogether the fault of Li Ting, for on the evening of the day on which she had received his present, she walked in the rice fields, and sitting down at the foot of a funereal cypress, whose highest branches pierced the Middle Air, she cried aloud:

"'I cannot control my bitterness. Of what use is it that I should be called the "White Pigeon among Golden Lilies," if my beauty is but for the hog-like eyes of the exceedingly objectionable Li Ting? Ah, Yung Chang, my unfortunate lover! what evil spirit pursues you that you cannot pass your examination for the second degree? My noble-minded but ambitious boy, why were you not content with an agricultural or even a manufacturing career and happiness? By aspiring to a literary degree, you have placed a barrier wider than the Whang Hai between us.'

"'As the earth seems small to the soaring swallow, so shall insuperable obstacles be overcome by the heart worn smooth with a fixed purpose,' said a voice beside her, and Yung Chang stepped from behind the cypress tree, where he had been waiting for Ning. 'O one more symmetrical than the chrysanthemum,' he continued, 'I shall yet, with the aid of my ancestors, pass the second degree, and even obtain a position of high trust in the public office at Peking.'

"'And in the meantime,' pouted Ning, 'I shall have partaken of the wedding-cake of the utterly unpresentable Li Ting.' And she exhibited the bracelets which she had that day received.

"'Alas!' said Yung Chang, 'there are times when one is tempted to doubt even the most efficacious and violent means. I had hoped that by this time Li Ting would have come to a sudden and most unseemly end; for I have drawn up and affixed in the most conspicuous places notifications of his character, similar to the one here.'

"Ning turned, and beheld fastened to the trunk of the cypress an exceedingly elegantly written and composed notice, which Yung read to her as follows:

"Beware of Incurring Death from Starvation

"'Let the distinguished inhabitants of this district observe the exceedingly ungraceful walk and bearing of the low person who calls himself Li Ting. Truthfully, it is that of a dog in the act of being dragged to the river because his sores and diseases render him objectionable in the house of his master. So will this hunchbacked person be dragged to the place of execution, and be bowstrung, to the great relief of all who respect the five senses; A Respectful Physiognomy, Passionless Reflexion, Soft Speech, Acute Hearing, Piercing Sight.

"'He hopes to attain to the Red Button and the Peacock's Feather; but the right hand of the Deity itches, and Li Ting will assuredly be removed suddenly.'

"'Li Ting must certainly be in league with the evil forces if he can withstand so powerful a weapon,' said Ning admiringly, when her lover had finished reading. 'Even now he is starting on a journey, nor will he return till the first day of the month when the sparrows go to the sea and are changed into oysters. Perhaps the fate will overtake him while he is away. If not —'

"'If not,' said Yung, taking up her words as she paused, 'then I have yet another hope. A moment ago you were regretting my choice of a literary career. Learn, then, the value of knowledge. By its aid (assisted, indeed, by the spirits of my ancestors) I have discovered a new and strange thing, for which I can find no word. By using this new system of reckoning, your illustrious but exceedingly narrow-minded and miserly father would be able to make five taels where he now makes one. Would he not, in consideration for this, consent to receive me as a son-in-law, and dismiss the inelegant and unworthy Li Ting?'

"'In the unlikely event of your being able to convince my illustrious parent of what you say, it would assuredly be so,' replied Ning. 'But in what way could you do so? My sublime and charitable father already employs all the means in his power to reap the full reward of his sacred industry. His "solid house-hold gods" are in reality mere shells of clay; higher-priced images are correspondingly constructed, and his clay gatherers and modellers are all paid on a "profit-sharing system." Nay, further, it is beyond likelihood that he should wish for more purchasers, for so great is his fame that those who come to buy have sometimes to wait for days in consequence of those before them; for my exceedingly methodical sire entrusts none with the receiving of money, and the exchanges are therefore made slowly. Frequently an unnaturally devout person will require as many as a hundred idols, and so the greater part of the day will be passed.'

"'In what way?' inquired Yung tremulously.

"'Why, in order that the countings may not get mixed, of course; it is necessary that when he has paid for one idol he should carry it to a place aside, and then return and pay for the second, carrying it to the first, and in such a manner to the end. In this way the sun sinks behind the mountains.'

"'But,' said Yung, his voice thick with his great discovery, 'if he could pay for the entire quantity at once, then it would take but a hundredth part of the time, and so more idols could be sold.'

"'How could this be done?' inquired Ning wonderingly. 'Surely it is impossible to conjecture the value of so many idols.'

"'To the unlearned it would indeed be impossible,' replied Yung proudly, 'but by the aid of my literary researches I have been enabled to discover a process by which such results would be not a matter of conjecture, but of certainty. These figures I have committed to tablets, which I am prepared to give to your mercenary and slow-witted father in return for your incomparable hand, a share of the profits, and the dismissal of the uninventive and morally threadbare Li Ting.'

"'When the earth-worm boasts of his elegant wings, the eagle can afford to be silent,' said a harsh voice behind them; and turning hastily they beheld Li Ting, who had come upon them unawares. 'Oh, most insignificant of table-spoilers,' he continued, 'it is very evident that much over-study has softened your usually well-educated brains. Were it not that you are obviously mentally afflicted, I should unhesitatingly persuade my beautiful and refined sword to introduce you to the spirits of your ignoble ancestors. As it is, I will merely cut off your nose and your left ear, so that people may not say that the Dragon of the Earth sleeps and wickedness goes unpunished.'

"Both had already drawn their swords, and very soon the blows were so hard and swift that, in the dusk of the evening, it seemed as though the air were filled with innumerable and many-coloured fireworks. Each was a practised swordsman, and there was no advantage gained on either side, when Ning, who had fled on the appearance of Li Ting, reappeared, urging on her father, whose usually leisurely footsteps were quickened by the dread that the duel must surely result in certain loss to himself, either of a valuable servant, or of the discovery which Ning had briefly explained to him, and of which he at once saw the value.

"'Oh, most distinguished and expert persons,' he exclaimed breathlessly, as soon as he was within hearing distance, 'do not trouble to give so marvellous an exhibition for the benefit of this unworthy individual, who is the only observer of your illustrious dexterity! Indeed, your honourable condescension so fills this illiterate person with shame that his hearing is thereby preternaturally sharpened, and he can plainly distinguish many voices from beyond the Hoang Ho, crying for the Heaven-sent representative of the degraded Ti Hung to bring them more idols. Bend, therefore, your refined footsteps in the direction of Poo Chow, O Li Ting, and leave me to make myself objectionable to this exceptional young man with my intolerable commonplaces.'

"'The shadow falls in such a direction as the sun wills,' said Li Ting, as he replaced his sword and departed.

"'Yung Chang,' said the merchant, 'I am informed that you have made a discovery that would be of great value to me, as it undoubtedly would if it is all that you say. Let us discuss the matter without ceremony. Can you prove to me that your system possesses the merit you claim for it? If so, then the matter of arrangement will be easy.'

"'I am convinced of the absolute certainty and accuracy of the discovery,' replied Yung Chang. 'It is not as though it were an ordinary matter of human intelligence, for this was discovered to me as I was worshipping at the tomb of my ancestors. The method is regulated by a system of squares, triangles, and cubes. But as the practical proof might be long, and as I hesitate to keep your adorable daughter out in the damp night air, may I not call at your inimitable dwelling in the morning, when we can go into the matter thoroughly?'

"I will not weary this intelligent gathering, each member of which doubtless knows all the books on mathematics off by heart, with a recital of the means by which Yung Chang proved to Ti Hung the accuracy of his tables and the value of his discovery of the multiplication table, which till then had been undreamt of," continued the story-teller. "It is sufficient to know that he did so, and that Ti Hung agreed to his terms, only stipulating that Li Ting should not be made aware of his dismissal until he had returned and given in his accounts. The share of the profits that Yung was to receive was cut down very low by Ti Hung, but the young man did not mind that, as he would live with his father-in-law for the future.

"With the introduction of this new system, the business increased like a river at flood-time. All rivals were left far behind, and Ti Hung put out this sign:

"*No Waiting Here!*

"Good-morning! Have you worshipped one of Ti Hung's refined ninety-nine cash idols?

"Let the purchasers of ill-constructed idols at other establishments, where they have grown old and venerable while waiting for the all-thumb proprietors to count up to ten, come to the shop of Ti Hung and regain their lost youth. Our ninety-nine cash idols are worth a tael a set. We do not, however, claim that they will do everything. The ninety-nine cash idols of Ti Hung will not, for example, purify linen, but even the most contented and frozen-brained person cannot be happy until he possesses one. What is happiness? The exceedingly well-educated Philosopher defines it as the accomplishment of all our desires. Everyone desires one of the Ti Hung's ninety-nine cash idols, therefore get one; but be sure that it is Ti Hung's.

"Have you a bad idol? If so, dismiss it, and get one of Ti Hung's ninety-nine cash specimens.

"Why does your idol look old sooner than your neighbours? Because yours is not one of Ti Hung's ninety-nine cash marvels.

"They bring all delights to the old and the young,
The elegant idols supplied by Ti Hung.

"N.B.—The 'Great Sacrifice' idol, forty-five cash; delivered, carriage free, in quantities of not less than twelve, at any temple, on the evening before the sacrifice.

"It was about this time that Li Ting returned. His journey had been more than usually successful, and he was well satisfied in consequence. It was not until he had made out his accounts and handed in his money that Ti Hung informed him of his agreement with Yung Chang.

"'Oh, most treacherous and excessively unpopular Ti Hung,' exclaimed Li Ting, in a terrible voice, 'this is the return you make for all my entrancing efforts in your services, then? It is in this way that you reward my exceedingly unconscientious recommendations of your very inferior and unendurable clay idols, with their goggle eyes and concave stomachs! Before I go, however, I request to be inspired to make the following remark-that I confidently predict your ruin. And now this low and undignified person will finally shake the elegant dust of your distinguished house from his thoroughly inadequate feet, and proceed to offer his incapable services to the rival establishment over the way.'

"'The machinations of such an evilly-disposed person as Li Ting will certainly be exceedingly subtle,' said Ti Hung to his son-in-law when the traveller had departed. 'I must counteract his omens. Herewith I wish to prophecy that henceforth I shall enjoy an unbroken run of good fortune. I have spoken, and assuredly I shall not eat my words.'

"As the time went on, it seemed as though Ti Hung had indeed spoken truly. The ease and celerity with which he transacted his business brought him customers and dealers from more remote regions than ever, for they could spend days on the journey and still save time. The army of clay-gatherers and modellers grew larger and larger, and the work-sheds stretched almost down to the river's edge. Only one thing troubled Ti Hung, and that was the uncongenial disposition of his son-in-law, for Yung took no further interest in the industry to which his discovery had given so great an impetus, but resolutely set to work again to pass his examination for the second degree.

"'It is an exceedingly distinguished and honourable thing to have failed thirty-five times, and still to be undiscouraged,' admitted Ti Hung; 'but I cannot cleanse my throat from bitterness when I consider that my noble and lucrative business must pass into the hands of strangers, perhaps even into the possession of the unendurable Li Ting.'

"But it had been appointed that this degrading thing should not happen, however, and it was indeed fortunate that Yung did not abandon his literary pursuits; for after some time it became very apparent to Ti Hung that there was something radically wrong with his business. It was not that his custom was falling off in any way; indeed, it had lately increased in a manner that was phenomenal, and when the merchant came to look into the matter, he found to his astonishment that the least order he had received in the past week had been for a hundred idols. All the sales had been large, and yet Ti Hung found himself most unaccountably deficient in taels. He was puzzled and alarmed, and for the next few days he looked into the business closely. Then it was that the reason was revealed, both for the falling off in the receipts and for the increase in the orders. The calculations of the unfortunate Yung Chang were correct up to a hundred, but at that number he had made a gigantic error-which, however, he was never able to detect and rectify-with the result that all transactions above that point worked out at a considerable loss to the seller. It was in vain that the panic-stricken Ti Hung goaded his miserable son-in-law to correct the mistake; it was equally in vain that he tried to stem the current of his enormous commercial popularity. He had competed for public favour, and he had won it, and every day his business increased till ruin grasped him by the pigtail. Then came an order from one firm at Peking for five millions of the ninety-nine cash idols, and at that Ti Hung put up his shutters, and sat down in the dust.

"'Behold!' he exclaimed, 'in the course of a lifetime there are many very disagreeable evils that may overtake a person. He may offend the Sacred Dragon, and be in consequence reduced to a fine dry powder; or he may incur the displeasure of the benevolent and pure-minded Emperor, and be condemned to death by roasting; he may also be troubled by demons or by the disturbed spirits of his ancestors, or be struck by thunderbolts. Indeed, there are numerous annoyances, but they become as Heaven-sent blessings in comparison to a self-opinionated and more than ordinarily weak-minded son-in-law. Of what avail is it that I have habitually sold one idol for the value of a hundred? The very objectionable man in possession sits in my delectable summer-house, and the unavoidable legal documents settle around me like a flock of pigeons. It is indeed necessary that I should declare myself to be in voluntary liquidation, and make an assignment of my book debts for the benefit of my creditors. Having accomplished this, I will proceed to the well-constructed tomb of my illustrious ancestors, and having kow-towed at their incomparable shrines, I will put an end to my distinguished troubles with this exceedingly well-polished sword.'

"'The wise man can adapt himself to circumstances as water takes the shape of the vase that contains it,' said the well-known voice of Li Ting. 'Let not the lion and the tiger fight at the bidding of the jackal. By combining our forces all may be well with you yet. Assist me to dispose of the entirely superfluous Yung Chang and to marry the elegant and symmetrical Ning, and in return I will allot to you a portion of my not inconsiderable income.'

"'However high the tree, the leaves fall to the ground, and your hour has come at last, O detestable Li Ting!' said Yung, who had heard the speakers and crept upon them unperceived. 'As for my distinguished and immaculate father-in-law, doubtless the heat has affected his indefatigable brains, or he would not have listened to your contemptible suggestion. For yourself, draw!'

"Both swords flashed, but before a blow could be struck the spirits of his ancestors hurled Li Ting lifeless to the ground, to avenge the memories that their unworthy descendant had so often reviled.

"'So perish all the enemies of Yung Chang,' said the victor. 'And now, my venerated but exceedingly short-sighted father-in-law, learn how narrowly you have escaped making yourself exceedingly objectionable to yourself. I have just received intelligence from Peking that I have passed the second degree, and have in consequence been appointed to a remunerative position under the Government. This will enable us to live in comfort, if not in affluence, and the rest of your engaging days can be peacefully spent in flying kites.'"

The Probation of Sen Heng

Related by Kai Lung, at Wu-Whei, as a Rebuke to Wang Yu and Certain Others Who Had Questioned the Practical Value of His Stories.

"It is an undoubted fact that this person has not realized the direct remunerative advantage which he confidently anticipated," remarked the idle and discontented pipe-maker Wang Yu, as, with a few other persons of similar inclination, he sat in the shade of the great mulberry tree at Wu-whei, waiting for the evil influence of certain very mysterious sounds, which had lately been heard, to pass away before he resumed his occupation. "When the seemingly proficient and trustworthy Kai Lung first made it his practice to journey to Wu-whei, and narrate to us the doings of persons of all classes of life," he continued, "it seemed to this one that by closely following the recital of how Mandarins obtained their high position, and exceptionally rich persons their wealth, he must, in the end, inevitably be rendered competent to follow in their illustrious footsteps. Yet in how entirely contrary a direction has the whole course of events tended! In spite of the honourable intention which involved a frequent absence from his place of commerce, those who journeyed thither with the set purpose of possessing one of his justly-famed opium pipes so perversely regarded the matter that, after two or three fruitless visits, they deliberately turned their footsteps towards the workshop of the inelegant Ming-yo, whose pipes are confessedly greatly inferior to those produced by the person who is now speaking. Nevertheless, the rapacious Kai Lung, to whose influence the falling off in custom was thus directly attributable, persistently declined to bear any share whatever in the loss which his profession caused, and, indeed, regarded the circumstance from so grasping and narrow-minded a point of observation that he would not even go to the length of suffering this much-persecuted one to join the circle of his hearers without on every occasion making the customary offering. In this manner a well-intentioned pursuit of riches has insidiously led this person within measurable distance of the bolted dungeon for those who do not meet their just debts, while the only distinction likely to result from his assiduous study of the customs and methods of those high in power is that of being publicly bowstrung as a warning to others. Manifestly the pointed finger of the unreliable Kai Lung is a very treacherous guide."

"It is related," said a dispassionate voice behind them, "that a person of limited intelligence, on being assured that he would certainly one day enjoy an adequate competence if he closely followed the industrious habits of the thrifty bee, spent the greater part of his life in anointing his thighs with the yellow powder which he laboriously collected from the flowers of the field. It is not so recorded; but doubtless the nameless one in question was by profession a maker of opium pipes, for this person has observed from time to time how that occupation, above all others, tends to degrade the mental faculties, and to debase its followers to a lower position than that of the beasts of labour. Learn therefrom, O superficial Wang Yu, that wisdom lies in an intelligent perception of great principles, and not in a slavish imitation of details which are, for the most part, beyond your simple and insufficient understanding."

"Such may, indeed, be the case, Kai Lung," replied Wang Yu sullenly-for it was the story-teller in question who had approached unperceived, and who now stood before them —"but it is none the less a fact that, on the last occasion when this misguided person joined the attending circle at your uplifted voice, a Mandarin of the third degree chanced to pass through Wu-whei, and halted at the door-step of 'The Fountain of Beauty,' fully intending to entrust this one with the designing and fashioning of a pipe of exceptional elaborateness. This matter, by his absence, has now passed from him, and to-day, through listening to the narrative of how the accomplished Yuin-Pel doubled his fortune, he is the poorer by many taels."

"Yet to-morrow, when the name of the Mandarin of the third degree appears in the list of persons who have transferred their entire property to those who are nearly related to them in order to avoid it being seized to satisfy the just claims made against them," replied Kai Lung, "you will be able to regard yourself the richer by so many taels."

At these words, which recalled to the minds of all who were present the not uncommon manner of behaving observed by those of exalted rank, who freely engaged persons to supply them with costly articles without in any way regarding the price to be paid, Wang Yu was silent.

"Nevertheless," exclaimed a thin voice from the edge of the group which surrounded Kai Lung, "it in nowise follows that the stories are in themselves excellent, or of such a nature that the hearing of their recital will profit a person. Wang Yu may be satisfied with empty words, but there are others present who were studying deep matters when Wang Yu was learning the art of walking. If Kai Lung's stories are of such remunerative benefit as the person in question claims, how does it chance that Kai Lung himself who is assuredly the best acquainted with them, stands before us in mean apparel, and on all occasions confessing an unassuming poverty?"

"It is Yan-hi Pung," went from mouth to mouth among the bystanders — "Yan-hi Pung, who traces on paper the words of chants and historical tales, and sells them to such as can afford to buy. And although his motive in exposing the emptiness of Kai Lung's stories may not be Heaven-sent — inasmuch as Kai Lung provides us with such matter as he himself purveys, only at a much more moderate price-yet his words are well considered, and must therefore be regarded."

"O Yan-hi Pung," replied Kai Lung, hearing the name from those who stood about him, and moving towards the aged person, who stood meanwhile leaning upon his staff, and looking from side to side with quickly moving eyelids in a manner very offensive towards the story-teller, "your just remark shows you to be a person of exceptional wisdom, even as your well-bowed legs prove you to be one of great bodily strength; for justice is ever obvious and wisdom hidden, and they who build structures for endurance discard the straight and upright and insist upon such an arch as you so symmetrically exemplify."

Speaking in this conciliatory manner, Kai Lung came up to Yan-hi Pung, and taking between his fingers a disc of thick polished crystal, which the aged and short-sighted chant-writer used for the purpose of magnifying and bringing nearer the letters upon which he was engaged, and which hung around his neck by an embroidered cord, the story-teller held it aloft, crying aloud:

"Observe closely, and presently it will be revealed and made clear how the apparently very conflicting words of the wise Yan-hi Pung, and those of this unassuming but nevertheless conscientious person who is now addressing you, are, in reality, as one great truth."

With this assurance Kai Lung moved the crystal somewhat, so that it engaged the sun's rays, and concentrated them upon the uncovered crown of the unsuspecting and still objectionably-engaged person before him. Without a moment's pause, Yan-hi Pung leapt high into the air, repeatedly pressing his hand to the spot thus selected and crying aloud:

"Evil dragons and thunderbolts! but the touch was as hot as a scar left by the uncut nail of the sublime Buddha!"

"Yet the crystal —" remarked Kai Lung composedly, passing it into the hands of those who stood near.

"Is as cool as the innermost leaves of the riverside sycamore," they declared.

Kai Lung said nothing further, but raised both his hands above his head, as if demanding their judgment. Thereupon a loud shout went up on his behalf, for the greater part of them loved to see the manner in which he brushed aside those who would oppose him; and the sight of the aged person Yan-hi Pung leaping far into the air had caused them to become exceptionally amused, and, in consequence, very amiably disposed towards the one who had afforded them the entertainment.

"The story of Sen Heng," began Kai Lung, when the discussion had terminated in the manner already recorded, "concerns itself with one who possessed an unsuspecting and ingenious nature, which ill-fitted him to take an ordinary part in the everyday affairs of life, no matter how engaging such a character rendered him among his friends and relations. Having at an early age been entrusted with a burden of rice and other produce from his father's fields to dispose of in the best possible manner at a neighbouring mart, and having completed the transaction in a manner extremely advantageous to those with whom he trafficked but very intolerable to the one who had sent him, it at once became apparent that some other means of gaining a livelihood must be discovered for him.

"'Beyond all doubt,' said his father, after considering the matter for a period, 'it is a case in which one should be governed by the wise advice and example of the Mandarin Poo-chow.'

"'Illustrious sire,' exclaimed Sen Heng, who chanced to be present, 'the illiterate person who stands before you is entirely unacquainted with the one to whom you have referred; nevertheless, he will, as you suggest, at once set forth, and journeying with all speed to the abode of the estimable Poo-chow, solicit his experience and advice.'

"'Unless a more serious loss should be occasioned,' replied the father coldly, 'there is no necessity to adopt so extreme a course. The benevolent Mandarin in question existed at a remote period of the Thang dynasty, and the incident to which an allusion has been made arose in the following way: To the public court of the enlightened Poo-chow there came one day a youth of very inferior appearance and hesitating manner, who besought his explicit advice, saying: "The degraded and unprepossessing being before you, O select and venerable Mandarin, is by nature and attainments a person of the utmost timidity and fearfulness. From this cause life itself has become a detestable observance in his eyes, for those who should be his companions of both sexes hold him in undisguised contempt, making various unendurable allusions to the colour and nature of his internal organs whenever he would endeavour to join them. Instruct him, therefore, the manner in which this cowardice may be removed, and no service in return will be esteemed too great." "There is a remedy," replied the benevolent Mandarin, without any hesitation whatever, "which if properly carried out is efficacious beyond the possibility of failure. Certain component parts of your body are lacking, and before the desired result can be obtained these must be supplied from without. Of all courageous things the tiger is the most fearless, and in consequence it combines all those ingredients which you require; furthermore, as the teeth of the tiger are the instruments with which it accomplishes its vengeful purpose, there reside the essential principles of its inimitable courage. Let the person who seeks instruction in the matter, therefore, do as follows: taking the teeth of a full-grown tiger as soon as it is slain, and before the essences have time to return into the body, he shall grind them to a powder, and mixing the powder with a portion of rice, consume it. After seven days he must repeat the observance, and yet again a third time, after another similar lapse. Let him, then, return for further guidance; for the present the matter interests this person no further." At these words the youth departed, filled with a new and inspired hope; for the wisdom of the sagacious Poo-chow was a matter which did not admit of any doubt whatever, and he had spoken with well-defined certainty of the success of the experiment. Nevertheless, after several days industriously spent in endeavouring to obtain by purchase the teeth of a newly-slain tiger, the details of the undertaking began to assume a new and entirely unforeseen aspect; for those whom he approached as being the most likely to possess what he required either became very immoderately and disagreeably amused at the nature of the request, or regarded it as a new and ill-judged form of ridicule, which they prepared to avenge by blows and by base remarks of the most personal variety. At length it became unavoidably obvious to the youth that if he was to obtain the articles in question it would first be necessary that he should become adept in the art of slaying tigers, for in no other way were the required conditions likely to be present. Although the prospect was one which did not greatly tend to allure him, yet he did not regard it with the utterly incapable emotions which would have been present on an earlier occasion; for the habit of continually guarding himself from the onslaughts of those who received his inquiry in an attitude of narrow-minded distrust had inspired him with a new-found valour, while his amiable and unrestrained manner of life increased his bodily vigour in every degree. First perfecting himself in the use of the bow and arrow, therefore, he betook himself to a wild and very extensive forest, and there concealed himself among the upper foliage of a tall tree standing by the side of a pool of water. On the second night of his watch, the youth perceived a large but somewhat ill-conditioned tiger approaching the pool for the purpose of quenching its thirst, whereupon he tremblingly fitted an arrow to his bowstring, and profiting by the instruction he had received, succeeded in piercing the creature to the heart. After fulfilling the observance laid upon him by the discriminating Poo-chow, the youth determined to remain in the forest, and sustain himself upon such food as fell to his weapons, until the time arrived when he should carry out the rite for the last time. At the end of seven days, so subtle had he become in all kinds of hunting, and so strengthened by the meat and herbs upon which he existed, that he disdained to avail himself of the shelter of a tree, but standing openly by the side of the water, he engaged the attention of the first tiger which came to drink, and discharged arrow after arrow into its body with unfailing power and precision. So entrancing, indeed, had the pursuit become that the next seven days lengthened out into the apparent period of as many moons, in such a leisurely manner did they rise and fall. On the appointed day, without waiting for the evening to arrive, the youth set out with the first appearance of light, and penetrated into the most inaccessible jungles, crying aloud words of taunt-laden challenge to all the beasts therein, and accusing the ancestors of their race of every imaginable variety of evil behaviour. Yet so great had become the renown of the one who stood forth, and so widely had the warning voice been passed from tree to tree, preparing all who dwelt in the forest against his anger, that not even the fiercest replied openly, though low growls and mutterings proceeded from every cave within a bow-shot's distance around. Wearying quickly of such feeble and timorous demonstrations, the youth rushed into the cave from which the loudest murmurs proceeded, and there discovered a tiger of unnatural size, surrounded by the bones of innumerable ones whom it had devoured; for from time to time its ravages became so great and unbearable, that armies were raised in the neighbouring villages and sent to destroy it, but more than a few stragglers never returned. Plainly recognizing that a just and inevitable vengeance had overtaken it, the tiger made only a very inferior exhibition of resistance, and the youth, having first stunned it with a blow of his closed hand, seized it by the middle, and repeatedly dashed its head against the rocky sides of its retreat. He then performed for the third time the ceremony enjoined by the Mandarin, and having cast upon the cringing and despicable forms concealed in the surrounding woods and caves a look of dignified and ineffable contempt, set out upon his homeward journey, and in the space of three days' time reached the town of the versatile Poo-chow. "Behold," exclaimed that person, when, lifting up his eyes, he saw the youth approaching laden with the skins of the tigers and other spoils, "now at least the youths and maidens of your native village will no longer withdraw themselves from the company of so undoubtedly heroic a person." "Illustrious Mandarin," replied the other, casting both his weapons and his trophies before his inspired adviser's feet, "what has this person to do with the little ones of either sex? Give him rather the foremost place in your ever-victorious company of bowmen, so that he may repay in part the undoubted debt under which he henceforth exists." This proposal found favour with the pure-minded Poo-chow, so that in course of time the unassuming youth who had come supplicating his advice became the valiant commander of his army, and the one eventually chosen to present plighting gifts to his only daughter.'

"When the father had completed the narrative of how the faint-hearted youth became in the end a courageous and resourceful leader of bowmen, Sen looked up, and not in any degree understanding the purpose of the story, or why it had been set forth before him, exclaimed:

"'Undoubtedly the counsel of the graceful and intelligent Mandarin Poo-chow was of inestimable service in the case recorded, and this person would gladly adopt it as his guide for the future, on the chance of it leading to a similar honourable career; but alas! there are no tigers to be found throughout this Province.'

"'It is a loss which those who are engaged in commerce in the city of Hankow strive to supply adequately,' replied his father, who had an assured feeling that it would be of no avail to endeavour to show Sen that the story which he had just related was one setting forth a definite precept rather than fixing an exact manner of behaviour. 'For that reason,' he continued, 'this person has concluded an arrangement by which you will journey to that place, and there enter into the house of commerce of an expert and conscientious vendor of moving contrivances. Among so rapacious and keen-witted a class of persons as they of Hankow, it is exceedingly unlikely that your amiable disposition will involve any individual one in an unavoidably serious loss, and even should such an unforeseen event come to pass, there will, at least, be the undeniable satisfaction of the thought that the unfortunate occurrence will in no way affect the prosperity of those to whom you are bound by the natural ties of affection.'

"'Benevolent and virtuous-minded father,' replied Sen gently, but speaking with an inspired conviction; 'from his earliest infancy this unassuming one has been instructed in an inviolable regard for the Five General Principles of Fidelity to the Emperor, Respect for Parents, Harmony between Husband and Wife, Agreement among Brothers, and Constancy in Friendship. It will be entirely unnecessary to inform so pious-minded a person as the one now being addressed that no evil can attend the footsteps of an individual who courteously observes these enactments.'

"'Without doubt it is so arranged by the protecting Deities,' replied the father; 'yet it is an exceedingly desirable thing for those who are responsible in the matter that the footsteps to which reference has been made should not linger in the neighbourhood of the village, but should, with all possible speed, turn in the direction of Hankow.'

"In this manner it came to pass that Sen Heng set forth on the following day, and coming without delay to the great and powerful city of Hankow, sought out the house of commerce known as 'The Pure Gilt Dragon of Exceptional Symmetry,' where the versatile King-y-Yang engaged in the entrancing occupation of contriving moving figures, and other devices of an ingenious and mirth-provoking character, which he entrusted into the hands of numerous persons to sell throughout the Province. From this cause, although enjoying a very agreeable recompense from the sale of the objects, the greatly perturbed King-y-Yang suffered continual internal misgivings; for the habit of behaving of those whom he appointed to go forth in the manner described was such that he could not entirely dismiss from his mind an assured conviction that the details were not invariably as they were represented to be. Frequently would one return in a very deficient and unpresentable condition of garment, asserting that on his return, while passing through a lonely and unprotected district, he had been assailed by an armed band of robbers, and despoiled of all he possessed. Another would claim to have been made the sport of evil spirits, who led him astray by means of false signs in the forest, and finally destroyed his entire burden of commodities, accompanying the unworthy act by loud cries of triumph and remarks of an insulting nature concerning King-y-Yang; for the honourable character and charitable actions of the person in question had made him very objectionable to that class of beings. Others continually accounted for the absence of the required number of taels by declaring that at a certain point of their journey they were made the object of marks of amiable condescension on the part of a high and dignified public official, who, on learning in whose service they were, immediately professed an intimate personal friendship with the estimable King-y-Yang, and, out of a feeling of gratified respect for him, took away all such contrivances as remained undisposed of, promising to arrange the payment with the refined King-y-Yang himself when they should next meet. For these reasons King-y-Yang was especially desirous of obtaining one whose spoken word could be received, upon all points, as an assured fact, and it was, therefore, with an emotion of internal lightness that he confidently heard from those who were acquainted with the person that Sen Heng was, by nature and endowments, utterly incapable of representing matters of even the most insignificant degree to be otherwise than what they really were.

Filled with an acute anxiety to discover what amount of success would be accorded to his latest contrivance, King-y-Yang led Sen Heng to a secluded chamber, and there instructed him in the method of selling certain apparently very ingeniously constructed ducks, which would have the appearance of swimming about on the surface of an open vessel of water, at the same time uttering loud and ever-increasing cries, after the manner of their kind. With ill-restrained admiration at the skilful nature of the deception, King-y-Yang pointed out that the ducks which were to be disposed of, and upon which a seemingly very low price was fixed, did not, in reality, possess any of these accomplishments, but would, on the contrary, if placed in water, at once sink to the bottom in a most incapable manner; it being part of Sen's duty to exhibit only a specially prepared creature which was restrained upon the surface by means of hidden cords, and, while bending over it, to simulate the cries as agreed upon. After satisfying himself that Sen could perform these movements competently, King-y-Yang sent him forth, particularly charging him that he should not return without a sum of money which fully represented the entire number of ducks entrusted to him, or an adequate number of unsold ducks to compensate for the deficiency.

"At the end of seven days Sen returned to King-y-Yang, and although entirely without money, even to the extent of being unable to provide himself with the merest necessities of a frugal existence, he honourably returned the full number of ducks with which he had set out. It then became evident that although Sen had diligently perfected himself in the sounds and movements which King-y-Yang had contrived, he had not fully understood that they were to be executed stealthily, but had, in consequence, manifested the accomplishment openly, not unreasonably supposing that such an exhibition would be an additional inducement to those who appeared to be well-disposed towards the purchase. From this cause it came about that although large crowds were attracted by Sen's manner of conducting the enterprise, none actually engaged to purchase even the least expensively-valued of the ducks, although several publicly complimented Sen on his exceptional proficiency, and repeatedly urged him to louder and more frequent cries, suggesting that by such means possible buyers might be attracted to the spot from remote and inaccessible villages in the neighbourhood.

"When King-y-Yang learned how the venture had been carried out, he became most intolerably self-opinionated in his expressions towards Sen's mental attainments and the manner of his bringing up. It was entirely in vain that the one referred to pointed out in a tone of persuasive and courteous restraint that he had not, down to the most minute particulars, transgressed either the general or the specific obligations of the Five General Principles, and that, therefore, he was blameless, and even worthy of commendation for the manner in which he had acted. With an inelegant absence of all refined feeling, King-y-Yang most incapably declined to discuss the various aspects of the controversy in an amiable manner, asserting, indeed, that for the consideration of as many brass cash as Sen had mentioned principles he would cause him to be thrown into prison as a person of unnatural ineptitude. Then, without rewarding Sen for the time spent in his service, or even inviting him to partake of food and wine, the insufferable deviser of very indifferent animated contrivances again sent him out, this time into the streets of Hankow with a number of delicately inlaid boxes, remarking in a tone of voice which plainly indicated an exactly contrary desire that he would be filled with an overwhelming satisfaction if Sen could discover any excuse for returning a second time without disposing of anything. This remark Sen's ingenuous nature led him to regard as a definite fact, so that when a passer-by, who tarried to examine the boxes chanced to remark that the colours might have been arranged to greater advantage, in which case he would certainly have purchased at least one of the articles, Sen hastened back, although in a distant part of the city, to inform King-y-Yang of the suggestion, adding that he himself had been favourably impressed with the improvement which could be effected by such an alteration.

"The nature of King-y-Yang's emotion when Sen again presented himself before him-and when by repeatedly applied tests on various parts of his body he understood that he was neither the victim of malicious demons, nor wandering in an insensible condition in the Middle Air, but that the cause of the return was such as had been plainly stated-was of so mixed and benumbing a variety, that for a considerable space of time he was quite unable to express himself in any way, either by words or by signs. By the time these attributes returned there had formed itself within King-y-Yang's mind a design of most contemptible malignity, which seemed to present to his enfeebled intellect a scheme by which Sen would be adequately punished, and finally disposed of, without causing him any further trouble in the matter. For this purpose he concealed the real condition of his sentiments towards Sen, and warmly expressed himself in terms of delicate flattery regarding that one's sumptuous and unfailing taste in the matter of the blending of the colours. Without doubt, he continued, such an alteration as the one proposed would greatly increase the attractiveness of the inlaid boxes, and the matter should be engaged upon without delay. In the meantime, however, not to waste the immediate services of so discriminating and persevering a servant, he would entrust Sen with a mission of exceptional importance, which would certainly tend greatly to his remunerative benefit. In the district of Yun, in the northwestern part of the Province, said the crafty and treacherous King-y-Yang, a particular kind of insect was greatly esteemed on account of the beneficent influence which it exercised over the rice plants, causing them to mature earlier, and to attain a greater size than ever happened in its absence. In recent years this creature had rarely been seen in the neighbourhood of Yun, and, in consequence, the earth-tillers throughout that country had been brought into a most disconcerting state of poverty, and would, inevitably, be prepared to exchange whatever they still possessed for even a few of the insects, in order that they might liberate them to increase, and so entirely reverse the objectionable state of things. Speaking in this manner, King-y-Yang entrusted to Sen a carefully prepared box containing a score of the insects, obtained at a great cost from a country beyond the Bitter Water, and after giving him further directions concerning the journey, and enjoining the utmost secrecy about the valuable contents of the box, he sent him forth.

"The discreet and sagacious will already have understood the nature of King-y-Yang's intolerable artifice; but, for the benefit of the amiable and unsuspecting, it is necessary to make it clear that the words which he had spoken bore no sort of resemblance to affairs as they really existed. The district around Yun was indeed involved in a most unprepossessing destitution, but this had been caused, not by the absence of any rare and auspicious insect, but by the presence of vast hordes of locusts, which had overwhelmed and devoured the entire face the country. It so chanced that among the recently constructed devices at 'The Pure Gilt Dragon of Exceptional Symmetry' were a number of elegant representations of rice fields and fruit gardens so skilfully fashioned that they deceived even the creatures, and attracted, among other living things, all the locusts in Hankow into that place of commerce. It was a number of these insects that King-y-Yang vindictively placed in the box which he instructed Sen to carry to Yun, well knowing that the reception which would be accorded to anyone who appeared there on such a mission would be of so fatally destructive a kind that the consideration of his return need not engage a single conjecture.

"Entirely tranquil in intellect-for the possibility of King-y-Yang's intention being in any way other than what he had represented it to be did not arise within Sen's ingenuous mind-the person in question cheerfully set forth on his long but unavoidable march towards the region of Yun. As he journeyed along the way, the nature of his meditation brought up before him the events which had taken place since his arrival at Hankow; and, for the first time, it was brought within his understanding that the story of the youth and the three tigers, which his father had related to him, was in the likeness of a proverb, by which counsel and warning is conveyed in a graceful and inoffensive manner. Readily applying the fable to his own condition, he could not doubt but that the first two animals to be overthrown were represented by the two undertakings which he had already conscientiously performed in the matter of the mechanical ducks and the inlaid boxes, and the conviction that he was even then engaged on the third and last trial filled him with an intelligent gladness so unobtrusive and refined that he could express his entrancing emotions in no other way that by lifting up his voice and uttering the far-reaching cries which he had used on the first of the occasions just referred to.

"In this manner the first part of the journey passed away with engaging celerity. Anxious as Sen undoubtedly was to complete the third task, and approach the details which, in his own case, would correspond with the command of the bowmen and the marriage with the Mandarin's daughter of the person in the story, the noontide heat compelled him to rest in the shade by the wayside for a lengthy period each day. During one of these pauses it occurred to his versatile mind that the time which was otherwise uselessly expended might be well disposed of in endeavouring to increase the value and condition of the creatures under his care by instructing them in the performance of some simple accomplishments, such as might not be too laborious for their feeble and immature understanding. In this he was more successful than he had imagined could possibly be the case, for the discriminating insects, from the first, had every appearance of recognizing that Sen was inspired by a sincere regard for their ultimate benefit, and was not merely using them for his own advancement. So assiduously did they devote themselves to their allotted tasks, that in a very short space of time there was no detail in connexion with their own simple domestic arrangements that was not understood and daily carried out by an appointed band. Entranced at this intelligent manner of conducting themselves, Sen industriously applied his time to the more congenial task of instructing them in the refined arts, and presently he had the enchanting satisfaction of witnessing a number of the most cultivated faultlessly and unhesitatingly perform a portion of the well-known gravity-removing play entitled "The Benevolent Omen of White Dragon Tea Garden; or, Three Times a Mandarin." Not even content with this elevating display, Sen ingeniously contrived, from various objects which he discovered at different points by the wayside, an effective and life-like representation of a war-junk, for which he trained a crew, who, at an agreed signal, would take up their appointed places and go through the required movements, both of sailing, and of discharging the guns, in a reliable and efficient manner.

"As Sen was one day educating the least competent of the insects in the simpler parts of banner-carriers, gong-beaters, and the like, to their more graceful and versatile companions, he lifted up his eyes and beheld, standing by his side, a person of very elaborately embroidered apparel and commanding personality, who had all the appearance of one who had been observing his movements for some space of time. Calling up within his remembrance the warning which he had received from King-y-Yang, Sen was preparing to restore the creatures to their closed box, when the stranger, in a loud and dignified voice, commanded him to refrain, adding:

"'There is, resting at a spot within the immediate neighbourhood, a person of illustrious name and ancestry, who would doubtless be gratified to witness the diverting actions of which this one has recently been a spectator. As the reward of a tael cannot be unwelcome to a person of your inferior appearance and unpresentable garments, take up your box without delay, and follow the one who is now before you.'

"With these words the richly-clad stranger led the way through a narrow woodland path, closely followed by Sen, to whom the attraction of the promised reward —a larger sum, indeed, than he had ever possessed-was sufficiently alluring to make him determined that the other should not, for the briefest possible moment, pass beyond his sight.

"Not to withhold that which Sen was entirely ignorant of until a later period, it is now revealed that the person in question was the official Provider of Diversions and Pleasurable Occupations to the sacred and illimitable Emperor, who was then engaged in making an unusually extensive march through the eight Provinces surrounding his Capital-for the acute and well-educated will not need to be reminded that Nanking occupied that position at the time now engaged with. Until his providential discovery of Sen, the distinguished Provider had been immersed in a most unenviable condition of despair, for his enlightened but exceedingly perverse-minded master had, of late, declined to be in any way amused, or even interested, by the simple and unpretentious entertainment which could be obtained in so inaccessible a region. The well-intentioned efforts of the followers of the Court, who engagingly endeavoured to divert the Imperial mind by performing certain feats which they remembered to have witnessed on previous occasions, but which, until the necessity arose, they had never essayed, were entirely without result of a beneficial order. Even the accomplished Provider's one attainment-that of striking together both the hands and the feet thrice simultaneously, while leaping into the air, and at the same time producing a sound not unlike that emitted by a large and vigorous bee when held captive in the fold of a robe, an action which never failed to throw the illustrious Emperor into a most uncontrollable state of amusement when performed within the Imperial Palace-now only drew from him the unsympathetic, if not actually offensive, remark that the attitude and the noise bore a marked resemblance to those produced by a person when being bowstrung, adding, with unprepossessing significance, that of the two entertainments he had an unevadable conviction that the bowstringing would be the more acceptable and gravity-removing.

"When Sen beheld the size and the silk-hung magnificence of the camp into which his guide led him, he was filled with astonishment, and at the same time recognized that he had acted in an injudicious and hasty manner by so readily accepting the offer of a tael; whereas, if he had been in possession of the true facts of the case, as they now appeared, he would certainly have endeavoured to obtain double that amount before consenting. As he was hesitating within himself whether the matter might not even yet be arranged in a more advantageous manner, he was suddenly led forward into the most striking and ornamental of the tents, and commanded to engage the attention of the one in whose presence he found himself, without delay.

"From the first moment when the inimitable creatures began, at Sen's spoken word, to go through the ordinary details of their domestic affairs, there was no sort of doubt as to the nature of the success with which their well-trained exertions would be received. The dark shadows instantly forsook the enraptured Emperor's select brow, and from time to time he expressed himself in words of most unrestrained and intimate encouragement. So exuberant became the overjoyed Provider's emotion at having at length succeeded in obtaining the services of one who was able to recall his Imperial master's unclouded countenance, that he came forward in a most unpresentable state of haste, and rose into the air uncommanded, for the display of his usually not unwelcome acquirement. This he would doubtless have executed competently had not Sen, who stood immediately behind him, suddenly and unexpectedly raised his voice in a very vigorous and proficient duck cry, thereby causing the one before him to endeavour to turn around in alarm, while yet in the air-an intermingled state of movements of both the body and the mind that caused him to abandon his original intention in a manner which removed the gravity of the Emperor to an even more pronounced degree than had been effected by the diverting attitudes of the insects.

"When the gratified Emperor had beheld every portion of the tasks which Sen had instilled into the minds of the insects, down even to the minutest detail, he called the well-satisfied Provider before him, and addressing him in a voice which might be designed to betray either sternness or an amiable indulgence, said:

"'You, O Shan-se, are reported to be a person of no particular intellect or discernment, and, for this reason, these ones who are speaking have a desire to know how the matter will present itself in your eyes. Which is it the more commendable and honourable for a person to train to a condition of unfailing excellence, human beings of confessed intelligence or insects of a low and degraded standard?'

"To this remark the discriminating Shan-se made no reply, being, indeed, undecided in his mind whether such a course was expected of him. On several previous occasions the somewhat introspective Emperor had addressed himself to persons in what they judged to be the form of a question, as one might say, 'How blue is the unapproachable air canopy, and how delicately imagined the colour of the clouds!' yet when they had expressed their deliberate opinion on the subjects referred to, stating the exact degree of blueness, and the like, the nature of their reception ever afterwards was such that, for the future, persons endeavoured to determine exactly the intention of the Emperor's mind before declaring themselves in words. Being exceedingly doubtful on this occasion, therefore, the very cautious Shan-se adopted the more prudent and uncompromising attitude, and smiling acquiescently, he raised both his hands with a self-deprecatory movement.

"'Alas!' exclaimed the Emperor, in a tone which plainly indicated that the evasive Shan-se had adopted a course which did not commend itself, 'how unendurable a condition of affairs is it for a person of acute mental perception to be annoyed by the inopportune behaviour of one who is only fit to mix on terms of equality with beggars, and low-caste street cleaners —'

"'Such a condition of affairs is indeed most offensively unbearable, illustrious Being,' remarked Shan-se, who clearly perceived that his former silence had not been productive of a delicate state of feeling towards himself.

"'It has frequently been said,' continued the courteous and pure-minded Emperor, only signifying his refined displeasure at Shan-se's really ill-considered observation by so arranging his position that the person in question on longer enjoyed the sublime distinction of gazing upon his benevolent face, 'that titles and offices have been accorded, from time to time, without any regard for the fitting qualifications of those to whom they were presented. The truth that such a state of things does occasionally exist has been brought before our eyes during the past few days by the abandoned and inefficient behaviour of one who will henceforth be a marked official; yet it has always been our endeavour to reward expert and unassuming merit, whenever it is discovered. As we were setting forth, when we were interrupted in a most obstinate and superfluous manner, the one who can guide and cultivate the minds of unthinking, and not infrequently obstinate and rapacious, insects would certainly enjoy an even greater measure of success if entrusted with the discriminating intellects of human beings. For this reason it appears that no more fitting person could be found to occupy the important and well-rewarded position of Chief Arranger of the Competitive Examinations than the one before us-provided his opinions and manner of expressing himself are such as commend themselves to us. To satisfy us on this point let Sen Heng now stand forth and declare his beliefs.'

"On this invitation Sen advanced the requisite number of paces, and not in any degree understanding what was required of him, determined that the occasion was one when he might fittingly declare the Five General Principles which were ever present in his mind. 'Unquestioning Fidelity to the Sacred Emperor —' he began, when the person in question signified that the trial was over.

"'After so competent and inspired an expression as that which has just been uttered, which, if rightly considered, includes all lesser things, it is unnecessary to say more,' he declared affably. 'The appointment which has already been specified is now declared to be legally conferred. The evening will be devoted to a repetition of the entrancing manoeuvres performed by the insects, to be followed by a feast and music in honour of the recognized worth and position of the accomplished Sen Heng. There is really no necessity for the apparently over-fatigued Shan-se to attend the festival.'

"In such a manner was the foundation of Sen's ultimate prosperity established, by which he came in the process of time to occupy a very high place in public esteem. Yet, being a person of honourably-minded conscientiousness, he did not hesitate, when questioned by those who made pilgrimages to him for the purpose of learning by what means he had risen to so remunerative a position, to ascribe his success, not entirely to his own intelligent perception of persons and events, but, in part, also to a never-failing regard for the dictates of the Five General Principles, and a discriminating subservience to the inspired wisdom of the venerable Poo-chow, as conveyed to him in the story of the faint-hearted youth and the three tigers. This story Sen furthermore caused to be inscribed in letters of gold, and displayed in a prominent position in his native village, where it has since doubtless been the means of instructing and advancing countless observant ones who have not been too insufferable to be guided by the experience of those who have gone before."

The Experiment of the Mandarin Chan Hung

Related by Kai Lung at Shan Tzu, on the Occasion of His Receiving a Very Unexpected Reward

"There are certainly many occasions when the principles of the Mandarin Chan Hung appear to find practical favour in the eyes of those who form this usually uncomplaining person's audiences at Shan Tzu," remarked Kai Lung, with patient resignation, as he took up his collecting-bowl and transferred the few brass coins which it held to a concealed place among his garments. "Has the village lately suffered from a visit of one of those persons who come armed with authority to remove by force or stratagem such goods as bear names other than those possessed by their holders? or is it, indeed-as they of Wu-whei confidently assert-that when the Day of Vows arrives the people of Shan Tzu, with one accord, undertake to deny themselves in the matter of gifts and free offerings, in spite of every conflicting impulse?"

"They of Wu-whei!" exclaimed a self-opinionated bystander, who had by some means obtained an inferior public office, and who was, in consequence, enabled to be present on all occasions without contributing any offering. "Well is that village named 'The Refuge of Unworthiness,' for its dwellers do little but rob and illtreat strangers, and spread evil and lying reports concerning better endowed ones than themselves."

"Such a condition of affairs may exist," replied Kai Lung, without any indication of concern either one way or the other; "yet it is an undeniable fact that they reward this commonplace story-teller's too often underestimated efforts in a manner which betrays them either to be of noble birth, or very desirous of putting to shame their less prosperous neighbouring places."

"Such exhibitions of uncalled-for lavishness are merely the signs of an ill-regulated and inordinate vanity," remarked a Mandarin of the eighth grade, who chanced to be passing, and who stopped to listen to Kai Lung's words. "Nevertheless, it is not fitting that a collection of decaying hovels, which Wu-whei assuredly is, should, in however small a detail, appear to rise above Shan Tzu, so that if the versatile and unassuming Kai Lung will again honour this assembly by allowing his well-constructed bowl to pass freely to and fro, this obscure and otherwise entirely superfluous individual will make it his especial care that the brass of Wu-whei shall be answered with solid copper, and its debased pewter with doubly refined silver."

With these encouraging words the very opportune Mandarin of the eighth grade himself followed the story-teller's collecting-bowl, observing closely what each person contributed, so that, although he gave nothing from his own store, Kai Lung had never before received so honourable an amount.

"O illustrious Kai Lung," exclaimed a very industrious and ill-clad herb-gatherer, who, in spite of his poverty, could not refrain from mingling with listeners whenever the story-teller appeared in Shan Tzu, "a single piece of brass money is to this person more than a block of solid gold to many of Wu-whei; yet he has twice made the customary offering, once freely, once because a courteous and pure-minded individual who possesses certain written papers of his connected with the repayment of some few taels walked behind the bowl and engaged his eyes with an unmistakable and very significant glance. This fact emboldens him to make the following petition: that in place of the not altogether unknown story of Yung Chang which had been announced the proficient and nimble-minded Kai Lung will entice our attention with the history of the Mandarin Chan Hung, to which reference has already been made."

"The occasion is undoubtedly one which calls for recognition to an unusual degree," replied Kai Lung with extreme affability. "To that end this person will accordingly narrate the story which has been suggested, notwithstanding the fact that it has been specially prepared for the ears of the sublime Emperor, who is at this moment awaiting this unseemly one's arrival in Peking with every mark of ill-restrained impatience, tempered only by his expectation of being the first to hear the story of the well-meaning but somewhat premature Chan Hung.

"The Mandarin in question lived during the reign of the accomplished Emperor Tsint-Sin, his Yamen being at Fow Hou, in the Province of Shan-Tung, of which place he was consequently the chief official. In his conscientious desire to administer a pure and beneficent rule, he not infrequently made himself a very prominent object for public disregard, especially by his attempts to introduce untried things, when from time to time such matters arose within his mind and seemed to promise agreeable and remunerative results. In this manner it came about that the streets of Fow Hou were covered with large flat stones, to the great inconvenience of those persons who had, from a very remote period, been in the habit of passing the night on the soft clay which at all seasons of the year afforded a pleasant and efficient resting-place. Nevertheless, in certain matters his engaging efforts were attended by an obvious success. Having noticed that misfortunes and losses are much less keenly felt when they immediately follow in the steps of an earlier evil, the benevolent and humane-minded Chan Hung devised an ingenious method of lightening the burden of a necessary taxation by arranging that those persons who were the most heavily involved should be made the victims of an attack and robbery on the night before the matter became due. By this thoughtful expedient the unpleasant duty of parting from so many taels was almost imperceptibly led up to, and when, after the lapse of some slight period, the first sums of money were secretly returned, with a written proverb appropriate to the occasion, the public rejoicing of those who, had the matter been left to its natural course, would still have been filling the air with bitter and unendurable lamentations, plainly testified to the inspired wisdom of the enlightened Mandarin.

"The well-merited success of this amiable expedient caused the Mandarin Chan Hung every variety of intelligent emotion, and no day passed without him devoting a portion of his time to the labour of discovering other advantages of a similar nature. Engrossed in deep and very sublime thought of this order, he chanced upon a certain day to be journeying through Fow Hou, when he met a person of irregular intellect, who made an uncertain livelihood by following the unassuming and charitably-disposed from place to place, chanting in a loud voice set verses recording their virtues, which he composed in their honour. On account of his undoubted infirmities this person was permitted a greater freedom of speech with those above him than would have been the case had his condition been merely ordinary; so that when Chan Hung observed him becoming very grossly amused on his approach, to such an extent indeed, that he neglected to perform any of the fitting acts of obeisance, the wise and noble-minded Mandarin did not in any degree suffer his complacency to be affected, but, drawing near, addressed him in a calm and dignified manner.

"'Why, O Ming-hi,' he said, 'do you permit your gravity to be removed to such an exaggerated degree at the sight of this in no way striking or exceptional person? and why, indeed, do you stand in so unbecoming an attitude in the presence of one who, in spite of his depraved inferiority, is unquestionably your official superior, and could, without any hesitation, condemn you to the tortures or even to bowstringing on the spot?'

"'Mandarin,' exclaimed Ming-hi, stepping up to Chan Hung, and, without any hesitation, pressing the gilt button which adorned the official's body garment, accompanying the action by a continuous muffled noise which suggested the repeated striking of a hidden bell, 'you wonder that this person stands erect on your approach, neither rolling his lowered head repeatedly from side to side, nor tracing circles in the dust of Fow Hou with his submissive stomach? Know then, the meaning of the proverb, "Distrust an inordinate appearance of servility. The estimable person who retires from your presence walking backwards may adopt that deferential manner in order to keep concealed the long double-edged knife with which he had hoped to slay you." The excessive amusement that seized this offensive person when he beheld your well-defined figure in the distance arose from his perception of your internal satisfaction, which is, indeed, unmistakably reflected in your symmetrical countenance. For, O Mandarin, in spite of your honourable endeavours to turn things which are devious into a straight line, the matters upon which you engage your versatile intellect-little as you suspect the fact-are as grains of the finest Foo-chow sand in comparison with that which escapes your attention.'

"'Strange are your words, O Ming-hi, and dark to this person your meaning,' replied Chan Hung, whose feelings were evenly balanced between a desire to know what thing he had neglected and a fear that his dignity might suffer if he were observed to remain long conversing with a person of Ming-hi's low mental attainments. 'Without delay, and with an entire absence of lengthy and ornamental forms of speech, express the omission to which you have made reference; for this person has an uneasy inside emotion that you are merely endeavouring to engage his attention to the end that you may make an unseemly and irrelevant reply, and thereby involve him in an undeserved ridicule.'

"'Such a device would be the pastime of one of immature years, and could have no place in this person's habit of conduct,' replied Ming-hi, with every appearance of a fixed sincerity. 'Moreover, the matter is one which touches his own welfare closely, and, expressed in the fashion which the proficient Mandarin has commanded, may be set forth as follows: By a wise and all-knowing divine system, it is arranged that certain honourable occupations, which by their nature cannot become remunerative to any marked degree, shall be singled out for special marks of reverence, so that those who engage therein may be compensated in dignity for what they must inevitably lack in taels. By this refined dispensation the literary occupations, which are in general the highroads to the Establishment of Public Support and Uniform Apparel, are held in the highest veneration. Agriculture, from which it is possible to wrest a competency, follows in esteem; while the various branches of commerce, leading as they do to vast possessions and the attendant luxury, are very justly deprived of all the attributes of dignity and respect. Yet observe, O justice-loving Mandarin, how unbecomingly this ingenious system of universal compensation has been debased at the instance of grasping and avaricious ones. Dignity, riches and ease now go hand in hand, and the highest rewarded in all matters are also the most esteemed, whereas, if the discriminating provision of those who have gone before and so arranged it was observed, the direct contrary would be the case.'

"'It is a state of things which is somewhat difficult to imagine in general matters of life, in spite of the fair-seemingness of your words,' said the Mandarin thoughtfully; 'nor can this rather obtuse and slow-witted person fully grasp the practical application of the system on the edge of the moment. In what manner would it operate in the case of ordinary persons, for example?'

"'There should be a fixed and settled arrangement that the low-minded and degrading occupations-such as that of following charitable persons from place to place, chanting verses composed in their honour, that of misleading travellers who inquire the way, so that they fall into the hands of robbers, and the like callings-should be the most highly rewarded to the end that those who are engaged therein may obtain some solace for the loss of dignity they experience, and the mean intellectual position which they are compelled to maintain. By this device they would be enabled to possess certain advantages and degrees of comfort which at present are utterly beyond their grasp, so that in the end they would escape being entirely debased. To turn to the other foot, those who are now high in position, and engaged in professions which enjoy the confidence of all persons, have that which in itself is sufficient to insure contentment. Furthermore, the most proficient and engaging in every department, mean or high-minded, have certain attributes of respect among those beneath them, so that they might justly be content with the lowest reward in whatever calling they professed, the least skilful and most left-handed being compensated for the mental anguish which they must undoubtedly suffer by receiving the greatest number of taels.'

"'Such a scheme would, as far as the matter has been expressed, appear to possess all the claims of respect, and to be, indeed, what was originally intended by those who framed the essentials of existence,' said Chan Hung, when he had for some space of time considered the details. 'In one point, however, this person fails to perceive how the arrangement could be amiably conducted in Fow Hou. The one who is addressing you maintains, as a matter of right, a position of exceptional respect, nor, if he must express himself upon such a detail, are his excessively fatiguing duties entirely unremunerative...'

"'In the case of the distinguished and unalterable Mandarin,' exclaimed Ming-hi, with no appearance of hesitation, 'the matter would of necessity be arranged otherwise. Being from that time, as it were, the controller of the destinies and remunerations of all those in Fow Hou, he would, manifestly, be outside the working of the scheme; standing apart and regulating, like the person who turns the handle of the corn-mill, but does not suffer himself to be drawn between the stones, he could still maintain both his respect and his remuneration unaltered.'

"'If the detail could honourably be regarded in such a light,' said Chan Hung, 'this person would, without delay, so rearrange matters in Fow Hou, and thereby create universal justice and an unceasing contentment within the minds of all.'

"'Undoubtedly such a course could be justly followed,' assented Ming-hi, 'for in precisely that manner of working was the complete scheme revealed to this highly-favoured person.'

"Entirely wrapped up in thoughts concerning the inception and manner of operation of this project Chan Hung began to retrace his steps towards the Yamen, failing to observe in his benevolent abstraction of mind, that the unaffectedly depraved person Ming-hi was stretching out his feet towards him and indulging in every other form of low-minded and undignified contempt.

"Before he reached the door of his residence the Mandarin overtook one who occupied a high position of confidence and remuneration in the Department of Public Fireworks and Coloured Lights. Fully assured of this versatile person's enthusiasm on behalf of so humane and charitable a device, Chan Hung explained the entire matter to him without delay, and expressly desired that if there were any details which appeared capable of improvement, he would declare himself clearly regarding them.

"'Alas!' exclaimed the person with whom the Mandarin was conversing, speaking in so un-feignedly disturbed and terrified a voice that several who were passing by stopped in order to learn the full circumstance, 'have this person's ears been made the object of some unnaturally light-minded demon's ill-disposed pastime, or does the usually well-balanced Chan Hung in reality contemplate so violent and un-Chinese an action? What but evil could arise from a single word of the change which he proposes to the extent of a full written book? The entire fixed nature of events would become reversed; persons would no longer be fully accountable to one another; and Fow Hou being thus thrown into a most unendurable state of confusion, the protecting Deities would doubtless withdraw their influence, and the entire region would soon be given over to the malicious guardianship of rapacious and evilly-disposed spirits. Let this person entreat the almost invariably clear-sighted Chan Hung to return at once to his adequately equipped and sumptuous Yamen, and barring well the door of his inner chamber, so that it can only be opened from the outside, partake of several sleeping essences of unusual strength, after which he will awake in an undoubtedly refreshed state of mind, and in a condition to observe matters with his accustomed diamond-like penetration.'

"'By no means!' cried one of those who had stopped to learn the occasion of the incident —a very inferior maker of unserviceable imitation pigtails —'the devout and conscientious-minded Mandarin Chan Hung speaks as the inspired mouth-piece of the omnipotent Buddha, and must, for that reason, be obeyed in every detail. This person would unhesitatingly counsel the now invaluable Mandarin to proceed to his well-constructed residence without delay, and there calling together his entire staff of those who set down his spoken words, put the complete Heaven-sent plan into operation, and beyond recall, before he retires to his inner chamber.'

"Upon this there arose a most inelegant display of undignified emotions on the part of the assembly which had by this time gathered together. While those who occupied honourable and remunerative positions very earnestly entreated the Mandarin to act in the manner which had been suggested by the first speaker, others-who had, in the meantime, made use of imagined figures, and thereby discovered that the proposed change would be greatly to their advantage-raised shouts of encouragement towards the proposal of the pigtail-maker, urging the noble Mandarin not to become small in the face towards the insignificant few who were ever opposed to enlightened reform, but to maintain an unflaccid upper lip, and carry the entire matter through to its destined end. In the course of this very unseemly tumult, which soon involved all persons present in hostile demonstrations towards each other, both the Mandarin and the official from the Fireworks and Coloured Lights Department found an opportunity to pass away secretly, the former to consider well the various sides of the matter, towards which he became better disposed with every thought, the latter to find a purchaser of his appointment and leave Fow Hou before the likelihood of Chan Hung's scheme became generally known.

"At this point an earlier circumstance, which affected the future unrolling of events to no insignificant degree, must be made known, concerning as it does Lila, the fair and very accomplished daughter of Chan Hung. Possessing no son or heir to succeed him, the Mandarin exhibited towards Lila a very unusual depth of affection, so marked, indeed, that when certain evil-minded ones endeavoured to encompass his degradation, on the plea of eccentricity of character, the written papers which they dispatched to the high ones at Peking contained no other accusation in support of the contention than that the individual in question regarded his daughter with an obvious pride and pleasure which no person of well-balanced intellect lavished on any but a son.

"It was his really conscientious desire to establish Lila's welfare above all things that had caused Chan Hung to become in some degree undecided when conversing with Ming-hi on the detail of the scheme; for, unaffected as the Mandarin himself would have been at the prospect of an honourable poverty, it was no part of his intention that the adorable and exceptionally-refined Lila should be drawn into such an existence. That, indeed, had been the essential of his reply on a certain and not far removed occasion, when two persons of widely differing positions had each made a formal request that he might be allowed to present marriage-pledging gifts to the very desirable Lila. Maintaining an enlightened openness of mind upon the subject, the Mandarin had replied that nothing but the merit of undoubted suitableness of a person would affect him in such a decision. As it was ordained by the wise and unchanging Deities that merit should always be fittingly rewarded, he went on to express himself, and as the most suitable person was obviously the one who could the most agreeably provide for her, the two circumstances inevitably tended to the decision that the one chosen should be the person who could amass the greatest number of taels. To this end he instructed them both to present themselves at the end of a year, bringing with them the entire profits of their undertakings between the two periods.

"This deliberate pronouncement affected the two persons in question in an entirely opposite manner, for one of them was little removed from a condition of incessant and most uninviting poverty, while the other was the very highly-rewarded picture-maker Pe-tsing. Both to this latter person, and to the other one, Lee Sing, the ultimate conclusion of the matter did not seem to be a question of any conjecture therefore, and, in consequence, the one became most offensively self-confident, and the other leaden-minded to an equal degree, neither remembering the unswerving wisdom of the proverb, 'Wait! all men are but as the black, horn-cased beetles which overrun the inferior cooking-rooms of the city, and even at this moment the heavily-shod and unerring foot of Buddha may be lifted.'

"Lee Sing was, by profession, one of those who hunt and ensnare the brilliantly-coloured winged insects which are to be found in various parts of the Empire in great variety and abundance, it being his duty to send a certain number every year to Peking to contribute to the amusement of the dignified Emperor. In spite of the not too intelligent nature of the occupation, Lee Sing took an honourable pride in all matters connected with it. He disdained, with well-expressed contempt, to avail himself of the stealthy and somewhat deceptive methods employed by others engaged in a similar manner of life. In this way he had, from necessity, acquired agility to an exceptional degree, so that he could leap far into the air, and while in that position select from a passing band of insects any which he might desire. This useful accomplishment was, in a measure, the direct means of bringing together the person in question and the engaging Lila; for, on a certain occasion, when Lee Sing was passing through the streets of Fow Hou, he heard a great outcry, and beheld persons of all ranks running towards him, pointing at the same time in an upward direction. Turning his gaze in the manner indicated,

Lee beheld, with every variety of astonishment, a powerful and unnaturally large bird of prey, carrying in its talons the lovely and now insensible Lila, to whom it had been attracted by the magnificence of her raiment. The rapacious and evilly-inspired creature was already above the highest dwelling-houses when Lee first beheld it, and was plainly directing its course towards the inaccessible mountain crags beyond the city walls. Nevertheless, Lee resolved upon an inspired effort, and without any hesitation bounded towards it with such well-directed proficiency, that if he had not stretched forth his hand on passing he would inevitably have been carried far above the desired object. In this manner he succeeded in dragging the repulsive and completely disconcerted monster to the ground, where its graceful and unassuming prisoner was released, and the presumptuous bird itself torn to pieces amid continuous shouts of a most respectful and engaging description in honour of Lee and of his versatile attainment.

"In consequence of this incident the grateful Lila would often deliberately leave the society of the rich and well-endowed in order to accompany Lee on his journeys in pursuit of exceptionally-precious winged insects. Regarding his unusual ability as the undoubted cause of her existence at that moment, she took an all-absorbing pride in such displays, and would utter loud and frequent exclamations of triumph when Lee leaped out from behind some rock, where he had lain concealed, and with unfailing regularity secured the object of his adroit movement. In this manner a state of feeling which was by no means favourable to the aspiring picture-maker Pe-tsing had long existed between the two persons; but when Lee Sing put the matter in the form of an explicit petition before Chan Hung (to which adequate reference has already been made), the nature of the decision then arrived at seemed to clothe the realization of their virtuous and estimable desires with an air of extreme improbability.

"'Oh, Lee,' exclaimed the greatly-disappointed maiden when her lover had explained to her the nature of the arrangement-for in her unassuming admiration of the noble qualities of Lee she had anticipated that Chan Hung would at once have received him with ceremonious embraces and assurances of his permanent affection —'how unendurable a state of things is this in which we have become involved! Far removed from this one's anticipations was the thought of becoming inalienably associated with that outrageous person Pe-tsing, or of entering upon an existence which will necessitate a feigned admiration of his really unpresentable efforts. Yet in such a manner must the entire circumstance complete its course unless some ingenious method of evading it can be discovered in the meantime. Alas, my beloved one! the occupation of ensnaring winged insects is indeed an alluring one, but as far as this person has observed, it is also exceedingly unproductive of taels. Could not some more expeditious means of enriching yourself be discovered? Frequently has the unnoticed but nevertheless very attentive Lila heard her father and the round-bodied ones who visit him speak of exploits which seem to consist of assuming the shapes of certain wild animals, and in that guise appearing from time to time at the place of exchange within the city walls. As this form of entertainment is undoubtedly very remunerative in its results, could not the versatile and ready-witted Lee conceal himself within the skin of a bear, or some other untamed beast, and in this garb, joining them unperceived, play an appointed part and receive a just share of the reward?'

"'The result of such an enterprise might, if the matter chanced to take an unforeseen development, prove of a very doubtful nature,' replied Lee Sing, to whom, indeed, the proposed venture appeared in a somewhat undignified light, although, with refined consideration, he withheld such a thought from Lila, who had proposed it for him, and also confessed that her usually immaculate father had taken part in such an exhibition. 'Nevertheless, do not permit the dark shadow of an inward cloud to reflect itself upon your almost invariably amiable countenance, for this person has become possessed of a valuable internal suggestion which, although he has hitherto neglected, being content with a small but assured competency, would doubtless bring together a serviceable number of taels if rightly utilized.'

"'Greatly does this person fear that the valuable internal suggestion of Lee Sing will weigh but lightly in the commercial balance against the very rapidly executed pictures of Pe-tsing,' said Lila, who had not fully recalled from her mind a disturbing emotion that Lee would have been well advised to have availed himself of her ingenious and well-thought-out suggestion. 'But of what does the matter consist?'

"'It is the best explained by a recital of the circumstances leading up to it,' said Lee. 'Upon an occasion when this person was passing through the streets of Fow Hou, there gathered around him a company of those who had, on previous occasions, beheld his exceptional powers of hurtling himself through the air in an upward direction, praying that he would again delight their senses by a similar spectacle. Not being unwilling to afford those estimable persons of the amusement they desired, this one, without any elaborate show of affected hesitancy, put himself into the necessary position, and would without doubt have risen uninterruptedly almost into the Middle Air, had he not, in making the preparatory movements, placed his left foot upon an over-ripe wampee which lay unperceived on the ground. In consequence of this really blameworthy want of caution the entire manner and direction of this short-sighted individual's movements underwent a sudden and complete change, so that to those who stood around it appeared as though he were making a well-directed endeavour to penetrate through the upper surface of the earth. This unexpected display had the effect of removing the gravity of even the most aged and severe-minded persons present, and for the space of some moments the behaviour and positions of those who stood around were such that they were quite unable to render any assistance, greatly as they doubtless wished to do so. Being in this manner allowed a period for inward reflexion of a very concentrated order, it arose within this one's mind that at every similar occurrence which he had witnessed, those who observed the event had been seized in a like fashion, being very excessively amused. The fact was made even more undoubted by the manner of behaving of an exceedingly stout and round-faced person, who had not been present from the beginning, but who was affected to a most incredible extent when the details, as they had occurred, were made plain to him, he declaring, with many references to the Sacred Dragon and the Seven Walled Temple at Peking, that he would willingly have contributed a specified number of taels rather than have missed the diversion. When at length this person reached his own chamber, he diligently applied himself to the task of carrying into practical effect the suggestion which had arisen in his mind. By an arrangement of transparent glasses and reflecting surfaces-which, were it not for a well-defined natural modesty, he would certainly be tempted to describe as highly ingenious-he ultimately succeeded in bringing about the effect he desired.'

"With these words Lee put into Lila's hands an object which closely resembled the contrivances by which those who are not sufficiently powerful to obtain positions near the raised platform, in the Halls of Celestial Harmony, are nevertheless enabled to observe the complexions and attire of all around them. Regulating it by means of a hidden spring, he requested her to follow closely the actions of a heavily-burdened passerby who was at that moment some little distance beyond them. Scarcely had Lila raised the glass to her eyes than she became irresistibly amused to a most infectious degree, greatly to the satisfaction of Lee, who therein beheld the realization of his hopes. Not for the briefest space of time would she permit the object to pass from her, but directed it at every person who came within her sight, with frequent and unfeigned exclamations of wonder and delight.

"'How pleasant and fascinating a device is this!' exclaimed Lila at length. 'By what means is so diverting and gravity-removing a result obtained?'

"'Further than that it is the concentration of much labour of continually trying with glasses and reflecting surfaces, this person is totally unable to explain it,' replied Lee. 'The chief thing, however, is that at whatever moving object it is directed-no matter whether a person so observed is being carried in a chair, riding upon an animal, or merely walking-at a certain point he has every appearance of being unexpectedly hurled to the ground in a most violent and mirth-provoking manner. Would not the stout and round-faced one, who would cheerfully have contributed a certain number of taels to see this person manifest a similar exhibition, unhesitatingly lay out that sum to secure the means of so gratifying his emotions whenever he felt the desire, even with the revered persons of the most dignified ones in the Empire? Is there, indeed, a single person between the Wall and the Bitter Waters on the South who is so devoid of ambition that he would miss the opportunity of subjecting, as it were, perhaps even the sacred Emperor himself to the exceptional feat?'

"'The temptation to possess one would inevitably prove overwhelming to any person of ordinary intelligence,' admitted Lila. 'Yet, in spite of this one's unassumed admiration for the contrivance, internal doubts regarding the ultimate happiness of the two persons who are now discussing the matter again attack her. She recollects, somewhat dimly, an almost forgotten, but nevertheless, very unassailable proverb, which declares that more contentment of mind can assuredly be obtained from the unexpected discovery of a tael among the folds of a discarded garment than could, in the most favourable circumstances, ensue from the well-thought-out construction of a new and hitherto unknown device. Furthermore, although the span of a year may seem unaccountably protracted when persons who reciprocate engaging sentiments are parted, yet when the acceptance or refusal of Pe-tsing's undesirable pledging-gifts hangs upon the accomplishment of a remote and not very probable object within that period, it becomes as a breath of wind passing through an autumn forest.'

"Since the day when Lila and Lee had sat together side by side, and conversed in this unrestrained and irreproachable manner, the great sky-lantern had many times been obscured for a period. Only an insignificant portion of the year remained, yet the affairs of Lee Sing were in no more prosperous a condition than before, nor had he found an opportunity to set aside any store of taels. Each day the unsupportable Pe-tsing became more and more obtrusive and self-conceited, even to the extent of throwing far into the air coins of insignificant value whenever he chanced to pass Lee in the street, at the same time urging him to leap after them and thereby secure at least one or two pieces of money against the day of calculating. In a similar but entirely opposite fashion, Lila and Lee experienced the acutest pangs of an ever-growing despair, until their only form of greeting consisted in gazing into each other's eyes with a soul-benumbing expression of self-reproach.

"Yet at this very time, when even the natural and unalterable powers seemed to be conspiring against the success of Lee's modest and inoffensive hopes, an event was taking place which was shortly to reverse the entire settled arrangement of persons and affairs, and involved Fow Hou in a very inextricable state of uncertainty. For, not to make a pretence of concealing a matter which has been already in part revealed, the Mandarin Chan Hung had by this time determined to act in the manner which Ming-hi had suggested; so that on a certain morning Lee Sing was visited by two persons, bearing between them a very weighty sack of taels, who also conveyed to him the fact that a like amount would be deposited within his door at the end of each succeeding seven days. Although Lee's occupation had in the past been very meagrely rewarded, either by taels or by honour, the circumstance which resulted in his now receiving so excessively large a sum is not made clear until the detail of Ming-hi's scheme is closely examined. The matter then becomes plain, for it had been suggested by that person that the most proficient in any occupation should be rewarded to a certain extent, and the least proficient to another stated extent, the original amounts being reversed. When those engaged by Chang Hung to draw up the various rates came to the profession of ensnaring winged insects, however, they discovered that Lee Sing was the only one of that description in Fow Hou, so that it became necessary in consequence to allot him a double portion, one amount as the most proficient, and a much larger amount as the least proficient.

"It is unnecessary now to follow the not altogether satisfactory condition of affairs which began to exist in Fow Hou as soon as the scheme was put into operation. The full written papers dealing with the matter are in the Hall of Public Reference at Peking, and can be seen by any person on the payment of a few taels to everyone connected with the establishment. Those who found their possessions reduced thereby completely overlooked the obvious justice of the arrangement, and immediately began to take most severe measures to have the order put aside; while those who suddenly and unexpectedly found themselves raised to positions of affluence tended to the same end by conducting themselves in a most incapable and undiscriminating manner. And during the entire period that this state of things existed in Fow Hou the really contemptible Ming-hi continually followed Chan Hung about from place to place, spreading out his feet towards him, and allowing himself to become openly amused to a most unseemly extent.

"Chief among those who sought to have the original manner of rewarding persons again established was the picture-maker, Pe-tsing, who now found himself in a condition of most abject poverty, so unbearable, indeed, that he frequently went by night, carrying a lantern, in the hope that he might discover some of the small pieces of money which he had been accustomed to throw into the air on meeting Lee Sing. To his pangs of hunger was added the fear that he would certainly lose Lila, so that from day to day he redoubled his efforts, and in the end, by using false statements and other artifices of a questionable nature, the party which he led was successful in obtaining the degradation of Chan Hung and his dismissal from office, together with an entire reversal of all his plans and enactments.

"On the last day of the year which Chan Hung had appointed as the period of test for his daughter's suitors, the person in question was seated in a chamber of his new abode—a residence of unassuming appearance but undoubted comfort-surrounded by Lila and Lee, when the hanging curtains were suddenly flung aside, and Pe-tsing, followed by two persons of low rank bearing sacks of money, appeared among them.

"'Chan Hung,' he said at length, 'in the past events arose which compelled this person to place himself against you in your official position. Nevertheless, he has always maintained towards you personally an unchanging affection, and understanding full well that you are one of those who maintain their spoken word in spite of all happenings, he has now come to exhibit the taels which he has collected together, and to claim the fulfilment of your deliberate promise.'

"With these words the commonplace picture-maker poured forth the contents of the sacks, and stood looking at Lila in a most confident and unprepossessing manner.

"'Pe-tsing,' replied Chan Hung, rising from his couch and speaking in so severe and impressive a voice that the two servants of Pe-tsing at once fled in great apprehension, 'this person has also found it necessary, in his official position, to oppose you; but here the similarity ends, for, on his part, he has never felt towards you the remotest degree of affection. Nevertheless, he is always desirous, as you say, that persons should regard their spoken word, and as you seem to hold a promise from the Chief Mandarin of Fow Hou regarding marriage-gifts towards his daughter, he would advise you to go at once to that person. A misunderstanding has evidently arisen, for the one whom you are addressing is merely Chan Hung, and the words spoken by the Mandarin have no sort of interest for him-indeed, he understands that all that person's acts have been reversed, so that he fails to see how anyone at all can regard you and your claim in other than a gravity-removing light. Furthermore, the maiden in question is now definitely and irretrievably pledged to this faithful and successful one by my side, who, as you will doubtless be gracefully overjoyed to learn, has recently disposed of a most ingenious and diverting contrivance for an enormous number of taels, so many, indeed, that both the immediate and the far-distant future of all the persons who are here before you are now in no sort of doubt whatever.'

"At these words the three persons whom he had interrupted again turned their attention to the matter before them; but as Pe-tsing walked away, he observed, though he failed to understand the meaning, that they all raised certain objects to their eyes, and at once became amused to a most striking and uncontrollable degree."

The Confession of Kai Lung

Related by Himself at Wu-Whei When Other Matter Failed Him.

As Kai Lung, the story-teller, unrolled his mat and selected, with grave deliberation, the spot under the mulberry-tree which would the longest remain sheltered from the sun's rays, his impassive eye wandered round the thin circle of listeners who had been drawn together by his uplifted voice, with a glance which, had it expressed his actual thoughts, would have betrayed a keen desire that the assembly should be composed of strangers rather than of his most consistent patrons, to whom his stock of tales was indeed becoming embarrassingly familiar. Nevertheless, when he began there was nothing in his voice but a trace of insufficiently restrained triumph, such as might be fitly assumed by one who has discovered and makes known for the first time a story by the renowned historian Lo Cha.

"The adventures of the enlightened and nobly-born Yuin-Pel—"

"Have already thrice been narrated within Wu-whei by the versatile but exceedingly uninventive Kai Lung," remarked Wang Yu placidly. "Indeed, has there not come to be a saying by which an exceptionally frugal host's rice, having undoubtedly seen the inside of the pot many times, is now known in this town as Kai-Pel?"

"Alas!" exclaimed Kai Lung, "well was this person warned of Wu-whei in the previous village, as a place of desolation and excessively bad taste, whose inhabitants, led by an evil-minded maker of very commonplace pipes, named Wang Yu, are unable to discriminate in all matters not connected with the cooking of food and the evasion of just debts. They at Shan Tzu hung on to my cloak as I strove to leave them, praying that I would again entrance their ears with what they termed the melodious word-music of this person's inimitable version of the inspired story of Yuin-Pel."

"Truly the story of Yuin-Pel is in itself excellent," interposed the conciliatory Hi Seng; "and Kai Lung's accomplishment of having three times repeated it here without deviating in the particular of a single word from the first recital stamps him as a story-teller of no ordinary degree. Yet the saying 'Although it is desirable to lose persistently when playing at squares and circles with the broad-minded and sagacious Emperor, it is none the less a fact that the observance of this etiquette deprives the intellectual diversion of much of its interest for both players,' is no less true today than when the all knowing H'sou uttered it."

"They well said-they of Shan Tzu-that the people of Wu-whei were intolerably ignorant and of low descent," continued Kai Lung, without heeding the interruption; "that although invariably of a timorous nature, even to the extent of retiring to the woods on the approach of those who select bowmen for the Imperial army, all they require in a story is that it shall be garnished with deeds of bloodshed and violence to the exclusion of the higher qualities of well-imagined metaphors and literary style which alone constitute true excellence."

"Yet it has been said," suggested Hi Seng, "that the inimitable Kai Lung can so mould a narrative in the telling that all the emotions are conveyed therein without unduly disturbing the intellects of the hearers."

"O amiable Hi Seng," replied Kai Lung with extreme affability, "doubtless you are the most expert of water-carriers, and on a hot and dusty day, when the insatiable desire of all persons is towards a draught of unusual length without much regard to its composition, the sight of your goat-skins is indeed a welcome omen; yet when in the season of Cold White Rains you chance to meet the belated chair-carrier who has been reluctantly persuaded into conveying persons beyond the limit of the city, the solitary official watchman who knows that his chief is not at hand, or a returning band of those who make a practise of remaining in the long narrow rooms until they are driven forth at a certain gong-stroke, can you supply them with the smallest portion of that invigorating rice spirit for which alone they crave? From this simple and homely illustration, specially conceived to meet the requirements of your stunted and meagre understanding, learn not to expect both grace and thorns from the willow-tree. Nevertheless, your very immature remarks on the art of story-telling are in no degree more foolish than those frequently uttered by persons who make a living by such a practice; in proof of which this person will relate to the select and discriminating company now assembled an entirely new and unrecorded story-that, indeed, of the unworthy, but frequently highly-rewarded Kai Lung himself."

"The story of Kai Lung!" exclaimed Wang Yu. "Why not the story of Ting, the sightless beggar, who has sat all his life outside the Temple of Miraculous Cures? Who is Kai Lung, that he should have a story? Is he not known to us all here? Is not his speech that of this Province, his food mean, his arms and legs unshaven? Does he carry a sword or wear silk raiment? Frequently have we seen him fatigued with journeying; many times has he arrived destitute of money; nor, on those occasions when a newly-appointed and unnecessarily officious Mandarin has commanded him to betake himself elsewhere and struck him with a rod has Kai Lung caused the stick to turn into a deadly serpent and destroy its master, as did the just and dignified Lu Fei. How, then, can Kai Lung have a story that is not also the story of Wang Yu and Hi Seng, and all others here?"

"Indeed, if the refined and enlightened Wang Yu so decides, it must assuredly be true," said Kai Lung patiently; "yet (since even trifles serve to dispel the darker thoughts of existence) would not the history of so small a matter as an opium pipe chain his intelligent consideration? such a pipe, for example, as this person beheld only today exposed for sale, the bowl composed of the finest red clay, delicately baked and fashioned, the long bamboo stem smoother than the sacred tooth of the divine Buddha, the spreading support patiently and cunningly carved with scenes representing the Seven Joys, and the Tenth Hell of unbelievers."

"Ah!" exclaimed Wang Yu eagerly, "it is indeed as you say, a Mandarin among masterpieces. That pipe, O most unobserving Kai Lung, is the work of this retiring and superficial person who is now addressing you, and, though the fact evidently escaped your all-seeing glance, the place where it is exposed is none other than his shop of 'The Fountain of Beauty,' which you have on many occasions endowed with your honourable presence."

"Doubtless the carving is the work of the accomplished Wang Yu, and the fitting together," replied Kai Lung; "but the materials for so refined and ornamental a production must of necessity have been brought many thousand li; the clay perhaps from the renowned beds of Honan, the wood from Peking, and the bamboo from one of the great forests of the North."

"For what reason?" said Wang Yu proudly. "At this person's very door is a pit of red clay, purer and infinitely more regular than any to be found at Honan; the hard wood of Wu-whei is extolled among carvers throughout the Empire, while no bamboo is straighter or more smooth than that which grows in the neighbouring woods."

"O most inconsistent Wang Yu!" cried the story-teller, "assuredly a very commendable local pride has dimmed your usually penetrating eyesight. Is not the clay pit of which you speak that in which you fashioned exceedingly unsymmetrical imitations of rat-pies in your childhood? How, then, can it be equal to those of Honan, which you have never seen? In the dark glades of these woods have you not chased the gorgeous butterfly, and, in later years, the no less gaily attired maidens of Wu-whei in the entrancing game of Kiss in the Circle? Have not the bamboo-trees to which you have referred provided you with the ideal material wherewith to roof over those cunningly-constructed pits into which it has ever been the chief delight of the young and audacious to lure dignified and unnaturally stout Mandarins? All these things you have seen and used ever since your mother made a successful offering to the Goddess Kum-Fa. How, then, can they be even equal to the products of remote Honan and fabulous Peking? Assuredly the generally veracious Wang Yu speaks this time with closed eyes and will, upon mature reflexion, eat his words."

The silence was broken by a very aged man who arose from among the bystanders.

"Behold the length of this person's pigtail," he exclaimed, "the whiteness of his moustaches and the venerable appearance of his beard! There is no more aged person present-if, indeed, there be such a one in all the Province. It accordingly devolves upon him to speak in this matter, which shall be as follows: The noble-minded and proficient Kai Lung shall relate the story as he has proposed, and the garrulous Wang Yu shall twice contribute to Kai Lung's bowl when it is passed round, once for himself and once for this person, in order that he may learn either to be more discreet or more proficient in the art of aptly replying."

"The events which it is this person's presumptuous intention to describe to this large-hearted and providentially indulgent gathering," began Kai Lung, when his audience had become settled, and the wooden bowl had passed to and fro among them, "did not occupy many years, although they were of a nature which made them of far more importance than all the remainder of his existence, thereby supporting the sage discernment of the philosopher Wen-weng, who first made the observation that man is greatly inferior to the meanest fly, inasmuch as that creature, although granted only a day's span of life, contrives during that period to fulfil all the allotted functions of existence.

"Unutterably to the astonishment and dismay of this person and all those connected with him (for several of the most expensive readers of the future to be found in the Empire had declared that his life would be marked by great events, his career a source of continual wonder, and his death a misfortune to those who had dealings with him) his efforts to take a degree at the public literary competitions were not attended with any adequate success. In view of the plainly expressed advice of his father it therefore became desirable that this person should turn his attention to some other method of regaining the esteem of those upon whom he was dependent for all the necessarys of existence. Not having the means wherewith to engage in any form of commerce, and being entirely ignorant of all matters save the now useless details of attempting to pass public examinations, he reluctantly decided that he was destined to become one of those who imagine and write out stories and similar devices for printed leaves and books.

"This determination was favourably received, and upon learning it, this person's dignified father took him aside, and with many assurances of regard presented to him a written sentence, which, he said, would be of incomparable value to one engaged in a literary career, and should in fact, without any particular qualifications, insure an honourable competency. He himself, he added, with what at the time appeared to this one as an unnecessary regard for detail, having taken a very high degree, and being in consequence appointed to a distinguished and remunerative position under the Board of Fines and Tortures, had never made any use of it.

"The written sentence, indeed, was all that it had been pronounced. It had been composed by a remote ancestor, who had spent his entire life in crystallizing all his knowledge and experience into a few written lines, which as a result became correspondingly precious. It defined in a very original and profound manner several undisputable principles, and was so engagingly subtle in its manner of expression that the most superficial person was irresistibly thrown into a deep inward contemplation upon reading it. When it was complete, the person who had contrived this ingenious masterpiece, discovering by means of omens that he still had ten years to live, devoted each remaining year to the task of reducing the sentence by one word without in any way altering its meaning. This unapproachable example of conciseness found such favour in the eyes of those who issue printed leaves that as fast as this person could inscribe stories containing it they were eagerly purchased; and had it not been for a very incapable want of foresight on this narrow-minded individual's part, doubtless it would still be affording him an agreeable and permanent means of living.

"Unquestionably the enlightened Wen-weng was well acquainted with the subject when he exclaimed, 'Better a frugal dish of olives flavoured with honey than the most sumptuously devised puppy-pie of which the greater portion is sent forth in silver-lined boxes and partaken of by others.' At that time, however, this versatile saying-which so gracefully conveys the truth of the undeniable fact that what a person possesses is sufficient if he restrain his mind from desiring aught else-would have been lightly treated by this self-conceited story-teller even if his immature faculties had enabled him fully to understand the import of so profound and well-digested a remark.

"At that time Tiao Ts'un was undoubtedly the most beautiful maiden in all Peking. So frequently were the verses describing her habits and appearances affixed in the most prominent places of the city, that many persons obtained an honourable livelihood by frequenting those spots and disposing of the sacks of written papers which they collected to merchants who engaged in that commerce. Owing to the fame attained by his written sentence, this really very much inferior being had many opportunities of meeting the incomparable maiden Tiao at flower-feasts, melon-seed assemblies, and those gatherings where persons of both sexes exhibit themselves in revolving attitudes, and are permitted to embrace openly without reproach; whereupon he became so subservient to her charms and virtues that he lost no opportunity of making himself utterly unendurable to any who might chance to speak to, or even gaze upon, this Heaven-sent creature.

"So successful was this person in his endeavour to meet the sublime Tiao and to gain her conscientious esteem that all emotions of prudence forsook him, or it would soon have become apparent even to his enfeebled understanding that such consistent good fortune could only be the work of unforgiving and malignant spirits whose ill-will he had in some way earned, and who were luring him on in order that they might accomplish his destruction. That object was achieved on a certain evening when this person stood alone with Tiao upon an eminence overlooking the city and watched the great sky-lantern rise from behind the hills. Under these delicate and ennobling influences he gave speech to many very ornamental and refined thoughts which arose within his mind concerning the graceful brilliance of the light which was cast all around, yet notwithstanding which a still more exceptional and brilliant light was shining in his own internal organs by reason of the nearness of an even purer and more engaging orb. There was no need, this person felt, to hide even his most inside thoughts from the dignified and sympathetic being at his side, so without hesitation he spoke-in what he believes even now must have been a very decorative manner-of the many thousand persons who were then wrapped in sleep, of the constantly changing lights which appeared in the city beneath, and of the vastness which everywhere lay around.

"'O Kai Lung,' exclaimed the lovely Tiao, when this person had made an end of speaking, 'how expertly and in what a proficient manner do you express yourself, uttering even the sentiments which this person has felt inwardly, but for which she has no words. Why, indeed, do you not inscribe them in a book?'

"Under her elevating influence it had already occurred to this illiterate individual that it would be a more dignified and, perhaps, even a more profitable course for him to write out and dispose of, to those who print such matters, the versatile and high-minded expressions which now continually formed his thoughts, rather than be dependent upon the concise sentence for which, indeed, he was indebted to the wisdom of a remote ancestor. Tiao's spoken word fully settled his determination, so that without delay he set himself to the task of composing a story which should omit the usual sentence, but should contain instead a large number of his most graceful and diamond-like thoughts. So engrossed did this near-sighted and superficial person become in the task (which daily seemed to increase rather than lessen as new and still more sublime images arose within his mind) that many months passed before the matter was complete. In the end, instead of a story, it had assumed the proportions of an important and many-volumed book; while Tiao had in the meantime accepted the wedding gifts of an objectionable and excessively round-bodied individual, who had amassed an inconceivable number of taels by inducing persons to take part in what at first sight appeared to be an ingenious but very easy competition connected with the order in which certain horses should arrive at a given and clearly defined spot. By that time, however, this unduly sanguine story-teller had become completely entranced in his work, and merely regarded Tiao-Ts'un as a Heaven-sent but no longer necessary incentive to his success. With every hope, therefore, he went forth to dispose of his written leaves, confident of finding some very wealthy person who would be in a condition to pay him the correct value of the work.

"At the end of two years this somewhat disillusionized but still undaunted person chanced to hear of a benevolent and unassuming body of men who made a habit of issuing works in which they discerned merit, but which, nevertheless, others were unanimous in describing as 'of no good.' Here this person was received with gracious effusion, and being in a position to impress those with whom he was dealing with his undoubted knowledge of the subject, he finally succeeded in making a very advantageous arrangement by which he was to pay one-half of the number of taels expended in producing the work, and to receive in return all the profits which should result from the undertaking. Those who were concerned in the matter were so engagingly impressed with the incomparable literary merit displayed in the production that they counselled a great number of copies being made ready in order, as they said, that this person should not lose by there being any delay when once the accomplishment became the one topic of conversation in tea-houses and yamens. From this cause it came about that the matter of taels to be expended was much greater than had been anticipated at the beginning, so that when the day arrived on which the volumes were to be sent forth this person found that almost his last piece of money had disappeared.

"Alas! how small a share has a person in the work of controlling his own destiny. Had only the necessarily penurious and now almost degraded Kai Lung been born a brief span before the great writer Lo Kuan Chang, his name would have been received with every mark of esteem from one end of the Empire to the other, while taels and honourable decorations would have been showered upon him. For the truth, which could no longer be concealed, revealed the fact that this inopportune individual possessed a mind framed in such a manner that his thoughts had already been the thoughts of the inspired Lo Kuan, who, as this person would not be so presumptuous as to inform this ornamental and well-informed gathering, was the most ingenious and versatile-minded composer of written words that this Empire-and therefore the entire world-has seen, as, indeed, his honourable title of 'The Many-hued Mandarin Duck of the Yang-tse' plainly indicates.

"Although this self-opinionated person had frequently been greatly surprised himself during the writing of his long work by the brilliance and manysidedness of the thoughts and metaphors which arose in his mind without conscious effort, it was not until the appearance of the printed leaves which make a custom of warning persons against being persuaded into buying certain books that he definitely understood how all these things had been fully expressed many dynasties ago by the all-knowing Lo Kuan Chang, and formed, indeed, the great national standard of unapproachable excellence. Unfortunately, this person had been so deeply engrossed all his life in literary pursuits that he had never found an opportunity to glance at the works in question, or he would have escaped the embarrassing position in which he now found himself.

"It was with a hopeless sense of illness of ease that this unhappy one reached the day on which the printed leaves already alluded to would make known their deliberate opinion of his writing, the extremity of his hope being that some would at least credit him with honourable motives, and perhaps a knowledge that if the inspired Lo Kuan Chan had never been born the entire matter might have been brought to a very different conclusion. Alas! only one among the many printed leaves which made reference to the venture contained any words of friendship or encouragement. This benevolent exception was sent forth from a city in the extreme Northern Province of the Empire, and contained many inspiring though delicately guarded messages of hope for the one to whom they gracefully alluded as 'this undoubtedly youthful, but nevertheless, distinctly promising writer of books.' While admitting that altogether they found the production undeniably tedious, they claimed to have discovered indications of an obvious talent, and therefore they unhesitatingly counselled the person in question to take courage at the prospect of a moderate competency which was certainly within his grasp if he restrained his somewhat over-ambitious impulses and closely observed the simple subjects and manner of expression of their own Chang Chow, whose 'Lines to a Wayside Chrysanthemum,' 'Mongolians who Have,' and several other composed pieces, they then set forth. Although it became plain that the writer of this amiably devised notice was, like this incapable person, entirely unacquainted with the masterpieces of Lo Kuan Chang, yet the indisputable fact remained that, entirely on its merit, the work had been greeted with undoubted enthusiasm, so that after purchasing many examples of the refined printed leaf containing it, this person sat far into the night continually reading over the one unprejudiced and discriminating expression.

"All the other printed leaves displayed a complete absence of good taste in dealing with the matter. One boldly asserted that the entire circumstance was the outcome of a foolish jest or wager on the part of a person who possessed a million taels; another predicted that it was a cunning and elaborately thought-out method of obtaining the attention of the people on the part of certain persons who claimed to vend a reliable and fragrantly-scented cleansing substance. The *Valley of Hoang Rose Leaves and Sweetness* hoped, in a spirit of no sincerity, that the ingenious Kai Lung would not rest on his tea-leaves, but would soon send forth an equally entertaining amended example of the *Sayings of Confucious* and other sacred works, while the *Pure Essence of the Seven Days' Happenings* merely printed side by side portions from the two books under the large inscription, 'IS THERE REALLY ANY NEED FOR US TO EXPRESS OURSELVES MORE CLEARLY?'

"The disappointment both as regards public esteem and taels-for, after the manner in which the work had been received by those who advise on such productions, not a single example was purchased-threw this ill-destined individual into a condition of most unendurable depression, from which he was only aroused by a remarkable example of the unfailing wisdom of the proverb which says 'Before hastening to secure a possible reward of five taels by dragging an unobservant person away from a falling building, examine well his features lest you find, when too late, that it is one to whom you are indebted for double that amount.' Disappointed in the hope of securing large gains from the sale of his great work, this person now turned his attention again to his former means of living, only to find, however, that the discredit in which he had become involved even attached itself to his concise sentence; for in place of the remunerative and honourable manner in which it was formerly received, it was now regarded on all hands with open suspicion. Instead of meekly kow-towing to an evidently pre-arranged doom, the last misfortune aroused this usually resigned story-teller to an ungovernable frenzy. Regarding the accomplished but at the same time exceedingly over-productive Lo Kuan Chang as the beginning of all his evils, he took a solemn oath as a mark of disapproval that he had not been content to inscribe on paper only half of his brilliant thoughts, leaving the other half for the benefit of this hard-striving and equally well-endowed individual, in which case there would have been a sufficiency of taels and of fame for both.

"For a very considerable space of time this person could conceive no method by which he might attain his object. At length, however, as a result of very keen and subtle intellectual searching, and many well-selected sacrifices, it was conveyed by means of a dream that one very ingenious yet simple way was possible. The renowned and universally-admired writings of the distinguished Lo Kuan for the most part take their action within a few dynasties of their creator's own time: all that remained for this inventive person to accomplish, therefore, was to trace out the entire matter, making the words and speeches to proceed from the mouths of those who existed in still earlier periods. By this crafty method it would at once appear as though the not-too-original Lo Kuan had been indebted to one who came before him for all his most subtle thoughts, and, in consequence, his tomb would become dishonoured and his memory execrated. Without any delay this person cheerfully set himself to the somewhat laborious task before him. Lo Kuan's well-known exclamation of the Emperor Tsing on the battlefield of Shih-ho, 'A sedan-chair! a sedan-chair! This person will unhesitatingly exchange his entire and well-regulated Empire for such an article,' was attributed to an Emperor who lived several thousand years before the treacherous and unpopular Tsing. The new matter of a no less frequently quoted portion ran: 'O nobly intentioned but nevertheless exceedingly morose Tung-shin, the object before you is your distinguished and evilly-disposed-of father's honourably-inspired demon,' the change of a name effecting whatever alteration was necessary; while the delicately-imagined speech beginning 'The person who becomes amused at matters resulting from double-edged knives has assuredly never felt the effect of a well-directed blow himself' was taken from the mouth of one person and placed in that of one of his remote ancestors. In such a manner, without in any great degree altering the matter of Lo Kuan's works, all the scenes and persons introduced were transferred to much earlier dynasties than those affected by the incomparable writer himself, the final effect being to give an air of extreme unoriginality to his really undoubtedly genuine conceptions.

"Satisfied with his accomplishment, and followed by a hired person of low class bearing the writings, which, by nature of the research necessary in fixing the various dates and places so that even the wary should be deceived, had occupied the greater part of a year, this now fully confident story-teller—unmindful of the well-tried excellence of the inspired saying, 'Money is hundred-footed; upon perceiving a tael lying apparently unobserved upon the floor, do not lose the time necessary in stooping, but quickly place your foot upon it, for one fails nothing in dignity thereby; but should it be a gold piece, distrust all things, and valuing dignity but as an empty name, cast your entire body upon it'—went forth to complete his great task of finally erasing from the mind and records of the Empire the hitherto venerated name of Lo Kuan Chang. Entering the place of commerce of the one who seemed the most favourable for the purpose, he placed the facts as they would in future be represented before him, explained the undoubtedly remunerative fame that would ensue to all concerned in the enterprise of sending forth the printed books in their new form, and, opening at a venture the written leaves which he had brought with him, read out the following words as an indication of the similarity of the entire work:

"'*Whai-Keng.* Friends, Chinamen, labourers who are engaged in agricultural pursuits, entrust to this person your acute and well-educated ears;

"'He has merely come to assist in depositing the body of Ko'ung in the Family Temple, not for the purpose of making remarks about him of a graceful and highly complimentary nature;

"'The unremunerative actions of which persons may have been guilty possess an exceedingly undesirable amount of endurance;

"'The successful and well-considered almost invariably are involved in a directly contrary course;

"'This person desires nothing more than a like fate to await Ko'ung.'

"When this one had read so far, he paused in order to give the other an opportunity of breaking in and offering half his possessions to be allowed to share in the undertaking. As he remained unaccountably silent, however, an inelegant pause occurred which this person at length broke by desiring an expressed opinion on the matter.

"'O exceedingly painstaking, but nevertheless highly inopportune Kai Lung,' he replied at length, while in his countenance this person read an expression of no-encouragement towards his venture, 'all your entrancing efforts do undoubtedly appear to attract the undesirable attention of some spiteful and tyrannical demon. This closely-written and elaborately devised work is in reality not worth the labour of a single stroke, nor is there in all Peking a sender forth of printed leaves who would encourage any project connected with its issue.'

"'But the importance of such a fact as that which would clearly show the hitherto venerated Lo Kuan Chang to be a person who passed off as his own the work of an earlier one!' cried this person in despair, well knowing that the deliberately expressed opinion of the one before him was a matter that would rule all others. 'Consider the interest of the discovery.'

"'The interest would not demand more than a few lines in the ordinary printed leaves,' replied the other calmly. 'Indeed, in a manner of speaking, it is entirely a detail of no consequence whether or not the sublime Lo Kuan ever existed. In reality his very commonplace name may have been simply Lung; his inspired work may have been written a score of dynasties before him by some other person, or they may have been composed by the enlightened Emperor of the period, who desired to conceal the fact, yet these matters would not for a moment engage the interest of any ordinary passer-by. Lo Kuan Chang is not a person in the ordinary expression; he is an embodiment of a distinguished and utterly unassailable national institution. The Heaven-sent works with which he is, by general consent, connected form the necessary unchangeable standard of literary excellence, and remain for ever above rivalry and above mistrust. For this reason the matter is plainly one which does not interest this person.'

"In the course of a not uneventful existence this self-deprecatory person has suffered many reverses and disappointments. During his youth the high-minded Empress on one occasion stopped and openly complimented him on the dignified outline presented by his body in profile, and when he was relying upon this incident to secure him a very remunerative public office, a jealous and powerful Mandarin substituted a somewhat similar, though really very much inferior, person for him at the interview which the Empress had commanded. Frequently in matters of commerce which have appeared to promise very satisfactorily at the beginning this person has been induced to entrust sums of money to others, when he had hoped from the indications and the manner of speaking that the exact contrary would be the case; and in one instance he was released at a vast price from the torture dungeon in Canton-where he had been thrown by the subtle and unconscientious plots of one who could not relate stories in so accurate and unvarying a manner as himself-on the day before that on which all persons were freely set at liberty on account of exceptional public rejoicing. Yet in spite of these and many other very unendurable incidents, this impetuous and ill-starred being never felt so great a desire to retire to a solitary place and there disfigure himself permanently as a mark of his unfeigned internal displeasure, as on the occasion when he endured extreme poverty and great personal inconvenience for an entire year in order that he might take away face from the memory of a person who was so placed that no one expressed any interest in the matter.

"Since then this very ill-clad and really necessitous person has devoted himself to the honourable but exceedingly arduous and in general unremunerative occupation of story-telling. To this he would add nothing save that not infrequently a nobly-born and highly-cultured audience is so entranced with his commonplace efforts to hold the attention, especially when a story not hitherto known has been related, that in order to afford it an opportunity of expressing its gratification, he has been requested to allow another offering to be made by all persons present at the conclusion of the entertainment."

The Vengeance of Tung Fel

For a period not to be measured by days or weeks the air of Ching-fow had been as unrestful as that of the locust plains beyond the Great Wall, for every speech which passed bore two faces, one fair to hear, as a greeting, but the other insidiously speaking behind a screen, of rebellion, violence, and the hope of overturning the fixed order of events. With those whom they did not mistrust of treachery persons spoke in low voices of definite plans, while at all times there might appear in prominent places of the city skilfully composed notices setting forth great wrongs and injustices towards which resignation and a lowly bearing were outwardly counselled, yet with the same words cunningly inflaming the minds, even of the patient, as no pouring out of passionate thoughts and undignified threatenings could have done. Among the people, unknown, unseen, and unsuspected, except to the proved ones to whom they desired to reveal themselves, moved the agents of the Three Societies. While to the many of Ching-fow nothing was desired or even thought of behind the downfall of their own officials, and, chief of all, the execution of the evil-minded and depraved Mandarin Ping Siang, whose cruelties and extortions had made his name an object of wide and deserved loathing, the agents only regarded the city as a bright spot in the line of blood and fire which they were fanning into life from Peking to Canton, and which would presumably burst forth and involve the entire Empire.

Although it had of late become a plain fact, by reason of the manner of behaving of the people, that events of a sudden and turbulent nature could not long be restrained, yet outwardly there was no exhibition of violence, not even to the length of resisting those whom Ping Siang sent to enforce his unjust demands, chiefly because a well-founded whisper had been sent round that nothing was to be done until Tung Fel should arrive, which would not be until the seventh day in the month of Winged Dragons. To this all persons agreed, for the more aged among them, who, by virtue of their years, were also the formers of opinion in all matters, called up within their memories certain events connected with the two persons in question which appeared to give to Tung Fel the privilege of expressing himself clearly when the matter of finally dealing with the malicious and self-willed Mandarin should be engaged upon.

Among the mountains which enclose Ching-fow on the southern side dwelt a jade-seeker, who also kept goats. Although a young man and entirely without relations, he had, by patient industry, contrived to collect together a large flock of the best-formed and most prolific goats to be found in the neighbourhood, all the money which he received in exchange for jade being quickly bartered again for the finest animals which he could obtain. He was dauntless in penetrating to the most inaccessible parts of the mountains in search of the stone, unfailing in his skilful care of the flock, in which he took much honourable pride, and on all occasions discreet and unassumingly restrained in his discourse and manner of life. Knowing this to be his invariable practice, it was with emotions of an agreeable curiosity that on the seventh day of the month of Winged Dragons those persons who were passing from place to place in the city beheld this young man, Yang Hu, descending the mountain path with unmistakable signs of profound agitation, and an entire absence of prudent care. Following him closely to the inner square of the city, on the continually expressed plea that they themselves had business in that quarter, these persons observed Yang Hu take up a position of unendurable dejection as he gazed reproachfully at the figure of the all-knowing Buddha which surmounted the Temple where it was his custom to sacrifice.

"Alas!" he exclaimed, lifting up his voice, when it became plain that a large number of people was assembled awaiting his words, "to what end does a person strive in this excessively evilly-regulated district? Or is it that this obscure and ill-destined one alone is marked out as with a deep white cross for humiliation and ruin? Father, and Sacred Temple of Ancestral Virtues, wherein the meanest can repose their trust, he has none; while now, being more destitute than the beggar at the gate, the hope of honourable marriage and a robust family of sons is more remote than the chance of finding the miracle-working Crystal Image which marks the last footstep of the Pure One. Yesterday this person possessed no secret store of silver or gold, nor had he knowledge of any special amount of jade hidden among the mountains, but to his call there responded four score goats, the most select and majestic to be found in all the Province, of which, nevertheless, it was his yearly custom to sacrifice one, as those here can testify, and to offer another as a duty to the Yamen of Ping Siang, in neither case opening his eyes widely when the hour for selecting arrived. Yet in what an unseemly manner is his respectful piety and courteous loyalty rewarded! To-day, before this person went forth on his usual quest, there came those bearing written papers by which they claimed, on the authority of Ping Siang, the whole of this person's flock, as a punishment and fine for his not contributing without warning to the Celebration of Kissing the Emperor's Face-the very obligation of such a matter being entirely unknown to him. Nevertheless, those who came drove off this person's entire wealth, the desperately won increase of a life full of great toil and uncomplainingly endured hardship, leaving him only his cave in the rocks, which even the most grasping of many-handed Mandarins cannot remove, his cloak of skins, which no beggar would gratefully receive, and a bright and increasing light of deep hate scorching within his mind which nothing but the blood of the obdurate extortioner can efficiently quench. No protection of charms or heavily-mailed bowmen shall avail him, for in his craving for just revenge this person will meet witchcraft with a Heaven-sent cause and oppose an unsleeping subtlety against strength. Therefore let not the innocent suffer through an insufficient understanding, O Divine One, but direct the hand of your faithful worshipper towards the heart that is proud in tyranny, and holds as empty words the clearly defined promise of an all-seeing justice."

Scarcely had Yang Hu made an end of speaking before there happened an event which could be regarded in no other light than as a direct answer to his plainly expressed request for a definite sign. Upon the clear air, which had become unnaturally still at Yang Hu's words, as though to remove any chance of doubt that this indeed was the requested answer, came the loud beating of many very powerful brass gongs, indicating the approach of some person of undoubted importance. In a very brief period the procession reached the square, the gong-beaters being followed by persons carrying banners, bowmen in armour, others bearing various weapons and instruments of torture, slaves displaying innumerable changes of raiment to prove the rank and consequence of their master, umbrella carriers and fan wavers, and finally, preceded by incense burners and surrounded by servants who cleared away all obstructions by means of their formidable and heavily knotted lashes, the unworthy and deceitful Mandarin Ping Siang, who sat in a silk-hung and elaborately wrought chair, looking from side to side with gestures and expressions of contempt and ill-restrained cupidity.

At the sign of this powerful but unscrupulous person all those who were present fell upon their faces, leaving a broad space in their midst, except Yang Hu, who stepped back into the shadow of a doorway, being resolved that he would not prostrate himself before one whom Heaven had pointed out as the proper object of his just vengeance.

When the chair of Ping Siang could no longer be observed in the distance, and the sound of his many gongs had died away, all the persons who had knelt at his approach rose to their feet, meeting each other's eyes with glances of assured and profound significance. At length there stepped forth an exceedingly aged man, who was generally believed to have the power of reading omens and forecasting futures, so that at his upraised hand all persons became silent.

"Behold!" he exclaimed, "none can turn aside in doubt from the deliberately pointed finger of Buddha. Henceforth, in spite of the well-intentioned suggestions of those who would shield him under the plea of exacting orders from high ones at Peking or extortions practised by slaves under him of which he is ignorant, there can no longer be any two voices concerning the guilty one. Yet what does the knowledge of the cormorant's cry avail the golden carp in the shallow waters of the Yuen-Kiang? A prickly mormosa is an adequate protection against a naked man armed only with a just cause, and a company of bowmen has been known to quench an entire city's Heaven-felt desire for retribution. This person, and doubtless others also, would have experienced a more heartfelt enthusiasm in the matter if the sublime and omnipotent Buddha had gone a step further, and pointed out not only the one to be punished, but also the instrument by which the destiny could be prudently and effectively accomplished."

From the mountain path which led to Yang Hu's cave came a voice, like an expressly devised reply to this speech. It was that of some person uttering the "Chant of Rewards and Penalties":

"How strong is the mountain sycamore!
"Its branches reach the Middle Air, and the eye of none can pierce its foliage;
"It draws power and nourishment from all around, so that weeds alone may flourish under its shadow.
"Robbers find safety within the hollow of its trunk; its branches hide vampires and all manner of evil things which prey upon the innocent;
"The wild boar of the forest sharpen their tusks against the bark, for it is harder than flint, and the axe of the woodsman turns back upon the striker.
"Then cries the sycamore, 'Hail and rain have no power against me, nor can the fiercest sun penetrate beyond my outside fringe;
"'The man who impiously raises his hand against me falls by his own stroke and weapon.
"'Can there be a greater or a more powerful than this one? Assuredly, I am Buddha; let all things obey me.'
"Whereupon the weeds bow their heads, whispering among themselves, 'The voice of the Tall One we hear, but not that of Buddha. Indeed, it is doubtless as he says.'
"In his musk-scented Heaven Buddha laughs, and not deigning to raise his head from the lap of the Phoenix Goddess, he thrusts forth a stone which lies by his foot.
"Saying, 'A god's present for a god. Take it carefully, O presumptuous Little One, for it is hot to the touch.'
"The thunderbolt falls and the mighty tree is rent in twain. 'They asked for my messenger,' said the Pure One, turning again to repose.
"Lo, *he comes!*"

With the last spoken word there came into the sight of those who were collected together a person of stern yet engaging appearance. His hands and face were the colour of mulberry stain by long exposure to the sun, while his eyes looked forth like two watch-fires outside a wolf-haunted camp. His long pigtail was tangled with the binding tendrils of the forest, and damp with the dew of an open couch. His apparel was in no way striking or brilliant, yet he strode with the dignity and air of a high official, pushing before him a covered box upon wheels.

"It is Tung Fel!" cried many who stood there watching his approach, in tones which showed those who spoke to be inspired by a variety of impressive emotions. "Undoubtedly this is the seventh day of the month of Winged Dragons, and, as he specifically stated would be the case, lo! he has come."

Few were the words of greeting which Tung Fel accorded even to the most venerable of those who awaited him.

"This person has slept, partaken of fruit and herbs, and devoted an allotted time to inward contemplation," he said briefly. "Other and more weighty matters than the exchange of dignified compliments and the admiration of each other's profiles remain to be accomplished. What, for example, is the significance of the written parchment which is displayed in so obtrusive a manner before our eyes? Bring it to this person without delay."

At these words all those present followed Tung Fel's gaze with astonishment, for conspicuously displayed upon the wall of the Temple was a written notice which all joined in asserting had not been there the moment before, though no man had approached the spot. Nevertheless it was quickly brought to Tung Fel, who took it without any fear or hesitation and read aloud the words which it contained.

"*To the Custom-Respecting Persons of Ching-Fow*

"Truly the span of existence of any upon this earth is brief and not to be considered; therefore, O unfortunate dwellers of Ching-fow, let it not affect your digestion that your bodies are in peril of sudden and most excruciating tortures and your Family Temples in danger of humiliating disregard.

"Why do your thoughts follow the actions of the noble Mandarin Ping Siang so insidiously, and why after each unjust exaction do your eyes look redly towards the Yamen?

"Is he not the little finger of those at Peking, obeying their commands and only carrying out the taxation which others have devised? Indeed, he himself has stated such to be the fact. If, therefore, a terrible and unforeseen fate overtook the usually cautious and well-armed Ping Siang, doubtless-perhaps after the lapse of some considerable time-another would be sent from Peking for a like purpose, and in this way, after a too-brief period of heaven-sent rest and prosperity, affairs would regulate themselves into almost as unendurable a condition as before.

"Therefore ponder these things well, O passer-by. Yesterday the only man-child of Huang the wood-carver was taken away to be sold into slavery by the emissaries of the most just Ping Siang (who would not have acted thus, we are assured, were it not for the insatiable ones at Peking), as it had become plain that the very necessitous Huang had no other possession to contribute to the amount to be expended in coloured lights as a mark of public rejoicing on the occasion of the moonday of the sublime Emperor. The illiterate and prosaic-minded Huang, having in a most unseemly manner reviled and even assailed those who acted in the matter, has been effectively disposed of, and his wife now alternately laughs and shrieks in the Establishment of Irregular Intellects.

"For this reason, gazer, and because the matter touches you more closely than, in your self-imagined security, you are prone to think, deal expediently with the time at your disposal. Look twice and lingeringly to-night upon the face of your first-born, and clasp the form of your favourite one in a closer embrace, for he by whose hand the blow is directed may already have cast devouring eyes upon their fairness, and to-morrow he may say to his armed men: 'The time is come; bring her to me.'"

"From the last sentence of the well-intentioned and undoubtedly moderately-framed notice this person will take two phrases," remarked Tung Fel, folding the written paper and placing it among his garments, "which shall serve him as the title of the lifelike and accurately-represented play which it is his self-conceited intention now to disclose to this select and unprejudiced gathering. The scene represents an enlightened and well-merited justice overtaking an arrogant and intolerable being who-need this person add? —existed many dynasties ago, and the title is:

"*The Time Is Come!*
By Whose Hand?"

Delivering himself in this manner, Tung Fel drew back the hanging drapery which concealed the front of his large box, and disclosed to those who were gathered round, not, as they had expected, a passage from the Record of the Three Kingdoms, or some other dramatic work of undoubted merit, but an ingeniously constructed representation of a scene outside the walls of their own Ching-fow. On one side was a small but minutely accurate copy of a wood-burner's hut, which was known to all present, while behind stood out the distant but nevertheless unmistakable walls of the city. But it was nearest part of the spectacle that first held the attention of the entranced beholders, for there disported themselves, in every variety of guileless and attractive attitude, a number of young and entirely unconcerned doves. Scarcely had the delighted onlookers fully observed the pleasing and effective scene, or uttered their expressions of polished satisfaction at the graceful and unassuming behaviour of the pretty creatures before them, than the view entirely changed, and, as if by magic, the massive and inelegant building of Ping Siang's Yamen was presented before them. As all gazed, astonished, the great door of the Yamen opened stealthily, and without a moment's pause a lean and ill-conditioned rat, of unnatural size and rapacity, dashed out and seized the most select and engaging of the unsuspecting prey in its hungry jaws. With the expiring cry of the innocent victim the entire box was immediately, and in the most unexpected manner, involved in a profound darkness, which cleared away as suddenly and revealed the forms of the despoiler and the victim lying dead by each other's side.

Tung Fel came forward to receive the well-selected compliments of all who had witnessed the entertainment.

"It may be objected," he remarked, "that the play is, in a manner of expressing one's self, incomplete; for it is unrevealed by whose hand the act of justice was accomplished. Yet in this detail is the accuracy of the representation justified, for though the time has come, the hand by which retribution is accorded shall never be observed."

In such a manner did Tung Fel come to Ching-fow on the seventh day of the month of Winged Dragons, throwing aside all restraint, and no longer urging prudence or delay. Of all the throng which stood before him scarcely one was without a deep offence against Ping Siang, while those who had not as yet suffered feared what the morrow might display.

A wandering monk from the Island of Irredeemable Plagues was the first to step forth in response to Tung Fel's plainly understood suggestion.

"There is no necessity for this person to undertake further acts of benevolence," he remarked, dropping the cloak from his shoulder and displaying the hundred and eight scars of extreme virtue; "nor," he continued, holding up his left hand, from which three fingers were burnt away, "have greater endurances been neglected. Yet the matter before this distinguished gathering is one which merits the favourable consideration of all persons, and this one will in no manner turn away, recounting former actions, while he allows others to press forward towards the accomplishment of the just and divinely-inspired act."

With these words the devout and unassuming person in question inscribed his name upon a square piece of rice-paper, attesting his sincerity to the fixed purpose for which it was designed by dipping his thumb into the mixed blood of the slain animals and impressing this unalterable seal upon the paper also. He was followed by a seller of drugs and subtle medicines, whose entire stock had been seized and destroyed by order of Ping Siang, so that no one in Ching-fow might obtain poison for his destruction. Then came an overwhelming stream of persons, all of whom had received some severe and well-remembered injury at the hands of the malicious and vindictive Mandarin. All these followed a similar observance, inscribing their names and binding themselves by the Blood Oath. Last of all Yang Hu stepped up, partly from a natural modesty which restrained him from offering himself when so many more versatile persons of proved excellence were willing to engage in the matter, and partly because an ill-advised conflict was taking place within his mind as to whether the extreme course which was contemplated was the most expedient to pursue. At last, however, he plainly perceived that he could not honourably withhold himself from an affair that was in a measure the direct outcome of his own unendurable loss, so that without further hesitation he added his obscure name to the many illustrious ones already in Tung Fel's keeping.

When at length dark fell upon the city and the cries of the watchmen, warning all prudent ones to bar well their doors against robbers, as they themselves were withdrawing until the morrow, no longer rang through the narrow ways of Ching-fow, all those persons who had pledged themselves by name and seal went forth silently, and came together at the place whereof Tung Fel had secretly conveyed them knowledge. There Tung Fel, standing somewhat apart, placed all the folded papers in the form of a circle, and having performed over them certain observances designed to insure a just decision and to keep away evil influences, submitted the selection to the discriminating choice of the Sacred Flat and Round Sticks. Having in this manner secured the name of the appointed person who should carry out the act of justice and retribution, Tung Fel unfolded the paper, inscribed certain words upon it, and replaced it among the others.

"The moment before great deeds," began Tung Fel, stepping forward and addressing himself to the expectant ones who were gathered round, "is not the time for light speech, nor, indeed, for sentences of dignified length, no matter how pleasantly turned to the ear they may be. Before this person stand many who are undoubtedly illustrious in various arts and virtues, yet one among them is pre-eminently marked out for distinction in that his name shall be handed down in imperishable history as that of a patriot of a pure-minded and uncompromising degree. With him there is no need of further speech, and to this end I have inscribed certain words upon his namepaper. To everyone this person will now return the paper which has been entrusted to him, folded so that the nature of its contents shall be an unwritten leaf to all others. Nor shall the papers be unfolded by any until he is within his own chamber, with barred doors, where all, save the one who shall find the message, shall remain, not venturing forth until daybreak. I, Tung Fel, have spoken, and assuredly I shall not eat my word, which is that a certain and most degrading death awaits any who transgress these commands."

It was with the short and sudden breath of the cowering antelope when the stealthy tread of the pitiless tiger approaches its lair, that Yang Hu opened his paper in the seclusion of his own cave; for his mind was darkened with an inspired inside emotion that he, the one doubting among the eagerly proffering and destructively inclined multitude, would be chosen to accomplish the high aim for which, indeed, he felt exceptionally unworthy. The written sentence which he perceived immediately upon unfolding the paper, instructing him to appear again before Tung Fel at the hour of midnight, was, therefore, nothing but the echo and fulfilment of his own thoughts, and served in reality to impress his mind with calmer feelings of dignified unconcern than would have been the case had he not been chosen. Having neither possessions nor relations, the occupation of disposing of his goods and making ceremonious and affectionate leavetakings of his family, against the occurrence of any unforeseen disaster, engrossed no portion of Yang Hu's time. Yet there was one matter to which no reference has yet been made, but which now forces itself obtrusively upon the attention, which was in a large measure responsible for many of the most prominent actions of Yang Hu's life, and, indeed, in no small degree influenced his hesitation in offering himself before Tung Fel.

Not a bowshot distance from the place where the mountain path entered the outskirts of the city lived Hiya-ai-Shao with her parents, who were persons of assured position, though of no particular wealth. For a period not confined to a single year it had been the custom of Yang Hu to offer to this elegant and refined maiden all the rarest pieces of jade which he could discover, while the most symmetrical and remunerative she-goat in his flock enjoyed the honourable distinction of bearing her incomparable name. Towards the almond garden of Hiya's abode Yang Hu turned his footsteps upon leaving his cave, and standing there, concealed from all sides by the white and abundant flower-laden foliage, he uttered a sound which had long been an agreed signal between them. Presently a faint perfume of choo-lan spoke of her near approach, and without delay Hiya herself stood by his side.

"Well-endowed one," said Yang Hu, when at length they had gazed upon each other's features and made renewals of their protestations of mutual regard, "the fixed intentions of a person have often been fitly likened to the seed of the tree-peony, so ineffectual are their efforts among the winds of constantly changing circumstance. The definite hope of this person had long pointed towards a small but adequate habitation, surrounded by sweet-smelling olive-trees and not far distant from the jade cliffs and pastures which would afford a sufficient remuneration and a means of living. This entrancing picture has been blotted out for the time, and in its place this person finds himself face to face with an arduous and dangerous undertaking, followed, perhaps, by hasty and immediate flight. Yet if the adorable Hiya will prove the unchanging depths of her constantly expressed intention by accompanying him as far as the village of Hing where suitable marriage ceremonies can be observed without delay, the exile will in reality be in the nature of a triumphal procession, and the emotions with which this person has hitherto regarded the entire circumstance will undergo a complete and highly accomplished change."

"Oh, Yang!" exclaimed the maiden, whose feelings at hearing these words were in no way different from those of her lover when he was on the point of opening the folded paper upon which Tung Fel had written; "what is the nature of the mission upon which you are so impetuously resolved? and why will it be followed by flight?"

"The nature of the undertaking cannot be revealed by reason of a deliberately taken oath," replied Yang Hu; "and the reason of its possible consequence is a less important question to the two persons who are here conversing together than of whether the amiable and graceful Hiya is willing to carry out her often-expressed desire for an opportunity of displaying the true depths of her emotions towards this one."

"Alas!" said Hiya, "the sentiments which this person expressed with irreproachable honourableness when the sun was high in the heavens and the probability of secretly leaving an undoubtedly well-appointed home was engagingly remote, seem to have an entirely different significance when recalled by night in a damp orchard, and on the eve of their fulfilment. To deceive one's parents is an ignoble prospect; furthermore, it is often an exceedingly difficult undertaking. Let the matter be arranged in this way: that Yang leaves the ultimate details of the scheme to Hiya's expedient care, he proceeding without delay to Hing, or, even more desirable, to the further town of Liyunnan, and there awaiting her coming. By such means the risk of discovery and pursuit will be lessened, Yang will be able to set forth on his journey with greater speed, and this one will have an opportunity of getting together certain articles without which, indeed, she would be very inadequately equipped."

In spite of his conscientious desire that Hiya should be by his side on the journey, together with an unendurable certainty that evil would arise from the course she proposed, Yang was compelled by an innate feeling of respect to agree to her wishes, and in this manner the arrangement was definitely concluded. Thereupon Hiya, without delay, returned to the dwelling, remarking that otherwise her absence might be detected and the entire circumstance thereby discovered, leaving Yang Hu to continue his journey and again present himself before Tung Fel, as he had been instructed.

Tung Fel was engaged with brush and ink when Yang Hu entered. Round him were many written parchments, some venerable with age, and a variety of other matters, among which might be clearly perceived weapons, and devices for reading the future. He greeted Yang with many tokens of dignified respect, and with an evidently restrained emotion led him towards the light of a hanging lantern, where he gazed into his face for a considerable period with every indication of exceptional concern.

"Yang Hu," he said at length, "at such a moment many dark and searching thoughts may naturally arise in the mind concerning objects and reasons, omens, and the moving cycle of events. Yet in all these, out of a wisdom gained by deep endurance and a hardly-won experience beyond the common lot, this person would say, Be content. The hand of destiny, though it may at times appear to move in a devious manner, is ever approaching its appointed aim. To this end were you chosen."

"The choice was openly made by wise and proficient omens," replied Yang Hu, without any display of uncertainty of purpose, "and this person is content."

Tung Fel then administered to Yang the Oath of Buddha's Face and the One called the Unutterable (which may not be further described in written words) thereby binding his body and soul, and the souls and repose of all who had gone before him in direct line and all who should in a like manner follow after, to the accomplishment of the design. All spoken matter being thus complete between them, he gave him a mask with which he should pass unknown through the streets and into the presence of Ping Siang, a variety of weapons to use as the occasion arose, and a sign by which the attendants at the Yamen would admit him without further questioning.

As Yang Hu passed through the streets of Ching-fow, which were in a great measure deserted owing to the command of Tung Fel, he was aware of many mournful and foreboding sounds which accompanied him on all sides, while shadowy faces, bearing signs of intolerable anguish and despair, continually formed themselves out of the wind. By the time he reached the Yamen a tempest of exceptional violence was in progress, nor were other omens absent which tended to indicate that matters of a very unpropitious nature were about to take place.

At each successive door of the Yamen the attendant stepped back and covered his face, so that he should by no chance perceive who had come upon so destructive a mission, the instant

Yang Hu uttered the sign with which Tung Fel had provided him. In this manner Yang quickly reached the door of the inner chamber upon which was inscribed: "Let the person who comes with a doubtful countenance, unbidden, or meditating treachery, remember the curse and manner of death which attended Lai Kuen, who slew the one over him; so shall he turn and go forth in safety." This unworthy safeguard at the hands of a person who passed his entire life in altering the fixed nature of justice, and who never went beyond his outer gate without an armed company of bowmen, inspired Yang Hu with so incautious a contempt, that without any hesitation he drew forth his brush and ink, and in a spirit of bitter signification added the words, "'Come, let us eat together,' said the wolf to the she-goat."

Being now within a step of Ping Siang and the completion of his undertaking, Yang Hu drew tighter the cords of his mask, tested and proved his weapons, and then, without further delay, threw open the door before him and stepped into the chamber, barring the door quickly so that no person might leave or enter without his consent.

At this interruption and manner of behaving, which clearly indicated the nature of the errand upon which the person before him had come, Ping Siang rose from his couch and stretched out his hand towards a gong which lay beside him.

"All summonses for aid are now unavailing, Ping Siang," exclaimed Yang, without in any measure using delicate or set phrases of speech; "for, as you have doubtless informed yourself, the slaves of tyrants are the first to welcome the downfall of their lord."

"The matter of your speech is as emptiness to this person," replied the Mandarin, affecting with extreme difficulty an appearance of no-concern. "In what manner has he fallen? And how will the depraved and self-willed person before him avoid the well-deserved tortures which certainly await him in the public square on the morrow, as the reward of his intolerable presumptions?"

"O Mandarin," cried Yang Hu, "the fitness and occasion for such speeches as the one to which you have just given utterance lie as far behind you as the smoke of yesterday's sacrifice. With what manner of eyes have you frequently journeyed through Ching-fow of late, if the signs and omens there have not already warned you to prepare a coffin adequately designed to receive your well-proportioned body? Has not the pungent vapour of burning houses assailed your senses at every turn, or the salt tears from the eyes of forlorn ones dashed your peach-tea and spiced foods with bitterness?"

"Alas!" exclaimed Ping Siang, "this person now certainly begins to perceive that many things which he has unthinkingly allowed would present a very unendurable face to others."

"In such a manner has it appeared to all Ching-fow," said Yang Hu; "and the justice of your death has been universally admitted. Even should this one fail there would be an innumerable company eager to take his place. Therefore, O Ping Siang, as the only favour which it is within this person's power to accord, select that which in your opinion is the most agreeable manner and weapon for your end."

"It is truly said that at the Final Gate of the Two Ways the necessity for elegant and well-chosen sentences ends," remarked Ping Siang with a sigh, "otherwise the manner of your address would be open to reproach. By your side this person perceives a long and apparently highly-tempered sword, which, in his opinion, will serve the purpose efficiently. Having no remarks of an improving but nevertheless exceedingly tedious nature with which to imprint the occasion for the benefit of those who come after, his only request is that the blow shall be an unhesitating and sufficiently well-directed one."

At these words Yang Hu threw back his cloak to grasp the sword-handle, when the Mandarin, with his eyes fixed on the naked arm, and evidently inspired by every manner of conflicting emotions, uttered a cry of unspeakable wonder and incomparable surprise.

"The Serpent!" he cried, in a voice from which all evenness and control were absent. "The Sacred Serpent of our Race! O mysterious one, who and whence are you?"

Engulfed in an all-absorbing doubt at the nature of events, Yang could only gaze at the form of the serpent which had been clearly impressed upon his arm from the earliest time of his remembrance, while Ping Siang, tearing the silk garment from his own arm and displaying thereon a similar form, continued:

"Behold the inevitable and unvarying birthmark of our race! So it was with this person's father and the ones before him; so it was with his treacherously-stolen son; so it will be to the end of all time."

Trembling beyond all power of restraint, Yang removed the mask which had hitherto concealed his face.

"Father or race has this person none," he said, looking into Ping Siang's features with an all-engaging hope, tempered in a measure by a soul-benumbing dread; "nor memory or tradition of an earlier state than when he herded goats and sought for jade in the southern mountains."

"Nevertheless," exclaimed the Mandarin, whose countenance was lightened with an interest and a benevolent emotion which had never been seen there before, "beyond all possibility of doubting, you are this person's lost and greatly-desired son, stolen away many years ago by the treacherous conduct of an unworthy woman, yet now happily and miraculously restored to cherish his declining years and perpetuate an honourable name and race."

"Happily!" exclaimed Yang, with fervent indications of uncontrollable bitterness. "Oh, my illustrious sire, at whose venerated feet this unworthy person now prostrates himself with well-merited marks of reverence and self-abasement, has the errand upon which an ignoble son entered-the every memory of which now causes him the acutest agony of the lost, but which nevertheless he is pledged to Tung Fel by the Unutterable Oath to perform-has this unnatural and eternally cursed thing escaped your versatile mind?"

"Tung Fel!" cried Ping Siang. "Is, then, this blow also by the hand of that malicious and vindictive person? Oh, what a cycle of events and interchanging lines of destiny do your words disclose!"

"Who, then, is Tung Fel, my revered Father?" demanded Yang.

"It is a matter which must be made clear from the beginning," replied Ping Siang. "At one time this person and Tung Fel were, by nature and endowments, united in the most amiable bonds of an inseparable friendship. Presently Tung Fel signed the preliminary contract of a marriage with one who seemed to be endowed with every variety of enchanting and virtuous grace, but who was, nevertheless, as the unrolling of future events irresistibly discovered, a person of irregular character and undignified habits. On the eve of the marriage ceremony this person was made known to her by the undoubtedly enraptured Tung Fel, whereupon he too fell into the snare of her engaging personality, and putting aside all thoughts of prudent restraint, made her more remunerative offers of marriage than Tung Fel could by any possible chance overbid. In such a manner-for after the nature of her kind riches were exceptionally attractive to her degraded imagination-she became this person's wife, and the mother of his only son. In spite of these great honours, however, the undoubted perversity of her nature made her an easy accomplice to the duplicity of Tung Fel, who, by means of various disguises, found frequent opportunity of uttering in her presence numerous well-thought-out suggestions specially designed to lead her imagination towards an existence in which this person had no adequate representation. Becoming at length terrified at the possibility of these unworthy emotions, obtruding themselves upon this person's notice, the two in question fled together, taking with them the one who without any doubt is now before me. Despite the most assiduous search and very tempting and profitable offers of reward, no information of a reliable nature could be obtained, and at length this dispirited and completely changed person gave up the pursuit as unavailing. With his son and heir, upon whose future he had greatly hoped, all emotions of a generous and high-minded nature left him, and in a very short space of time he became the avaricious and deservedly unpopular individual against whose extortions the amiable and long-suffering ones of Ching-fow have for so many years protested mildly. The sudden and not altogether unexpected fate which is now on the point of reaching him is altogether too lenient to be entirely adequate."

"Oh, my distinguished and really immaculate sire!" cried Yang Hu, in a voice which expressed the deepest feelings of contrition. "No oaths or vows, however sacred, can induce this person to stretch forth his hand against the one who stands before him."

"Nevertheless," replied Ping Siang, speaking of the matter as though it were one which did not closely concern his own existence, "to neglect the Unutterable Oath would inevitably involve not only the two persons who are now conversing together, but also those before and those who are to come after in direct line, in a much worse condition of affairs. That is a fate which this person would by no means permit to exist, for one of his chief desires has ever been to establish a strong and vigorous line, to which end, indeed, he was even now concluding a marriage arrangement with the beautiful and refined Hiya-ai-Shao, whom he had at length persuaded into accepting his betrothal tokens without reluctance."

"Hiya-ai-Shao!" exclaimed Yang; "she has accepted your silk-bound gifts?"

"The matter need not concern us now," replied the Mandarin, not observing in his complicated emotions the manner in which the name of Hiya had affected Yang, revealing as it undoubtedly did the treachery of his beloved one. "There only appears to be one honourable way in which the full circumstances can be arranged, and this person will in no measure endeavour to avoid it."

"Such an end is neither ignoble nor painful," he said, in an unchanging voice; "nor will this one in any way shrink from so easy and honourable a solution."

"The affairs of the future do not exhibit themselves in delicately coloured hues to this person," said Yang Hu; "and he would, if the thing could be so arranged, cheerfully submit to a similar fate in order that a longer period of existence should be assured to one who has every variety of claim upon his affection."

"The proposal is a graceful and conscientious one," said Ping Siang, "and is, moreover, a gratifying omen of the future of our race, which must of necessity be left in your hands. But, for that reason itself, such a course cannot be pursued. Nevertheless, the events of the past few hours have been of so exceedingly prosperous and agreeable a nature that this short-sighted and frequently desponding person can now pass beyond with a tranquil countenance and every assurance of divine favour."

With these words Ping Siang indicated that he was desirous of setting forth the Final Expression, and arranging the necessary matters upon the table beside him, he stretched forth his hands over Yang Hu, who placed himself in a suitable attitude of reverence and abasement.

"Yang Hu," began the Mandarin, "undoubted son, and, after the accomplishment of the intention which it is our fixed purpose to carry out, fitting representative of the person who is here before you, engrave well within your mind the various details upon which he now gives utterance. Regard the virtues; endeavour to pass an amiable and at the same time not unremunerative existence; and on all occasions sacrifice freely, to the end that the torments of those who have gone before may be made lighter, and that others may be induced in turn to perform a like benevolent charity for yourself. Having expressed himself upon these general subjects, this person now makes a last and respectfully-considered desire, which it is his deliberate wish should be carried to the proper deities as his final expression of opinion: That Yang Hu may grow as supple as the dried juice of the bending-palm, and as straight as the most vigorous bamboo from the forests of the North. That he may increase beyond the prolificness of the white-necked crow and cover the ground after the fashion of the binding grass. That in battle his sword may be as a vividly-coloured and many-forked lightning flash, accompanied by thunderbolts as irresistible as Buddha's divine wrath; in peace his voice as resounding as the rolling of many powerful drums among the Khingan Mountains. That when the kindled fire of his existence returns to the great Mountain of Pure Flame the earth shall accept again its component parts, and in no way restrain the divine essence from journeying to its destined happiness. These words are Ping Siang's last expression of opinion before he passes beyond, given in the unvarying assurance that so sacred and important a petition will in no way be neglected."

Having in this manner completed all the affairs which seemed to be of a necessary and urgent nature, and fixing his last glance upon Yang Hu with every variety of affectionate and estimable emotion, the Mandarin drank a sufficient quantity of the liquid, and placing himself upon a couch in an attitude of repose, passed in this dignified and unassuming manner into the Upper Air.

After the space of a few moments spent in arranging certain objects and in inward contemplation, Yang Hu crossed the chamber, still holding the half-filled vessel of gold-leaf in his hand, and drawing back the hanging silk, gazed over the silent streets of Ching-fow and towards the great sky-lantern above.

"Hiya is faithless," he said at length in an unspeaking voice; "this person's mother a bitter-tasting memory, his father a swiftly passing shadow that is now for ever lost." His eyes rested upon the closed vessel in his hand. "Gladly would —" his thoughts began, but with this unworthy image a new impression formed itself within his mind. "A clearly-expressed wish was uttered," he concluded, "and Tung Fel still remains." With this resolution he stepped back into the chamber and struck the gong loudly.

The Career of the Charitable Quen-Ki-Tong

First Period: The Public Official

"The motives which inspired the actions of the devout Quen-Ki-Tong have long been ill-reported," said Kai Lung the story-teller, upon a certain occasion at Wu-whei, "and, as a consequence, his illustrious memory has suffered somewhat. Even as the insignificant earth-worm may bring the precious and many coloured jewel to the surface, so has it been permitted to this obscure and superficially educated one to discover the truth of the entire matter among the badly-arranged and frequently really illegible documents preserved at the Hall of Public Reference at Peking. Without fear of contradiction, therefore, he now sets forth the credible version.

"Quen-Ki-Tong was one who throughout his life had been compelled by the opposing force of circumstances to be content with what was offered rather than attain to that which he desired. Having been allowed to wander over the edge of an exceedingly steep crag, while still a child, by the aged and untrustworthy person who had the care of him, and yet suffering little hurt, he was carried back to the city in triumph, by the one in question, who, to cover her neglect, declared amid many chants of exultation that as he slept a majestic winged form had snatched him from her arms and traced magical figures with his body on the ground in token of the distinguished sacred existence for which he was undoubtedly set apart. In such a manner he became famed at a very early age for an unassuming mildness of character and an almost inspired piety of life, so that on every side frequent opportunity was given him for the display of these amiable qualities. Should it chance that an insufficient quantity of puppy-pie had been prepared for the family repast, the undesirable but necessary portion of cold dried rat would inevitably be allotted to the uncomplaining Quen, doubtless accompanied by the engaging but unnecessary remark that he alone had a Heaven-sent intellect which was fixed upon more sublime images than even the best constructed puppy-pie. Should the number of sedan-chairs not be sufficient to bear to the Exhibition of Kites all who were desirous of becoming entertained in such a fashion, inevitably would Quen be the one left behind, in order that he might have adequate leisure for dignified and pure-minded internal reflexion.

"In this manner it came about that when a very wealthy but unnaturally avaricious and evil-tempered person who was connected with Quen's father in matters of commerce expressed his fixed determination that the most deserving and enlightened of his friend's sons should enter into a marriage agreement with his daughter, there was no manner of hesitation among those concerned, who admitted without any questioning between themselves that Quen was undeniably the one referred to.

"Though naturally not possessing an insignificant intellect, a continuous habit, together with a most irreproachable sense of filial duty, subdued within Quen's internal organs whatever reluctance he might have otherwise displayed in the matter, so that as courteously as was necessary he presented to the undoubtedly very ordinary and slow-witted maiden in question the gifts of irretrievable intention, and honourably carried out his spoken and written words towards her.

"For a period of years the circumstances of the various persons did not in any degree change, Quen in the meantime becoming more pure-souled and inward-seeing with each moon-change, after the manner of the sublime Lien-ti, who studied to maintain an unmoved endurance in all varieties of events by placing his body to a greater extent each day in a vessel of boiling liquid. Nevertheless, the good and charitable deities to whom Quen unceasingly sacrificed were not altogether unmindful of his virtues; for a son was born, and an evil disease which arose from a most undignified display of uncontrollable emotion on her part ended in his wife being deposited with becoming ceremony in the Family Temple.

"Upon a certain evening, when Quen sat in his inner chamber deliberating upon the really beneficent yet somewhat inexplicable arrangement of the all-seeing ones to whom he was very amiably disposed in consequence of the unwonted tranquillity which he now enjoyed, yet who, it appeared to him, could have set out the entire matter in a much more satisfactory way from the beginning, he was made aware by the unexpected beating of many gongs, and by other signs of refined and deferential welcome, that a person of exalted rank was approaching his residence. While he was still hesitating in his uncertainty regarding the most courteous and delicate form of self-abasement with which to honour so important a visitor-whether to rush forth and allow the chair-carriers to pass over his prostrate form, to make a pretence of being a low-caste slave, and in that guise doing menial service, or to conceal himself beneath a massive and overhanging table until his guest should have availed himself of the opportunity to examine at his leisure whatever the room contained-the person in question stood before him. In every detail of dress and appointment he had the undoubted appearance of being one to whom no door might be safely closed.

"'Alas!' exclaimed Quen, 'how inferior and ill-contrived is the mind of a person of my feeble intellectual attainments. Even at this moment, when the near approach of one who obviously commands every engaging accomplishment might reasonably be expected to call up within it an adequate amount of commonplace resource, its ill-destined possessor finds himself entirely incapable of conducting himself with the fitting outward marks of his great internal respect. This residence is certainly unprepossessing in the extreme, yet it contains many objects of some value and of great rarity; illiterate as this person is, he would not be so presumptuous as to offer any for your acceptance, but if you will confer upon him the favour of selecting that which appears to be the most priceless and unreplaceable, he will immediately, and with every manifestation of extreme delight, break it irredeemably in your honour, to prove the unaffected depth of his gratified emotions.'

"'Quen-Ki-Tong,' replied the person before him, speaking with an evident sincerity of purpose, 'pleasant to this one's ears are your words, breathing as they do an obvious hospitality and a due regard for the forms of etiquette. But if, indeed, you are desirous of gaining this person's explicit regard, break no articles of fine porcelain or rare inlaid wood in proof of it, but immediately dismiss to a very distant spot the three-score gong-beaters who have enclosed him within two solid rings, and who are now carrying out their duties in so diligent a manner that he greatly doubts if the unimpaired faculties of hearing will ever be fully restored. Furthermore, if your exceedingly amiable intentions desire fuller expression, cause an unstinted number of vessels of some uninflammable liquid to be conveyed into your chrysanthemum garden and there poured over the numerous fireworks and coloured lights which still appear to be in progress. Doubtless they are well-intentioned marks of respect, but they caused this person considerable apprehension as he passed among them, and, indeed, give to this unusually pleasant and unassuming spot the by no means inviting atmosphere of a low-class tea-house garden during the festivities attending the birthday of the sacred Emperor.'

"'This person is overwhelmed with a most unendurable confusion that the matters referred to should have been regarded in such a light,' replied Quen humbly. 'Although he himself had no knowledge of them until this moment, he is confident that they in no wise differ from the usual honourable manifestations with which it is customary in this Province to welcome strangers of exceptional rank and titles.'

"'The welcome was of a most dignified and impressive nature,' replied the stranger, with every appearance of not desiring to cause Quen any uneasy internal doubts; 'yet the fact is none the less true that at the moment this person's head seems to contain an exceedingly powerful and well-equipped band; and also, that as he passed through the courtyard an ingeniously constructed but somewhat unmanageable figure of gigantic size, composed entirely of jets of many-coloured flame, leaped out suddenly from behind a dark wall and made an almost successful attempt to embrace him in its ever-revolving arms. Lo Yuen greatly fears that the time when he would have rejoiced in the necessary display of agility to which the incident gave rise has for ever passed away.'

"'Lo Yuen!' exclaimed Quen, with an unaffected mingling of the emotions of reverential awe and pleasureable anticipation. 'Can it indeed be an uncontroversial fact that so learned and ornamental a person as the renowned Controller of Unsolicited Degrees stands beneath this inelegant person's utterly unpresentable roof! Now, indeed, he plainly understands why this ill-conditioned chamber has the appearance of being filled with a Heaven-sent brilliance, and why at the first spoken words of the one before him a melodious sound, like the rushing waters of the sacred Tien-Kiang, seemed to fill his ears.'

"'Undoubtedly the chamber is pervaded by a very exceptional splendour,' replied Lo Yuen, who, in spite of his high position, regarded graceful talk and well-imagined compliments in a spirit of no-satisfaction; 'yet this commonplace-minded one has a fixed conviction that it is caused by the crimson-eyed and pink-fire-breathing dragon which, despite your slave's most assiduous efforts, is now endeavouring to climb through the aperture behind you. The noise which still fills his ears, also, resembles rather the despairing cries of the Ten Thousand Lost Ones at the first sight of the Pit of Liquid and Red-hot Malachite, yet without question both proceed from the same cause. Laying aside further ceremony, therefore, permit this greatly over-estimated person to disclose the object of his inopportune visit. Long have your amiable virtues been observed and appreciated by the high ones at Peking, O Quen-Ki-Tong. Too long have they been unrewarded and passed over in silence. Nevertheless, the moment of acknowledgement and advancement has at length arrived; for, as the Book of Verses clearly says, "Even the three-legged mule may contrive to reach the agreed spot in advance of the others, provided a circular running space has been selected and the number of rounds be sufficiently ample." It is this otherwise uninteresting and obtrusive person's graceful duty to convey to you the agreeable intelligence that the honourable and not ill-rewarded office of Guarder of the Imperial Silkworms has been conferred upon you, and to require you to proceed without delay to Peking, so that fitting ceremonies of admittance may be performed before the fifteenth day of the month of Feathered Insects.'

"Alas! how frequently does the purchaser of seemingly vigorous and exceptionally low-priced flower-seeds discover, when too late, that they are, in reality, fashioned from the root of the prolific and valueless tzu-ka, skilfully covered with a disguising varnish! Instead of presenting himself at the place of commerce frequented by those who entrust money to others on the promise of an increased repayment when certain very probable events have come to pass (so that if all else failed he would still possess a serviceable number of taels), Quen-Ki-Tong entirely neglected the demands of a most ordinary prudence, nor could he be induced to set out on his journey until he had passed seven days in public feasting to mark his good fortune, and then devoted fourteen more days to fasting and various acts of penance, in order to make known the regret with which he acknowledged his entire unworthiness for the honour before him. Owing to this very conscientious, but nevertheless somewhat short-sighted manner of behaving, Quen found himself unable to reach Peking before the day preceding that to which Lo Yuen had made special reference. From this cause it came about that only sufficient time remained to perform the various ceremonies of admission, without in any degree counselling Quen as to his duties and procedure in the fulfilment of his really important office.

"Among the many necessary and venerable ceremonies observed during the changing periods of the year, none occupy a more important place than those for which the fifteenth day of the month of Feathered Insects is reserved, conveying as they do a respectful and delicately-fashioned petition that the various affairs upon which persons in every condition of life are engaged may arrive at a pleasant and remunerative conclusion. At the earliest stroke of the gong the versatile Emperor, accompanied by many persons of irreproachable ancestry and certain others, very elaborately attired, proceeds to an open space set apart for the occasion. With unassuming dexterity the benevolent Emperor for a brief span of time engages in the menial occupation of a person of low class, and with his own hands ploughs an assigned portion of land in order that the enlightened spirits under whose direct guardianship the earth is placed may not become lax in their disinterested efforts to promote its fruitfulness. In this charitable exertion he is followed by various other persons of recognized position, the first being, by custom, the Guarder of the Imperial Silkworms, while at the same time the amiably-disposed Empress plants an allotted number of mulberry trees, and deposits upon their leaves the carefully reared insects which she receives from the hands of their Guarder. In the case of the accomplished Emperor an ingenious contrivance is resorted to by which the soil is drawn aside by means of hidden strings as the plough passes by, the implement in question being itself constructed from paper of the highest quality, while the oxen which draw it are, in reality, ordinary persons cunningly concealed within masks of cardboard. In this thoughtful manner the actual labours of the sublime Emperor are greatly lessened, while no chance is afforded for an inauspicious omen to be created by the rebellious behaviour of a maliciously-inclined ox, or by any other event of an unforeseen nature. All the other persons, however, are required to make themselves proficient in the art of ploughing, before the ceremony, so that the chances of the attendant spirits discovering the deception which has been practised upon them in the case of the Emperor may not be increased by its needless repetition. It was chiefly for this reason that Lo Yuen had urged Quen to journey to Peking as speedily as possible, but owing to the very short time which remained between his arrival and the ceremony of ploughing, not only had the person in question neglected to profit by instruction, but he was not even aware of the obligation which awaited him. When, therefore, in spite of every respectful protest on his part, he was led up to a massively-constructed implement drawn by two powerful and undeniably evilly-intentioned-looking animals, it was with every sign of great internal misgivings, and an entire absence of enthusiasm in the entertainment, that he commenced his not too well understood task. In this matter he was by no means mistaken, for it soon became plain to all observers-of whom an immense concourse was assembled-that the usually self-possessed Guarder of the Imperial Silkworms was conducting himself in a most undignified manner; for though he still clung to the plough-handles with an inspired tenacity, his body assumed every variety of base and uninviting attitude. Encouraged by this inelegant state of affairs, the evil spirits which are ever on the watch to turn into derision the charitable intentions of the pure-minded entered into the bodies of the oxen and provoked within their minds a sudden and malignant confidence that the time had arrived when they might with safety break into revolt and throw off the outward signs of their dependent condition. From these various causes it came about that Quen was, without warning, borne with irresistible certainty against the majestic person of the sacred Emperor, the inlaid box of Imperial silkworms, which up to that time had remained safely among the folds of his silk garment, alone serving to avert an even more violent and ill-destined blow.

"Well said the wise and deep-thinking Ye-te, in his book entitled *Proverbs of Everyday Happenings*, 'Should a person on returning from the city discover his house to be in flames, let him examine well the change which he has received from the chair-carrier before it is too late; for evil never travels alone.' Scarcely had the unfortunate Quen recovered his natural attributes from the effect of the disgraceful occurrence which has been recorded (which, indeed, furnished the matter of a song and many unpresentable jests among the low-class persons of the city), than the magnanimous Empress reached that detail of the tree-planting ceremony when it was requisite that she should deposit the living emblems of the desired increase and prosperity upon the leaves. Stretching forth her delicately-proportioned hand to Quen for this purpose, she received from the still greatly confused person in question the Imperial silkworms in so unseemly a condition that her eyes had scarcely rested upon them before she was seized with the rigid sickness, and in that state fell to the ground. At this new and entirely unforeseen calamity a very disagreeable certainty of approaching evil began to take possession of all those who stood around, many crying aloud that every omen of good was wanting, and declaring that unless something of a markedly propitiatory nature was quickly accomplished, the agriculture of the entire Empire would cease to flourish, and the various departments of the commerce in silk would undoubtedly be thrown into a state of most inextricable confusion. Indeed, in spite of all things designed to have a contrary effect, the matter came about in the way predicted, for the Hoang-Ho seven times overcame its restraining barriers, and poured its waters over the surrounding country, thereby gaining for the first time its well-deserved title of 'The Sorrow of China,' by which dishonourable but exceedingly appropriate designation it is known to this day.

"The manner of greeting which would have been accorded to Quen had he returned to the official quarter of the city, or the nature of his treatment by the baser class of the ordinary people if they succeeded in enticing him to come among them, formed a topic of such uninviting conjecture that the humane-minded Lo Yuen, who had observed the entire course of events from an elevated spot, determined to make a well-directed effort towards his safety. To this end he quickly purchased the esteem of several of those who make a profession of their strength, holding out the hope of still further reward if they conducted the venture to a successful termination. Uttering loud cries of an impending vengeance, as Lo Yuen had instructed them in the matter, and displaying their exceptional proportions to the astonishment and misgivings of all beholders, these persons tore open the opium-tent in which Quen had concealed himself, and, thrusting aside all opposition, quickly dragged him forth. Holding him high upon their shoulders, in spite of his frequent and ill-advised endeavours to cast himself to the ground, some surrounded those who bore him-after the manner of disposing his troops affected by a skilful leader when the enemy begin to waver-and crying aloud that it was their unchanging purpose to submit him to the test of burning splinters and afterwards to torture him, they succeeded by this stratagem in bringing him through the crowd; and hurling back or outstripping those who endeavoured to follow, conveyed him secretly and unperceived to a deserted and appointed spot. Here Quen was obliged to remain until other events caused the recollection of the many to become clouded and unconcerned towards him, suffering frequent inconveniences in spite of the powerful protection of Lo Yuen, and not at all times being able to regard the most necessary repast as an appointment of undoubted certainty. At length, in the guise of a wandering conjurer who was unable to display his accomplishments owing to an entire loss of the power of movement in his arms, Quen passed undetected from the city, and safely reaching the distant and unimportant town of Lu-Kwo, gave himself up to a protracted period of lamentation and self-reproach at the unprepossessing manner in which he had conducted his otherwise very inviting affairs.

Second Period: The Temple Builder

Two hand-counts of years passed away and Quen still remained at Lu-kwo, all desire of returning either to Peking or to the place of his birth having by this time faded into nothingness. Accepting the inevitable fact that he was not destined ever to become a person with whom taels were plentiful, and yet being unwilling to forego the charitable manner of life which he had always been accustomed to observe, it came about that he spent the greater part of his time in collecting together such sums of money as he could procure from the amiable and well-disposed, and with them building temples and engaging in other benevolent works. From this cause it arose the Quen obtained around Lu-kwo a reputation for high-minded piety, in no degree less than that which had been conferred upon him in earlier times, so that pilgrims from far distant places would purposely contrive their journey so as to pass through the town containing so unassuming and virtuous a person.

"During this entire period Quen had been accompanied by his only son, a youth of respectful personality, in whose entertaining society he took an intelligent interest. Even when deeply engaged in what he justly regarded as the crowning work of his existence-the planning and erecting of an exceptionally well-endowed marble temple, which was to be entirely covered on the outside with silver paper, and on the inside with gold-leaf—he did not fail to observe the various conditions of Liao's existence, and the changing emotions which from time to time possessed him. Therefore, when the person in question, without displaying any signs of internal sickness, and likewise persistently denying that he had lost any considerable sum of money, disclosed a continuous habit of turning aside with an unaffected expression of distaste from all manner of food, and passed the entire night in observing the course of the great sky-lantern rather than in sleep, the sage and discriminating Quen took him one day aside, and asked him, as one who might aid him in the matter, who the maiden was, and what class and position her father occupied.

"'Alas!' exclaimed Liao, with many unfeigned manifestations of an unbearable fate, 'to what degree do the class and position of her entirely unnecessary parents affect the question? or how little hope can this sacrilegious one reasonably have of ever progressing as far as earthly details of a pecuniary character in the case of so adorable and far-removed a Being? The uttermost extent of this wildly-hoping person's ambition is that when the incomparably symmetrical Ts'ain learns of the steadfast light of his devotion, she may be inspired to deposit an emblematic chrysanthemum upon his tomb in the Family Temple. For such a reward he will cheerfully devote the unswerving fidelity of a lifetime to her service, not distressing her gentle and retiring nature by the expression of what must inevitably be a hopeless passion, but patiently and uncomplainingly guarding her footsteps as from a distance.'

"Being in this manner made aware of the reason of Liao's frequent and unrestrained exclamations of intolerable despair, and of his fixed determination with regard to the maiden Ts'ain (which seemed, above all else, to indicate a resolution to shun her presence) Quen could not regard the immediately-following actions of his son with anything but an emotion of confusion. For when his eyes next rested upon the exceedingly contradictory Liao, he was seated in the open space before the house in which Ts'ain dwelt, playing upon an instrument of stringed woods, and chanting verses into which the names of the two persons in question had been skilfully introduced without restraint, his whole manner of behaving being with the evident purpose of attracting the maiden's favourable attention. After an absence of many days, spent in this graceful and complimentary manner, Liao returned suddenly to the house of his father, and, prostrating his body before him, made a specific request for his assistance.

"'As regards Ts'ain and myself,' he continued, 'all things are arranged, and but for the unfortunate coincidence of this person's poverty and of her father's cupidity, the details of the wedding ceremony would undoubtedly now be in a very advanced condition. Upon these entrancing and well-discussed plans, however, the shadow of the grasping and commonplace Ah-Ping has fallen like the inopportune opium-pipe from the mouth of a person examining substances of an explosive nature; for the one referred to demands a large and utterly unobtainable amount of taels before he will suffer his greatly-sought-after daughter to accept the gifts of irretrievable intention.'

"'Grievous indeed is your plight,' replied Quen, when he thus understood the manner of obstacle which impeded his son's hopes; 'for in the nature of taels the most diverse men are to be measured through the same mesh. As the proverb says, "'All money is evil,' exclaimed the philosopher with extreme weariness, as he gathered up the gold pieces in exchange, but presently discovering that one among them was such indeed has he had described, he rushed forth without tarrying to take up a street garment; and with an entire absence of dignity traversed all the ways of the city in the hope of finding the one who had defrauded him." Well does this person know the mercenary Ah-Ping, and the unyielding nature of his closed hand; for often, but always fruitlessly, he has entered his presence on affairs connected with the erecting of certain temples. Nevertheless, the matter is one which does not admit of any incapable faltering, to which end this one will seek out the obdurate Ah-Ping without delay, and endeavour to entrap him by some means in the course of argument.'

"From the time of his earliest youth Ah-Ping had unceasingly devoted himself to the object of getting together an overwhelming number of taels, using for this purpose various means which, without being really degrading or contrary to the written law, were not such as might have been cheerfully engaged in by a person of high-minded honourableness. In consequence of this, as he grew more feeble in body, and more venerable in appearance, he began to express frequent and bitter doubts as to whether his manner of life had been really well arranged; for, in spite of his great wealth, he had grown to adopt a most inexpensive habit on all occasions, having no desire to spend; and an ever-increasing apprehension began to possess him that after he had passed beyond, his sons would be very disinclined to sacrifice and burn money sufficient to keep him in an affluent condition in the Upper Air. In such a state of mind was Ah-Ping when Quen-Ki-Tong appeared before him, for it had just been revealed to him that his eldest and favourite son had, by flattery and by openly praising the dexterity with which he used his brush and ink, entrapped him into inscribing his entire name upon certain unwritten sheets of parchment, which the one in question immediately sold to such as were heavily indebted to Ah-Ping.

"'If a person can be guilty of this really unfilial behaviour during the lifetime of his father,' exclaimed Ah-Ping, in a tone of unrestrained vexation, 'can it be prudently relied upon that he will carry out his wishes after death, when they involve the remitting to him of several thousand taels each year? O estimable Quen-Ki-Tong, how immeasurably superior is the celestial outlook upon which you may safely rely as your portion! When you are enjoying every variety of sumptuous profusion, as the reward of your untiring charitable exertions here on earth, the spirit of this short-sighted person will be engaged in doing menial servitude for the inferior deities, and perhaps scarcely able, even by those means, to clothe himself according to the changing nature of the seasons.'

"'Yet,' replied Quen, 'the necessity for so laborious and unremunerative an existence may even now be averted by taking efficient precautions before you pass to the Upper Air.'

"'In what way?' demanded Ah-Ping, with an awakening hope that the matter might not be entirely destitute of cheerfulness, yet at the same time preparing to examine with even unbecoming intrusiveness any expedient which Quen might lay before him. 'Is it not explicitly stated that sacrifices and acts of a like nature, when performed at the end of one's existence by a person who to that time has professed no sort of interest in such matters, shall in no degree be entered as to his good, but rather regarded as examples of deliberate presumptuousness, and made the excuse for subjecting him to more severe tortures and acts of penance than would be his portion if he neglected the custom altogether?'

"'Undoubtedly such is the case,' replied Quen; 'and on that account it would indicate a most regrettable want of foresight for you to conduct your affairs in the manner indicated. The only undeniably safe course is for you to entrust the amount you will require to a person of exceptional piety, receiving in return his written word to repay the full sum whenever you shall claim it from him in the Upper Air. By this crafty method the amount will be placed at the disposal of the person in question as soon as he has passed beyond, and he will be held by his written word to return it to you whenever you shall demand it.'

"So amiably impressed with this ingenious scheme was Ah-Ping that he would at once have entered more fully into the detail had the thought not arisen in his mind that the person before him was the father of Liao, who urgently required a certain large sum, and that for this reason he might with prudence inquire more fully into the matter elsewhere, in case Quen himself should have been imperceptibly led aside, even though he possessed intentions of a most unswerving honourableness. To this end, therefore, he desired to converse again with Quen on the matter, pleading that at that moment a gathering of those who direct enterprises of a commercial nature required his presence. Nevertheless, he would not permit the person referred to depart until he had complimented him, in both general and specific terms, on the high character of his life and actions, and the intelligent nature of his understanding, which had enabled him with so little mental exertion to discover an efficient plan.

"Without delay Ah-Ping sought out those most skilled in all varieties of law-forms, in extorting money by devices capable of very different meanings, and in expedients for evading just debts; but all agreed that such an arrangement as the one he put before them would be unavoidably binding, provided the person who received the money alluded to spent it in the exercise of his charitable desires, and provided also that the written agreement bore the duty seal of the high ones at Peking, and was deposited in the coffin of the lender. Fully satisfied, and rejoicing greatly that he could in this way adequately provide for his future and entrap the avaricious ones of his house, Ah-Ping collected together the greater part of his possessions, and converting it into pieces of gold, entrusted them to Quen on the exact understanding that has already been described, he receiving in turn Quen's written and thumb-signed paper of repayment, and his assurance that the whole amount should be expended upon the silver-paper and gold-leaf Temple with which he was still engaged.

"It is owing to this circumstance that Quen-Ki-Tong's irreproachable name has come to be lightly regarded by many who may be fitly likened to the latter person in the subtle and experienced proverb, 'The wise man's eyes fell before the gaze of the fool, fearing that if he looked he must cry aloud, "Thou hopeless one!" "There," said the fool to himself, "behold this person's power!"' These badly educated and undiscriminating persons, being entirely unable to explain the ensuing train of events, unhesitatingly declare that Quen-Ki-Tong applied a portion of the money which he had received from Ah-Ping in the manner described to the object of acquiring Ts'ain for his son Liao. In this feeble and incapable fashion they endeavour to stigmatize the pure-minded Quen as one who acted directly contrary to his deliberately spoken word, whereas the desired result was brought about in a much more artful manner; they describe the commercially successful Ah-Ping as a person of very inferior prudence, and one easily imposed upon; while they entirely pass over, as a detail outside the true facts, the written paper preserved among the sacred relics in the Temple, which announces, among other gifts of a small and uninviting character, 'Thirty thousand taels from an elderly ginseng merchant of Lu-kwo, who desires to remain nameless, through the hand of Quen-Ki-Tong.' The full happening in its real and harmless face is now set forth for the first time.

"Some weeks after the recorded arrangement had been arrived at by Ah-Ping and Quen, when the taels in question had been expended upon the Temple and were, therefore, infallibly beyond recall, the former person chanced to be passing through the public garden in Lu-kwo when he heard a voice lifted up in the expression of every unendurable feeling of dejection to which one can give utterance. Stepping aside to learn the cause of so unprepossessing a display of unrestrained agitation, and in the hope that perhaps he might be able to use the incident in a remunerative manner, Ah-Ping quickly discovered the unhappy being who, entirely regardless of the embroidered silk robe which he wore, reclined upon a raised bank of uninviting earth, and waved his hands from side to side as his internal emotions urged him.

"'Quen-Ki-Tong!' exclaimed Ah-Ping, not fully convinced that the fact was as he stated it in spite of the image clearly impressed upon his imagination; 'to what unpropitious occurrence is so unlooked-for an exhibition due? Are those who traffic in gold-leaf demanding a high and prohibitive price for that commodity, or has some evil and vindicative spirit taken up its abode within the completed portion of the Temple, and by its offensive but nevertheless diverting remarks and actions removed all semblance of gravity from the countenances of those who daily come to admire the construction?'

"'O thrice unfortunate Ah-Ping,' replied Quen when he observed the distinguishing marks of the person before him, 'scarcely can this greatly overwhelmed one raise his eyes to your open and intelligent countenance; for through him you are on the point of experiencing a very severe financial blow, and it is, indeed, on your account more than on his own that he is now indulging in these outward signs of a grief too far down to be expressed in spoken words.' And at the memory of his former occupation, Quen again waved his arms from side to side with untiring assiduousness.

"'Strange indeed to this person's ears are your words,' said Ah-Ping, outwardly unmoved, but with an apprehensive internal pain that he would have regarded Quen's display of emotion with an easier stomach if his own taels were safely concealed under the floor of his inner chamber. 'The sum which this one entrusted to you has, without any pretence been expended upon the Temple, while the written paper concerning the repayment bears the duty seal of the high ones at Peking. How, then, can Ah-Ping suffer a loss at the hands of Quen-Ki-Tong?'

"'Ah-Ping,' said Quen, with every appearance of desiring that both persons should regard the matter in a conciliatory spirit, 'do not permit the awaiting demons, which are ever on the alert to enter into a person's mind when he becomes distressed out of the common order of events, to take possession of your usually discriminating faculties until you have fully understood how this affair has come about. It is no unknown thing for a person of even exceptional intelligence to reverse his entire manner of living towards the end of a long and consistent existence; the far-seeing and not lightly-moved Ah-Ping himself has already done so. In a similar, but entirely contrary manner, the person who is now before you finds himself impelled towards that which will certainly bear a very unpresentable face when the circumstances become known; yet by no other means is he capable of attaining his greatly-desired object.'

"'And to what end does that trend?' demanded Ah-Ping, in no degree understanding how the matter affected him.

"'While occupied with enterprises which those of an engaging and complimentary nature are accustomed to refer to as charitable, this person has almost entirely neglected a duty of scarcely less importance-that of establishing an unending line, through which his name and actions shall be kept alive to all time,' replied Quen. 'Having now inquired into the matter, he finds that his only son, through whom alone the desired result can be obtained, has become unbearably attached to a maiden for whom a very large sum is demanded in exchange. The thought of obtaining no advantage from an entire life of self-denial is certainly unprepossessing in the extreme, but so, even to a more advanced degree, is the certainty that otherwise the family monuments will be untended, and the temple of domestic virtues become an early ruin. This person has submitted the dilemma to the test of omens, and after considering well the reply, he has decided to obtain the price of the maiden in a not very honourable manner, which now presents itself, so that Liao may send out his silk-bound gifts without delay.'

"'It is an unalluring alternative,' said Ah-Ping, whose only inside thought was one of gratification that the exchange money for Ts'ain would so soon be in his possession, 'yet this person fails to perceive how you could act otherwise after the decision of the omens. He now understands, moreover, that the loss you referred to on his part was in the nature of a figure of speech, as one makes use of thunderbolts and delicately-scented flowers to convey ideas of harsh and amiable passions, and alluded in reality to the forthcoming departure of his daughter, who is, as you so versatilely suggested, the comfort and riches of his old age.'

"'O venerable, but at this moment somewhat obtuse, Ah-Ping,' cried Quen, with a recurrence to his former method of expressing his unfeigned agitation, 'is your evenly-balanced mind unable to grasp the essential fact of how this person's contemplated action will affect your own celestial condition? It is a distressing but entirely unavoidable fact, that if this person acts in the manner which he has determined upon, he will be condemned to the lowest place of torment reserved for those who fail at the end of an otherwise pure existence, and in this he will never have an opportunity of meeting the very much higher placed Ah-Ping, and of restoring to him the thirty-thousand taels as agreed upon.'

"At these ill-destined words, all power of rigidness departed from Ah-Ping's limbs, and he sank down upon the forbidding earth by Quen's side.

"'O most unfortunate one who is now speaking,' he exclaimed, when at length his guarding spirit deemed it prudent to restore his power of expressing himself in words, 'happy indeed would have been your lot had you been content to traffic in ginseng and other commodities of which you have actual knowledge. O amiable Quen, this matter must be in some way arranged without causing you to deviate from the entrancing paths of your habitual virtue. Could not the very reasonable Liao be induced to look favourably upon the attractions of some low-priced maiden, in which case this not really hard-stomached person would be willing to advance the necessary amount, until such time as it could be restored, at a very low and unremunerative rate of interest?'

"'This person has observed every variety of practical humility in the course of his life,' replied Quen with commendable dignity, 'yet he now finds himself totally unable to overcome an inward repugnance to the thought of perpetuating his honoured name and race through the medium of any low-priced maiden. To this end has he decided.'

"Those who were well acquainted with Ah-Ping in matters of commerce did not hesitate to declare that his great wealth had been acquired by his consistent habit of forming an opinion quickly while others hesitated. On the occasion in question he only engaged his mind with the opposing circumstances for a few moments before he definitely fixed upon the course which he should pursue.

"'Quen-Ki-Tong,' he said, with an evident intermingling of many very conflicting emotions, 'retain to the end this well-merited reputation for unaffected honourableness which you have so fittingly earned. Few in the entire Empire, with powers so versatilely pointing to an eminent position in any chosen direction, would have been content to pass their lives in an unremunerative existence devoted to actions of charity. Had you selected an entirely different manner of living, this person has every confidence that he, and many others in Lu-kwo, would by this time be experiencing a very ignoble poverty. For this reason he will make it his most prominent ambition to hasten the realization of the amiable hopes expressed both by Liao and by Ts'ain, concerning their future relationship. In this, indeed, he himself will be more than exceptionally fortunate should the former one prove to possess even a portion of the clear-sighted sagaciousness exhibited by his engaging father.'

> *"Verses Composed by a Musician of Lu-Kwo,*
> *on the Occasion of the Wedding Ceremony of*
> *Liao And Ts'ain*
>
> "Bright hued is the morning, the dark clouds have fallen;
> At the mere waving of Quen's virtuous hands they melted away.
> Happy is Liao in the possession of so accomplished a parent,
> Happy also is Quen to have so discriminating a son.
>
> "The two persons in question sit, side by side, upon an embroidered couch,
> Listening to the well-expressed compliments of those who pass to and fro.
> From time to time their eyes meet, and glances of a very significant amusement pass between them;
> Can it be that on so ceremonious an occasion they are recalling events of a gravity-removing nature?
>
> "The gentle and rainbow-like Ts'ain has already arrived,
> With the graceful motion of a silver carp gliding through a screen of rushes, she moves among those who are assembled.
> On the brow of her somewhat contentious father there rests the shadow of an ill-repressed sorrow;
> Doubtless the frequently-misjudged Ah-Ping is thinking of his lonely hearth, now that he is for ever parted from that which he holds most precious.
>
> "In the most commodious chamber of the house the elegant wedding-gifts are conspicuously displayed; let us stand beside the one which we have contributed, and point out its excellence to those who pass by.
> Surely the time cannot be far distant when the sound of many gongs will announce that the very desirable repast is at length to be partaken of."

The Vision of Yin, the Son of Yat Huang

When Yin, the son of Yat Huang, had passed beyond the years assigned to the pursuit of boyhood, he was placed in the care of the hunchback Quang, so that he might be fully instructed in the management of the various weapons used in warfare, and also in the art of stratagem, by which a skilful leader is often enabled to conquer when opposed to an otherwise overwhelming multitude. In all these accomplishments Quang excelled to an exceptional degree; for although unprepossessing in appearance he united matchless strength to an untiring subtlety. No other person in the entire Province of Kiang-si could hurl a javelin so unerringly while uttering sounds of terrifying menace, or could cause his sword to revolve around him so rapidly, while his face looked out from the glittering circles with an expression of ill-intentioned malignity that never failed to inspire his adversary with irrepressible emotions of alarm. No other person could so successfully feign to be devoid of life for almost any length of time, or by his manner of behaving create the fixed impression that he was one of insufficient understanding, and therefore harmless. It was for these reasons that Quang was chosen as the instructor of Yin by Yat Huang, who, without possessing any official degree, was a person to whom marks of obeisance were paid not only within his own town, but for a distance of many li around it.

At length the time arrived when Yin would in the ordinary course of events pass from the instructorship of Quang in order to devote himself to the commerce in which his father was engaged, and from time to time the unavoidable thought arose persistently within his mind that although Yat Huang doubtless knew better than he did what the circumstances of the future required, yet his manner of life for the past years was not such that he could contemplate engaging in the occupation of buying and selling porcelain clay with feelings of an overwhelming interest. Quang, however, maintained with every manifestation of inspired assurance that Yat Huang was to be commended down to the smallest detail, inasmuch as proficiency in the use of both blunt and sharp-edged weapons, and a faculty for passing undetected through the midst of an encamped body of foemen, fitted a person for the every-day affairs of life above all other accomplishments.

"Without doubt the very accomplished Yat Huan is well advised on this point," continued Quang, "for even this mentally short-sighted person can call up within his understanding numerous specific incidents in the ordinary career of one engaged in the commerce of porcelain clay when such attainments would be of great remunerative benefit. Does the well-endowed Yin think, for example, that even the most depraved person would endeavour to gain an advantage over him in the matter of buying or selling porcelain clay if he fully understood the fact that the one with whom he was trafficking could unhesitatingly transfix four persons with one arrow at the distance of a hundred paces? Or to what advantage would it be that a body of unscrupulous outcasts who owned a field of inferior clay should surround it with drawn swords by day and night, endeavouring meanwhile to dispose of it as material of the finest quality, if the one whom they endeavoured to ensnare in this manner possessed the power of being able to pass through their ranks unseen and examine the clay at his leisure?"

"In the cases to which reference has been made, the possession of those qualities would undoubtedly be of considerable use," admitted Yin; yet, in spite of his entire ignorance of commercial matters, this one has a confident feeling that it would be more profitable to avoid such very doubtful forms of barter altogether rather than spend eight years in acquiring the arts by which to defeat them. "That, however, is a question which concerns this person's virtuous and engaging father more than his unworthy self, and his only regret is that no opportunity has offered by which he might prove that he has applied himself diligently to your instruction and example, O amiable Quang."

It had long been a regret to Quang also that no incident of a disturbing nature had arisen whereby Yin could have shown himself proficient in the methods of defence and attack which he had taught him. This deficiency he had endeavoured to overcome, as far as possible, by constructing life-like models of all the most powerful and ferocious types of warriors and the fiercest and most relentless animals of the forest, so that Yin might become familiar with their appearance and discover in what manner each could be the most expeditiously engaged.

"Nevertheless," remarked Quang, on an occasion when Yin appeared to be covered with honourable pride at having approached an unusually large and repulsive-looking tiger so stealthily that had the animal been really alive it would certainly have failed to perceive him, "such accomplishments are by no means to be regarded as conclusive in themselves. To steal insidiously upon a destructively-included wild beast and transfix it with one well-directed blow of a spear is attended by difficulties and emotions which are entirely absent in the case of a wickerwork animal covered with canvas-cloth, no matter how deceptive in appearance the latter may be."

To afford Yin a more trustworthy example of how he should engage with an adversary of formidable proportions, Quang resolved upon an ingenious plan. Procuring the skin of a grey wolf, he concealed himself within it, and in the early morning, while the mist-damp was still upon the ground, he set forth to meet Yin, who had on a previous occasion spoken to him of his intention to be at a certain spot at such an hour. In this conscientious enterprise, the painstaking Quang would doubtless have been successful, and Yin gained an assured proficiency and experience, had it not chanced that on the journey Quang encountered a labourer of low caste who was crossing the enclosed ground on his way to the rice field in which he worked. This contemptible and inopportune person, not having at any period of his existence perfected himself in the recognized and elegant methods of attack and defence, did not act in the manner which would assuredly have been adopted by Yin in similar circumstances, and for which Quang would have been fully prepared. On the contrary, without the least indication of what his intention was, he suddenly struck Quang, who was hesitating for a moment what action to take, a most intolerable blow with a formidable staff which he carried. The stroke in question inflicted itself upon Quang upon that part of the body where the head becomes connected with the neck, and would certainly have been followed by others of equal force and precision had not Quang in the meantime decided that the most dignified course for him to adopt would be to disclose his name and titles without delay. Upon learning these facts, the one who stood before him became very grossly and offensively amused, and having taken from Quang everything of value which he carried among his garments, went on his way, leaving Yin's instructor to retrace his steps in unendurable dejection, as he then found that he possessed no further interest whatever in the undertaking.

When Yat Huang was satisfied that his son was sufficiently skilled in the various arts of warfare, he called him to his inner chamber, and having barred the door securely, he placed Yin under a very binding oath not to reveal, until an appointed period, the matter which he was going to put before him.

"From father to son, in unbroken line for ten generations, has such a custom been observed," he said, "for the course of events is not to be lightly entered upon. At the commencement of that cycle, which period is now fully fifteen score years ago, a very wise person chanced to incur the displeasure of the Emperor of that time, and being in consequence driven out of the capital, he fled to the mountains. There his subtle discernment and the pure and solitary existence which he led resulted in his becoming endowed with faculties beyond those possessed by ordinary beings. When he felt the end of his earthly career to be at hand he descended into the plain, where, in a state of great destitution and bodily anguish, he was discovered by the one whom this person has referred to as the first of the line of ancestors. In return for the care and hospitality with which he was unhesitatingly received, the admittedly inspired hermit spent the remainder of his days in determining the destinies of his rescuer's family and posterity. It is an undoubted fact that he predicted how one would, by well-directed enterprise and adventure, rise to a position of such eminence in the land that he counselled the details to be kept secret, lest the envy and hostility of the ambitious and unworthy should be raised. From this cause it has been customary to reveal the matter fully from father to son, at stated periods, and the setting out of the particulars in written words has been severely discouraged. Wise as this precaution certainly was, it has resulted in a very inconvenient state of things; for a remote ancestor-the fifth in line from the beginning-experienced such vicissitudes that he returned from his travels in a state of most abandoned idiocy, and when the time arrived that he should, in turn, communicate to his son, he was only able to repeat over and over again the name of the pious hermit to whom the family was so greatly indebted, coupling it each time with a new and markedly offensive epithet. The essential details of the undertaking having in this manner passed beyond recall, succeeding generations, which were merely acquainted with the fact that a very prosperous future awaited the one who fulfilled the conditions, have in vain attempted to conform to them. It is not an alluring undertaking, inasmuch as nothing of the method to be pursued can be learned, except that it was the custom of the early ones, who held the full knowledge, to set out from home and return after a period of years. Yet so clearly expressed was the prophecy, and so great the reward of the successful, that all have eagerly journeyed forth when the time came, knowing nothing beyond that which this person has now unfolded to you."

When Yat Huang reached the end of the matter which it was his duty to disclose, Yin for some time pondered the circumstances before replying. In spite of a most engaging reverence for everything of a sacred nature, he could not consider the inspired remark of the well-intentioned hermit without feelings of a most persistent doubt, for it occurred to him that if the person in question had really been as wise as he was represented to be, he might reasonably have been expected to avoid the unaccountable error of offending the enlightened and powerful Emperor under whom he lived. Nevertheless, the prospect of engaging in the trade of porcelain clay was less attractive in his eyes than that of setting forth upon a journey of adventure, so that at length he expressed his willingness to act after the manner of those who had gone before him.

This decision was received by Yat Huang with an equal intermingling of the feelings of delight and concern, for although he would have by no means pleasurably contemplated Yin breaking through a venerable and esteemed custom, he was unable to put entirely from him the thought of the degrading fate which had overtaken the fifth in line who made the venture. It was, indeed, to guard Yin as much as possible against the dangers to which he would become exposed, if he determined on the expedition, that the entire course of his training had been selected. In order that no precaution of a propitious nature should be neglected, Yat Huang at once despatched written words of welcome to all with whom he was acquainted, bidding them partake of a great banquet which he was preparing to mark the occasion of his son's leave-taking. Every variety of sacrifice was offered up to the controlling deities, both good and bad; the ten ancestors were continuously exhorted to take Yin under their special protection, and sets of verses recording his virtues and ambitions were freely distributed among the necessitous and low-caste who could not be received at the feast.

The dinner itself exceeded in magnificence any similar event that had ever taken place in Ching-toi. So great was the polished ceremony observed on the occasion, that each guest had half a score of cups of the finest apricot-tea successively placed before him and taken away untasted, while Yat Huang went to each in turn protesting vehemently that the honour of covering such pure-minded and distinguished persons was more than his badly designed roof could reasonably bear, and wittingly giving an entrancing air of reality to the spoken compliment by begging them to move somewhat to one side so that they might escape the heavy central beam if the event which he alluded to chanced to take place. After several hours had been spent in this congenial occupation, Yat Huang proceeded to read aloud several of the sixteen discourses on education which, taken together, form the discriminating and infallible example of conduct known as the Holy Edict. As each detail was dwelt upon Yin arose from his couch and gave his deliberate testimony that all the required tests and rites had been observed in his own case. The first part of the repast was then partaken of, the nature of the ingredients and the manner of preparing them being fully explained, and in a like manner through each succeeding one of the four-and-forty courses. At the conclusion Yin again arose, being encouraged by the repeated uttering of his name by those present, and with extreme modesty and brilliance set forth his manner of thinking concerning all subjects with which he was acquainted.

Early on the morning of the following day Yin set out on his travels, entirely unaccompanied, and carrying with him nothing beyond a sum of money, a silk robe, and a well-tried and reliable spear. For many days he journeyed in a northerly direction, without encountering anything sufficiently unusual to engage his attention. This, however, was doubtless part of a pre-arranged scheme so that he should not be drawn from a destined path, for at a small village lying on the southern shore of a large lake, called by those around Silent Water, he heard of the existence of a certain sacred island, distant a full day's sailing, which was barren of all forms of living things, and contained only a single gigantic rock of divine origin and majestic appearance. Many persons, the villagers asserted, had sailed to the island in the hope of learning the portent of the rock, but none ever returned, and they themselves avoided coming even within sight of it; for the sacred stone, they declared, exercised an evil influence over their ships, and would, if permitted, draw them out of their course and towards itself. For this reason Yin could find no guide, whatever reward he offered, who would accompany him; but having with difficulty succeeded in hiring a small boat of inconsiderable value, he embarked with food, incense, and materials for building fires, and after rowing consistently for nearly the whole of the day, came within sight of the island at evening. Thereafter the necessity of further exertion ceased, for, as they of the village had declared would be the case, the vessel moved gently forward, in an unswerving line, without being in any way propelled, and reaching its destination in a marvellously short space of time, passed behind a protecting spur of land and came to rest. It then being night, Yin did no more than carry his stores to a place of safety, and after lighting a sacrificial fire and prostrating himself before the rock, passed into the Middle Air.

In the morning Yin's spirit came back to the earth amid the sound of music of a celestial origin, which ceased immediately he recovered full consciousness. Accepting this manifestation as an omen of Divine favour, Yin journeyed towards the centre of the island where the rock stood, at every step passing the bones of innumerable ones who had come on a similar quest to his, and perished. Many of these had left behind them inscriptions on wood or bone testifying their deliberate opinion of the sacred rock, the island, their protecting deities, and the entire train of circumstances, which had resulted in their being in such a condition. These were for the most part of a maledictory and unencouraging nature, so that after reading a few, Yin endeavoured to pass without being in any degree influenced by such ill-judged outbursts.

"Accursed be the ancestors of this tormented one to four generations back!" was prominently traced upon an unusually large shoulder-blade. "May they at this moment be simmering in a vat of unrefined dragon's blood, as a reward for having so undiscriminatingly reared the person who inscribes these words only to attain this end!" "Be warned, O later one, by the signs around!" Another and more practical-minded person had written: "Retreat with all haste to your vessel, and escape while there is yet time. Should you, by chance, again reach land through this warning, do not neglect, out of an emotion of gratitude, to burn an appropriate amount of sacrifice paper for the lessening of the torments of the spirit of Li-Kao," to which an unscrupulous one, who was plainly desirous of sharing in the benefit of the requested sacrifice, without suffering the exertion of inscribing a warning after the amiable manner of Li-Kao, had added the words, "and that of Huan Sin."

Halting at a convenient distance from one side of the rock which, without being carved by any person's hand, naturally resembled the symmetrical countenance of a recumbent dragon (which he therefore conjectured to be the chief point of the entire mass), Yin built his fire and began an unremitting course of sacrifice and respectful ceremony. This manner of conduct he observed conscientiously for the space of seven days. Towards the end of that period a feeling of unendurable dejection began to possess him, for his stores of all kinds were beginning to fail, and he could not entirely put behind him the memory of the various well-intentioned warnings which he had received, or the sight of the fleshless ones who had lined his path. On the eighth day, being weak with hunger and, by reason of an intolerable thirst, unable to restrain his body any longer in the spot where he had hitherto continuously prostrated himself nine-and-ninety times each hour without ceasing, he rose to his feet and retraced his steps to the boat in order that he might fill his water-skins and procure a further supply of food.

With a complicated emotion, in which was present every abandoned and disagreeable thought to which a person becomes a prey in moments of exceptional mental and bodily anguish, he perceived as soon as he reached the edge of the water that the boat, upon which he was confidently relying to carry him back when all else failed, had disappeared as entirely as the smoke from an extinguished opium pipe. At this sight Yin clearly understood the meaning of Li-Kao's unregarded warning, and recognized that nothing could now save him from adding his incorruptible parts to those of the unfortunate ones whose unhappy fate had, seven days ago, engaged his refined pity. Unaccountably strengthened in body by the indignation which possessed him, and inspired with a virtuous repulsion at the treacherous manner of behaving on the part of those who guided his destinies, he hastened back to his place of obeisance, and perceiving that the habitually placid and introspective expression on the dragon face had imperceptibly changed into one of offensive cunning and unconcealed contempt, he snatched up his spear and, without the consideration of a moment, hurled it at a score of paces distance full into the sacred but nevertheless very unprepossessing face before him.

At the instant when the presumptuous weapon touched the holy stone the entire intervening space between the earth and the sky was filled with innumerable flashes of forked and many-tongued lightning, so that the island had the appearance of being the scene of a very extensive but somewhat badly-arranged display of costly fireworks. At the same time the thunder rolled among the clouds and beneath the sea in an exceedingly disconcerting manner. At the first indication of these celestial movements a sudden blindness came upon Yin, and all power of thought or movement forsook him; nevertheless, he experienced an emotion of flight through the air, as though borne upwards upon the back of a winged creature. When this emotion ceased, the blindness went from him as suddenly and entirely as if a cloth had been pulled away from his eyes, and he perceived that he was held in the midst of a boundless space, with no other object in view than the sacred rock, which had opened, as it were, revealing a mighty throng within, at the sight of whom Yin's internal organs trembled as they would never have moved at ordinary danger, for it was put into his spirit that these in whose presence he stood were the sacred Emperors of his country from the earliest time until the usurpation of the Chinese throne by the devouring Tartar hordes from the North.

As Yin gazed in fear-stricken amazement, a knowledge of the various Pure Ones who composed the assembly came upon him. He understood that the three unclad and commanding figures which stood together were the Emperors of the Heaven, Earth, and Man, whose reigns covered a space of more than eighty thousand years, commencing from the time when the world began its span of existence. Next to them stood one wearing a robe of leopard-skin, his hand resting upon a staff of a massive club, while on his face the expression of tranquillity which marked his predecessors had changed into one of alert wakefulness; it was the Emperor of Houses, whose reign marked the opening of the never-ending strife between man and all other creatures. By his side stood his successor, the Emperor of Fire, holding in his right hand the emblem of the knotted cord, by which he taught man to cultivate his mental faculties, while from his mouth issued smoke and flame, signifying that by the introduction of fire he had raised his subjects to a state of civilized life.

On the other side of the boundless chamber which seemed to be contained within the rocks were Fou-Hy, Tchang-Ki, Tcheng-Nung, and Huang, standing or reclining together. The first of these framed the calendar, organized property, thought out the eight Essential Diagrams, encouraged the various branches of hunting, and the rearing of domestic animals, and instituted marriage. From his couch floated melodious sounds in remembrance of his discovery of the property of stringed woods. Tchang-Ki, who manifested the property of herbs and growing plants, wore a robe signifying his attainments by means of embroidered symbols. His hand rested on the head of the dragon, while at his feet flowed a bottomless canal of the purest water. The discovery of written letters by Tcheng-Nung, and his ingenious plan of grouping them after the manner of the constellations of stars, was emblemized in a similar manner, while Huang, or the Yellow Emperor, was surrounded by ores of the useful and precious metals, weapons of warfare, written books, silks and articles of attire, coined money, and a variety of objects, all testifying to his ingenuity and inspired energy.

These illustrious ones, being the greatest, were the first to take Yin's attention, but beyond them he beheld an innumerable concourse of Emperors who not infrequently outshone their majestic predecessors in the richness of their apparel and the magnificence of the jewels which they wore. There Yin perceived Hung-Hoang, who first caused the chants to be collected, and other rulers of the Tcheon dynasty; Yong-Tching, who compiled the Holy Edict; Thang rulers whose line is rightly called "the golden," from the unsurpassed excellence of the composed verses which it produced; renowned Emperors of the versatile Han dynasty; and, standing apart, and shunned by all, the malignant and narrow-minded Tsing-Su-Hoang, who caused the Sacred Books to be burned.

Even while Yin looked and wondered, in great fear, a rolling voice, coming from one who sat in the midst of all, holding in his right hand the sun, and in his left the moon, sounded forth, like the music of many brass instruments playing in unison. It was the First Man who spoke.

"Yin, son of Yat Huang, and creature of the Lower Part," he said, "listen well to the words I speak, for brief is the span of your tarrying in the Upper Air, nor will the utterance I now give forth ever come unto your ears again, either on the earth, or when, blindly groping in the Middle Distance, your spirit takes its nightly flight. They who are gathered around, and whose voices I speak, bid me say this: Although immeasurably above you in all matters, both of knowledge and of power, yet we greet you as one who is well-intentioned, and inspired with honourable ambition. Had you been content to entreat and despair, as did all the feeble and incapable ones whose white bones formed your pathway, your ultimate fate would have in no wise differed from theirs. But inasmuch as you held yourself valiantly, and, being taken, raised an instinctive hand in return, you have been chosen; for the day to mute submission has, for the time or for ever, passed away, and the hour is when China shall be saved, not by supplication, but by the spear."

"A state of things which would have been highly unnecessary if I had been permitted to carry out my intention fully, and restore man to his prehistoric simplicity," interrupted Tsin-Su-Hoang. "For that reason, when the voice of the assemblage expresses itself, it must be understood that it represents in no measure the views of Tsin-Su-Hoang."

"In the matter of what has gone before, and that which will follow hereafter," continued the Voice dispassionately, "Yin, the son of Yat-Huang, must concede that it is in no part the utterance of Tsin-Su-Hoang—Tsin-Su-Hoang who burned the Sacred Books."

At the mention of the name and offence of this degraded being a great sound went up from the entire multitude—a universal cry of execration, not greatly dissimilar from that which may be frequently heard in the crowded Temple of Impartiality when the one whose duty it is to take up, at a venture, the folded papers, announces that the sublime Emperor, or some mandarin of exalted rank, has been so fortunate as to hold the winning number in the Annual State Lottery. So vengeance-laden and mournful was the combined and evidently preconcerted wail, that Yin was compelled to shield his ears against it; yet the inconsiderable Tsin-Su-Hoang, on whose account it was raised, seemed in no degree to be affected by it, he, doubtless, having become hardened by hearing a similar outburst, at fixed hours, throughout interminable cycles of time.

When the last echo of the cry had passed away the Voice continued to speak.

"Soon the earth will again receive you, Yin," it said, "for it is not respectful that a lower one should be long permitted to gaze upon our exalted faces. Yet when you go forth and stand once more among men this is laid on you: that henceforth you are as a being devoted to a fixed and unchanging end, and whatever moves towards the restoring of the throne of the Central Empire the outcast but unalterably sacred line of its true sovereigns shall have your arm and mind. By what combination of force and stratagem this can be accomplished may not be honourably revealed by us, the all-knowing. Nevertheless, omens and guidance shall not be lacking from time to time, and from the beginning the weapon by which you have attained to this distinction shall be as a sign of our favour and protection over you."

When the Voice made an end of speaking the sudden blindness came upon Yin, as it had done before, and from the sense of motion which he experienced, he conjectured that he was being conveyed back to the island. Undoubtedly this was the case, for presently there came upon him the feeling that he was awakening from a deep and refreshing sleep, and opening his eyes, which he now found himself able to do without any difficulty, he immediately discovered that he was reclining at full length on the ground, and at a distance of about a score of paces from the dragon head. His first thought was to engage in a lengthy course of self-abasement before it, but remembering the words which had been spoken to him while in the Upper Air, he refrained, and even ventured to go forward with a confident but somewhat self-deprecatory air, to regain the spear, which he perceived lying at the foot of the rock. With feelings of a reassuring nature he then saw that the very undesirable expression which he had last beheld upon the dragon face had melted into one of encouraging urbanity and benignant esteem.

Close by the place where he had landed he discovered his boat, newly furnished with wine and food of a much more attractive profusion than that which he had purchased in the village. Embarking in it, he made as though he would have returned to the south, but the spear which he held turned within his grasp, and pointed in an exactly opposite direction. Regarding this fact as an express command on the part of the Deities, Yin turned his boat to the north, and in the space of two days' time-being continually guided by the fixed indication of the spear-he reached the shore and prepared to continue his travels in the same direction, upheld and inspired by the knowledge that henceforth he moved under the direct influence of very powerful spirits.

The Ill-Regulated Destiny of Kin Yen, the Picture-Maker

As Recorded by Himself Before His Sudden Departure From Peking, Owing to Circumstances Which Are Made Plain in the Following Narrative.

There are moments in the life of a person when the saying of the wise Ni-Hyu that "Misfortune comes to all men and to most women" is endowed with double force. At such times the faithful child of the Sun is a prey to the whitest and most funereal thoughts, and even the inspired wisdom of his illustrious ancestors seems more than doubtful, while the continued inactivity of the Sacred Dragon appears for the time to give colour to the scoffs of the Western barbarian. A little while ago these misgivings would have found no resting-place in the bosom of the writer. Now, however-but the matter must be made clear from the beginning.

The name of the despicable person who here sets forth his immature story is Kin Yen, and he is a native of Kia-Lu in the Province of Che-Kiang. Having purchased from a very aged man the position of Hereditary Instructor in the Art of Drawing Birds and Flowers, he gave lessons in these accomplishments until he had saved sufficient money to journey to Peking. Here it was his presumptuous intention to learn the art of drawing figures in order that he might illustrate printed leaves of a more distinguished class than those which would accept what true politeness compels him to call his exceedingly unsymmetrical pictures of birds and flowers. Accordingly, when the time arrived, he disposed of his Hereditary Instructorship, having first ascertained in the interests of his pupils that his successor was a person of refined morals and great filial piety.

Alas! it is well written, "The road to eminence lies through the cheap and exceedingly uninviting eating-houses." In spite of this person's great economy, and of his having begged his way from Kia-Lu to Peking in the guise of a pilgrim, journeying to burn incense in the sacred Temple of Truth near that city, when once within the latter place his taels melted away like the smile of a person of low class when he discovers that the mandarin's stern words were not intended as a jest. Moreover, he found that the story-makers of Peking, receiving higher rewards than those at Kia-Lu, considered themselves bound to introduce living characters into all their tales, and in consequence the very ornamental drawings of birds and flowers which he had entwined into a legend entitled "The Last Fight of the Heaven-sent Tcheng" —a story which had been entrusted to him for illustration as a test of his skill-was returned to him with a communication in which the writer revealed his real meaning by stating contrary facts. It therefore became necessary that he should become competent in the art of drawing figures without delay, and with this object he called at the picture-room of Tieng Lin, a person whose experience was so great that he could, without discomfort to himself, draw men and women of all classes, both good and bad. When the person who is setting forth this narrative revealed to Tieng Lin the utmost amount of money he could afford to give for instruction in the art of drawing living figures, Tieng Lin's face became as overcast as the sky immediately before the Great Rains, for in his ignorance of this incapable person's poverty he had treated him with equality and courtesy, nor had he kept him waiting in the mean room on the plea that he was at that moment closeted with the Sacred Emperor. However, upon receiving an assurance that a rumour would be spread in which the number of taels should be multiplied by ten, and that the sum itself should be brought in advance, Tieng Lin promised to instruct this person in the art of drawing five characters, which, he said, would be sufficient to illustrate all stories except those by the most expensive and highly-rewarded story-tellers—men who have become so proficient that they not infrequently introduce a score or more of living persons into their tales without confusion.

After considerable deliberation, this unassuming person selected the following characters, judging them to be the most useful, and the most readily applicable to all phases and situations of life:

117

1. A bad person, wearing a long dark pigtail and smoking an opium pipe. His arms to be folded, and his clothes new and very expensive.

2. A woman of low class. One who removes dust and useless things from the rooms of the over-fastidious and of those who have long nails; she to be carrying her trade-signs.

3. A person from Pe-ling, endowed with qualities which cause the beholder to be amused. This character to be especially designed to go with the short sayings which remove gravity.

4. One who, having incurred the displeasure of the sublime Emperor, has been decapitated in consequence.

5. An ordinary person of no striking or distinguished appearance. One who can be safely introduced in all places and circumstances without great fear of detection.

After many months spent in constant practice and in taking measurements, this unenviable person attained a very high degree of proficiency, and could draw any of the five characters without hesitation. With renewed hope, therefore, he again approached those who sit in easy-chairs, and concealing his identity (for they are stiff at bending, and when once a picture-maker is classed as "of no good" he remains so to the end, in spite of change), he succeeded in getting entrusted with a story by the elegant and refined Kyen Tal. This writer, as he remembered with distrust, confines his distinguished efforts entirely to the doings of sailors and of those connected with the sea, and this tale, indeed, he found upon reading to be the narrative of how a Hang-Chow junk and its crew, consisting mostly of aged persons, were beguiled out of their course by an exceedingly ill-disposed dragon, and wrecked upon an island of naked barbarians. It was, therefore, with a somewhat heavy stomach that this person set himself the task of arranging his five characters as so to illustrate the words of the story.

The sayings of the ancient philosopher Tai Loo are indeed very subtle, and the truth of his remark, "After being disturbed in one's dignity by a mandarin's foot it is no unusual occurrence to fall flat on the face in crossing a muddy street," was now apparent. Great as was the disadvantage owing to the nature of the five characters, this became as nothing when it presently appeared that the avaricious and clay-souled Tieng Lin, taking advantage of the blindness of this person's enthusiasm, had taught him the figures so that they all gazed in the same direction. In consequence of this it would have been impossible that two should be placed as in the act of conversing together had not the noble Kyen Tal been inspired to write that "his companions turned from him in horror." This incident the ingenious person who is recording these facts made the subject of three separate drawings, and having in one or two other places effected skilful changes in the writing, so similar in style to the strokes of the illustrious Kyen Tal as to be undetectable, he found little difficulty in making use of all his characters. The risks of the future, however, were too great to be run with impunity; therefore it was arranged, by means of money-for this person was fast becoming acquainted with the ways of Peking-that an emissary from one who sat in an easy-chair should call upon him for a conference, the narrative of which appeared in this form in the Peking Printed Leaves of Thrice-distilled Truth:

The brilliant and amiable young picture-maker Kin Yen, in spite of the immediate and universal success of his accomplished efforts, is still quite rotund in intellect, nor is he, if we may use a form of speaking affected by our friends across the Hoang Hai, "suffering from swollen feet." A person with no recognized position, but one who occasionally does inferior work of this nature for us, recently surprised Kin Yen without warning, and found him in his sumptuously appointed picture-room, busy with compasses and tracing-paper. About the place were scattered in elegant confusion several of his recent masterpieces. From the subsequent conversation we are in a position to make it known that in future this refined and versatile person will confine himself entirely to illustrations of processions, funerals, armies on the march, persons pursued by others, and kindred subjects which appeal strongly to his imagination. Kin Yen has severe emotions on the subject of individuality in art, and does not hesitate to express himself forcibly with reference to those who are content to degrade the names of their ancestors by turning out what he wittily describes as "so much of varied mediocrity."

The prominence obtained by this pleasantly-composed notice-for it was copied by others who were unaware of the circumstance of its origin-had the desired effect. In future, when one of those who sit in easy-chairs wished for a picture after the kind mentioned, he would say to his lesser one: "Oh, send to the graceful and versatile Kin Yen; he becomes inspired on the subject of funerals," or persons escaping from prison, or families walking to the temple, or whatever it might be. In that way this narrow-minded and illiterate person was soon both looked at and rich, so that it was his daily practice to be carried, in silk garments, past the houses of those who had known him in poverty, and on these occasions he would puff out his cheeks and pull his moustaches, looking fiercely from side to side.

True are the words written in the elegant and distinguished Book of Verses: "Beware lest when being kissed by the all-seeing Emperor, you step upon the elusive banana-peel." It was at the height of eminence in this altogether degraded person's career that he encountered the being who led him on to his present altogether too lamentable condition.

Tien Nung is the earthly name by which is known she who combines all the most illustrious attributes which have been possessed of women since the days of the divine Fou-Hy. Her father is a person of very gross habits, and lives by selling inferior merchandise covered with some of good quality. Upon past occasions, when under the direct influence of Tien, and in the hope of gaining some money benefit, this person may have spoken of him in terms of praise, and may even have recommended friends to entrust articles of value to him, or to procure goods on his advice. Now, however, he records it as his unalterable decision that the father of Tien Nung is by profession a person who obtains goods by stratagem, and that, moreover, it is impossible to gain an advantage over him on matters of exchange.

The events that have happened prove the deep wisdom of Li Pen when he exclaimed "The whitest of pigeons, no matter how excellent in the silk-hung chamber, is not to be followed on the field of battle." Tien herself was all that the most exacting of persons could demand, but her opinions on the subject of picture-making were not formed by heavy thought, and it would have been well if this had been borne in mind by this person. One morning he chanced to meet her while carrying open in his hands four sets of printed leaves containing his pictures.

"I have observed," said Tien, after the usual personal inquiries had been exchanged, "that the renowned Kin Yen, who is the object of the keenest envy among his brother picture-makers, so little regards the sacredness of his accomplished art that never by any chance does he depict persons of the very highest excellence. Let not the words of an impetuous maiden disarrange his digestive organs if they should seem too bold to the high-souled Kin Yen, but this matter has, since she has known him, troubled the eyelids of Tien. Here," she continued, taking from this person's hand one of the printed leaves which he was carrying, "in this illustration of persons returning from extinguishing a fire, is there one who appears to possess those qualities which appeal to all that is intellectual and competitive within one? Can it be that the immaculate Kin Yen is unacquainted with the subtle distinction between the really select and the vastly ordinary? Ah, undiscriminating Kin Yen! are not the eyelashes of the person who is addressing you as threads of fine gold to junk's cables when compared with those of the extremely commonplace female who is here pictured in the art of carrying a bucket? Can the most refined lack of vanity hide from you the fact that your own person is infinitely rounder than this of the evilly-intentioned-looking individual with the opium pipe? O blind Kin Yen!"

Here she fled in honourable confusion, leaving this person standing in the street, astounded, and a prey to the most distinguished emotions of a complicated nature.

"Oh, Tien," he cried at length, "inspired by those bright eyes, narrower than the most select of the three thousand and one possessed by the sublime Buddha, the almost fallen Kin Yen will yet prove himself worthy of your esteemed consideration. He will, without delay, learn to draw two new living persons, and will incorporate in them the likenesses which you have suggested."

Returning swiftly to his abode, he therefore inscribed and despatched this letter, in proof of his resolve:

"To the Heaven-sent human chrysanthemum, in whose body reside the Celestial Principles and the imprisoned colours of the rainbow.

"From the very offensive and self-opinionated picture-maker.

"Henceforth this person will take no rest, nor eat any but the commonest food, until he shall have carried out the wishes of his one Jade Star, she whose teeth he is not worthy to blacken.

"When Kin Yen has been entrusted with a story which contains a being in some degree reflecting the character of Tien, he will embellish it with her irreproachable profile and come to hear her words. Till then he bids her farewell."

From that moment most of this person's time was necessarily spent in learning to draw the two new characters, and in consequence of this he lost much work, and, indeed, the greater part of the connexion which he had been at such pains to form gradually slipped away from him. Many months passed before he was competent to reproduce persons resembling Tien and himself, for in this he was unassisted by Tieng Lin, and his progress was slow.

At length, being satisfied, he called upon the least fierce of those who sit in easy-chairs, and requested that he might be entrusted with a story for picture-making.

"We should have been covered with honourable joy to set in operation the brush of the inspired Kin Yen," replied the other with agreeable condescension; "only at the moment, it does not chance that we have before us any stories in which funerals, or beggars being driven from the city, form the chief incidents. Perhaps if the polished Kin Yen should happen to be passing this ill-constructed office in about six months' time —"

"The brush of Kin Yen will never again depict funerals, or labourers arranging themselves to receive pay or similar subjects," exclaimed this person impetuously, "for, as it is well said, 'The lightning discovers objects which the paper-lantern fails to reveal.' In future none but tales dealing with the most distinguished persons shall have his attention."

"If this be the true word of the dignified Kin Yen, it is possible that we may be able to animate his inspired faculties," was the response. "But in that case, as a new style must be in the nature of an experiment, and as our public has come to regard Kin Yen as the great exponent of Art Facing in One Direction, we cannot continue the exceedingly liberal payment with which we have been accustomed to reward his elegant exertions."

"Provided the story be suitable, that is a matter of less importance," replied this person.

"The story," said the one in the easy-chair, "is by the refined Tong-king, and it treats of the high-minded and conscientious doubts of one who would become a priest of Fo. When preparing for this distinguished office he discovers within himself leanings towards the religion of Lao-Tse. His illustrious scruples are enhanced by his affection for Wu Ping, who now appears in the story."

"And the ending?" inquired this person, for it was desirable that the two should marry happily.

"The inimitable stories of Tong-king never have any real ending, and this one, being in his most elevated style, has even less end than most of them. But the whole narrative is permeated with the odour of joss-sticks and honourable high-mindedness, and the two characters are both of noble birth."

As it might be some time before another story so suitable should be offered, or one which would afford so good an opportunity of wafting incense to Tien, and of displaying her incomparable outline in dignified and magnanimous attitudes, this was eagerly accepted, and for the next week this obscure person spent all his days and nights in picturing the lovely Tien and his debased self in the characters of the nobly-born young priest of Fo and Wu Ping. The pictures finished, he caused them to be carefully conveyed to the office, and then, sitting down, spent many hours in composing the following letter, to be sent to Tien, accompanying a copy of the printed leaves wherein the story and his drawing should appear:

"When the light has for a period been hidden from a person, it is no uncommon thing for him to be struck blind on gazing at the sun; therefore, if the sublime Tien values the eyes of Kin Yen, let her hide herself behind a gauze screen on his approach.

"The trembling words of Tien have sunk deep into the inside of Kin Yen and become part of his being. Never again can he depict persons of the quality and in the position he was wont to do.

"With this he sends his latest efforts. In each case he conceives his drawings to be the pictures of the written words; in the noble Tien's case it is undoubtedly so, in his own he aspires to it. Doubtless the unobtrusive Tien would make no claim to the character and manner of behaving of the one in the story, yet Kin Yen confidently asserts that she is to the other as the glove is to the hand, and he is filled with the most intelligent delight at being able to exhibit her in her true robes, by which she will be known to all who see her, in spite of her dignified protests. Kin Yen hopes; he will come this evening after sunset."

The week which passed between the finishing of the pictures and the appearance of the eminent printed leaves containing them was the longest in this near-sighted person's ill-spent life. But at length the day arrived, and going with exceedingly mean haste to the place of sale, he purchased a copy and sent it, together with the letter of his honourable intention, on which he had bestowed so much care, to Tien.

Not till then did it occur to this inconsiderable one that the impetuousness of his action was ill-judged; for might it not be that the pictures were evilly-printed, or that the delicate and fragrant words painting the character of the one who now bore the features of Tien had undergone some change?

To satisfy himself, scarce as taels had become with him, he purchased another copy.

There are many exalted sayings of the wise and venerable Confucious constructed so as to be of service and consolation in moments of strong mental distress. These for the greater part recommend tranquillity of mind, a complete abnegation of the human passions and the like behaviour. The person who is here endeavouring to bring this badly-constructed account of his dishonourable career to a close pondered these for some moments after twice glancing through the matter in the printed leaves, and then, finding the faculties of speech and movement restored to him, procured a two-edged knife of distinguished brilliance and went forth to call upon the one who sits in an easy-chair.

"Behold," said the lesser one, insidiously stepping in between this person an the inner door, "my intellectual and all-knowing chief is not here to-day. May his entirely insufficient substitute offer words of congratulation to the inspired Kin Yen on his effective and striking pictures in this week's issue?"

"His altogether insufficient substitute," answered this person, with difficulty mastering his great rage, "may and shall offer words of explanation to the inspired Kin Yen, setting forth the reason of his pictures being used, not with the high-minded story of the elegant Tong-king for which they were executed, but accompanying exceedingly base, foolish, and ungrammatical words written by Klan-hi, the Peking remover of gravity-words which will evermore brand the dew-like Tien as a person of light speech and no refinement"; and in his agony this person struck the lacquered table several times with his elegant knife.

"O Kin Yen," exclaimed the lesser one, "this matter rests not here. It is a thing beyond the sphere of the individual who is addressing you. All he can tell is that the graceful Tong-king withdrew his exceedingly tedious story for some reason at the final moment, and as your eminent drawings had been paid for, my chief of the inner office decided to use them with this story of Klan-hi. But surely it cannot be that there is aught in the story to displease your illustrious personality?"

"Judge for yourself," this person said, "first understanding that the two immaculate characters figuring as the personages of the narrative are exact copies of this dishonoured person himself and of the willowy Tien, daughter of the vastly rich Pe-li-Chen, whom he was hopeful of marrying."

Selecting one of the least offensive of the passages in the work, this unhappy person read the following immature and inelegant words:

"This well-satisfied writer of printed leaves had a highly-distinguished time last night. After Chow had departed to see about food, and the junk had been fastened up at the lock of Kilung, on the Yang-tse-Kiang, he and the round-bodied Shang were journeying along the narrow path by the river-side when the right leg of the graceful and popular person who is narrating these events disappeared into the river. Suffering no apprehension in the dark, but that the vanishing limb was the left leg of Shang, this intelligent writer allowed his impassiveness to melt away to an exaggerated degree; but at that moment the circumstance became plain to the round-bodied Shang, who was in consequence very grossly amused at the mishap and misapprehension of your good lord, the writer, at the same time pointing out the matter as it really was. Then it chanced that there came by one of the maidens who carry tea and jest for small sums of money to the sitters at the little tables with round white tops, at which this remarkable person, the confidant of many mandarins, ever desirous of displaying his priceless power of removing gravity, said to her:

"'How much of gladness, Ning-Ning? By the Sacred Serpent this is plainly your night out.'

"Perceiving the true facts of the predicament of this commendable writer, she replied:

"'Suffer not your illustrious pigtail to be removed, venerable Wang; for in this maiden's estimation it is indeed your night in.'

"There are times when this valued person wonders whether his method of removing gravity be in reality very antique or quite new. On such occasions the world, with all its schools, and those who interfere in the concerns of others, continues to revolve around him. The wondrous sky-lanterns come out silently two by two like to the crystallized music of stringed woods. Then, in the mystery of no-noise, his head becomes greatly enlarged with celestial and highly-profound thoughts; his groping hand seems to touch matter which may be written out in his impressive style and sold to those who print leaves, and he goes home to write out such."

When this person looked up after reading, with tears of shame in his eyes, he perceived that the lesser one had cautiously disappeared. Therefore, being unable to gain admittance to the inner office, he returned to his home.

Here the remark of the omniscient Tai Loo again fixes itself upon the attention. No sooner had this incapable person reached his house than he became aware that a parcel had arrived for him from the still adorable Tien. Retiring to a distance from it, he opened the accompanying letter and read:

"When a virtuous maiden has been made the victim of a heartless jest or a piece of coarse stupidity at a person's hands, it is no uncommon thing for him to be struck blind on meeting her father. Therefore, if the degraded and evil-minded Kin Yen values his eyes, ears, nose, pigtail, even his dishonourable breath, let him hide himself behind a fortified wall at Pe-li-Chen's approach.

"With this Tien returns everything she has ever accepted from Kin Yen. She even includes the brace of puppies which she received anonymously about a month ago, and which she did not eat, but kept for reasons of her own-reasons entirely unconnected with the vapid and exceedingly conceited Kin Yen."

As though this letter, and the puppies of which this person now heard for the first time, making him aware of the existence of a rival lover, were not enough, there almost immediately arrived a letter from Tien's father:

"This person has taken the advice of those skilled in extorting money by means of law forms, and he finds that Kin Yen has been guilty of a grave and highly expensive act. This is increased by the fact that Tien had conveyed his seemingly distinguished intentions to all her friends, before whom she now stands in an exceedingly ungraceful attitude. The machinery for depriving Kin Yen of all the necessaries of existence shall be put into operation at once."

At this point, the person who is now concluding his obscure and commonplace history, having spent his last piece of money on joss-sticks and incense-paper, and being convinced of the presence of the spirits of his ancestors, is inspired to make the following prophecies: That Tieng Lin, who imposed upon him in the matter of picture-making, shall come to a sudden end, accompanied by great internal pains, after suffering extreme poverty; that the one who sits in an easy-chair, together with his lesser one and all who make stories for them, shall, while sailing to a rice feast during the Festival of Flowers, be precipitated into the water and slowly devoured by sea monsters, Klan-hi in particular being tortured in the process; that Pel-li-Chen, the father of Tien, shall be seized with the dancing sickness when in the presence of the august Emperor, and being in consequence suspected of treachery, shall, to prove the truth of his denials, be submitted to the tests of boiling tar, red-hot swords, and of being dropped from a great height on to the Sacred Stone of Goodness and Badness, in each of which he shall fail to convince his judges or to establish his innocence, to the amusement of all beholders.

These are the true words of Kin Yen, the picture-maker, who, having unweighed his mind and exposed the avaricious villainy of certain persons, is now retiring by night to a very select and hidden spot in the Khingan Mountains.

The End

KAI LUNG'S GOLDEN HOURS

The Encountering of Six Within a Wood

Only at one point along the straight earth-road leading from Loo-chow to Yu-ping was there any shade, a wood of stunted growth, and here Kai Lung cast himself down in refuge from the noontide sun and slept.

When he woke it was with the sound of discreet laughter trickling through his dreams. He sat up and looked around. Across the glade two maidens stood in poised expectancy within the shadow of a wild fig-tree, both their gaze and their manner denoting a fixed intention to be prepared for any emergency. Not being desirous that this should tend towards their abrupt departure, Kai Lung rose guardedly to his feet, with many gestures of polite reassurance, and having bowed several times to indicate his pacific nature, he stood in an attitude of deferential admiration. At this display the elder and less attractive of the maidens fled, uttering loud and continuous cries of apprehension in order to conceal the direction of her flight. The other remained, however, and even moved a few steps nearer to Kai Lung, as though encouraged by his appearance, so that he was able to regard her varying details more appreciably. As she advanced she plucked a red blossom from a thorny bush, and from time to time she shortened the broken stalk between her jade teeth.

"Courteous loiterer," she said, in a very pearl-like voice, when they had thus regarded one another for a few beats of time, "what is your honourable name, and who are you who tarry here, journeying neither to the east nor to the west?"

"The answer is necessarily commonplace and unworthy of your polite interest," was the diffident reply. "My unbecoming name is Kai, to which has been added that of Lung. By profession I am an incapable relater of imagined tales, and to this end I spread my mat wherever my uplifted voice can entice together a company to listen. Should my feeble efforts be deemed worthy of reward, those who stand around may perchance contribute to my scanty store, but sometimes this is judged superfluous. For this cause I now turn my expectant feet from Loo-chow towards the untried city of Yu-ping, but the undiminished li stretching relentlessly before me, I sought beneath these trees a refuge from the noontide sun."

"The occupation is a dignified one, being to no great degree removed from that of the Sages who compiled The Books," remarked the maiden, with an encouraging smile. "Are there many stories known to your retentive mind?"

"In one form or another, all that exist are within my mental grasp," admitted Kai Lung modestly. "Thus equipped, there is no arising emergency for which I am unprepared."

"There are other things that I would learn of your craft. What kind of story is the most favourably received, and the one whereby your collecting bowl is the least ignored?"

"That depends on the nature and condition of those who stand around, and therein lies much that is essential to the art," replied Kai Lung, not without an element of pride. "Should the company be chiefly formed of the illiterate and the immature of both sexes, stories depicting the embarrassment of unnaturally round-bodied mandarins, the unpremeditated flight of eccentrically-garbed passers-by into vats of powdered rice, the despair of guardians of the street when assailed by showers of eggs and overripe lo-quats, or any other variety of humiliating pain inflicted upon the innocent and unwary, never fail to win approval. The prosperous and substantial find contentment in hearing of the unassuming virtues and frugal lives of the poor and unsuccessful. Those of humble origin, especially tea-house maidens and the like, are only really at home among stories of the exalted and quick-moving, the profusion of their robes, the magnificence of their palaces, and the general high-minded depravity of their lives. Ordinary persons require stories dealing lavishly with all the emotions, so that they may thereby have a feeling of sufficiency when contributing to the collecting bowl."

"These things being so," remarked the maiden, "what story would you consider most appropriate to a company composed of such as she who is now conversing with you?"

"Such a company could never be obtained," replied Kai Lung, with conviction in his tone. "It is not credible that throughout the Empire could be found even another possessing all the engaging attributes of the one before me. But should it be my miraculous fortune to be given the opportunity, my presumptuous choice for her discriminating ears alone would be the story of the peerless Princess Taik and of the noble minstrel Ch'eng, who to regain her presence chained his wrist to a passing star and was carried into the assembly of the gods."

"Is it," inquired the maiden, with an agreeable glance towards the opportune recumbence of a fallen tree, "is it a narration that would lie within the passage of the sun from one branch of this willow to another?"

"Adequately set forth, the history of the Princess Taik and of the virtuous youth occupies all the energies of an agile story-teller for seven weeks," replied Kai Lung, not entirely gladdened that she should deem him capable of offering so meagre an entertainment as that she indicated. "There is a much-flattened version which may be compressed within the narrow limits of a single day and night, but even that requires for certain of the more moving passages the accompaniment of a powerful drum or a hollow wooden fish."

"Alas!" exclaimed the maiden, "though the time should pass like a flash of lightning beneath the allurement of your art, it is questionable if those who await this one's returning footsteps would experience a like illusion. Even now —" With a magnanimous wave of her well-formed hand she indicated the other maiden, who, finding that the danger of pursuit was not sustained, had returned to claim her part.

"One advances along the westward road," reported the second maiden. "Let us fly elsewhere, O allurer of mankind! It may be —"

"Doubtless in Yu-ping the sound of your uplifted voice —" But at this point a noise upon the earth-road, near at hand, impelled them both to sudden flight into the deeper recesses of the wood.

Thus deprived, Kai Lung moved from the shadow of the trees and sought the track, to see if by chance he from whom they fled might turn to his advantage. On the road he found one who staggered behind a laborious wheel-barrow in the direction of Loo-chow. At that moment he had stopped to take down the sail, as the breeze was bereft of power among the obstruction of the trees, and also because he was weary.

"Greeting," called down Kai Lung, saluting him. "There is here protection from the fierceness of the sun and a stream wherein to wash your feet."

"Haply," replied the other; "and a greatly over-burdened one would gladly leave this ill-nurtured earth-road even for the fields of hell, were it not that all his goods are here contained upon an utterly intractable wheel-barrow."

Nevertheless he drew himself up from the road to the level of the wood and there reclined, yet not permitting the wheel-barrow to pass beyond his sight, though he must thereby lie half in the shade and half in the heat beyond. "Greeting, wayfarer."

"Although you are evidently a man of some wealth, we are for the time brought to a common level by the forces that control us," remarked Kai Lung. "I have here two onions, a gourd and a sufficiency of millet paste. Partake equally with me, therefore, before you resume your way. In the meanwhile I will procure water from the stream near by, and to this end my collecting bowl will serve."

When Kai Lung returned he found that the other had added to their store a double handful of dates, some snuff and a little jar of oil. As they ate together the stranger thus disclosed his mind:

"The times are doubtful and it behoves each to guard himself. In the north the banners of the 'Spreading Lotus' and the 'Avenging Knife' are already raised and pressing nearer every day, while the signs and passwords are so widely flung that every man speaks slowly and with a double tongue. Lately there have been slicings and other forms of vigorous justice no farther distant than Loo-chow, and now the Mandarin Shan Tien comes to Yu-ping to flatten any signs of discontent. The occupation of this person is that of a maker of sandals and coverings for the head, but very soon there will be more wooden feet required than leather sandals in Yu-ping, and artificial ears will be greater in demand than hats. For this reason he has got together all his goods, sold the more burdensome, and now ventures on an untried way."

"Prosperity attend your goings. Yet, as one who has set his face towards Yu-ping, is it not possible for an ordinary person of simple life and unassuming aims to escape persecution under this same Shan Tien?"

"Of the Mandarin himself those who know speak with vague lips. What is done is done by the pressing hand of one Ming-shu, who takes down his spoken word; of whom it is truly said that he has little resemblance to a man and still less to an angel."

"Yet," protested the story-teller hopefully, "it is wisely written: 'He who never opens his mouth in strife can always close his eyes in peace.'"

"Doubtless," assented the other. "He can close his eyes assuredly. Whether he will ever again open them is another matter."

With this timely warning the sandal-maker rose and prepared to resume his journey. Nor did he again take up the burden of his task until he had satisfied himself that the westward road was destitute of traffic.

"A tranquil life and a painless death," was his farewell parting. "Jung, of the line of Hai, wishes you well." Then, with many imprecations on the relentless sun above, the inexorable road beneath, and on every detail of the evilly-balanced load before him, he passed out on his way.

It would have been well for Kai Lung had he also forced his reluctant feet to raise the dust, but his body clung to the moist umbrage of his couch, and his mind made reassurance that perchance the maiden would return. Thus it fell that when two others, who looked from side to side as they hastened on the road, turned as at a venture to the wood they found him still there.

"Restrain your greetings," said the leader of the two harshly, in the midst of Kai Lung's courteous obeisance; "and do not presume to disparage yourself as if in equality with the one who stands before you. Have two of the inner chamber, attired thus and thus, passed this way? Speak, and that to a narrow edge."

"The road lies beyond the perception of my incapable vision, chiefest," replied Kai lung submissively. "Furthermore, I have slept."

"Unless you would sleep more deeply, shape your stubborn tongue to a specific point," commanded the other, touching a meaning sword. "Who are you who loiter here, and for what purpose do you lurk? Speak fully, and be assured that your word will be put to a corroding test."

Thus encouraged, Kai Lung freely disclosed his name and ancestry, the means whereby he earned a frugal sustenance and the nature of his journey. In addition, he professed a willingness to relate his most recently-acquired story, that entitled "Wu-yong: or The Politely Inquiring Stranger", but the offer was thrust ungracefully aside.

"Everything you say deepens the suspicion which your criminal-looking face naturally provokes," said the questioner, putting away his tablets on which he had recorded the replies. "At Yu-ping the matter will be probed with a very definite result. You, Li-loe, remain about this spot in case she whom we seek should pass. I return to speak of our unceasing effort."

"I obey," replied the dog-like Li-loe. "What men can do we have done. We are no demons to see through solid matter."

When they were alone, Li-loe drew nearer to Kai Lung and, allowing his face to assume a more pacific bend, he cast himself down by the story-teller's side.

"The account which you gave of yourself was ill contrived," he said. "Being put to the test, its falsity cannot fail to be discovered."

"Yet," protested Kai Lung earnestly, "in no single detail did it deviate from the iron line of truth."

"Then your case is even more desperate than before," exclaimed Li-loe. "Know now that the repulsive-featured despot who has just left us is Ming-shu, he who takes down the Mandarin Shan Tien's spoken word. By admitting that you are from Loo-chow, where disaffection reigns, you have noosed a rope about your neck, and by proclaiming yourself as one whose habit it is to call together a company to listen to your word, you have drawn it tight."

"Every rope has two ends," remarked Kai Lung philosophically, "and to-morrow is yet to come. Tell me rather, since that is our present errand, who is she whom you pursue and to what intent?"

"That is not so simple as to be contained within the hollow of an acorn sheath. Let it suffice that she has the left ear of Shan Tien, even as Ming-shu has the right, but on which side his hearing is better it might be hazardous to guess."

"And her meritorious name?"

"She is of the house of K'ang, her name being Hwa-mei, though from the nature of her charm she is ofttime called the Golden Mouse. But touching this affair of your own immediate danger: we being both but common men of the idler sort, it is only fitting that when high ones threaten I should stand by you."

"Speak definitely," assented Kai Lung, "yet with the understanding that the full extent of my store does not exceed four or five strings of cash."

"The soil is somewhat shallow for the growth of deep friendship, but what we have we will share equally between us." With these auspicious words Li-loe possessed himself of three of the strings of cash and displayed an empty sleeve. "I, alas, have nothing. The benefits I have in mind are of a subtler and more priceless kind. At Yu-ping my office will be that of the keeper of the doors of the yamen, including that of the prison-house. Thus I shall doubtless be able to render you frequent service of an inconspicuous kind. Do not forget the name of Li-loe."

By this time the approaching sound of heavy traffic, heralded by the beating of drums, the blowing of horns and the discharge of an occasional firework, indicated the passage of some dignified official. This, declared Li-loe, could be none other than the Mandarin Shan Tien, resuming his march towards Yu-ping, and the doorkeeper prepared to join the procession at his appointed place. Kai Lung, however, remained unseen among the trees, not being desirous of obtruding himself upon Ming-shu unnecessarily. When the noise had almost died away in the distance he came forth, believing that all would by this time have passed, and approached the road. As he reached it a single chair was hurried by, its carriers striving by increased exertion to regain their fellows. It was too late for Kai Lung to retreat, whoever might be within. As it passed a curtain moved somewhat, a symmetrical hand came discreetly forth, and that which it held fell at his feet. Without varying his attitude he watched the chair until it was out of sight, then stooped and picked something up—a red blossom on a thorny stalk, the flower already parched but the stem moist and softened to his touch.

The Inexorable Justice of the Mandarin Shan Tien

"By having access to this enclosure you will be able to walk where otherwise you must stand. That in itself is cheap at the price of three reputed strings of inferior cash. Furthermore, it is possible to breathe."

"The outlook, in one direction, is an extensive one," admitted Kai Lung, gazing towards the sky. "Here, moreover, is a shutter through which the vista doubtless lengthens."

"So long as there is no chance of you exploring it any farther than your neck, it does not matter," said Li-loe. "Outside lies a barren region of the yamen garden where no one ever comes. I will now leave you, having to meet one with whom I would traffic for a goat. When I return be prepared to retrace your steps to the prison cell."

"The shadow moves as the sun directs," replied Kai Lung, and with courteous afterthought he added the wonted parting: "Slowly, slowly; walk slowly."

In such a manner the story-teller found himself in a highly-walled enclosure, lying between the prison-house and the yamen garden, a few days after his arrival in Yu-ping. Ming-shu had not eaten his word.

The yard itself possessed no attraction for Kai Lung. Almost before Li-loe had disappeared he was at the shutter in the wall, had forced it open and was looking out. Thus long he waited, motionless, but observing every leaf that stirred among the trees and shrubs and neglected growth beyond. At last a figure passed across a distant glade and at the sight Kai Lung lifted up a restrained voice in song:

> "At the foot of a bleak and inhospitable mountain
> An insignificant stream winds its uncared way;
> Although inferior to the Yangtze-kiang in every detail
> Yet fish glide to and fro among its crannies
> Nor would they change their home for the depths of the widest river.
>
> The palace of the sublime Emperor is made rich with hanging curtains.
> While here rough stone walls forbid repose.
> Yet there is one who unhesitatingly prefers the latter;
> For from an open shutter here he can look forth,
> And perchance catch a glimpse of one who may pass by.
>
> The occupation of the Imperial viceroy is both lucrative and noble;
> While that of a relater of imagined tales is by no means esteemed.
> But he who thus expressed himself would not exchange with the other;
> For around the identity of each heroine he can entwine the personality of one whom he has encountered.
> And thus she is ever by his side."

"Your uplifted voice comes from an unexpected quarter, minstrel," said a melodious voice, and the maiden whom he had encountered in the wood stood before him. "What crime have you now committed?"

"An ancient one. I presumed to raise my unworthy eyes—"

"Alas, story-teller," interposed the maiden hastily, "it would seem that the star to which you chained /your/ wrist has not carried you into the assembly of the gods."

"Yet already it has borne me half-way—into a company of malefactors. Doubtless on the morrow the obliging Mandarin Shan Tien will arrange for the journey to be complete."

"Yet have you then no further wish to continue in an ordinary existence?" asked the maiden.

"To this person," replied Kai Lung, with a deep-seated look, "existence can never again be ordinary. Admittedly it may be short."

As they conversed together in this inoffensive manner she whom Li-loe had called the Golden Mouse held in her delicately-formed hands a priceless bowl filled with ripe fruit of the rarer kinds which she had gathered. These from time to time she threw up to the opening, rightly deciding that one in Kai Lung's position would stand in need of sustenance, and he no less dexterously held and retained them. When the bowl was empty she continued for a space to regard it silently, as though exploring the many-sided recesses of her mind.

"You have claimed to be a story-teller and have indeed made a boast that there is no arising emergency for which you are unprepared," she said at length. "It now befalls that you may be put to a speedy test. Is the nature of this imagined scene"—thus she indicated the embellishment of the bowl—"familiar to your eyes?"

"It is that known as 'The Willow,'" replied Kai Lung. "There is a story—"

"There is a story!" exclaimed the maiden, loosening from her brow the overhanging look of care. "Thus and thus. Frequently have I importuned him before whom you will appear to explain to me the meaning of the scene. When you are called upon to plead your cause, see to it well that your knowledge of such a tale is clearly shown. He before whom you kneel, craftily plied meanwhile by my unceasing petulance, will then desire to hear it from your lips...At the striking of the fourth gong the day is done. What lies between rests with your discriminating wit."

"You are deep in the subtler kinds of wisdom, such as the weak possess," confessed Kai Lung. "Yet how will this avail to any length?"

"That which is put off from to-day is put off from to-morrow," was the confident reply. "For the rest-at a corresponding gong-stroke of each day it is this person's custom to gather fruit. Farewell, minstrel."

When Li-loe returned a little later Kai Lung threw his two remaining strings of cash about that rapacious person's neck and embraced him as he exclaimed:

"Chieftain among doorkeepers, when I go to the Capital to receive the all-coveted title 'Leaf-crowned' and to chant ceremonial odes before the Court, thou shalt accompany me as forerunner, and an agile tribe of selected goats shall sport about thy path."

"Alas, manlet," replied the other, weeping readily, "greatly do I fear that the next journey thou wilt take will be in an upward or a downward rather than a sideway direction. This much have I learned, and to this end, at some cost admittedly, I enticed into loquacity one who knows another whose brother holds the key of Ming-shu's confidence: that to-morrow the Mandarin will begin to distribute justice here, and out of the depths of Ming-shu's malignity the name of Kai Lung is the first set down."

"With the title," continued Kai Lung cheerfully, "there goes a sufficiency of taels; also a vat of a potent wine of a certain kind."

"If," suggested Li-loe, looking anxiously around, "you have really discovered hidden about this place a secret store of wine, consider well whether it would not be prudent to entrust it to a faithful friend before it is too late."

It was indeed as Li-loe had foretold. On the following day, at the second gong-stroke after noon, the order came and, closely guarded, Kai Lung was led forth. The middle court had been duly arranged, with a formidable display of chains, weights, presses, saws, branding irons and other implements for securing justice. At the head of a table draped with red sat the Mandarin Shan Tien, on his right the secretary of his hand, the contemptible Ming-shu. Round about were positioned others who in one necessity or another might be relied upon to play an ordered part. After a lavish explosion of fire-crackers had been discharged, sonorous bells rung and gongs beaten, a venerable geomancer disclosed by means of certain tests that all doubtful influences had been driven off and that truth and impartiality alone remained.

"Except on the part of the prisoners, doubtless," remarked the Mandarin, thereby imperilling the gravity of all who stood around.

"The first of those to prostrate themselves before your enlightened clemency, Excellence, is a notorious assassin who, under another name, has committed many crimes," began the execrable Ming-shu. "He confesses that, now calling himself Kai Lung, he has recently journeyed from Loo-chow, where treason ever wears a smiling face."

"Perchance he is saddened by our city's loyalty," interposed the benign Shan Tien, "for if he is smiling now it is on the side of his face removed from this one's gaze."

"The other side of his face is assuredly where he will be made to smile ere long," acquiesced Ming-shu, not altogether to his chief's approval, as the analogy was already his. "Furthermore, he has been detected lurking in secret meeting-places by the wayside, and on reaching Yu-ping he raised his rebellious voice inviting all to gather round and join his unlawful band. The usual remedy in such cases during periods of stress, Excellence, is strangulation."

"The times are indeed pressing," remarked the agile-minded Mandarin, "and the penalty would appear to be adequate." As no one suffered inconvenience at his attitude, however, Shan Tien's expression assumed a more unbending cast.

"Let the witnesses appear," he commanded sharply.

"In so clear a case it has not been thought necessary to incur the expense of hiring the usual witnesses," urged Ming-shu; "but they are doubtless clustered about the opium floor and will, if necessary, testify to whatever is required."

"The argument is a timely one," admitted the Mandarin. "As the result cannot fail to be the same in either case, perhaps the accommodating prisoner will assist the ends of justice by making a full confession of his crimes?"

"High Excellence," replied the story-teller, speaking for the first time, "it is truly said that that which would appear as a mountain in the evening may stand revealed as a mud-hut by the light of day. Hear my unpainted word. I am of the abject House of Kai and my inoffensive rice is earned as a narrator of imagined tales. Unrolling my threadbare mat at the middle hour of yesterday, I had raised my distressing voice and announced an intention to relate the Story of Wong Ts'in, that which is known as 'The Legend of the Willow Plate Embellishment,' when a company of armed warriors, converging upon me —"

"Restrain the melodious flow of your admitted eloquence," interrupted the Mandarin, veiling his arising interest. "Is the story, to which you have made reference, that of the scene widely depicted on plates and earthenware?"

"Undoubtedly. It is the true and authentic legend as related by the eminent Tso-yi."

"In that case," declared Shan Tien dispassionately, "it will be necessary for you to relate it now, in order to uphold your claim. Proceed."

"Alas, Excellence," protested Ming-shu from a bitter throat, "this matter will attenuate down to the stroke of evening rice. Kowtowing beneath your authoritative hand, that which the prisoner only had the intention to relate does not come within the confines of his evidence."

"The objection is superficial and cannot be sustained," replied Shan Tien. "If an evilly-disposed one raised a sword to strike this person, but was withheld before the blow could fall, none but a leper would contend that because he did not progress beyond the intention thereby he should go free. Justice must be impartially upheld and greatly do I fear that we must all submit."

With these opportune words the discriminating personage signified to Kai Lung that he should begin.

The Story of Wong T'sin and the Willow Plate Embellishment

Wong Ts'in, the rich porcelain maker, was ill at ease within himself. He had partaken of his customary midday meal, flavoured the repast by unsealing a jar of matured wine, consumed a little fruit, a few sweetmeats and half a dozen cups of unapproachable tea, and then retired to an inner chamber to contemplate philosophically from the reposeful attitude of a reclining couch.

But upon this occasion the merchant did not contemplate restfully. He paced the floor in deep dejection and when he did use the couch at all it was to roll upon it in a sudden access of internal pain. The cause of his distress was well known to the unhappy person thus concerned, nor did it lessen the pangs of his emotion that it arose entirely from his own ill-considered action.

When Wong Ts'in had discovered, by the side of a remote and obscure river, the inexhaustible bed of porcelain clay that ensured his prosperity, his first care was to erect adequate sheds and labouring-places; his next to build a house sufficient for himself and those in attendance round about him.

So far prudence had ruled his actions, for there is a keen edge to the saying: "He who sleeps over his workshop brings four eyes into the business," but in one detail Wong T'sin's head and feet went on different journeys, for with incredible oversight he omitted to secure the experience of competent astrologers and omen-casters in fixing the exact site of his mansion.

The result was what might have been expected. In excavating for the foundations, Wong T'sin's slaves disturbed the repose of a small but rapacious earth-demon that had already been sleeping there for nine hundred and ninety-nine years. With the insatiable cunning of its kind, this vindictive creature waited until the house was completed and then proceeded to transfer its unseen but formidable presence to the quarters that were designed for Wong Ts'in himself. Thenceforth, from time to time, it continued to revenge itself for the trouble to which it had been put by an insidious persecution. This frequently took the form of fastening its claws upon the merchant's digestive organs, especially after he had partaken of an unusually rich repast (for in some way the display of certain viands excited its unreasoning animosity), pressing heavily upon his chest, invading his repose with dragon-dreams while he slept, and the like. Only by the exercise of an ingenuity greater than its own could Wong Ts'in succeed in baffling its ill-conditioned spite.

On this occasion, recognizing from the nature of his pangs what was taking place, Wong Ts'in resorted to a stratagem that rarely failed him. Announcing in a loud voice that it was his intention to refresh the surface of his body by the purifying action of heated vapour, and then to proceed to his mixing-floor, the merchant withdrew. The demon, being an earth-dweller with the ineradicable objection of this class of creatures towards all the elements of moisture, at once relinquished its hold, and going direct to the part of the works indicated, it there awaited its victim with the design of resuming its discreditable persecution.

Wong Ts'in had spoken with a double tongue. On leaving the inner chamber he quickly traversed certain obscure passages of his house until he reached an inferior portal. Even if the demon had suspected his purpose it would not have occurred to a creature of its narrow outlook that anyone of Wong Ts'in's importance would make use of so menial an outway. The merchant therefore reached his garden unperceived and thenceforward maintained an undeviating face in the direction of the Outer Expanses. Before he had covered many li he was assured that he had indeed succeeded for the time in shaking off his unscrupulous tormentor. His internal organs again resumed their habitual calm and his mind was lightened as from an overhanging cloud.

There was another reason why Wong Ts'in sought the solitude of the thinly-peopled outer places, away from the influence and distraction of his own estate. For some time past a problem that had once been remote was assuming dimensions of increasing urgency. This detail concerns Fa Fai, who had already been referred to by a person of literary distinction, in a poetical analogy occupying three written volumes, as a pearl-tinted peach-blossom shielded and restrained by the silken net-work of wise parental affection (and recognizing the justice of the comparison, Wong

Ts'in had been induced to purchase the work in question). Now that Fa Fai had attained an age when she could fittingly be sought in marriage the contingency might occur at any time, and the problem confronting her father's decision was this: owing to her incomparable perfection Fa Fai must be accounted one of Wong Ts'in's chief possessions, the other undoubtedly being his secret process of simulating the lustrous effect of pure gold embellishment on china by the application of a much less expensive substitute. Would it be more prudent to concentrate the power of both influences and let it become known that with Fa Fai would go the essential part of his very remunerative clay enterprise, or would it be more prudent to divide these attractions and secure two distinct influences, both concerned about his welfare? In the first case there need be no reasonable limit to the extending vista of his ambition, and he might even aspire to greet as a son the highest functionary of the province-an official of such heavily-sustained importance that when he went about it required six chosen slaves to carry him, and of late it had been considered more prudent to employ eight.

If, on the other hand, Fa Fai went without any added inducement, a mandarin of moderate rank would probably be as high as Wong Ts'in could look, but he would certainly be able to adopt another of at least equal position, at the price of making over to him the ultimate benefit of his discovery. He could thus acquire either two sons of reasonable influence, or one who exercised almost unlimited authority. In view of his own childlessness, and of his final dependence on the services of others, which arrangement promised the most regular and liberal transmission of supplies to his expectant spirit when he had passed into the Upper Air, and would his connection with one very important official or with two subordinate ones secure him the greater amount of honour and serviceable recognition among the more useful deities?

To Wong Ts'in's logical mind it seemed as though there must be a definite answer to this problem. If one manner of behaving was right the other must prove wrong, for as the wise philosopher Ning-hy was wont to say: "Where the road divides, there stand two Ning-hys." The decision on a matter so essential to his future comfort ought not to be left to chance. Thus it had become a habit of Wong Ts'in's to penetrate the Outer Spaces in the hope of there encountering a specific omen.

Alas, it has been well written: "He who thinks that he is raising a mound may only in reality be digging a pit." In his continual search for a celestial portent among the solitudes Wong Ts'in had of late necessarily somewhat neglected his earthly (as it may thus be expressed) interests. In these emergencies certain of the more turbulent among his workers had banded themselves together into a confederacy under the leadership of a craftsman named Fang. It was the custom of these men, who wore a badge and recognized a mutual oath and imprecation, to present themselves suddenly before Wong Ts'in and demand a greater reward for their exertions than they had previously agreed to, threatening that unless this was accorded they would cast down the implements of their labour in unison and involve in idleness those who otherwise would have continued at their task. This menace Wong Ts'in bought off from time to time by agreeing to their exactions, but it began presently to appear that this way of appeasing them resembled Chou Hong's method of extinguishing a fire by directing jets of wind against it. On the day with which this related story has so far concerned itself, a band of the most highly remunerated and privileged of the craftsmen had appeared before Wong Ts'in with the intolerable Fang at their head. These men were they whose skill enabled them laboriously to copy upon the surfaces of porcelain a given scene without appreciable deviation from one to the other, for in those remote cycles of history no other method was yet known or even dreamed of.

"Suitable greetings, employer of our worthless services," remarked their leader, seating himself upon the floor unbidden. "These who speak through the mouth of the cringing mendicant before you are the Bound-together Brotherhood of Colour-mixers and Putters-on of Thought-out Designs, bent upon a just cause."

"May their Ancestral Tablets never fall into disrepair," replied Wong Ts'in courteously. "For the rest-let the mouth referred to shape itself into the likeness of a narrow funnel, for the lengthening gong-strokes press round about my unfinished labours."

"That which in justice requires the amplitude of a full-sized cask shall be pressed down into the confines of an inadequate vessel," assented Fang. "Know then, O batterer upon our ill-requited skill, how it has come to our knowledge that one who is not of our Brotherhood moves among us and performs an equal task for a less reward. This is our spoken word in consequence: in place of one tael every man among us shall now take two, and he who before has laboured eight gongs to receive it shall henceforth labour four. Furthermore, he who is speaking shall, as their recognized head and authority, always be addressed by the honourable title of 'Polished,' and the dog who is not one of us shall be cast forth."

"My hand itches to reward you in accordance with the inner prompting of a full heart," replied the merchant, after a well-sustained pause. "But in this matter my very deficient ears must be leading my threadbare mind astray. The moon has not been eaten up since the day when you stood before me in a like attitude and bargained that every man should henceforth receive a full tael where hitherto a half had been his portion, and that in place of the toil of sixteen gong-strokes eight should suffice. Upon this being granted all bound themselves by spoken word that the matter should stand thus and thus between us until the gathering-in of the next rice harvest."

"That may have been so at the time," admitted Fang, with dog-like obstinacy, "but it was not then known that you had pledged yourself to Hien Nan for tenscore embellished plates of porcelain within a stated time, and that our services would therefore be essential to your reputation. There has thus arisen what may be regarded as a new vista of eventualities, and this frees us from the bondage of our spoken word. Having thus moderately stated our unbending demand, we will depart until the like gong-stroke of to-morrow, when, if our claim be not agreed to, all will cast down their implements of labour with the swiftness of a lightning-flash and thereby involve the whole of your too-profitable undertaking in well-merited stagnation. We go, venerable head; auspicious omens attend your movements!"

"May the All-Seeing guide your footsteps," responded Wong Ts'in, and with courteous forbearance he waited until they were out of hearing before he added —"into a vat of boiling sulphur!"

Thus may the position be outlined when Wei Chang, the unassuming youth whom the black-hearted Fang had branded with so degrading a comparison, sat at his appointed place rather than join in the discreditable conspiracy, and strove by his unaided dexterity to enable Wong Ts'in to complete the tenscore embellished plates by the appointed time. Yet already he knew that in this commendable ambition his head grew larger than his hands, for he was the slowest-working among all Wong Ts'in's craftsmen, and even then his copy could frequently be detected from the original. Not to overwhelm his memory with unmerited contempt it is fitting now to reveal somewhat more of the unfolding curtain of events.

Wei Chang was not in reality a worker in the art of applying coloured designs to porcelain at all. He was a student of the literary excellences and had decided to devote his entire life to the engaging task of reducing the most perfectly matched analogy to the least possible number of words when the unexpected appearance of Fa Fai unsettled his ambitions. She was restraining the impatience of a powerful horse and controlling its movements by means of a leather thong, while at the same time she surveyed the landscape with a disinterested glance in which Wei Chang found himself becoming involved. Without stopping even to consult the spirits of his revered ancestors on so important a decision, he at once burned the greater part of his collection of classical analogies and engaged himself, as one who is willing to become more proficient, about Wong Ts'in's earth-yards. Here, without any reasonable intention of ever becoming in any way personally congenial to her, he was in a position occasionally to see the distant outline of Fa Fai's movements, and when a day passed and even this was withheld he was content that the shadow of the many-towered building that contained her should obscure the sunlight from the window before which he worked.

While Wei Chang was thus engaged the door of the enclosure in which he laboured was thrust cautiously inwards, and presently he became aware that the being whose individuality was never completely absent from his thoughts was standing in an expectant attitude at no great distance from him. As no other person was present, the craftsmen having departed in order to consult an oracle that dwelt beneath an appropriate sign, and Wong Ts'in being by this time among the Outer Ways seeking an omen as to Fa Fai's disposal, Wei Chang did not think it respectful to become aware of the maiden's presence until a persistent distress of her throat compelled him to recognize the incident.

"Unapproachable perfection," he said, with becoming deference, "is it permissible that in the absence of your enlightened sire you should descend from your golden eminence and stand, entirely unattended, at no great distance from so ordinary a person as myself?"

"Whether it be strictly permissible or not, it is only on like occasions that she ever has the opportunity of descending from the solitary pinnacle referred to," replied Fa Fai, not only with no outward appearance of alarm at being directly addressed by one of a different sex, but even moving nearer to Wei Chang as she spoke. "A more essential detail in the circumstances concerns the length of time that he may be prudently relied upon to be away?"

"Doubtless several gong-strokes will intervene before his returning footsteps gladden our expectant vision," replied Wei Chang. "He is spoken of as having set his face towards the Outer Ways, there perchance to come within the influence of a portent."

"Its probable object is not altogether unknown to the one who stands before you," admitted Fa Fai, "and as a dutiful and affectionate daughter it has become a consideration with her whether she ought not to press forward, as it were, to a solution on her own account.... If the one whom I am addressing could divert his attention from the embellishment of the very inadequate claw of a wholly superfluous winged dragon, possibly he might add his sage counsel on that point."

"It is said that a bull-frog once rent his throat in a well-meant endeavour to advise an eagle in the art of flying," replied Wei Chang, concealing the bitterness of his heart beneath an easy tongue. "For this reason it is inexpedient for earthlings to fix their eyes on those who dwell in very high places."

"To the intrepid, very high places exist solely to be scaled; with others, however, the only scaling they attempt is lavished on the armour of preposterous flying monsters, O youth of the House of Wei!"

"Is it possible," exclaimed Wei Chang, moving forward with so sudden an ardour that the maiden hastily withdrew herself several paces from beyond his enthusiasm, "is it possible that this person's hitherto obscure and execrated name is indeed known to your incomparable lips?"

"As the one who periodically casts up the computations of the sums of money due to those who labour about the earth-yards, it would be strange if the name had so far escaped my notice," replied Fa Fai, with a distance in her voice that the few paces between them very inadequately represented. "Certain details engrave themselves upon the tablets of recollection by their persistence. For instance, the name of Fang is generally at the head of each list; that of Wei Chang is invariably at the foot."

"It is undeniable," admitted Wei Chang, in a tone of well-merited humiliation; "and the attainment of never having yet applied a design in such a manner that the copy might be mistaken for the original has entirely flattened-out this person's self-esteem."

"Doubtless," suggested Fa Fai, with delicate encouragement, "there are other pursuits in which you would disclose a more highly developed proficiency-as that of watching the gyrations of untamed horses, for example. Our more immediate need, however, is to discover a means of defeating the malignity of the detestable Fang. With this object I have for some time past secretly applied myself to the task of contriving a design which, by blending simplicity with picturesque effect, will enable one person in a given length of time to achieve the amount of work hitherto done by two."

With these auspicious words the accomplished maiden disclosed a plate of translucent porcelain, embellished in the manner which she had described. At the sight of the ingenious way in which trees and persons, stream and buildings, and objects of a widely differing nature had been so arranged as to give the impression that they all existed at the same time, and were equally visible without undue exertion on the part of the spectator who regarded them, Wei Chang could not restrain an exclamation of delight.

"How cunningly imagined is the device by which objects so varied in size as an orange and an island can be depicted within the narrow compass of a porcelain plate without the larger one completely obliterating the smaller or the smaller becoming actually invisible by comparison with the other! Hitherto this unimaginative person had not considered the possibility of showing other than dragons, demons, spirits, and the forces which from their celestial nature may be regarded as possessing no real thickness of substance and therefore being particularly suitable for treatment on a flat surface. But this engaging display might indeed be a scene having an actual existence at no great space away."

"Such is assuredly the case," admitted Fa Fai. "Within certain limitations, imposed by this new art of depicting realities as they are, we may be regarded as standing before an open window. The important-looking building on the right is that erected by this person's venerated father. Its prosperity is indicated by the luxurious profusion of the fruit-tree overhanging it. Pressed somewhat to the back, but of dignified proportion, are the outer buildings of those who labour among the clay."

"In a state of actuality, they are of measurably less dignified dimensions," suggested Wei Chang.

"The objection is inept," replied Fa Fai. "The buildings in question undoubtedly exist at the indicated position. If, therefore, the actuality is to be maintained, it is necessary either to raise their stature or to cut down the trees obscuring them. To this gentle-minded person the former alternative seemed the less drastic. As, however, it is regarded in a spirit of no-satisfaction —"

"Proceed, incomparable one, proceed," implored Wei Chang. "It was but a breath of thought, arising from a recollection of the many times that this incapable person has struck his unworthy head against the roof-beams of those nobly-proportioned buildings."

"The three stunted individuals crossing the bridge in undignified attitudes are the debased Fang and two of his mercenary accomplices. They are, as usual, bending their footsteps in the direction of the hospitality of a house that announces its purpose beneath the sign of a spreading bush. They are positioned as crossing the river to a set purpose, and the bridge is devoid of a rail in the hope that on their return they may all fall into the torrent in a helpless condition and be drowned, to the satisfaction of the beholders."

"It would be a fitting conclusion to their ill-spent lives," agreed Wei Chang. "Would it not add to their indignity to depict them as struggling beneath the waves?"

"It might do so," admitted Fa Fai graciously, "but in order to express the arisement adequately it would be necessary to display them twice-first on the bridge with their faces turned towards the west, and then in the flood with their faces towards the east; and the superficial might hastily assume that the three on the bridge would rescue the three in the river."

"You are all-wise," said Wei Chang, with well-marked admiration in his voice. "This person's suggestion was opaque."

"In any case," continued Fa Fai, with a reassuring glance, "it is a detail that is not essential to the frustration of Fang's malignant scheme, for already well on its way towards Hien Nan may be seen a trustworthy junk, laden with two formidable crates, each one containing fivescore plates of the justly esteemed Wong Ts'in porcelain."

"Nevertheless," maintained Wei Chang mildly, "the out-passing of Fang would have been a satisfactory detail of the occurrence."

"Do not despair," replied Fa Fai. "Not idly is it written: 'Destiny has four feet, eight hands and sixteen eyes: how then shall the ill-doer with only two of each hope to escape?' An even more ignominious end may await Fang, should he escape drowning, for, conveniently placed by the side of the stream, this person has introduced a spreading willow-tree. Any of its lower branches is capable of sustaining Fang's weight, should a reliable rope connect the two."

"There is something about that which this person now learns is a willow that distinguishes it above all the other trees of the design," remarked Wei Chang admiringly. "It has a wild and yet a romantic aspect."

"This person had not yet chanced upon a suitable title for the device," said Fa Fai, "and a distinguishing name is necessary, for possibly scores of copies may be made before its utility is exhausted. Your discriminating praise shall be accepted as a fortunate omen, and henceforth this shall be known as the Willow Pattern Embellishment."

"The honour of suggesting the title is more than this commonplace person can reasonably carry," protested Wei Chang, feeling that very little worth considering existed outside the earth-shed. "Not only scores, but even hundreds of copies may be required in the process of time, for a crust of rice-bread and handful of dried figs eaten from such a plate would be more satisfying than a repast of many-coursed richness elsewhere."

In this well-sustained and painless manner Fa Fai and Wei Chang continued to express themselves agreeably to each other, until the lengthening gong-strokes warned the former person that her absence might inconvenience Wong Ts'in's sense of tranquillity on his return, nor did Wei Chang contest the desirability of a great space intervening between them should the merchant chance to pass that way. In the meanwhile Chang had explained many of the inner details of his craft so that Fa Fai should the better understand the requirements of her new art.

"Yet where is the Willow plate itself?" said the maiden, as she began to arrange her mind towards departure. "As the colours were still in a receptive state this person placed it safely aside for the time. It was somewhat near the spot where you —"

During the amiable exchange of shafts of polished conversation Wei Chang had followed Fa Fai's indication and had seated himself upon a low bench without any very definite perception of his movements. He now arose with the unstudied haste of one who has inconvenienced a scorpion.

"Alas!" he exclaimed, in a tone of the acutest mental distress; "can it be possible that this utterly profane outcast has so desecrated —"

"Certainly comment of an admittedly crushing nature has been imposed on this one's well-meant handiwork," said Fa Fai. With these lightly-barbed words, which were plainly devised to restore the other person's face towards himself, the magnanimous maiden examined the plate which Wei Chang's uprising had revealed.

"Not only has the embellishment suffered no real detriment," she continued, after an adequate glance, "but there has been imparted to the higher lights-doubtless owing to the nature of the fabric in which your lower half is encased —a certain nebulous quality that adds greatly to the successful effect of the various tones."

At the first perception of the indignity to which he had subjected the entrancing Fa Fai's work, and the swift feeling that much more than the coloured adornment of a plate would thereby be destroyed, all power of retention had forsaken Wei Chang's incapable knees and he sank down heavily upon another bench. From this dejection the maiden's well-chosen encouragement recalled him to a position of ordinary uprightness.

"A tombstone is lifted from this person's mind by your gracefully-placed words," he declared, and he was continuing to indicate the nature of his self-reproach by means of a suitable analogy when the expression of Fa Fai's eyes turned him to a point behind himself. There, lying on the spot from which he had just risen, was a second Willow plate, differing in no detail of resemblance from the first.

"Shadow of the Great Image!" exclaimed Chang, in an awe-filled voice. "It is no marvel that miracles should attend your footsteps, celestial one, but it is incredible that this clay-souled person should be involved in the display."

"Yet," declared Fa Fai, not hesitating to allude to things as they existed, in the highly-raised stress of the discovery, "it would appear that the miracle is not specifically connected with this person's feet. Would you not, in furtherance of this line of suggestion, place yourself in a similar attitude on yet another plate, Wei Chang?"

Not without many protests that it was scarcely becoming thus to sit repeatedly in her presence, Chang complied with the request, and upon Fa Fai's further insistence he continued to impress himself, as it were, upon a succession of porcelain plates, with a like result. Not until the eleventh process was reached did the Willow design begin to lose its potency.

"Ten perfect copies produced within as many moments, and not one distinguishable from the first!" exclaimed Wei Chang, regarding the array of plates with pleasurable emotion. "Here is a means of baffling Fang's crafty confederacy that will fill Wong Ts'in's ears with waves of gladness on his return."

"Doubtless," agreed Fa Fai, with a dark intent. She was standing by the door of the enclosure in the process of making her departure, and she regarded Wei Chang with a set deliberation. "Yet," she continued definitely, "if this person possessed that which was essential to Wong Ts'in's prosperity, and Wong Ts'in held that which was necessary for this one's tranquillity, a locked bolt would be upon the one until the other was pledged in return."

With these opportune words the maiden vanished, leaving Wei Chang prostrating himself in spirit before the many-sidedness of her wisdom.

Wong T'sin was not altogether benevolently inclined towards the universe on his return a little later. The persistent image of Fang's overthreatening act still corroded the merchant's throat with bitterness, for on his right he saw the extinction of his business as unremunerative if he agreed, and on his left he saw the extinction of his business as undependable if he refused to agree.

Furthermore, the omens were ill-arranged.

On his way outwards he had encountered an aged man who possessed two fruit-trees, on which he relied for sustenance. As Wong Ts'in drew near, this venerable person carried from his dwelling two beaten cakes of dog-dung and began to bury them about the root of the larger tree. This action, on the part of one who might easily be a disguised wizard, aroused Wong Ts'in's interest.

"Why," he demanded, "having two cakes of dung and two fruit-trees, do you not allot one to each tree, so that both may benefit and return to you their produce in the time of your necessity?"

"The season promises to be one of rigour and great need," replied the other. "A single cake of dung might not provide sufficient nourishment for either tree, so that both should wither away. By reducing life to a bare necessity I could pass from one harvest to another on the fruit of this tree alone, but if both should fail I am undone. To this end I safeguard my existence by ensuring that at least the better of the two shall thrive."

"Peace attend your efforts!" said Wong Ts'in, and he began to retrace his footsteps, well content.

Yet he had not covered half the distance back when his progress was impeded by an elderly hag who fed two goats, whose milk alone preserved her from starvation. One small measure of dry grass was all that she was able to provide them with, but she divided it equally between them, to the discontent of both.

"The season promises to be one of rigour and great need," remarked Wong Ts'in affably, for the being before him might well be a creature of another part who had assumed that form for his guidance. "Why do you not therefore ensure sustenance to the better of the two goats by devoting to it the whole of the measure of dry grass? In this way you would receive at least some nourishment in return and thereby safeguard your own existence until the rice is grown again."

"In the matter of the two goats," replied the aged hag, "there is no better, both being equally stubborn and perverse, though one may be finer-looking and more vainglorious than the other. Yet should I foster this one to the detriment of her fellow, what would be this person's plight if haply the weaker died and the stronger broke away and fled! By treating both alike I retain a double thread on life, even if neither is capable of much."

"May the Unseen weigh your labours!" exclaimed Wong Ts'in in a two-edged voice, and he departed.

When he reached his own house he would have closed himself in his own chamber with himself had not Wei Chang persisted that he sought his master's inner ear with a heavy project. This interruption did not please Wong Ts'in, for he had begun to recognize the day as being unlucky, yet Chang succeeded by a device in reaching his side, bearing in his hands a guarded burden.

Though no written record of this memorable interview exists, it is now generally admitted that Wei Chang either involved himself in an unbearably attenuated caution before he would reveal his errand, or else that he made a definite allusion to Fa Fai with a too sudden conciseness, for the slaves who stood without heard Wong Ts'in clear his voice of all restraint and express himself freely on a variety of subjects. But this gave place to a subdued murmur, ending with the ceremonial breaking of a plate, and later Wong Ts'in beat on a silver bell and called for wine and fruit.

The next day Fang presented himself a few gong-strokes later than the appointed time, and being met by an unbending word he withdrew the labour of those whom he controlled. Thenceforth these men, providing themselves with knives and axes, surrounded the gate of the earth-yards and by the pacific argument of their attitudes succeeded in persuading others who would willingly have continued at their task that the air of Wong Ts'in's sheds was not congenial to their health. Towards Wei Chang, whose efforts they despised, they raised a cloud of derision, and presently noticing that henceforth he invariably clad himself in lower garments of a dark blue material (to a set purpose that will be as crystal to the sagacious), they greeted his appearance with cries of: "Behold the sombre one! Thou dark leg!" so that this reproach continues to be hurled even to this day at those in a like case, though few could answer why.

Long before the stipulated time the tenscore plates were delivered to Hien Nan. So greatly were they esteemed, both on account of their accuracy of unvarying detail and the ingenuity of their novel embellishment, that orders for scores, hundreds and even thousands began to arrive from all quarters of the Empire. The clay enterprise of Wong Ts'in took upon itself an added lustre, and in order to deal adequately with so vast an undertaking the grateful merchant adopted Wei Chang and placed him upon an equal footing with himself. On the same day Wong Ts'in honourably fulfilled his spoken word and the marriage of Wei Chang and Fa Fai took place, accompanied by the most lavish display of fireworks and coloured lights that the province had ever seen. The controlling deities approved, and they had seven sons, one of whom had seven fingers upon each hand. All these sons became expert in Wei Chang's process of transferring porcelain embellishment, for some centuries elapsed before it was discovered that it was not absolutely necessary to sit upon each plate to produce the desired effect.

This chronicle of an event that is now regarded as almost classical would not be complete without an added reference to the ultimate end of the sordid Fang.

Fallen into disrepute among his fellows owing to the evil plight towards which he had enticed them, it became his increasing purpose to frequent the house beyond the river. On his return at nightfall he invariably drew aside on reaching the bridge, well knowing that he could not prudently rely upon his feet among so insecure a crossing, and composed himself to sleep amid the rushes. While in this position one night he was discovered and pushed into the river by a devout ox (an instrument of high destinies), where he perished incapably.

Those who found his body, not being able to withdraw so formidable a weight direct, cast a rope across the lower branch of a convenient willow-tree and thus raised it to the shore. In this striking manner Fa Fai's definite opinion achieved a destined end.

The Degraded Persistence of the Effete Ming-Shu

At about the same gong-stroke as before, Kai Lung again stood at the open shutter, and to him presently came the maiden Hwa-mei, bearing in her hands a gift of fruit.

"The story of the much-harassed merchant Wong Ts'in and of the assiduous youth Wei Chang has reached this person's ears by a devious road, and though it doubtless lost some of the subtler qualities in the telling, the ultimate tragedy had a convincing tone," she remarked pleasantly.

"It is scarcely to be expected that one who has spent his life beneath an official umbrella should have at his command the finer analogies of light and shade," tolerantly replied Kai Lung. "Though by no means comparable with the unapproachable history of the Princess Taik and the minstrel Ch'eng as a means for conveying the unexpressed aspirations of the one who relates towards the one who is receptive, there are many passages even in the behaviour of Wei Chang into which this person could infuse an unmistakable stress of significance were he but given the opportunity."

"The day of that opportunity has not yet dawned," replied the Golden Mouse; "nor has the night preceding it yet run its gloomy course. Foiled in his first attempt, the vindictive Ming-shu now creeps towards his end by a more tortuous path. Whether or not dimly suspecting something of the strategy by which your imperishable life was preserved to-day, it is no part of his depraved scheme that you should be given a like opportunity again. To-morrow another will be led to judgment, one Cho-kow, a tribesman of the barbarian land of Khim."

"With him I have already conversed and shared rice," interposed Kai Lung. "Proceed, elegance."

"Accused of plundering mountain tombs and of other crimes now held in disrepute, he will be offered a comparatively painless death if he will implicate his fellows, of whom you will be held to be the chief. By this ignoble artifice you will be condemned on his testimony in your absence, nor will you have any warning of your fate until you are led forth to suffer."

Then replied Kai Lung, after a space of thought: "Not ineptly is it written: 'When the leading carriage is upset the next one is more careful,' and Ming-shu has taken the proverb to his heart. To counteract his detestable plot will not be easy, but it should not be beyond our united power, backed by a reasonable activity on the part of our protecting ancestors."

"The devotional side of the emergency has had this one's early care," remarked Hwa-mei. "From daybreak to-morrow six zealous and deep-throated monks will curse Ming-shu and all his ways unceasingly, while a like number will invoke blessings and success upon your enlightened head. In the matter of noise and illumination everything that can contribute has been suitably prepared."

"It is difficult to conjecture what more could be done in that direction," confessed Kai Lung gratefully.

"Yet as regards a more material effort —?" suggested the maiden, amid a cloud of involving doubt.

"If there is a subject in which the imagination of the Mandarin Shan Tien can be again enmeshed it might be yet accomplished," replied Kai Lung. "Have you a knowledge of any such deep concern?"

"Truly there is a matter that disturbs his peace of late. He has dreamed a dream three times, and its meaning is beyond the skill of any man to solve. Yet how shall this avail you who are no geomancer?"

"What is the nature of the dream?" inquired Kai Lung. "For remember, 'Though Shen-fi has but one gate, many roads lead to it.'"

"The substance of the dream is this: that herein he who sleeps walks freely in the ways of men wearing no robe or covering of any kind, yet suffering no concern or indignity therefrom; that the secret and hidden things of the earth are revealed to his seeing eyes; and that he can float in space and project himself upon the air at will. These three things are alien to his nature, and being three times repeated, the uncertainty assails his ease."

"Let it, under your persistent care, assail him more and that unceasingly," exclaimed Kai Lung, with renewed lightness in his voice. "Breathe on the surface of his self-repose as a summer breeze moves the smooth water of a mountain lake-not deeply, but never quite at rest. Be assured: it is no longer possible to doubt that powerful Beings are interested in our cause."

"I go, oppressed one," replied Hwa-mei. "May this period of your ignoble trial be brought to a distinguished close."

On the following day at the appointed hour Cho-kow was led before the Mandarin Shan Tien, and the nature of his crimes having been explained to him by the contemptible Ming-shu, he was bidden to implicate Kai Lung and thus come to an earlier and less painful end.

"All-powerful," he replied, addressing himself to the Mandarin, "the words that have been spoken are bent to a deceptive end. They of our community are a simple race and doubtless in the past their ways were thus and thus. But, as it is truly said, 'Tian went bare, his eyes could pierce the earth and his body float in space, but they of his seed do but dream the dream.' We, being but the puny descendants —"

"You have spoken of one Tian whose attributes were such, and of those who dream thereof," interrupted the Mandarin, as one who performs a reluctant duty. "That which you adduce to uphold your cause must bear the full light of day."

"Alas, omnipotence," replied Cho-kow, "this concerns the doing of the gods and those who share their line. Now I am but an ill-conditioned outcast from the obscure land of Khim, and possess no lore beyond what happens there. Haply the gods that rule in Khim have a different manner of behaving from those in the Upper Air above Yu-ping, and this person's narration would avoid the semblance of the things that are and he himself would thereby be brought to disrepute."

"Suffer not that apprehension to retard your impending eloquence," replied Shan Tien affably. "Be assured that the gods have exactly the same manner of behaving in every land."

"Furthermore," continued Cho-kow, with patient craft, "I am a man of barbarian tongue, the full half of my speech being foreign to your ear. The history of the much-accomplished Tian and the meaning of the dreams that mark those of his race require for a full understanding the subtle analogies of an acquired style. Now that same Kai Lung whom you have implicated to my band —"

"Excellence!" protested Ming-shu, with a sudden apprehension in his throat, "yesterday our labours dissolved in air through the very doubtful precedent of allowing one to testify what he had had the intention to relate. Now we are asked to allow a tomb-haunter to call a parricide to disclose that which he himself is ignorant of. Press down your autocratic thumb —"

"Alas, instructor," interposed Shan Tien compassionately, "the sympathetic concern of my mind overflows upon the spectacle of your ill-used forbearance, yet you having banded together the two in a common infamy, it is the ancient privilege of this one to call the other to his cause. We are but the feeble mouthpieces of a benevolent scheme of all-embracing justice and greatly do I fear that we must again submit."

With these well-timed words the broad-minded personage settled himself more reposefully among his cushions and signified that Kai Lung should be led forward and begin.

The Story of Ning, the Captive God, and the Dreams that Mark his Race

I. The Malice of the Demon, Leou

When Sun Wei definitely understood that the deities were against him (for on every occasion his enemies prospered and the voice of his own authority grew less), he looked this way and that with a well-considering mind.

He did nothing hastily, but when once a decision was reached it was as unbending as iron and as smoothly finished as polished jade. At about the evening hour when others were preparing to offer sacrifice he took the images and the altars of his Rites down from their honourable positions and cast them into a heap on a waste expanse beyond his courtyard. Then with an axe he unceremoniously detached their incomparable limbs from their sublime bodies and flung the parts into a fire that he had prepared.

"It is better," declared Sun Wei, standing beside the pile, his hands buried within his sleeves—"it is better to be struck down at once, rather than to wither away slowly like a half-uprooted cassia-tree."

When this act of defiance was reported in the Upper World the air grew thick with the cries of indignation of the lesser deities, and the sound of their passage as they projected themselves across vast regions of space and into the presence of the supreme N'guk was like the continuous rending of innumerable pieces of the finest silk.

In his musk-scented heaven, however, N'guk slept, as his habit was at the close of each celestial day. It was with some difficulty that he could be aroused and made to understand the nature of Sun Wei's profanity, for his mind was dull with the smoke of never-ending incense.

"To-morrow," he promised, with a benignant gesture, turning over again on his crystal throne, "some time to-morrow impartial justice shall be done. In the meanwhile-courteous dismissal attend your opportune footsteps."

"He is becoming old and obese," murmured the less respectful of the demons. "He is not the god he was, even ten thousand cycles ago. It were well—"

"But, omnipotence," protested certain conciliatory spirits, pressing to the front, "consider, if but for a short breath of time. A day here is as threescore of their years as these mortals live. By to-morrow night not only Sun Wei, but most of those now dwelling down below, will have Passed Beyond. But the story of his unpunished infamy will live. We shall become discredited and our altar fires extinct. Sacrifice of either food or raiment will cease to reach us. The Season of White Rain is approaching and will find us ill provided. We who speak are but Beings of small part—"

"Peace!" commanded N'guk, now thoroughly disturbed, for the voices of the few had grown into a tumult; "how is it possible to consider with a torrent like the Hoang-Ho in flood pouring through my very ordinary ears? Your omniscient but quite inadequate Chief would think."

At this rebuke the uproar ceased. So deep became the nature of N'guk's profound thoughts that they could be heard rolling like thunder among the caverns of his gigantic brain. To aid the process, female slaves on either side fanned his fiery head with celestial lotus leaves. On the earth, far beneath, cyclones, sand-storms and sweeping water-spouts were forced into being.

"Hear the contemptible wisdom of my ill-formed mouth," said N'guk at length. "If we at once put forth our strength, the degraded Wun Sei is ground—"

"Sun Wei, All-knowing One," murmured an attending spirit beneath his breath.

"—the unmentionable outcast whom we are discussing is immediately ground into powder," continued the Highest, looking fixedly at a distant spot situated directly beyond his painstaking attendant. "But what follows? Henceforth no man can be allowed to whisper ill of us but we must at once seek him out and destroy him, or the obtuse and superficial will exclaim: 'It was not so in the days of-of So-and-So. Behold'"—here the Great One bent a look of sudden resentment on the band of those who would have reproached him —"'behold the gods become old and obese. They are not the Powers they were. It would be better to address ourselves to other altars.'"

At this prospect many of the more venerable spirits began to lose their enthusiasm. If every mortal who spoke ill of them was to be pursued what leisure for dignified seclusion would remain?

"If, however," continued the dispassionate Being, "the profaner is left to himself he will, sooner or later, in the ordinary course of human intelligence, become involved in some disaster of his own contriving. Then they who dwell around will say: 'He destroyed the alters! Truly the hands of the Unseen are slow to close, but their arms are very long. Lo, we have this day ourselves beheld it. Come, let us burn incense lest some forgotten misdeed from the past lurk in our path.'"

When he had finished speaking all the more reputable of those present extolled his judgment. Some still whispered together, however, whereupon the sagacious N'guk opened his mouth more fully and shot forth tongues of consuming fire among the murmurers so that they fled howling from his presence.

Now among the spirits who had stood before the Pearly Ruler without taking any share in the decision were two who at this point are drawn into the narration, Leou and Ning. Leou was a revengeful demon, ever at enmity with one or another of the gods and striving how he might enmesh his feet in destruction. Ning was a better-class deity, voluptuous but well-meaning, and little able to cope with Leou's subtlety. Thus it came about that the latter one, seeing in the outcome a chance to achieve his end, at once dropped headlong down to earth and sought out Sun Wei.

Sun Wei was reclining at his evening rice when Leou found him. Becoming invisible, the demon entered a date that Sun Wei held in his hand and took the form of a stone. Sun Wei recognized the doubtful nature of the stone as it passed between his teeth, and he would have spat it forth again, but Leou had the questionable agility of the serpent and slipped down the other's throat. He was thus able to converse familiarly with Sun Wei without fear of interruption.

"Sun Wei," said the voice of Leou inwardly, "the position you have chosen is a desperate one, and we of the Upper Air who are well disposed towards you find the path of assistance fringed with two-edged swords."

"It is well said: 'He who lacks a single tael sees many bargains,'" replied Sun Wei, a refined bitterness weighing the import of his words. "Truly this person's friends in the Upper Air are a never-failing lantern behind his back."

At this justly-barbed reproach Leou began to shake with disturbed gravity until he remembered that the motion might not be pleasing to Sun Wei's inner feelings.

"It is not that the well-disposed are slow to urge your claims, but that your enemies number some of the most influential demons in all the Nine Spaces," he declared, speaking with a false smoothness that marked all his detestable plans. "Assuredly in the past you must have led a very abandoned life, Sun Wei, to come within the circle of their malignity."

"By no means," replied Sun Wei. "Until driven to despair this person not only duly observed the Rites and Ceremonies, but he even avoided the Six Offences. He remained by the side of his parents while they lived, provided an adequate posterity, forbore to tread on any of the benevolent insects, safeguarded all printed paper, did not consume the meat of the industrious ox, and was charitable towards the needs of hungry and homeless ghosts."

"These observances are well enough," admitted Leou, restraining his narrow-minded impatience; "and with an ordinary number of written charms worn about the head and body they would doubtless carry you through the lesser contingencies of existence. But by, as it were, extending contempt, you have invited the retaliatory propulsion of the sandal of authority."

"To one who has been pushed over the edge of a precipice, a rut across the path is devoid of menace; nor do the destitute tremble at the departing watchman's cry: 'Sleep warily; robbers are about.'"

"As regards bodily suffering and material extortion, it is possible to attain such a limit as no longer to excite the cupidity of even the most rapacious deity," admitted Leou. "Other forms of flattening-out a transgressor's self-content remain however. For instance, it has come within the knowledge of the controlling Powers that seven generations of your distinguished ancestors occupy positions of dignified seclusion in the Upper Air."

For the first time Sun Wei's attitude was not entirely devoid of an emotion of concern.

"They would not—?"

"To mark their sense of your really unsupportable behaviour it has been decided that all seven shall return to the humiliating scenes of their former existences in admittedly objectionable forms," replied the outrageous Leou. "Sun Chen, your venerated sire, will become an agile grasshopper; your incomparable grandfather, Yuen, will have the similitude of a yellow goat; as a tortoise your leisurely-minded ancestor Huang, the high public official—"

"Forbear!" exclaimed the conscience-stricken Sun Wei; "rather would this person suffer every imaginable form of torture than that the spirit of one of his revered ancestors should be submitted to so intolerable a bondage. Is there no amiable form of compromise whereby the ancestors of some less devoted and liberally-inspired son might be imperceptibly, as it were, substituted?"

"In ordinary cases some such arrangement is generally possible," conceded Leou; "but not idly is it written: 'There is a time to silence an adversary with the honey of logical persuasion, and there is a time to silence him with the argument of a heavily-directed club.' In your extremity a hostage is the only efficient safeguard. Seize the person of one of the gods themselves and raise a strong wall around your destiny by holding him to ransom."

"'Ho Tai, requiring a light for his pipe, stretched out his hand towards the great sky-lantern,'" quoted Sun Wei.

"'Do not despise Ching To because his armour is invisible,'" retorted Leou, with equal point. "Your friends in the Above are neither feeble nor inept. Do as I shall instruct you and no less a Being than Ning will be delivered into your hand."

Then replied Sun Wei dubiously: "A spreading mango-tree affords a pleasant shade within one's courtyard, and a captive god might for a season undoubtedly confer an enviable distinction. But presently the tree's encroaching roots may disturb the foundation of the house so that the walls fall and crush those who are within, and the head of a restrained god would in the end certainly displace my very inadequate roof-tree."

"A too-prolific root can be pruned back," replied Leou, "and the activities of a bondaged god may be efficiently curtailed. How this shall be accomplished will be revealed to you in a dream: take heed that you do not fail by the deviation of a single hair."

Having thus prepared his discreditable plot, Leou twice struck the walls enclosing him, so that Sun Wei coughed violently. The demon was thereby enabled to escape, and he never actually appeared in a tangible form again, although he frequently communicated, by means of signs and omens, with those whom he wished to involve in his sinister designs.

II. The Part Played by the Slave-Girl, Hia

Among the remaining possessions that the hostility of the deities still left to Sun Wei at the time of these happenings was a young slave of many-sided attraction. The name of Hia had been given to her, but she was generally known as Tsing-ai on account of the extremely affectionate gladness of her nature.

On the day following that in which Sun Wei and the demon Leou had conversed together, Hia was disporting herself in the dark shades of a secluded pool, as her custom was after the heat of her labours, when a phoenix, flying across the glade, dropped a pearl of unusual size and lustre into the stream. Possessing herself of the jewel and placing it in her mouth, so that it should not impede the action of her hands, Hia sought the bank and would have drawn herself up when she became aware of the presence of one having the guise of a noble commander. He was regarding her with a look in which well-expressed admiration was blended with a delicate intimation that owing to the unparalleled brilliance of her eyes he was unable to perceive any other detail of her appearance, and was, indeed, under the impression that she was devoid of ordinary outline. At the same time, without permitting her glance to be in any but an entirely opposite direction, Hia was able to satisfy herself that the stranger was a person on whom she might prudently lavish the full depths of her regard if the necessity arose. His apparel was rich, voluminous and of colours then unknown within the Empire; his hair long and abundant; his face placid but sincere. He carried no weapons, but wherever he trod there came a yellow flame from below his right foot and a white vapour from beneath his left. His insignia were those of a royal prince, and when he spoke his voice resembled the noise of arrows passing through the upper branches of a prickly forest. His long and pointed nails indicated the high and dignified nature of all his occupations; each nail was protected by a solid sheath, there being amethyst, ruby, topaz, ivory, emerald, white jade, iron, chalcedony, gold and malachite.

When the distinguished-looking personage had thus regarded Hia for some moments he drew an instrument of hollow tubes from a fold of his garment and began to sing of two who, as the outcome of a romantic encounter similar to that then existing, had professed an agreeable attachment for one another and had, without unnecessary delay, entered upon a period of incomparable felicity. Doubtless Hia would have uttered words of high-minded rebuke at some of the more detailed analogies of the recital had not the pearl deprived her of the power of expressing herself clearly on any subject whatever, nor did it seem practicable to her to remove it without withdrawing her hands from the modest attitudes into which she had at once distributed them. Thus positioned, she was compelled to listen to the stranger's well-considered flattery, and this (together with the increasing coldness of the stream as the evening deepened) convincingly explains her ultimate acquiescence to his questionable offers.

Yet it cannot be denied that Ning (as he may now fittingly be revealed) conducted the enterprise with a seemly liberality; for upon receiving from Hia a glance not expressive of discouragement he at once caused the appearance of a suitably-furnished tent, a train of Nubian slaves offering rich viands, rare wine and costly perfumes, companies of expert dancers and musicians, a retinue of discreet elderly women to robe her and to attend her movements, a carpet of golden silk stretching from the water's edge to the tent, and all the accessories of a high-class profligacy.

When the night was advanced and Hia and Ning, after partaking of a many-coursed feast, were reclining on an ebony couch, the Being freely expressed the delight that he discovered in her amiable society, incautiously adding: "Demand any recompense that is within the power of this one to grant, O most delectable of water-nymphs, and its accomplishment will be written by a flash of lightning." In this, however, he merely spoke as the treacherous Leou (who had enticed him into the adventure) had assured him was usual in similar circumstances, he himself being privately of the opinion that the expenditure already incurred was more than adequate to the occasion.

Then replied Hia, as she had been fully instructed against the emergency: "The word has been spoken. But what is precious metal after listening to the pure gold of thy lips, or who shall again esteem gems while gazing upon the full round radiance of thy moon-like face? One thing only remains: remove the various sheaths from off thy hands, for they not only conceal the undoubted perfection of the nails within, but their massive angularity renders the affectionate ardour of your embrace almost intolerable."

At this very ordinary request a sudden flatness overspread Ning's manner and he began to describe the many much more profitable rewards that Hia might fittingly demand. As none of these appeared to entice her imagination, he went on to rebuke her want of foresight, and, still later, having unsuccessfully pointed out to her the inevitable penury and degradation in which her thriftless perversity would involve her later years, to kick the less substantial appointments across the tent.

"The night thickens, with every indication of a storm," remarked Hia pleasantly. "Yet that same impending flash of promised lightning tarries somewhat."

"Truly is it written: 'A gracious woman will cause more strife than twelve armed men can quell,'" retorted Ning bitterly.

"Not, perchance, if one of them bares his nails?" Thus she lightly mocked him, but always with a set intent, as a poised dragon-fly sips water yet does not wet his wings. Whereupon, finally, Ning tore the sheaths from off his fingers and cast them passionately about her feet, immediately afterwards sinking into a profound sleep, for both the measure and the potency of the wine he had consumed exceeded his usual custom. Otherwise he would scarcely have acted in this incapable manner, for each sheath was inscribed with one symbol of a magic charm and in the possession of the complete sentence resided the whole of the Being's authority and power.

Then Hia, seeing that he could no longer control her movements, and that the end to which she had been bending was attained, gathered together the fruits of her conscientious strategy and fled.

When Ning returned to the condition of ordinary perceptions he was lying alone in the field by the river-side. The great sky-fire made no pretence of averting its rays from his uncovered head, and the lesser creatures of the ground did not hesitate to walk over his once sacred form. The tent and all the other circumstances of the quest of Hia had passed into a state of no-existence, for with a somewhat narrow-minded economy the deity had called them into being with the express provision that they need only be of such a quality as would last for a single night.

With this recollection, other details began to assail his mind. His irreplaceable nail-sheaths—there was no trace of one of them. He looked again. Alas! his incomparable nails were also gone, shorn off to the level of his finger-ends. For all their evidence he might be one who had passed his days in discreditable industry. Each moment a fresh point of degradation met his benumbed vision. His profuse and ornamental locks were reduced to a single roughly-plaited coil; his sandals were inelegant and harsh; in place of his many-coloured flowing robes a scanty blue gown clothed his form. He who had been a god was undistinguishable from the labourers of the fields. Only in one thing did the resemblance fail: about his neck he found a weighty block of wood controlled by an iron ring: while they at least were free he was a captive slave.

A shadow on the grass caused him to turn. Sun Wei approached, a knotted thong in one hand, in the other a hoe. He pointed to an unweeded rice-field and with many ceremonious bows pressed the hoe upon Ning as one who confers high honours. As Ning hesitated, Sun Wei pressed the knotted thong upon him until it would have been obtuse to disregard his meaning. Then Ning definitely understood that he had become involved in the workings of very powerful forces, hostile to himself, and picking up the hoe he bent his submissive footsteps in the direction of the laborious rice-field.

III. The In-Coming of the Youth, Tian

It was dawn in the High Heaven and the illimitable N'guk, waking to his labours for the day, looked graciously around on the assembled myriads who were there to carry his word through boundless space. Not wanting are they who speak two-sided words of the Venerable One from behind fan-like hands, but when his voice takes upon it the authority of a brazen drum knees become flaccid.

"There is a void in the unanimity of our council," remarked the Supreme, his eye resting like a flash of lightning on a vacant place. "Wherefore tarries Ning, the son of Shin, the Seed-sower?"

For a moment there was an edging of N'guk's inquiring glance from each Being to his neighbour. Then Leou stood audaciously forth.

"He is reported to be engaged on a private family matter," he replied gravely. "Haply his feet have become entangled in a mesh of hair."

N'guk turned his benevolent gaze upon another-one higher in authority.

"Perchance," admitted the superior Being tolerantly. "Such things are. How comes it else that among the earth-creatures we find the faces of the deities-both the good and the bad?"

"How long has he been absent from our paths?"

They pressed another forward-keeper of the Outer Path of the West Expanses, he.

"He went, High Excellence, in the fifteenth of the earth-ruler Chun, whom your enlightened tolerance has allowed to occupy the lower dragon throne for twoscore years, as these earthlings count. Thus and thus—"

"Enough!" exclaimed the Supreme. "Hear my iron word. When the buffoon-witted Ning rises from his congenial slough this shall be his lot: for sixty thousand ages he shall fail to find the path of his return, but shall, instead, thread an aimless flight among the frozen ambits of the outer stars, carrying a tormenting rain of fire at his tail. And Leou, the Whisperer," added the Divining One, with the inscrutable wisdom that marked even his most opaque moments, "Leou shall meanwhile perform Ning's neglected task."

* * *

For five and twenty years Ning had laboured in the fields of Sun Wei with a wooden collar girt about his neck, and Sun Wei had prospered. Yet it is to be doubted whether this last detail deliberately hinged on the policy of Leou or whether Sun Wei had not rather been drawn into some wider sphere of destiny and among converging lines of purpose. The ways of the gods are deep and sombre, and water once poured out will flow as freely to the north as to the south. The wise kowtows acquiescently whatever happens and thus his face is to the ground. "Respect the deities," says the imperishable Sage, "but do not become familiar with them." Sun Wei was clearly wrong.

To Ning, however, standing on a grassy space on the edge of a flowing river, such thoughts do not extend. He is now a little hairy man of gnarled appearance, and his skin of a colour and texture like a ripe lo-quat. As he stands there, something in the outline of the vista stirs the retentive tablets of his mind: it was on this spot that he first encountered Hia, and from that involvement began the cycle of his unending ill.

As he stood thus, implicated with his own inner emotions, a figure emerged from the river at its nearest point and, crossing the intervening sward, approached. He had the aspect of being a young man of high and dignified manner, and walked with the air of one accustomed to a silk umbrella, but when Ning looked more closely, to see by his insignia what amount of reverence he should pay, he discovered that the youth was destitute of the meagrest garment.

"Rise, venerable," said the stranger affably, for Ning had prostrated himself as being more prudent in the circumstances. "The one before you is only Tian, of obscure birth, and himself of no particular merit or attainment. You, doubtless, are of considerably more honourable lineage?"

"Far from that being the case," replied Ning, "the one who speaks bears now the commonplace name of Lieu, and is branded with the brand of Sun Wei. Formerly, indeed, he was a god, moving in the Upper Space and known to the devout as Ning, but now deposed by treachery."

"Unless the subject is one that has painful associations," remarked Tian considerately, "it is one on which this person would willingly learn somewhat deeper. What, in short, are the various differences existing between gods and men?"

"The gods are gods; men are men," replied Ning. "There is no other difference."

"Yet why do not the gods now exert their strength and raise from your present admittedly inferior position one who is of their band?"

"Behind their barrier the gods laugh at all men. How much more, then, is their gravity removed at the sight of one of themselves who has fallen lower than mankind?"

"Your plight would certainly seem to be an ill-destined one," admitted Tian, "for, as the Verses say: 'Gold sinks deeper than dross.' Is there anything that an ordinary person can do to alleviate your subjection?"

"The offer is a gracious one," replied Ning, "and such an occasion undoubtedly exists. Some time ago a pearl of unusual size and lustre slipped from its setting about this spot. I have looked for it in vain, but your acuter eyes, perchance—"

Thus urged, the youth Tian searched the ground, but to no avail. Then chancing to look upwards, he exclaimed:

"Among the higher branches of the tallest bamboo there is an ancient phoenix nest, and concealed within its wall is a pearl such as you describe."

"That manifestly is what I seek," said Ning. "But it might as well be at the bottom of its native sea, for no ladder could reach to such a height nor would the slender branch support a living form."

"Yet the emergency is one easily disposed of." With these opportune words the amiable person rose from the ground without any appearance of effort or conscious movement, and floating upward through the air he procured the jewel and restored it to Ning.

When Ning had thus learned that Tian possessed these three attainments which are united in the gods alone-that he could stand naked before others without consciousness of shame, that his eyes were able to penetrate matter impervious to those of ordinary persons, and that he controlled the power of rising through the air unaided-he understood that the one before him was a deity of some degree. He therefore questioned him closely about his history, the various omens connected with his life and the position of the planets at his birth. Finding that these presented no element of conflict, and that, furthermore, the youth's mother was a slave, formerly known as Hia, Ning declared himself more fully and greeted Tian as his undoubted son.

"The absence of such a relation is the one thing that has pressed heavily against this person's satisfaction in the past, and the deficiency is now happily removed," exclaimed Tian. "The distinction of having a deity for a father outweighs even the present admittedly distressing condition in which he reveals himself. His word shall henceforth be my law."

"The sentiment is a dutiful one," admitted Ning, "and it is possible that you are now thus discovered in pursuance of some scheme among my more influential accomplices in the Upper Air for restoring to me my former eminence."

"In so meritorious a cause this person is prepared to immerse himself to any depth," declared Tian readily. "Nothing but the absence of precise details restrains his hurrying feet."

"Those will doubtless be communicated to us by means of omens and portents as the requirement becomes more definite. In the meanwhile the first necessity is to enable this person's nails to grow again; for to present himself thus in the Upper Air would be to cover him with ridicule. When the Emperor Chow-sin endeavoured to pass himself off as a menial by throwing aside his jewelled crown, the rebels who had taken him replied: 'Omnipotence, you cannot throw away your knees.' To claim kinship with those Above and at the same time to extend towards them a hand obviously inured to probing among the stony earth would be to invite the averted face of recognition."

"Let recognition be extended in other directions and the task of returning to a forfeited inheritance will be lightened materially," remarked a significant voice.

"Estimable mother," exclaimed Tian, "this opportune stranger is my venerated father, whose continuous absence has been an overhanging cloud above my gladness, but now happily revealed and restored to our domestic altar."

"Alas!" interposed Ning, "the opening of this enterprise forecasts a questionable omen. Before this person stands the one who enticed him into the beginning of all his evil; how then —"

"Let the word remain unspoken," interrupted Hia. "Women do not entice men-though they admittedly accompany them, with an extreme absence of reluctance, in any direction. In her youth this person's feet undoubtedly bore her occasionally along a light and fantastic path, for in the nature of spring a leaf is green and pliable, and in the nature of autumn it is brown and austere, and through changeless ages thus and thus. But, as it is truly said: 'Milk by repeated agitation turns to butter,' and for many years it has been this one's ceaseless study of the Arts whereby she might avert that which she helped to bring about in her unstable youth."

"The intention is a commendable one, though expressed with unnecessary verbiage," replied Ning. "To what solution did your incantations trend?"

"Concealed somewhere within the walled city of Ti-foo are the sacred nail-sheaths on which your power so essentially depends, sent thither by Sun Wei at the crafty instance of the demon Leou, who hopes at a convenient time to secure them for himself. To discover these and bear them forth will be the part allotted to Tian, and to this end has the training of his youth been bent. By what means he shall strive to the accomplishment of the project the unrolling curtain of the future shall disclose."

"It is as the destinies shall decide and as the omens may direct," said Tian. "In the meanwhile this person's face is inexorably fixed in the direction of Ti-foo."

"Proceed with all possible discretion," advised Ning. "In so critical an undertaking you cannot be too cautious, but at the same time do not suffer the rice to grow around your advancing feet."

"A moment," conselled Hia. "Tarry yet a moment. Here is one whose rapidly-moving attitude may convey a message."

"It is Lin Fa!" exclaimed Ning, as the one alluded to drew near —"Lin Fa who guards the coffers of Sun Wei. Some calamity pursues him."

"Hence!" cried Lin Fa, as he caught sight of them, yet scarcely pausing in his flight: "flee to the woods and caves until the time of this catastrophe be past. Has not the tiding reached you?"

"We be but dwellers on the farther bounds and no word has reached our ear, O great Lin Fa. Fill in, we pray you, the warning that has been so suddenly outlined."

"The usurper Ah-tang has lit the torch of swift rebellion and is flattening-down the land that bars his way. Already the villages of Yeng, Leu, Liang-li and the Dwellings by the Three Pure Wells are as dust beneath his trampling feet, and they who stayed there have passed up in smoke. Sun Wei swings from the roof-tree of his own ruined yamen. Ah-tang now lays siege to walled Ti-foo so that he may possess the Northern Way. Guard this bag of silver meanwhile, for what I have is more than I can reasonably bear, and when the land is once again at peace, assemble to meet me by the Five-Horned Pagoda, ready with a strict account."

"All this is plainly part of an orderly scheme for my advancement, brought about by my friends in the Upper World," remarked Ning, with some complacency. "Lin Fa has been influenced to the extent of providing us with the means for our immediate need; Sun Wei has been opportunely removed to the end that this person may now retire to a hidden spot and there suffer his dishonoured nails to grow again: Ah-tang has been impelled to raise the banner of insurrection outside Ti-foo so that Tian may make use of the necessities of either side in pursuit of his design. Assuredly the long line of our misfortunes is now practically at an end."

IV. Events Round Walled Ti-Foo

Nevertheless, the alternative forced on Tian was not an alluring one. If he joined the band of Ah-tang and the usurper failed, Tian himself might never get inside Ti-foo; if, however, he allied himself with the defenders of Ti-foo and Ah-tang did not fail, he might never get out of Ti-foo. Doubtless he would have reverently submitted his cause to the inspired decision of the Sticks, or some other reliable augur, had he not, while immersed in the consideration, walked into the camp of Ah-tang. The omen of this occurrence was of too specific a nature not to be regarded as conclusive.

Ah-tang was one who had neglected the Classics from his youth upwards. For this reason his detestable name is never mentioned in the Histories, and the various catastrophes he wrought are charitably ascribed to the action of earthquakes, thunderbolts and other admitted forces. He himself, with his lamentable absence of literary style, was wont to declare that while confessedly weak in analogies he was strong in holocausts. In the end he drove the sublime emperor from his capital and into the Outer Lands; with true refinement the annalists of the period explain that the condescending monarch made a journey of inspection among the barbarian tribes on the confines of his Empire.

When Tian, charged with being a hostile spy, was led into the presence of Ah-tang, it was the youth's intention to relate somewhat of his history, but the usurper, excusing himself on the ground of literary deficiency, merely commanded five of his immediate guard to bear the prisoner away and to return with his head after a fitting interval. Misunderstanding the exact requirement, Tian returned at the appointed time with the heads of the five who had charge of him and the excuse that in those times of scarcity it was easier to keep one head than five. This aptitude so pleased Ah-tang (who had expected at the most a farewell apophthegm) that he at once made Tian captain of a chosen band.

Thus was Tian positioned outside the city of Ti-foo, materially contributing to its ultimate surrender by the resourceful courage of his arms. For the first time in the history of opposing forces he tamed the strength and swiftness of wild horses to the use of man, and placing copper loops upon their feet and iron bars between their teeth, he and his band encircled Ti-foo with an ever-moving shield through which no outside word could reach the town. Cut off in this manner from all hope of succour, the stomachs of those within the walls grew very small, and their eyes became weary of watching for that which never came. On the third day of the third moon of their encirclement they sent a submissive banner, and one bearing a written message, into the camp of Ah-tang.

> "We are convinced" (it ran) "of the justice of your cause. Let six of your lordly nobles appear unarmed before our ill-kept Lantern Gate at the middle gong-stroke of to-morrow and they will be freely admitted within our midst. Upon receiving a bound assurance safeguarding the limits of our temples, the persons and possessions of our chiefs, and the undepreciated condition of the first wives and virgin daughters of such as be of mandarin rank or literary degree, the inadequate keys of our broken-down defences will be laid at their sumptuous feet.
>
> "With a fervent hand-clasp as of one brother to another, and a passionate assurance of mutual good-will, Ko'En Cheng, Important Official."

"It is received," replied Ah-tang, when the message had been made known to him. "Six captains will attend."

Alas! it is well written: "There is often a space between the fish and the fish-plate." Mentally inflated at the success of their efforts and the impending surrender of Ti-foo, Tian's band suffered their energies to relax. In the dusk of that same evening one disguised in the skin of a goat browsed from bush to bush until he reached the town. There, throwing off all restraint, he declared his errand to Ko'en Cheng.

"Behold!" he exclaimed, "the period of your illustrious suffering is almost at an end. With an army capable in size and invincible in determination, the ever-victorious Wu Sien is marching to your aid. Defy the puny Ah-tang for yet three days more and great glory will be yours."

"Doubtless," replied Ko'en Cheng, with velvet bitterness: "but the sun has long since set and the moon is not yet risen. The appearance of a solitary star yesterday would have been more foot-guiding than the forecast of a meteor next week. This person's thumb-signed word is passed and to-morrow Ah-tang will hold him to it."

Now there was present among the council one wrapped in a mantle made of rustling leaves, who spoke in a smooth, low voice, very cunning and persuasive, with a plan already shaped that seemed to offer well and to safeguard Ko'en Cheng's word. None remembered to have seen him there before, and for this reason it is now held by some that this was Leou, the Whisperer, perturbed lest the sacred nail-sheaths of Ning should pass beyond his grasp. As to this, says not the Wise One: "When two men cannot agree over the price of an onion who shall decide what happened in the time of Yu?" But the voice of the unknown prevailed, all saying: "At the worst it is but as it will be; perchance it may be better."

That night there was much gladness in the camp of Ah-tang, and men sang songs of victory and cups of wine were freely passed, though in the outer walks a strict watch was kept. When it was dark the word was passed that an engaging company was approaching from the town, openly and with lights. These being admitted revealed themselves as a band of maidens, bearing gifts of fruit and wine and assurances of their agreeable behaviour. Distributing themselves impartially about the tents of the chiefs and upper ones, they melted the hours of the night in graceful accomplishments and by their seemly compliance dispelled all thought of treachery. Having thus gained the esteem of their companions, and by the lavish persuasion of bemusing wine dimmed their alertness, all this band, while it was still dark, crept back to the town, each secretly carrying with her the arms, robes and insignia of the one who had possessed her.

When the morning broke and the sound of trumpets called each man to an appointed spot, direful was the outcry from the tents of all the chiefs, and though many heads were out-thrust in rage of indignation, no single person could be prevailed upon wholly to emerge. Only the lesser warriors, the slaves and the bearers of the loads moved freely to and fro and from between closed teeth and with fluttering eyelids tossed doubtful jests among themselves.

It was close upon the middle gong-stroke of the day when Ah-tang, himself clad in a shred torn from his tent (for in all the camp there did not remain a single garment bearing a sign of noble rank), got together a council of his chiefs. Some were clad in like attire, others carried a henchman's shield, a paper lantern or a branch of flowers; Tian alone displayed himself without reserve.

"There are moments," said Ah-tang, "when this person's admitted accomplishment of transfixing three foemen with a single javelin at a score of measured paces does not seem to provide a possible solution. Undoubtedly we are face to face with a crafty plan, and Ko'en Cheng has surely heard that Wu Sien is marching from the west. If we fail to knock upon the outer gate of Ti-foo at noon to-day Ko'en Cheng will say: 'My word returns. It is as naught.' If they who go are clad as underlings, Ko'en Cheng will cry: 'What slaves be these! Do men break plate with dogs? Our message was for six of noble style. Ah-tang but mocks.'" He sat down again moodily. "Let others speak."

"Chieftain"—Tian threw forth his voice—"your word must be as iron—'Six captains shall attend.' There is yet another way."

"Speak on," Ah-tang commanded.

"The quality of Ah-tang's chiefs resides not in a cloak of silk nor in a silver-hilted sword, but in the sinews of their arms and the lightning of their eyes. If they but carry these they proclaim their rank for all to see. Let six attend taking neither sword nor shield, neither hat nor sandal, nor yet anything between. 'There are six thousand more,' shall be their taunt, 'but Ko'en Cheng's hospitality drew rein at six. He feared lest they might carry arms; behold they have come naked. Ti-foo need not tremble."

"It is well," agreed Ah-tang. "At least, nothing better offers. Let five accompany you."

Seated on a powerful horse Tian led the way. The others, not being of his immediate band, had not acquired the necessary control, so that they walked in a company. Coming to the Lantern Gate Tian turned his horse suddenly so that its angry hoof struck the gate. Looking back he saw the others following, with no great space between, and so passed in.

When the five naked captains reached the open gate they paused. Within stood a great concourse of the people, these being equally of both sexes, but they of the inner chambers pressing resolutely to the front. Through the throng of these their way must lead, and at the sight the hearts of all became as stagnant water in the sun.

"Tarry not for me, O brothers," said the one who led. "A thorn has pierced my foot. Take honourable precedence while I draw it forth."

"Never," declared the second of the band, "never shall it be cast abroad that Kang of the House of Ka failed his brother in necessity. I sustain thy shoulder, comrade."

"Alas!" exclaimed the third. "This person broke his fast on rhubarb stewed in fat. Inopportunely—" So he too turned aside.

"Have we considered well," said they who remained, "whether this be not a subtle snare, and while the camp is denuded of its foremost warriors a strong force—?"

Unconscious of these details, Tian went on alone. In spite of the absence of gravity on the part of the more explicit portion of the throng he suffered no embarrassment, partly because of his position, but chiefly through his inability to understand that his condition differed in any degree from theirs; for, owing to the piercing nature of his vision, they were to him as he to them. In this way he came to the open space known as the Space of the Eight Directions, where Ko'en Cheng and his nobles were assembled.

"One comes alone," they cried. "This guise is as a taunt." "Naked to a naked town–the analogy is plain." "Shall the mocker be suffered to return?"

Thus the murmur grew. Then one, more impetuous than the rest, swung clear his sword and drew it. For the first time Tian understood that treachery was afoot. He looked round for any of his band, but found that he was as a foam-tossed cork upon a turbulent Whang Hai. Cries of anger and derision filled the air; threatening arms waved encouragement to each other to begin. The one with drawn sword raised it above his head and made a step. Then Tian, recognizing that he was unarmed, and that a decisive moment had arrived, stooped low and tore a copper hoop from off his horse's foot. High he swung its polished brightness in the engaging sun, resolutely brought it down, so that it pressed over the sword-warrior's shattered head and hung about his neck. Having thus effected as much bloodshed as could reasonably be expected in the circumstances, Tian curved his feet about his horse's sides and imparting to it the virtue of his own condition they rose into the air together. When those who stood below were able to exert themselves a flight of arrows, spears and every kind of weapon followed, but horse and rider were by that time beyond their reach, and the only benevolent result attained was that many of their band were themselves transfixed by the falling shafts.

In such a manner Tian continued his progress from the town until he came above the Temple of Fire and Water Forces, where on a high tower a strong box of many woods was chained beneath a canopy, guarded by an incantation laid upon it by Leou, that no one should lift it down. Recognizing the contents as the object of his search, Tian brought his horse to rest upon the tower, and breaking the chains he bore the magic sheaths away, the charm (owing to Leou's superficial habits) being powerless against one who instead of lifting the box down carried it up.

In spite of this distinguished achievement it was many moons before Tian was able to lay the filial tribute of restored power at Ning's feet, for with shallow-witted obstinacy Ti-foo continued to hold out, and, scarcely less inept, Ah-tang declined to release Tian even to carry on so charitable a mission. Yet when the latter one ultimately returned and was, as the reward of his intrepid services, looking forward to a period of domestic reunion under the benevolent guidance of an affectionate father, it was but to point the seasoned proverb: "The fuller the cup the sooner the spill," for scarcely had Ning drawn on the recovered sheaths and with incautious joy repeated the magic sentence than he was instantly projected across vast space and into the trackless confines of the Outer Upper Paths. If this were an imagined tale, framed to entice the credulous, herein would its falseness cry aloud, but even in this age Ning may still be seen from time to time with a tail of fire in his wake, missing the path of his return as N'guk ordained.

Thus bereft, Tian was on the point of giving way to a seemly despair when a message concerned with Mu, the only daughter of Ko'en Cheng, reached him. It professed a high-minded regard for his welfare, and added that although the one who was inspiring the communication had been careful to avoid seeing him on the occasion of his entry into Ti-foo, it was impossible for her not to be impressed by the dignity of his bearing. Ko'en Cheng having become vastly wealthy as the result of entering into an arrangement with Ah-tang before Ti-foo was sacked, it did not seem unreasonable to Tian that Ning was in some way influencing his destiny from afar. On this understanding he ultimately married Mu, and thereby founded a prolific posterity who inherited a great degree of his powers. In the course of countless generations the attributes have faded, but even to this day the true descendants of the line of Ning are frequently vouchsafed dreams in which they stand naked and without shame, see gems or metals hidden or buried in the earth and float at will through space.

The Inopportune Behaviour of the Covetous Li-Loe

It was upon the occasion of his next visit to the shutter in the wall that Kai Lung discovered the obtuse-witted Li-loe moving about the enclosure. Though docile and well-meaning on the whole, the stunted intelligence of the latter person made him a doubtful accomplice, and Kai Lung stood aside, hoping to be soon alone.

Li-loe held in his hand an iron prong, and with this he industriously searched the earth between the rocks and herbage. Ever since their previous encounter upon that same spot it had been impossible to erase from his deformed mind the conviction that a store of rare and potent wine lay somewhere concealed within the walls of the enclosure. Continuously he besought the story-teller to reveal the secret of its hiding-place, saying: "What an added bitterness will assail your noble throat if, when you are led forth to die, your eye closes upon the one who has faithfully upheld your cause lying with a protruded tongue panting in the noonday sun."

"Peace, witless," Kai Lung usually replied; "there is no such store."

"Nevertheless," the doorkeeper would stubbornly insist, "the cask cannot yet be empty. It is beyond your immature powers."

Thus it again befell, for despite Kai Lung's desire to escape, Li-loe chanced to look up suddenly and observed him.

"Alas, brother," he remarked reproachfully, when they had thus contended, "the vessel that returns whole the first time is chipped the second and broken at the third essay, and it will yet be too late between us. If it be as you claim, to what end did you boast of a cask of wine and of running among a company of goats with leaves entwined in your hair?"

"That," replied Kai Lung, "was in the nature of a classical allusion, too abstruse for your deficient wit. It concerned the story of Kiau Sun, who first attained the honour."

"Be that as it may," replied Li-loe, with mulish iteration, "five deficient strings of home-made cash are a meagre return for a friendship such as mine."

"There is a certain element of truth in what you claim," confessed Kai Lung, "but until my literary style is more freely recognized it will be impossible to reward you adequately. In anything not of a pecuniary nature, however, you may lean heavily upon my gratitude."

"In the meanwhile, then," demanded Li-loe, "relate to me the story to which reference has been made, thereby proving the truth of your assertion, and at the same time affording an entertainment of a somewhat exceptional kind."

"The shadows lengthen," replied Kai Lung, "but as the narrative in question is of an inconspicuous span I will raise no barrier against your flattering request, especially as it indicates an awakening taste hitherto unsuspected."

"Proceed, manlet, proceed," said Li-loe, with a final probe among the surrounding rocks before selecting one to lean against. "Yet if this person could but lay his hand —"

The Story of Wong Pao and the Minstrel

To Wong Pao, the merchant, pleasurably immersed in the calculation of an estimated profit on a junk-load of birds' nests, sharks' fins and other seasonable delicacies, there came a distracting interruption occasioned by a wandering poet who sat down within the shade provided by Wong Pao's ornamental gate in the street outside. As he reclined there he sang ballads of ancient valour, from time to time beating a hollow wooden duck in unison with his voice, so that the charitable should have no excuse for missing the entertainment.

Unable any longer to continue his occupation, Wong Pao struck an iron gong.

"Bear courteous greetings to the accomplished musician outside our gate," he said to the slave who had appeared, "and convince him-by means of a heavily-weighted club if necessary-that the situation he has taken up is quite unworthy of his incomparable efforts."

When the slave returned it was with an entire absence of the enthusiasm of one who has succeeded in an enterprise.

"The distinguished mendicant outside disarmed the one who is relating the incident by means of an unworthy stratagem, and then struck him repeatedly on the head with the image of a sonorous wooden duck," reported the slave submissively.

Meanwhile the voice with its accompaniment continued to chant the deeds of bygone heroes.

"In that case," said Wong Pao coldly, "entice him into this inadequate chamber by words suggestive of liberal entertainment."

This device was successful, for very soon the slave returned with the stranger. He was a youth of studious appearance and an engaging openness of manner. Hung about his neck by means of a cord were a variety of poems suitable to most of the contingencies of an ordinary person's existence. The name he bore was Sun and he was of the house of Kiau.

"Honourable greeting, minstrel," said Wong Pao, with dignified condescension. "Why do you persist in exercising your illustrious talent outside this person's insignificant abode?"

"Because," replied Sun modestly, "the benevolent mandarin who has just spoken had not then invited me inside. Now, however, he will be able to hear to greater advantage the very doubtful qualities of my entertainment."

With these words Kiau Sun struck the duck so proficiently that it emitted a life-like call, and prepared to raise his voice in a chant.

"Restrain your undoubted capacity," exclaimed Wong Pao hastily. "The inquiry presented itself to you at an inaccurate angle. Why, to restate it, did you continue before this uninviting hovel when, under the external forms of true politeness, my slave endeavoured to remove you hence?"

"In the circumstances this person may have overlooked the delicacy of the message, for, as it is well written, 'To the starving, a blow from a skewer of meat is more acceptable than a caress from the hand of a maiden,'" said Kiau Sun. "Whereunto remember, thou two-stomached merchant, that although the house in question is yours, the street is mine."

"By what title?" demanded Wong Pao contentiously.

"By the same that confers this well-appointed palace upon you," replied Sun: "because it is my home."

"The point is one of some subtlety," admitted Wong Pao, "and might be pursued to an extreme delicacy of attenuation if it were argued by those whose profession it is to give a variety of meanings to the same thing. Yet even allowing the claim, it is none the less an unendurable affliction that your voice should disturb my peacefully conducted enterprise."

"As yours would have done mine, O concave-witted Wong Pao!"

"That," retorted the merchant, "is a disadvantage that you could easily have averted by removing yourself to a more distant spot."

"The solution is equally applicable to your own case, mandarin," replied Kiau Sun affably.

"Alas!" exclaimed Wong Pao, with an obvious inside bitterness, "it is a mistake to argue with persons of limited intelligence in terms of courtesy. This, doubtless, was the meaning of

155

the philosopher Nhy-hi when he penned the observation, 'Death, a woman and a dumb mute always have the last word,' Why did I have you conducted hither to convince you dispassionately, rather than send an armed guard to force you away by violence?"

"Possibly," suggested the minstrel, "because my profession is a legally recognized one, and, moreover, under the direct protection of the exalted Mandarin Shen-y-ling."

"Profession!" retorted Wong Pao, stung by the reference to Shen-y-ling, for that powerful official's attitude was indeed the inner reason why he had not pushed violence to a keener edge against Kiau Sun, "an abject mendicancy, yielding two hands' grasp of copper cash a day on a stock composed of half a dozen threadbare odes."

"Compose me half a dozen better and one hand-count of cash shall be apportioned to you each evening," suggested Sun.

"A handful of cash for /my/ labour!" exclaimed the indignant Wong Pao. "Learn, puny wayfarer, that in a single day the profit of my various enterprises exceeds a hundred taels of silver."

"That is less than the achievement of my occupation," said Kiau Sun.

"Less!" repeated the merchant incredulously. "Can you, O boaster, display a single tael?"

"Doubtless I should be the possessor of thousands if I made use of the attributes of a merchant-three hands and two faces. But that was not the angle of my meaning: your labour only compels men to remember; mine enables them to forget."

Thus they continued to strive, each one contending for the pre-eminence of his own state, regardless of the sage warning: "In three moments a labourer will remove an obstructing rock, but three moons will pass without two wise men agreeing on the meaning of a vowel"; and assuredly they would have persisted in their intellectual entertainment until the great sky-lantern rose and the pangs of hunger compelled them to desist, were it not for the manifestation of a very unusual occurrence.

The Emperor, N'ang Wei, then reigning, is now generally regarded as being in no way profound or inspired, but possessing the faculty of being able to turn the dissensions among his subjects to a profitable account, and other accomplishments useful in a ruler. As he passed along the streets of his capital he heard the voices of two raised in altercation, and halting the bearer of his umbrella, he commanded that the persons concerned should be brought before him and state the nature of their dispute.

"The rivalry is an ancient one," remarked the Emperor when each had made his claim. "Doubtless we ourselves could devise a judgment, but in this cycle of progress it is more usual to leave decision to the pronouncement of the populace-and much less exacting to our Imperial ingenuity. An edict will therefore be published, stating that at a certain hour Kiau Sun will stand upon the Western Hill of the city and recite one of his incomparable epics, while at the same gong-stroke Wong Pao will take his station on the Eastern Hill, let us say for the purpose of distributing pieces of silver among any who are able to absent themselves from the competing attraction. It will then be clearly seen which entertainment draws the greater number."

"Your mind, O all-wisest, is only comparable to the peacock's tail in its spreading brilliance!" exclaimed Wong Pao, well assured of an easy triumph.

Kiau Sun, however, remained silent, but he observed closely the benignly impartial expression of the Emperor's countenance.

When the indicated time arrived, only two persons could have been observed within the circumference of the Western Hill of the city—a blind mendicant who had lost his way and an extremely round-bodied mandarin who had been abandoned there by his carriers when they heard the terms of the edict. But about the Eastern Hill the throng was so great that for some time after it was unusual to meet a person whose outline had not been permanently altered by the occasion. Even Kiau Sun was present.

On a protected eminence stood N'ang Wei. Near him was Wong Pao, confidently awaiting the moment when the Emperor should declare himself. When, therefore, the all-wisest graciously made a gesture of command, Wong Pao hastened to his side, an unbecoming elation gilding the fullness of his countenance.

"Wong Pao," said the Illimitable, "the people are here in gratifying profusion. The moment has thus arrived for you to consummate your triumph over Kiau Sun."

"Omnipotence?" queried Wong Pao.

"The silver that you were to distribute freely to all who came. Doubtless you have a retinue of slaves in attendance with weighty sacks of money for the purpose?"

"But that was only in the nature of an imagined condition, Sublime Being, designed to test the trend of their preference," said Wong Pao, with an incapable feeling of no-confidence in the innermost seat of his self-esteem. "This abject person did not for a single breathing-space contemplate or provide for so formidable an outlay."

A shadow of inquiry appeared above the eyebrows of the Sublimest, although his refined imperturbability did not permit him to display any acute emotion.

"It is not entirely a matter of what you contemplated, merchant, but what this multitudinous and, as we now perceive, generally well-armed concourse imagined. Greatly do we fear that when the position has been explained to them, the breathing-space remaining, O Wong Pao, will not be in your body. What," continued the liberal-minded sovereign, turning to one of his attending nobles, "what was it that happened to Ning-lo who failed to satisfy the lottery ticket holders in somewhat similar circumstances?"

"The scorpion vat, Serenest," replied the vassal.

"Ah," commented the Enlightened One, "for the moment we thought it was the burning sulphur plaster."

"That was Ching Yan, who lost approval in the inlaid coffin raffle, Benign Head," prompted the noble.

"True-there is a certain oneness in these cases. Well, Wong Pao, we are entirely surrounded by an expectant mob and their attitude, after much patient waiting, is tending towards a clearly-defined tragedy. By what means is it your intention to extricate us all from the position into which your insatiable vanity has thrust us?"

"Alas, Imperishable Majesty, I only appear to have three pieces of silver and a string of brass cash in my sleeve," confessed Wong Pao tremblingly.

"And that would not go very far-even if flung into the limits of the press," commented the Emperor. "We must look elsewhere for deliverance, then. Kiau Sun, stand forth and try your means."

Upon this invitation Sun appeared from the tent in which he had awaited the summons and advanced to the edge of the multitude. With no appearance of fear or concern, he stood before them, and bending his energies to the great task imposed upon him, he struck the hollow duck so melodiously that the note of expectancy vibrated into the farthest confines of the crowd. Then modulating his voice in unison Kiau Sun began to chant.

At first the narration was of times legendary, when dragons and demons moved about the earth in more palpable forms than they usually maintain to-day. A great mist overspread the Empire and men's minds were vaporous, nor was their purpose keen. Later, deities and well-disposed Forces began to exercise their powers. The mist was turned into a benevolent system of rivers and canals, and iron, rice and the silk-worm then appeared. Next, heroes and champions, whose names have been preserved, arose. They fought the giants and an era of literature and peaceful tranquillity set in. After this there was the Great Invasion from the north, but the people rallied and by means of a war lasting five years, five moons and five days the land was freed again. This prefaced the Golden Age when chess was invented, printed books first made and the Examination System begun.

So far Kiau Sun had only sung of things that men knew dimly through a web of time, but the melody of his voice and the valours of the deeds he told had held their minds. Now he began skilfully to intertwine among the narration scenes and doings that were near to all-of the coming of Spring across the mountains that surround the capital; sunrise on the great lagoon, with the splash of oars and the cormorants in flight; the appearance of the blossom in the peach orchards; the Festival of Boats and of Lanterns, their daily task, and the reward each saw beyond. Finally he spoke quite definitely of the homes awaiting their return, the mulberry-tree about the gate, the fire then burning on the hearth, the pictures on the walls, the ancestral tablets, and the voices calling each. And as he spoke and made an end of speaking the people began silently to melt away, until none remained but Kiau, Wong Pao and the Emperor and his band.

"Kiau Sun," said the discriminating N'ang Wei, "in memory of this day the office of Chanter of Congratulatory Odes in the Palace ceremonial is conferred on you, together with the title 'Leaf-crowned' and the yearly allowance of five hundred taels and a jar of rice wine. And Wong Pao," he added thoughtfully —"Wong Pao shall be permitted to endow the post-also in memory of this day."

The Timely Intervention of the Mandarin Shan Tien's Lucky Day

When Kai Lung at length reached the shutter, after the delay caused by Li-loe's inopportune presence, he found that Hwa-mei was already standing there beneath the wall.

"Alas!" he exclaimed, in an access of self-reproach, "is it possible that I have failed to greet your arriving footsteps? Hear the degrading cause of my—"

"Forbear," interrupted the maiden, with a magnanimous gesture of the hand that was not engaged in bestowing a gift of fruit. "There is a time to scatter flowers and a time to prepare the soil. To-morrow a further trial awaits you, for which we must conspire."

"I am in your large and all-embracing grasp," replied Kai Lung. "Proceed to spread your golden counsel."

"The implacable Ming-shu has deliberated with himself, and deeming it unlikely that you should a third time allure the imagination of the Mandarin Shan Tien by your art, he has ordered that you are again to be the first led out to judgment. On this occasion, however, he has prepared a cloud of witnesses who will, once they are given a voice, quickly overwhelm you in a flood of calumny."

"Even a silver trumpet may not prevail above a score of brazen horns," confessed the story-teller doubtfully. "Would it not be well to engage an even larger company who will outlast the first?"

"The effete Ming-shu has hired all there are," replied Hwa-mei, with a curbing glance. "Nevertheless, do not despair. At a convenient hour a trusty hand will let fall a skin of wine at their assembling place. Their testimony, should any arrive, will entail some conflict."

"I bow before the practical many-sidedness of your mind, enchanting one," murmured Kai Lung, in deep-felt admiration.

"To-morrow, being the first of the Month of Gathering-in, will be one of Shan Tien's lucky days," continued the maiden, her look acknowledging the fitness of the compliment, but at the same time indicating that the moment was not a suitable one to pursue the detail further. "After holding court the Mandarin will accordingly proceed to hazard his accustomed stake upon the chances of certain of the competitors in the approaching examinations. His mind will thus be alertly watchful for a guiding omen. The rest should lie within your persuasive tongue."

"The story of Lao Ting—" began Kai Lung.

"Enough," replied Hwa-mei, listening to a distant sound. "Already has this one strayed beyond her appointed limit. May your virtuous cause prevail!"

With this auspicious message the maiden fled, leaving Kai Lung more than ever resolved to conduct the enterprise in a manner worthy of her high regard.

On the following day, at the appointed hour, Kai Lung was again led before the Mandarin Shan Tien. To the alert yet downcast gaze of the former person it seemed as if the usually inscrutable expression of that high official was not wholly stern as it moved in his direction. Ming-shu, on the contrary, disclosed all his voracious teeth without restraint.

"Calling himself Kai Lung," began the detestable accuser, in a voice even more repulsive than its wont, "and claiming—"

"The name has a somewhat familiar echo," interrupted the Fountain of Justice, with a genial interest in what was going on, rare in one of his exalted rank. "Have we not seen the ill-conditioned thing before?"

"He has tasted of your unutterable clemency in the past," replied Ming-shu, "this being by no means his first appearance thus. Claiming to be a story-teller—"

"What," demanded the enlightened law-giver with leisurely precision, "is a story-teller, and how is he defined?"

"A story-teller, Excellence," replied the inscriber of his spoken word, with the concise manner of one who is not entirely grateful to another, "is one who tells stories. Having on—"

"The profession must be widely spread," remarked the gracious administrator thoughtfully. "All those who supplicate in this very average court practise it to a more or less degree."

"The prisoner," continued the insufferable Ming-shu, so lost to true refinement that he did not even relax his dignity at a remark handed down as gravity-removing from times immemorial, "has already been charged and made his plea. It only remains, therefore, to call the witnesses and to condemn him."

"The usual band appears to be more retiring than their custom is," observed Shan Tien, looking around. "Their lack of punctual respect does not enlarge our sympathy towards their cause."

"They are all hard-striving persons of studious or commercial habits," replied Ming-shu, "and have doubtless become immersed in their various traffics."

"Should the immersion referred to prove to be so deep—"

"A speedy messenger has already gone, but his returning footsteps tarry," urged Ming-shu anxiously. "In this extremity, Excellence, I will myself—"

"High Excellence," appealed Kai Lung, as soon as Ming-shu's departing sandals were obscured to view, "out of the magnanimous condescension of your unworldly heart hear an added plea. Taught by the inoffensive example of that Lao Ting whose success in the literary competitions was brought about by a conjunction of miraculous omens—"

"Arrest the stream of your acknowledged oratory for a single breathing-space," commanded the Mandarin dispassionately, yet at the same time unostentatiously studying a list that lay within his sleeve. "What was the auspicious name of the one of whom you spoke?"

"Lao Ting, exalted; to whom at various periods were subjoined those of Li, Tzu, Sun, Chu, Wang and Chin."

"Assuredly. Your prayer for a fuller hearing will reach our lenient ears. In the meanwhile, in order to prove that the example upon which you base your claim is a worthy one, proceed to narrate so much of the story of Lao Ting as bears upon the means of his success."

The Story of Lao Ting and the Luminous Insect

It is of Lao Ting that the saying has arisen, "He who can grasp Opportunity as she slips by does not need a lucky dream."

So far, however, Lao Ting may be judged to have had neither opportunities nor lucky dreams. He was one of studious nature and from an early age had devoted himself to a veneration of the Classics. Yet with that absence of foresight on the part of the providing deities (for this, of course, took place during an earlier, and probably usurping, dynasty), which then frequently resulted in the unworthy and illiterate prospering, his sleeve was so empty that at times it seemed almost impossible for him to continue in his high ambition.

As the date of the examinations drew near, Lao Ting's efforts increased, and he grudged every moment spent away from books. His few available cash scarcely satisfied his ever-moving brush, and his sleeve grew so light that it seemed as though it might become a balloon and carry him into the Upper Air; for, as the Wisdom has it, "A well-filled purse is a trusty earth anchor." On food he spent even less, but the inability to procure light after the sun had withdrawn his benevolence from the narrow street in which he lived was an ever-present shadow across his hopes. On this extremity he patiently and with noiseless skill bored a hole through the wall into the house of a wealthy neighbour, and by this inoffensive stratagem he was able to distinguish the imperishable writings of the Sages far into the night. Soon, however, the gross hearted person in question discovered the device, owing to the symmetrical breathing of Lao Ting, and applying himself to the opening unperceived, he suddenly blew a jet of water through and afterwards nailed in a wooden skewer. This he did because he himself was also entering for the competitions, though he did not really fear Lao Ting.

Thus denied, Lao Ting sought other means to continue his study, if for only a few minutes longer daily, and it became his custom to leave his ill-equipped room when it grew dusk and to walk into the outer ways, always with his face towards the west, so that he might prolong the benefit of the great luminary to the last possible moment. When the time of no-light definitely arrived he would climb up into one of the high places to await the first beam of the great sky-lantern, and also in the reasonable belief that the nearer he got to it the more powerful would be its light.

It was upon such an occasion that Lao Ting first became aware of the entrancing presence of Chun Hoa-mi, and although he plainly recognized from the outset that the graceful determination with which she led a water-buffalo across the landscape by means of a slender cord attached to its nose was not conducive to his taking a high place in the competitions, he soon found that he was unable to withdraw himself from frequenting the spot at the same hour on each succeeding day. Presently, however, he decided that his previous misgiving was inaccurate, as her existence inspired him with an all-conquering determination to outdistance every other candidate in so marked a manner that his name would at once become famous throughout the province, to attain high office without delay, to lead a victorious army against the encroaching barbarian foe and thus to save the Empire in a moment of emergency, to acquire vast riches (in a not clearly defined manner), to become the intimate counsellor of the grateful Emperor, and finally to receive posthumous honours of unique distinction, the harmonious personality of Hoa-Mi being inextricably entwined among these achievements.

At other times, however, he became subject to a funereal conviction that he would fail discreditably in the examinations to an accompaniment of the ridicule and contempt of all who knew him, that he would never succeed in acquiring sufficient brass cash to ensure a meagre sustenance even for himself, and that he would probably end his lower existence by ignominious decapitation, so that his pale and hungry ghost would be unable to find its way from place to place and be compelled to remain on the same spot through all eternity. Yet so quickly did these two widely diverging vistas alternate in Lao Ting's mind that on many occasions he was under the influence of both presentiments at the same time.

It will thus be seen that Lao Ting was becoming involved in emotions of a many-sided hue, by which his whole future would inevitably be affected, when an event took place which greatly tended to restore his tranquillity of mind. He was, at the usual hour, lurking unseen on the path of Hoa-mi's approach when the water-buffalo, with the perversity of its kind, suddenly withdrew itself from the amiable control of its attendant's restraining hand and precipitated its resistless footsteps towards the long grass in which Lao Ting lay concealed. Recognizing that a decisive moment in the maiden's esteem lay before him, the latter, in spite of an incapable doubt as to the habits and manner of behaviour of creatures of this part, set out resolutely to subdue it... . At a later period, by clinging tenaciously to its tail, he undoubtedly impeded its progress, and thereby enabled Hoa-mi to greet him as one who had a claim upon her gratitude.

"The person who has performed this slight service is Ting, of the outcast line of Lao," said the student with an admiring bow in spite of a benumbing pain that involved all his lower attributes. "Having as yet achieved nothing, the world lies before him."

"She who speaks is Hoa-mi, her father's house being Chun," replied the maiden agreeably. "In addition to the erratic but now repentant animal that has thus, as it were, brought us within the same narrow compass, he possesses a wooden plough, two wheel-barrows, a red bow with threescore arrows, and a rice-field, and is therefore a person of some consequence."

"True," agreed Lao Ting, "though perhaps the dignity is less imposing than might be imagined in the eye of one who, by means of successive examinations, may ultimately become the Right hand of the Emperor."

"Is the contingency an impending one?" inquired Hoa-mi, with polite interest.

"So far," admitted Lao Ting, "it is more in the nature of a vision. There are, of necessity, many trials, and few can reach the ultimate end. Yet even the Yangtze-kiang has a source."

"Of your unswerving tenacity this person has already been witness," said the maiden, with a glance of refined encouragement.

"Your words are more inspiring than the example of the aged woman of Shang-li to the student Tsung," declared Lao Ting gratefully. "Unless the Omens are asleep they should tend to the same auspicious end."

"The exact instance of the moment escapes my recollection." Probably Hoa-mi was by no means willing that one of studious mind should associate her exclusively with water-buffaloes. "Is it related in the Classics?"

"Possibly, though in which actual masterpiece just now evades my grasp. The youth referred to was on the point of abandoning a literary career, appalled at the magnitude of the task before him, when he encountered an aged woman who was employed in laboriously rubbing away the surface of an iron crowbar on a block of stone. To his inquiry she cheerfully replied: 'The one who is thus engaged required a needle to complete a task. Being unable to procure one she was about to give way to an ignoble despair when chance put into her hands this bar, which only requires bringing down to the necessary size.' Encouraged by this painstaking example Tsung returned to his books and in due course became a high official."

"Doubtless in the time of his prosperity he retraced his footsteps and lavishly rewarded the one to whom he was thus indebted," suggested Hoa-mi gracefully.

"Doubtless," admitted Lao Ting, "but the detail is not pursued to so remote an extremity in the Classic. The delicate poise of the analogy is what is chiefly dwelt upon, the sign for a needle harmonizing with that for official, and there being a similar balance between crowbar and books."

"Your words are like a page written in vermilion ink," exclaimed Hoa-mi, with a sideway-expressed admiration.

"Alas!" he declared, with conscious humility, "my style is meagre and almost wholly threadbare. To remedy this, each day I strive to perfect myself in the correct formation of five new written signs. When equipped with a knowledge of every one there is I shall be competent to write so striking and original an essay on any subject that it will no longer be possible to exclude my name from the list of official appointments."

"It will be a day of well-achieved triumph for the spirits of your expectant ancestors," said Hoa-mi sympathetically.

"It will also have a beneficial effect on my own material prospects," replied Lao Ting, with a commendable desire to awaken images of a more specific nature in the maiden's imagination. "Where hitherto it has been difficult to support one, there will then be a lavish profusion for two. The moment the announcement is made, my impatient feet will carry me to this spot. Can it be hoped —?"

"It has long been this one's favourite resort also," confessed Hoa-mi, with every appearance of having adequately grasped Lao Ting's desired inference, "Yet to what number do the written signs in question stretch?"

"So highly favoured is our unapproachable language that the number can only be faintly conjectured. Some claim fivescore thousand different written symbols; the least exacting agree to fourscore thousand."

"You are all-knowing," responded the maiden absently. With her face in an opposing direction her lips moved rapidly, as though she might be in the act of addressing some petition to a Power. Yet it is to be doubted if this accurately represents the nature of her inner thoughts, for when she again turned towards Lao Ting the engaging frankness of her expression had imperceptibly deviated, as she continued:

"In about nine and forty years, then, O impetuous one, our converging footsteps will doubtless again encounter upon this spot. In the meanwhile, however, this person's awaiting father is certainly preparing something against her tardy return which the sign for a crowbar would fittingly represent."

Then urging the water-buffalo to increased exertion she fled, leaving Lao Ting a prey to emotions of a very distinguished intensity.

In spite of the admittedly rough-edged nature of Hoa-mi's leave-taking, Lao Ting retraced his steps in an exalted frame of mind. He had spoken to the maiden and heard her incomparable voice. He now knew her name and the path leading to her father's house. It only remained for him to win a position worthy of her acceptance (if the Empire could offer such a thing), and their future happiness might be regarded as assured.

Thus engaged, Lao Ting walked on, seeing within his head the arrival of the bridal chair, partaking of the well-spread wedding feast, hearing the felicitations of the guests: "A hundred sons and a thousand grandsons!" Something white fluttering by the wayside recalled him to the realities of the day. He had reached the buildings of the outer city, and on a wall before him a printed notice was displayed.

It has already been set forth that the few solitary cash which from time to time fell into the student's sleeve were barely sufficient to feed his thirsty brush with ink. For the material on which to write and to practise the graceful curves essential to a style he was driven to various unworthy expedients. It had thus become his habit to lurk in the footsteps of those who affix public proclamations in the ways and spaces of the city, and when they had passed on to remove, as unostentatiously as possible, the more suitable pronouncements and to carry them to his own abode. For this reason he regarded every notice from a varying angle, being concerned less with what appeared upon it than with what did not appear. Accordingly he now crossed the way and endeavoured to secure the sheet that had attracted his attention. In this he was unsuccessful, however, for he could only detach a meagre fragment.

When Lao Ting reached his uninviting room the last pretence of daylight had faded. He recognized that he had lost many precious moments in Hoa-mi's engaging society, and although he would willingly have lost many more, there was now a deeper pang in his regret that he could not continue his study further into the night. As this was impossible, he drew his scanty night coverings around him and composed his mind for sleep, conscious of an increasing rigour in the air; for, as he found when the morning came, one who wished him well, passing in his absence, had written a lucky saying on a stone and cast it through the paper window.

When Lao Ting awoke it was still night, but the room was no longer entirely devoid of light. As his custom was, an open page lay on the floor beside him, ready to be caught up eagerly with the first gleam of day; above this a faint but sufficient radiance now hung, enabling him to read the written signs. At first the student regarded the surroundings with some awe, not doubting that this was in the nature of a visitation, but presently he discovered that the light was provided by a living creature, winged but docile, which carried a glowing lustre in its tail. When he had read to the end, Lao Ting endeavoured to indicate by a sign that he wished to turn the page. To his delight he found that the winged creature intelligently grasped the requirement and at once transferred its presence to the required spot. All through the night the youth eagerly read on, nor did this miraculously endowed visitor ever fail him. By dawn he had more than made up the time in which the admiration of Hoa-mi had involved him. If such a state of things could be assured for the future, the vista would stretch like a sunlit glade before his feet.

Early in the day he set out to visit an elderly monk, who lived in a cave on the mountain above. Before he went, however, he did not fail to procure a variety of leaves and herbs, and to display them about the room in order to indicate to his unassuming companion that he had a continued interest in his welfare. The venerable hermit received him hospitably, and after inviting him to sit upon the floor and to partake of such food as he had brought with him, listened attentively to his story.

"Your fear that in this manifestation you may be the sport of a malicious Force, conspiring to some secret ill, is merely superstition," remarked Tzu-lu when Lao Ting had reached an end. "Although creatures such as you describe are unknown in this province, they undoubtedly exist in outer barbarian lands, as do apes with the tails of peacocks, ducks with their bones outside their skins, beings whose pale green eyes can discover the precious hidden things of the earth, and men with a hole through their chests so that they require no chair to carry them, but are transposed from spot to spot by means of poles."

"Your mind is widely opened, esteemed," replied Lao Ting respectfully. "Yet the omen must surely tend towards a definite course?"

"Be guided by the mature philosophy of the resolute Heng-ki, who, after an unfortunate augury, exclaimed to his desponding warriors: 'Do your best and let the Omens do their worst!' What has happened is as clear as the iridescence of a dragon's eye. In the past you have lent a sum of money to a friend who has thereupon passed into the Upper Air, leaving you unrequited."

"A friend receiving a sum of money from this person would have every excuse for passing away suddenly."

"Or," continued the accommodating recluse, "you have in some other way placed so formidable an obligation upon one now in the Beyond that his disturbed spirit can no longer endure the burden. For this reason it has taken the form of a luminous insect, and has thus returned to earth in order that it may assist you and thereby discharge the debt."

"The explanation is a convincing one," replied Lao Ting. "Might it not have been more satisfactory in the end, however, if the gracious person in question had clothed himself with the attributes of the examining chancellor or some high mandarin, so that he could have upheld my cause in any extremity?"

Without actually smiling, a form of entertainment that was contrary to his strict vow, the patriarchal anchorite moved his features somewhat at the youth's innocence.

"Do not forget that it is written: 'Though you set a monkey on horseback yet will his hands and feet remain hairy,'" he remarked. "The one whose conduct we are discussing may well be aware of his own deficiencies, and know that if he adopted such a course a humiliating exposure would await him. Do not have any fear for the future, however: thus protected, this person is inspired to prophesy that you will certainly take a high place in the examinations... . Indeed," he added thoughtfully, "it might be prudent to venture a string of cash upon your lucky number."

With this auspicious leave-taking Tzu-lu dismissed him, and Lao Ting returned to the city greatly refreshed in spirit by the encounter. Instead of retiring to his home he continued into the more reputable ways beyond, it then being about the hour at which the affixers of official notices were wont to display their energies.

So it chanced indeed, but walking with his feet off the ground, owing to the obliging solitary's encouragement, Lao Ting forgot his usual caution, and came suddenly into the midst of a band of these men at an angle of the paths.

"Honourable greetings," he exclaimed, feeling that if he passed them by unregarded his purpose might be suspected. "Have you eaten your rice?"

"How is your warmth and cold?" they replied courteously. "Yet why do you arrest your dignified footsteps to converse with outcasts so illiterate as ourselves?"

"The reason," admitted Lao Ting frankly, "need not be buried in a well. Had I avoided the encounter you might have said among yourselves: 'Here is one who shuns our gaze. This, perchance, is he who of late has lurked within the shadow of our backs to bear away our labour.' Not to create this unworthy suspicion I freely came among you, for, as the Ancient Wisdom says: 'Do not adjust your sandals while passing through a melon-field, nor yet arrange your hat beneath an orange-tree.'"

"Yet," said the leader of the band, "we were waiting thus in expectation of the one whom you describe. The incredible leper who rules our goings has, even at this hour and notwithstanding that now is the appointed day and time for the gathering together of the Harmonious Constellation of Paste Appliers and Long Brush Wielders, thrust within our hands a double task."

"May bats defile his Ancestral Tablets and goats propagate within his neglected tomb!" chanted the band in unison. "May the sinews of his hams snap suddenly in moments of achievement! May the principles of his warmth and cold never be properly adjusted but —"

"Thus positioned," continued the leader, indicating by a gesture that while he agreed with these sentiments the moment was not opportune for their full recital, "we await. If he who lurks in our past draws near he will doubtless accept from our hands that which he will assuredly possess behind our backs. Thus mutual help will lighten the toil of all."

"The one whom you require dwells beneath my scanty roof," said the youth. "He is now, however, absent on a secret mission. Entrust to me the burden of your harassment and I will answer, by the sanctity of the Four-eyed Image, that it shall reach his speedy hand."

When Lao Ting gained his own room, bowed down but rejoicing beneath the weight of his unexpected fortune, his eyes were gladdened by the soft light that hung about his books. Although it was not yet dark, the radiance of the glow seemed greater than before. Going to the spot the delighted student saw that in place of one there were now four, the grateful insect having meanwhile summoned others to his cause. All these stood in an expectant attitude awaiting his control, so that through the night he plied an untiring brush and leapt onward in the garden of similitudes.

From this time forward Lao Ting could not fail to be aware that the faces of those whom he familiarly encountered were changed towards him. Men greeted him as one worthy of their consideration, and he even heard his name spoken of respectfully in the society of learned strangers. More than once he found garlands of flowers hung upon his outer door, harmonious messages, and —once —a gift of food. Incredible as it seemed to him it had come to be freely admitted that the unknown scholar Lao Ting would take a very high place in the forthcoming competition, and those who were alert and watchful did not hesitate to place him first. To this general feeling a variety of portents had contributed. Doubtless the beginning was the significant fact, known to the few at first, that the miracle-working Tzu-lu had staked his inner garment on Lao Ting's success. Brilliant lights were seen throughout the night to be moving in the meagre dwelling (for the four efficacious creatures had by this time greatly added to their numbers), and the one within was credited with being assisted by the Forces. It is well said that that which passes out of one mouth passes into a hundred ears, and before dawn had become dusk all the early and astute were following the inspired hermit's example. They who conducted the lotteries, becoming suddenly aware of the burden of the hazard they incurred, thereat declared that upon the venture of Lao Ting's success there must be set two taels in return for one. Whereupon the desire of those who had refrained waxed larger than before, and thus the omens grew.

When the days that remained before the opening of the trial could be counted on the fingers of one hand, there came, at a certain hour, a summons on the outer door of Lao Ting's house, and in response to his spoken invitation there entered one, Sheng-yin, a competitor.

"Lao Ting," said this person, when they had exchanged formalities, "in spite of the flattering attentions of the shallow" —he here threw upon the floor a garland which he had conveyed from off Lao Ting's door —"it is exceedingly unlikely that at the first attempt your name will be among those of the chosen, and the possibility of it heading the list may be dismissed as vapid."

"Your experience is deep and wide," replied Lao Ting, the circumstance that Sheng-yin had already tried and failed three and thirty times adding an edge to the words; "yet if it is written it is written."

"Doubtless," retorted Sheng-yin no less capably; "but it will never be set to music. Now, until your inconsiderate activities prevailed, this person was confidently greeted as the one who would be first."

"The names of Wang-san and Yin Ho were not unknown to the expectant," suggested Lao Ting mildly.

"The mind of Wang-san is only comparable with a wastepaper basket," exclaimed the visitor harshly; "and Yin Ho is in reality as dull as split ebony. But in your case, unfortunately, there is nothing to go on, and, unlikely though it be, it is just possible that this person's well-arranged ambitions may thereby be brought to a barren end. For that reason he is here to discuss this matter as between virtuous friends."

"Let your auspicious mouth be widely opened," replied Lao Ting guardedly. "My ears will not refrain."

"Is there not, perchance, some venerable relative in a distant part of the province whose failing eyes crave, at this juncture, to rest upon your wholesome features before he passes Upwards?"

"Assuredly some such inopportune person might be forthcoming," admitted Lao Ting. "Yet the cost of so formidable a journey would be far beyond this necessitous one's means."

"In so charitable a cause affluent friends would not be lacking. Depart on the third day and remain until the ninth and twenty taels of silver will glide imperceptibly into your awaiting sleeve."

"The prospect of not taking the foremost place in the competition-added to the pangs of those who have hazarded their store upon the unworthy name of Lao-is an ignoble one," replied the student, after a moment's thought. "The journey will be a costly task at this season of the rains; it cannot possibly be accomplished for less than fifty taels."

"It is well said, 'Do not look at robbers sharing out their spoil: look at them being executed,' " urged Sheng-yin. "Should you be so ill-destined as to compete, and, as would certainly be the case, be awarded a position of contempt, how unendurable would be your anguish when, amidst the execrations of the deluded mob, you remembered that thirty taels of the purest had slipped from your effete grasp."

"Should the Bridge of the Camel Back be passable, five and forty might suffice," mused Lao Tung to himself.

"Thirty-seven taels, five hundred cash, are the utmost that your obliging friends would hazard in the quest," announced Sheng-yin definitely. "On the day following that of the final competition the sum will be honourably —"

"By no means," interrupted the other, with unswerving firmness. "How thus is the journey to be defrayed? In advance, assuredly."

"The requirement is unusual. Yet upon satisfactory oaths being offered —"

"This person will pledge the repose of the spirits of his venerated ancestors practically back to prehistoric times," agreed Lao Ting readily. "From the third to the ninth day he will be absent from the city and will take no part in anything therein. Should he eat his words, may his body be suffocated beneath five cart-loads of books and his weary ghost chained to that of a leprous mule. It is spoken."

"Truly. But it may as well be written also." With this expression of narrow-minded suspicion Sheng-yin would have taken up one from a considerable mass of papers lying near at hand, had not Lao Ting suddenly restrained him.

"It shall be written with clarified ink on paper of a special excellence," declared the student. "Take the brush, Seng-yin, and write. It almost repays this person for the loss of a degree to behold the formation of signs so unapproachable as yours."

"Lao Ting," replied the visitor, pausing in his task, "you are occasionally inspired, but the weakness of your character results in a lack of caution. In this matter, therefore, be warned: 'The crocodile opens his jaws; the rat-trap closes his; keep yours shut.'"

When Lao Ting returned after a scrupulously observed six days of absence he could not fail to become aware that the city was in an uproar, and the evidence of this increased as he approached the cheap and lightly esteemed quarter in which those of literary ambitions found it convenient to reside. Remembering Sheng-yin's parting, he forbore to draw attention to himself by questioning any, but when he reached the door of his own dwelling he discovered the one of whom he was thinking, standing, as it were, between the posts.

"Lao Ting," exclaimed Sheng-yin, without waiting to make any polite reference to the former person's food or condition, "in spite of this calamity you are doubtless prepared to carry out the spirit of your oath?"

"Doubtless," replied Lao Ting affably. "Yet what is the nature of the calamity referred to, and how does it affect the burden of my vow?"

"Has not the tiding reached your ear? The examinations, alas! have been withheld for seven full days. Your journey has been in vain!"

"By no means!" declared the youth. "Debarred by your enticement from a literary career this person turned his mind to other aims, and has now gained a deep insight into the habits and behaviour of water-buffaloes."

"They who control the competitions from the Capital," continued Sheng-yin, without even hearing the other's words, "when all had been arranged, learned from the Chief Astrologer (may subterranean fires singe his venerable moustaches!) that a forgotten obscuration of the sun would take place on the opening day of the test. In the face of so formidable a portent they acted thus and thus."

"How then fares it that due warning of the change was not set forth?"

"The matter is as long as The Wall and as deep as seven wells," grumbled Sheng-yin, "and the Hoang Ho in flood is limpid by its side. Proclamations were sent forth, yet none appeared, and they entrusted with their wide disposal have a dragon-story of a shining lordly youth who ever followed in their steps... . Thus in a manner of expressing it, the spirit —"

"Sheng-yin," said Lao Ting, with courteous firmness, yet so moving the door so that while he passed in the former person remained outside, "you have sought, at the expenditure of thirty-seven taels five hundred cash, to deflect Destiny from her appointed line. The result has been lamentable to all-or nearly all-concerned. The lawless effort must not be repeated, for when heaven itself goes out of its way to set a correcting omen in the sky, who dare disobey?"

When the list and order of the competition was proclaimed, the name of Wang-san stood at the very head and that of Yin Ho was next. Lao Ting was the very last of those who were successful; Sheng-yin was the next, and was thus the first of those who were unsuccessful. It was as much as the youth had secretly dared to hope, and much better than he had generally feared. In Sheng-yin's case, however, it was infinitely worse than he had ever contemplated. Regarding Lao Ting as the cause of his disgrace he planned a sordid revenge. Waiting until night had fallen he sought the student's door-step and there took a potent drug, laying upon his ghost a strict injunction to devote itself to haunting and thwarting the ambitions of the one who dwelt within. But even in this he was inept, for the poison was less speedy than he thought, and Lao Ting returned in time to convey him to another door.

On the strength of his degree Lao Ting found no difficulty in earning a meagre competence by instructing others who wished to follow in his footsteps. He was also now free to compete for the next degree, where success would bring him higher honour and a slightly less meagre competence. In the meanwhile he married Hoa-mi, being able to display thirty-seven taels and nearly five hundred cash towards that end. Ultimately he rose to a position of remunerative ease, but it is understood that he attained this more by a habit of acting as the necessities of the moment required than by his literary achievements.

Over the door of his country residence in the days of his profusion he caused the image of a luminous insect to be depicted, and he engraved its semblance on his seal. He would also have added the presentment of a water-buffalo, but Hoa-mi deemed this inexpedient.

The High-Minded Strategy of the Amiable Hwa-Mei

Warned by the mischance attending his previous meeting with Hwa-mei, Kai Lung sought the walled enclosure at the earliest moment of his permitted freedom, and secreting himself among the interlacing growth he anxiously awaited the maiden's coming.

Presently a movement in the trees without betrayed a presence, and the story-teller was on the point of disclosing himself at the shutter when the approaching one displayed an unfamiliar outline. Instead of a maiden of exceptional symmetry and peach-like charm an elderly and deformed hag drew near. As she might be hostile to his cause, Kai Lung deemed it prudent to remain concealed; but in case she should prove to be an emissary from Hwa-mei seeking him, his purpose was to stand revealed. To combine these two attitudes until she should declare herself was by no means an easy task, but she looked neither near nor far in scrutiny until she stood, mumbling and infirm, beneath the shutter.

"It is well, minstrel," she called aloud. "She whom you await bid me greet you with a sign." At Kai Lung's feet there fell a crimson flower, growing on a thorny stem. "What word shall I in turn bear back? Speak freely, for her mind is as my open hand."

"Tell me rather," said Kai Lung, looking out, "how she fares and what averts her footsteps?"

"That will appear in due time," replied the aged one. "In the meanwhile I have her message to declare. Three times foiled in his malignant scheme the now obscene Ming-shu sets all the Axioms at naught. Distrusting you and those about your path, it is his sinister intention to call up for judgment Kai-moo, who lies within the women's cell beyond the Water Way."

"What is her crime and how will this avail him?"

"Charged with the murder of her man by means of the supple splinter her condemnation is assured. The penalty is piecemeal slicing, and in it are involved those of her direct line, in the humane effort to eradicate so treacherous a strain."

"That is but just," agreed Kai Lung.

"Truly. But on the slender ligament of a kindred name you will be joined with her in that end. Ming-shu will see to it that records of your kinship are not lacking. Being accused of no crime on your own behalf there will be nothing for you to appear against."

"It is written: 'Even leprosy may be cured, but the enmity of an official underling can never be dispelled,' and the malice of the persistent Ming-shu certainly points to the wisdom of the verse. Is the person of Kai-moo known to you, and where is the prison-house you speak of?"

To this the venerable creature replied that the cell in question was in a distant quarter of the city. Kai-moo, she continued, might be regarded as fashioned like herself, being deformed in shape and repellent in appearance. Furthermore, she was of deficient understanding, these things aiding Ming-shu's plan, as she would be difficult to reach and impossible to instruct when reached.

"The extremity is almost hopeless enough to be left to the ever-protecting spirits of one's all-powerful Ancestors," declared Kai Lung at length. "Did she from whom you come forecast any confidence?"

"She had some assurance in a certain plan, which it is my message to declare to you."

"Her wisdom is to be computed neither by a rule nor by a measure. Say on."

"The keeper of the women's prison-house lies within her hollowed hand, nor will silver be wanting to still any arising doubt. Wrapped in prison garb, and with her face disguised by art, she whose word I bear will come forth at the appointed call and, taking her place before Shan Tien, will play a fictitious part."

"Alas! dotard," interrupted Kai Lung impatiently, "it would be well if I spent my few remaining hours in kowtowing to the Powers whom I shall shortly meet. An aged and unsightly hag! Know you not, O venerable bat, that the smooth perfection of the one you serve would shine dazzling through a beaten mask of tempered steel? Her matchless hair, glossier than a starling's wing, floats like an autumn cloud. Her eyes strike fire from damp clay, or make the touch of velvet harsh and stubborn, according to her several moods. Peach-bloom held against her cheek withers incapably by comparison. Her feet, if indeed she has such commonplace attributes at all, are smaller —"

"Yet," interrupted the hag, in a changed and quite melodious voice, "if it is possible to delude the imagination of one whose longing eyes dwell so constantly on these threadbare charms, what then will be the position of the obtuse Ming-shu and the superficial Mandarin Shan Tien, burdened as they now are by outside cares?"

"There are times when the classical perfection of our graceful tongue is strangely inadequate to express emotion," confessed Kai Lung, colouring deeply, as Hwa-mei stood revealed before him. "It is truly said: 'The ingenuity of a guileless woman will undermine nine mountains.' You have cut off all the words of my misgivings."

"To that end have I wrought, for in this I also need your skill. Listen well and think deeply as I speak. Everywhere the outcome of the strife grows more uncertain day by day and no man really knows which side to favour yet. In this emergency each plays a double part. While visibly loyal to the Imperial cause, the Mandarin Shan Tien fans the whisper that in secret he upholds the rebellious banners. Ming-shu now openly avers that if this and that are thus and thus the rising has justice in its ranks, while at the same time he has it put abroad that this is but a cloak the better to serve the state. Thus every man maintains a double face in the hope that if the one side fails the other will preserve him, and as a band all pledge to save (or if need be to betray) each other."

"This is the more readily understood as it is the common case on every like occasion."

"Then doubtless there are instances waiting on your lips. Teach me such a story whereby the hope of those who are thus swayed may be engaged and leave the rest to my arranging hand."

On the following day at the appointed hour a bent and forbidding hag was brought before Shan Tien, and the nature of her offence proclaimed.

"It is possible to find an excuse for almost everything, regarding it from one angle or another," remarked the Mandarin impartially; "but the crime of destroying a husband-and by a means so unpleasantly insinuating-really seems to leave nothing to be said."

"Yet, imperishable, even a bad coin must have two sides," replied the hag. "That I should be guilty and yet innocent would be no more wonderful than the case of Weng Cho, who, when faced with the alternative of either defying the Avenging Societies or of opposing fixed authority found a way out of escaping both."

"That should be worth-that is to say, if you base your defence upon an existing case —"

"Providing the notorious thug Kai Lung is not thereby brought in," suggested the narrow-minded Ming-shu, who equally desired to learn the stratagem involved.

"Weng Cho was the only one concerned," replied the ancient obtusely —"he who escaped the consequences. Is it permitted to this one to make clear her plea?"

"If the fatigue is not more than your venerable personality can reasonably bear," replied Shan Tien courteously.

"To bear is the lot of every woman, be she young or old," replied the one before them. "I comply, omnipotence."

The Story of Weng Cho; or, the One Devoid of Name

There was peach-blossom in the orchards of Kien-fi, a blue sky above, and in the air much gladness; but in Wu Chi's yamen gloom hung like the herald of a thunderstorm. At one end of a table in the ceremonial hall sat Wu Chi, heaviness upon his brow, deceit in his eyes, and a sour enmity about the lines of his mouth; at the other end stood his son Weng, and between them, as it were, his whole life lay.

Wu Chi was an official of some consequence and had two wives, as became him. His union with the first had failed in its essential purpose; therefore he had taken another to carry on the direct line which alone could bring him contentment in this world and a reputable existence in the next. This degree of happiness was supplied by Weng's mother, yet she must ever remain but a "secondary wife," with no rights and a very insecure position. In the heart of the chief wife smouldered a most bitter hatred, but the hour of her ascendancy came, for after many years she also bore her lord a son. Thenceforward she was strong in her authority; but Weng's mother remained, for she was very beautiful, and despite all the arts of the other woman Wu Chi could not be prevailed upon to dismiss her. The easy solution of this difficulty was that she soon died-the "white powder death" was the shrewd comment of the inner chambers of Kien-fi.

Wu Chi put on no mourning, custom did not require it; and now that the woman had Passed Beyond he saw no necessity to honour her memory at the expense of his own domestic peace. His wife donned her gayest robes and made a feast. Weng alone stood apart, and in funereal sackcloth moved through the house like an accusing ghost. Each day his father met him with a frown, the woman whom alone he must regard as his mother with a mocking smile, but he passed them without any word of dutiful and submissive greeting. The period of all seemly mourning ended-it touched that allotted to a legal parent; still Weng cast himself down and made no pretence to hide his grief. His father's frown became a scowl, his mother's smile framed a biting word. A wise and venerable friend who loved the youth took him aside one day and with many sympathetic words counselled restraint.

"For," he said, "your conduct, though affectionate towards the dead, may be urged by the ill-disposed as disrespectful towards the living. If you have a deeper end in view, strive towards it by a less open path."

"You are subtle and esteemed in wisdom," replied Weng, "but neither of those virtues can restore a broken jar. The wayside fountain must one day dry up at its source, but until then not even a mountain placed upon its mouth can pen back its secret stores. So is it with unfeigned grief."

"The analogy may be exact," replied the aged friend, shaking his head, "but it is no less truly said: 'The wise tortoise keeps his pain inside.' Rest assured, on the disinterested advice of one who has no great experience of mountains and hidden springs, but a life-long knowledge of Wu Chi and of his amiable wife, that if you mourn too much you will have reason to mourn more."

His words were pointed to a sharp edge. At that moment Wu Chi was being confronted by his wife, who stood before him in his inner chamber. "Who am I?" she exclaimed vehemently, "that my authority should be denied before my very eyes? Am I indeed Che of the house of Meng, whose ancestors wore the Yellow Scabbard, or am I some nameless one? Or does my lord sleep, or has he fallen blind upon the side by which Weng approaches?"

"His heart is bad and his instincts perverted," replied Wu Chi dully. "He ignores the rites, custom, and the Emperor's example, and sets at defiance all the principles of domestic government. Do not fear that I shall not shortly call him to account with a very heavy call."

"Do so, my lord," said his wife darkly, "or many valiant champions of the House of Meng may press forward to make a cast of that same account. To those of our ancient line it would not seem a trivial thing that their daughter should share her rights with a purchased slave."

"Peace, cockatrice! the woman was well enough," exclaimed Wu Chi, with slow resentment. "But the matter of this obstinacy touches the dignity of my own authority, and before to-day has passed Weng shall bring up his footsteps suddenly before a solid wall."

Accordingly, when Weng returned at his usual hour he found his father awaiting him with curbed impatience. That Wu Chi should summon him into his presence in the great hall was of itself an omen that the matter was one of moment, but the profusion of lights before the Ancestral Tablets and the various symbols arranged upon the table showed that the occasion was to be regarded as one involving irrevocable issues.

"Weng Cho," said his father dispassionately, from his seat at the head of the table, "draw near, and first pledge the Ancient Ones whose spirits hover above their Tablets in a vessel of wine."

"I am drinking affliction and move under the compact of a solemn vow," replied Weng fixedly, "therefore I cannot do this; nor, as signs are given me to declare, will the forerunners of our line, who from their high places look down deep into the mind and measure the heart with an impartial rod, deem this an action of disrespect to their illustrious shades."

"It is well to be a sharer of their councils," said Wu Chi, with pointed insincerity. "But," he continued, in the same tone, "for whom can Weng Cho of the House of Wu mourn? His father is before him in his wonted health; in the inner chamber his mother plies an unfaltering needle; while from the Dragon Throne the supreme Emperor still rules the world. Haply, however, a thorn has pierced his little finger, or does he perchance bewail the loss of a favourite bird?"

"That thorn has sunk deeply into his existence, and the memory of that loss still dims his eyes with bitterness," replied Weng. "Bid the rain cease to fall when the clouds are heavy."

"The comparison is ill-chosen," cried Whu Chi harshly. "Rather should the allusion be to the evil tendency of a self-willed branch which, in spite of the continual watering of precept and affection, maintains its perverted course, and must henceforth either submit to be bound down into an appointed line, or be utterly cut off so that the tree may not suffer. Long and patiently have I marked your footsteps, Weng Cho, and they are devious. This is not a single offence, but it is no light one. Appointed by the Board of Ceremony, approved of by the Emperor, and observed in every loyal and high-minded subject are the details of the rites and formalities which alone serve to distinguish a people refined and humane from those who are rude and barbarous. By setting these observances at defiance you insult their framers, act traitorously towards your sovereign, and assail the foundations of your House; for your attitude is a direct reflection upon others; and if you render such a tribute to one who is incompetent to receive it, how will you maintain a seemly balance when a greater occasion arises?"

"When the earth that has nourished it grows cold the leaves of the branch fall-doubtless the edicts of the Board referred to having failed to reach their ears," replied Weng bitterly. "Revered father, is it not permitted that I should now depart? Behold I am stricken and out of place."

"You are evil and your heart is fat with presumptuous pride!" exclaimed Wu Chi, releasing the cords of his hatred and anger so that they leapt out from his throat like the sudden spring of a tiger from a cave. "Evil in birth, grown under an evil star and now come to a full maturity. Go you shall, Weng Cho, and that on a straight journey forthwith or else bend your knees with an acquiescent face." With these words he beat furiously on a gong, and summoning the entire household he commanded that before Weng should be placed a jar of wine and two glass vessels, and on the other side a staff and a pair of sandals. From an open shutter the face of the woman Che looked down in mocking triumph.

The alternatives thus presented were simple and irrevocable. On the one hand Weng must put from him all further grief, ignore his vows, and join in mirth and feast; on the other he must depart, never to return, and be deprived of every tie of kinship, relinquishing ancestry, possessions and name. It was a course severer than anything that Wu Chi had intended when he sent for his son, but resentment had distorted his eyesight. It was a greater test than Weng had anticipated, but his mind was clear, and his heart charged with fragrant memories of his loss. Deliberately but with silent dignity he poured the untasted wine upon the ground, drew his sword and touched the vessels lightly so that they broke, took from off his thumb the jade ring inscribed with the sign of the House of Wu, and putting on the sandals grasped the staff and prepared to leave the hall.

"Weng Cho, for the last time spoken of as of the House of Wu, now alienated from that noble line, and henceforth and for ever an outcast, you have made a choice and chosen as befits your rebellious life. Between us stretches a barrier wider and deeper than the Yellow Sea, and throughout all future time no sign shall pass from that distant shore to this. From every record of our race your name shall be cut out; no mention of it shall profane the Tablets, and both in this world and the next it shall be to us as though you have never been. As I break this bowl so are all ties broken, as I quench this candle so are all memories extinguished, and as, when you go, the space is filled with empty air, so shall it be."

"Ho, nameless stranger," laughed the woman from above, "here is food and drink to bear you on your way"; and from the grille she threw a withered fig and spat.

"The fruit is the cankered effort of a barren tree," cast back Weng over his shoulder. "Look to your own offspring, basilisk. It is given me to speak." Even as he spoke there was a great cry from the upper part of the house, the sound of many feet and much turmoil, but he went on his way without another word.

Thus it was that Weng Cho came to be cut off from the past. From his father's house he stepped out into the streets of Kien-fi a being without a name, destitute, and suffering the pangs of many keen emotions. Friends whom he encountered he saluted distantly, not desirous of sharing their affection until they should have learned his state; but there was one who stood in his mind as removed above the possibility of change, and to the summer-house of Tiao's home he therefore turned his steps.

Tiao was the daughter of a minor official, an unsuccessful man of no particular descent. He had many daughters, and had encouraged Weng's affection, with frequent professions that he regarded only the youth's virtuous life and discernment, and would otherwise have desired one not so highly placed. Tiao also had spoken of rice and contentment in a ruined pagoda. Yet as she listened to Weng's relation a new expression gradually revealed itself about her face, and when he had finished many paces lay between them.

"A breaker of sacred customs, a disobeyer of parents and an outcast! How do you disclose yourself!" she exclaimed wildly. "What vile thing has possessed you?"

"One hitherto which now rejects me," replied Weng slowly. "I had thought that here alone I might find a familiar greeting, but that also fails."

"What other seemly course presents itself?" demanded the maiden unsympathetically. "How degrading a position might easily become that of the one who linked her lot with yours if all fit and proper sequences are to be reversed! What menial one might supplant her not only in your affections but also in your Rites! He had defied the Principles!" she exclaimed, as her father entered from behind a screen.

"He has lost his inheritance," muttered the little old man, eyeing him contemptuously. "Weng Cho," he continued aloud, "you have played a double part and crossed our step with only half your heart. Now the past is past and the future an unwritten sheet."

"It shall be written in vermilion ink," replied Weng, regaining an impassive dignity; "and upon that darker half of my heart can now be traced two added names."

He had no aim now, but instinct drove him towards the mountains, the retreat of the lost and despairing. A three days' journey lay between. He went forward vacantly, without food and without rest. A falling leaf, as it is said, would have turned the balance of his destiny, and at the wayside village of Li-yong so it chanced. The noisome smell of burning thatch stung his face as he approached, and presently the object came into view. It was the bare cabin of a needy widow who had become involved in a lawsuit through the rapacity of a tax-gatherer. As she had the means neither to satisfy the tax nor to discharge the dues, the powerful Mandarin before whom she had been called ordered all her possessions to be seized, and that she should then be burned within her hut as a warning to others. This was the act of justice being carried out, and even as Weng heard the tale the Mandarin in question drew near, carried in his state chair to satisfy his eyes that his authority was scrupulously maintained. All those villagers who had not drawn off unseen at once fell upon their faces, so that Weng alone remained standing, doubtful what course to take.

"Ill-nurtured dog!" exclaimed the Mandarin, stepping up to him, "prostrate yourself! Do you not know that I am of the Sapphire Button, and have fivescore bowmen at my yamen, ready to do my word?" And he struck the youth across the face with a jewelled rod.

"I have only one sword, but it is in my hand," cried Weng, reckless beneath the blow, and drawing it he at one stroke cut down the Mandarin before any could raise a hand. Then breaking in the door of the hovel he would have saved the woman, but it was too late, so he took the head and body and threw them into the fire, saying: "There, Mandarin, follow to secure justice. They shall not bear witness against you Up There in your absence."

The chair-carriers had fled in terror, but the villagers murmured against Weng as he passed through them. "It was a small thing that one house and one person should be burned; now, through this, the whole village will assuredly be consumed. He was a high official and visited justice impartially on us all. It was our affair, and you, who are a stranger, have done ill."

"I did you wrong, Mandarin," said Weng, resuming his journey; "you took me for one of them. I pass you the parting of the woman Che, burrowers in the cow-heap called Li-yong."

"Oi-ye!" exclaimed a voice behind, "but yonder earth-beetles haply have not been struck off the Tablets and found that a maiden with well-matched eyes can watch two ways at once, all of a morning: and thereby death through red spectacles is not that same death through blue spectacles. Things in their appointed places, noble companion."

"Greetings, wayfarer," said Weng, stopping. "The path narrows somewhat inconveniently hereabout. Take honourable precedence."

"The narrower the better to defend then," replied the stranger good-humouredly. "Whereto, also, two swords cut a larger slice than one. Without doubt fivescore valiant bowmen will soon be a-ranging when they hear that the enemy goes upon two feet, and then ill befall who knows not the passes." As he spoke an arrow, shot from a distance, flew above their heads.

"Why should you bear a part with me, and who are you who know these recent things?" demanded Weng doubtfully.

"I am one of many, we being a branch of that great spreading lotus the Triad, though called by the tillers here around the League of Tomb-Haunters, because we must be sought in secret places. The things I have spoken I know because we have many ears, and in our care a whisper passes from east to west and from north to south without a word being spilled."

"And the price of your sword is that I should join the confederacy?" asked Weng thoughtfully.

"I had set out to greet you before the estimable Mandarin who is now saluting his ancestors was so inopportune as to do so," replied the emissary. "Yet it is not to be denied that we offer an adequate protection among each other, while at the same time punishing guilt and administering a rigorous justice secretly."

"Lead me to your meeting-place, then," said Weng determinedly. "I have done with the outer things."

The guide pointed to a rock, shaped like a locust's head, which marked the highest point of the steep mountain before them. Soon the fertile lowlands ended and they passed beyond the limit of the inhabitable region. Still ascending they reached the Tiger's High Retreat, which defines the spot where even the animal kind turn back and where watercourses cease to flow. Beyond this the most meagre indication of vegetable sustenance came to an end, and thenceforward their passage was rendered more slow and laborious by frequent snow-storms, barriers of ice, and sudden tempests which strove to hurl them to destruction. Nevertheless, by about the hour of midnight they reached the rock shaped like a locust's head, which stood in the wildest and most inaccessible part of the mountain, and masked the entrance to a strongly-guarded cave. Here Weng suffered himself to be blindfolded, and being led forward he was taken into the innermost council. Closely questioned, he professed a spontaneous desire to be admitted into their band, to join in their dangers and share their honours; whereupon the oath was administered to him, the passwords and secret signs revealed, and he was bound from that time forth, under the bonds of a most painful death and torments in the afterworld, to submerge all passions save those for the benefit of their community, and to cherish no interests, wrongs or possessions that did not affect them all alike.

For the space of seven years Weng remained about the shadow of the mountain, carrying out, together with the other members of the band, the instructions which from time to time they received from the higher circles of the Society, as well as such acts of retributive justice as they themselves determined upon, and in this quiet and unostentatious manner maintaining peace and greatly purifying the entire province. In this passionless subservience to the principles of the Order none exceeded him; yet at no time have men been forbidden to burn joss-sticks to the spirit of the destinies, and who shall say?

At the end of seven years the first breath from out of the past reached Weng (or Thang, as he had announced himself to be when cast out nameless). One day he was summoned before the chief of their company and a mission laid upon him.

"You have proved yourself to be capable and sincere in the past, and this matter is one of delicacy," said the leader. "Furthermore, it is reported that you know something of the paths about Kien-fi?"

"There is not a forgotten turn within those paths by which I might stumble in the dark," replied Weng, striving to subdue his mind.

"See that out of so poignant a memory no more formidable barrier than a forgotten path arises," said the leader, observing him closely. "Know you, then a house bearing as a sign the figure of a golden ibis?"

"Truly; I have noted it," replied Weng, changing his position, so that he now leaned against a rock. "There dwelt an old man of some lower official rank, who had no son but many daughters."

"He has Passed, and one of those—Tiao by name," said the other, referring to a parchment — "has schemingly driven out the rest and held the patrimony. Crafty and ambitious, she has of late married a high official who has ever been hostile to ourselves. Out of a private enmity the woman seeks the lives of two who are under our most solemn protection, and now uses her husband's wealth and influence to that end. It is on him that the blow must fall, for men kill only men, and she, having no son, will then be discredited and impotent."

"And concerning this official?" asked Weng.

"It has not been thought prudent to speak of him by name," replied the chief. "Stricken with a painful but not dangerous malady he has retired for a time to the healthier seclusion of his wife's house, and there he may be found. The woman you will know with certainty by a crescent scar-above the right eye."

"Beneath the eye," corrected Weng instantly.

"Assuredly, beneath: I misread the sign," said the head, appearing to consult the scroll. "Yet, out of a keen regard for your virtues, Thang, let me point a warning that it is antagonistic to our strict rule to remember these ancient scars too well. Further, in accordance with that same esteem, do not stoop too closely nor too long to identify the mark. By our pure and exacting standard no high attainment in the past can justify defection. The pains and penalties of failure you well know."

"I bow, chieftain," replied Weng acquiescently.

"It is well," said the chief. "Your strategy will be easy. To cure this lord's disorder a celebrated physician is even now travelling from the Capital towards Kien-fi. A day's journey from that place he will encounter obstacles and fall into the hands of those who will take away his robes and papers. About the same place you will meet one with a bowl on the roadside who will hail you, saying, 'Charity, out of your superfluity, noble mandarin coming from the north!' To him you will reply, 'Do mandarins garb thus and thus and go afoot? It is I who need a change of raiment and a chair; aye, by the token of the Locust's Head!' He will then lead you to a place where you will find all ready and a suitable chair with trusty bearers. The rest lies beneath your grinding heel. Prosperity!"

Weng prostrated himself and withdrew. The meeting by the wayside befell as he had received assurance-they who serve the Triad do not stumble-and at the appointed time he stood before Tiao's door and called for admission. He looked to the right and the left as one who examines a new prospect, and among the azalea flowers the burnished roof of the summer-house glittered in the sun.

"Lucky omens attend your coming, benevolence," said the chief attendant obsequiously; "for since he sent for you an unpropitious planet has cast its influence upon our master, so that his power languishes."

"Its malignity must be controlled," said Weng, in a feigned voice, for he recognized the one before him. "Does any watch?"

"Not now," replied the attendant; "for he has slept since these two hours. Would your graciousness have speech with the one of the inner chamber?"

"In season perchance. First lead me to your lord's side and then see that we are undisturbed until I reappear. It may be expedient to invoke a powerful charm without delay."

In another minute Weng stood alone in the sick man's room, between them no more barrier than the silk-hung curtains of the couch. He slid down his right hand and drew a keen-edged knife; about his left he looped the even more fatal cord; then advancing with a noiseless step he pulled back the drapery and looked down. It was the moment for swift and silent action; nothing but hesitation and delay could imperil him, yet in that supreme moment he stepped back, released the curtain from his faltering grasp and, suffering the weapons to fall unheeded to the floor, covered his face with his hands, for lying before him he had seen the outstretched form, the hard contemptuous features, of his father.

Yet most solemnly alienated from him in every degree. By Wu Chi's own acts every tie of kinship had been effaced between them: the bowl had been broken, the taper blown out, empty air had filled his place. Wu Chi acknowledged no memory of a son; he could claim no reverence as a father.... Tiao's husband.... Then he was doubly childless.... The woman and her seed had withered, as he had prophesied.

On the one hand stood the Society, powerful enough to protect him in every extremity, yet holding failure as treason; most terrible and inexorable towards set disobedience. His body might find a painless escape from their earthly torments, but by his oaths his spirit lay in their keeping to be punished through all eternity.

That he was no longer Wu Chi's son, that he had no father-this conviction had been strong enough to rule him in every contingency of life save this. By every law of men and deities the ties between them had been dissolved, and they stood as a man and man; yet the salt can never be quite washed out of sea-water.

For a time which ceased to be hours or minutes, but seemed as a fragment broken off eternity, he stood, motionless but most deeply racked. With an effort he stooped to take the cord, and paused again; twice he would have seized the dagger, but doubt again possessed him. From a distant point of the house came the chant of a monk singing a prayer and beating upon a wooden drum. The rays of the sun falling upon the gilded roof in the garden again caught his eyes; nothing else stirred.

"These in their turn have settled great issues lightly," thought Weng bitterly. "Must I wait upon an omen?"

"...submitting oneself to purifying scars," droned the voice far off; "propitiating if need be by even greater self-inflictions..."

"It suffices," said Weng dispassionately, and picking up the knife he turned to leave the room.

At the door he paused again, but not in an arising doubt. "I will leave a token for Tiao to wear as a jest," was the image that had sprung from his new abasement, and taking a sheet of parchment he quickly wrote thereon: "A wave has beat from that distant shore to this, and now sinks in the unknown depths."

Again he stepped noiselessly to the couch, drew the curtain and dropped the paper lightly on the form. As he did so his breath stopped; his fingers stiffened. Cautiously, on one knee, he listened intently, lightly touched the face; then recklessly taking a hand he raised the arm and suffered it to fall again. No power restrained it; no alertness of awakening life came into the dull face. Wu Chi had already Passed Beyond.

Not Concerned With Any Particular Attribute of Those Who Are Involved

Unendurable was the intermingling of hopes and fears with which Kai Lung sought the shutter on the next occasion after the avowal of Hwa-mei's devoted strategy. While repeatedly assuring himself that it would have been better to submit to piecemeal slicing without a protesting word rather than that she should incur so formidable a risk, he was compelled as often to admit that when once her mind had formed its image no effort on his part would have held her back. Doubtless Hwa-mei readily grasped the emotion that would possess the one whose welfare was now her chief concern, for without waiting to gum her hair or to gild her lips she hastened to the spot beneath the wall at the earliest moment that Kai Lung could be there.

"Seven marble tombstones are lifted from off my chest!" exclaimed the story-teller when he could greet her. "How did your subterfuge proceed, and with what satisfaction was the history of Weng Cho received?"

"That," replied Hwa-mei modestly, "will provide the matter for an autumn tale, when seated around a pine-cone fire. In the meanwhile this protracted ordeal takes an ambiguous bend."

"To what further end does the malignity of the ill-made Ming-shu now shape itself? Should it entail a second peril to your head—"

"The one whom you so justly name fades for a moment out of our concern. Burdened with a secret mission he journeys to Hing-poo, nor does the Mandarin Shan Tien hold another court until the day of his return."

"That gives a breathing space of time to our ambitions?"

"So much is assured. Yet even in that a subtle danger lurks. Certain contingencies have become involved in the recital of your admittedly ingenious stories which the future unfolding of events may not always justify. For instance, the very speculative Shan Tien, casting his usual moderate limit to the skies, has accepted the Luminous Insect as a beckoning omen, and immersed himself deeply in the chances of every candidate bearing the name of Lao, Ting, Li, Tzu, Sung, Chu, Wang or Chin. Should all these fail incapably at the trials a very undignified period in the Mandarin's general manner of expressing himself may intervene."

"Had the time at the disposal of this person been sufficiently enlarged he would not have omitted the various maxims arising from the tale," admitted Kai Lung, with a shadow of remorse. "That suited to the need of a credulous and ill-balanced mind would doubtless be the proverb: 'He who believes in gambling will live to sell his sandals.' It is regrettable if the well-intending Mandarin took the wrong one. Fortunately another moon will fade before the results are known—"

"In the meantime," continued the maiden, indicating by a glance that what she had to relate was more essential to the requirements of the moment than anything he was saying: "Shan Tien is by no means indisposed towards your cause. Your unassuming attitude and deep research have enlarged your wisdom in his eyes. To-morrow he will send for you to lean upon your well-stored mind."

"Is the emergency one for which any special preparation is required?" questioned Kai Lung.

"That is the message of my warning. Of late a company of grateful friends has given the Mandarin an inlaid coffin to mark the sense of their indebtedness, the critical nature of the times rendering the gift peculiarly appropriate. Thus provided, Shan Tien has cast his eyes around to secure a burial robe worthy of the casket. The merchants proffer many, each endowed with all the qualities, but meanwhile doubts arise, and now Shan Tien would turn to you to learn what is the true and ancient essential of the garment, and wherein its virtue should reside."

"The call will not find me inept," replied Kai Lung. "The story of Wang Ho —"

"It is enough," exclaimed the maiden warningly. "The time for wandering together in the garden of the imagination has not yet arrived. Ming-shu's feet are on a journey, it is true, but his eyes are doubtless left behind. Until a like hour to-morrow gladdens our expectant gaze, farewell!"

On the following day, at about the stroke of the usual court, Li-loe approached Kai Lung with a grievous look.

"Alas, manlet," he exclaimed, "here is one direct from the presence of our high commander, requiring you against his thumb-signed bond. Go you must, and that alone, whether it be for elevation on a tree or on a couch. Out of an insatiable friendship this one would accompany you, were it possible, equally to hold your hand if you are to die or hold your cup if you are to feast. Yet touching that same cask of hidden wine there is still time —"

"Cease, mooncalf," replied Kai Lung reprovingly. "This is but an eddy on the surface of a moving stream. It comes, it goes; and the waters press on as before."

Then Kai Lung, neither bound nor wearing the wooden block, was led into the presence of Shan Tien, and allowed to seat himself upon the floor as though he plied his daily trade.

"Sooner or later it will certainly devolve upon this person to condemn you to a violent end," remarked the far-seeing Mandarin reassuringly. "In the ensuing interval, however, there is no need for either of us to dwell upon what must be regarded as an unpleasant necessity."

"Yet no crime has been committed, beneficence," Kai Lung ventured to protest; "nor in his attitude before your virtuous self has this one been guilty of any act of disrespect."

"You have shown your mind to be both wide and deep, and suitably lined," declared Shan Tien, dexterously avoiding the weightier part of the story-teller's plea. "A question now arises as to the efficacy of embroidered coffin cloths, and wherein their potent merit lies. Out of your well-stored memory declare your knowledge of this sort, conveying the solid information in your usual palatable way."

"I bow, High Excellence," replied Kai Lung. "This concerns the story of Wang Ho."

The Story of Wang Ho and the Burial Robe

There was a time when it did not occur to anyone in this pure and enlightened Empire to question the settled and existing order of affairs. It would have been well for the merchant Wang Ho had he lived in that happy era. But, indeed, it is now no unheard-of thing for an ordinary person to suggest that customs which have been established for centuries might with advantage be changed —a form of impiety which is in no degree removed from declaring oneself to be wiser or more profound than one's ancestors! Scarcely more seemly is this than irregularity in maintaining the Tablets or observing the Rites; and how narrow is the space dividing these delinquencies from the actual crimes of overturning images, counselling rebellion, joining in insurrection and resorting to indiscriminate piracy and bloodshed.

Certainly the merchant Wang Ho would be a thousand taels wealthier to-day if he had fully considered this in advance. Nor would Cheng Lin-but who attempts to eat an orange without first disposing of the peel, or what manner of a dwelling could be erected unless an adequate foundation be first provided?

Wang Ho, then, let it be stated, was one who had early in life amassed a considerable fortune by advising those whose intention it was to hazard their earnings in the State Lotteries as to the numbers that might be relied upon to be successful, or, if not actually successful, those at least that were not already predestined by malign influences to be absolutely incapable of success. These chances Wang Ho at first forecast by means of dreams, portents and other manifestations of an admittedly supernatural tendency, but as his name grew large and the number of his clients increased vastly, while his capacity for dreaming remained the same, he found it no less effective to close his eyes and to become inspired rapidly of numbers as they were thus revealed to him.

Occasionally Wang Ho was the recipient of an appropriate bag of money from one who had profited by his advice, but it was not his custom to rely upon this contingency as a source of income, nor did he in any eventuality return the amount which had been agreed upon (and invariably deposited with him in advance) as the reward of his inspired efforts. To those who sought him in a contentious spirit, inquiring why he did not find it more profitable to secure the prizes for himself, Wang Ho replied that his enterprise consisted in forecasting the winning numbers for State Lotteries and not in solving enigmas, writing deprecatory odes, composing epitaphs or conducting any of the other numerous occupations that could be mentioned. As this plausible evasion was accompanied by the courteous display of the many weapons which he always wore at different convenient points of his attire, the incident invariably ended in a manner satisfactory to Wang Ho.

Thus positioned Wang Ho prospered, and had in the course of years acquired a waist of honourable proportions, when the unrolling course of events influenced him to abandon his lucrative enterprise. It was not that he failed in any way to become as inspired as before; indeed, with increasing practice he attained a fluency that enabled him to outdistance every rival, so that on the occasion of one lottery he afterwards privately discovered that he had predicted the success of every possible combination of numbers, thus enabling those who followed his advice (as he did not fail to announce in inscriptions of vermilion assurance) to secure-among them-every variety of prize offered.

But, about this time, the chief wife of Wang Ho having been greeted with amiable condescension by the chief wife of a high official of the Province, and therefrom in an almost equal manner by the wives of even higher officials, the one in question began to abandon herself to a more rapidly outlined manner of existence than formerly, and to involve Wang Ho in a like attitude, so that presently this ill-considering merchant, who but a short time before would have unhesitatingly cast himself bodily to earth on the approach of a city magistrate, now acquired the habit of alluding to mandarins in casual conversation by names of affectionate abbreviation. Also, being advised of the expediency by a voice speaking in an undertone, he sought still further to extend beyond himself by suffering his nails to grow long and obliterating his name from the public announcements upon the city walls.

In spite of this ambitious sacrifice Wang Ho could not entirely shed from his habit a propensity to associate with those requiring advice on matters involving financial transactions. He could no longer conduct enterprises which entailed many clients and the lavish display of his name, but in the society of necessitous persons who were related to others of distinction he allowed it to be inferred that he was benevolently disposed and had a greater sufficiency of taels than he could otherwise make use of. He also involved himself, for the benefit of those whom he esteemed, in transactions connected with pieces of priceless jade, jars of wine of an especially fragrant character, and pictures of reputable antiquity. In the written manner of these transactions (for it is useless to conceal the fact that Wang Ho was incapable of tracing the characters of his own name) he employed a youth whom he never suffered to appear from beyond the background. Cheng Lin is thus brought naturally and unobtrusively into the narrative.

Had Cheng Lin come into the world when a favourably disposed band of demons was in the ascendant he would certainly have merited an earlier and more embellished appearance in this written chronicle. So far, however, nothing but omens of an ill-destined obscurity had beset his career. For many years two ambitions alone had contained his mind, both inextricably merged into one current and neither with any appearance of ever flowing into its desired end. The first was to pass the examination of the fourth degree of proficiency in the great literary competitions, and thereby qualify for a small official post where, in the course of a few years, he might reasonably hope to be forgotten in all beyond the detail of being allotted every third moon an unostentatious adequacy of taels. This distinction Cheng Lin felt to be well within his power of attainment could he but set aside three uninterrupted years for study, but to do this would necessitate the possession of something like a thousand taels of silver, and Lin might as well fix his eyes upon the great sky-lantern itself.

Dependent on this, but in no great degree removed from it, was the hope of being able to entwine into that future the actuality of Hsi Mean, a very desirable maiden whom it was Cheng Lin's practice to meet by chance on the river bank when his heavily-weighted duties for the day were over.

To those who will naturally ask why Cheng Lin, if really sincere in his determination, could not imperceptibly acquire even so large a sum as a thousand taels while in the house of the wealthy Wang Ho, immersed as the latter person was with the pursuit of the full face of high mandarins and further embarrassed by a profuse illiteracy, it should be sufficient to apply the warning: "Beware of helping yourself to corn from the manger of the blind mule."

In spite of his preoccupation Wang Ho never suffered his mind to wander when sums of money were concerned, and his inability to express himself by written signs only engendered in his alert brain an ever-present decision not to be entrapped by their use. Frequently, Cheng Lin found small sums of money lying in such a position as to induce the belief that they had been forgotten, but upon examining them closely he invariably found upon them marks by which they could be recognized if the necessity arose; he therefore had no hesitation in returning them to Wang Ho with a seemly reference to the extreme improbability of the merchant actually leaving money thus unguarded, and to the lack of respect which it showed to Cheng Lin himself to expect that a person of his integrity should be tempted by so insignificant an amount. Wang Ho always admitted the justice of the reproach, but he did not on any future occasion materially increase the sum in question, so that it is to be doubted if his heart was sincere.

It was on the evening of such an incident that Lin walked with Mean by the side of the lotus-burdened Hoang-keng expressing himself to the effect that instead of lilies her hair was worthy to be bound up with pearls of a like size, and that beneath her feet there should be spread a carpet not of verdure, but of the finest Chang-hi silk, embroidered with five-clawed dragons and other emblems of royal authority, nor was Mean in any way displeased by this indication of extravagant taste on her lover's part, though she replied:

"The only jewels that this person desires are the enduring glances of pure affection with which you, O my phoenix one, entwined the lilies about her hair, and the only carpet that she would crave would be the embroidered design created by the four feet of the two persons who are now conversing together for ever henceforth walking in uninterrupted harmony."

"Yet, alas!" exclaimed Lin, "that enchanting possibility seems to be more remotely positioned than ever. Again has the clay-souled Wang Ho, on the pretext that he can no longer make his in and out taels meet, sought to diminish the monthly inadequacy of cash with which he rewards this person's conscientious services."

"Undoubtedly that opaque-eyed merchant will shortly meet a revengeful fire-breathing vampire when walking alone on the edge of a narrow precipice," exclaimed Mean sympathetically. "Yet have you pressingly laid the facts before the spirits of your distinguished ancestors with a request for their direct intervention?"

"The expedient has not been neglected," replied Lin, "and appropriate sacrifices have accompanied the request. But even while in the form of an ordinary existence the venerable ones in question were becoming distant in their powers of hearing, and doubtless with increasing years the ineptitude has grown. It would almost seem that in the case of a person so obtuse as Wang Ho is, more direct means would have to be employed."

"It is well said," assented Mean, "that those who are unmoved by the thread of a vat of flaming sulphur in the Beyond, rend the air if they chance to step on a burning cinder here on earth."

"The suggestion is a timely one," replied Lin. "Wang Ho's weak spot lies between his hat and his sandals. Only of late, feeling the natural infirmities of time pressing about him, he has expended a thousand taels in the purchase of an elaborate burial robe, which he wears on every fit occasion, so that the necessity for its ultimate use may continue to be remote."

"A thousand taels!" repeated Mean. "With that sum you could—"

"Assuredly. The coincidence may embody something in the nature of an omen favourable to ourselves. At the moment, however, this person has not any clear-cut perception of how the benefit may be attained."

"The amount referred to has already passed into the hands of the merchant in burial robes?"

"Irrevocably. In the detail of the transference of actual sums of money Wang Ho walks hand in hand with himself from door to door. The pieces of silver are by this time beneath the floor of Shen Heng's inner chamber."

"Shen Heng?"

"The merchant in silk and costly fabrics, who lives beneath the sign of the Golden Abacus. It was from him—"

"Truly. It is for him that this person's sister Min works the finest embroideries. Doubtless this very robe—"

"It is of blue silk edged with sand pearls in a line of three depths. Felicitations on long life and a list of the most venerable persons of all times serve to remind the controlling deities to what length human endurance can proceed if suitably encouraged. These are designed in letters of threaded gold. Inferior spirits are equally invoked in characters of silver."

"The description is sharp-pointed. It is upon this robe that the one referred to has been ceaselessly engaged for several moons. On account of her narrow span of years, no less than her nimble-jointed dexterity, she is justly esteemed among those whose wares are guaranteed to be permeated with the spirit of rejuvenation."

"Thereby enabling the enterprising Shen Heng to impose a special detail into his account: 'For employing the services of one who will embroider into the fabric of the robe the vital principles of youth and long-life-to-come—an added fifty taels.' Did she of your house benefit to a proportionate extent?"

Mean indicated a contrary state of things by a graceful movement of her well-arranged eyebrows.

"Not only that," she added, "but the sordid-minded Shen Heng, on a variety of pretexts, has diminished the sum Min was to receive at the completion of the work, until that which should have required a full hand to grasp could be efficiently covered by two attenuated fingers. From this cause Min is vindictively inclined towards him and, steadfastly refusing to bend her feet in the direction of his workshop, she has, between one melancholy and another, involved herself in a dark distemper."

As Mean unfolded the position lying between her sister Min and the merchant Shen Heng, Lin grew thoughtful, and, although it was not his nature to express the changing degrees of emotion by varying the appearance of his face, he did not conceal from Mean that her words had fastened themselves upon his imagination.

"Let us rest here a while," he suggested presently. "That which you say, added to what I already know, may, under the guidance of a sincere mind, put a much more rainbow-like outlook on our combined future than hitherto appeared probable."

So they composed themselves about the bank of the river, while Lin questioned her more closely as to those things of which she had spoken. Finally, he laid certain injunctions upon her for her immediate guidance. Then, it being now the hour of middle light, they returned, Mean accompanying her voice to the melody of stringed wood, as she related songs of those who have passed through great endurances to a state of assured contentment. To Lin it seemed as though the city leapt forward to meet them, so narrow was the space of time involved in reaching it.

A few days later Wang Ho was engaged in the congenial occupation of marking a few pieces of brass cash before secreting them where Cheng Lin must inevitably displace them, when the person in question quietly stood before him. Thereupon Wang Ho returned the money to his inner sleeve, ineptly remarking that when the sun rose it was futile to raise a lantern to the sky to guide the stars.

"Rather is it said, 'From three things cross the road to avoid: a falling tree, your chief and second wives whispering in agreement, and a goat wearing a leopard's tail,'" replied Lin, thus rebuking Wang Ho, not only for his crafty intention, but also as to the obtuseness of the proverb he had quoted. "Nevertheless, O Wang Ho, I approach you on a matter of weighty consequence."

"To-morrow approaches," replied the merchant evasively. "If it concerns the detail of the reduction of your monthly adequacy, my word has become unbending iron."

"It is written: 'Cho Sing collected feathers to make a garment for his canary when it began to moult,'" replied Lin acquiescently. "The care of so insignificant a person as myself may safely be left to the Protecting Forces, esteemed. This matter touches your own condition."

"In that case you cannot be too specific." Wang Ho lowered himself into a reclining couch, thereby indicating that the subject was not one for hasty dismissal, at the same time motioning to Lin that he should sit upon the floor. "Doubtless you have some remunerative form of enterprise to suggest to me?"

"Can a palsied finger grasp a proffered coin? The matter strikes more deeply at your very existence, honoured chief."

"Alas!" exclaimed Wang Ho, unable to retain the usual colour of his appearance, "the attention of a devoted servant is somewhat like Tohen-hi Yang's spiked throne-it torments those whom it supports. However, the word has been spoken-let the sentence be filled in."

"The full roundness of your illustrious outline is as a display of coloured lights to gladden my commonplace vision," replied Lin submissively. "Admittedly of late, however, an element of dampness has interfered with the brilliance of the display."

"Speak clearly and regardless of polite evasion," commanded Wang Ho. "My internal organs have for some time suspected that hostile influences were at work. For how long have you noticed this, as it may be expressed, falling off?"

"My mind is as refined crystal before your compelling glance," admitted Lin. "Ever since it has been your custom to wear the funeral robe fashioned by Shen Heng has your noble shadow suffered erosion."

This answer, converging as it did upon the doubts that had already assailed the merchant's satisfaction, convinced him of Cheng Lin's discrimination, while it increased his own suspicion. He had for some little time found that after wearing the robe he invariably suffered pangs that could only be attributed to the influence of malign and obscure Beings. It is true that the occasions of his wearing the robe were elaborate and many-coursed feasts, when he and his guests had partaken lavishly of birds' nests, sharks' fins, sea snails and other viands of a rich and glutinous nature. But if he could not both wear the funeral robe and partake unstintingly of well-spiced food, the harmonious relation of things was imperilled; and, as it was since the introduction of the funeral robe into his habit that matters had assumed a more poignant phase, it was clear that the influence of the funeral robe was at the root of the trouble.

"Yet," protested Wang Ho, "the Mandarin Ling-ni boasts that he has already lengthened the span of his natural life several years by such an expedient, and my friend the high official T'cheng asserts that, while wearing a much less expensive robe than mine, he feels the essence of an increased vitality passing continuously into his being. Why, then, am I marked out for this infliction, Cheng Lin?"

"Revered," replied Lin, with engaging candour, "the inconveniences of living in a country so densely populated with demons, vampires, spirits, ghouls, dragons, omens, forces and influences, both good and bad, as our own unapproachably favoured Empire is, cannot be evaded from one end of life to the other. How much greater is the difficulty when the prescribed forms for baffling the ill-disposed among the unseen appear to have been wrongly angled by those framing the Rites!"

Wang Ho made a gesture of despair. It conveyed to Lin's mind the wise reminder of N'sy-hing: "When one is inquiring for a way to escape from an advancing tiger, flowers of speech assume the form of noisome bird-weed." He therefore continued:

"Hitherto it has been assumed that for a funeral robe to exercise its most beneficial force it should be the work of a maiden of immature years, the assumption being that, having a prolonged period of existence before her, the influence of longevity would pass through her fingers into the garment and in turn fortify the wearer."

"Assuredly," agreed Wang Ho anxiously. "Thus was the analogy outlined to me by one skilled in the devices, and the logic of it seems unassailable."

"Yet," objected Lin, with sympathetic concern in his voice, "how unfortunate must be the position of a person involved in a robe that has been embroidered by one who, instead of a long life, has been marked out by the Destinies for premature decay and an untimely death! For in that case the influence —"

"Such instances," interrupted Wang Ho, helping himself profusely to rice-spirit from a jar near at hand, "must providentially be of rare occurrence?"

"Esteemed head," replied Lin, helping Wang Ho to yet another superfluity of rice-spirit, "there are moments when it behoves each of us to maintain an unflaccid outline. Suspecting the true cause of your declining radiance, I have, at an involved expenditure of seven taels and three hand counts of brash cash, pursued this matter to its ultimate source. The robe in question owes its attainment to one Min, of the obscure house of Hsi, who recently ceased to have an existence while her years yet numbered short of a score. Not only was it the last work upon which she was engaged, but so closely were the two identified that her abrupt Passing Beyond must certainly exercise a corresponding effect upon any subsequent wearer."

"Alas!" exclaimed Wang Ho, feeling many of the symptoms of contagion already manifesting themselves about his body. "Was the infliction of a painless nature?"

"As to whether it was leprosy, the spotted plague, or acute demoniacal possession, the degraded Shen Heng maintains an unworthy silence. Indeed, at the mention of Hsi Min's name he wraps his garment about his head and rolls upon the floor-from which the worst may be inferred. They of Min's house, however, are less capable of guile, and for an adequate consideration, while not denying that Shen Heng has paid them to maintain a stealthy silence, they freely admit that the facts are as they have been stated."

"In that case, Shen Heng shall certainly return the thousand taels in exchange for this discreditable burial robe," exclaimed Wang Ho vindictively.

"Venerated personality," said Lin, with unabated loyalty, "the essential part of the development is to safeguard your own incomparable being against every danger. Shen Heng may be safely left to the avenging demons that are ever lying in wait for the contemptible."

"The first part of your remark is inspired," agreed Wang Ho, his incapable mind already beginning to assume a less funereal forecast. "Proceed, regardless of all obstacles."

"Consider the outcome of publicly compelling Shen Heng to undo the transaction, even if it could be legally achieved! Word of the calamity would pass on heated breath, each succeeding one becoming more heavily embroidered than the robe itself. The yamens and palaces of your distinguished friends would echo with the once honoured name of Wang Ho, now associated with every form of malignant distemper and impending fate. All would hasten to withdraw themselves from the contagion of your overhanging end."

"Am I, then," demanded Wang Ho, "to suffer the loss of a thousand taels and retain an inadequate and detestable burial robe that will continue to exercise its malign influence over my being?"

"By no means," replied Lin confidently. "But be warned by the precept: 'Do not burn down your house in order to inconvenience even your chief wife's mother.' Sooner or later a relation of Shen Heng's will turn his steps towards your inner office. You can then, without undue effort, impose on him the thousand taels that you have suffered loss from those of his house. In the meantime a device must be sought for exchanging your dangerous but imposing-looking robe for one of proved efficiency."

"It begins to assume a definite problem in this person's mind as to whether such a burial robe exists," declared Wang Ho stubbornly.

"Yet it cannot be denied, when a reliable system is adopted in the fabrication," protested Lin. "For a score and five years the one to whom this person owes his being has worn such a robe."

"To what age did your venerated father attain?" inquired the merchant, with courteous interest.

"Fourscore years and three parts of yet another score."

"And the robe in question eventually accompanied him when he Passed Beyond?"

"Doubtless it will. He is still wearing it," replied Lin, as one who speaks of casual occurrences.

"Is he, then, at so advanced an age, in the state of an ordinary existence?"

"Assuredly. Fortified by the virtue emanating from the garment referred to, it is his deliberate intention to continue here for yet another score of years at least."

"But if such robes are of so dubious a nature how can reliance be placed on any one?"

"Esteemed," replied Lin, "it is a matter that has long been suspected among the observant. Unfortunately, the Ruby Buttons of the past mistakenly formulated that the essence of continuous existence was imparted to a burial robe through the hands of a young maiden-hence so many deplorable experiences. The proper person to be so employed is undoubtedly one of ripe attainment, for only thereby can the claim to possess the vital principle be assured."

"Was the robe which has so effectively sustained your meritorious father thus constructed?" inquired Wang Ho, inviting Lin to recline himself upon a couch by a gesture as of one who discovers for the first time that an honoured guest has been overlooked.

"It is of ancient make, and thereby in the undiscriminating eye perhaps somewhat threadbare; but to the desert-traveller all wells are sparkling," replied Lin. "A venerable woman, inspired of certain magic wisdom, which she wove into the texture, to the exclusion of the showier qualities, designed it at the age of threescore years and three short of another score. She was engaged upon its fabrication yet another seven, and finally Passed Upwards at an attainment of three hundred and thirty-three years, three moons, and three days, thus conforming to all the principles of allowed witchcraft."

"Cheng Lin," said Wang Ho amiably, pouring out for the one whom he addressed a full measure of rice-spirit, "the duty that an obedient son owes even to a grasping and self-indulgent father has in the past been pressed to a too-conspicuous front, at the expense of the harmonious relation that should exist between a comfortably-positioned servant and a generous and broad-minded master. Now in the matter of these two coffin cloths —"

"My ears are widely opened towards your auspicious words, benevolence," replied Lin.

"You, Cheng Lin, are still too young to be concerned with the question of Passing Beyond; your imperishable father is, one is compelled to say, already old enough to go. As regards both persons, therefore, the assumed virtue of one burial robe above another should be merely a matter of speculative interest. Now if some arrangement should be suggested, not unprofitable to yourself, by which one robe might be imperceptibly substituted for another-and, after all, one burial robe is very like another —"

"The prospect of deceiving a trustful and venerated sire is so ignoble that scarcely any material gain would be a fitting compensation-were it not for the fact that an impending loss of vision renders the deception somewhat easy to accomplish. Proceed, therefore, munificence, towards a precise statement of your open-handed prodigality."

* * *

Indescribable was the bitterness of Shen Heng's throat when Cheng Lin unfolded his burden and revealed the Wang Ho thousand-tael burial robe, with an unassuming request for the return of the purchase money, either in gold or honourable paper, as the article was found unsuitable. Shen Heng shook the rafters of the Golden Abacus with indignation, and called upon his domestic demons, the spirits of eleven generations of embroidering ancestors, and the illuminated tablets containing the High Code and Authority of the Distinguished Brotherhood of Coffin Cloth and Burial Robe Makers in protest against so barbarous an innovation.

Bowing repeatedly and modestly expressing himself to the effect that it was incredible that he was not justly struck dead before the sublime spectacle of Shen Heng's virtuous indignation, Cheng Lin carefully produced the written lines of the agreement, gently directing the Distinguished Brother's fire-kindling eyes to an indicated detail. It was a provision that the robe should be returned and the purchase money restored if the garment was not all that was therein stipulated: with his invariable painstaking loyalty Lin had insisted upon this safeguard when he drew up the form, although, probably from a disinclination to extol his own services, he had omitted mentioning the fact to Wang Ho in their recent conversation.

With deprecating firmness Lin directed Shen Heng's reluctant eyes to another line-the unfortunate exaction of fifty taels in return for the guarantee that the robe should be permeated with the spirit of rejuvenation. As the undoubted embroiderer of the robe-one Min of the family of Hsi-had admittedly Passed Beyond almost with the last stitch, it was evident that she could only have conveyed by her touch an entirely contrary emanation. If, as Shen Heng never ceased to declare, Min was still somewhere alive, let her be produced and a fitting token of reconciliation would be forthcoming; otherwise, although with the acutest reluctance, it would be necessary to carry the claim to the court of the chief District Mandarin, and (Cheng Lin trembled at the sacrilegious thought) it would be impossible to conceal the fact that Shen Heng employed persons of inauspicious omen, and the high repute of coffin cloths from the Golden Abacus would be lost. The hint arrested Shen Heng's fingers in the act of tearing out a handful of his beautiful pigtail. For the first time he noticed, with intense self-reproach, that Lin was not reclining on a couch.

The amiable discussion that followed, conducted with discriminating dignity by Shen Heng and conscientious humility on the part of Cheng Lin, extended from one gong-stroke before noon until close upon the time for the evening rice. The details arrived at were that Shen Heng should deliver to Lin eight-hundred and seventy-five taels against the return of the robe. He would also press upon that person a silk purse with an onyx clasp, containing twenty-five taels, as a deliberate mark of his individual appreciation and quite apart from anything to do with the transaction on hand. All suggestions of anything other than the strictest high-mindedness were withdrawn from both sides. In order that the day should not be wholly destitute of sunshine at the Golden Abacus, Lin declared his intention of purchasing, at a price not exceeding three taels and a half, the oldest and most unattractive burial robe that the stock contained. So moved was Shen Heng by this delicate consideration that he refused to accept more than two taels and three-quarters. Moreover, he added for Lin's acceptance a small jar of crystallized limpets.

To those short-sighted ones who profess to discover in the conduct of Cheng Lin (now an official of the seventeenth grade and drawing his quarterly sufficiency of taels in a distant province) something not absolutely honourably arranged, it is only necessary to display the ultimate end as it affected those persons in any way connected.

Wang Ho thus obtained a burial robe in which he was able to repose absolute confidence. Doubtless it would have sustained him to an advanced age had he not committed self-ending, in the ordinary way of business, a few years later.

Shen Heng soon disposed of the returned garment for two thousand taels to a person who had become prematurely wealthy owing to the distressed state of the Empire. In addition he had sold, for more than two taels, a robe which he had no real expectation of ever selling at all.

Min, made welcome at the house of Mean and Lin, removed with them to that distant province. There she found that the remuneration for burial robe embroidery was greater than she had ever obtained before. With the money thus amassed she was able to marry an official of noble rank.

The father of Cheng Lin had passed into the Upper Air many years before the incidents with which this related narrative concerns itself. He is thus in no way affected. But Lin did not neglect, in the time of his prosperity, to transmit to him frequent sacrifices of seasonable delicacies suited to his condition.

The Timely Disputation Among Those of an Inner Chamber of Yu-Ping

For the space of three days Ming-shu remained absent from Yu-ping, and the affections of Kai Lung and Hwa-mei prospered. On the evening of the third day the maiden stood beneath the shutter with a more definite look, and Kai Lung understood that a further period of unworthy trial was now at hand.

"Behold!" she explained, "at dawn the corrupt Ming-shu will pass within our gates again, nor is it prudent to assume that his enmity has lessened."

"On the contrary," replied Kai Lung, "like that unnatural reptile that lives on air, his malice will have grown upon the voidness of its cause. As the wise Ling-kwang remarks: 'He who plants a vineyard with one hand —'"

"Assuredly, beloved," interposed Hwa-mei dexterously. "But our immediate need is less to describe Ming-shu's hate in terms of classical analogy than to find a potent means of baffling its venom."

"You are all-wise as usual," confessed Kai Lung, with due humility. "I will restrain my much too verbose tongue."

"The invading Banners from the north have for the moment failed and those who drew swords in their cause are flying to the hills. In Yu-ping, therefore, loyalty wears a fully round face and about the yamen of Shan Tien men speak almost in set terms. While these conditions prevail, justice will continue to be administered precisely as before. We have thus nothing to hope in that direction."

"Yet in the ideal state of purity aimed at by the illustrious founders of our race —" began Kai Lung, and ceased abruptly, remembering.

"As it is, we are in the state of Tsin in the fourteenth of the heaven-sent Ching," retorted Hwa-mei capably. "The insatiable Ming-shu will continue to seek your life, calling to his aid every degraded subterfuge. When the nature of these can be learned somewhat in advance, as the means within my power have hitherto enabled us to do, a trusty shield is raised in your defence."

Kai Lung would have spoken of the length and the breadth of his indebtedness, but she who stood below did not encourage this.

"Ming-shu's absence makes this plan fruitless here to-day, and as a consequence he may suddenly disclose a subtle snare to which your feet must bend. In this emergency my strategy has been towards safeguarding your irreplaceable life to-morrow at all hazard. Should this avail, Ming-shu's later schemes will present no baffling veil."

"Your virtuous little finger is as strong as Ming-shu's offensive thumb," remarked Kai Lung. "This person has no fear."

"Doubtless," acquiesced Hwa-mei. "But she who has spun the thread knows the weakness of the net. Heed well to the end that no ineptness may arise. Shan Tien of late extols your art, claiming that in every circumstance you have a story fitted to the need."

"He measures with a golden rule," agreed Kai Lung. "Left to himself, Shan Tien is a just, if superficial, judge."

The knowledge of this boast, Hwa-mei continued to relate, had spread to the inner chambers of the yamen, where the lesser ones vied with each other in proclaiming the merit of the captive minstrel. Amid this eulogy Hwa-mei moved craftily and played an insidious part, until she who was their appointed head was committed to the claim. Then the maiden raised a contentious voice.

"Our lord's trout were ever salmon," she declared, "and lo! here is another great and weighty fish! Assuredly no living man is thus and thus; or are the T'ang epicists returned to earth? Truly our noble one is easily pleased-in many ways!" With these well-fitted words she fixed her eyes upon the countenance of Shan Tien's chief wife and waited.

"The sun shines through his words and the moon adorns his utterances," replied the chief wife, with unswerving loyalty, though she added, no less suitably: "That one should please him easily and another therein fail, despite her ceaseless efforts, is as the Destinies provide."

"You are all-seeing," admitted Hwa-mei generously; "nor is a locked door any obstacle to your discovering eye. Let this arisement be submitted to a facile test. Dependent from my ill-formed ears are rings of priceless jade that have ever tinged your thoughts, while about your shapely neck is a crystal charm, to which an unclouded background would doubtless give some lustre. I will set aside the rings and thou shalt set aside the charm. Then, at a chosen time, this vaunted one shall attend before us here, and I having disclosed the substance of a theme, he shall make good the claim. If he so does, capably and without delay, thou shalt possess the jewels. But if, in the judgment of these around, he shall fail therein, then are both jewels mine. Is it so agreed?"

"It is agreed!" cried those who were the least concerned, seeing some entertainment to themselves. "Shall the trial take place at once?"

"Not so," replied Hwa-mei. "A sufficient space must be allowed for this one wherein to select the matter of the test. To-morrow let it be, before the hour of evening rice. And thou?"

"Inasmuch as it will enlarge the prescience of our lord in minds that are light and vaporous, I also do consent," replied the chief wife. "Yet must he too be of our company, to be witness of the upholding of his word and, if need be, to cast a decisive voice."

"Thus," continued Hwa-mei, as she narrated these events, "Shan Tien is committed to the trial and thereby he must preserve you until that hour. Tell me now the answer to the test, that I may frame the question to agree."

Kai Lung thought a while, then said:

"There is the story of Chang Tao. It concerns one who, bidden to do an impossible task, succeeded though he failed, and shows how two identically similar beings may be essentially diverse. To this should be subjoined the apophthegm that that which we are eager to obtain may be that which we have striven to avoid."

"It suffices," agreed Hwa-mei. "Bear well your part."

"Still," suggested Kai Lung, hoping to detain her retiring footsteps for yet another span, "were it not better that I should fall short at the test, thus to enlarge your word before your fellows?"

"And in so doing demean yourself, darken the face of Shan Tien's present regard, and alienate all those who stand around! O most obtuse Kai Lung!"

"I will then bare my throat," confessed Kai Lung. "The barbed thought had assailed my mind that perchance the rings of precious jade lay coiled around your heart. Thus and thus I spoke."

"Thus also will I speak," replied Hwa-mei, and her uplifted eyes held Kai Lung by the inner fibre of his being. "Did I value them as I do, and were they a single hair of my superfluous head, the whole head were freely offered to a like result."

With these noticeable words, which plainly testified the strength of her emotion, the maiden turned and hastened on her way, leaving Kai Lung gazing from the shutter in a very complicated state of disquietude.

The Story of Chang Tao, Melodious Vision and the Dragon

After Chang Tao had reached the age of manhood his grandfather took him apart one day and spoke of a certain matter, speaking as a philosopher whose mind has at length overflowed.

"Behold!" he said, when they were at a discreet distance aside, "your years are now thus and thus, but there are still empty chairs where there should be occupied cradles in your inner chamber, and the only upraised voice heard in this spacious residence is that of your esteemed father repeating the Analects. The prolific portion of the tree of our illustrious House consists of its roots; its existence onwards narrows down to a single branch which as yet has put forth no blossoms."

"The loftiest tower rises from the ground," remarked Chang Tao evasively, not wishing to implicate himself on either side as yet.

"Doubtless; and as an obedient son it is commendable that you should close your ears, but as a discriminating father there is no reason why I should not open my mouth," continued the venerable Chang in a voice from which every sympathetic modulation was withdrawn. "It is admittedly a meritorious resolve to devote one's existence to explaining the meaning of a single obscure passage of one of the Odes, but if the detachment necessary to the achievement results in a hitherto carefully-preserved line coming to an incapable end, it would have been more satisfactory to the dependent shades of our revered ancestors that the one in question should have collected street garbage rather than literary instances, or turned somersaults in place of the pages of the Classics, had he but given his first care to providing you with a wife and thereby safeguarding our unbroken continuity."

"My father is all-wise," ventured Chang Tao dutifully, but observing the nature of the other's expression he hastened to add considerately, "but my father's father is even wiser."

"Inevitably," assented the one referred to; "not merely because he is the more mature by a generation, but also in that he is thereby nearer to the inspired ancients in whom the Cardinal Principles reside."

"Yet, assuredly, there must be occasional exceptions to this rule of progressive deterioration?" suggested Chang Tao, feeling that the process was not without a definite application to himself.

"Not in our pure and orthodox line," replied the other person firmly. "To suggest otherwise is to admit the possibility of a son being the superior of his own father, and to what a discordant state of things would that contention lead! However immaturely you may think at present, you will see the position at its true angle when you have sons of your own."

"The contingency is not an overhanging one," said Chang Tao. "On the last occasion when I reminded my venerated father of my age and unmarried state, he remarked that, whether he looked backwards or forwards, extinction seemed to be the kindest destiny to which our House could be subjected."

"Originality, carried to the length of eccentricity, is a censurable accomplishment in one of official rank," remarked the elder Chang coldly. "Plainly it is time that I should lengthen the authority of my own arm very perceptibly. If a father is so neglectful of his duty, it is fitting that a grandfather should supply his place. This person will himself procure a bride for you without delay."

"The function might perhaps seem an unusual one," suggested Chang Tao, who secretly feared the outcome of an enterprise conducted under these auspices.

"So, admittedly, are the circumstances. What suitable maiden suggests herself to your doubtless better-informed mind? Is there one of the house of Tung?"

"There are eleven," replied Chang Tao, with a gesture of despair, "all reputed to be untiring with their needle, skilled in the frugal manipulation of cold rice, devout, discreet in the lines of their attire, and so sombre of feature as to be collectively known to the available manhood of the city as the Terror that Lurks for the Unwary. Suffer not your discriminating footsteps to pause before that house, O father of my father! Now had you spoken of Golden Eyebrows, daughter of Kuo Wang —"

"It would be as well to open a paper umbrella in a thunderstorm as to seek profit from an alliance with Kuo Wang. Crafty and ambitious, he is already deep in questionable ventures, and high as he carries his head at present, there will assuredly come a day when Kuo Wang will appear in public with his feet held even higher than his crown."

"The rod!" exclaimed Chang Tao in astonishment. "Can it really be that one who is so invariably polite to me is not in every way immaculate?"

"Either bamboo will greet his feet or hemp adorn his neck," persisted the other, with a significant movement of his hands in the proximity of his throat. "Walk backwards in the direction of that house, son of my son. Is there not one Ning of the worthy line of Lo, dwelling beneath the emblem of a Sprouting Aloe?"

"Truly," agreed the youth, "but at an early age she came under the malign influence of a spectral vampire, and in order to deceive the creature she was adopted to the navigable portion of the river here, and being announced as having Passed Above was henceforth regarded as a red mullet."

"Yet in what detail does that deter you?" inquired Chang, for the nature of his grandson's expression betrayed an acute absence of enthusiasm towards the maiden thus concerned.

"Perchance the vampire was not deceived after all. In any case this person dislikes red mullet," replied the youth indifferently.

The venerable shook his head reprovingly.

"It is imprudent to be fanciful in matters of business," he remarked. "Lo Chiu, her father, is certainly the possessor of many bars of silver, and, as it is truly written: 'With wealth one may command demons; without it one cannot summon even a slave.'"

"It is also said: 'When the tree is full the doubtful fruit remains upon the branch,'" retorted Chang Tao. "Are not maidens in this city as the sand upon a broad seashore? If one opens and closes one's hands suddenly out in the Ways on a dark night, the chances are that three or four will be grasped. A stone cast at a venture —"

"Peace!" interrupted the elder. "Witless spoke thus even in the days of this person's remote youth-only the virtuous did not then open and close their hands suddenly in the Ways on dark nights. Is aught reported of the inner affairs of Shen Yi, a rich philosopher who dwells somewhat remotely on the Stone Path, out beyond the Seven Terraced Bridge?"

Chang Tao looked up with a sharply awakening interest.

"It is well not to forget that one," he replied. "He is spoken of as courteous but reserved, in that he drinks tea with few though his position is assured. Is not his house that which fronts on a summer-seat domed with red copper?"

"It is the same," agreed the other. "Speak on."

"What I recall is meagre and destitute of point. Nevertheless, it so chanced that some time ago this person was proceeding along the further Stone Path when an aged female mendicant, seated by the wayside, besought his charity. Struck by her destitute appearance he bestowed upon her a few unserviceable broken cash, such as one retains for the indigent, together with an appropriate blessing, when the hag changed abruptly into the appearance of a young and alluring maiden, who smilingly extended to this one her staff, which had meanwhile become a graceful branch of flowering lotus. The manifestation was not sustained, however, for as he who is relating the incident would have received the proffered flower he found that his hand was closing on the neck of an expectant serpent, which held in its mouth an agate charm. The damsel had likewise altered, imperceptibly merging into the form of an overhanging fig-tree, among whose roots the serpent twined itself. When this person would have eaten one of the ripe fruit of the tree he found that the skin was filled with a bitter dust, whereupon he withdrew, convinced that no ultimate profit was likely to result from the encounter. His departure was accompanied by the sound of laughter, mocking yet more melodious than a carillon of silver gongs hung in a porcelain tower, which seemed to proceed from the summer-seat domed with red copper."

"Some omen doubtless lay within the meeting," said the elder Chang. "Had you but revealed the happening fully on your return, capable geomancers might have been consulted. In this matter you have fallen short."

"It is admittedly easier to rule a kingdom than to control one's thoughts," confessed Chang Tao frankly. "A great storm of wind met this person on his way back, and when he had passed through it, all recollection of the incident had, for the time, been magically blown from his mind."

"It is now too late to question the augurs. But in the face of so involved a portent it would be well to avert all thought from Melodious Vision, wealthy Shen Yi's incredibly attractive daughter."

"It is unwise to be captious in affairs of negotiation," remarked the young man thoughtfully. "Is the smile of the one referred to such that at the vision of it the internal organs of an ordinary person begin to clash together, beyond the power of all control?"

"Not in the case of the one who is speaking," replied the grandfather of Chang Tao, "but a very illustrious poet, whom Shen Yi charitably employed about his pig-yard, certainly described it as a ripple on the surface of a dark lake of wine, when the moon reveals the hidden pearls beneath; and after secretly observing the unstudied grace of her movements, the most celebrated picture-maker of the province burned the implements of his craft, and began life anew as a trainer of performing elephants. But when maidens are as numerous as the grains of sand —"

"Esteemed," interposed Chang Tao, with smooth determination, "wisdom lurks in the saying: 'He who considers everything decides nothing.' Already this person has spent an unprofitable score of years through having no choice in the matter; at this rate he will spend yet another score through having too much. Your timely word shall be his beacon. Neither the disadvantage of Shen Yi's oppressive wealth nor the inconvenience of Melodious Vision's excessive beauty shall deter him from striving to fulfil your delicately expressed wish."

"Yet," objected the elder Chang, by no means gladdened at having the decision thus abruptly lifted from his mouth, "so far, only a partially formed project —"

"To a thoroughly dutiful grandson half a word from your benevolent lips carries further than a full-throated command does from a less revered authority."

"Perchance. This person's feet, however, are not liable to a similar acceleration, and a period of adequate consideration must intervene before they are definitely moving in the direction of Shen Yi's mansion. 'Where the road bends abruptly take short steps,' Chang Tao."

"The necessity will be lifted from your venerable shoulders, revered," replied Chang Tao firmly. "Fortified by your approving choice, this person will himself confront Shen Yi's doubtful countenance, and that same bend in the road will be taken at a very sharp angle and upon a single foot."

"In person! It is opposed to the Usages!" exclaimed the venerable; and at the contemplation of so undignified a course his voice prudently withdrew itself, though his mouth continued to open and close for a further period.

"'As the mountains rise, so the river winds,'" replied Chang Tao, and with unquenchable deference he added respectfully as he took his leave, "Fear not, eminence; you will yet remain to see five generations of stalwart he-children, all pressing forward to worship your imperishable memory."

In such a manner Chang Tao set forth to defy the Usages and-if perchance it might be-to speak to Shen Yi face to face of Melodious Vision. Yet in this it may be that the youth was not so much hopeful of success by his own efforts as that he was certain of failure by the elder Chang's. And in the latter case the person in question might then irrevocably contract him to a maiden of the house of Tung, or to another equally forbidding. Not inaptly is it written: "To escape from fire men will plunge into boiling water."

Nevertheless, along the Stone Path many doubts and disturbances arose within Chang Tao's mind. It was not in this manner that men of weight and dignity sought wives. Even if Shen Yi graciously overlooked the absence of polite formality, would not the romantic imagination of Melodious Vision be distressed when she learned that she had been approached with so indelicate an absence of ceremony? "Here, again," said Chang Tao's self-reproach accusingly, "you have, as usual, gone on in advance of both your feet and of your head. 'It is one thing to ignore the Rites: it is quite another to expect the gods to ignore the Penalties.' Assuredly you will suffer for it."

It was at this point that Chang Tao was approached by one who had noted his coming from afar, and had awaited him, for passers-by were sparse and remote.

"Prosperity attend your opportune footsteps," said the stranger respectfully. "A misbegotten goat-track enticed this person from his appointed line by the elusive semblance of an avoided li. Is there, within your enlightened knowledge, the house of one Shen Yi, who makes a feast to-day, positioned about this inauspicious region? It is further described as fronting on a summer-seat domed with red copper."

"There is such a house as you describe, at no great distance to the west," replied Chang Tao. "But that he marks the day with music had not reached these superficial ears."

"It is but among those of his inner chamber, this being the name-day of one whom he would honour in a refined and at the same time inexpensive manner. To that end am I bidden."

"Of what does your incomparable exhibition consist?" inquired Chang Tao.

"Of a variety of quite commonplace efforts. It is entitled 'Half-a-gong-stroke among the No-realities; or Gravity-removing devoid of Inelegance.' Thus, borrowing the neck-scarf of the most dignified-looking among the lesser ones assembled I will at once discover among its folds the unsuspected presence of a family of tortoises; from all parts of the person of the roundest-bodied mandarin available I will control the appearance of an inexhaustible stream of copper cash, and beneath the scrutinizing eyes of all a bunch of paper chrysanthemums will change into the similitude of a crystal bowl in whose clear depth a company of gold and silver carp glide from side to side."

"These things are well enough for the immature, and the sight of an unnaturally stout official having an interminable succession of white rabbits produced from the various recesses of his waistcloth admittedly melts the austerity of the superficial of both sexes. But can you, beneath the undeceptive light of day, turn a sere and unattractive hag into the substantial image of a young and beguiling maiden, and by a further complexity into a fruitful fig-tree; or induce a serpent so far to forsake its natural instincts as to poise on the extremity of its tail and hold a charm within its mouth?"

"None of these things lies within my admitted powers," confessed the stranger. "To what end does your gracious inquiry tend?"

"It is in the nature of a warning, for within the shadow of the house you seek manifestations such as I describe pass almost without remark. Indeed it is not unlikely that while in the act of displaying your engaging but simple skill you may find yourself transformed into a chameleon or saddled with the necessity of finishing your gravity-removing entertainment under the outward form of a Manchurian ape."

"Alas!" exclaimed the other. "The eleventh of the moon was ever this person's unlucky day, and he would have done well to be warned by a dream in which he saw an unsuspecting kid walk into the mouth of a voracious tiger."

"Undoubtedly the tiger was an allusion to the dangers awaiting you, but it is not yet too late for you to prove that you are no kid," counselled Chang Tao. "Take this piece of silver so that the enterprise of the day may not have been unfruitful and depart with all speed on a homeward path. He who speaks is going westward, and at the lattice of Shen Yi he will not fail to leave a sufficient excuse for your no-appearance."

"Your voice has the compelling ring of authority, beneficence," replied the stranger gratefully. "The obscure name of the one who prostrates himself is Wo, that of his degraded father being Weh. For this service he binds his ghost to attend your ghost through three cycles of time in the After."

"It is remitted," said Chang Tao generously, as he resumed his way. "May the path be flattened before your weary feet."

Thus, unsought as it were, there was placed within Chang Tao's grasp a staff that might haply bear his weight into the very presence of Melodious Vision herself. The exact strategy of the undertaking did not clearly yet reveal itself, but "When fully ripe the fruit falls of its own accord," and Chang Tao was content to leave such detail to the guiding spirits of his destinies. As he approached the outer door he sang cheerful ballads of heroic doings, partly because he was glad, but also to reassure himself.

"One whom he expects awaits," he announced to the keeper of the gate. "The name of Wo, the son of Weh, should suffice."

"It does not," replied the keeper, swinging his roomy sleeve specifically. "So far it has an empty, short-stopping sound. It lacks sparkle; it has no metallic ring... . He sleeps."

"Doubtless the sound of these may awaken him," said Chang Tao, shaking out a score of cash.

"Pass in munificence. Already his expectant eyes rebuke the unopen door."

Although he had been in a measure prepared by Wo, Chang Tao was surprised to find that three persons alone occupied the chamber to which he was conducted. Two of these were Shen Yi and a trusted slave; at the sight of the third Chang Tao's face grew very red and the deficiencies of his various attributes began to fill his mind with dark forebodings, for this was Melodious Vision and no man could look upon her without her splendour engulfing his imagination. No record of her pearly beauty is preserved beyond a scattered phrase or two; for the poets and minstrels of the age all burned what they had written, in despair at the inadequacy of words. Yet it remains that whatever a man looked for, that he found, and the measure of his requirement was not stinted.

"Greeting," said Shen Yi, with easy-going courtesy. He was a more meagre man than Chang Tao had expected, his face not subtle, and his manner restrained rather than oppressive. "You have come on a long and winding path; have you taken your rice?"

"Nothing remains lacking," replied Chang Tao, his eyes again elsewhere. "Command your slave, Excellence."

"In what particular direction do your agreeable powers of leisure-beguiling extend?"

So far Chang Tao had left the full consideration of this inevitable detail to the inspiration of the moment, but when the moment came the prompting spirits did not disclose themselves. His hesitation became more elaborate under the expression of gathering enlightenment that began to appear in Melodious Vision's eyes.

"An indifferent store of badly sung ballads," he was constrained to reply at length, "and—perchance —a threadbare assortment of involved questions and replies."

"Was it your harmonious voice that we were privileged to hear raised beneath our ill-fitting window a brief space ago?" inquired Shen Yi.

"Admittedly at the sight of this noble palace I was impelled to put my presumptuous gladness into song."

"Then let it fain be the other thing," interposed the maiden, with decision. "Your gladness came to a sad end, minstrel."

"Involved questions are by no means void of divertisement," remarked Shen Yi, with conciliatory mildness in his voice. "There was one, turning on the contradictory nature of a door which under favourable conditions was indistinguishable from an earthenware vessel, that seldom failed to baffle the unalert in the days before the binding of this person's hair."

"That was the one which it had been my feeble intention to propound," confessed Chang Tao.

"Doubtless there are many others equally enticing," suggested Shen Yi helpfully.

"Alas," admitted Chang Tao with conscious humiliation; "of all those wherein I retain an adequate grasp of the solution, the complication eludes me at the moment, and thus in a like but converse manner with the others."

"Esteemed parent," remarked Melodious Vision, without emotion, "this is neither a minstrel nor one in any way entertaining. It is merely Another."

"Another!" exclaimed Chang Tao in refined bitterness. "Is it possible that after taking so extreme and unorthodox a course as to ignore the Usages and advance myself in person I am to find that I have not even the mediocre originality of being the first, as a recommendation?"

"If the matter is thus and thus, so far from being the first, you are only the last of a considerable line of worthy and enterprising youths who have succeeded in gaining access to the inner part of this not really attractive residence on one pretext or another," replied the tolerant Shen Yi. "In any case you are honourably welcome. From the position of your various features I now judge you to be Tao, only son of the virtuous house of Chang. May you prove more successful in your enterprise than those who have preceded you."

"The adventure appears to be tending in unforeseen directions," said Chang Tao uneasily. "Your felicitation, benign, though doubtless gold at heart, is set in a doubtful frame."

"It is for your stalwart endeavour to assure a happy picture," replied Shen Yi, with undisturbed cordiality. "You bear a sword."

"What added involvement is this?" demanded Chang Tao. "This one's thoughts and intention were not turned towards savagery and arms, but in the direction of a pacific union of two distinguished lines."

"In such cases my attitude has invariably been one of sympathetic unconcern," declared Shen Yi. "The weight of either side produces an atmosphere of absolute poise that cannot fail to give full play to the decision of the destinies."

"But if this attitude is maintained on your part how can the proposal progress to a definite issue?" inquired Chang Tao.

"So far, it never has so progressed," admitted Shen Yi. "None of the worthy and hard-striving young men-any of whom I should have been overjoyed to greet as a son-in-law had my inopportune sense of impartiality permitted it-has yet returned from the trial to claim the reward."

"Even the Classics become obscure in the dark. Clear your throat of all doubtfulness, O Shen Yi, and speak to a definite end."

"That duty devolves upon this person, O would-be propounder of involved questions," interposed Melodious Vision. Her voice was more musical than a stand of hanging jewels touched by a rod of jade, and each word fell like a separate pearl. "He who ignores the Usages must expect to find the Usages ignored. Since the day when K'ung-tsz framed the Ceremonies much water has passed beneath the Seven Terraced Bridge, and that which has overflowed can never be picked up again. It is no longer enough that you should come and thereby I must go; that you should speak and I be silent; that you should beckon and I meekly obey. Inspired by the uprisen sisterhood of the outer barbarian lands, we of the inner chambers of the Illimitable Kingdom demand the right to express ourselves freely on every occasion and on every subject, whether the matter involved is one that we understand or not."

"Your clear-cut words will carry far," said Chang Tao deferentially, and, indeed, Melodious Vision's voice had imperceptibly assumed a penetrating quality that justified the remark. "Yet is it fitting that beings so superior in every way should be swayed by the example of those who are necessarily uncivilized and rude?"

"Even a mole may instruct a philosopher in the art of digging," replied the maiden, with graceful tolerance. "Thus among those uncouth tribes it is the custom, when a valiant youth would enlarge his face in the eyes of a maiden, that he should encounter forth and slay dragons, to the imperishable glory of her name. By this beneficent habit not only are the feeble and inept automatically disposed of, but the difficulty of choosing one from among a company of suitors, all apparently possessing the same superficial attributes, is materially lightened."

"The system may be advantageous in those dark regions," admitted Chang Tao reluctantly, "but it must prove unsatisfactory in our more favoured land."

"In what detail?" demanded the maiden, pausing in her attitude of assured superiority.

"By the essential drawback that whereas in those neglected outer parts there really are no dragons, here there really are. Thus —"

"Doubtless there are barbarian maidens for those who prefer to encounter barbarian dragons, then," exclaimed Melodious Vision, with a very elaborately sustained air of no-concern.

"Doubtless," assented Chang Tao mildly. "Yet having set forth in the direction of a specific Vision it is this person's intention to pursue it to an ultimate end."

"The quiet duck puts his foot on the unobservant worm," murmured Shen Yi, with delicate encouragement, adding "This one casts a more definite shadow than those before."

"Yet," continued the maiden, "to all, my unbending word is this: he who would return for approval must experience difficulties, overcome dangers and conquer dragons. Those who do not adventure on the quest will pass outward from this person's mind."

"And those who do will certainly Pass Upward from their own bodies," ran the essence of the youth's inner thoughts. Yet the network of her unevadable power and presence was upon him; he acquiescently replied:

"It is accepted. On such an errand difficulties and dangers will not require any especial search. Yet how many dragons slain will suffice to win approval?"

"Crocodile-eyed one!" exclaimed Melodious Vision, surprised into wrathfulness. "How many —" Here she withdrew in abrupt vehemence.

"Your progress has been rapid and profound," remarked Shen Yi, as, with flattering attention, he accompanied Chang Tao some part of the way towards the door. "Never before has that one been known to leave a remark unsaid; I do not altogether despair of seeing her married yet. As regards the encounter with the dragon-well, in the case of the one whispering in your ear there was the revered mother of the one whom he sought. After all, a dragon is soon done with-one way or the other."

In such a manner Chang Tao set forth to encounter dragons, assured that difficulties and dangers would accompany him on either side. In this latter detail he was inspired, but as the great light faded and the sky-lantern rose in interminable succession, while the unconquerable li ever stretched before his expectant feet, the essential part of the undertaking began to assume a dubious facet. In the valleys and fertile places he learned that creatures of this part now chiefly inhabited the higher fastnesses, such regions being more congenial to their wild and intractable natures. When, however, after many laborious marches he reached the upper peaks of pathless mountains the scanty crag-dwellers did not vary in their assertion that the dragons had for some time past forsaken those heights for the more settled profusion of the plains. Formerly, in both places they had been plentiful, and all those whom Chang Tao questioned spoke openly of many encounters between their immediate forefathers and such Beings.

It was in the downcast frame of mind to which the delays in accomplishing his mission gave rise that Chang Tao found himself walking side by side with one who bore the appearance of an affluent merchant. The northernward way was remote and solitary, but seeing that the stranger carried no outward arms Chang Tao greeted him suitably and presently spoke of the difficulty of meeting dragons, or of discovering their retreats from dwellers in that region.

"In such delicate matters those who know don't talk, and those who talk don't know," replied the other sympathetically. "Yet for what purpose should one who would pass as a pacific student seek to encounter dragons?"

"For a sufficient private reason it is necessary that I should kill a certain number," replied Chang Tao freely. "Thus their absence involves me in much ill-spared delay."

At this avowal the stranger's looks became more sombre, and he breathed inwards several times between his formidable teeth before he made reply.

"This is doubtless your angle, but there is another; nor is it well to ignore the saying, 'Should you miss the tiger be assured that he will not miss you,'" he remarked at length. "Have you sufficiently considered the eventuality of a dragon killing you?"

"It is no less aptly said: 'To be born is in the course of nature, but to die is according to the decree of destiny.'"

"That is a two-edged weapon, and the dragon may be the first to apply it."

"In that case this person will fall back upon the point of the adage: 'It is better to die two years too soon than to live one year too long,'" replied Chang Tao. "Should he fail in the adventure and thus lose all hope of Melodious Vision, of the house of Shen, there will be no further object in prolonging a wearisome career."

"You speak of Melodious Vision, she being of the house of Shen," said the stranger, regarding his companion with an added scrutiny. "Is the unmentioned part of her father's honourable name Yi, and is his agreeable house so positioned that it fronts upon a summer-seat domed with red copper?"

"The description is exact," admitted Chang Tao. "Have you, then, in the course of your many-sided travels, passed that way?"

"It is not unknown to me," replied the other briefly. "Learn now how incautious had been your speech, and how narrowly you have avoided the exact fate of which I warned you. The one speaking to you is in reality a powerful dragon, his name being Pe-lung, from the circumstance that the northern limits are within his sway. Had it not been for a chance reference you would certainly have been struck dead at the parting of our ways."

"If this is so it admittedly puts a new face upon the matter," agreed Chang Tao. "Yet how can reliance be spontaneously placed upon so incredible a claim? You are a man of moderate cast, neither diffident nor austere, and with no unnatural attributes. All the dragons with which history is concerned possess a long body and a scaly skin, and have, moreover, the power of breathing fire at will."

"That is easily put to the test." No sooner had Pe-lung uttered these words than he faded, and in his place appeared a formidable monster possessing all the terror-inspiring characteristics of his kind. Yet in spite of his tree-like eyebrows, fiercely-moving whiskers and fire-breathing jaws, his voice was mild and pacific as he continued: "What further proof can be required? Assuredly, the self-opinionated spirit in which you conduct your quest will bring you no nearer to a desired end."

"Yet this will!" exclaimed Chang Tao, and suddenly drawing his reliable sword he drove it through the middle part of the dragon's body. So expertly was the thrust weighted that the point of the weapon protruded on the other side and scarred the earth. Instead of falling lifeless to the ground, however, the Being continued to regard its assailant with benignant composure, whereupon the youth withdrew the blade and drove it through again, five or six times more. As this produced no effect beyond rendering the edge of the weapon unfit for further use, and almost paralysing the sinews of his own right arm, Chang Tao threw away the sword and sat down on the road in order to recall his breath. When he raised his head again the dragon had disappeared and Pe-lung stood there as before.

"Fortunately it is possible to take a broad-minded view of your uncourteous action, owing to your sense of the fitnesses being for the time in abeyance through allegiance to so engaging a maiden as Melodious Vision," said Pe-lung in a voice not devoid of reproach. "Had you but confided in me more fully I should certainly have cautioned you in time. As it is, you have ended by notching your otherwise capable weapon beyond repair and seriously damaging the scanty cloak I wear"—indicating the numerous rents that marred his dress of costly fur. "No wonder dejection sits upon your downcast brow."

"Your priceless robe is a matter of profuse regret and my self-esteem can only be restored by your accepting in its place this threadbare one of mine. My rust-eaten sword is unworthy of your second thought. But certainly neither of these two details is the real reason of my dark despair."

"Disclose yourself more openly," urged Pe-lung.

"I now plainly recognize the futility of my well-intentioned quest. Obviously it is impossible to kill a dragon, and I am thus the sport either of Melodious Vision's deliberate ridicule or of my own ill-arranged presumption."

"Set your mind at rest upon that score: each blow was competently struck and convincingly fatal. You may quite fittingly claim to have slain half a dozen dragons at the least-none of the legendary champions of the past has done more."

"Yet how can so arrogant a claim be held, seeing that you stand before me in the unimpaired state of an ordinary existence?"

"The explanation is simple and assuring. It is, in reality, very easy to kill a dragon, but it is impossible to keep him dead. The reason for this is that the Five Essential Constituents of fire, water, earth, wood and metal are blended in our bodies in the Sublime or Indivisible proportion. Thus although it is not difficult by extreme violence to disturb the harmonious balance of the Constituents, and so bring about the effect of no-existence, they at once re-tranquillize again, and all effect of the ill usage is spontaneously repaired."

"That is certainly a logical solution, but it stands in doubtful stead when applied to the familiar requirements of life; nor is it probable that one so acute-witted as Melodious Vision would greet the claim with an acquiescent face," replied Chang Tao. "Not unnaturally is it said: 'He who kills tigers does not wear rat-skin sleeves.' It would be one thing to make a boast of having slain six dragons; it would be quite another to be bidden to bring in their tails."

"That is a difficulty which must be considered," admitted Pe-lung, "but a path round it will inevitably be found. In the meantime night is beginning to encircle us, and many dark Powers will be freed and resort to these inaccessible slopes. Accompany me, therefore, to my bankrupt hovel, where you will be safe until you care to resume your journey."

To this agreeable proposal Chang Tao at once assented. The way was long and laborious, "For," remarked Pe-lung, "in an ordinary course I should fly there in a single breath of time; but to seize an honoured guest by the body-cloth and thus transfer him over the side of a mountain is toilsome to the one and humiliating to the other."

To beguile the time he spoke freely of the hardships of his lot.

"We dragons are frequently objects of envy at the hands of the undiscriminating, but the few superficial privileges we enjoy are heavily balanced by the exacting scope of our duties. Thus to-night it is my degraded task to divert the course of the river flowing below us, so as to overwhelm the misguided town of Yang, wherein swells a sordid outcast who has reviled the Sacred Claw. In order to do this properly it will be my distressing part to lie across the bed of the stream, my head resting upon one bank and my tail upon the other, and so remain throughout the rigour of the night."

As they approached the cloudy pinnacle whereon was situated the dragon's cave, one came forth at a distance to meet them. As she drew near, alternating emotions from time to time swayed Chang Tao's mind. From beneath a well-ruled eyebrow Pe-lung continued to observe him closely.

"Fuh-sang, the unattractive daughter of my dwindling line," remarked the former person, with refined indifference. "I have rendered you invisible, and she, as her custom is, would advance to greet me."

"But this enchanting apparition is Melodious Vision!" exclaimed Chang Tao. "What new bewilderment is here?"

"Since you have thus expressed yourself, I will now throw off the mask and reveal fully why I have hitherto spared your life, and for what purpose I have brought you to these barren heights," replied Pe-lung. "In the past Shen Yi provoked the Deities, and to mark their displeasure it was decided to take away his she-child and to substitute for it one of demoniac birth. Accordingly Fuh-sang, being of like age, was moulded to its counterpart, and an attendant gnome was despatched with her secretly to make the change. Becoming overwhelmed with the fumes of rice-spirit, until then unknown to his simple taste, this clay-brained earth-pig left the two she-children alone for a space while he slept. Discovering each other to be the creature of another part, they battled together and tore from one another the signs of recognition. When the untrustworthy gnome recovered from his stupor he saw what he had done, but being terror-driven he took up one of the she-children at a venture and returned with a pliant tale. It was not until a few moons ago that while in a close extremity he confessed his crime. Meanwhile Shen Yi had made his peace with those Above and the order being revoked the she-children had been exchanged again. Thus the matter rests."

"Which, then, of the twain is she inherent of your house and which Melodious Vision?" demanded Chang Tao in some concern. "The matter can assuredly not rest thus."

"That," replied Pe-lung affably, "it will be your engaging task to unravel, and to this end will be your opportunity of closely watching Fuh-sang's unsuspecting movements in my absence through the night."

"Yet how should I, to whom the way of either maiden is as yet no more than the title-page of a many-volumed book, succeed where the father native to one has failed?"

"Because in your case the incentive will be deeper. Destined, as you doubtless are, to espouse Melodious Vision, the Forces connected with marriage and its Rites will certainly endeavour to inspire you. This person admittedly has no desire to nurture one who should prove to be of merely human seed, but your objection to propagating a race of dragonets turns on a keener edge. Added to all, a not unnatural disinclination to be dropped from so great a height as this into so deep and rocky a valley as that will conceivably lend wings to your usually nimble-footed mind."

While speaking to Chang Tao in this encouraging strain, Pe-lung was also conversing suitably with Fuh-sang, who had by this time joined them, warning her of his absence until the dawn, and the like. When he had completed his instruction he stroked her face affectionately, greeting Chang Tao with a short but appropriate farewell, and changing his form projected himself downwards into the darkness of the valley below. Recognizing that the situation into which he had been drawn possessed no other outlet, Chang Tao followed Fuh-sang on her backward path, and with her passed unsuspected into the dragon's cave.

Early as was Pe-lung's return on the ensuing morning, Chang Tao stood on a rocky eminence to greet him, and the outline of his face, though not altogether free of doubt, was by no means hopeless. Pe-lung still retained the impressive form of a gigantic dragon as he cleft the Middle Air, shining and iridescent, each beat of his majestic wings being as a roll of thunder and the skittering of sand and water from his crepitant scales leaving blights and rain-storms in his wake. When he saw Chang Tao he drove an earthward angle and alighting near at hand considerably changed into the semblance of an affluent merchant as he approached.

"Greeting," he remarked cheerfully. "Did you find your early rice?"

"It has sufficed," replied Chang Tao. "How is your own incomparable stomach?"

Pe-lung pointed to the empty bed of the deflected river and moved his head from side to side as one who draws an analogy to his own condition. "But of your more pressing enterprise," he continued, with sympathetic concern: "have you persevered to a fruitful end, or will it be necessary —?" And with tactful feeling he indicated the gesture of propelling an antagonist over the side of a precipice rather than allude to the disagreeable contingency in spoken words.

"When the oil is exhausted the lamp goes out," admitted Chang Tao, "but my time is not yet come. During the visionary watches of the night my poising mind was sustained by Forces as you so presciently foretold, and my groping hand was led to an inspired solution of the truth."

"This points to a specific end. Proceed," urged Pe-lung, for Chang Tao had hesitated among his words as though their import might not be soothing to the other's mind.

"Thus it is given me to declare: she who is called Melodious Vision is rightly of the house of Shen, and Fuh-sang is no less innate of your exalted tribe. The erring gnome, in spite of his misdeed, was but a finger of the larger hand of destiny, and as it is, it is."

"This assurance gladdens my face, no less for your sake than for my own," declared Pe-lung heartily. "For my part, I have found a way to enlarge you in the eyes of those whom you solicit. It is a custom with me that every thousand years I should discard my outer skin-not that it requires it, but there are certain standards to which we better-class dragons must conform. These sloughs are hidden beneath a secret stone, beyond the reach of the merely vain or curious. When you have disclosed the signs by which I shall have securance of Fuh-sang's identity I will pronounce the word and the stone being thus released you shall bear away six suits of scales in token of your prowess."

Then replied Chang Tao: "The signs, assuredly. Yet, omnipotence, without your express command the specific detail would be elusive to my respectful tongue."

"You have the authority of my extended hand," conceded Pe-lung readily, raising it as he spoke. "Speak freely."

"I claim the protection of its benignant shadow," said Chang Tao, with content. "You, O Pe-lung, are one who has mingled freely with creatures of every kind in all the Nine Spaces. Yet have you not, out of your vast experience thus gained, perceived the essential wherein men and dragons differ? Briefly and devoid of graceful metaphor, every dragon, esteemed, would seem to possess a tail; beings of my part have none."

For a concise moment the nature of Pe-lung's reflection was clouded in ambiguity, though the fact that he became entirely enveloped in a dense purple vapour indicated feelings of more than usual vigour. When this cleared away it left his outer form unchanged indeed, but the affable condescension of his manner was merged into one of dignified aloofness.

"Certainly all members of our enlightened tribe have tails," he replied, with distant precision, "nor does this one see how any other state is possible. Changing as we constantly do, both male and female, into Beings, Influences, Shadows and unclothed creatures of the lower parts, it is essential for our mutual self-esteem that in every manifestation we should be thus equipped. At this moment, though in the guise of a substantial trader, I possess a tail-small but adequate. Is it possible that you and those of your insolvent race are destitute?"

"In this particular, magnificence, I and those of my threadbare species are most lamentably deficient. To the proving of this end shall I display myself?"

"It is not necessary," said Pe-lung coldly. "It is inconceivable that, were it otherwise, you would admit the humiliating fact."

"Yet out of your millenaries of experience you must already —"

"It is well said that after passing a commonplace object a hundred times a day, at nightfall its size and colour are unknown to one," replied Pe-lung. "In this matter, from motives which cannot have been otherwise than delicate, I took too much for granted it would seem... . Then you-all-Shen Yi, Melodious Vision, the military governor of this province, even the sublime Emperor-all —?"

"All tailless," admitted Chang Tao, with conscious humility. "Nevertheless there is a tradition that in distant aeons —"

"Doubtless on some issue you roused the High Ones past forgiveness and were thus deprived as the most signal mark of their displeasure."

"Doubtless," assented Chang Tao, with unquenchable politeness.

"Coming to the correct attitude that you have maintained throughout, it would appear that during the silent gong-strokes of the night, by some obscure and indirect guidance it was revealed to you that Fuh-that any Being of my superior race was, on the contrary —" The menace of Pe-lung's challenging eye, though less direct and assured than formerly, had the manner of being uncertainly restrained by a single much-frayed thread, but Chang Tao continued to meet it with respectful self-possession.

"The inference is unflinching," he replied acquiescently. "I prostrate myself expectantly."

"You have competently performed your part," admitted Pe-lung, although an occasional jet of purple vapour clouded his upper person and the passage of his breath among his teeth would have been distasteful to one of sensitive refinement. "Nothing remains but the fulfilling of my iron word."

Thereupon he pronounced a mystic sign and revealing the opening to a cave he presently brought forth six sets of armoured skin. Binding these upon Chang Tao's back, he dismissed him, yet the manner of his parting was as of one who is doubtful even to the end.

Thus equipped —

But who having made a distant journey into Outer Land speaks lengthily of the level path of his return, or of the evening glow upon the gilded roof of his awaiting home? Thus, this limit being reached in the essential story of Chang Tao, Melodious Vision and the Dragon, he who relates their commonplace happenings bows submissively.

Nevertheless it is true that once again in a later time Chang Tao encountered in the throng one whom he recognized. Encouraged by the presence of so many of his kind, he approached the other and saluted him.

"Greeting, O Pe-lung," he said, with outward confidence. "What bends your footsteps to this busy place of men?"

"I come to buy an imitation pig-tail to pass for one," replied Pe-lung, with quiet composure. "Greeting, valorous champion! How fares Melodious Vision?"

"Agreeably so," admitted Chang Tao, and then, fearing that so far his reply had been inadequate, he added: "Yet, despite the facts, there are moments when this person almost doubts if he did not make a wrong decision in the matter after all."

"That is a very common complaint," said Pe-lung, becoming most offensively amused.

The Propitious Dissension Between Two Whose General Attributes Have Already Been Sufficiently Described

When Kai Lung had related the story of Chang Tao and had made an end of speaking, those who were seated there agreed with an undivided voice that he had competently fulfilled his task. Nor did Shan Tien omit an approving word, adding:

"On one point the historical balance of a certain detail seemed open to contention. Accompany me, therefore, to my own severe retreat, where this necessarily flat and unentertaining topic can be looked at from all round."

When they were alone together the Mandarin unsealed a jar of wine, apportioned melon seeds, and indicated to Kai Lung that he should sit upon the floor at a suitable distance from himself.

"So long as we do not lose sight of the necessity whereby my official position will presently involve me in condemning you to a painful death, and your loyal subjection will necessitate your whole-hearted co-operation in the act, there is no reason why the flower of literary excellence should wither for lack of mutual husbandry," remarked the broad-minded official tolerantly.

"Your enlightened patronage is a continual nourishment to the soil of my imagination," replied the story teller.

"As regards the doings of Chang Tao and of the various other personages who unite with him to form the fabric of the narrative, would not a strict adherence to the fable in its classical simplicity require the filling in of certain details which under your elusive tongue seemed, as you proceeded, to melt imperceptibly into a discreet background?"

"Your voice is just," confessed Kai Lung, "and your harmonious ear corrects the deficiencies of my afflicted style. Admittedly in the story of Chang Tao there are here and there analogies which may be fittingly left to the imagination as the occasion should demand. Is it not rightly said: 'Discretion is the handmaiden of Truth'? and in that spacious and well-appointed palace there is every kind of vessel, but the meaner are not to be seen in the more ceremonial halls. Thus he who tells a story prudently suits his furnishing to the condition of his hearers."

"Wisdom directs your course," replied Shan Tien, "and propriety sits beneath your supple tongue. As the necessity for this very seemly expurgation is now over, I would myself listen to your recital of the fullest and most detailed version-purely, let it be freely stated, in order to judge whether its literary qualities transcend those of the other."

"I comply, benevolence," replied Kai Lung. "This rendering shall be to the one that has gone before as a spreading banyan-tree overshadowing an immature shrub."

"Forbear!" exclaimed a discordant voice, and the sour-eyed Ming-shu revealed his inopportune presence from behind a hanging veil. "Is it meet, O eminence, that in this person's absence you should thus consort on terms of fraternity with tomb-riflers and grain-thieves?"

"The reproach is easily removed," replied Shan Tien hospitably. "Join the circle of our refined felicity and hear at full length by what means the ingenious Chang Tao —"

"There are moments when one despairs before the spectacle of authority thus displayed," murmured Ming-shu, his throat thickening with acrimony. "Understand, pre-eminence," he continued more aloud, "that not this one's absence but your own presence is the distressing feature, as being an obstacle in the path of that undeviating justice in which our legal system is embedded. From the first moment of our encountering it had been my well-intentioned purpose that loyal confidence should be strengthened and rebellion cowed by submitting this opportune but otherwise inoffensive stranger to a sordid and degrading end. Yet how shall this beneficent example be attained if on every occasion —"

"Your design is a worthy and enlightened one," interposed the Mandarin, with dignity. "What you have somewhat incapably overlooked, Ming-shu, is the fact that I never greet this intelligent and painstaking young man without reminding him of the imminence of his fate and of his suitability for it."

"Truth adorns your lips and accuracy anoints your palate," volunteered Kai Lung.

"Be this as the destinies permit, there is much that is circuitous in the bending of events," contended Ming-shu stubbornly. "Is it by chance or through some hidden tricklage that occasion always finds Kai Lung so adequately prepared?"

"It is, as the story of Chang Tao has this day justified, and as this discriminating person has frequently maintained, that the one in question has a story framed to meet the requirement of every circumstance," declared Shan Tien.

"Or that each requirement is subtly shaped to meet his preparation," retorted Ming-shu darkly. "Be that as it shall perchance ultimately appear, it is undeniable that your admitted weaknesses —"

"Weaknesses!" exclaimed the astonished Mandarin, looking around the room as though to discover in what crevice the unheard-of attributes were hidden. "This person's weaknesses? Can the sounding properties of this ill-constructed roof thus pervert one word into the semblance of another? If not, the bounds set to the admissible from the taker-down of the spoken word, Ming-shu, do not in their most elastic moods extend to calumny and distortion... . The one before you has no weaknesses... . Doubtless before another moon has changed you will impute to him actual faults!"

"Humility directs my gaze," replied Ming-shu, with downcast eyes, and he plainly recognized that his presumption had been too maintained. "Yet," he added, with polished irony, "there is a well-timed adage that rises to the lips: 'Do not despair; even Yuen Yan once cast a missile at the Tablets!'"

"Truly," agreed Shan Tien, with smooth concurrence, "the line is not unknown to me. Who, however, was the one in question and under what provocation did he so behave?"

"That is beyond the province of the saying," replied Ming-shu. "Nor is it known to my remembrance."

"Then out of your own mouth a fitting test is set, which if Kai Lung can agreeably perform will at once demonstrate a secret and a guilty confederacy between you both. Proceed, O storyteller, to incriminate Ming-shu together with yourself!"

"I proceed, High Excellence, but chiefly to the glorification of your all-discerning mind," replied Kai Lung.

The Story of Yuen Yan, of the Barber Chou-hu, and His Wife Tsae-che

"Do not despair; even Yuen Yan once cast a missile at the Tablets," is a proverb of encouragement well worn throughout the Empire; but although it is daily on the lips of some it is doubtful if a single person could give an intelligent account of the Yuen Yan in question beyond repeating the outside facts that he was of a humane and consistent disposition and during the greater part of his life possessed every desirable attribute of wealth, family and virtuous esteem. If more closely questioned with reference to the specific incident alluded to, these persons would not hesitate to assert that the proverb was not to be understood in so superficial a sense, protesting, with much indignation, that Yuen Yan was of too courteous and lofty a nature to be guilty of so unseemly an action, and contemptuously inquiring what possible reason one who enjoyed every advantage in this world and every prospect of an unruffled felicity in The Beyond could have for behaving in so outrageous a manner. This explanation by no means satisfied the one who now narrates, and after much research he has brought to light the forgotten story of Yuen Yan's early life, which may be thus related.

At the period with which this part of the narrative is concerned, Yuen Yan dwelt with his mother in one of the least attractive of the arches beneath the city wall. As a youth it had been his intention to take an exceptionally high place in the public examinations, and, rising at once to a position of responsible authority, to mark himself out for continual promotion by the exercise of unfailing discretion and indomitable zeal. Having saved his country in a moment of acute national danger, he contemplated accepting a title of unique distinction and retiring to his native province, where he would build an adequate palace which he had already planned out down to the most trivial detail. There he purposed spending the remainder of his life, receiving frequent tokens of regard from the hand of the gratified Emperor, marrying an accomplished and refined wife who would doubtless be one of the princesses of the Imperial House, and conscientiously regarding The Virtues throughout. The transition from this sumptuously contrived residence to a damp arch in the city wall, and from the high destiny indicated to the occupation of leading from place to place a company of sightless mendicants, had been neither instantaneous nor painless, but Yuen Yan had never for a moment wavered from the enlightened maxims which he had adopted as his guiding principles, nor did he suffer unending trials to lessen his reverence for The Virtues. "Having set out with the full intention of becoming a wealthy mandarin, it would have been a small achievement to have reached that position with unshattered ideals," he frequently remarked; "but having thus set out it is a matter for more than ordinary congratulation to have fallen to the position of leading a string of blind beggars about the city and still to retain unimpaired the ingenuous beliefs and aspirations of youth."

"Doubtless," replied his aged mother, whenever she chanced to overhear this honourable reflection, "doubtless the foolish calf who innocently puts his foot into the jelly finds a like consolation. This person, however, would gladly exchange the most illimitable moral satisfaction engendered by acute poverty for a few of the material comforts of a sordid competence, nor would she hesitate to throw into the balance all the aspirations and improving sayings to be found within the Classics."

"Esteemed mother," protested Yan, "more than three thousand years ago the royal philosopher Nin-hyo made the observation: 'Better an earth-lined cave from which the stars are visible than a golden pagoda roofed over with iniquity,' and the saying has stood the test of time."

"The remark would have carried a weightier conviction if the broad-minded sovereign had himself first stood the test of lying for a few years with enlarged joints and afflicted bones in the abode he so prudently recommended for others," replied his mother, and without giving Yuen Yan any opportunity of bringing forward further proof of their highly-favoured destiny she betook herself to her own straw at the farthest end of the arch.

Up to this period of his life Yuen Yan's innate reverence and courtesy of manner had enabled him to maintain an impassive outlook in the face of every discouragement, but now he was exposed to a fresh series of trials in addition to the unsympathetic attitude which his mother never failed to unroll before him. It has already been expressed that Yuen Yan's occupation and the manner by which he gained his livelihood consisted in leading a number of blind mendicants about the streets of the city and into the shops and dwelling-places of those who might reasonably be willing to pay in order to be relieved of their presence. In this profession Yan's venerating and custom-regarding nature compelled him to act as leaders of blind beggars had acted throughout all historical times and far back into the dim recesses of legendary epochs and this, in an era when the leisurely habits of the past were falling into disuse, and when rivals and competitors were springing up on all sides, tended almost daily to decrease the proceeds of his labour and to sow an insidious doubt even in his unquestioning mind.

In particular, among those whom Yan regarded most objectionably was one named Ho. Although only recently arrived in the city from a country beyond the Bitter Water, Ho was already known in every quarter both to the merchants and stallkeepers, who trembled at his approaching shadow, and to the competing mendicants who now counted their cash with two fingers where they had before needed both hands. This distressingly active person made no secret of his methods and intention; for, upon his arrival, he plainly announced that his object was to make the foundations of benevolence vibrate like the strings of a many-toned lute, and he compared his general progress through the haunts of the charitably disposed to the passage of a highly-charged firework through an assembly of meditative turtles. He was usually known, he added, as "the rapidly-moving person," or "the one devoid of outline," and it soon became apparent that he was also quite destitute of all dignified restraint. Selecting the place of commerce of some wealthy merchant, Ho entered without hesitation and thrusting aside the waiting customers he continued to strike the boards impatiently until he gained the attention of the chief merchant himself. "Honourable salutations," he would say, "but do not entreat this illiterate person to enter the inner room, for he cannot tarry to discuss the movements of the planets or the sublime Emperor's health. Behold, for half-a-tael of silver you may purchase immunity from his discreditable persistence for seven days; here is the acknowledgement duly made out and attested. Let the payment be made in pieces of metal and not in paper obligations." Unless immediate compliance followed Ho at once began noisily to cast down the articles of commerce, to roll bodily upon the more fragile objects, to become demoniacally possessed on the floor, and to resort to a variety of expedients until all the customers were driven forth in panic.

In the case of an excessively stubborn merchant he had not hesitated to draw a formidable knife and to gash himself in a superficial but very imposing manner; then he had rushed out uttering cries of terror, and sinking down by the door had remained there for the greater part of the day, warning those who would have entered to be upon their guard against being enticed in and murdered, at the same time groaning aloud and displaying his own wounds. Even this seeming disregard of time was well considered, for when the tidings spread about the city other merchants did not wait for Ho to enter and greet them, but standing at their doors money in hand they pressed it upon him the moment he appeared and besought him to remove his distinguished presence from their plague-infected street. To the ordinary mendicants of the city this stress of competition was disastrous, but to Yuen Yan it was overwhelming. Thoroughly imbued with the deferential systems of antiquity, he led his band from place to place with a fitting regard for the requirements of ceremonial etiquette and a due observance of leisurely unconcern. Those to whom he addressed himself he approached with obsequious tact, and in the face of refusal to contribute to his store his most violent expedient did not go beyond marshalling his company of suppliants in an orderly group upon the shop floor, where they sang in unison a composed chant extolling the fruits of munificence and setting forth the evil plight which would certainly attend the flinty-stomached in the Upper Air. In this way Yuen Yan had been content to devote several hours to a single shop in the hope of receiving finally a few pieces of brass money; but now his persecutions were so mild that the merchants and vendors rather welcomed him by comparison with the intolerable Ho, and would on no account pay to be relieved of the infliction of his presence. "Have we not disbursed in one day to the piratical Ho thrice the sum which we had set by to serve its purpose for a hand-count of moons; and do we possess the Great Secret?" they cried. "Nevertheless, dispose your engaging band of mendicants about the place freely until it suits your refined convenience to proceed elsewhere, O meritorious Yuen Yan, for your unassuming qualities have won our consistent regard; but an insatiable sponge has already been laid upon the well-spring of our benevolence and the tenacity of our closed hand is inflexible."

Even the passive mendicants began to murmur against his leadership, urging him that he should adopt some of the simpler methods of the gifted Ho and thereby save them all from an otherwise inevitable starvation. The Emperor Kai-tsing, said the one who led their voices (referring in his malignant bitterness to a sovereign of the previous dynasty), was dead, although the fact had doubtless escaped Yuen Yan's deliberate perception. The methods of four thousand years ago were becoming obsolete in the face of a strenuous competition, and unless Yuen Yan was disposed to assume a more highly-coiled appearance they must certainly address themselves to another leader.

It was on this occasion that the incident took place which has passed down in the form of an inspiriting proverb. Yuen Yan had conscientiously delivered at the door of his abode the last of his company and was turning his footsteps towards his own arch when he encountered the contumelious Ho, who was likewise returning at the close of a day's mendicancy-but with this distinction: that, whereas Ho was followed by two stalwart attendants carrying between them a sack full of money, Yan's share of his band's enterprise consisted solely of one base coin of a kind which the charitable set aside for bestowing upon the blind and quite useless for all ordinary purposes of exchange. A few paces farther on Yan reached the Temple of the Unseen Forces and paused for a moment, as his custom was, to cast his eyes up to the tablets engraved with The Virtues, before which some devout person nightly hung a lantern. Goaded by a sudden impulse, Yan looked each way about the deserted street, and perceiving that he was alone he deliberately extended his out-thrust tongue towards the inspired precepts. Then taking from an inner sleeve the base coin he flung it at the inscribed characters and observed with satisfaction that it struck the verse beginning, "The Rewards of a Quiescent and Mentally-introspective Life are Unbounded —"

When Yan entered his arch some hours later his mother could not fail to perceive that a subtle change had come over his manner of behaving. Much of the leisurely dignity had melted out of his footsteps, and he wore his hat and outer garments at an angle which plainly testified that he was a person who might be supposed to have a marked objection to returning home before the early hours of the morning. Furthermore, as he entered he was chanting certain melodious words by which he endeavoured to convey the misleading impression that his chief amusement consisted in defying the official watchers of the town, and he continually reiterated a claim to be regarded as "one of the beardless goats." Thus expressing himself, Yan sank down in his appointed corner and would doubtlessly soon have been floating peacefully in the Middle Distance had not the door been again thrown open and a stranger named Chou-hu entered.

"Prosperity!" said Chou-hu courteously, addressing himself to Yan's mother. "Have you eaten your rice? Behold, I come to lay before you a very attractive proposal regarding your son."

"The flower attracts the bee, but when he departs it is to his lips that the honey clings," replied the woman cautiously; for after Yan's boastful words on entering she had a fear lest haply this person might be one on behalf of some guardian of the night whom her son had flung across the street (as he had specifically declared his habitual treatment of them to be) come to take him by stratagem.

"Does the pacific lamb become a wolf by night?" said Chou-hu, displaying himself reassuringly. "Wrap your ears well round my words, for they may prove very remunerative. It cannot be a matter outside your knowledge that the profession of conducting an assembly of blind mendicants from place to place no longer yields the wage of even a frugal existence in this city. In the future, for all the sympathy that he will arouse, Yan might as well go begging with a silver bowl. In consequence of his speechless condition he will be unable to support either you or himself by any other form of labour, and your line will thereupon become extinct and your standing in the Upper Air be rendered intolerable."

"It is a remote contingency, but, as the proverb says, 'The wise hen is never too old to dread the Spring,'" replied Yan's mother, with commendable prudence. "By what means, then, may this calamity be averted?"

"The person before you," continued Chou-hu, "is a barber and embellisher of pig-tails from the street leading to the Three-tiered Pagoda of Eggs. He has long observed the restraint and moderation of Yan's demeanour and now being in need of one to assist him his earliest thought turns to him. The affliction which would be an insuperable barrier in all ordinary cases may here be used to advantage, for being unable to converse with those seated before him, or to hear their salutations, Yan will be absolved from the necessity of engaging in diffuse and refined conversation, and in consequence he will submit at least twice the number of persons to his dexterous energies. In that way he will secure a higher reward than this person could otherwise afford and many additional comforts will doubtless fall into the sleeve of his engaging mother."

At this point the woman began to understand that the sense in which Chou-hu had referred to Yan's speechless condition was not that which she had at the time deemed it to be. It may here be made clear that it was Yuen Yan's custom to wear suspended about his neck an inscribed board bearing the words, "Speechless, and devoid of the faculty of hearing," but this originated out of his courteous and deferential nature (for to his self-obliterative mind it did not seem respectful that he should appear to be better endowed than those whom he led), nor could it be asserted that he wilfully deceived even the passing stranger, for he would freely enter into conversation with anyone whom he encountered. Nevertheless an impression had thus been formed in Chou-hu's mind and the woman forbore to correct it, thinking that it would be scarcely polite to assert herself better informed on any subject than he was, especially as he had spoken of Yan thereby receiving a higher wage. Yan himself would certainly have revealed something had he not been otherwise employed. Hearing the conversation turn towards his afflictions, he at once began to search very industriously among the straw upon which he lay for the inscribed board in question; for to his somewhat confused imagination it seemed at the time that only by displaying it openly could he prove to Chou-hu that he was in no way deficient. As the board was found on the following morning nailed to the great outer door of the Hall of Public Justice (where it remained for many days owing to the official impression that so bold and undeniable a pronouncement must have received the direct authority of the sublime Emperor), Yan was not unnaturally engaged for a considerable time, and in the meanwhile his mother contrived to impress upon him by an unmistakable sign that he should reveal nothing, but leave the matter in her hands.

Then said Yan's mother: "Truly the proposal is not altogether wanting in alluring colours, but in what manner will Yan interpret the commands of those who place themselves before him, when he has attained sufficient proficiency to be entrusted with the knife and the shearing irons?"

"The objection is a superficial one," replied Chou-hu. "When a person seats himself upon the operating stool he either throws back his head, fixing his eyes upon the upper room with a set and resolute air, or inclines it slightly forward as in a reverent tranquillity. In the former case he requires his uneven surfaces to be made smooth; in the latter he is desirous that his pig-tail should be drawn out and trimmed. Do not doubt Yan's capability to conduct himself in a discreet and becoming manner, but communicate to him, by the usual means which you adopt, the offer thus laid out, and unless he should be incredibly obtuse or unfilial to a criminal degree he will present himself at the Sign of the Gilt Thunderbolt at an early hour to-morrow."

There is a prudent caution expressed in the proverb, "The hand that feeds the ox grasps the knife when it is fattened: crawl backwards from the presence of a munificent official." Chou-hu, in spite of his plausible pretext, would have experienced no difficulty in obtaining the services of one better equipped to assist him than was Yuen Yan, so that in order to discover his real object it becomes necessary to look underneath his words. He was indeed, as he had stated, a barber and an embellisher of pig-tails, and for many years he had grown rich and round-bodied on the reputation of being one of the most skilful within his quarter of the city. In an evil moment, however, he had abandoned the moderation of his past life and surrounded himself with an atmosphere of opium smoke and existed continually in the mind-dimming effects of rice-spirit. From this cause his custom began to languish; his hand no longer swept in the graceful and unhesitating curves which had once been the admiration of all beholders, but displayed on the contrary a very disconcerting irregularity of movement, and on the day of his visit he had shorn away the venerable moustaches of the baker Heng-cho under a mistaken impression as to the reality of things and a wavering vision of their exact position. Now the baker had been inordinately proud of his long white moustaches and valued them above all his possessions, so that, invoking the spirits of his ancestors to behold his degradation and to support him in his resolve, and calling in all the passers-by to bear witness to his oath, he had solemnly bound himself either to cut down Chou-hu fatally, or, should that prove too difficult an accomplishment, to commit suicide within his shop. This twofold danger thoroughly stupefied Chou-hu and made him incapable of taking any action beyond consuming further and more unstinted portions of rice-spirit and rending article after article of his apparel until his wife Tsae-che modestly dismissed such persons as loitered, and barred the outer door.

"Open your eyes upon the facts by which you are surrounded, O contemptible Chou-hu," she said, returning to his side and standing over him. "Already your degraded instincts have brought us within measurable distance of poverty, and if you neglect your business to avoid Heng-cho, actual want will soon beset us. If you remain openly within his sight you will certainly be removed forcibly to the Upper Air, leaving this inoffensive person destitute and abandoned, and if by the exercise of unfailing vigilance you escape both these dangers, you will be reserved to an even worse plight, for Heng-cho in desperation will inevitably carry out the latter part of his threat, dedicating his spirit to the duty of continually haunting you and frustrating your ambitions here on earth and calling to his assistance myriads of ancestors and relations to torment you in the Upper Air."

"How attractively and in what brilliantly-coloured outlines do you present the various facts of existence!" exclaimed Chou-hu, with inelegant resentment. "Do not neglect to add that, to-morrow being the occasion of the Moon Festival, the inexorable person who owns this residence will present himself to collect his dues, that, in consequence of the rebellion in the south, the sagacious viceroy has doubled the price of opium, that some irredeemable outcast has carried away this person's blue silk umbrella, and then doubtless the alluring picture of internal felicity around the Ancestral Altar of the Gilt Thunderbolt will be complete."

"Light words are easily spoken behind barred doors," said his wife scornfully. "Let my lord, then, recline indolently upon the floor of his inner chamber while this person sumptuously lulls him into oblivion with the music of her voice, regardless of the morrow and of the fate in which his apathy involves us both."

"By no means!" exclaimed Chou-hu, rising hastily and tearing away much of his elaborately arranged pigtail in his uncontrollable rage; "there is yet a more pleasurable alternative than that and one which will ensure to this person a period of otherwise unattainable domestic calm and at the same time involve a detestable enemy in confusion. Anticipating the dull-witted Heng-cho /this/ one will now proceed across the street and, committing suicide within /his/ door, will henceforth enjoy the honourable satisfaction of haunting /his/ footsteps and rending his bakehouses and ovens untenable." With this assurance Chou-hu seized one of his most formidable business weapons and caused it to revolve around his head with great rapidity, but at the same time with extreme carefulness.

"There is a ready saying: 'The new-born lamb does not fear a tiger, but before he becomes a sheep he will flee from a wolf,'" said Tsae-che without in any way deeming it necessary to arrest Chou-hu's hand. "Full confidently will you set out, O Chou-hu, but to reach the shop of Heng-cho it is necessary to pass the stall of the dealer in abandoned articles, and next to it are enticingly spread out the wares of Kong, the merchant in distilled spirits. Put aside your reliable scraping iron while you still have it, and this not ill-disposed person will lay before you a plan by which you may even yet avoid all inconveniences and at the same time regain your failing commerce."

"It is also said: 'The advice of a wise woman will ruin a walled city,'" replied Chou-hu, somewhat annoyed at his wife so opportunely comparing him to a sheep, but still more concerned to hear by what possible expedient she could successfully avert all the contending dangers of his position. "Nevertheless, proceed."

"In one of the least reputable quarters of the city there dwells a person called Yuen Yan," said the woman. "He is the leader of a band of sightless mendicants and in this position he has frequently passed your open door, though-probably being warned by the benevolent-he has never yet entered. Now this Yuen Yan, save for one or two unimportant details, is the reflected personification of your own exalted image, nor would those most intimate with your form and outline be able to pronounce definitely unless you stood side by side before them. Furthermore, he is by nature unable to hear any remark addressed to him, and is incapable of expressing himself in spoken words. Doubtless by these indications my lord's locust-like intelligence will already have leapt to an inspired understanding of the full project?"

"Assuredly," replied Chou-hu, caressing himself approvingly. "The essential details of the scheme are built about the ease with which this person could present himself at the abode of Yuen Yan in his absence and, gathering together that one's store of wealth unquestioned, retire with it to a distant and unknown spot and thereby elude the implacable Heng-cho's vengeance."

"Leaving your menial one in the 'walled city' referred to, to share its fate, and, in particular, to undertake the distressing obligation of gathering up the atrocious Heng-cho after he has carried his final threat into effect? Truly must the crystal stream of your usually undimmed intelligence have become vaporized. Listen well. Disguising your external features slightly so that the resemblance may pass without remark, present yourself openly at the residence of the Yuen Yan in question—"

"First learning where it is situated?" interposed Chou-hu, with a desire to grasp the details competently.

"Unless a person of your retrospective taste would prefer to leave so trivial a point until afterwards," replied his wife in a tone of concentrated no-sincerity. "In either case, however, having arrived there, bargain with the one who has authority over Yuen Yan's movements, praising his demeanour and offering to accept him into the honours and profits of your craft. The words of acquiescence should spring to meet your own, for the various branches of mendicancy are languishing, and Yuen Yan can have no secret store of wealth. Do not hesitate to offer a higher wage than you would as an affair of ordinary commerce, for your safety depends upon it. Having secured Yan, teach him quickly the unpolished outlines of your business and then clothing him in robes similar to your own let him take his stand within the shop and withdraw yourself to the inner chamber. None will suspect the artifice, and Yuen Yan is manifestly incapable of betraying it. Heng-cho, seeing him display himself openly, will not deem it necessary to commit suicide yet, and, should he cut down Yan fatally, the officials of the street will seize him and your own safety will be assured. Finally, if nothing particular happens, at least your prosperity will be increased, for Yuen Yan will prove /industrious/, /frugal/, /not addicted to excesses/ and in every way /reliable/, and towards the shop of so exceptional a barber customers will turn in an unending stream."

"Alas!" exclaimed Chou-hu, "when you boasted of an inspired scheme this person for a moment foolishly allowed his mind to contemplate the possibility of your having accidentally stumbled upon such an expedient haply, but your suggestion is only comparable with a company of ducks attempting to cross an ice-bound stream-an excessive outlay of action but no beneficial progress. Should Yuen Yan freely present himself here on the morrow, pleading destitution and craving to be employed, this person will consider the petition with an open head, but it is beneath his dignity to wait upon so low-class an object." Affecting to recollect an arranged meeting of some importance, Chou-hu then clad himself in other robes, altered the appearance of his face, and set out to act in the manner already described, confident that the exact happening would never reach his lesser one's ears.

On the following day Yuen Yan presented himself at the door of the Gilt Thunderbolt, and quickly perfecting himself in the simpler methods of smoothing surfaces and adorning pig-tails he took his stand within the shop and operated upon all who came to submit themselves to his embellishment. To those who addressed him with salutations he replied by a gesture, tactfully bestowing an agreeable welcome yet at the same time conveying the impression that he was desirous of remaining undisturbed in the philosophical reflection upon which he was engaged. In spite of this it was impossible to lead his mind astray from any weighty detail, and those who, presuming upon his absorbed attitude, endeavoured to evade a just payment on any pretext whatever invariably found themselves firmly but courteously pressed to the wall by the neck, while a highly polished smoothing blade was flashed to and fro before their eyes with an action of unmistakable significance. The number of customers increased almost daily, for Yan quickly proved himself to be expert above all comparison, while others came from every quarter of the city to test with their own eyes and ears the report that had reached them, to the effect that in the street leading to the Three-tiered Pagoda of Eggs there dwelt a barber who made no pretence of elegant and refined conversation and who did not even press upon those lying helpless in his power miraculous ointments and infallible charm-waters. Thus Chou-hu prospered greatly, but Yan still obeyed his mother's warning and raised a mask before his face so that Chou-hu and his wife never doubted the reality of his infirmities. From this cause they did not refrain from conversing together freely before him on subjects of the most poignant detail, whereby Yan learned much of their past lives and conduct while maintaining an attitude of impassive unconcern.

Upon a certain evening in the month when the grass-blades are transformed into silk-worms Yan was alone in the shop, improving the edge and reflecting brilliance of some of his implements, when he heard the woman exclaim from the inner room: "Truly the air from the desert is as hot and devoid of relief as the breath of the Great Dragon. Let us repose for the time in the outer chamber." Whereupon they entered the shop and seating themselves upon a couch resumed their occupations, the barber fanning himself while he smoked, his wife gumming her hair and coiling it into the semblance of a bird with outstretched wings.

"The necessity for the elaborate caution of the past no longer exists," remarked Chou-hu presently. "The baker Heng-cho is desirous of becoming one of those who select the paving-stones and regulate the number of hanging lanterns for the district lying around the Three-tiered Pagoda. In this ambition he is opposed by Kong, the distilled-spirit vendor, who claims to be a more competent judge of paving-stones and hanging lanterns and one who will exercise a lynx-eyed vigilance upon the public outlay and especially devote himself to curbing the avarice of those bread-makers who habitually mix powdered white earth with their flour. Heng-cho is therefore very concerned that many should bear honourable testimony of his engaging qualities when the day of trial arrives, and thus positioned he has inscribed and sent to this person a written message offering a dignified reconciliation and adding that he is convinced of the necessity of an enactment compelling all persons to wear a smooth face and a neatly braided pig-tail."

"It is a creditable solution of the matter," said Tsae-che, speaking between the ivory pins which she held in her mouth. "Henceforth, then, you will take up your accustomed stand as in the past?"

"Undoubtedly," replied Chou-hu. "Yuen Yan is painstaking, and has perhaps done as well as could be expected of one of his shallow intellect, but the absence of suave and high-minded conversation cannot fail to be alienating the custom of the more polished. Plainly it is a short-sighted policy for a person to try and evade his destiny. Yan seems to have been born for the express purpose of leading blind beggars about the streets of the city and to that profession he must return."

"O distressingly superficial Chou-hu!" exclaimed his wife, "do men turn willingly from wine to partake of vinegar, or having been clothed in silk do they accept sackcloth without a struggle? Indeed, your eyes, which are large to regard your own deeds and comforts, grow small when they are turned towards the attainments of another. In no case will Yan return to his mendicants, for his band is by this time scattered and dispersed. His sleeve being now well lined and his hand proficient in every detail of his craft, he will erect a stall, perchance even directly opposite or next to ourselves, and by subtlety, low charges and diligence he will draw away the greater part of your custom."

"Alas!" cried Chou-hu, turning an exceedingly inferior yellow, "there is a deeper wisdom in the proverb, 'Do not seek to escape from a flood by clinging to a tiger's tail,' than appears at a casual glance. Now that this person is contemplating gathering again into his own hands the execution of his business, he cannot reasonably afford to employ another, yet it is an intolerable thought that Yan should make use of his experience to set up a sign opposed to the Gilt Thunderbolt. Obviously the only really safe course out of an unpleasant dilemma will be to slay Yan with as little delay as possible. After receiving continuous marks of our approval for so long it is certainly very thoughtless of him to put us to so unpardonable an inconvenience."

"It is not an alluring alternative," confessed Tsae-che, crossing the room to where Yan was seated in order to survey her hair to greater advantage in a hanging mirror of three sides composed of burnished copper; "but there seems nothing else to be done in the difficult circumstances."

"The street is opportunely empty and there is little likelihood of anyone approaching at this hour," suggested Chou-hu. "What better scheme could be devised than that I should indicate to Yan by signs that I would honour him, and at the same time instruct him further in the correct pose of some of the recognized attitudes, by making smooth the surface of his face? Then during the operation I might perchance slip upon an overripe whampee lying unperceived upon the floor; my hand —"

"Ah-/ah/!" cried Tsae-che aloud, pressing her symmetrical fingers against her gracefully-proportioned ears; "do not, thou dragon-headed one, lead the conversation to such an extremity of detail, still less carry the resolution into effect before the very eyes of this delicately-susceptible person. Now to-morrow, after the midday meal, she will be journeying as far as the street of the venders of woven fabrics in order to procure a piece of silk similar to the pearl-grey robe which she is wearing. The opportunity will be a favourable one, for to-morrow is the weekly occasion on which you raise the shutters and deny customers at an earlier hour; and it is really more modest that one of my impressionable refinement should be away from the house altogether and not merely in the inner chamber when that which is now here passes out."

"The suggestion is well timed," replied Chou-hu. "No interruption will then be possible."

"Furthermore," continued his wife, sprinkling upon her hair a perfumed powder of gold which made it sparkle as it engaged the light at every point with a most entrancing lustre, "would it not be desirable to use a weapon less identified with your own hand? In the corner nearest to Yan there stands a massive and heavily knotted club which could afterwards be burned. It would be an easy matter to call the simple Yan's attention to some object upon the floor and then as he bent down suffer him to Pass Beyond."

"Assuredly," agreed Chou-hu, at once perceiving the wisdom of the change; "also, in that case, there would be less —"

"/Ah/!" again cried the woman, shaking her upraised finger reprovingly at Chou-hu (for so daintily endowed was her mind that she shrank from any of the grosser realities of the act unless they were clothed in the very gilded flowers of speech). "Desist, O crimson-minded barbarian! Let us now walk side by side along the river bank and drink in the soul-stirring melody of the musicians who at this hour will be making the spot doubly attractive with the concord of stringed woods and instruments of brass struck with harmonious unison."

The scheme for freeing Chou-hu from the embarrassment of Yan's position was not really badly arranged, nor would it have failed in most cases, but the barber was not sufficiently broad-witted to see that many of the inspired sayings which he used as arguments could be taken in another light and conveyed a decisive warning to himself. A pleasantly devised proverb has been aptly compared to a precious jewel, and as the one has a hundred light-reflecting surfaces, so has the other a diversity of applications, until it is not infrequently beyond the comprehension of an ordinary person to know upon which side wisdom and prudence lie. On the following afternoon Yan was seated in his accustomed corner when Chou-hu entered the shop with uneven feet. The barriers against the street had been raised and the outer door was barred so that none might intrude, while Chou-hu had already carefully examined the walls to ensure that no crevices remained unsealed. As he entered he was seeking, somewhat incoherently, to justify himself by assuring the deities that he had almost changed his mind until he remembered the many impious acts on Yan's part in the past, to avenge which he felt himself to be their duly appointed instrument. Furthermore, to convince them of the excellence of his motive (and also to protect himself against the influence of evil spirits) he advanced repeating the words of an invocation which in his youth he had been accustomed to say daily in the temple, and thereupon Yan knew that the moment was at hand.

"Behold, master!" he exclaimed suddenly, in clearly expressed words, "something lies at your feet."

Chou-hu looked down to the floor and lying before him was a piece of silver. To his dull and confused faculties it sounded an inaccurate detail of his pre-arranged plan that Yan should have addressed him, and the remark itself seemed dimly to remind him of something that he had intended to say, but he was too involved with himself to be able to attach any logical significance to the facts and he at once stooped greedily to possess the coin. Then Yan, who had an unfaltering grasp upon the necessities of each passing second, sprang agilely forward, swung the staff, and brought it so proficiently down upon Chou-hu's lowered head that the barber dropped lifeless to the ground and the weapon itself was shattered by the blow. Without a pause Yan clothed himself with his master's robes and ornaments, wrapped his own garment about Chou-hu instead, and opening a stone door let into the ground rolled the body through so that it dropped down into the cave beneath. He next altered the binding of his hair a little, cut his lips deeply for a set purpose, and then reposing upon the couch of the inner chamber he took up one of Chou-hu's pipes and awaited Tsae-che's return.

"It is unendurable that they of the silk market should be so ill-equipped," remarked Tsae-che discontentedly as she entered. "This pitiable one has worn away the heels of her sandals in a vain endeavour to procure a suitable embroidery, and has turned over the contents of every stall to no material end. How have the events of the day progressed with you, my lord?"

"To the fulfilling of a written destiny. Yet in a measure darkly, for a light has gone out," replied Yuen Yan.

"There was no unanticipated divergence?" inquired the woman with interest and a marked approval of this delicate way of expressing the operation of an unpleasant necessity.

"From detail to detail it was as this person desired and contrived," said Yan.

"And, of a surety, this one also?" claimed Tsae-che, with an internal emotion that something was insidiously changed in which she had no adequate part.

"The language may be fully expressed in six styles of writing, but who shall read the mind of a woman?" replied Yan evasively. "Nevertheless, in explicit words, the overhanging shadow has departed and the future is assured."

"It is well," said Tsae-che. "Yet how altered is your voice, and for what reason do you hold a cloth before your mouth?"

"The staff broke and a splinter flying upwards pierced my lips," said Yan, lowering the cloth. "You speak truly, for the pain attending each word is by no means slight, and scarcely can this person recognize his own voice."

"Oh, incomparable Chou-hu, how valiantly do you bear your sufferings!" exclaimed Tsae-che remorsefully. "And while this heedless one has been passing the time pleasantly in handling rich brocades you have been lying here in anguish. Behold now, without delay she will prepare food to divert your mind, and to mark the occasion she had already purchased a little jar of gold-fish gills, two eggs branded with the assurance that they have been earth-buried for eleven years, and a small serpent preserved in oil."

When they had eaten for some time in silence Yuen Yan again spoke. "Attend closely to my words," he said, "and if you perceive any disconcerting oversight in the scheme which I am about to lay before you do not hesitate to declare it. The threat which Heng-cho the baker swore he swore openly, and many reputable witnesses could be gathered together who would confirm his words, while the written message of reconciliation which he sent will be known to none. Let us therefore take that which lies in the cave beneath and clothing it in my robes bear it unperceived as soon as the night has descended and leave it in the courtyard of Heng-cho's house. Now Heng-cho has a fig plantation outside the city, so that when he rises early, as his custom is, and finds the body, he will carry it away to bury it secretly there, remembering his impetuous words and well knowing the net of entangling circumstances which must otherwise close around him. At that moment you will appear before him, searching for your husband, and suspecting his burden raise an outcry that may draw the neighbours to your side if necessary. On this point, however, be discreetly observant, for if the tumult calls down the official watch it will go evilly with Heng-cho, but we shall profit little. The greater likelihood is that as soon as you lift up your voice the baker will implore you to accompany him back to his house so that he may make a full and honourable compensation. This you will do, and hastening the negotiation as much as is consistent with a seemly regard for your overwhelming grief, you will accept not less than five hundred taels and an undertaking that a suitable funeral will be provided."

"O thrice-versatile Chou-hu!" exclaimed Tsae-che, whose eyes had reflected an ever-increasing sparkle of admiration as Yan unfolded the details of his scheme, "how insignificant are the minds of others compared with yours! Assuredly you have been drinking at some magic well in this one's absence, for never before was your intellect so keen and lustreful. Let us at once carry your noble stratagem into effect, for this person's toes vibrate to bear her on a project of such remunerative ingenuity."

Accordingly they descended into the cave beneath and taking up Chou-hu they again dressed him in his own robes. In his inner sleeve Yan placed some parchments of slight importance; he returned the jade bracelet to his wrist and by other signs he made his identity unmistakable; then lifting him between them, when the night was well advanced, they carried him through unfrequented ways and left him unperceived within Heng-cho's gate.

"There is yet another precaution which will ensure to you the sympathetic voices of all if it should become necessary to appeal openly," said Yuen Yan when they had returned. "I will make out a deed of final intention conferring all I possess upon Yuen Yan as a mark of esteem for his conscientious services, and this you can produce if necessary in order to crush the niggard baker in the wine-press of your necessitous destitution." Thereupon Yan drew up such a document as he had described, signing it with Chou-hu's name and sealing it with his ring, while Tsae-che also added her sign and attestation. He then sent her to lurk upon the roof, strictly commanding her to keep an undeviating watch upon Heng-cho's movements.

It was about the hour before dawn when Heng-cho appeared, bearing across his back a well-filled sack and carrying in his right hand a spade. His steps were turned towards the fig orchard of which Yan had spoken, so that he must pass Chou-hu's house, but before he reached it Tsae-che had glided out and with loosened hair and trailing robes she sped along the street. Presently there came to Yuen Yan's waiting ear a long-drawn cry and the sounds of many shutters being flung open and the tread of hurrying feet. The moments hung about him like the wings of a dragon-dream, but a prudent restraint chained him to the inner chamber.

It was fully light when Tsae-che returned, accompanied by one whom she dismissed before she entered. "Felicity," she explained, placing before Yan a heavy bag of silver. "Your word has been accomplished."

"It is sufficient," replied Yan in a tone from which every tender modulation was absent, as he laid the silver by the side of the parchment which he had drawn up. "For what reason is the outer door now barred and they who drink tea with us prevented from entering to wish Yuen Yan prosperity?"

"Strange are my lord's words, and the touch of his breath is cold to his menial one," said the woman in doubting reproach.

"It will scarcely warm even the roots of Heng-cho's fig-trees," replied Yuen Yan with unveiled contempt. "Stretch across your hand."

In trembling wonder Tsae-che laid her hand upon the ebony table which stood between them and slowly advanced it until Yan seized it and held it firmly in his own. For a moment he held it, compelling the woman to gaze with a soul-crushing dread into his face, then his features relaxed somewhat from the effort by which he had controlled them, and at the sight Tsae-che tore away her hand and with a scream which caused those outside to forget the memory of every other cry they had ever heard, she cast herself from the house and was seen in the city no more.

These are the pages of the forgotten incident in the life of Yuen Yan which this narrator has sought out and discovered. Elsewhere, in the lesser Classics, it may be read that the person in question afterwards lived to a venerable age and finally Passed Above surrounded by every luxury, after leading an existence consistently benevolent and marked by an even exceptional adherence to the principles and requirements of The Virtues.

The Incredible Obtuseness of Those Who Had Opposed the Virtuous Kai Lung

It was later than the appointed hour that same day when Kai Lung and Hwa-mei met about the shutter, for the Mandarin's importunity had disturbed the harmonious balance of their fixed arrangement. As the story-teller left the inner chamber a message of understanding, veiled from those who stood around, had passed between their eyes, and so complete was the sympathy that now directed them that without a spoken word their plans were understood. Li-loe's acquiescence had been secured by the bestowal of a flask of wine (provided already by Hwa-mei against such an emergency), and though the door-keeper had indicated reproach by a variety of sounds, he forbore from speaking openly of any vaster store.

"Let the bitterness of this one's message be that which is first spoken, so that the later and more enduring words of our remembrance may be devoid of sting. A star has shone across my mediocre path which now an envious cloud has conspired to obscure. This meeting will doubtless be our last."

Then replied Kai Lung from the darkness of the space above, his voice unhurried as its wont:

"If this is indeed the end, then to the spirits of the destinies I prostrate myself in thanks for those golden hours that have gone before, and had there been no others to recall then would I equally account myself repaid in life and death by this."

"My words ascend with yours in a pale spiral to the bosom of the universal mother," Hwa-mei made response. "I likewise am content, having tasted this felicity."

"There is yet one other thing, esteemed, if such a presumption is to be endured," Kai Lung ventured to request. "Each day a stone has been displaced from off the wall and these now lie about your gentle feet. If you should inconvenience yourself to the extent of standing upon the mound thus raised, and would stretch up your hand, I, leaning forth, could touch it with my finger-tips."

"This also will I dare to do and feel it no reproach," replied Hwa-mei; thus for the first time their fingers met.

"Let me now continue the ignoble message that my unworthy lips must bear," resumed the maiden, with a gesture of refined despair. "Ming-shu and Shan Tien, recognizing a mutual need in each, have agreed to forego their wordy strife and have entered upon a common cause. To mark this reconciliation the Mandarin to-morrow night will make a feast of wine and song in honour of Ming-shu and into this assembly you will be led, bound and wearing the wooden cang, to contribute to their offensive mirth. To this end you will not be arraigned to-morrow, but on the following morning at a special court swift sentence will be passed and carried out, neither will Shan Tien suffer any interruption nor raise an arresting hand."

The darkness by this time encompassed them so that neither could see the other's face, but across the scent-laden air Hwa-mei was conscious of a subtle change, as of a poise or the tightening of a responsive cord.

"This is the end?" she whispered up, unable to sustain. "Ah, is it not the end?"

"In the high wall of destiny that bounds our lives there is ever a hidden gap to which the Pure Ones may guide our unconscious steps perchance, if they see fit to intervene... . So that to-morrow, being the eleventh of the Moon of Gathering-in, is to be celebrated by the noble Mandarin with song and wine? Truly the nimble-witted Ming-shu must have slumbered by the way!"

"Assuredly he has but now returned from a long journey."

"Haply he may start upon a longer. Have the musicians been commanded yet?"

"Even now one goes to inform the leader of their voices and to bid him hold his band in readiness."

"Let it be your continual aim that nothing bars their progress. Where does that just official dwell of whom you lately spoke?"

"The Censor K'o-yih, he who rebuked Shan Tien's ambitions and made him mend his questionable life? His yamen is about the Three-eyed Gate of Tai, a half-day's journey to the south."

"The lines converge and the issues of Shan Tien, Ming-shu and we who linger here will presently be brought to a very decisive point where each must play a clear-cut part. To that end is your purpose firm?"

"Lay your commands," replied Hwa-mei steadfastly, "and measure not the burden of their weight."

"It is well," agreed Kai Lung. "Let Shan Tien give the feast and the time of acquiescence will have passed... . The foothold of to-morrow looms insecure, yet a very pressing message must meanwhile reach your hands."

"At the feast?"

"Thus: about the door of the inner hall are two great jars of shining brass, one on either side, and at their approach a step. Being led, at that step I shall stumble... . the message you will thereafter find in the jar from which I seek support."

"It shall be to me as your spoken word. Alas! the moment of recall is already here."

"Doubt not; we stand on the edge of an era that is immeasurable. For that emergency I now go to consult the spirits who have so far guided us."

On the following day at an evening hour Kai Lung received an imperious summons to accompany one who led him to the inner courts. Yet neither the cords about his arms nor the pillory around his neck could contain the gladness of his heart. From within came the sounds of instruments of wood and string with the measured beating of a drum; nothing had fallen short, for on that forbidden day, incredibly blind to the depths of his impiety, the ill-starred Mandarin Shan Tien was having music!

"Gall of a misprocured she-mule!" exclaimed the unsympathetic voice of the one who had charge of him, and the rope was jerked to quicken his loitering feet. In an effort to comply Kai Lung missed the step that crossed his path and stumbling blindly forward would have fallen had he not struck heavily against a massive jar of lacquered brass, one of two that flanked the door.

"Thy province is to tell a tale rather than to dance a grotesque, as I understand the matter," said the attendant, mollified by the amusement. "In any case, restrain thy admitted ardour for a while; the call is not yet for us."

From a group that stood apart some distance from the door one moved forth and leisurely crossed the hall. Kai Lung's wounded head ceased to pain him.

"What slave is this," she demanded of the other in a slow and level tone, "and wherefore do the two of you intrude on this occasion?"

"The exalted lord commands that this one of the prisoners should attend here thus, to divert them with his fancies, he having a certain wit of the more foolish kind. Kai Lung, the dog's name is."

"Approach yet nearer to the inner door," enjoined the maiden, indicating the direction; "so that when the message comes there shall be no inept delay." As they moved off to obey she stood in languid unconcern, leaning across the opening of a tall brass vase, one hand swinging idly in its depths, until they reached their station. Kai Lung did not need his eyes to know.

Presently the music ceased, and summoned to appear in turn, Kai Lung stood forth among the guests. On the right hand of the Mandarin reclined the base Ming-shu, his mind already vapoury with the fumes of wine, the secret malice of his envious mind now boldly leaping from his eyes.

"The overrated person now about to try your refined patience to its limit is one who calls himself Kai Lung," declared Ming-shu offensively. "From an early age he has combined minstrelsy with other and more lucrative forms of crime. It is the boast of this contumacious mendicant that he can recite a story to fit any set of circumstances, this, indeed, being the only merit claimed for his feeble entertainment. The test selected for your tolerant amusement on this very second-rate occasion is that he relates the story of a presuming youth who fixes his covetous hopes upon one so far above his degraded state that she and all who behold his uncouth efforts are consumed by helpless laughter. Ultimately he is to be delivered to a severe but well-earned death by a conscientious official whose leisurely purpose is to possess the maiden for himself. Although occasionally bordering on the funereal, the details of the narrative are to be of a light and gravity-removing nature on the whole. Proceed."

The story-teller made obeisance towards the Mandarin, whose face meanwhile revealed a complete absence of every variety of emotion.

"Have I your genial permission to comply, nobility?" he asked.

"The word is spoken," replied Shan Tien unwillingly. "Let the vaunt be justified."

"I obey, High Excellence. This involves the story of Hien and the Chief Examiner."

The Story of Hien and the Chief Examiner

In the reign of the Emperor K'ong there lived at Ho Chow an official named Thang-li, whose degree was that of Chief Examiner of Literary Competitions for the district. He had an only daughter, Fa Fei, whose mind was so liberally stored with graceful accomplishments as to give rise to the saying that to be in her presence was more refreshing than to sit in a garden of perfumes listening to the wisdom of seven elderly philosophers, while her glossy floating hair, skin of crystal lustre, crescent nails and feet smaller and more symmetrical than an opening lotus made her the most beautiful creature in all Ho Chow. Possessing no son, and maintaining an open contempt towards all his nearer relations, it had become a habit for Thang-li to converse with his daughter almost on terms of equality, so that she was not surprised on one occasion, when, calling her into his presence, he graciously commanded her to express herself freely on whatever subject seemed most important in her mind.

"The Great Middle Kingdom in which we live is not only inhabited by the most enlightened, humane and courteous-minded race, but is itself fittingly the central and most desirable point of the Universe, surrounded by other less favoured countries peopled by races of pig-tailless men and large-footed women, all destitute of refined intelligence," replied Fa Fei modestly. "The sublime Emperor is of all persons the wisest, purest and —"

"Undoubtedly," interrupted Thang-li. "These truths are of gem-like brilliance, and the ears of a patriotic subject can never be closed to the beauty and music of their ceaseless repetition. Yet between father and daughter in the security of an inner chamber there not unnaturally arise topics of more engrossing interest. For example, now that you are of a marriageable age, have your eyes turned in the direction of any particular suitor?"

"Oh, thrice-venerated sire!" exclaimed Fa Fei, looking vainly round for some attainable object behind which to conceal her honourable confusion, "should the thoughts of a maiden dwell definitely on a matter of such delicate consequence?"

"They should not," replied her father; "but as they invariably do, the speculation is one outside our immediate concern. Nor, as it is your wonted custom to ascend upon the outside roof at a certain hour of the morning, is it reasonable to assume that you are ignorant of the movements of the two young men who daily contrive to linger before this in no way attractive residence without any justifiable pretext."

"My father is all-seeing," replied Fa Fei in a commendable spirit of dutiful acquiescence, and also because it seemed useless to deny the circumstance.

"It is unnecessary," said Thang-li. "Surrounded, as he is, by a retinue of eleven female attendants, it is enough to be all-hearing. But which of the two has impressed you in the more favourable light?"

"How can the inclinations of an obedient daughter affect the matter?" said Fa Fei evasively. "Unless, O most indulgent, it is your amiable intention to permit me to follow the inspiration of my own unfettered choice?"

"Assuredly," replied the benevolent Thang-li. "Provided, of course, that the choice referred to should by no evil mischance run in a contrary direction to my own maturer judgment."

"Yet if such an eventuality did haply arise?" persisted Fa Fei.

"None but the irredeemably foolish spend their time in discussing the probable sensation of being struck by a thunderbolt," said Thang-li more coldly. "From this day forth, also, be doubly guarded in the undeviating balance of your attitude. Restrain the swallow-like flights of your admittedly brilliant eyes, and control the movements of your expressive fan within the narrowest bounds of necessity. This person's position between the two is one of exceptional delicacy and he has by no means yet decided which to favour."

"In such a case," inquired Fa Fei, caressing his pig-tail persuasively, "how does a wise man act, and by what manner of omens is he influenced in his decision?"

"In such a case," replied Thang-li, "a very wise man does not act; but maintaining an impassive countenance, he awaits the unrolling of events until he sees what must inevitably take place. It is thus that his reputation for wisdom is built up."

"Furthermore," said Fa Fei hopefully, "the ultimate pronouncement rests with the guarding deities?"

"Unquestionably," agreed Thang-li. "Yet, by a venerable custom, the esteem of the maiden's parents is the detail to which the suitors usually apply themselves with the greatest diligence."

* * *

Of the two persons thus referred to by Thang-li, one, Tsin Lung, lived beneath the sign of the Righteous Ink Brush. By hereditary right Tsin Lung followed the profession of copying out the more difficult Classics in minute characters upon parchments so small that an entire library could be concealed among the folds of a garment, in this painstaking way enabling many persons who might otherwise have failed at the public examination, and been driven to spend an idle and perhaps even dissolute life, to pass with honourable distinction to themselves and widespread credit to his resourceful system. One gratified candidate, indeed, had compared his triumphal passage through the many grades of the competition to the luxurious ease of being carried in a sedan-chair, and from that time Tsin Lung was jestingly referred to as a "sedan-chair."

It might reasonably be thought that a person enjoying this enviable position would maintain a loyal pride in the venerable traditions of his house and suffer the requirements of his craft to become the four walls of his ambition. Alas! Tsin Lung must certainly have been born under the influence of a very evil planet, for the literary quality of his profession did not entice his imagination at all, and his sole and frequently-expressed desire was to become a pirate. Nothing but the necessity of obtaining a large sum of money with which to purchase a formidable junk and to procure the services of a band of capable and bloodthirsty outlaws bound him to Ho Chow, unless, perchance, it might be the presence there of Fa Fei after he had once cast his piratical eye upon her overwhelming beauty.

The other of the two persons was Hien, a youth of studious desires and unassuming manner. His father had been the chief tax-collector of the Chunling mountains, beyond the town, and although the exact nature of the tax and the reason for its extortion had become forgotten in the process of interminable ages, he himself never admitted any doubt of his duty to collect it from all who passed over the mountains, even though the disturbed state of the country made it impossible for him to transmit the proceeds to the capital. To those who uncharitably extended the envenomed tongue of suspicion towards the very existence of any Imperial tax, the father of Hien replied with unshaken loyalty that in such a case the sublime Emperor had been very treacherously served by his advisers, as the difficulty of the paths and the intricate nature of the passes rendered the spot peculiarly suitable for the purpose, and as he was accompanied by a well-armed and somewhat impetuous band of followers, his arguments were inevitably successful. When he Passed Beyond, Hien accepted the leadership, but solely out of a conscientious respect for his father's memory, for his heart was never really in the occupation. His time was almost wholly taken up in reading the higher Classics, and even before he had seen Fa Fei his determination had been taken that when once he had succeeded in passing the examination for the second degree and thereby become entitled to an inferior mandarinship he would abandon his former life forever. From this resolution the entreaties of his devoted followers could not shake him, and presently they ceased to argue, being reassured by the fact that although Hien presented himself unfailingly for every examination his name appeared at the foot of each successive list with unvarying frequency. It was at this period that he first came under the ennobling spell of Fa Fei's influence and from that time forth he redoubled his virtuous efforts.

After conversing with her father, as already related, Fa Fei spent the day in an unusually thoughtful spirit. As soon as it was dark she stepped out from the house and veiling her purpose under the pretext of gathering some herbs to complete a charm she presently entered a grove of overhanging cedars where Hien had long been awaiting her footsteps.

"Rainbow of my prosaic existence!" he exclaimed, shaking hands with himself courteously, "have you yet carried out your bold suggestion?" and so acute was his anxiety for her reply that he continued to hold his hand unconsciously until Fa Fei turned away her face in very becoming confusion.

"Alas, O my dragon-hearted one," she replied at length, "I have indeed dared to read the scroll, but how shall this person's inelegant lips utter so detestable a truth?"

"It is already revealed," said Hien, striving to conceal from her his bitterness. "When the list of competitors at the late examination is publicly proclaimed to-morrow at the four gates of the city, the last name to be announced will again, and for the eleventh time, be that of the degraded Hien."

"Beloved," exclaimed Fa Fei, resolved that as she could not honourably deny that her Hien's name was again indeed the last one to appear she would endeavour to lead his mind subtly away to the contemplation of more pleasurable thoughts, "it is as you have said, but although your name is the last, it is by far the most dignified and romantic-sounding of all, nor is there another throughout the list which can be compared to it for the ornamental grace of its flowing curves."

"Nevertheless," replied Hien, in a violent access of self-contempt, "it is a name of abandoned omen and is destined only to reach the ears of posterity to embellish the proverb of scorn, 'The lame duck should avoid the ploughed field.' Can there-can there by no chance have been some hope-inspiring error?"

"Thus were the names inscribed on the parchment which after the public announcement will be affixed to the Hall of Ten Thousand Lustres," replied Fa Fei. "With her own unworthy eyes this incapable person beheld it."

"The name 'Hien' is in no way striking or profound," continued the one in question, endeavouring to speak as though the subject referred to some person standing at a considerable distance away. "Furthermore, so commonplace and devoid of character are its written outlines that it has very much the same appearance whichever way up it is looked at... . The possibility that in your graceful confusion you held the list in such a position that what appeared to be the end was in reality the beginning is remote in the extreme, yet —"

In spite of an absorbing affection Fa Fei could not disguise from herself that her feelings would have been more pleasantly arranged if her lover had been inspired to accept his position unquestioningly. "There is a detail, hitherto unrevealed, which disposes of all such amiable suggestions," she replied. "After the name referred to, someone in authority had inscribed the undeniable comment 'As usual.'"

"The omen is a most encouraging one," exclaimed Hien, throwing aside all his dejection. "Hitherto this person's untiring efforts had met with no official recognition whatever. It is now obvious that far from being lost in the crowd he is becoming an object of honourable interest to the examiners."

"One frequently hears it said, 'After being struck on the head with an axe it is a positive pleasure to be beaten about the body with a wooden club,'" said Fa Fei, "and the meaning of the formerly elusive proverb is now explained. Would it not be prudent to avail yourself at length of the admittedly outrageous Tsin Lung's services, so that this period of unworthy trial may be brought to a distinguished close?"

"It is said, 'Do not eat the fruit of the stricken branch,'" replied Hien, "and this person will never owe his success to one who is so detestable in his life and morals that with every facility for a scholarly and contemplative existence he freely announces his barbarous intention of becoming a pirate. Truly the Dragon of Justice does but sleep for a little time, and when he awakens all that will be left of the mercenary Tsin Lung and those who associate with him will scarcely be enough to fill an orange skin."

"Doubtless it will be so," agreed Fa Fei, regretting, however, that Hien had not been content to prophesy a more limited act of vengeance, until, at least, her father had come to a definite decision regarding her own future. "Alas, though, the Book of Dynasties expressly says, 'The one-legged never stumble,' and Tsin Lung is so morally ill-balanced that the proverb may even apply to him."

"Do not fear," said Hien. "It is elsewhere written, 'Love and leprosy few escape,' and the spirit of Tsin Lung's destiny is perhaps even at this moment lurking unsuspected behind some secret place."

"If," exclaimed a familiar voice, "the secret place alluded to should chance to be a hollow cedar-tree of inadequate girth, the unfortunate spirit in question will have my concentrated sympathy."

"Just and magnanimous father!" exclaimed Fa Fei, thinking it more prudent not to recognize that he had learned of their meeting-place and concealing himself there had awaited their coming, "when your absence was discovered a heaven-sent inspiration led me to this spot. Have I indeed been permitted here to find you?"

"Assuredly you have," replied Thang-li, who was equally desirous of concealing the real circumstances, although the difficulty of the position into which he had hastily and incautiously thrust his body on their approach compelled him to reveal himself. "The same inspiration led me to lose myself in this secluded spot, as being the one which you would inevitably search."

"Yet by what incredible perversity does it arise, venerable Thang-li, that a leisurely and philosophical stroll should result in a person of your dignified proportions occupying so unattractive a position?" said Hien, who appeared to be too ingenuous to suspect Thang-li's craft, in spite of a warning glance from Fa Fei's expressive eyes.

"The remark is a natural one, O estimable youth," replied Thang-li, doubtless smiling benevolently, although nothing of his person could be actually seen by Hien or Fa Fei, "but the recital is not devoid of humiliation. While peacefully studying the position of the heavens this person happened to glance into the upper branches of a tree and among them he beheld a bird's nest of unusual size and richness-one that would promise to yield a dish of the rarest flavour. Lured on by the anticipation of so sumptuous a course, he rashly trusted his body to an unworthy branch, and the next moment, notwithstanding his unceasing protests to the protecting Powers, he was impetuously deposited within this hollow trunk."

"Not unreasonably is it said, 'A bird in the soup is better than an eagle's nest in the desert,'" exclaimed Hien. "The pursuit of a fair and lofty object is set about with hidden pitfalls to others beyond you, O noble Chief Examiner! By what nimble-witted act of adroitness is it now your enlightened purpose to extricate yourself?"

At this admittedly polite but in no way inspiring question a silence of a very acute intensity seemed to fall on that part of the forest. The mild and inscrutable expression of Hien's face did not vary, but into Fa Fei's eyes there came an unexpected but not altogether disapproving radiance, while, without actually altering, the appearance of the tree encircling Thang-li's form undoubtedly conveyed the impression that the benevolent smile which might hitherto have been reasonably assumed to exist within had been abruptly withdrawn.

"Your meaning is perhaps well-intentioned, gracious Hien," said Thang-li at length, "but as an offer of disinterested assistance your words lack the gong-like clash of spontaneous enthusiasm. Nevertheless, if you will inconvenience yourself to the extent of climbing this not really difficult tree for a short distance you will be able to grasp some outlying portion of this one's body without any excessive fatigue."

"Mandarin," replied Hien, "to touch even the extremity of your incomparable pig-tail would be an honour repaying all earthly fatigue —"

"Do not hesitate to seize it, then," said Thang-li, as Hien paused. "Yet, if this person may without ostentation continue the analogy, to grasp him firmly by the shoulders must confer a higher distinction and would be even more agreeable to his own feelings."

"The proposal is a flattering one," continued Hien, "but my hands are bound down by the decree of the High Powers, for among the most inviolable of the edicts is it not written: 'Do the lame offer to carry the footsore; the blind to protect the one-eyed? Distrust the threadbare person who from an upper back room invites you to join him in an infallible process of enrichment; turn aside from the one devoid of pig-tail who says, "Behold, a few drops daily at the hour of the morning sacrifice and your virtuous head shall be again like a well-sown rice-field at the time of harvest"; and towards the passing stranger who offers you that mark of confidence which your friends withhold close and yet again open a different eye. So shall you grow obese in wisdom'?"

"Alas!" exclaimed Thang-li, "the inconveniences of living in an Empire where a person has to regulate the affairs of his everyday life by the sacred but antiquated proverbial wisdom of his remote ancestors are by no means trivial. Cannot this possibly mythical obstacle be flattened-out by the amiable acceptance of a jar of sea snails or some other seasonable delicacy, honourable Hien?"

"Nothing but a really well-grounded encouragement as regards Fa Fei can persuade this person to regard himself as anything but a solitary outcast," replied Hien, "and one paralysed in every useful impulse. Rather than abandon the opportunity of coming to such an arrangement he would almost be prepared to give up all idea of ever passing the examination for the second degree."

"By no means," exclaimed Thang-li hastily. "The sacrifice would be too excessive. Do not relinquish your sleuth-hound-like persistence, and success will inevitably reward your ultimate end."

"Can it really be," said Hien incredulously, "that my contemptible efforts are a matter of sympathetic interest to one so high up in every way as the renowned Chief Examiner?"

"They are indeed," replied Thang-li, with that ingratiating candour that marked his whole existence. "Doubtless so prosaic a detail as the system of remuneration has never occupied your refined thoughts, but when it is understood that those in the position of this person are rewarded according to the success of the candidates you will begin to grasp the attitude."

"In that case," remarked Hien, with conscious humiliation, "nothing but a really sublime tolerance can have restrained you from upbraiding this obscure competitor as a thoroughly corrupt egg."

"On the contrary," replied Thang-li reassuringly, "I have long regarded you as the auriferous fowl itself. It is necessary to explain, perhaps, that the payment by result alluded to is not based on the number of successful candidates, but-much more reasonably as all those have to be provided with lucrative appointments by the authorities-on the economy effected to the State by those whom I can conscientiously reject. Owing to the malignant Tsin Lung's sinister dexterity these form an ever-decreasing band, so that you may now be fittingly deemed the chief prop of a virtuous but poverty-afflicted line. When you reflect that for the past eleven years you have thus really had the honour of providing the engaging Fa Fei with all the necessities of her very ornamental existence you will see that you already possess practically all the advantages of matrimony. Nevertheless, if you will now bring our agreeable conversation to an end by releasing this inauspicious person he will consider the matter with the most indulgent sympathies."

"Withhold!" exclaimed a harsh voice before Hien could reply, and from behind a tree where he had heard Thang-li's impolite reference to himself Tsin Lung stood forth. "How does it chance, O two-complexioned Chief Examiner, that after weighing this one's definite proposals-even to the extent of demanding a certain proportion in advance-you are now engaged in holding out the same alluring hope to another? Assuredly, if your existence is so critically imperilled this person and none other will release you and claim the reward."

"Turn your face backwards, imperious Tsin Lung," cried Hien. "These incapable hands alone shall have the overwhelming distinction of drawing forth the illustrious Thang-li."

"Do not get entangled among my advancing footsteps, immature one," contemptuously replied Tsin Lung, shaking the massive armour in which he was encased from head to foot. "It is inept for pigmies to stand before one who has every intention of becoming a rapacious pirate shortly."

"The sedan-chair is certainly in need of new shafts," retorted Hien, and drawing his sword with an expression of ferocity he caused it to whistle around his head so loudly that a flock of migratory doves began to arrive, under the impression that others of their tribe were calling them to assemble.

"Alas!" exclaimed Thang-li, in an accent of despair, "doubtless the wise Nung-yu was surrounded by disciples all eager that no other should succour him when he remarked: 'A humble friend in the same village is better than sixteen influential brothers in the Royal Palace.' In all this illimitable Empire is there not room for one whose aspirations are bounded by the submerged walls of a predatory junk and another whose occupation is limited to the upper passes of the Chunling mountains? Consider the poignant nature of this person's vain regrets if by a couple of evilly directed blows you succeeded at this inopportune moment in exterminating one another!"

"Do not fear, exalted Thang-li," cried Hien, who, being necessarily somewhat occupied in preparing himself against Tsin Lung's attack, failed to interpret these words as anything but a direct encouragement to his own cause. "Before the polluting hands of one who disdains the Classics shall be laid upon your sacred extremities this tenacious person will fix upon his antagonist with a serpent-like embrace and, if necessary, suffer the spirits of both to Pass Upward in one breath." And to impress Tsin Lung with his resolution he threw away his scabbard and picked it up again several times.

"Grow large in hope, worthy Chief Examiner," cried Tsin Lung, who from a like cause was involved in a similar misapprehension. "Rather shall your imperishable bones adorn the interior of a hollow cedar-tree throughout all futurity than you shall suffer the indignity of being extricated by an earth-nurtured sleeve-snatcher." And to intimidate Hien by the display he continued to clash his open hand against his leg armour until the pain became intolerable.

"Honourable warriors!" implored Thang-li in so agonized a voice-and also because they were weary of the exercise-that Hien and Tsin Lung paused, "curb your bloodthirsty ambitions for a breathing-space and listen to what will probably be a Last Expression. Believe the passionate sincerity of this one's throat when he proclaims that there would be nothing repugnant to his very keenest susceptibilities if an escaping parricide, who was also guilty of rebellion, temple-robbing, book-burning, murder and indiscriminate violence, and the pollution of tombs, took him familiarly by the hand at this moment. What, therefore, would be his gratified feelings if two such nobly-born subjects joined forces and drew him up dexterously by the body-cloth? Accept his definite assurance that without delay a specific pronouncement would be made respecting the bestowal of the one around whose jade-like personality this encounter has arisen."

"The proposal casts a reasonable shadow, gracious Hien," remarked Tsin Lung, turning towards the other with courteous deference. "Shall we bring a scene of irrational carnage to an end and agree to regard the incomparable Thang-li's benevolent tongue as an outstretched olive branch?"

"It is admittedly said, 'Every road leads in two directions,' and the alternative you suggest, O virtue-loving Tsin Lung, is both reputable and just," replied Hien pleasantly. In this amiable spirit they extricated Thang-li and bore him to the ground. At an appointed hour he received them with becoming ceremony and after a many-coursed repast rose to fulfil the specific terms of his pledge.

"The Line of Thang," he remarked with inoffensive pride, "has for seven generations been identified with a high standard of literary achievement. Undeniably it is a very creditable thing to control the movements of an ofttime erratic vessel and to emerge triumphantly from a combat with every junk you encounter, and it is no less worthy of esteem to gather round about one, on the sterile slopes of the Chunlings, a devoted band of followers. Despite these virtues, however, neither occupation is marked by any appreciable literary flavour, and my word is, therefore, that both persons shall present themselves for the next examination, and when in due course the result is declared the more successful shall be hailed as the chosen suitor. Lo, I have spoken into a sealed bottle, and my voice cannot vary."

Then replied Tsin Lung: "Truly, it is as it is said, astute Thang-li, though the encircling wall of a hollow cedar-tree, for example, might impart to the voice in question a less uncompromising ring of finality than it possesses when raised in a silk-lined chamber and surrounded by a band of armed retainers. Nevertheless the pronouncement is one which appeals to this person's sense of justice, and the only improvement he can suggest is that the superfluous Hien should hasten that ceremony at which he will be an honoured guest by now signifying his intention of retiring from so certain a defeat. For by what expedient," he continued, with arrogant persistence, "can you avert that end, O ill-destined Hien? Have you not burned joss-sticks to the deities, both good and bad, for eleven years unceasingly? Can you, as this person admittedly can, inscribe the Classics with such inimitable delicacy that an entire volume of the Book of Decorum, copied in his most painstaking style, may be safely carried about within a hollow tooth, a lengthy ode, traced on a shred of silk, wrapped undetectably around a single eyelash?"

"It is true that the one before you cannot bend his brush to such deceptive ends," replied Hien modestly. "A detail, however, has escaped your reckoning. Hitherto Hien has been opposed by a thousand, and against so many it is true that the spirits of his ancestors have been able to afford him very little help. On this occasion he need regard one adversary alone. Giving those Forces which he invokes clearly to understand that they need not concern themselves with any other, he will plainly intimate that after so many sacrifices on his part something of a really tangible affliction is required to overwhelm Tsin Lung. Whether this shall take the form of mental stagnation, bodily paralysis, demoniacal possession, derangement of the internal faculties, or being changed into one of the lower animals, it might be presumptuous on this person's part to stipulate, but by invoking every accessible power and confining himself to this sole petition a very definite tragedy may be expected. Beware, O contumacious Lung, 'However high the tree the shortest axe can reach its trunk.'"

* * *

As the time for the examination drew near the streets of Ho Chow began to wear a fuller and more animated appearance both by day and night. Tsin Lung's outer hall was never clear of anxious suppliants all entreating him to supply them with minute and reliable copies of the passages which they found most difficult in the selected works, but although his low and avaricious nature was incapable of rejecting this means of gain he devoted his closest energies and his most inspired moments to his own personal copies, a set of books so ethereal that they floated in the air without support and so cunningly devised in the blending of their colour as to be, in fact, quite invisible to any but his microscopic eyes. Hien, on the other hand, devoted himself solely to interesting the Powers against his rival's success by every variety of incentive, omen, sacrifice, imprecation, firework, inscribed curse, promise, threat or combination of inducements. Through the crowded streets and by-ways of Ho Chow moved the imperturbable Thang-li, smiling benevolently on those whom he encountered and encouraging each competitor, and especially Hien and Tsin Lung, with a cheerful proverb suited to the moment.

An outside cause had further contributed to make this period one of the most animated in the annals of Ho Chow, for not only was the city, together with the rest of the imperishable Empire, celebrating a great and popular victory, but, as a direct consequence of that event, the sublime Emperor himself was holding his court at no great distance away. An armed and turbulent rabble of illiterate barbarians had suddenly appeared in the north and, not giving a really sufficient indication of their purpose, had traitorously assaulted the capital. Had he followed the prompting of his own excessive magnanimity, the charitable Monarch would have refused to take any notice whatever of so puny and contemptible a foe, but so unmistakable became the wishes of the Ever-victorious Army that, yielding to their importunity, he placed himself at their head and resolutely led them backward. Had the opposing army been more intelligent, this crafty move would certainly have enticed them on into the plains, where they would have fallen an easy victim to the Imperial troops and all perished miserably. Owing to their low standard of reasoning, however, the mule-like invaders utterly failed to grasp the advantage which, as far as the appearance tended, they might reasonably be supposed to reap by an immediate pursuit. They remained incapably within the capital slavishly increasing its defences, while the Ever-victorious lurked resourcefully in the neighbourhood of Ho Chow, satisfied that with so dull-witted an adversary they could, if the necessity arose, go still further.

Upon a certain day of the period thus indicated there arrived at the gate of the royal pavilion one having the appearance of an aged seer, who craved to be led into the Imperial Presence.

"Lo, Mightiest," said a slave, bearing in this message, "there stands at the outer gate one resembling an ancient philosopher, desiring to gladden his failing eyesight before he Passes Up with a brief vision of your illuminated countenance."

"The petition is natural but inopportune," replied the agreeable Monarch. "Let the worthy soothsayer be informed that after an exceptionally fatiguing day we are now snatching a few short hours of necessary repose, from which it would be unseemly to recall us."

"He received your gracious words with distended ears and then observed that it was for your All-wisdom to decide whether an inspired message which he had read among the stars was not of more consequence than even a refreshing sleep," reported the slave, returning.

"In that case," replied the Sublimest, "tell the persevering wizard that we have changed our minds and are religiously engaged in worshipping our ancestors, so that it would be really sacrilegious to interrupt us."

"He kowtowed profoundly at the mere mention of your charitable occupation and proceeded to depart, remarking that it would indeed be corrupt to disturb so meritorious an exercise with a scheme simply for your earthly enrichment," again reported the message-bearer.

"Restrain him!" hastily exclaimed the broadminded Sovereign. "Give the venerable necromancer clearly to understand that we have worshipped them enough for one day. Doubtless the accommodating soothsayer has discovered some rare jewel which he is loyally bringing to embellish our crown."

"There are rarer jewels than those which can be pasted in a crown, Supreme Head," said the stranger, entering unperceived behind the attending slave. He bore the external signs of an infirm magician, while his face was hidden in a cloth to mark the imposition of a solemn vow. "With what apter simile," he continued, "can this person describe an imperishable set of verses which he heard this morning falling from the lips of a wandering musician like a seven-roped cable of pearls pouring into a silver bucket? The striking and original title was 'Concerning Spring,' and although the snow lay deep at the time several bystanders agreed that an azalea bush within hearing came into blossom at the eighty-seventh verse."

"We have heard of the poem to which you refer with so just a sense of balance," said the impartial Monarch encouragingly. (Though not to create a two-sided impression it may be freely stated that he himself was the author of the inspired composition.) "Which part, in your mature judgment, reflected the highest genius and maintained the most perfectly-matched analogy?"

"It is aptly said: 'When it is dark the sun no longer shines, but who shall forget the colours of the rainbow?'" replied the astrologer evasively. "How is it possible to suspend topaz in one cup of the balance and weigh it against amethyst in the other; or who in a single language can compare the tranquillizing grace of a maiden with the invigorating pleasure of witnessing a well-contested rat-fight?"

"Your insight is clear and unbiased," said the gracious Sovereign. "But however entrancing it is to wander unchecked through a garden of bright images, are we not enticing your mind from another subject of almost equal importance?"

"There is yet another detail, it is true," admitted the sage, "but regarding its comparative importance a thoroughly loyal subject may be permitted to amend the remark of a certain wise Emperor of a former dynasty: 'Any person in the City can discover a score of gold mines if necessary, but One only could possibly have written "Concerning Spring."'"

"The arts may indeed be regarded as lost," acquiesced the magnanimous Head, "with the exception of a solitary meteor here and there. Yet in the trivial matter of mere earthly enrichment —"

"Truly," agreed the other. "There is, then, a whisper in the province that the floor of the Imperial treasury is almost visible."

"The rumour, as usual, exaggerates the facts grossly," replied the Greatest. "The floor of the Imperial treasury is quite visible."

"Yet on the first day of the next moon the not inconsiderable revenue contributed by those who present themselves for the examination will flow in."

"And by an effete and unworthy custom almost immediately flow out again to reward the efforts of the successful," replied the Wearer of the Yellow in an accent of refined bitterness. "On other occasions it is possible to assist the overworked treasurer with a large and glutinous hand, but from time immemorial the claims of the competitors have been inviolable."

"Yet if by a heaven-sent chance none, or very few, reached the necessary standard of excellence—?"

"Such a chance, whether proceeding from the Upper Air or the Other Parts would be equally welcome to a very hard-lined Ruler," replied the one who thus described himself.

"Then listen, O K'ong-hi, of the imperishable dynasty of Chung," said the stranger. "Thus was it laid upon me in the form of a spontaneous dream. For seven centuries the Book of the Observances has been the unvarying Classic of the examinations because during that period it has never been surpassed. Yet as the Empire has admittedly existed from all time, and as it would be impious not to agree that the immortal System is equally antique, it is reasonable to suppose that the Book of the Observances displaced an earlier and inferior work, and is destined in the cycle of time to be itself laid aside for a still greater."

"The inference is self-evident," acknowledged the Emperor uneasily, "but the logical development is one which this diffident Monarch hesitates to commit to spoken words."

"It is not a matter for words but for a stroke of the Vermilion Pencil," replied the other in a tone of inspired authority. "Across the faint and puny effusions of the past this person sees written in very large and obliterating strokes the words 'Concerning Spring.' Where else can be found so novel a conception combined with so unique a way of carrying it out? What other poem contains so many thoughts that one instinctively remembers as having heard before, so many involved allusions that baffle the imagination of the keenest, and so much sound in so many words? With the possible exception of Meng-hu's masterpiece, 'The Empty Coffin,' what other work so skilfully conveys the impression of being taken down farther than one can ever again come up and then suddenly upraised beyond the possible descent? Where else can be found so complete a defiance of all that has hitherto been deemed essential, and, to insert a final wedge, what other poem is half so long?"

"Your criticism is severe but just," replied the Sovereign, "except that part having reference to Meng-hu. Nevertheless, the atmosphere of the proposal, though reasonable, looms a degree stormily into a troubled future. Can it be permissible even for—"

"Omnipotence!" exclaimed the seer.

"The title is well recalled," confessed the Emperor. "Yet although unquestionably omnipotent there must surely be some limits to our powers in dealing with so old established a system as that of the examinations."

"Who can doubt a universal admission that the composer of 'Concerning Spring' is capable of doing anything?" was the profound reply. "Let the mandate be sent out-but, to an obvious end, let it be withheld until the eve of the competitions."

"The moment of hesitancy has faded; go forth in the certainty, esteemed," said the Emperor reassuringly. "You have carried your message with a discreet hand. Yet before you go, if there is any particular mark of Imperial favour that we can show-something of a special but necessarily honorary nature-do not set an iron screen between your ambition and the light of our favourable countenance."

"There is indeed such a signal reward," assented the aged person, with an air of prepossessing diffidence. "A priceless copy of the immortal work—"

"By all means," exclaimed the liberal-minded Sovereign, with an expression of great relief. "Take three or four in case any of your fascinating relations have large literary appetites. Or, still more conveniently arranged, here is an unopened package from the stall of those who send forth the printed leaves —'thirteen in the semblance of twelve,' as the quaint and harmonious phrase of their craft has it. Walk slowly, revered, and a thousand rainbows guide your retiring footsteps."

Concerning the episode of this discreetly-veiled personage the historians who have handed down the story of the imperishable affection of Hien and Fa Fei have maintained an illogical silence. Yet it is related that about the same time, as Hien was walking by the side of a bamboo forest of stunted growth, he was astonished by the maiden suddenly appearing before him from the direction of the royal camp. She was incomparably radiant and had the appearance of being exceptionally well satisfied with herself. Commanding him that he should stand motionless with closed eyes, in order to ascertain what the presiding deities would allot him, she bound a somewhat weighty object to the end of his pig-tail, at the same time asking him in how short a period he could commit about nineteen thousand lines of atrociously ill-arranged verse to the tablets of his mind.

"Then do not suffer the rice to grow above your ankles," she continued, when Hien had modestly replied that six days with good omens should be sufficient, "but retiring to your innermost chamber bar the door and digest this scroll as though it contained the last expression of an eccentric and vastly rich relation," and with a laugh more musical than the vibrating of a lute of the purest Yun-nan jade in the Grotto of Ten Thousand Echoes she vanished.

It has been sympathetically remarked that no matter how painstakingly a person may strive to lead Destiny along a carefully-prepared path and towards a fit and thoroughly virtuous end there is never lacking some inopportune creature to thrust his superfluous influence into an opposing balance. This naturally suggests the intolerable Tsin Lung, whose ghoulish tastes led him to seek the depths of that same glade on the following day. Walking with downcast eyes, after his degraded custom, he presently became aware of an object lying some distance from his way. To those who have already fathomed the real character of this repulsive person it will occasion no surprise to know that, urged on by the insatiable curiosity that was deeply grafted on to his avaricious nature, he turned aside to probe into a matter with which he had no possible concern, and at length succeeded in drawing a package from the thick bush in which it had been hastily concealed. Finding that it contained twelve lengthy poems entitled "Concerning Spring", he greedily thrust one in his sleeve, and upon his return, with no other object than the prompting of an ill-regulated mind, he spent all the time that remained before the contest in learning it from end to end.

There have been many remarkable scenes enacted in the great Examination Halls and in the narrow cells around, but it can at once be definitely stated that nothing either before or since has approached the unanimous burst of frenzy that shook the dynasty of Chung when in the third year of his reign the well-meaning but too-easily-led-aside Emperor K'ong inopportunely sought to replace the sublime Classic then in use with a work that has since been recognized to be not only shallow but inept. At Ho Chow nine hundred and ninety-eight voices blended into one soul-benumbing cry of rage, having all the force and precision of a carefully drilled chorus, when the papers were opened, and had not the candidates been securely barred within their solitary pens a popular rising must certainly have taken place. There they remained for three days and nights, until the clamour had subsided into a low but continuous hum, and they were too weak to carry out a combined effort.

Throughout this turmoil Hien and Tsin Lung each plied an unfaltering brush. It may here be advantageously stated that the former person was not really slow or obtuse and his previous failures were occasioned solely by the inequality he strove under in relying upon his memory alone when every other competitor without exception had provided himself with a concealed scrip. Tsin Lung also had a very retentive mind. The inevitable consequence was, therefore, that when the papers were collected Hien and Tsin Lung had accomplished an identical number of correct lines and no other person had made even an attempt.

In explaining Thang-li's subsequent behaviour it has been claimed by many that the strain of being compelled, in the exercise of his duty, to remain for three days and three nights in the middle of the Hall surrounded by that ferocious horde, all clamouring to reach him, and the contemplation of the immense sum which he would gain by so unparalleled a batch of rejections, contorted his faculties of discrimination and sapped the resources of his usually active mind. Whatever cause is accepted, it is agreed that as soon as he returned to his house he summoned Hien and Tsin Lung together and leaving them for a moment presently returned, leading Fa Fei by the hand. It is further agreed by all that these three persons noticed upon his face a somewhat preoccupied expression, and on the one side much has been made of the admitted fact that as he spoke he wandered round the room catching flies, an occupation eminently suited to his age and leisurely tastes but, it may be confessed, not altogether well chosen at so ceremonious a moment.

"It has been said," he began at length, withdrawing his eyes reluctantly from an unusually large insect upon the ceiling and addressing himself to the maiden, "that there are few situations in life that cannot be honourably settled, and without loss of time, either by suicide, a bag of gold, or by thrusting a despised antagonist over the edge of a precipice upon a dark night. This inoffensive person, however, has striven to arrive at the conclusion of a slight domestic arrangement both by passively waiting for the event to unroll itself and, at a later period, by the offer of a definite omen. Both of the male persons concerned have applied themselves so tenaciously to the ordeal that the result, to this simple one's antique mind, savours overmuch of the questionable arts. The genial and light-witted Emperor appears to have put his foot into the embarrassment ineffectually; and Destiny herself has every indication of being disinclined to settle so doubtful a point. As a last resort it now remains for you yourself to decide which of these strenuous and evenly-balanced suitors I may acclaim with ten thousand felicitations."

"In that case, venerated and commanding sire," replied Fa Fei simply, yet concealing her real regard behind the retiring mask of a modest indifference, "it shall be Hien, because his complexion goes the more prettily with my favourite heliotrope silk."

When the results of the examination were announced it was at once assumed by those with whom he had trafficked that Tsin Lung had been guilty of the most degraded treachery. Understanding the dangers of his position, that person decided upon an immediate flight. Disguised as a wild-beast tamer, and leading several apparently ferocious creatures by a cord, he succeeded in making his way undetected through the crowds of competitors watching his house, and hastily collecting his wealth together he set out towards the coast. But the evil spirits which had hitherto protected him now withdrew their aid. In the wildest passes of the Chunlings Hien's band was celebrating his unexpected success by a costly display of fireworks, varied with music and dancing.... So heavily did they tax him that when he reached his destination he was only able to purchase a small and dilapidated junk and to enlist the services of three thoroughly incompetent mercenaries. The vessels which he endeavoured to pursue stealthily in the hope of restoring his fortunes frequently sailed towards him under the impression that he was sinking and trying to attract their benevolent assistance. When his real intention was at length understood both he and his crew were invariably beaten about the head with clubs, so that although he persevered until the three hired assassins rebelled, he never succeeded in committing a single act of piracy. Afterwards he gained a precarious livelihood by entering into conversation with strangers, and still later he stood upon a board and dived for small coins which the charitable threw into the water. In this pursuit he was one day overtaken by a voracious sea-monster and perished miserably.

The large-meaning but never fully-accomplishing Emperor K'ong reigned for yet another year, when he was deposed by the powerful League of the Three Brothers. To the end of his life he steadfastly persisted that the rebellion was insidiously fanned, if not actually carried out, by a secret confederacy of all the verse-makers of the Empire, who were distrustful of his superior powers. He spent the years of his exile in composing a poetical epitaph to be carved upon his tomb, but his successor, the practical-minded Liu-yen, declined to sanction the expense of procuring so fabulous a supply of marble.

* * *

When Kai Lung had repeated the story of the well- intentioned youth Hien and of the Chief Examiner Thang-li and had ceased to speak, a pause of questionable import filled the room, broken only by the undignified sleep-noises of the gross Ming-shu. Glances of implied perplexity were freely passed among the guests, but it remained for Shan Tien to voice their doubt.

"Yet wherein is the essence of the test maintained," he asked, "seeing that the one whom you call Hien obtained all that which he desired and he who chiefly opposed his aims was himself involved in ridicule and delivered to a sudden end?"

"Beneficence," replied Kai Lung, with courteous ease, despite the pinions that restrained him, "herein it is one thing to demand and another to comply, for among the Platitudes is the admission made: 'No needle has two sharp points.' The conditions which the subtlety of Ming-shu imposed ceased to bind, for their corollary was inexact. In no romance composed by poet or sage are the unassuming hopes of virtuous love brought to a barren end or the one who holds them delivered to an ignominious doom. That which was called for does not therefore exist, but the story of Hien may be taken as indicating the actual course of events should the case arise in an ordinary state of life."

This reply was not deemed inept by most of those who heard, and they even pressed upon the one who spoke slight gifts of snuff and wine. The Mandarin Shan Tien, however, held himself apart.

"It is doubtful if your lips will be able thus to frame so confident a boast when to-morrow fades," was his dark forecast.

"Doubtless their tenor will be changed, revered, in accordance with your far-seeing word," replied Kai Lung submissively as he was led away.

Of Which It Is Written: "in Shallow Water Dragons Become the Laughing-Stock of Shrimps"

At an early gong-stroke of the following day Kai Lung was finally brought up for judgment in accordance with the venomous scheme of the reptilian Ming-shu. In order to obscure their guilty plans all justice-loving persons were excluded from the court, so that when the story-teller was led in by a single guard he saw before him only the two whose enmity he faced, and one who stood at a distance prepared to serve their purpose.

"Committer of every infamy and inceptor of nameless crimes," began Ming-shu, moistening his brush, "in the past, by the variety of discreditable subterfuges, you have parried the stroke of a just retribution. On this occasion, however, your admitted powers of evasion will avail you nothing. By a special form of administration, designed to meet such cases, your guilt will be taken as proved. The technicalities of passing sentence and seeing it carried out will follow automatically."

"In spite of the urgency of the case," remarked the Mandarin, with an assumption of the evenly-balanced expression that at one time threatened to obtain for him the title of "The Just", "there is one detail which must not be ignored-especially as our ruling will doubtless become a lantern to the feet of later ones. You appear, malefactor, to have committed crimes-and of all these you have been proved guilty by the ingenious arrangement invoked by the learned recorder of my spoken word-which render you liable to hanging, slicing, pressing, boiling, roasting, grilling, freezing, vatting, racking, twisting, drawing, compressing, inflating, rending, spiking, gouging, limb-tying, piecemeal-pruning and a variety of less tersely describable discomforts with which the time of this court need not be taken up. The important consideration is, in what order are we to proceed and when, if ever, are we to stop?"

"Under your benumbing eye, Excellence," suggested Ming-shu resourcefully, "the precedent of taking first that for which the written sign is the longest might be established. Failing that, the names of all the various punishments might be inscribed on separate shreds of parchment and these deposited within your state umbrella. The first withdrawn by an unbiased —"

"High Excellence," Kai Lung ventured to interrupt, "a further plan suggests itself which —"

"If," exclaimed Ming-shu in irrational haste, "if the criminal proposes to narrate a story of one who in like circumstances —"

"Peace!" interposed Shan Tien tactfully. "The felon will only be allowed the usual ten short measures of time for his suggestion, nor must he, under that guise, endeavour to insert an imagined tale."

"Your ruling shall keep straight my bending feet, munificence," replied Kai Lung. "Hear now my simplifying way. In place of cited wrongs-which, after all, are comparatively trivial matters, as being merely offences against another or in defiance of a local usage-substitute one really overwhelming crime for which the penalty is sharp and explicit."

"To that end you would suggest —?" Uncertainty sat upon the brow of both Shan Tien and Ming-shu.

"To straighten out the entangled thread this person would plead guilty to the act-in a lesser capacity and against his untrammelled will-of rejoicing musically on a day set apart for universal woe: a crime aimed directly at the sacred person of the Sublime Head and all those of his Line."

At this significant admission the Mandarin's expression faded; he stroked the lower part of his face several times and unostentatiously indicated to the two attendants that they should retire to a more distant obscurity. Then he spoke.

"When did this-this alleged indiscretion occur, Kai Lung?" he asked in a considerate voice.

"It is useless to raise a cloud of evasion before the sun of your penetrating intellect," replied the story-teller. "The eleventh day of the existing moon was its inauspicious date."

"That being yesterday? Ming-shu, you upon whom the duty of regulating my admittedly vagarious mind devolves, what happened officially on the eleventh day of the Month of Gathering-in?" demanded the Mandarin in an ominous tone.

"On such and such a day, benevolence, threescore and fifteen years ago, the imperishable founder of the existing dynasty ascended on a fiery dragon to be a guest on high," confessed the conscience-stricken scribe, after consulting his printed tablets. "Owing to the stress of a sudden journey significance of the date had previously escaped my weed-grown memory, tolerance."

"Alas!" exclaimed Shan Tien bitterly, "among the innumerable drawbacks of an exacting position the enforced reliance upon an unusually inept and more than ordinarily self-opinionated inscriber of the spoken word is perhaps the most illimitable. Owing to your profuse incompetence that which began as an agreeable prelude to a busy day has turned into a really serious matter."

"Yet, lenience," pleaded the hapless Ming-shu, lowering his voice for the Mandarin's private ear, "so far the danger resides in this one throat alone. That disposed of—"

"Perchance," replied Shan Tien; then turning to Kai Lung: "Doubtless, O story-teller, you were so overcome by the burden of your guilt that until this moment you have hidden the knowledge of it deep within your heart?"

"Magnificence, the commanding quality of your enduring voice would draw the inner matter from a marrow-bone," frankly replied Kai Lung. "Fearful lest this crime might go unconfessed and my weak and trembling ghost therefrom be held to bear its weight unto the end of time, I set out the full happening in a written scroll and sent it at daybreak by a sure and secret hand to a scrupulous official to deal with as he sees fit."

"Your worthy confidant would assuredly be a person of incorruptible integrity?"

"The repute of the upright Censor K'o-yih had reached even these stunted ears."

"Inevitably: the Censor K'o-yih!" Shan Tien's hasty glance took in the angle of the sun and for a moment rested on the door leading to the part where his swiftest horses lay. "By this time the message will have reached him?"

"Omnipotence," replied Kai Lung, spreading out his hands to indicate the full extent of his submission, "not even a piece of the finest Ping-hi silk could be inserted between the deepest secret of this person's heart and your all-extracting gaze. Should you, in your meritorious sense of justice, impose upon me a punishment that would seem to be adequate, it would be superfluous to trouble the obliging Censor in the matter. To this end the one who bears the message lurks in a hidden corner of Tai until a certain hour. If I am in a position to intercept him there he will return the message to my hand; if not, he will straightway bear it to the integritous K'o-yih."

"May the President of Hades reward you—I am no longer in a position to do so!" murmured Shan Tien with concentrated feeling. "Draw near, Kai Lung," he continued sympathetically, "and indicate-with as little delay as possible-what in your opinion would constitute a sufficient punishment."

Thus invited and with his cords unbound, Kai Lung advanced and took his station near the table, Ming-shu noticeably making room for him.

"To be driven from your lofty presence and never again permitted to listen to the wisdom of your inspired lips would undoubtedly be the first essential of my penance, High Excellence."

"It is gran-inflicted," agreed Shan Tien, with swift decision.

"The necessary edict may conveniently be drafted in the form of a safe-conduct for this person and all others of his band to a point beyond the confines of your jurisdiction-when the usually agile-witted Ming-shu can sufficiently shake off the benumbing torpor now assailing him so as to use his brush."

"It is already begun, O virtuous harbinger of joy," protested the dazed Ming-shu, overturning all the four precious implements in his passion to comply. "A mere breath of time—"

"Let it be signed, sealed and thumb-pressed at every available point of ambiguity," enjoined Shan Tien.

"Having thus oppressed the vainglory of my self-willed mind, the presumption of this unworthy body must be subdued likewise. The burden of five hundred taels of silver should suffice. If not—"

"In the form of paper obligations, estimable Kai Lung, the same amount would go more conveniently within your scrip," suggested the Mandarin hopefully.

"Not convenience, O Mandarin, but bodily exhaustion is the essence of my task," reproved the story-teller.

"Yet consider the anguish of my internal pang, if thus encumbered, you sank spent by the wayside, and being thereby unable to withhold the message, you were called upon to endure a further ill."

"That, indeed, is worthy of our thought," confessed Kai Lung. "To this end I will further mortify myself by adventuring upon the uncertain apex of a trustworthy steed (a mode of progress new to my experience) until I enter Tai."

"The swiftest and most reputable awaits your guiding hand," replied Shan Tien.

"Let it be enticed forth into a quiet and discreet spot. In the interval, while the obliging Ming-shu plies an unfaltering brush, the task of weighing out my humiliating burden shall be ours."

In an incredibly short space of time, being continually urged on by the flattering anxiety of Shan Tien (whose precipitancy at one point became so acute that he mistook fourscore taels for five), all things were prepared. With the inscribed parchment well within his sleeve and the bags of silver ranged about his body, Kai Lung approached the platform that had been raised to enable him to subdue the expectant animal.

"Once in the desired position, weighted down as you are, there is little danger of your becoming displaced," remarked the Mandarin auspiciously.

"Your words are, as usual, many-sided in their wise application, benignity," replied Kai Lung. "One thing only yet remains. It is apart from the expression of this one's will, but as an act of justice to yourself and in order to complete the analogy —" And he indicated the direction of Ming-shu.

"Nevertheless you are agreeably understood," declared Shan Tien, moving apart. "Farewell."

As those who controlled the front part of the horse at this moment relaxed their tenacity, Kai Lung did not deem it prudent to reply, nor was he specifically observant of the things about. But a little later, while in the act of permitting the creature whose power he ruled to turn round for a last look at its former home, he saw that the unworthy no longer flourished. Ming-shu, with his own discarded cang around his vindictive neck, was being led off in the direction of the prison-house.

The Out-Passing Into a State of Assured Felicity of the Much-Enduring Two With Whom These Printed Leaves Have Chiefly Been Concerned

Although it was towards sunset, the heat of the day still hung above the dusty earth-road, and two who tarried within the shadow of an ancient arch were loath to resume their way. They had walked far, for the uncertain steed, having revealed a too contentious nature, had been disposed of in distant Tai to an honest stranger who freely explained the imperfection of its ignoble outline.

"Let us remain another space of time," pleaded Hwa-mei reposefully, "and as without your all-embracing art the course of events would undoubtedly have terminated very differently from what it has, will you not, out of an emotion of gratitude, relate a story for my ear alone, weaving into it the substance of this ancient arch whose shade proves our rest?"

"Your wish is the crown of my attainment, unearthly one," replied Kai Lung, preparing to obey. "This concerns the story of Ten-teh, whose name adorns the keystone of the fabric."

The Story of the Loyalty of Ten-teh, the Fisherman
"Devotion to the Emperor…." —*The Five Great Principles*

The reign of the enlightened Emperor Tung Kwei had closed amid scenes of treachery and lust, and in his perfidiously-spilled blood was extinguished the last pale hope of those faithful to his line. His only son was a nameless fugitive-by ceaseless report already Passed Beyond-his party scattered and crushed out like the sparks from his blackened Capital, while nothing that men thought dare pass their lips. The usurper Fuh-chi sat upon the dragon throne and spake with the voice of brass cymbals and echoing drums, his right hand shedding blood and his left hand spreading fire. To raise an eye before him was to ape with death, and a whisper in the outer ways foreran swift torture. With harrows he uprooted the land until no household could gather round its ancestral tablets, and with marble rollers he flattened it until none dare lift his head. For the body of each one who had opposed his ambition there was offered an equal weight of fine silver, and upon the head of the child-prince was set the reward of ten times his weight in pure gold. Yet in noisome swamps and forests, hidden in caves, lying on desolate islands, and concealing themselves in every kind of solitary place were those who daily prostrated themselves to the memory of Tung Kwei and by a sign acknowledged the authority of his infant son Kwo Kam. In the Crystal City there was a great roar of violence and drunken song, and men and women lapped from deep lakes filled up with wine; but the ricesacks of the poor had long been turned out and shaken for a little dust; their eyes were closing and in their hearts they were as powder between the mill-stones. On the north and the west the barbarians had begun to press forward in resistless waves, and from The Island to The Beak pirates laid waste the coast.

I. Under the Dragon's Wing

Among the lagoons of the Upper Seng river a cormorant fisher, Ten-teh by name, daily followed his occupation. In seasons of good harvest, when they of the villages had grain in abundance and money with which to procure a more varied diet, Ten-teh was able to regard the ever-changeful success of his venture without anxiety, and even to add perchance somewhat to his store; but when affliction lay upon the land the carefully gathered hoard melted away and he did not cease to upbraid himself for adopting so uncertain a means of livelihood. At these times the earth-tillers, having neither money to spend nor crops to harvest, caught such fish as they could for themselves. Others in their extremity did not scruple to drown themselves and their dependents in Ten-teh's waters, so that while none contributed to his prosperity the latter ones even greatly added to the embarrassment of his craft. When, therefore, his own harvest failed him in addition, or tempests drove him back to a dwelling which was destitute of food either for himself, his household, or his cormorants, his self-reproach did not appear to be ill-reasoned. Yet in spite of all Ten-teh was of a genial disposition, benevolent, respectful and incapable of guile. He sacrificed adequately at all festivals, and his only regret was that he had no son of his own and very scanty chances of ever becoming rich enough to procure one by adoption.

The sun was setting one day when Ten-teh reluctantly took up his propelling staff and began to urge his raft towards the shore. It was a season of parched crops and destitution in the villages, when disease could fondle the bones of even the most rotund and leprosy was the insidious condiment in every dish; yet never had the Imperial dues been higher, and each succeeding official had larger hands and a more inexorable face than the one before him. Ten-teh's hoarded resources had already followed the snows of the previous winter, his shelf was like the heart of a despot to whom the oppressed cry for pity, and the contents of the creel at his feet were too insignificant to tempt the curiosity even of his hungry cormorants. But the mists of the evening were by this time lapping the surface of the waters and he had no alternative but to abandon his fishing for the day.

"Truly they who go forth to fish, even in shallow waters, experience strange things when none are by to credit them," suddenly exclaimed his assistant —a mentally deficient youth of the villages whom Ten-teh charitably employed because all others rejected him. "Behold, master, a spectre bird approaches."

"Peace, witless," replied Ten-teh, not turning from his occupation, for it was no uncommon incident for the deficient youth to mistake widely-differing objects for one another or to claim a demoniacal insight into the most trivial happenings. "Visions do not materialize for such as thou and I."

"Nevertheless," continued the weakling, "if you will but slacken your agile proficiency with the pole, chieftain, our supper to-night may yet consist of something more substantial than the fish which it is our intention to catch to-morrow."

When the defective youth had continued for some time in this meaningless strain Ten-teh turned to rebuke him, when to his astonishment he perceived that a strange cormorant was endeavouring to reach them, its progress being impeded by an object which it carried in its mouth. Satisfying himself that his own birds were still on the raft, Ten-teh looked round in expectation for the boat of another fisherman, although none but he had ever within his memory sought those waters, but as far as he could see the wide-stretching lagoon was deserted by all but themselves. He accordingly waited, drawing in his pole, and inciting the bird on by cries of encouragement.

"A nobly-born cormorant without doubt," exclaimed the youth approvingly. "He is lacking the throat-strap, yet he holds his prey dexterously and makes no movement to consume it. But the fish itself is outlined strangely."

As the bird drew near Ten-teh also saw that it was devoid of the usual strap which in the exercise of his craft was necessary as a barrier against the gluttonous instincts of the race. It was unnaturally large, and even at a distance Ten-teh could see that its plumage was smoothed to a polished lustre, its eye alert, and the movement of its flight untamed. But, as the youth had said, the fish it carried loomed mysteriously.

"The Wise One and the Crafty Image-behold they prostrate themselves!" cried the youth in a tone of awe-inspired surprise, and without a pause he stepped off the raft and submerged himself beneath the waters.

It was even as he asserted; Ten-teh turned his eyes and lo, his two cormorants, instead of rising in anger, as their contentious nature prompted, had sunk to the ground and were doing obeisance. Much perturbed as to his own most prudent action, for the bird was nearing the craft, Ten-teh judged it safest to accept this token and falling down he thrice knocked his forehead submissively. When he looked up again the majestic bird had vanished as utterly as the flame that is quenched, and lying at his feet was a naked man-child.

"O master," said the voice of the assistant, as he cautiously protruded his head above the surface of the raft, "has the vision faded, or do creatures of the air before whom even their own kind kowtow still haunt the spot?"

"The manifestation has withdrawn," replied Ten-teh reassuringly, "but like the touch of the omnipotent Buddha it has left behind it that which proves its reality," and he pointed to the man-child.

"Beware, alas!" exclaimed the youth, preparing to immerse himself a second time if the least cause arose; "and on no account permit yourself to be drawn into the snare. Inevitably the affair tends to evil from the beginning and presently that which now appears as a man-child will assume the form of a devouring vampire and consume us all. Such occurrences are by no means uncommon when the great sky-lantern is at its full distension."

"To maintain otherwise would be impious," admitted his master, "but at the same time there is nothing to indicate that the beneficial deities are not the ones responsible for this apparition." With these humane words the kindly-disposed Ten-teh wrapped his outer robe about the man-child and turned to lay him in the empty creel, when to his profound astonishment he saw that it was now filled with fish of the rarest and most unapproachable kinds.

"Footsteps of the dragon!" exclaimed the youth, scrambling back on to the raft hastily; "undoubtedly your acuter angle of looking at the visitation was the inspired one. Let us abandon the man-child in an unfrequented spot and then proceed to divide the result of the adventure equally among us."

"An agreed portion shall be allotted," replied Ten-teh, "but to abandon so miraculously-endowed a being would cover even an outcast with shame."

"'Shame fades in the morning; debts remain from day to day,'" replied the youth, the allusion of the proverb being to the difficulty of sustaining life in times so exacting, when men pledged their household goods, their wives, even their ancestral records for a little flour or a jar of oil. "To the starving the taste of a grain of corn is more satisfying than the thought of a roasted ox, but as many years must pass as this creel now holds fish before the little one can disengage a catch or handle the pole."

"It is as the Many-Eyed One sees," replied Ten-teh, with unmoved determination. "This person has long desired a son, and those who walk into an earthquake while imploring heaven for a sign are unworthy of consideration. Take this fish and depart until the morrow. Also, unless you would have the villagers regard you as not only deficient but profane, reveal nothing of this happening to those whom you encounter." With these words Ten-teh dismissed him, not greatly disturbed at the thought of whatever he might do; for in no case would any believe a word he spoke, while the greater likelihood tended towards his forgetting everything before he had reached his home.

As Ten-teh approached his own door his wife came forth to meet him. "Much gladness!" she cried aloud before she saw his burden; "tempered only by a regret that you did not abandon your chase at an earlier hour. Fear not for the present that the wolf-tusk of famine shall gnaw our repose or that the dreaded wings of the white and scaly one shall hover about our house-top. Your wealthy cousin, journeying back to the Capital from the land of the spice forests, has been here in your absence, leaving you gifts of fur, silk, carved ivory, oil, wine, nuts and rice and rich foods of many kinds. He would have stayed to embrace you were it not that his company of bearers awaited him at an arranged spot and he had already been long delayed."

Then said Ten-teh, well knowing that he had no such desirable relative, but drawn to secrecy by the unnatural course of events: "The years pass unperceived and all changes but the heart of man; how appeared my cousin, and has he greatly altered under the enervating sun of a barbarian land?"

"He is now a little man, with a loose skin the colour of a finely-lacquered apricot," replied the woman. "His teeth are large and jagged, his expression open and sincere, and the sound of his breathing is like the continuous beating of waves upon a stony beach. Furthermore, he has ten fingers upon his left hand and a girdle of rubies about his waist."

"The description is unmistakable," said Ten-teh evasively. "Did he chance to leave a parting message of any moment?"

"He twice remarked: 'When the sun sets the moon rises, but to-morrow the drawn will break again,'" replied his wife. "Also, upon leaving he asked for ink, brushes and a fan, and upon it he inscribed certain words." She thereupon handed the fan to Ten-teh, who read, written in characters of surpassing beauty and exactness, the proverb: "Well-guarded lips, patient alertness and a heart conscientiously discharging its accepted duty: these three things have a sure reward."

At that moment Ten-teh's wife saw that he carried something beyond his creel and discovering the man-child she cried out with delight, pouring forth a torrent of inquiries and striving to possess it. "A tale half told is the father of many lies," exclaimed Ten-teh at length, "and of the greater part of what you ask this person knows neither the beginning nor the end. Let what is written on the fan suffice." With this he explained to her the meaning of the characters and made their significance clear. Then without another word he placed the man-child in her arms and led her back into the house.

From that time Hoang, as he was thenceforward called, was received into the household of Ten-teh, and from that time Ten-teh prospered. Without ever approaching a condition of affluence or dignified ease, he was never exposed to the penury and vicissitudes which he had been wont to experience; so that none had need to go hungry or ill-clad. If famine ravaged the villages Ten-teh's store of grain was miraculously maintained; his success on the lagoons was unvaried, fish even leaping on to the structure of the raft. Frequently in dark and undisturbed parts of the house he found sums of money and other valuable articles of which he had no remembrance, while it was no uncommon thing for passing merchants to leave bales of goods at his door in mistake and to meet with some accident which prevented them from ever again visiting that part of the country. In the meanwhile Hoang grew from infancy into childhood, taking part with Ten-teh in all his pursuits, yet even in the most menial occupation never wholly shaking off the air of command and nobility of bearing which lay upon him. In strength and endurance he outpaced all the youths around, while in the manipulation of the raft and the dexterous handling of the cormorants he covered Ten-teh with gratified shame. So excessive was the devotion which he aroused in those who knew him that the deficient youth wept openly if Hoang chanced to cough or sneeze; and it is even asserted that on more than one occasion high officials, struck by the authority of his presence, though he might be in the act of carrying fish along the road, hastily descended from their chairs and prostrated themselves before him.

In the fourteenth year of the reign of the usurper Fuh-chi a little breeze rising in the Province of Sz-chuen began to spread through all the land and men's minds were again agitated by the memory of a hope which had long seemed dead. At that period the tyrannical Fuh-chi finally abandoned the last remaining vestige of restraint and by his crimes and excesses alienated even the protection of the evil spirits and the fidelity of his chosen guard; so that he conspired with himself to bring about his own destruction. One discriminating adviser alone had stood at the foot of the throne, and being no less resolute than far-seeing, he did not hesitate to warn Fuh-chi and to hold the prophetic threat of rebellion before his eyes. Such sincerity met with the reward not difficult to conjecture.

"Who are our enemies?" exclaimed Fuh-chi, turning to a notorious flatterer at his side, "and where are they who are displeased with our too lenient rule?"

"Your enemies, O Brother of the Sun and Prototype of the Red-legged Crane, are dead and unmourned. The living do naught but speak of your clemency and bask in the radiance of your eye-light," protested the flatterer.

"It is well said," replied Fuh-chi. "How is it, then, that any can eat of our rice and receive our bounty and yet repay us with ingratitude and taunts, holding their joints stiffly in our presence? Lo, even lambs have the grace to suck kneeling."

"Omnipotence," replied the just minister, "if this person is deficient in the more supple graces of your illustrious Court it is because the greater part of his life has been spent in waging your wars in uncivilized regions. Nevertheless, the alarm can be as competently sounded upon a brass drum as by a silver trumpet, and his words came forth from a sincere throat."

"Then the opportunity is by no means to be lost," exclaimed Fuh-chi, who was by this time standing some distance from himself in the effects of distilled pear juice; "for we have long desired to see the difference which must undoubtedly exist between a sincere throat and one bent to the continual use of evasive flattery."

Without further consideration he ordered that both persons should be beheaded and that their bodies should be brought for his inspection. From that time there was none to stay his hand or to guide his policy, so that he mixed blood and wine in foolishness and lust until the land was sick and heaved.

The whisper starting from Sz-chuen passed from house to house and from town to town until it had cast a network over every province, yet no man could say whence it came or by whom the word was passed. It might be in the manner of a greeting or the pledging of a cup of tea, by the offer of a coin to a blind beggar at the gate, in the fold of a carelessly-worn garment, or even by the passing of a leper through a town. Oppression still lay heavily upon the people; but it was without aim and carried no restraint; famine and pestilence still went hand in hand, but the message rode on their backs and was hospitably received. Soon, growing bolder, men stood face to face and spoke of settled plans, gave signs, and openly declared themselves. On all sides proclamations began to be affixed; next weapons were distributed, hands were made proficient in their uses, until nothing remained but definite instruction and a swift summons for the appointed day. At intervals omens had appeared in the sky and prophecies had been put into the mouths of sooth-sayers, so that of the success of the undertaking and of its justice none doubted. On the north and the west entire districts had reverted to barbarism, and on the coasts the pirates anchored by the water-gates of walled cities and tossed jests to the watchmen on the towers.

Throughout this period Ten-teh had surrounded Hoang with an added care, never permitting him to wander beyond his sight, and distrusting all men in spite of his confiding nature. One night, when a fierce storm beyond the memory of man was raging, there came at the middle hour a knocking upon the outer wall, loud and insistent; nevertheless Ten-teh did not at once throw open the door in courteous invitation, but drawing aside a shutter he looked forth. Before the house stood one of commanding stature, clad from head to foot in robes composed of plaited grasses, dyed in many colours. Around him ran a stream of water, while the lightning issuing in never-ceasing flashes from his eyes revealed that his features were rugged and his ears pierced with many holes from which the wind whistled until the sound resembled the shrieks of ten thousand tortured ones under the branding-iron. From him the tempest proceeded in every direction, but he stood unmoved among it, without so much as a petal of the flowers he wore disarranged.

In spite of these indications, and of the undoubted fact that the Being could destroy the house with a single glance, Ten-teh still hesitated.

"The night is dark and stormy, and robbers and evil spirits are certainly about in large numbers, striving to enter unperceived by any open door," he protested, but with becoming deference. "With what does your welcome and opportune visit concern itself, honourable stranger?"

"The one before you is not accustomed to be questioned in his doings, or even to be spoken to by ordinary persons," replied the Being. "Nevertheless, Ten-teh, there is that in your history for the past fourteen years which saves you from the usual fatal consequences of so gross an indiscretion. Let it suffice that it is concerned with the flight of the cormorant."

Upon this assurance Ten-teh no longer sought evasion. He hastened to throw open the outer door and the stranger entered, whereupon the tempest ceased, although the thunder and lightning still lingered among the higher mountains. In passing through the doorway the robe of plaited grasses caught for a moment on the staple and pulling aside revealed that the Being wore upon his left foot a golden sandal and upon his right foot one of iron, while embedded in his throat was a great pearl. Convinced by this that he was indeed one of the Immortal Eight, Ten-teh prostrated himself fittingly, and explained that the apparent disrespect of his reception arose from a conscientious interest in the safety of the one committed to his care.

"It is well," replied the Being affably; "and your unvarying fidelity shall not go unrewarded when the proper time arrives. Now bring forward the one whom hitherto you have wisely called Hoang."

In secret during the past years Ten-teh had prepared for such an emergency a yellow silk robe bearing embroidered on it the Imperial Dragon with Five Claws. He had also provided suitable ornaments, fur coverings for the hands and face, and a sword and shield. Waking Hoang, he quickly dressed him, sprinkled a costly perfume about his head and face, and taking him for the last time by the hand he led him into the presence of the stranger.

"Kwo Kam, chosen representative of the sacred line of Tang," began the Being, when he and Hoang had exchanged signs and greetings of equality in an obscure tongue, "the grafted peach-tree on the Crystal Wall is stricken and the fruit is ripe and rotten to the touch. The flies that have fed upon its juice are drunk with it and lie helpless on the ground; the skin is empty and blown out with air, the leaves withered, and about the root is coiled a great worm which has secretly worked to this end. From the Five Points of the kingdom and beyond the Outer Willow Circle the Sheaf-binders have made a full report and it has been judged that the time is come for the tree to be roughly shaken. To this destiny the Old Ones of your race now call you; but beware of setting out unless your face should be unchangingly fixed and your heart pure from all earthly desires and base considerations."

"The decision is too ever-present in my mind to need reflection," replied Hoang resolutely. "To grind to powder that presumptuous tyrant utterly, to restore the integrity of the violated boundaries of the land, and to set up again the venerable Tablets of the true Tang line-these desires have long since worn away the softer portion of this person's heart by constant thought."

"The choice has been made and the words have been duly set down," said the Being. "If you maintain your high purpose to a prosperous end nothing can exceed your honour in the Upper Air; if you fail culpably, or even through incapacity, the lot of Fuh-chi himself will be enviable compared with yours."

Understanding that the time had now come for his departure, Hoang approached Ten-teh as though he would have embraced him, but the Being made a gesture of restraint.

"Yet, O instructor, for the space of fourteen years —" protested Hoang.

"It has been well and discreetly accomplished," replied the Being in a firm but not unsympathetic voice, "and Ten-teh's reward, which shall be neither slight nor grudging, is awaiting him in the Upper Air, where already his immediate ancestors are very honourably regarded in consequence. For many years, O Ten-teh, there has dwelt beneath your roof one who from this moment must be regarded as having passed away without leaving even a breath of memory behind. Before you stands your sovereign, to whom it is seemly that you should prostrate yourself in unquestioning obeisance. Do not look for any recompense or distinction here below in return for that which you have done towards a nameless one; for in the State there are many things which for high reasons cannot be openly proclaimed for the ill-disposed to use as feathers in their darts. Yet take this ring; the ears of the Illimitable Emperor are never closed to the supplicating petition of his children and should such a contingency arise you may freely lay your cause before him with the full assurance of an unswerving justice."

A moment later the storm broke out again with redoubled vigour, and raising his face from the ground Ten-teh perceived that he was again alone.

II. The Message from the Outer Land

After the departure of Hoang the affairs of Ten-teh ceased to prosper. The fish which for so many years had leaped to meet his hand now maintained an unparalleled dexterity in avoiding it; continual storms drove him day after day back to the shore, and the fostering beneficence of the deities seemed to be withdrawn, so that he no longer found forgotten stores of wealth nor did merchants ever again mistake his door for that of another to whom they were indebted.

In the year that followed there passed from time to time through the secluded villages lying in the Upper Seng valley persons who spoke of the tumultuous events progressing everywhere. In such a manner those who had remained behind learned that the great rising had been honourably received by the justice-loving in every province, but that many of official rank, inspired by no friendship towards Fuh-chi, but terror-stricken at the alternatives before them, had closed certain strong cities against the Army of the Avenging Pure. It was at this crisis, when the balance of the nation's destiny hung poised, that Kwo Kam, the only son of the Emperor Tung Kwei, and rightful heir of the dynasty of the glorious Tang, miraculously appeared at the head of the Avenging Pure and being acclaimed their leader with a unanimous shout led them on through a series of overwhelming and irresistible victories. At a later period it was told how Kwo Kam had been crowned and installed upon his father's throne, after receiving a mark of celestial approbation in the Temple of Heaven, how Fuh-chi had escaped and fled and how his misleading records had been publicly burned and his detestable name utterly blotted out.

At this period an even greater misfortune than his consistent ill success met Ten-teh. A neighbouring mandarin, on a false pretext, caused him to be brought before him, and speaking very sternly of certain matters in the past, which, he said, out of a well-intentioned regard for the memory of Ten-teh's father he would not cast abroad, he fined him a much larger sum than all he possessed, and then at once caused the raft and the cormorants to be seized in satisfaction of the claim. This he did because his heart was bad, and the sight of Ten-teh bearing a cheerful countenance under continual privation had become offensive to him.

The story of this act of rapine Ten-teh at once carried to the appointed head of the village communities, assuring him that he was ignorant of the cause, but that no crime or wrong-doing had been committed to call for so overwhelming an affliction in return, and entreating him to compel a just restitution and liberty to pursue his inoffensive calling peaceably in the future.

"Listen well, O unassuming Ten-teh, for you are a person of discernment and one with a mature knowledge of the habits of all swimming creatures," said the headman after attending patiently to Ten-teh's words. "If two lean and insignificant carp encountered a voracious pike and one at length fell into his jaws, by what means would the other compel the assailant to release his prey?"

"So courageous an emotion would serve no useful purpose," replied Ten-teh. "Being ill-equipped for such a conflict, it would inevitably result in the second fish also falling a prey to the voracious pike, and recognizing this, the more fortunate of the two would endeavour to escape by lying unperceived among the reeds about."

"The answer is inspired and at the same time sufficiently concise to lie within the hollow bowl of an opium pipe," replied the headman, and turning to his bench he continued in his occupation of beating flax with a wooden mallet.

"Yet," protested Ten-teh, when at length the other paused, "surely the matter could be placed before those in authority in so convincing a light by one possessing your admitted eloquence that Justice would stumble over herself in her haste to liberate the oppressed and to degrade the guilty."

"The phenomenon has occasionally been witnessed, but latterly it would appear that the conscientious deity in question must have lost all power of movement, or perhaps even fatally injured herself, as the result of some such act of rash impulsiveness in the past," replied the headman sympathetically.

"Alas, then," exclaimed Ten-teh, "is there, under the most enlightened form of government in the world, no prescribed method of obtaining redress?"

"Assuredly," replied the headman; "the prescribed method is the part of the system that has received the most attention. As the one of whom you complain is a mandarin of the fifth degree, you may fittingly address yourself to his superiors of the fourth, third, second and first degrees. Then there are the city governors, the district prefects, the provincial rulers, the Imperial Assessors, the Board of Censors, the Guider of the Vermilion Pencil, and, finally, the supreme Emperor himself. To each of these, if you are wealthy enough to reach his actual presence, you may prostrate yourself in turn, and each one, with many courteous expressions of intolerable regret that the matter does not come within his office, will refer you to another. The more prudent course, therefore, would seem to be that of beginning with the Emperor rather than reaching him as the last resort, and as you are now without means of livelihood if you remain here there is no reason why you should not journey to the Capital and make the attempt."

"The Highest!" exclaimed Ten-teh, with a pang of unfathomable emotion. "Is there, then, no middle way? Who is Ten-teh, the obscure and illiterate fisherman, that he should thrust himself into the presence of the Son of Heaven? If the mother of the dutiful Chou Yii could destroy herself and her family at one blow to the end that her son might serve his sovereign with a single heart, how degraded an outcast must he be who would obtrude his own trivial misfortunes at so critical a time?"

"'A thorn in one's own little finger is more difficult to endure than a sword piercing the sublime Emperor's arm,'" replied the headman, resuming his occupation. "But if your angle of regarding the various obligations is as you have stated it, then there is obviously nothing more to be said. In any case it is more than doubtful whether the Fountain of Justice would raise an eyelash if you, by every combination of fortunate circumstance, succeeded in reaching his presence."

"The headman has spoken, and his word is ten times more weighty than that of an ill-educated fisherman," replied Ten-teh submissively, and he departed.

From that time Ten-teh sought to sustain life upon roots and wild herbs which he collected laboriously and not always in sufficient quantities from the woods and rank wastes around. Soon even this resource failed him in a great measure, for a famine of unprecedented harshness swept over that part of the province. All supplies of adequate food ceased, and those who survived were driven by the pangs of hunger to consume weeds and the bark of trees, fallen leaves, insects of the lowest orders and the bones of wild animals which had died in the forest. To carry a little rice openly was a rash challenge to those who still valued life, and a loaf of chaff and black mould was guarded as a precious jewel. No wife or daughter could weigh in the balance against a measure of corn, and men sold themselves into captivity to secure the coarse nourishment which the rich allotted to their slaves. Those who remained in the villages followed in Ten-teh's footsteps, so that the meagre harvest that hitherto had failed to supply one household now constituted the whole provision for many. At length these persons, seeing a lingering but inevitable death before them all, came together and spoke of how this might perchance be avoided.

"Let us consider well," said one of their number, "for it may be that succour would not be withheld did we but know the precise manner in which to invoke it."

"Your words are light, O Tan-yung, and your eyes too bright in looking at things which present no encouragement whatever," replied another. "We who remain are old, infirm, or in some way deficient, or we would ere this have sold ourselves into slavery or left this accursed desert in search of a more prolific land. Therefore our existence is of no value to the State, so that they will not take any pains to preserve it. Furthermore, now being beyond the grasp of the most covetous extortion, the district officials have no reason for maintaining an interest in our lives. Assuredly there is no escape except by the White Door of which each one himself holds the key."

"Yet," objected a third, "the aged Ning has often recounted how in the latter years of the reign of the charitable Emperor Kwong, when a similar infliction lay upon the land, a bullock-load of rice was sent daily into the villages of the valley and freely distributed by the headman. Now that same munificent Kwong was a direct ancestor to the third degree of our own Kwo Kam."

"Alas!" remarked a person who had lost many of his features during a raid of brigands, "since the days of the commendable Kwong, while the feet of our lesser ones have been growing smaller the hands of our greater ones have been growing larger. Yet even nowadays, by the protection of the deities, the bullock might reach us."

"The wheel-grease of the cart would alone make the day memorable," murmured another.

"O brothers," interposed one who had not yet spoken, "do not cause our throats to twitch convulsively; nor is it in any way useful to leave the date of solid reflection in pursuit of the stone of light and versatile fancy. Is it thought to be expedient that we should send an emissary to those in authority, pleading our straits?"

"Have not two already journeyed to Kuing-yi in our cause, and to what end?" replied the second one who had raised his voice.

"They did but seek the city mandarin and failed to reach his ear, being empty-handed," urged Tan-yung. "The distance to the Capital is admittedly great, yet it is no more than a persevering and resolute-minded man could certainly achieve. There prostrating himself before the Sublime One and invoking the memory of the imperishable Kwong he could so outline our necessity and despair that the one wagon-load referred to would be increased by nine and the unwieldy oxen give place to relays of swift horses."

"The Emperor!" exclaimed the one who had last spoken, in tones of undisguised contempt towards Tan-yung. "Is the eye of the Unapproachable Sovereign less than that of a city mandarin, that having failed to come near the one we should now strive to reach the other; or are we, peradventure, to fill the sleeves of our messenger with gold and his inner scrip with sapphires!" Nevertheless the greater part of those who stood around zealously supported Tan-yung, crying aloud: "The Emperor! The suggestion is inspired! Undoubtedly the beneficent Kwo Kam will uphold our cause and our troubles may now be considered as almost at an end."

"Yet," interposed a faltering voice, "who among us is to go?"

At the mention of this necessary detail of the plan the cries which were the loudest raised in exultation suddenly leapt back upon themselves as each person looked in turn at all the others and then at himself. The one who had urged the opportune but disconcerting point was lacking in the power of movement in his lower limbs and progressed at a pace little advanced to that of a shell-cow upon two slabs of wood. Tan-yung was subject to a disorder which without any warning cast him to the ground almost daily in a condition of writhing frenzy; the one who had opposed him was paralysed in all but his head and feet, while those who stood about were either blind, lame, camel-backed, leprous, armless, misshapen, or in some way mentally or bodily deficient in an insuperable degree. "Alas!" exclaimed one, as the true understanding of their deformities possessed him, "not only would they of the Court receive it as a most detestable insult if we sent such as ourselves, but the probability of anyone so harassed overcoming the difficulties of river, desert and mountain barrier is so remote that this person is more than willing to stake his entire share of the anticipated bounty against a span-length of succulent lotus root or an embossed coffin handle."

"Let unworthy despair fade!" suddenly exclaimed Tan-yung, who nevertheless had been more downcast than any other a moment before; "for among us has been retained one who has probably been especially destined for this very service. There is yet Ten-teh. Let us seek him out."

With this design they sought for Ten-teh and finding him in his hut they confidently invoked his assistance, pointing out how he would save all their lives and receive great honour. To their dismay Ten-teh received them with solemn curses and drove them from his door with blows, calling them traitors, ungrateful ones, and rebellious subjects whose minds were so far removed from submissive loyalty that rather than perish harmlessly they would inopportunely thrust themselves in upon the attention of the divine Emperor when his mind was full of great matters and his thoughts tenaciously fixed upon the scheme for reclaiming the abandoned outer lands of his forefathers. "Behold," he cried, "when a hand is raised to sweep into oblivion a thousand earthworms they lift no voice in protest, and in this matter ye are less than earthworms. The dogs are content to starve dumbly while their masters feast, and ye are less than dogs. The dutiful son cheerfully submits himself to torture on the chance that his father's sufferings may be lessened, and the Emperor, as the supreme head, is more to be venerated than any father; but your hearts are sheathed in avarice and greed." Thus he drove them away, and their last hope being gone they wandered back to the forest, wailing and filling the air with their despairing moans; for the brief light that had inspired them was extinguished and the thought that by a patient endurance they might spare the Emperor an unnecessary pang was not a sufficient recompense in their eyes.

The time of warmth and green life passed. With winter came floods and snow-storms, great tempests from the north and bitter winds that cut men down as though they had been smitten by the sword. The rivers and lagoons were frozen over; the meagre sustenance of the earth lay hidden beneath an impenetrable crust of snow and ice, until those who had hitherto found it a desperate chance to live from day to day now abandoned the unequal struggle for the more attractive certainty of a swift and painless death. One by one the fires went out in the houses of the dead; the ever-increasing snow broke down the walls. Wild beasts from the mountains walked openly about the deserted streets, thrust themselves through such doors as were closed against them and lurked by night in the most sacred recesses of the ruined temples. The strong and the wealthy had long since fled, and presently out of all the eleven villages of the valley but one man remained alive and Ten-teh lay upon the floor of his inner chamber, dying.

"There was a sign–there was a sign in the past that more was yet to be accomplished," ran the one thought of his mind as he lay there helpless, his last grain consumed and the ashes on his hearthstone black. "Can it be that so solemn an omen has fallen unfulfilled to the ground; or has this person long walked hand in hand with shadows in the Middle Air?"

"Dwellers of Yin; dwellers of Chung-yo; of Wei, Shan-ta, Feng, the Rock of the Bleak Pagoda and all the eleven villages of the valley!" cried a voice from without. "Ho, inhospitable sleeping ones, I have reached the last dwelling of the plain and no one has as yet bidden me enter, no voice invited me to unlace my sandals and partake of tea. Do they fear that this person is a robber in disguise, or is this the courtesy of the Upper Seng valley?"

"They sleep more deeply," said Ten-teh, speaking back to the full extent of his failing power; "perchance your voice was not raised high enough, O estimable wayfarer. Nevertheless, whether you come in peace or armed with violence, enter here, for the one who lies within is past help and beyond injury."

Upon this invitation the stranger entered and stood before Ten-teh. He was of a fierce and martial aspect, carrying a sword at his belt and a bow and arrows slung across his back, but privation had set a deep mark upon his features and his body bore unmistakable traces of a long and arduous march. His garments were ragged, his limbs torn by rocks and thorny undergrowth, while his ears had fallen away before the rigour of the ice-laden blasts. In his right hand he carried a staff upon which he leaned at every step, and glancing to the ground Ten-teh perceived that the lower part of his sandals were worn away so that he trod painfully upon his bruised and naked feet.

"Greeting," said Ten-teh, when they had regarded each other for a moment; "yet, alas, no more substantial than of the lips, for the hospitality of the eleven villages is shrunk to what you see before you," and he waved his arm feebly towards the empty bowl and the blackened hearth. "Whence come you?"

"From the outer land of Im-kau," replied the other. "Over the Kang-ling mountains."

"It is a moon-to-moon journey," said Ten-teh. "Few travellers have ever reached the valley by that inaccessible track."

"More may come before the snow has melted," replied the stranger, with a stress of significance. "Less than seven days ago this person stood upon the northern plains."

Ten-teh raised himself upon his arm. "There existed, many cycles ago, a path-of a single foot's width, it is said-along the edge of the Pass called the Ram's Horn, but it has been lost beyond the memory of man."

"It has been found again," said the stranger, "and Kha-hia and his horde of Kins, joined by the vengeance-breathing Fuh-chi, lie encamped less than a short march beyond the Pass."

"It can matter little," said Ten-teh, trembling but speaking to reassure himself. "The people are at peace among themselves, the Capital adequately defended, and an army sufficiently large to meet any invasion can march out and engage the enemy at a spot most convenient to ourselves."

"A few days hence, when all preparation is made," continued the stranger, "a cloud of armed men will suddenly appear openly, menacing the western boundaries. The Capital and the fortified places will be denuded, and all who are available will march out to meet them. They will be but as an empty shell designed to serve a crafty purpose, for in the meanwhile Kha-hia will creep unsuspected through the Kang-lings by the Ram's Horn and before the army can be recalled he will swiftly fall upon the defenceless Capital and possess it."

"Alas!" exclaimed Ten-teh, "why has the end tarried thus long if it be but for this person's ears to carry to the grave so tormenting a message! Yet how comes it, O stranger, that having been admitted to Kha-hia's innermost council you now betray his trust, or how can reliance be placed upon the word of one so treacherous?"

"Touching the reason," replied the stranger, with no appearance of resentment, "that is a matter which must one day lie between Kha-hia, this person, and one long since Passed Beyond, and to this end have I uncomplainingly striven for the greater part of a lifetime. For the rest, men do not cross the King-langs in midwinter, wearing away their lives upon those stormy heights, to make a jest of empty words. Already sinking into the Under World, even as I am now powerless to raise myself above the ground, I, Nau-Kaou, swear and attest what I have spoken."

"Yet, alas!" exclaimed Ten-teh, striking his breast bitterly in his dejection, "to what end is it that you have journeyed? Know that out of all the eleven villages by famine and pestilence not another man remains. Beyond the valley stretch the uninhabited sand plains, so that between here and the Capital not a solitary dweller could be found to bear the message."

"The Silent One laughs!" replied Nau-Kaou dispassionately; and drawing his cloak more closely about him he would have composed himself into a reverent attitude to Pass Beyond.

"Not so!" cried Ten-teh, rising in his inspired purpose and standing upright despite the fever that possessed him; "the jewel is precious beyond comparison and the casket mean and falling to pieces, but there is none other. This person will bear the warning."

The stranger looked up from the ground in an increasing wonder. "You do but dream, old man," he said in a compassionate voice. "Before me stands one of trembling limbs and infirm appearance. His face is the colour of potter's clay; his eyes sunken and yellow. His bones protrude everywhere like the points of armour, while his garment is scarcely fitted to afford protection against a summer breeze."

"Such dreams do not fade with the light," replied Ten-teh resolutely. "His feet are whole and untired; his mind clear. His heart is as inflexibly fixed as the decrees of destiny, and, above all, his purpose is one which may reasonably demand divine encouragement."

"Yet there are the Han-sing mountains, flung as an insurmountable barrier across the way," said Nau-Kaou.

"The wind passes over them," replied Ten-teh, binding on his sandals.

"The Girdle," continued the other, thereby indicating the formidable obstacle presented by the tempestuous river, swollen by the mountain snows.

"The fish, moved by no great purpose, swim from bank to bank," again replied Ten-teh. "Tell me rather, for the time presses when such issues hang on the lips of dying men, to what extent Kha-hia's legions stretch?"

"In number," replied Nau-Kaou, closing his eyes, "they are as the stars on a very clear night, when the thousands in front do but serve to conceal the innumerable throng behind. Yet even a small and resolute army taking up its stand secretly in this valley and falling upon them unexpectedly when half were crossed could throw them into disorder and rout, and utterly destroy the power of Kha-hia for all time."

"So shall it be," said Ten-Teh from the door. "Pass Upward with a tranquil mind, O stranger from the outer land. The torch which you have borne so far will not fail until his pyre is lit."

"Stay but a moment," cried Nau-Kaou. "This person, full of vigour and resource, needed the spur of a most poignant hate to urge his trailing footsteps. Have you, O decrepit one, any such incentive to your failing powers?"

"A mightier one," came back the voice of Ten-teh, across the snow from afar. "Fear not."

"It is well; they are the great twin brothers," exclaimed Nau-Kaou. "Kha-hia is doomed!" Then twice beating the ground with his open hand he loosened his spirit and passed contentedly into the Upper Air.

III. The Last Service

The wise and accomplished Emperor Kwo Kam (to whom later historians have justly given the title "Profound") sat upon his agate throne in the Hall of Audience. Around him were gathered the most illustrious from every province of the Empire, while emissaries from the courts of other rulers throughout the world passed in procession before him, prostrating themselves in token of the dependence which their sovereigns confessed, and imploring his tolerant acceptance of the priceless gifts they brought. Along the walls stood musicians and singers who filled the air with melodious visions, while fan-bearing slaves dexterously wafted perfumed breezes into every group. So unparalleled was the splendour of the scene that rare embroidered silks were trodden under foot and a great fountain was composed of diamonds dropping into a jade basin full of pearls, but Kwo Kam outshone all else by the dignity of his air and the magnificence of his apparel.

Suddenly, and without any of the heralding strains of drums and cymbals by which persons of distinction had been announced, the arras before the chief door was plucked aside and a figure, blinded by so much jewelled brilliance, stumbled into the chamber, still holding thrust out before him the engraved ring bearing the Imperial emblem which alone had enabled him to pass the keepers of the outer gates alive. He had the appearance of being a very aged man, for his hair was white and scanty, his face deep with shadows and lined like a river bank when the waters have receded, and as he advanced, bent down with infirmity, he mumbled certain words in ceaseless repetition. From his feet and garment there fell a sprinkling of sand as he moved, and blood dropped to the floor from many an unhealed wound, but his eyes were very bright, and though sword-handles were grasped on all sides at the sight of so presumptuous an intrusion, yet none opposed him. Rather, they fell back, leaving an open passage to the foot of the throne; so that when the Emperor lifted his eyes he saw the aged man moving slowly forward to do obeisance.

"Ten-teh, revered father!" exclaimed Kwo Kam, and without pausing a moment he leapt down from off his throne, thrust aside those who stood about him and casting his own outer robe of state about Ten-teh's shoulders embraced him affectionately.

"Supreme ruler," murmured Ten-teh, speaking for the Emperor's ear alone, and in such a tone of voice as of one who has taught himself a lesson which remains after all other consciousness has passed away, "an army swiftly to the north! Let them dispose themselves about the eleven villages and, overlooking the invaders as they assemble, strike when they are sufficiently numerous for the victory to be lasting and decisive. The passage of the Ram's Horn has been found and the malignant Fuh-chi, banded in an unnatural alliance with the barbarian Kins, lies with itching feet beyond the Kang-lings. The invasion threatening on the west is but a snare; let a single camp, feigning to be a multitudinous legion, be thrown against it. Suffer delay from no cause. Weigh no alternative. He who speaks is Ten-teh, at whose assuring word the youth Hoang was wont to cast himself into the deepest waters fearlessly. His eyes are no less clear to-day, but his heart is made small with overwhelming deference or in unshrinking loyalty he would cry: 'Hear and obey! All, all-Flags, Ironcaps, Tigers, Braves-all to the Seng valley, leaving behind them the swallow in their march and moving with the guile and secrecy of the ringed tree-snake.'" With these words Ten-teh's endurance passed its drawn-out limit and again repeating in a clear and decisive voice, "All, all to the north!" he released his joints and would have fallen to the ground had it not been for the Emperor's restraining arms.

When Ten-teh again returned to a knowledge of the lower world he was seated upon the throne to which the Emperor had borne him. His rest had been made easy by the luxurious cloaks of the courtiers and emissaries which had been lavishly heaped about him, while during his trance the truly high-minded Kwo Kam had not disdained to wash his feet in a golden basin of perfumed water, to shave his limbs, and to anoint his head. The greater part of the assembly had been dismissed, but some of the most trusted among the ministers and officials still waited in attendance about the door.

"Great and enlightened one," said Ten-teh, as soon as his stupor was lifted, "has this person delivered his message competently, for his mind was still a seared vision of snow and sand and perchance his tongue has stumbled?"

"Bend your ears to the wall, O my father," replied the Emperor, "and be assured."

A radiance of the fullest satisfaction lifted the settling shadows for a moment from Ten-teh's countenance as from the outer court came at intervals the low and guarded words of command, the orderly clashing of weapons as they fell into their appointed places, and the regular and unceasing tread of armed men marching forth. "To the Seng valley-by no chance to the west?" he demanded, trembling between anxiety and hope, and drinking in the sound of the rhythmic tramp which to his ears possessed a more alluring charm than if it were the melody of blind singing girls.

"Even to the eleven villages," replied the Emperor. "At your unquestioned word, though my kingdom should hang upon the outcome."

"It is sufficient to have lived so long," said Ten-teh. Then perceiving that it was evening, for the jade and crystal lamps were lighted, he cried out: "The time has leapt unnoted. How many are by this hour upon the march?"

"Sixscore companies of a hundred spearmen each," said Kwo Kam. "By dawn four times that number will be on their way. In less than three days a like force will be disposed about the passes of the Han-sing mountains and the river fords, while at the same time the guards from less important towns will have been withdrawn to take their place upon the city walls."

"Such words are more melodious than the sound of many marble lutes," said Ten-teh, sinking back as though in repose. "Now is mine that peace spoken of by the philosopher Chi-chey as the greatest: 'The eye closing upon its accomplished work.'"

"Assuredly do you stand in need of the healing sleep of nature," said the Emperor, not grasping the inner significance of the words. "Now that you are somewhat rested, esteemed sire, suffer this one to show you the various apartments of the palace so that you may select for your own such as most pleasingly attract your notice."

"Yet a little longer," entreated Ten-teh. "A little longer by your side and listening to your voice alone, if it may be permitted, O sublime one."

"It is for my father to command," replied Kwo Kam. "Perchance they of the eleven villages sent some special message of gratifying loyalty which you would relate without delay?"

"They slept, omnipotence, or without doubt it would be so," replied Ten-teh.

"Truly," agreed the Emperor. "It was night when you set forth, my father?"

"The shadows had fallen deeply upon the Upper Seng Valley," said Ten-teh evasively.

"The Keeper of the Imperial Stores has frequently conveyed to us their expressions of unfeigned gratitude for the bounty by which we have sought to keep alive the memory of their hospitality and our own indebtedness," said the Emperor.

"The sympathetic person cannot have overstated their words," replied Ten-teh falteringly. "Never, as their own utterances bear testimony, never was food more welcome, fuel more eagerly sought for, and clothing more necessary than in the years of the most recent past."

"The assurance is as dew upon the drooping lotus," said Kwo Kam, with a lightening countenance. "To maintain the people in an unshaken prosperity, to frown heavily upon extortion and to establish justice throughout the land-these have been the achievements of the years of peace. Yet often, O my father, this one's mind has turned yearningly to the happier absence of strife and the simple abundance which you and they of the valley know."

"The deities ordain and the balance weighs; your reward will be the greater," replied Ten-teh. Already he spoke with difficulty, and his eyes were fast closing, but he held himself rigidly, well knowing that his spirit must still obey his will.

"Do you not crave now to partake of food and wine?" inquired the Emperor, with tender solicitude. "A feast has long been prepared of the choicest dishes in your honour. Consider well the fatigue through which you have passed."

"It has faded," replied Ten-teh, in a voice scarcely above a whisper, "the earthly body has ceased to sway the mind. A little longer, restored one; a very brief span of time."

"Your words are my breath, my father," said the Emperor, deferentially. "Yet there is one matter which we had reserved for affectionate censure. It would have spared the feet of one who is foremost in our concern if you had been content to send the warning by one of the slaves whose acceptance we craved last year, while you followed more leisurely by the chariot and the eight white horses which we deemed suited to your use."

Ten-teh was no longer able to express himself in words, but at this indication of the Emperor's unceasing thought a great happiness shone on his face. "What remains?" must reasonably have been his reflection; "or who shall leave the shade of the fruitful palm-tree to search for raisins?" Therefore having reached so supreme an eminence that there was nothing human above, he relaxed the effort by which he had so long sustained himself, and suffering his spirit to pass unchecked, he at once fell back lifeless among the cushions of the throne.

That all who should come after might learn by his example, the history of Ten-teh was inscribed upon eighteen tablets of jade, carved patiently and with graceful skill by the most expert stone-cutters of the age. A triumphal arch of seven heights was also erected outside the city and called by his name, but the efforts of story-tellers and poets will keep alive the memory of Ten-teh even when these imperishable monuments shall have long fallen from their destined use.

* * *

When Kai Lung had completed the story of the loyalty of Ten- teh and had pointed out the forgotten splendour of the crumbling arch, the coolness of the evening tempted them to resume their way. Moving without discomfort to themselves before nightfall they reached a small but seemly cottage conveniently placed upon the mountain-side. At the gate stood an aged person whose dignified appearance was greatly added to by his long white moustaches. These possessions he pointed out to Hwa-mei with inoffensive pride as he welcomed the two who stood before him.

"Venerated father," explained Kai Lung dutifully, "this is she who has been destined from the beginning of time to raise up a hundred sons to keep your line extant."

"In that case," remarked the patriarch, "your troubles are only just beginning. As for me, since all that is now arranged, I can see about my own departure —'Whatever height the tree, its leaves return to the earth at last.'"

"It is thus at evening-time —to-morrow the light will again shine forth," whispered Kai Lung. "Alas, radiance, that you who have dwelt about a palace should be brought to so mean a hut!"

"If it is small, your presence will pervade it; in a palace there are many empty rooms," replied Hwa-mei, with a reassuring glance. "I enter to prepare our evening rice."

The End

KAI LUNG UNROLLS HIS MAT

**Part I
The Protecting Ancestors**

The Malignity of the Depraved Ming-Shu Rears Its Offensive Head

As Kai Lung turned off the dusty earth road and took the woodland path that led to his small but seemly cottage on the higher slope, his exultant heart rose up in song. His quest, indeed, had not been prolific of success, and he was returning with a sleeve as destitute of silver taels as when he had first set out, but the peach tree about his gate would greet him with a thousand perfumed messages of welcome, and standing expectant at the door he would perchance presently espy the gracefully outlined form of Hwa-mei, once called the Golden Mouse.

"As I climb the precipitous hillside,"
"My thoughts persistently dwell on the one who awaits my coming;
Though her image has never been wholly absent from my mind,
For our affections are as the two ends of a stretching cable — united by what divides them;
And harmony prevails.
Each sunrise renews the pearly splendour of her delicate being;
And floating weed recalls her abundant hair.
In the slender willows of the Yengtse valley I see her silken eye-lashes,
And the faint tint of the waving moon-flower tells of her jade-rivalled cheek.
Where is the exactitude of her matchless perfection —"

"There is a time to speak in hyperbole and a time to frame words to the limit of a narrow edge," interposed a contentious voice and Shen Hing, an elderly neighbour, appeared in the way. "What manner of man are you, Kai Lung, or does some alien Force possess you that you should reveal this instability of mind on the very threshold of misfortune?"

"Greetings, estimable wood-cutter," replied Kai Lung, who knew the other's morose habit; "yet wherefore should despondency arise? It is true that the outcome of my venture has been concave in the extreme, but, whatever befall, the produce of a single field will serve our winter need; while now the air is filled with gladness and the song of insects, and, shortly, Hwa-mei will discern me on the homeward track and come hurriedly to meet me with a cup of water in her hand. How, then, can heaviness prevail?"

At this, Shen Hing turned half aside, under the pretext that he required to spit, but he coughed twice before he could recompose his voice.

"Whence are you, amiable Kai Lung?" he asked with unaccustomed mildness; "and have you of late had speech with none?"

"I am, last of all, from Shun, which lies among the Seven Water-heads," was the reply. "Thinking to shorten the path of my return, I chose the pass known as the Locust's Leap, and from this cause I have encountered few. Haply you have some gratifying tidings that you would impart-yet should not these await another's telling, when seated around our own domestic hearth?"

"Haply," replied Shen Hing, with the same evasive bearing, "but there is a fall no less than a rise to every tide, and is it not further said that of three words that reach our ears two will be evil?"

"Does famine then menace the province?" demanded Kai Lung uneasily.

"There is every assurance of an abundant harvest, and already the sound of many blades being whetted is not unknown to us."

"It can scarcely be that the wells are failing our community again? Fill in the essential detail of your shadowy warning, O dubious Shen Hing, for I am eager to resume my homeward way, whatever privation threatens."

"It is better to come empty handed than to be the bearer of ill news," answered the sombre woodman, "but since you lay the burden on my head, it is necessary that you should turn your impatient feet aside to ascend yonder slight incline," and he pointed to a rocky crag that rose above the trees. "From this height, minstrel, now bend your discriminating gaze a few li to the west and then declare what there attracts your notice."

"That is the direction in which my meagre hut is placed," admitted Kai Lung, after he had searched the distance long and anxiously, "but, although the landmarks are familiar, that which I most look for eludes my mediocre eyes. It must be that the setting sun —"

"Even a magician cannot see the thing that is not there," replied Shen Hing meaningly. "Doubtless your nimble-witted mind will now be suitably arranged for what is to follow."

"Say on," adjured Kai Lung, taking a firmer hold upon the inner fibre of his self control. "If it should be more than an ordinary person can reasonably bear, I call upon the shades of all my virtuous ancestors to rally to my aid."

"Had but one of them put in a appearance a week ago, it might have served you better, for, as it is truly written, 'A single humble friend with rice when you are hungry is better than fifteen influential kinsmen coming to a feast,' " retorted Shen Hing. "Hear my lamentable word, however. It has for some time been rumoured that the banners of insurrection were being trimmed and the spears of revolt made ready."

"There was a whisper trickling through the land when I set forth," murmured Kai Lung. "But in this sequestered region, surely —"

"The trickle meanwhile grew into a swiftly moving stream, although the torrent seemed as though it would spare our peaceful valley. Like a faint echo from some far-off contest we heard that the standard of the Avenging Knife had been definitely raised and all men were being pressed into this scale or that of the contending causes.... High among the rebel council stood one who had, it is said, suffered an indignity at your requiting hand in the days gone by-Ming-shu his forbidding name."

"Ming-shu!" exclaimed Kai Lung, falling back a step before the ill-omened menace of that malignant shadow. "Can it be that the enmity of the inscriber of the Mandarin's spoken word has pursued me to this retreat?"

"It is, then, even as men told," declared Shen Hing, with no attempt to forego an overhanging bitterness, "and you, Kai Lung, whom we received in friendship, have brought this disaster to our doors. Could demons have done more?"

"Speak freely," invoked Kai Lung, averting his face, "and do not seek to spare this one's excessive self-reproach. What next occurred?"

"We of our settlement are a peaceful race, neither vainglorious nor trained to the use of arms, and the opposing camps of warriors had so far passed us by, going either on the Eastern or the Western Route and none turning aside. But in a misbegotten moment Ming-shu fell under a deep depression while in his tent at no great space away, and one newly of his band, thinking to disclose a fount of gladness, spoke of your admitted capacity as a narrator of imagined tales, with a special reference to the serviceable way in which the aptitude had extricated you from a variety of unpleasant transactions in the past."

"That would undoubtedly refresh the wells of Ming-shu's memory," remarked Kai Lung. "How did he testify the fullness of his joy?"

"It is related that, when those who stood outside heard the grinding of his ill assorted teeth, the rumour spread that the river banks were giving way. At a later period the clay-souled out-law was seen to rub his offensive hands pleasurably together and heard to remark that there is undoubtedly a celestial influence that moulds our ultimate destinies even though we ourselves may appear to trim the edges somewhat. He then directed a chosen company of his repulsive guard to surprise and surround our dwellings and to bring you a bound captive to his feet."

"Alas!" exclaimed Kai Lung. "It would have been more in keeping with the classical tradition that they should have taken me, rather than that others must suffer in my stead."

"There can be no two opinions on that score," replied the scrupulous Shen Hing, "but a literary aphorism makes a poor defense against a suddenly propelled battle axe, and before mutual politeness was restored a score of our tribe had succumbed to the force of the opposing argument. Then, on the plea that a sincere reconciliation demanded the interchange of gifts, they took whatever we possessed, beat us heavily about the head and body with clubs in return, and departed, after cutting down your orchard and setting fire to your very inflammably constructed hut, in order, as their leader courteously expressed it, 'to lighten the path of your return.'"

"But she-Hwa-mei," urged Kai Lung thickly. "Speak to a point now that the moment must be faced-the cord is at my heart."

"In that you are well matched, for another was about her neck when she went forth," replied Shen Hing concisely. "Thus, Ming-shu may be said to possess a double hold upon your destiny."

"And thereafter? She —?"

"Why, as to that, the outlook is obscure. But a brigand with whom I conversed-albeit one-sidedly, he standing upon this person's prostrate form meanwhile-boasted of the exploit. Hwa-mei would seem to be a lure by which it is hoped to attract some high official's shifting allegiance to the rebel cause, she having held a certain sway upon him in the past."

"The Mandarin Shan Tien-now a provincial governor!" exclaimed Kai Lung. "Thus our ancient strife asserts itself again, though the angles ever change. But she lives-at least that is assured."

"She lives," agreed Shen Hing dispassionately, "but so likewise does Ming-shu. If he was your avowed enemy, minstrel, you did wrong to spare him in the past, for 'If you leave the stricken bull his horns, he will yet contrive to gore you.'"

"It is no less written, 'The malice of the unworthy is more to be prized than an illuminated vellum,'" replied Kai Lung. "Furthermore, the ultimate account has not yet been cast. In which direction did Ming-shu's force proceed, and how long are they gone?"

"One who overlooked their camp spoke of them as marching to the west, and for three days now have we been free of their corroding presence. That being so, the more valiant among us are venturing down from about the treetops, and tomorrow life will begin afresh, doubtless as before. Have no fear therefore, storyteller; Ming-shu will not return."

"It is on that very issue that I am troubled," was Kai Lung's doubtful answer. "Ming-shu may still return."

"Then at least do not show it, for we are all in the same plight," urged the woodman. "To-morrow we assemble to repair the broken walls and fences, so that in the association of our numbers you may gain assurance."

"The spirit you display is admittedly contagious," agreed Kai Lung. "In the meanwhile, I will seek my devastated ruin to see if haply anything remains. There was a trivial store of some few bars of silver hidden about the roof. Should that hope fail, I am no worse off than he who possesses nothing."

"I will accompany and sustain you, neighbour," declared Shen Hing more cheerfully. "In sudden fortune, whether good or bad, men become as brothers."

"Do so if you feel you must," replied Kai Lung, "though I would rather be alone. But, in any case, I will do the actual searching-it would be the reverse of hospitable to set you to a task."

When they reached the ruin of his once befitting home, Kai Lung could not forbear an emotion of despair, but he indicated to Shen Hing how that one should stand a reasonable distance away while he himself sought among the ashes.

"A steady five cash a day is better than the prospect of a fortune." Shen Hing busied himself looking for earth-nuts, but in spite of the apt proverb his sombre look returned.

"Even this slender chance has faded," reported Kai Lung at length, approaching Shen Hing again. "Nothing remains, and I must now adventure forth on an untried way with necessity alone to be my guide. Farewell, compassionate Shen Hing."

"But what new vagary is here?" exclaimed Shen Hing, desisting from his search. "Is it not your purpose to join in the toil of restoring our settlement, when we, in turn, will support you in the speedy raising of your fallen roof?"

"There is a greater need that calls me, and every day Hwa-mei turns her expectant eyes toward the path of rescue," replied Kai Lung.

"Hwa-mei! But she is surrounded by a rebel guard in Ming-shu's camp, a hundred li or more away by now. Consider well, storyteller. It is very easy on an unknown road to put your foot into a trap or your head into a noose, but by patient industry one can safely earn enough to replace a wife with a few successful harvests."

"When this one lay captive in Ming-shu's power, she whom you would so readily forsake did not weigh the hazards of snare or rope with an appraising eye, but came hastening forward, offering life itself in two outstretched hands. Would a dog do less than follow now?"

"That is as it may be, and I have certainly heard some account of the affair at various times," replied Shen Hing craftily, for he well knew that Kai Lung's reciting voice would lighten the task of each succeeding day. "But even a beggar will not cross a shaking bridge by night, and how are you, who have neither gold wherewith to purchase justice nor force by which to compel it, to out-do the truculent Ming-shu, armed at every point?"

"I have sandals for my feet, a well-tried staff between my hands, a story on my lips, and the divine assurance that integrity will in the end prevail," was Kai Lung's modest boast. "What, therefore, can I lack?"

" 'In the end'?" repeated Shen Hing darkly. "Admittedly. But an ordinary person inclines to something less ambitious provided it can be relied upon more toward the middle. You are one who is prone to resort to analogies and signs, Kai Lung, to guide you in the emergencies of life. How can you then justify a journey entered upon so suddenly and without reference to the omens?"

"He who moves toward the light has no need of the glow of joss-sticks," replied Kai Lung, indicating the brightness that still lingered in the sky. "The portent will not fail."

"It is certainly a point to be noted," confessed Shen Hing, "and I cannot altogether expect to dissuade you in the circumstances. But do not overlook the fact that the sun has already set and nothing but dark and forbidding clouds now fill the heavens."

"We can see only the clouds, but the clouds can see the sun," was the confident reply. "Success is a matter of luck, but every man obeys his destiny."

With this inspired pronouncement, Kai Lung turned his back upon the ruin of his unassuming home and set out again, alone and destitute, upon an unknown path. Shen Hing pressed into his sleeve the few inferior nuts that he had laboriously collected, but he did not offer to accompany the storyteller on his way. Indeed, as soon as he was reasonably sure that he was free from interruption, the discriminating wood-cutter began to search the ashes on his own account, to see if haply there was not something of value that Kai Lung had perchance overlooked.

The Difficult Progression of the Virtuous Kai Lung Assumes a Concrete Form

It was Kai Lung's habit, as he approached any spot where it seemed as though his mat might be profitably unrolled, to beat upon a small wooden drum and even to discharge an occasional firework, so that the leisurely and indulgent should have no excuse for avoiding his entertainment. As darkness was fast approaching when he reached the village of Ching, it would have been prudent first of all to obtain shelter for the night and a little rice to restore his failing powers, for three days had passed since the parting from Shen Hing, and with scarcely a pause Kai Lung had pressed relentlessly on toward the west, journeying through a barren upland waste where nothing to sustain life offered beyond the roots of herbs and a scanty toll of honey. But the rocky path that he had followed was scarcely less harsh and forbidding than the faces of those to whom the storyteller now spoke of food and shelter, with an assumed payment at some future time, and however ill-fitted he felt his attributes to be, he had no alternative but to retrace his faltering steps to the deserted open space and there to spread his mat and lift up his voice in the hope of enticing together one or two who would contribute even a few brass pieces to his bowl.

When Kai Lung had beat upon his drum for as long as it was prudent and had expended the last firecracker of his slender store, he looked around so that he might estimate what profit the enterprise held out and judge therefrom what variety of story would be adequate. To his gratified surprise, he now perceived that, so far from attracting only a meagre sprinkling of the idle and necessitous, about him stood a considerable throng, and persons of even so dignified a position as an official chair bearer and an assistant tax collector had not scrupled to draw near. At least two full strings of negotiable cash might be looked for, and Kai Lung brushed aside his hunger and fatigue as he resolved to justify so auspicious an occasion.

"It is well said," he remarked with becoming humility, "that the more insignificant the flower the handsomer the bees that are attracted to it, and the truth of the observation is borne out by this distinguished gathering of influential noblemen all condescending to listen to the second rate elocution of so ill endowed a person as the one who is now speaking. Nevertheless, in order to start the matter on a satisfactory basis, attention is now drawn to this very inadequate collecting bowl. When even its lower depth is hidden beneath the impending shower of highclass currency, these deficient lips will be stimulated to recite the story of Ling Tso and the Golden Casket of the Lady Wu."

For a few beats of time there was an impressive pause, which Kai Lung ascribed to a pleased anticipation of what was to follow, but no shower of coins ensued. Then a venerable person stood forth and raised a forbidding hand.

"Refrain from this ineptitude and tell us the thing that we have come to hear," he remarked in an unappreciative voice. "Is it to be thought that persons of such importance as an official chair bearer and an assistant tax collector "—here he indicated the two, who assumed expressions of appropriate severity—"would bend their weighty ears to the painted insincerity of a fictitious tale?"

"Yet wherein can offence be taken at the history of Ling Tso and the virtuous Lady Wu?" asked Kai Lung in pained surprise. "None the less, it is reasonably said that he who hires the carriage picks the road, and should another tale be indicated, this one will cheerfully endeavour to comply with the demand."

"Alas," exclaimed the one who had constituted himself the leader of their voices, "can obliquity go further? Why should we who are assembled to hear what relief Ang-Liang can send us in our straits be withheld in this extraneous manner? Deliver your message competently, O townsman of Ang-Liang, so that we may quickly know."

At this reversal of his hopes and all that it foreshadowed, Kai Lung suddenly felt the cords of his restraint give way, and for a discreditable moment he covered his face with his hands, lest his anguish should appear there.

"It is very evident that an unfortunate misconception has arisen," he said, when he had recovered his inner possession. "The one before you has journeyed from the east, nor has he any part with the township of Ang-Liang, neither does he bear with him a message."

"Then how arises it," demanded the foremost of the throng acrimoniously, "that you have come to this very spot, beating upon a wooden drum and bearing other signs of him whom we expect?"

"I had sought this open space thinking to earn a narrow sufficiency of the means whereby to secure food and shelter before the darkness closes in," replied Kai Lung freely. "My discreditable calling is that of a minstrel and a relater of imagined tales, my abject name being Lung, and Kai that of my offensive father's ill-conditioned Line. Being three days' journey from my bankrupt home, I have nothing but my own distressing voice and the charitable indulgence of your unsullied hearts to interpose between myself and various unpleasant ways of Passing Upward. To that end I admittedly beat upon this hollow drum and discharged an occasional cracker, as my harmless custom is."

"Were it not possible to take a lenient view of the offence by reason of your being a stranger, it is difficult to say what crime you may not have committed," declared the spokesman with obtuse persistence. "As it is, it would be well that you should return to your own place without delay and avoid the boundaries of Ching in future. Justice may not close an eye twice in the same direction."

"Nothing could be more agreeably expressed, and this one will not fail to profit by your broad-minded toleration," meekly replied Kai Lung. "Yet inexperienced wayfarers have been known to wander in a circle after nightfall and so to return to the point of their departure. To avoid this humiliating transgression, the one who is now striving to get away at the earliest possible moment will restrain his ardour until daybreak. In the meanwhile, to satisfy your natural demand that he should justify the claim to be as he asserts, he will now relate the story of Wan and the Remarkable Shrub — a narrative which, while useful to ordinary persons as indicative of what may be reasonably expected in a variety of circumstances, does not impose so severe a strain upon the imagination as does the history of Ling Tso and the Golden Casket."

"Any strain upon the imagination is capable of sympathetic adjustment," put forward one of the circle, evidently desirous of sharing in some form of entertainment. "As regards the claim of the collecting bowl to which reference has been made —"

"Cease, witling," interposed the leader in a tone of no-encouragement. "Having been despoiled by Ming-shu's insatiable horde, are we now to be beguiled into contributing to a strolling musician's scarcely less voracious bowl? Understand, mountebank, that by flood, fire, and famine, culminating in this last iniquity at the hands of a rebel band, our village is not only cashless but is already destitute of food and fuel for itself, so that we have even sent imploring messages to less deficient neighbours."

"In that case, the historical legend of Wan and the Remarkable Shrub is exceptionally appropriate, conveying as it does the inspiring maxim that misfortune may be turned to a final gain, and indicating-on broad lines-how this desirable result may be attained."

"A recital of that nature cannot be deemed to be merely light and indulgent," contended the one who had favoured the amusement, "and, indeed, may be regarded as a definite commercial asset. It is true that among us we have not the wherewithal to line even the bottom of the accomodating Kai Lung's unassuming bowl, but if a mat upon my misshapen sleeping bench should be judged an equivalent share —"

"In the matter of your evening rice this person chances to have a superfluous portion of meat upon a skewer," remarked the official chair bearer. "Lean and unappetizing as it will doubtless prove, it is freely offered as a proportionate bestowal."

"Meat of itself requires the savour of mixed herbs," interposed the assistant tax collector, not desirous of being outdone by others, "and in that respect this one will not prove lacking."

"When the tide turns, it carries all before it," grumbled the head-man of the community, with a supine glance at the many who were pressing forward. "As regards tea to any reasonable amount, the name of Thang stands to that detail."

"An onion to refresh your supple throat," came from another.

"A little snuff to bring out the flavor of each dish"; "Look to Wei Ho, for mien paste to form a staple"; "A small dried fish, well steeped in oil"; "The gratuitous shaving of your noble footsore limbs" —these and a variety of inspiring cries were raised on every side.

"It is necessary to test silver on a block, but hospitality proclaims itself," replied Kai Lung agreeably. "This brings in the legendary tale of Wan and what befell him."

The Story of Wan and the Remarkable Shrub

I

The story of Wan and the Remarkable Shrub is commendable in that it shows how, under a beneficent scheme of government, such as that of our unapproachably enlightened Empire admittedly is, impartial justice will sooner or later be accomplished. When a contrary state of things seems to prevail, and the objectionable appear to triumph while the worthy are reduced to undignified expedients, it will generally be found that powerful demoniacal influences are at work or else that the retributive forces have been counter-balanced by an unfortunate conjunction of omens acting on the lives of those concerned. If neither of these causes is responsible, it may be that a usurpatory and unauthorized dynasty has secured the sacred dragon throne (a not unusual occurrence in our distinguished history), and virtue is thereby for a time superseded from its function; or, possibly, a closer scrutiny will reveal that those whom we had hitherto regarded as tending toward one extreme were not in reality such as we deemed them to be, and that the destinies meted out to them were therefore both adequate and just. Thus, whatever happens, it is always more prudent to assume that the integrities have been suitably maintained all round and that the inspired system initiated by the Sages ten thousand years ago continues even today to enshrine the highest wisdom of mankind and is yet administered by the most scrupulous body of officials in what is still the best possible among the nations of the earth.

For this reason the story of Wan and his associates, badly told and commonplace as it must inevitably sound when narrated by this incompetent person, is appropriate for the mental nourishment of the young and impressionable, while even the ill intentioned and austere may be discreetly influenced along a desired path by its opportune recital at convenient intervals.

At a period so remote that it would be impious to doubt whatever happened then, a venerable and prosperous philosopher, Ah-shoo by name, dwelt at the foot of a mountain in a distant province. His outward life was simple but reserved, and although he spent large sums of money on fireworks and other forms of charity, he often professed his indifference to wealth and position. Yet it must not be supposed that Ah-shoo was unmindful of the essentials, for upon it being courteously pointed out to him, by a well disposed neighbour who had many daughters of his own, that in failing to provide a reliable posterity he was incurring a grave risk of starvation in the Upper World, he expressed a seemly regret for the oversight and at once arranged to marry an elderly person who chanced at the time to be returning his purified wearing apparel. It was to this incident that the one with whom this related story is chiefly concerned owned his existence, and when the philosopher's attention was diverted to the occurrence, he bestowed on him the name of Wan, thereby indicating that he was born toward the evening of his begetter's life, and also conveying the implication that the achievement was one that could scarcely be expected to be repeated. On this point he was undoubtedly inspired.

When Wan reached the age of manhood, the philosopher abruptly Passed Above without any interval of preparation. It had been his custom to engage Wan in philosophical discussion at the close of each day, and on this occasion he was contrasting the system of Ka-ping, who maintained that the world has suspended from a powerful fibrous rope, with that of Ta-u, who contended that it was supported upon a substantial bamboo pole. With the clear insight of an original and discerning mind, Ah-shoo had already detected the fundamental weakness of both theories.

"If the earth was indeed dependent on the flexible retention of an unstable cord, it is inevitable that, during the season of Much Wind, it must from time to time have been blown into a reversed position, with the distressing result that what was the east when we composed ourselves to sleep would be the west when we awoke from our slumber, to the confusion of all ordinary process of observation and the well-grounded annoyance of those who, being engaged upon a journey, found themselves compelled to return and set out again in the opposite direction. As there exists no tradition of this having ever happened, it is certain that the ingenious Ka-ping did not walk in step with the verities."

"Then the system of the profound Ta-u is the one to be regarded?" inquired Wan respectfully.

"'Because Hi is in the wrong, it does not automatically follow that Ho is necessarily right,'" quoted Ah-shoo, referring to the example of two celebrated astrologers who were equally involved in error. "The ill-conceived delusion of the obsolete Ta-u is no less open to logical disproval than the grotesque fallacy of the badly informed Ka-ping. If a rigid and unyielding staff of wood upheld the world it is obvious that when the ground became dry and crumbling the upper end of the pole would enlarge the socket in which it was embedded, and the earth, thus deprived of a firm and stable basis, would oscillate with every considerable movement upon its upper side. Even more disturbing would be the outcome of a season of continuous flood, such as our agreeable land frequently enjoys, for then, owing to the soft and pliant nature of the soil, and the ever increasing weight of the impending structure, the pole would continue to sink deeper and deeper into the mass, until at length it would protrude upon the upper side, when the earth, deprived of all support, would slide down the pole until it plunged into the impenetrable gloom of the Beneath-Parts."

"Yet," suggested Wan with becoming deference, "if the point of the staff concerned should have been resourcefully embedded in a a formidable block of stone —?"

"The system of the self-opinionated Ta-u contains no reference to any such block of stone," replied Ah-shoo coldly, for it was not wholly agreeable to his sense of the harmonies that the one who was his son should seek to supply Ta-u's deficiency. "Furthermore, the difficulty of hewing out the necessary incision for the head of the pole to fit into, in view of the hardness of the rock and the inverted position in which the workers must necessarily toil, would be insuperable. Consider well another time, O Wan, before you intervene. 'None but a nightingale should part his lips merely to emit sound.'"

"Your indulgent censure will henceforth stimulate my powers of silence," declared the dutiful Wan in a straightforward voice. "Otherwise it would have been my inopportune purpose to learn of your undoubted omniscience what actually does support the earth."

"The inquiry is a natural one," replied Ah-shoo more genially, for it was a desire to set forth his own opinion on the subject that had led him to approach the problem, "and your instinct in referring it to me is judicious. The world is kept in its strict and inflexible position by —"

Who having found a jewel lifts his voice to proclaim the fact, thereby inviting one and all to claim a share? Rather does he put an unassuming foot upon the spot and direct attention to the auspicious movements of a distant flock of birds or the like, until he can prudently stoop to secure what he has seen. Certainly, the analogy may not be exact at all its angles, but in any case Ah-shoo would have been well advised to speak with lowered voice. It is to be inferred that the philosopher did not make a paper boast when he spoke of possessing the fundamental secret of the earth's stability, but that the High Powers were unwilling, at that early stage of our civilization, for the device to become generally understood. Ah-shoo was therefore fated to suffer for his indiscretion, and this took the form of a general stagnation of the attributes, so that although he lingered for a further period before he Passed Above he was unable to express himself in a coherent form. Being deprived of the power of speech, he remembered, when too late, that he had neglected to initiate Wan into any way of applying his philosophical system to a remunerative end, while it so happened that his store of wealth was unusually low owing to an imprudently generous contribution to a scheme for permanently driving evil beings out of the neighbourhood by a serious of continuous explosions.

It is no longer necessary to conceal the fact that throughout his life Ah-shoo had in reality played a somewhat two-faced part. In addition to being a profound philosopher and a polite observer of the forms he was, in secret, an experienced magician, and in that capacity he was able to transmute base matter into gold. For this purpose he kept a variety of coloured fluids in a shuttered recess of the wall, under a strict injunction. Having now a natural craving to assure Wan's future comfort, he endeavoured by a gesture to indicate this source of affluence, confident that the one in question would not fail to grasp the significance of anything brought to his notice at so precise a moment, and thus be led to test the properties of the liquids and in the end to discover their potency. Unfortunately, Ah-shoo's vigour was by this time unequal to the required strain and his inefficient hand could not raise itself higher than to point toward an inscribed tablet suspended at a lower level upon the wall. This chancing to be the delineation of the Virtues, warning the young against the pursuit of wealth, against trafficking with doubtful Forces, and so forth, Wan readily accepted the gesture as a final encouragement toward integrity on the part of an affectionate and pure-minded father, and dutifully prostrating himself, he specifically undertook to avoid the enticements described. It was in vain that the distracted Ah-shoo endeavoured to remove this impression and to indicate his meaning more exactly. His feeble limb was incapable of more highly sustained effort, and the more desperately he strove to point, the more persistently Wan kow-towed acquiescently and bound himself by an ever increasing array of oaths and penalties to shun the snare of riches and to avoid all connection with the forbidden. Finally, this inability to make himself understood engendered a fatal acridity within the magician's throat, so that, with an expression of scarcely veiled contempt on his usually benevolent features, he rolled from side to side several times in despair and then passed out into the Upper Region.

It was not long before Wan began to experience an uncomfortable deficiency of taels. The more ordinary places of concealment were already familiar to his investigating thumb, but even the most detailed search failed to disclose Ah-shoo's expected hoard. When at length very little of the structural portion of the house remained intact, Wan was reluctantly compelled to admit that no such store existed.

"It is certainly somewhat inconsiderate of the one to whom my very presence here is due, to have inculcated in me a contempt for riches and a fixed regard for the Virtues, and then to have Passed Away without making any adequate provision for maintaining the position," remarked Wan to the sharer of his inner chamber, as he abandoned his search as hopeless. "Tastes such as these are by no means easy to support."

"Perchance," suggested Lan-yen, the one referred to, helpfully, "it was part of an ordered scheme, thereby to inspire a confidence in your own exertions."

"The confidence inspired by the possession of a well-filled vault of silver will last an ordinary person a lifetime," replied Wan, with an entire absence of enthusiasm. "Further, the philosophical outfit, which so capably enables one to despise riches in the midst of affluence, seems to have overlooked any system of procuring them when destitution threatens."

"Yet are there not other methods of enrichment?" persisted the well-meaning but not altogether gracefully animated one in question.

"Undoubtedly," replied Wan, with a self-descriptive smile, "the processes are many and diffuse. There are, to example them, those who remove uncongenial teeth for the afflicted; others who advance the opposing claims of the litigiously inclined; and forecasters of the future. But in order to succeed in these various enterprises, it is desirable to be able to extract an indicated fang, to entice the confidence of the disputations, or to be able to make what has been predicted bear some recognizable semblance to what has come to pass. Then there are merchants in gems and precious stones, builders of palaces, and robbers in the Ways, but here again it is first advantageous to possess the costly traffic of a merchant's stall, to have some experience in erecting palaces, or to be able to divest wayfarers of their store in the face of their sustained resistance. Still endeavouring to extract the priceless honey from the garden of your inspired suggestion, there are those who collect the refuse of the public streets, but in order to be received into the band it is necessary to have been born one of the Hereditary Confederacy of Superfluity Removers and Abandoned Oddment Gatherers. Aspire to wisdom, O peerless one, but in the meanwhile emulate the pattern of the ruminative ox. This person will now proceed to frequent the society of those best acquainted with the less guarded moments of the revered ascended, and endeavour to learn perchance something more of his inner business methods."

With this resolve, Wan sought out a body of successful merchants and the like whose custom it was to meet together beneath the Sign of Harmonious Ease, where they chiefly spoke in two breaths alternatively of their wealth and their poverty, and there strove to attach himself to the more leisurely inclined. In this he experienced no difficulty, it being for the most part their continual despair that none would give heed to their well-displayed views on things in general, but when he spoke of the one for whom he dressed in white and endeavoured to ascertain by what means he had earned his facile wealth, even the most sympathetic held out no encouraging hope.

"The same problem has occasioned this person many sleepless nights," admitted the one on whose testimony Wan had placed the most reliance. "In a spirit of disinterested friendship he strove, by every possible expedient that a fertile and necessity-driven imagination could devise, to inveigle your venerated sire into a disclosure of the facts but to the end he maintained a deluded and narrow-minded silence. The opinion of some here was that he secretly controlled a band of river pirates; others held that he associated with ghouls who despoiled the hidden treasure of the earth. My own opinion was that he had stumbled upon some discreditable fact connected with the past life of one now high in power. Properly developed, any of these three lines of suggestion should lead you to an honourable competence, but if the one whose foresight we are discussing has neglected to provide you with the essential clue before he Journeyed Hence, the line you incautiously chose might leave you suspended in quite another position. Your obvious policy would therefore tend toward neglecting to sacrifice for him the commodities of which he must now stand most in need. Under this humane pressure, his distinguished preoccupation may perhaps be brought to an enlightened end, and in the form of a dream or through the medium of an opportune vision he may find a means to remedy his omission."

"It is easy to close a door that none is holding open," replied Wan freely, for the period had already come when it was difficult for him to provide for the maintenance of his own requirements, "and the course that you suggest is like Ho Chow's selection in the analogy that bears his name."

"It is always a privilege to be able to counsel the young and inexperienced," observed the other, rising and shaking hands with himself benevolently as the beating of a gong announced that the evening rice was laid out near at hand. "Do not hesitate to bend your inquiring footsteps in the direction of my receptive ear whenever you stand in need of intellectual sustenance. In the meanwhile, may your capacious waist-cloth always be distended to repletion."

"May the pearls of wisdom continue to germinate in the nutritious soil of your well-watered brain," replied Wan no less appropriately, as he set out on a homeward path.

II

There can be little doubt that the Mandarin Hin Ching was an official of the most offensive type: rich, powerful, and in every way successful at this period of his career. Nevertheless, it is truly written, "Destroy the root and the branches wither of their own accord," and it will go hard with this obscure person's power of relating history, if toward the close, Hin Ching shall not be brought to a plight that will be both sharp and ignominious.

Among the other degraded attributes of the concave Hin Ching was a disposition to direct his acquisitive glances toward objects with which he could have no legitimate concern, and in this way it had become a custom for him to loiter, on a variety of unworthy pretexts, in the region of Wan's not specially attractive home at such hours as those when Lan-yen might reasonably be encountered there alone. For her part, the one in question dutifully endeavoured to create the impression that she was unaware of his repulsively expressed admiration, and even of his presence, but owing to his obtuse persistence there were occasions when to have done this consistently would have become inept. Thus and thus Wan had more than once discovered him, but with his usual ill-conditioned guile Hin Ching had never yet failed to have his feet arranged in an appropriate position when they encountered.

On his return from the Abode of Harmonious Ease, where the outcome of his quest has already been so insipidly described, Wan presently became aware that the chair of a person of some consequence lurked in the shadow of his decrepit door, the bearers, after the manner of their supine tribe, having composed themselves to sleep. Wan was thereby given the opportunity to enter unperceived, which he did in an attitude of introspective reverie, this enabling him to linger abstractedly for an appreciable moment at the curtain of the ceremonial hall before he disclosed his presence. In this speculative poise he was able to listen, without any loss of internal face, to the exact terms of the deplorable Hin Ching's obscene allurement, and, slightly later, to Lan-yen's virtuous and dignified rejoinder. Rightly assuming that there would be no further arisement likely to outweigh the disadvantages of being detected there, Wan then stepped forth.

"O perverse and double-dealing Mandarin!" he exclaimed reproachfully; "is this the way that justice is displayed about the limits of the Ia-ling Mountains? Or how shall the shepherd that assails the flock by night control his voice to sentence those ravage it by day?"

"It is well to be reminded of my exalted office," replied Hin Ching, recovering his composure and arrogantly displaying the insignia of his rank. "Knees such as yours were made to bend, presumptuous Wan, and the rebellious head that has grown too tall to do obeisance can be shortened," and he indicated by a gesture that the other should prostrate himself.

"When the profound Ng-tai made the remark, 'Beneath an integritous roof all men are equal,' he was entertaining an imitator of official seals, three sorcerers, and a celebrated viceroy. Why then should this person depart from the high principle in favour of one merely of the crystal button?"

"Four powerful reasons may be brought to bear upon the argument," replied Hin Ching, and he moved toward the door to summon his attendants.

"They do not apply to the case as I present it," retorted Wan, drawing his self-reliant sword and intervening its persuasive edge between the other and his purpose. "Let us confine the issue to essential points, O crafty Mandarin."

At this determined mien Hin Ching lost the usual appearance of his face somewhat, though he made a misbegotten attempt to gather reassurance by grinding his ill-arranged teeth aggressively. As Wan still persisted in an unshaken front, however, the half-stomached person facing him very soon began to retire behind himself and to raise a barrier of evasive subterfuge-first by the claim that as the undoubted thickness of his body afforded a double target he should be permitted to return two blows for each one aimed against him, and later with a demand that he should be allowed to stand upon a dais during the encounter by virtue of his high position. Whatever might have been the issue of his strategy, the conflict was definitely averted by a melodious wail of anguish from Lan-yen as she suddenly composed herself into a gracefully displayed rigidity at the impending scene of bloodshed. In the ensuement, the detestable Hin Ching imperceptibly faded out, the last indiciation of his contaminating presence being the apophthegm that were more ways of killing a dragon than that of holding its head under water.

As the time went on, the deeper meaning of the contemptible Hin Ching's sinister remark gradually came up to the surface. Those who in the past had not scrupled to associate with Wan now began to alienate themselves from his society, and when closely pressed spoke from behind well-guarded lips of circumspection and the submission to authority that the necessities of an increased posterity entailed. Others raised a lukewarm finger as he passed where before there had been two insistent outstretched hands, and everywhere there was a disposition to remember neglected tasks on his approach.

In other and more sombre shapes, the inauspicious shadow of this corrupt official darkened Wan's blameless path. Merchants with whom he had been wont to traffic on the general understanding that he would requite them in a more propitious hour now disclosed a concentration of adverse circumstances that obliged them to withhold their store, so that gradually the bare necessities of the least elaborate life ceased to be within his reach. From time to time heavy rocks, moved by no apparent cause, precipitated themselves around his footsteps, hitherto reliant bridges burst asunder at the exact moment when he might be expected to be crossing them, and immutable laws governing the recurrence of a stated hazard seemed for a time to be suspended from their function. "The egregious Hin Ching certainly does not intend to eat his words," remarked Wan impassively as a triumphant arch which lay beyond his gate crumbled for the fourth time as he passed through.

III

Who has not proved the justice of the saying, "She who breaks the lid by noon will crack the dish ere nightfall?" Wan was already suffering from the inadequacy of a misguided father, the depravity of an unscrupulous official, and the flaccidity of a weak-kneed band of neighbours. To these must now be added a cessation of the ordinary source of nature and the intervention of the correcting gods. Under their avenging rule, a prolonged drought assailed the land, so that where fruitfulness and verdure had hitherto prevailed, there was soon nothing to be found but barrenness and dust. Wan and Lan-yen began to look into each other's eyes with a benumbing dread, and each in turn secretly replaced among their common store something from the allotted portion and strove unseen to dull the natural pangs of hunger by countless unstable wiles. The meagre strip of cultivated land they held, perforce their sole support, was ill-equipped against the universal famine, and it was with halting feet and downcast face that Wan returned each day to display his slender gain. "A few parched fruit I bring," it might be, or, "This cup of earth-nuts must suffice," perchance. Soon, "Naught remains now but bitter-tasting herbs," he was compelled to say, and Lan-yen waited for the time when there would come the presage of their fate, "There now is nothing more."

In the most distant corner of the garden there stood two shrubs of a kind then unfamiliar to the land, not tall but very sturdy in their growth. Once when they walked together in that part, Lan-yen had drawn Wan aside, and being of a thrifty and sententious mind, had pointed to them, saying:

"Here are two shrubs which neither bear fruit nor serve a useful purpose in some other way. Put out your hand, proficient one, and hew them down so that their wood may feed our scanty hearth and a more profitable herbage occupy their place."

At this request Wan changed countenance, and although he cleared his throat repeatedly, it was some time before he could frame a suitable reply.

"There is a tradition connected with this spot," he said at length, "which would make it extremely ill-advised to do as you suggest."

"How then does it chance that the story has never yet reached my all-embracing ears?" inquired Lan-yen in some confusion. "What mystery is here?"

"That," replied Wan tactfully, "is because your conversation is mainly with the ephemeral and slight. The legend was received from the lips of the most venerable dweller in this community, who had in turn acquired it from the mental storehouse of his predecessor."

"The words of a patriarch, though generally diffuse and sometimes incoherent, are worth of regard," admitted Lan-yen gracefully. "Proceed to unfold your reminiscent mood."

"Upon this spot in bygone years there lived a pious anchorite who sought to attain perfection by repeating the names of the Pure Ones an increasing number of times each day. Devoting himself wholly to this sacred undertaking, and being by nature generously equipped toward the task, he at length formed the meritorious project of continuing without intermission either by night or day, and, in this tenacious way outstripping all rival and competing anchorites, of being received finally into a higher state of total obliteration in the Ultimate Beyond than any recluse had hitherto attained. Every part of his being responded to the exalted call made on it, save only one, but in each case, just as the permanent achievement lay within his grasp, his rebellious eyelids fell from the high standard of perfection and betrayed him into sleep. All ordinary methods of correction having failed, the conscientious solitary took a knife of distinguishing sharpness, and resolutely slicing off the effete members of his house, he cast them from him out into the night. The watchful Powers approved, and to mark the sacrifice a tree sprang up where each lid fell and by the contour of its leaf proclaimed the symbol of its origin."

This incident occurred to Lan-yen's mind when their extremity had passed all normal bounds and every kind of cultivated food had ceased. The time had now come when Wan returned an empty bowl into her waiting hands, and with mute gestures and uncertain steps had sought to go, rather than speak the message of despair. It was then that Lan-yen detained him by her gentle voice to urge a last resort.

"There still remain the two mysterious trees, whose rich and glossy leaves suggest a certain juicy nourishment. Should they happen to prove deadly in effect, then our end will only be more sharply ruled than would otherwise be the case; if, on the contrary, they are of innocuous growth, they may sustain us until some other form of succour intervenes."

"If you are willing to embark on so doubtful an adventure, it would cover me with secret humiliation to refrain," replied Wan acquiescently. "Give me the bowl again."

When she heard his returning step, Lan-yen went out to meet him, and seeing his downcast look she hailed him from a distance.

"Do not despond," she cried. "The sting of a whip indicates its end and your menial one is inspired to prophesy a very illustrious close to all our trials. Further, she has procured the flavour of an orange and a sprinkling of snuff wherewith to spice the dish."

"In that case," replied Wan, displaying what he had brought, "the savouring will truly be the essence of our feast. The produce of the shrubs has at length shared the common fate," and he made to throw away the dry and withered leaves that the bowl contained.

"Forbear!" exclaimed Lan-yen, restraining him. " 'It is no farther on than back again when the halfway house is reached.' Who knows what hidden virtues may diffuse from so miraculous a root?"

In this agreeable spirit the accomodating person took up the task, and with such patient skill as if a banquet of ceremonial swallows had been involved, she prepared a dish of the withered leaves from the unknown shrubs. When all was ready, she set the alien fare before Wan and took her place beside the chair to serve his hand.

"Eat," she exhorted, "and may the Compassionate Ones protect you."

"I lean against their sympathetic understanding," responded Wan devoutly as he looked beneath the cover. "Nevertheless," he added graciously, "on so momentous an occasion priority shall be yours."

"By no means," replied Lan-yen hastily, at the same time pressing him back into the seat he would vacate. "Not until you have slaked your noble appetite shall my second rate lips partake."

"It is proverbial that from a hungry tiger and an affectionate woman there is no escape," murmured Wan, and taking up a portion of the food he swallowed it.

"Your usually expressive eye has assumed a sudden glassy lustre," exclaimed Lan-yen, who had not ceased to regard him anxiously. "What is the outstanding flavour of the dish?"

"It has no discernible flavour of any kind," declared Wan, speaking with considerable emotion, "but the general effect it produces is undistinguishable from suffocation. A cup of water, adored, before it is too late!"

"Alas," admitted Lan-yen, looking round in a high-minded access of refined dismay, "none now remains! There is nothing here but the dark and austere liquor in which the herb has boiled."

"So long as it is liquid it suffices," replied Wan in an extremity, and seizing the proffered vessel from her misgiving hand he took a well-sustained grasp of its contents.

"The remedy would appear to be a protracted one," remarked Lan-yen in some surprise, as Wan maintained the steady rhythm of his action. "Surely the obstruction is by now dispersed?"

"Phoenix-eyed one," replied Wan, pausing with some reluctance; "not only is that obstruction now removed, but every other impediment is likewise brushed away. Observe this person's sudden rise of vigour, his unexpected store of energy, the almost alarming air of general proficiency radiating from his system. It becomes plain now that from the beginning of our oppression everything has been working in an ordered scheme to lead us to an end. This is no earthly liquid, such as you might brew, but a special nectar sent down by the gods to sustain mankind in every sort of trial. From this moment our future prosperity is assured."

As he finished speaking, there was a sudden outcry from the Way beyond, a blending of heavy steps and upraised voices; the door was thrust widely open, and with a deplorable absence of seemly ostentation the sublime Emperor of the land, accompanied by a retinue of agitated nobles, pressed into the room.

IV

Let it be freely admitted that a really capable narrator of events would have led up to this badly arranged crisis more judiciously and in a manner less likely to distress the harmonious balance of his hearers' feelings. Yet there is a certain fitness in the stress, however ineptly reached, for that august sovereign now involved was so rapidly outlined in all his movements that between his conception of a course and the moment when he embarked upon it there was very little opportunity for those chiefly concerned to engage in preparation. Thus steps into the record Ming Wang, last of his royal line.

When the famine had cankered the land for seven full moons, there appeared before the Palace gate a stranger clad in fur. Without deigning to reply to any man of those confronting him with words of this or that, he loftily took down the brazen trident from among the instruments that hung there and struck on it a loud, compelling note with the fingers of his open hand. At this defiant challenge, in compliance with the Ancient Usage, he was led into the presence of Ming Wang at once.

"Speak without fear," said the sympathetic ruler affably, "for the iron law of Yu protects you."

At the mention of this heroic name, the stranger's expression varied in its tenor, and he drew up the covering of his face a little, although the day was warm.

"In the north and the south, on the east and the west, there is a famine in the land, for the resentful gods withhold their natural moisture," he proclaimed; and it was afterward agreed that the sound of his voice was like the whetting of a sickle on a marble hone. "For seven moons and seven more days has this affliction been, and you who stand regently between the Upper and the Lower Worlds have suffered it to be."

"What you say is very surprising," replied Ming Wang, "and the more so as no appreciable scarcity has been apparent at our royal table for the time you name. Be assured that due inquiry shall be made however."

"Let it be made forthwith and justice measured out," said the intruder sternly, and he turned away and stood so that none might see the working of his complicated thoughts.

"When two minds are agreed, what matter which tongue speaks?" remarked the liberally endowed monarch to the scandalized officials hovering round, and with truly imperial large-handedness he ordered the immediate presence of the four chancellors of the regions named, despite the fact that they were then residing in their several distant capitals. No stronger proof of the efficiency of Ming Wang's vigorous rule need be sought, for no sooner was the command issued than four chancellors immediately appeared.

"It is obligingly reported by an unnamed well-wisher that a scarcity exists in all the corners of our boundless realm," remarked the Illimitable, in so encouraging a voice that the four chancellors began to beat their heads upon the granite floor in an access of misgiving. "Doubtless each has a wholly adequate reply?"

"Omnipotence," pleaded the first, "there has been a slight temporary derangement of transport in the Province of the North, with the unfortunate arisement that here and there a luxury is scarce."

"All-seeing," replied the next, "certain grain in a restricted area of the Province of the South has been consumed by subterranean Beings. Yet what are southern men that they should not turn from rice to millet with a cheerful face?"

"In the Province of the East, Benevolence," declared the third, "a fiery omen shot across the sky, corroding the earth to barrenness that lay within its sphere. To judgments such as this the faithful can but bend an acquiescent neck."

"Father of all mercies," stammered the last, who being slow-witted had no palliation ready to his tongue, "that same blazing menace then passed onward to the Province of the West where it wrought a like disaster."

"Nothing could be more convincing," agreed the Mouthpiece of Wisdom heartily. "We were sure that something of the sort would be at once forthcoming. It will certainly be a fountain of consolation to your sorrowing friends, even in the most poignant moments of their grief, that your crime-despite its regrettable consequence-was purely of a technical description."

"High Majesty?" besought the four in harmony.

"It would appear," explained the Supreme indulgently, "that by withholding all mention of this distressing state of things (doubtless to spare our too warmhearted ears) you have each inadvertently come within the Code of Yao-u and Shun, under the Section: 'Conduct in an official whereby disaffection of the Outer Lands may be engendered.' In that imperishable Statute every phase of misdoing is crystallized with unfailing legal skill into this shining principle of universal justice: one crime, one responsible official. That firmly grasped, the administration of an otherwise complex judicial system becomes purely a matter of elementary mathematics. In this case, as there are clearly four crimes to be atoned, four responsible officials suffer the usual fatal expiation."

"Enough," exclaimed the stranger, emerging from his reverie and confronting Ming Wang again. "In that respect, no doubt, a fit example will be made. But what of the greatest need besetting you, or who will persuade the seasons to resume their normal courses?"

"As to that," replied the Emperor agreeably, "we are waiting to tread in your illuminating footsteps in whatever direction you may indicate."

"He who brings the word is not thereby required to go the way," replied the one who thus described himself. "You, Younger Brother, hold the Line of the Immortal Eight. See to it that you do not fail their now expectant eyes."

"It is one thing to hold the line; it is quite another to obtain a message from the farther end," murmured the Sublime rebelliously, but when he would have again applied for more explicit guidance, it was discovered that the stranger had withdrawn, though none had marked the moment of his going.

"All-knowing," urged a faithful slave who bore the Emperor's cup, "if you seek enlightenment, wherefore are The Books?"

"It is well said," exclaimed the Monarch, casting off his gloom. "What more in keeping with the theme than that a vassal youth should recall what the trusted keepers of our Inner Council have forgot!"

"Revered," returned the spokesman of the Elder Branch, by no means disposed to have their prescience questioned thus, "if we who guard the dark secrets of the Books forebore, it was not that our minds were tardy in your need, but rather because our passionate devotion shrank from the thought of finding what we may."

The Divine made a gesture of reconciliation.

"Your loyalty is clear and deep, Tso Paik, nor has its source yet been reached," he admitted freely. "But what does the somewhat heavily scored music of your genial voice forecast?"

"That is as will presently appear," replied the other sombrely, "for since the day of your great progenitor Shan-ti (who chose self-ending in consequence of what he learned) the restraining cords have not been cut nor the wisdom of The Books displayed."

"Certainly there are strong arguments against doing anything of the sort in an idle spirit," admitted Ming Wang hastily, at the same time spilling the larger portion of his wine upon the kneeling cupbearer. "Perhaps after all —"

"The requirement has gone forth: the issue must be met," pronounced the custodian firmly. "Even the lower-class demons have their feelings in such matters." Then, raising his voice, as his especial office permitted him to do, he called for the attendance of all his satellites and for the bringing of The Books. At this unusual cry, general business of every sort was immediately suspended within the limits of the Palace walls and an interminable stream of augurs, sorcerers, diviners, astrologers, forecasters, necromancers, haruspices, magicians, incantators, soothsayers, charm-workers, illusionists, singers and dancers, thought-readers, contortionists, and the like rallied to his side, bringing with them birds, serpents, fruit, ashes, flat and rounded sticks, cords, fire, entrails, perfumed wax, salt, coloured earth, dung of the sacred apes, crystal spheres, and the other necessary utensils of their enlightened arts. So great was the press that very few ordinary persons gained admittance, and of these only the outspoken and robust. When order was restored, the splendid ceremony of Bringing in The Books was formally observed, the casket opened, and the cords released.

"Ming Wang," pronounced the one who had made himself conspicuous throughout, "this is the Wisdom of The Books and thus stands the passage on the bamboo slip to which my necessarily inspired finger has been led: 'Drought, excessive, to assuage. Should a pestilential drought continue unappeased, a palatable extract may be made of the fermented grain of rice —' "

"Tso Paik," muttered another of the Inner Council, from about his sleeve, "what the Evil Dragon has assailed your mental balance?"

"Imperishable," pleaded Tso Paik in servile confusion, "dazzled by the brilliance of your shining condescension, this illiterate person misread the initial sign and diverged to an inappropriate line. Yet his arresting finger was not deceived, for the jewelled passage that relates appears on the next slip."

"Continue, discriminating Tso Paik," said the Emperor pleasantly. "Nor suffer your finger yet to lose that selfsame place."

"Sublimity, the guidance sought is that entitled: 'Drought, caused by Good or Bad Spirits, to disperse,'" resumed Tso Paik in a less compelling voice. "Thus and thus the message is pronounced: 'He who stands between the Upper and the Lower Planes alone can intervene when the Immortals have so far declared their wrath' —there follows much of a circumlocutory nature connected wit the Inherent Principle of Equipoise, and so forth."

"That can fittingly be served for our leisurely delectation at some future date," put in the Highest. "Insert your chop-stick in the solid meat, Tso Paik. What have we got to do?"

"Putting aside these gems of philosophical profundity, Benign, the nature of your submission is neither palatable nor light." At these foreboding words a thrill of apprehension swayed the vast concourse, but it was widely noticed that the crude Tso Paik's lamentable voice took upon itself a pleasurable shade. "Decked to the likeness of a sacrificial ox, shorn both of hair and rank-denoting nails, and riding in a farmyard cart, it is your unpleasant lot to be taken to the highest point of the sacred Ia-ling range and there confess your sins to Heaven and undertake reform. When this humane sacrifice has been achieved (providing no untoward omen intervenes meanwhile) the healing rain will fall."

At the full understanding of this direful penance, an awestruck silence fell upon the throng. The first to break it was the captain of the Emperor's chosen guard, and although he was incapable of producing more than an attenuated whisper, his words expressed the thoughts of every loyal subject there.

"Sins! Who speaks of sins?" he murmured in a maze. "How can that which is not, be? The Ever-righteous has no sins!"

Never was the profundity of the All-grasping more lucidly displayed than in that exacting pause when, whatever else happened, a popular rising, in one direction or another, seemed inevitable.

"Peace, worthy Sung," he cried, in a voice that carried to the public square outside, where it was rapturously acclaimed, although at that distance it was, of course, impossible to distinguish a word he said; "restrain your generous zeal and whet your docile ears to an acuter edge. The obligation is to confess sins: not to possess them. Admittedly we have no sins, for, little as the censorious credit it, your Unapproachable is often denied what the meanest outcast in his realm can wallow in. Nothing that we may do is, or can be, wrong; but the welfare of the people is our chief concern, and to secure that end there is no catalogue of vice that we shall not cheerfully subscribe to."

So unutterable was the effect produced by this truly regal magnaminity that all who heard its terms were rendered speechless. Those outside, on the contrary, hastily assuming that Ming Wang had said all that he had intended, testified their satisfaction more joyfully than before, and loud cries of "A thousand years!" filled the air.

"In the detail of promising amendment, also, there is nothing to which the most arbitrary need take exception," continued the enlightened Monarch when his voice could once more be heard. "What, after all, is a promise of amendment but an affirmation that the one who makes it will be more worthy of homage tomorrow than today? There is nothing new about that in your Immaculate's career; every day finds him better than before."

"Your words are like a string of hanging lanterns, when the way has hitherto been dark," fervently declared an aged counsellor. "But, Pre ̈

eminence, your polished nails, your cultivated hair —!"

"It is better to lose two spans outward than one span inward," replied the practical-minded Sovereign, dropping his voice for that one's ear alone. "Yet," he continued, turning to Tso Paik again, "in one respect the limit of compliance has been reached, and he who opens a hand so freely on the right may close one as tightly on the left. 'The likeness of an ox,' is doubtless a picturesque analogy, and the similitude is not bereft of a certain massive dignity. But if at the extremity of your prolific mind, Tso Paik, you cherish the questionable ambition of displaying your confiding Ruler to a superstitious though by no means simpleminded populace, wearing horns —"

"Mirror of felicity!" protested Tso Paik, as one who is maligned; "if my crude tongue offends, let it cease. You wear a sword and my head has but a single neck."

"In our romantic land there should be room both for your tongue and my sword to move without any overlapping," reassured Ming Wang. "Proceed, in your sublime office, therefore, to the exactitude of detail, and let harmony prevail."

V

Thus in the third year of his short but glorious reign the well disposed Ming Wang set out to free his people from the evil that oppressed them, draped in the semblance of a sacrificial ox (the metaphor, it was found, did not demand more than a screen of rushes to enclose his lower half), shorn, and riding in a dung-cart through the land. With so liberal-minded a prince, in so ambiguous a guise, it was impossible that the journey should be devoid of incident, but this is the essential story of Wan, and he who, while gathering mast, suffers his mind to dwell on the thought of peaches, will return with an empty sack.

In due course the company reached the lower slopes of the Ia-ling Mountains and thenceforward all progress was on foot. Tso Paik, who was gross by nature and very sluggish on his feet, would willingly have remained below to offer up (he said) an invocation to the gods, but Ming Wang would not suffer this, claiming that if he did their appetites might become satiate before his own chance came. Being of a slight and strenuous cast, this mode of progress was more congenial to the Emperor's taste than the restricted freedom of the dung-cart, and from time to time he inspired his train by pointing out to them that what they deemed to be the highest point was an imposition of the eye, and that yet another peak lay beyond. Finally, Tso Paik rolled bodily on the ground and declared that, as he could go no farther, where he lay in his official rank as Chief Custodian of The Books must constitute the limit, and this was then agreed to.

No complete record of Ming Wang's confession now exists, all those who accompanied him having entered into a deep compact to preserve a stubborn silence. It is admitted, however, that it was of inordinate length, very explicit in its details, and that it implicated practically every courtier and official of any standing. In a final access of self reproach, the Emperor penitently admitted that he was the guilty head of a thoroughly decayed and criminal autocracy, that he weakly surrounded himself with greedy and incompetent officials, and that he had thoughtlessly permitted sycophantry, bribery, and peculation to abound.

Almost before he had begun to speak, heavy clouds were seen to drift up from the west; with the final words of definite submission, a few drops fell, and the ceremony was concluded in a steady downpour. The conscientious Monarch did not allow the undoubted discomfort of all concerned to stem the flow of his inspired penitence, but when the last atrocity that he could lay to his own and, even more pointedly, to his ministers' charge had been revealed, he called up on Tso Paik.

"You, Tso Paik, as Ceremonial Director of the Enterprise, have accomplished an end. Yet, no longer to maintain a poise, does not the copious promptness of the response astonish even you?"

"Omnipotence," replied Tso Paik, looking steadily before him, "my faith was like an elephant tethered to a rock."

"It is well," agreed the Greatest, endeavouring to shake his scanty outer garment free of moisture. "Bring forward now our largest state umbrella."

At this sudden but in no way unreasonable command, a very concentrated silence engaged the company, and those who had not the opportunity to withdraw in unstudied abstraction sought to anticipate any call upon themselves by regarding the one involved expectantly.

"Alas," confessed the dense Tso Paik, "it had not occurred to this one's bankrupt mind that there would be any likelihood —" But at that point, understanding the snare to which he had enticed himself, he stopped ineptly.

A passing shiver disturbed the royal frame, though with high-born delicacy he endeavoured to conceal it. Only a faint elevation of the celestial eyebrows betrayed the generous emotion at the painful obligation laid upon him.

"It wrings my tenderest parts with hooks of bitterness," he said, "that so loyal and trustworthy a subject should have brought himself within the Code of Yao-u and Shun, under the Section: 'Conduct in an official whereby the wellbeing of his Sovereign is directly or indirectly menaced.' Li Tung, you are a dignitary of high justice; receive the unfortunate Tso Paik into your charge until the Palace executioner shall require him at your hands. Let us now strive to avert, so far as we can, the ill consequences of this fatal indiscretion by seeking the nearest shelter."

VI

In this remarkable manner, two of the most notable characters of any age, Wan the son of Ah-shoo, and Ming Wang (to whose memory posterity has dedicated as a title "The Knowing") at last encountered, for it was to the penurious home of the former person that destiny inclined the Emperor's footsteps. Recognizing the languished fortunes of the one whose roof he sought, the considerate Monarch forebore to stand on ceremony, merely requiring a reclining stool before the charcoal fire.

"Beneficence," exclaimed Wan, falling on his face to the best of his ability as he offered a steaming cup, "admittedly the hearth will warm the muscles of your lordly body, but here is that which will invigorate the cockles of your noble heart."

For a perceptible moment the Imperishable wavered-certainly the balance of the analogy might have been more classically maintained, or possibly he remembered the long succession of food-tasters who had fallen lifeless at his feet-but in that pause the exquisite aroma of the fragrant liquid assailed his auspicious nose. He took the cup and emptied it, returned it to Wan's hand with an appropriate gesture, and continued thus and thus until the latter person had to confess that his store was destitute. Not until then did Ming Wang devote his throat to speech.

"What is this enchanted beverage?" he demanded, "and why has it been withheld from us until now?"

"It is the produce of a sacred tree, high Majesty, and its use but lately revealed to me by special favour of the Powers. Never before, from the legendary days of the First Man until this hour, has it been brewed on earth, and save for the necessary tests, your own distinguished lips are the first to taste it."

"It is certainly miraculous," agreed Ming Wang ecstatically, and unable to contain himself he began to cross and recross the room, to the embarassment of the assembled nobles who were thus also kept in a continual state of flux. "It has a perfection hitherto unknown among the liquids of the world. It cheers yet without any disconcerting effect upon the speech or movements. It warms where one is cold and cools where one is hot. Already every trace of fatigue and despondency has vanished, leaving us inspired for further deeds of public usefulness, eager to accomplish other acts of justice. It stimulates, invigorates, rejuvenates, animates, lubricates —"

"Sublimest of Potentates," pleaded the recorder of his voice, "retard the torrent of your melodious soliloquy! How else shall this clay-fingered menial take down your priceless words which it is his design presently to set to appropriate music?"

"It will be as acceptable at the earliest gong-stroke of the yet unawakened morn, as it will become the inevitable accompaniment to the afternoon rice. Into the inner office of the commercially inclined it will be brought to smooth the progress of each bargain, and in the dim recesses of our departmental activities it will produce harmony and discreet mirth among the abstemious yet sprightly of both sexes. In the chambers of our lesser ones its name is destined to rank as a synonym of all that is confidential and inexact. The weary student, endeavouring to banish sleep; the minor priest, striving to maintain enthusiasm amid an inadequacy of taels; the harassed and ill-requited inscriber of the spoken word —"

"Proceed, O Taproot of Eloquence, proceed!" murmured the one who plied a hurrying brush. "To an accompaniment of drums, horns, and metallic serpents —"

"To cope the final pinnacle, it is an entirely new thing; indeed it is the new thing, and unless our experience of an imitative and docile people is signally astray it will soon become 'the thing.'" It is hardly necessary to insist at this late date how noticeably the prescient Ming Wang's words have been literally fulfilled. Known for many centuries as "the new thing," the popular decoction passed by a natural stage into "the thing," and then, in affectionate abbreviation, to "the." By this appropriate designation it is recognized in every land to which our flowery civilization carries, though doubtless on barbaric tongues the melodious word is bent to many uncouth similarities.

"It now only remains," continued the evenhanded lawgiver, "to reward virtue and to eradicate vice. The former is personified before us-the latter we shall doubtless very soon discover in some form or another. What, O benefactor of mankind, is your upright name?"

"My low-class appellation is Wan, that of my mentally defective father being Ah-shoo, we springing from the lowly house of Lam," replied the other suitably. "The inconspicuous shadow lurking in the background is Lan-yen, whose name entwines with mine."

"Yet how comes it that you, who are evidently under the direct protection of the higher Forces, are in so-as it may be expressed —?" and with commendable tact the humane Emperor merely indicated the threadbare walls and Wan's immemorial garb.

"Formerly, Magnificence, my state was thus and thus, lacking nothing and having slaves to stand before my presence," admitted Wan. "But of late one in authority has oppressed me for no cause, save that the proverb aptly says, 'Should you touch a rat upon the tail be assured that he will turn and bite you,' and in this latter end his malice has prevailed.

"Ah," commented the Enlightened with a meaning nod at each of his suite in turn, to which they duly responded an apt glance of cognizance. "What is this corrupt official's name and the sign of his condition?"

"He is of the crystal button, lord, and his forbidding name is Hin Ching. Furthermore, led on by an insatiable curiosity, he is at this moment standing about this person's crumbling gate, striving to peer through the prickly hedge toward us."

"Let him be brought in at once," was the command, and with no opportunity to prepare an evasive tale Hin Ching was hurried forward.

"Hin Ching," said the Emperor, who had meanwhile taken up an imposing station, "all your duplicity is known to us and no defense will serve you. How comes it that you have so pursued this meritorious youth who has our royal favor?"

"Tolerance," pleaded the terror-stricken culprit, seeing no other course before him, and kowtowing so passionately that his words could scarcely be heard above the steady clashing of his head upon the sonorous floor, "be clement in your strength, for it has long been suspected that this person's heart is touched."

"In that case," decided the Sun of Impartiality, "the marks should certainly be visible so that the innocent may be warned thereby." Then turning to his retinue he continued: "Procure a reasonable abundance of supple bamboo rods, and without disturbing the afflicted Mandarin from the position which he has so conveniently assumed, remove his lower robe."

At this awful presage of the nature of the correction shortly to be laid upon Hin Ching, a shudder went up from the assembled host and even Wan vacillated in his strict resentment.

"Brother of the peacock," he pleaded, "suffer justice this once to drowse. He is a man of middle years and obese beyond his age."

"It has ever been the privilege of the wronged to condone the guilty," replied Ming Wang, "and to that extent your plea must hold. Yet wherein shall Hin Ching's penance lie, in this case being outside the Code of Yao-u and Shun? What, Mandarin, is your strict equivalent?"

"Your entirely humble ranks equal with a district prefect, High Excellence — equal and above."

"Henceforth you will rank equal and below, thus degrading you appreciably and at the same time enabling you to save a portion of your face. On the unbending line of pure romantic justice all your belongings should divert to Wan, but as this would probably result in your becoming a dangerous criminal, the special requirements will be met by allotting to him half. To prevent any mutual delusion, you will divide all you possess into two equal mounds-and Wan will make his choice."

"May your life span ten thousand ages and your grandsons rule the world!" exclaimed Wan. "It is enough to have seen this day." And even Hin Ching contributed an appropriate, though a shorter, blessing from within his teeth.

"It only remains to define your duties," continued the Ever-thoughtful, addressing himself to Wan. "Your style will be that of 'Protector of the Tree,' and the scroll confirming this will follow in due season. Your chief function will, of course, be that of assuring an unfailing supply of the beverage to your royal Palaces at all times. In your spare moments you can transmit offshoots of the trees to every point of our boundless Empire, so that the seed shall never fail. The office, which will be strictly hereditary, will naturally be quite honorary, what you receive from Hin Ching being sufficient to maintain your state. It will, however, carry with it a salute of three trumpets and the emblem of a steaming cup."

"Majesty," reported an attending slave, entering at this pause, "a relay of swift horses from the Capital awaits your commanding voice without."

The All-accomplishing rose and moved toward the door with the well-satisfied smile of a person who has achieved his worthy end.

"Everything has been set right here," he remarked pleasantly, "and the usual edicts will follow within a moon." Then to his suite: "Come, let us press forward with all haste to scatter the germs of promiscuous justice elsewhere."

The Further Continuance of Kai Lung's Quest and His Opportune Encounter With an Outcast Band, All Ignorant of the Classical Examples of the Past

The next day, as soon as it was light, Kai Lung resumed his toilsome way, sustained by the cordial leave-takings of the villagers to whom his unassuming qualities as a relater of events had proved of interest, and no less encouraged by the tactful bestowal of such gifts as they had no further use for.

"Even a meatless bone should be tendered with both hands," apologized one bereft of reason, as he indicated all that he could offer—a pipe containing only ashes, and in the same harmonious spirit Kai Lung placed the stem between his lips for a few moments with the equally polite assurance, "It is not necessary to pluck the fruit in order to admire the tree."

At the parting of the roads a patriarchal figure was seated on the earth. As the one with whom this narration is essentially concerned approached, the inopportune person indicated that the other should retard his footsteps so that they might converse at leisure and with ease. Unwelcome as the delay would prove, Kai Lung had no alternative but to defer to the wishes of a venerable whose long white moustaches almost touched the ground. He stopped and saluted him with deference.

"What is passing through your mind is by no means so hidden as you may think," remarked the stranger, with a penetrating glance; "nor, considering the mission upon which you are embarked, is your reluctance to be wondered at."

"Your insight is both clear and deep," confessed Kai Lung. "What you infer is all the more surprising, as no word of this has so far escaped my docile tongue."

The ancient smiled slightly in a self-approving manner and caressed the more accessible portions of his virtuous moustache.

"It is not necessary for a philosopher to light a torch to catch glow-worms at midday," he replied profoundly. "The one before you, in spite of his admittedly quite ordinary appearance, is really an experienced wizard. Last night, in return for the gratifying entertainment afforded by your study of the vicissitudinous Wan, he spent the hours of darkness in drawing up the fundamentals of your lucky system. From these it would appear that the numbers 4 and 14 are inimical to your prospects, while 7 and 41 point directly to success. The mango is a tree to be avoided, but a golden bud set on a leafless stem leads to your achievement. Finally, should you encounter two hyenas and an infirm tiger disputing for the possession of a sick cow's bones, do not hesitate."

"It is well expressed," replied Kai Lung gratefully. "Yet in what precise direction should the recommended lack of indecision tend?"

The gifted necromancer raised his inspired eyebrows somewhat, as though this stress of detail did not altogether merit his approval.

"It is one thing to forecast contingencies," was his reply; "it is another branch of the occupation to explain what takes place thereafter. If you have led a consistent life, doubtless some benignant Influence will be told off to direct you in the crisis."

"I can make no particular claim to anything excessive," admitted Kai Lung with due humility. "My usual practice has been to avoid treading on bees, ants, silkworms, and industrious creatures generally, and there is a suitable hole cut in my outer door and a bowl of rice always set within so that any passing homeless ghost need not go hungry through the night. The care of ancestral spirits need not be specified."

The aged made a gesture expressive of some doubt.

"It may be deemed sufficient in your hour of trial," he conceded, "but a few authentic charms, written with perfumed ink and worn at the more vulnerable angles of the body, might well be added."

With this warning in his ears, the storyteller passed forward on his way, for the pious anchorite had immediately fallen into a deep introspective haze from which it would have been unseemly to recall him. Profiting by the directions readily disclosed to him by dwellers in those parts, Kai Lung steadily followed in Ming-shu's offensive wake, not forming any very clear perception of how to act when the moment of their meeting should arrive, but content meanwhile to leave the matter to the all-directing wisdom of the forerunners of his Line.

After enduring many hardships and suffering occasional inconvenience through the really flattering but too excessively persistent attentions of brigands, outlaws, underling officials, wild beasts of various kinds, snakes and scorpions, swollen rivers, broken paths, and thunder-stones, Kai Lung came on the seventh day at evening to the outskirt of a trackless morass that barred his further progress. The scanty dwellers in that sterile waste were persons of a low standard of intelligence whose sole means of livelihood consisted of the occasional wayfarer who sought their aid. These it was their custom, by immemorial use, to rob and then fatally dispose of, or to guide along the secret morass paths for an agreed reward-according to the arrangement which they found the more convenient. The appearance of Kai Lung was disconcerting to a tribe of so regular a habit.

"For here is one who has nothing in his sleeve and whose apparel is inferior to the worst among ourselves," they said. "Thus he is secure from our extracting thumbs, and having no complaint to carry hence against us there is no reason why we should put ourselves to the trouble of disposing of him fatally," and they continued to look at one another askance.

"That is a matter very easily arranged," interposed Kai Lung. "In accordance with a certain vow, it is necessary that I should cross these voracious swamps in pursuit of Ming-shu's host. By guiding me among the secret ways, you will fulfil one of your essential purposes, and by supplying me with such meagre food as will enable me to justify my oath, you will acquire merit of a very special kind."

To this solution of their difficulty, the better-class murderers at once agreed, but some of the more sordid-minded, who by reason of their deficient literary attainments could not follow the balance of the synthesis, began to murmur from behind their fanlike hands.

"It is all very well," they implied, "but Ming-shu, who began by putting us to death to exact our service, was forced in the end to succumb to our terms. Why, then, should we guide this alien wayfarer, who is plainly banded with Ming-shu, merely to gain some hypothetical distinction in a future state?"

"The reply to that is easy and concise," was Kai Lung's ready answer. "This being the seventh day of my pursuit, it falls within my lucky zone, and thereby I cannot fail. Should you neglect to profit by my auspicious presence here, another will snatch this godsend from your grasp, for in the circumstances a powerful friend will certainly arise to foster me, even as that high official the Mandarin Wong Tsoi came to the aid of Keu Chun, the needy actor."

"We who are men of the bog land of Ying-tze pay allegiance to the Mandarin Ho Hung alone," the ill-contents replied. "What is this new official with whom you threaten us?"

"The word is inexact," maintained Kai Lung, "nor would a throat so obsequious as mine bend to the line of menace. The Mandarin Wong Tsoi is one who had no actual existence in this world, he being but a fictitious creation of an imagined tale."

At this the tribesmen conferred together apart and it was plain that even the boldest were shaken. Then the spokesman stood forth again.

"If the Mandarin Wong Tsoi was such as you affirm, how is it possible to say what words he used or the manner of his behaviour in any contingency of life?"

"That constitutes the storyteller's art," replied the one before them, "and therein lie the essentials of this craft. But is it possible," he added, scarcely daring to voice so incredible a thought, "that you are unacquainted with the crystalline scintillation and many-petalled efflorescence of a well-related legendary occurrence?"

"We are but the untutored brigands of this lonely waste, whose immature ideas have hitherto been bounded by the arrival of inoffensive travellers from the east and the manner of their passing out toward the west," confessed the tribe. "The form of entertainment to which you allude lies quite beyond our sphere."

"Yet it would seem incredible," lamented Kai Lung sadly, "that within the furthest confines of our classic-loving Empire there should be tribes so barbarous and deficient in the rudiments of a literary veneer as not to be acquainted with the 'Romance of Three Kingdoms' or the more austere 'Wilderness of Pearls,' and to whom the graceful apophthegm-spangled masterpieces of the sublime period of T'ang are a never-opened book."

"We certainly begin to become conscious of a hitherto-unsuspected void," agreed the leaders. "But how can a community living so remote aspire to correct our fault?"

"As to that," replied Kai Lung modestly, "the one before you is himself a very third-rate relater of fabricated legends. On the understanding that you will guide him through the hidden byways of your prepossessing swamp and will supply his present need, he will, to the best of his quite unsatisfactory ability, endeavour to waste your priceless time with the narrative entitled 'The Story of Wong Tsoi and the Merchant Teen King's Thumb.'"

"Is that a noteworthy example of your inimitable style?" asked the chieftain of the band politely.

"It is neither better nor worse than any other threadbare makeshift of my superannuated stock," replied Kai Lung no less reciprocally. "It maintains, however, a certain harmonious parallelity to our existing state in that a discreditable outcast finds a beneficent protector in his hour of need, and the one who thus upheld his cause is himself rewarded for his virtuous action."

"If that is the case, we will constitute your circle," agreed the others, "and when you have honourable fulfilled your word you will find no disposition on our part to recede from ours." Kai Lung accordingly unrolled his well-worn mat and indicated that his simple preparation was complete.

The Story of Wong Tsoi and the Merchant Teen King's Thumb

It was the custom of the Mandarin Wong Tsoi to move about the streets of Hoo-Yang at night unattended and by stealth. Sometimes he chanced upon an encounter of a kind that was not strictly within his province as a magistrate, at others he heard a whisper that enabled him to influence justice toward those whom he distrusted without the necessity of invoking the more elaborate forms of law, and upon one occasion — But having thus brought to the notice of a select and proverbially open-handed band of listeners the most distinguished person of this very ordinary recital (according to the dictates of the refined models of the past), it is now permissible to begin in a more convenient manner.

When Chun, the son of Keu, returning to his father's house from a lengthy absence, made his first inquiry, after the protestations of regard and filial devotion, it was of Fragrant Petal he spoke. Recalling little of what had gone before, they told him freely, with, perchance, an added jest that one so old and unwieldy in his bunk as Teen King, the rich produce merchant, should seek to possess a butterfly. When he knew all, Chun reached for his hat and staff and unlatched the door.

"I would look again upon the Ways and well-remembered quarters of the city," he remarked evasively.

"Yet it is now dark," they reminded him, "and you are but just restored to us. Tomorrow —"

"There is still light enough to show me what I seek," was his reply.

As Chun turned into a convenient byway that led down to one of the deep places of the river, he met two men running and heard a cry from the darkness of the water. The great sky lantern at that moment directing a propitious beam, he discovered one struggling vainly to regain the shore, and thrusting a long pole toward him, Keu Chun succeeded at length in bringing him to safety.

"Your aid was timely," remarked the stranger when he was somewhat recovered, "and the measure of this one's gratitude will not be stinted. In what particular direction does your necessity lie?"

"This is in the nature of things, seeing that the origin of our meeting is your desire to avoid drowning and my determination to encounter it," replied Keu Chun sombrely. "Thus the foreshore of the river on which we stand becomes, as it were, a common ground to both. If you will but continue your footsteps to the north and leave me equally to press forward to the south, our various purposes will thereby be effected."

"What you say is sufficiently surprising, and I would gladly learn something more of your condition," exclaimed the other. "The dilapidated hut that shelters me stands but a short li distant from this spot. Even if your mind is set on drowning, courtesy demands that I who am concerned shall at least provide you with a change of dry apparel in which to do so more agreeably. Should you still be in the same mood after this slight civility, there will be nothing lost, for, as the proverb says, 'Felicity slips quickly by, but affliction walks side by side along our path.'"

"If you feel that the omission would leave you under an intolerable obligation, I cannot reasonably deny you what you ask," admitted Chun with an emotion of no-enthusiasm toward any arisement. "Therefore, lead on."

With this encouragement the stranger professed himself content, and together they sought the higher ground. Presently the more noisome district of the city, where beggars, criminals, and the literary classes had their quarter, was left behind, the better-reputed parts frequented by the industrious and sincere were likewise passed, and soon the spacious ways and well-spread gardens of successful merchants and officials marked their further progress.

"Admittedly the path that seems long to a person when fleeing from justice appears incredibly short when he is led down to execution," remarked Keu Chun at length. "Nevertheless, this small li of yours —"

"We are even now at the poverty-stricken gate," replied the guide, stopping before the largest and most lavishly ornamented of the mansions, and with a key that he drew from his inner sleeve he unlocked a door leading to the courtyard and stood aside. "Pass in, nobility."

"Before one whose ancestors doubtless wore the peacock feather?" protested Chun no less agreeably. "These rebellious knees would refuse their sustenance should I attempt so impolite and act," and he also moved farther away.

"The circumstances are not happily arranged for a really well-kept-up display of mutual refinement," remarked the other, speaking with some discomfort through his chattering teeth and at the same time stooping to wring an excess of moisture from his body-cloth. "In the name of the Viceroy of Hades let us go in together."

On this understanding, they went forward side by side, though with some difficulty, the way being narrow and the one who led Chun a person of outstanding attitude.

"This is evidently an underling in the service of some noble," thought Chun. "His easy manner proclaims that he is not altogether without influence." But the one concerned did not turn aside toward the living huts. He led the way up to the great house itself, and again drawing forth a key, he unlocked a door.

"This is certainly a personal attendant upon a high official," next considered Chun, "and unless my memory is grossly is at fault, the ya-men of the district mandarin should he hereabout. If I have rendered this service to one who has the ear of Wong Tsoi, it may turn, if not actually to my advantage, at least to the disadvantage of Teen King."

"Let us now rearrange ourselves more in comfort," said the stranger affably, and with the tone of authority, he struck an imperious gong. "Two changes of fine raiment here without delay," he cried to the slave who hurried at the call. "Later, let a repast be laid out in my inner room —a display suited to the entertainment of an honoured guest."

"I hear and obey, high excellence," replied the slave, retiring.

"Excellence!" repeated Keu Chen, falling back several paces from so august a presence. "Can it be that you are —?"

The broad minded official made a gesture implying caution.

"The wise duck keeps his mouth shut when he smells frogs," he remarked significantly. "Be discreet, and you may rely upon the advancement of your righteous cause. But should you be so shortsighted as to maintain a special claim on this one's succour it would be his duty, as an incorruptible upholder of the law, to sentence you to a variety of unpleasant exertions for attempted blackmail."

"So presumptuous a thought never entered this ill-nourished mind," replied Keu Chun.

"It is well said," agreed Wong Tsoi; "and among virtuous friends a slight inclination of the head is as efficacious as the more painful admonition from an iron-shod foot."

With discriminating courtesy, the tolerantly inclined mandarin forebore to question Keu Chun more closely until a rich and varied abundance had restored their energies. Then, reclining with dignified ease among the cushions of his couch, Wong Tsoi indicated to his guest that he should seat himself upon the floor at a respectful distance away and disclose his past.

"For," he added, "it concerns one who is responsible for the administration of the best-regulated city of our Celestial Empire to discover what flaw in an otherwise perfect judicial code prompted you to so distressing a remedy."

"Yet, eminence," Chun ventured to remind him, "if your benevolent condescension is moved by so slight a matter as this obscure person's mere misfortune, with what refined anguish must you regard actual crime! The two unseemly outcasts who ventured to lay their sacrilegious hands upon your honored person—"

"Cherish no apprehension on that score," replied the farseeing Wong Tsoi capably. "In cases of absolute wrongdoing, it is impossible for even the least experienced official to deviate from the iron rule of conduct. Cause and effect; effect and cause: these two facets of an integral system corollarate with absolute precision. Two persons having committed a Category One crime, two persons will automatically suffer a Category One punishment, and the Essential Equipoise of Justice will thereby be painlessly maintained."

"It is what the scrupulous would look for," assented Chun.

"It is what they will inevitably see," replied Wong Tsoi. "Should your leisurely footsteps chance to turn in the direction of the public execution ground on the occasion of the next general felicity, your discriminating eyes will receive assurance that the feet of the depraved find no resting-place on the upright soil of Hoo-yang."

"It is indeed a matter for rejoicing that your penetrating gaze recognized the degraded miscreants who will thus be brought to an appropriate end."

A faint absence of agreement for the moment obscured the well-balanced exactness of the lawgiver's expression.

"If," he remarked profoundly, "so sublime a principle as Justice should depend on so fallible a thread as a single human attribute, all feeling of security would be gone forever. The two misbegotten harbingers of shame who submitted this hard-striving person to the indignity of thrusting him down into a polluted stream will sooner or later meet with a fate that will be both painful and grotesque. In the meanwhile, the wholesome moral of retribution will be inculcated in the throng by two others (doubtless quite as abandoned in their several ways) demonstrating that authority does not slumber."

"It has been claimed that there is equally one law for the just and for the unjust," assented Chun, "and in a certain guise —"

"Your loyal approbation nourishes the roots of our endeavour," interposed Wong Tsoi, rewarding the speaker with a handful of melon seeds cast in his direction. "Now disclose your own involvement."

"Beneficence," replied Chun readily, "my obscure happening may be likened to a scorpion's tail, in that it is short but sharply pointed. My lowly name is Chun, that of my father's meagre house being Keu, and having ever been of a wayward bend, I earn my scanty rice as an inefficient Brother of the Peach Orchard."

"An actor," exclaimed Wong Tsoi, regarding his guest with a special interest.

"Alas, exalted," confessed Chun, "such is my offensive calling."

The leniently inspired official made a gesture of dissent, after satisfying himself that no attendant lingered.

"That which would brand you as an outcast in the eyes of the tightly buttoned, to me contains an added flavour," he admitted. "In the security of this inner chamber I will confide to your specific ear that I also am of a straggling and romantic nature, though the dignity of office makes it impossible for me to go very far in any impropriety. Nevertheless, half a cycle of years ago, when I had failed for the third time to attain the degree of Budding Genius in the competitions, I had all but decided to throw up an official career and go upon the wooden platform.... . Does your refined gift lie in the portrayal of noble youths of exalted lineage who are for a time alienated from the path of happiness by the machination of an elderly vampire?"

"At one time my ambition reached in that direction, but, as the saying has it, 'One learns to itch where one can scratch,' and my unworthy talents are considered most effective in the delineation of club-armed guardians of the street who slip heavily backward on over-ripe loquats, and similar devices of a gravity-removing nature."

"Proceed with the recital of your story," commanded the Mandarin briefly.

"Over against my lowborn father's bankrupt hovel there stands the home of Fragrant Petal, the graceful and entrancing offspring of the autumnal widow Le-she. From an early period it has been the habit of the sympathetic maiden and the calamitous earthworm now before you to meet unostentatiously in a convenient spot that was suitably screened from the windows of both houses. Here a binding arrangement was mutually exchanged, that each would remain faithful to the other. Fortified with this incentive, nothing seemed too excessive, and a score of moons ago the one who is now relating his sordid experience set forth to achieve distinction and to win an agreeable superfluity of taels. Today he returned —"

"Doubtless to entrust a few bars of gold to a discreet friend's keeping?" suggested Wong Tsoi politely, as the other paused.

"To recover a still serviceable pair of sandals that he remembered leaving in an outer shed, esteemed," replied Keu Chun with conscious diffidence. "Then only did he learn of the grossly unfit-to-live Le-she's perfidy. Taking advantage of this one's absence and of the obscene Teen King's infatuation, she had bartered Fragrant Petal to be that glutinous-eyed produce monger's possession at the price of a hundred taels of silver."

"In these close-handed times, a hundred taels are not to be spat at," remarked the Mandarin judicially.

"Excellence!" cried Keu Chun springing to his feet, "it is not the equivalent of a single hair among the ten thousand glossy ones that go to crown her high perfection. When she smiles, her eyes throw out continuous beams of violet light — even sideways. At every step her classically proportioned feet leave the impress of a golden lily. The Imperial treasury within the Purple City does not contain sufficient store to buy one glance of approbation —"

"It was thus with this one also in the days of his own brightly coloured youth," sighed Wong Tsoi reminiscently, as he removed the outer skin of a choice apricot. "There was Che-Che who danced on pigeon's eggs at the 'Melodious Resort of Virtue' in Chiang-foo, and another, whose attractive name has escaped my weed-grown memory, who was reputed to have invisible wings, for in no other way could her graceful unconcern, as she progressed upon one foot along a distended cord, be accounted for. But maidens are no longer what they were in the days before they gummed their hair. Doubtless this Fragrant Petal —"

"If your own distinguished eyes could but see —"

"Enough!" interposed Wong Tsoi decisively. "Shall one measure the bounty of the Yangtse-kiang by a teacup? But for your graceful versatility with a perverse-willed steering pole, the misshapen eyes to which you so fittingly allude would at this moment be unable to regard anything beyond the ill-made bed of an offensive watercourse."

"Then, benevolence —?" begged Chun, stirred by new hope.

"The engaging qualities you display-added to the fact that the low-conditioned Teen King recently deluded this confiding person in a matter affecting the quality of some reputed swallows' nests-establish the justice of your cause. How to proceed is another matter, for the contaminating refuse-blender has both wealth and legality on his side. Speaking strictly as one loyal subject to another, it may well be admitted that it is not infeasible to outstrip legal forms by means of a well-lined sleeve, nor yet to get the better of mere riches by a dexterous use of lawful methods. But to defeat both of these while possessing neither would melt the tenacity of demons."

"Could you not," suggested Keu Chun helpfully, "in the exercise of your exalted office, denounce the unclean Teen King to vigilant authority as one worthy of immediate death, without disclosing too exactly the nature of his crime?"

"Undoubtedly," agreed Wong Tsoi. "It is by no means as unusual course, and it has the merit of ruling out a mass of evidence which is wholly irrelevant when the result has already been decided. But by a most corrupt enactment, it is necessary for any official submitting a complaint to begin it with a full recital of the various times that he himself has been degraded."

"Degraded!" exclaimed Keu Chun, incredulous of so harsh an infliction toward one so spotless. "Surely these blameworthy ears —"

"On seven misjudged occasions-thrice charged with 'ordinariness of character' and on yet four times more for 'displaying originality of conduct unseemly in a high official.' " replied Wong Tsoi dispassionately. "Rearrange your composure, worthy Keu Chun; these are but formalities in the daily life of a zealous servant of the state and merely indicate that another would gladly wear his button."

"Why, then, graciousness —?"

"It nevertheless bars your well-meant plan. So inauspiciously sired a plaint would be consigned by the merest official pencil-moistener to the eternal oblivion of the dove's retreat," explained the Mandarin, with a meaning flicker of his wrist. "If you hope to look forward to a hundred strong sons to venerate your name, Keu Chun, something more apt must emerge from our mutual endeavour."

"Benevolence," confessed Keu Chun with some dejection, "the one before you would cheerfully face the torments to achieve his quest, but in matters involving guile he is as devoid of wisdom as a new-laid egg is destitute of feathers."

"Certainly the enterprise will need qualities of no common order," agreed Wong Tsoi ungrudgingly. "To your knowledge, did the maiden go unwillingly, and is she still allegiant to your cause?"

Chun put a hand within his sleeve, and from a hidden fold he offered to the Mandarin a sheaf of polished bamboo slips tied together with a crimson thread. A score and five there would be in all, or even more.

"This missive awaited my discovering thumb within a certain hollow cypress which often served our need," he said. "Read freely, excellence, of her gracefully expressed affection and of the high-minded repugnance with which she regards her detested lot."

"Your meritorious word suffices," replied the Mandarin hastily, as he recognized the formidable proportion of the letter. "It is scarcely meet that another eye should rest upon the context of so privileged a message. Doubtless, after this avowal, you sought to approach beneath Teen King's inner window?"

"That would have served no profitable end, esteemed. For a reason not yet clear, Fragrant Petal has been straightway conveyed to that corrupt spice adulterator's summer seat, a lonely tower lying off the northern earth-road, where she is strictly held."

"Yet Teen King himself has not passed beyond the city gates during the present moon," observed Wong Tsoi shrewdly. "His ardour has a strangely tardy bend that it must loiter so."

"Perchance the chief one of his inner chamber has raised a contentious voice —"

"There you have struck the wooden skewer on its thicker end, Keu Chun!" exclaimed the other with conviction. "Her forbidding name is Tsoo, and hitherto she has allowed no secondary to share her place. Teen King, stricken with this corroding passion of his unsavoury old age, has acted thus and thus, hoping doubtless to sway Tsoo on one plea or another, or, perchance, failing that, to dispose of her inoffensively by some simple but well-tried method."

"If that is indeed the case, then Fragrant Petal may still —"

"May still be yours, you would say? Yet, should that come to pass, is there any secure retreat into which you and the ornamentally described one could imperceptibly fade? Assuredly, in so amiable a cause, some unnamed well-wisher would be forthcoming to contribute a double hand-count of taels to your virtuous success."

"Munificence," replied Keu Chun, "to elude pursuit would then be easy. A propitious friend, lying at no great distance from this spot, trades a commodious junk far into the lower reaches of the river. Once there —"

"Truly. As well look for an eel in a cartload of live adders. Forego despair, Keu Chun. I am by no means desirous that my care-word ghost should be under the burden of this obligation to your exacting ghost in the Hereafter. What a far from slow-witted official can do to readjust the balance now will be discreetly effected."

"I am in your large and never-failing hand," replied Keu Chun submissively.

Wong Tsoi waved a gesture of benevolent dismissal and closed his eyes to indicate tactfully that a concentrated reverie was necessary in which to mature his plans. So deep indeed became the profundity of his thoughts that neither Keu Chun's deferential leave-taking nor yet the various gong-strokes of the night were suffered to obtrude, and the early light of dawn found him with his eyes still closed in meditation and his body in the same pliant attitude of introspective calm.

Let it be freely admitted that, when Wong Tsoi stepped forth from his ya-men on the following day, he had not the most shadowy idea of how to bring about Keu Chun's desire and thus fulfil the obligation that the saving of his life-at the risk of incurring the malignity of the presiding demon of the river-had imposed upon him.

"Yet," he remarked self-reliantly as he set out, "I am pledged to the undertaking, and as the wise philosopher of Ts'i has so observantly remarked, 'Where the head has already gone, the hind quarters are bound to follow.'"

In pursuit of a guiding omen, the scrupulous official dismissed his chair and bearers presently and bent his not entirely reluctant feet in the direction of the "Abode of Harmony and Well-seasoned Dishes" at about the time of the evening rice. Beneath this auspicious sign might be found at that hour many of his more opulent and mentionable neighbours within Hoo-yang. The honour of an unceremonious visit from so high a dignitary was a conspicuous event, and the gratified Comptroller of the Table, meeting Wong Tsoi at the door, preceded him backward to his place, chanting meanwhile a happily arranged song in his honour, into which the versatile person gradually blended the names of the various delicacies available as they neared the highest seat. Wong Tsoi having made an appropriate choice, the one who had attended him retired in the same becoming order, extolling the guest's discernment in another set of verses, wherein he pronounced the selected viands in a louder key, thus to apprise the Custodian of the Grill of what was required of him. When the first dish duly arrived, following the dictates of ordinary courtesy, the latest guest stood up and pressed everyone around to join him in partaking of it.

"The one before you is a thoroughly inadequate host," he announced, bowing graciously in the four directions; "a worse combination of courses than those that he has chosen could not well be hit upon, and, as is quite befitting, the most inferior portion of each dish has been specially reserved for him. How great, therefore, will be your amiable condescension if you will but leave your own attractively arranged tables and endure the unappetizing deficiencies of his."

"On the contrary," came from every side, "your nimble-minded wit makes you so desirable a guest that we must really implore your company here with us instead. As for the assorting of the dishes and the quality of the food, we can assure your high excellence that you are pleasurably mistaken in thinking that yours are worse than ours. Do, therefore —" The remainder of the graceful compliment was lost in the agreeable rattle of chopsticks as all resumed their interrupted occupation precisely as before.

Now, although Wong Tsoi had evolved no definite plan, he had come to the "Abode of Harmony" in the full expectation of finding the unsightly produce merchant also there. Toward the outcome of that incident he had not neglected to burn a liberal supply of joss-sticks, so that, when his entirely expressionless gaze noted the gross outline of the objectionable Teen King seated at no great space away, he recognized that, so far as the Doubtful Forces were concerned, he was not ill-equipped for an encounter.

Teen King, for his part, fancied that the dignified inclination sent in his direction was perceptibly warmer than the other three. Wong Tsoi recognized as the loudest voice raised in complimentary greeting that of Teen King. The omens pointed to the mutual recriminations in the matter of a few kin of debatable birds' nests being forgotten, but so far neither was committed beyond one side of his face.

When Teen King rose to go, it was not inevitable that he should pass Wong Tsoi's table, but with absentminded detachment he took that course. Seeing this, the Mandarin's preoccupied foot thoughtlessly moved a vacant seat so that it barred the way.

"Ten thousand sincere regrets that your honourable progress should be impeded in this manner," exclaimed Wong Tsoi, drawing the chair aside with his own obliging hand. "Have you appeased your virtuous stomach?"

"Rather it is my own incommodious bulk that disturbs your well-intentioned chair," replied Teen King deferentially. "Are they gratifying your enlightened palate?"

"Since an unlooked-for felicity has delayed you at this spot, will you not occupy the seat so auspiciously provided?" suggested the other. "After your laborious passage of this badly arranged room, doubtless a moment's rest —" and he pushed his snuff-bottle of priceless jade across the table for Teen King's use.

"Excellence," began Teen King, after he had helped himself liberally from the snout of the recumbent pig that formed the bottle, "with the exception of ordinary business transactions, the one before you had led an integritous life. Why, then, should the path of his endeavour be edged with sharp afflictions?"

"It is truly said that a rogue may sit under a scaffolding all day, but if a righteous man ventures to pass beneath a ladder, something offensive is sure to fall upon his meritorious head," remarked Wong Tsoi with ready sympathy. "Unload your overweighted mind, Teen King."

"Your warm compassion melts the crust of my underbred reluctance," confessed the merchant. "Furthermore, I desire to lean somewhat upon your official counsel."

"Speak freely," replied Wong Tsoi, with but one thought, "for in matters affecting the relationship of the inner circle —"

"That is a crow of quite another colour," interrupted Teen King, his face not entirely gladdened by the plain allusion. "Upon questions of that sort, it is seldom necessary for a really humane and affectionate head to raise the shutter of his domestic interior."

"Yet," urged the exalted, "the one before you, as high official of the district, stands in the position of a benevolent father toward every family within his province."

"Assuredly," agreed Teen King, "but the truly considerate son hides a great deal of what might be unnecessarily distressing from a venerated parent's eyes. In the direction to which you are obviously leading, excellence, be satisfied that by patience and the use of a stick no thicker than that which is legally permissible, the most opinioned of our lesser ones can ultimately be persuaded to bask in the light of reason."

"This concerns Tsoo and the one called Fragrant Petal," reflected Wong Tsoi in the pause that followed, "and it clearly indicates that I was right in my conjecture. But with what other adversity is the misshapen thing before me harassed?" Aloud, however, he said:

"With your usual crystalline logic, Teen King, you compass an entire social system to within the narrow limits of an acorn-shell. Yet you spoke —"

"It is of it that I would speak further," replied the merchant, lowering his naturally repulsive voice and arranging his ill-balanced form so that they should not be overlooked. "Pass your esteemed judgment upon this obligation, highness."

Wong Tsoi took the folded parchment that was offered him and submitted it to the test of a close scrutiny, even to the length of using an enlarging-glass to supplement his eyes.

"There is no ambiguity at any point of this, Teen King," he said, courteously veiling his regret that it was not some tiding of disaster. "Herein you authorize your secondary to recompense ten taels of silver and a like amount of store to the one presenting this, he having already rendered its equivalent to you."

"Do you find no questionable line about the thumb-sign?" almost implored the merchant.

"I am as familiar with the signet of your pliant thumb as with the details of your prepossessing face," freely replied Wong Tsoi. "Should I fail to recognize you when we encounter in the Ways, or would I greet another by your ever-welcome name? Thus and thus. In every thread and indent is this your accepted impress."

"Yet," protested Teen King, so overwrought because he dare not shout aloud his frenzy or kick any of the lavish arrangements of the room that his always unbecoming neck increased to several times its wonted thickness, "yet, high puissance, it is not the impression of my own authentic thumb, nor had I ever seen the thrice accursed draft until the mentally weak-kneed Chin discharged the obligation. What an infamy is here residing within Hoo-yang!"

At this disclosure, Wong Tsoi achieved a sympathetic noise among his teeth, but he bent his face above the writing so that Teen King should not misread the signs of his compassion.

"This is an unheard-of thing to come about," he remarked impartially. "Hitherto it has been assumed that by a benevolent dispensation for the safeguarding of commercial intercourse, no two thumbs would be created of identical design. It now becomes evident that something essential has been overlooked. Is there any more of this, as it were, questionable paper upon the market, merchant?"

"It is that qualmous thought that is eroding the walls of my tranquility," confessed the effete Teen King. "Three misprocured drafts have I so far honoured, and I tremble at the possibility of what may yet appear."

"But," objected the Mandarin, "if you are the victim of a well-laid plot, why should you not proclaim the falsity, repudiate the impression of this alien thumb, and warn the merchants of our city to be alert?"

"Therein you speak as an official and not as a man of commerce," replied Teen King with feeling. "Were I to do as you advise, I might as well throw open the doors of all my marts for the four winds to blow in and out. My thumb-sign is the evidence of an inviolable word. To proclaim openly that it is henceforth more than doubtful would be to put the profitable house of Teen into the 'formerly existed' class."

"What then do you contemplate? To submit to this iniquity forever?"

"That is the purpose of my confidence in you," replied Teen King. "As the ruler of the city, you will assuredly put forth your straightforward hand and the sacrilegious dog will cease to prosper."

Wong Tsoi thought for a few moments under the pretext of having inhaled a superfluity of snuff. Then his face resumed its usual expression of inscrutable profundity, and he turned toward Teen King with a gesture of open-minded assent.

"Agreeably so," he replied pleasantly. "Deliver the abandoned leper into my keeping, and your unblemishable name will be free from the shadow of this taint forever."

"Therein lies the key of this one's hardship," exclaimed Teen King with some annoyance, for he began to describe Wong Tsoi to himself as a person of very stunted outlook. "Could I but discover and take the offender myself, one of my refining vats would very quickly adjust the difference between us. As it is, I rely on your authority to transact justice."

"The one before you is a high official," returned Wong Tsoi with appreciable coldness. "Were he a dog, doubtless he could follow a trail from this paper in his hand to the lair of the aggressor. Or were he a demon in some barbarian fable he might, perchance, regard a little dust beneath an enlarging-glass and then, stretching out his hand into the void, withdraw it with the miscreant attached."

"Nevertheless," persisted the merchant stubbornly, "it behooves you for your own wellbeing not to suffer the rice to grow around your tardy ankles in the matter."

"Teen King undoubtedly has something in his sleeve, or he would not press me to this limit," pondered Wong Tsoi. "Perhaps it would be as well to tempt the distressing mountebank into disclosing himself more fully. An apt saying should serve here." Accordingly he added: "Anything to do with your graceful personality admittedly has weight, Teen King, but in questions of authority mere bulk is not everything. It might be prudent to take to heart the adage, 'A toad has to pass a very severe examination before he can become a dragon.'"

At this allusion, Teen King changed colour several times and for a moment it seemed inevitable that the chair in which he sat must fail incapably under the weight of his displeasure. Seeing this, the one concerned rose abruptly to his feet.

"It is also written, 'A pointed tongue, however keen a sword, makes an insufficient shield,' and you, O contemptible Wong Tsoi, will soon be putting the analogy to a desperate trial," he replied with vigour. "Learn now how that incorruptible official, Kao-tse of the Board of Censors, has been deputed to visit Hoo-yang before the next full moon. As he is somewhat heavily in this person's debt, the nature of his report, should you maintain your headstrong front, need not tax your imagination. It is one thing to be technically degraded seven times, Mandarin; it is quite another to be actually shortened at both ends, even once."

With this illiberal forecast, the outrageous Teen King shook hands with himself in a disagreeable manner and withdrew his contaminating presence.

"A person of true refinement would have expressed much of that very differently, but nothing will ever make up for the lack of a classical education," reflected Wong Tsoi when he was again alone. "However," he added self-capably, "though it will obviously become necessary to do something to counteract his malicious influence, there is no reason why the incident should be allowed to mar an otherwise well-arranged repast. This business clearly concerns Ho Hung, and he will doubtless be at home throughout the night."

Ho Hung now steps into the narration, and in order to explain the unfolding of events, it is as well to describe his outline. He was of middle stature and not ill-cast, but with the essentials of an appearance spoiled somewhat by his face. His ears were loose and ragged, his teeth as large as those of a moderate horse but of several different colours, while his nose resembled a toucan's beak. One of his eyes was elsewhere; the other had a deceptive bend which enabled Ho Hung frequently to observe persons closely without their appreciation of the fact. At this period he was the admitted head and chief of all the thieves and assassins in Hoo-yang, but formerly he had conducted lotteries.

When Wong Tsoi, late that same night, knocked in a special way upon a certain door in the least reputed quarter of the city, it was opened by Ho Hung himself. When he recognized the one who stood outside, the natural repugnance of his features changed to a look of welcome not unmixed with an arising lack of gravity.

"You do well to greet me cordially, Ho Hung," remarked the official as he glanced cautiously about before he entered, "for if I should be recognized in this doubtful situation, it would certainly cost me my button."

"As to that, Mandarin," replied Ho Hung with simple familiarity, "should you ever be put to it, there are half-a-dozen openings I could tell you of, in which dignity combines with ease, and in any capacity you would very soon excel us all. But will you not honour this one's bankrupt home by entering, and there-if you can but put up with its longstanding deficiency-partake of tea?"

" 'For wine the top of the bottle; for tea the bottom of the pot,'" quoted Wong Tsoi pleasantly as he stepped within. "May worthiness never forsake your rooftree, valiant Hung."

"May winning numbers come to you in dreams," responded Ho Hung heartily, standing aside in hospitable respect.

As they sat together and drank, Ho Hung broached the subject that had shaken his dignity on the Mandarin's arrival.

"Some word of the inept misadventure that involved your conscientious secretary last night has already reached my threadbare ears," he remarked discreetly, affecting to turn aside to catch a passing winged insect as he spoke. "Doubtless it is upon that quest that you are here at all?"

"Up to a certain point the deduction is exact," replied Wong Tsoi, sprinkling a little snuff into Ho Hung's tea to mark his appreciation of that one's tact. "But, as the saying is, 'Although the T'ang road is long, it does not lead everywhere.' What is this that is being told of one whose thumb simulates the natural signature of Teen King, the produce merchant?"

At this inquiry Ho Hung became so excessively disturbed in gravity that he could only with difficulty retain his seat, while his endeavour to imply the reason of his mirth by rapidly opening and closing his missing eye began to have a disquieting effect upon Wong Tsoi's imagination.

"Thang-I the rogue's name is, and he has but lately come among us from the Waste Lands to the south," replied Ho Hung when he could speak with ease. "The witling has no ready parts beyond this facile thumb, he being of the mulish sort. But Tong, the fabricator of salt-due seals, who chanced upon this gift, has put the business through. Tong it is who does all Teen King's resealing when he mixes-your nobility will understand-so that he was well familiar with that aggressive merchant's thumb-sign."

"This is likely enough," replied Wong Tsoi, "but wherein lurks the essence of the jest?"

"It is not to be expected that a high official will have so gross an appetite for gravity removal as a mere sleeve-snatcher," pleaded Ho Hung. "The obese Teen King has ever been wont to press down an acrimonious thumb upon the feeble in Hoo-yang so that now the way that it has been turned against him has passed into a variety of questionable sayings. Indeed, it is become the matter of a most objectionable song that is being taken up by the river boatman to the rhythm of their task."

"Even the humblest of the muses is to be encouraged," tolerantly observed Wong Tsoi. "Should a superfluous copy of that ballad come your way—"

"It shall reach your discriminating hand without delay," promised the other, marking a sign upon his tablets.

"There still remains the question of justice," continued the high official. "For the harmonious relation of our several interests, it is vital that the overstepping of certain limits should not be unredressed."

"That is admitted," agreed Ho Hung, with a dutiful obeisance. "Your hand is that of a benevolent corrector, eminence, and this one will not, for his part, fail."

"In assaulting, as you have so correctly been informed, the person of the one who takes down my spoken word, two unmentionable outcasts have been guilty of an attack-by deputy-on me, thereby-obliquely-against the State, and thus — by analogy-have finally as it were submitted the venerated person of the Sublime Emperor himself to the extreme indignity of being projected into the tempestuous waters of an unclean stream. For this iniquity two malefactors must suffer the fullest penalty in order to appease the justly outraged feelings of a loyal people."

"Authority must be maintained," replied the congenial Ho, "or whereon do we stand? The very foundation of the Joined-together Band of Superfluity Adjusters and Excrescence Removers of Hoo-yang, with this one at its head, is menaced."

"We have always so far been able to arrange these necessary formalities in mutual concord," remarked Wong Tsoi. So amiable at these recollections became the condescension of this truly broad minded being that, after wiping the traces of tea from off his lips, he did not disdain to press the same cloth upon Ho Hung. "Nor," he continued, "is there any reason why we should not now. As regards this slow-witted Thang-I: has the lowly clown friends of any standing?"

"He is a stranger among us here, and therefore not of our fraternity," was the reply. "Had this case not been thus and thus, he would have been driven forth ere this. Disclose your mind, exalted."

"To earmark Thang-I for this needful expiation would effect a double turn. Have I your acquiescent word?'"

"The dog has served an end, but the jest has all but run its course," considered Ho Hung. "there is none to raise a voice against what you propose-save, perhaps, Tong, and he is of slight account."

"Tong-would he so do? Then nothing could be better regulated. Two culprits are required: that being the case, why should not Tong be coupled with Thang-I and so still every murmur?"

"Eminence," interposed Ho Hung, "even a goat and an ox must keep in step if they would plow together, and, as you have said, in matters of this sort we stand on a common footing. Let Thang-I fall to your deciding voice; for this one's share The-tang will serve."

Wong Tsoi accorded a motion of dignified assent, for he had no concern in Tong, the seal counterfeiter, either one way or the other.

"But The-tang?" he asked with polite interest. "Is not one of that name the prop of your right hand?"

"He was, he is, but he will not henceforth be. Of late Teh-tang's eyes have been fixed on a point somewhat above his head. It is as well that he should be removed before his aspiring footsteps seek to follow."

"That is a detail that concerns your own internal state, nor would this one seek to probe into the routine of your well-conducted band," declared the liberal-minded official.

Then as he turned to go he gave the courteous farewell: "May your deserving path be smooth, even to the grave-side."

"May your warmth and cold always be correctly balanced," replied Ho Hung, with no less feeling.

It was at a later date that the keeper of the door of Teen King's summer-house was roused from a profound meditation by an insistent knocking at the grille. The night being dark and stormy, the menial did not hasten to comply, but a still more urgent summons brought him to his feet.

"Should corrosion reward your acrimonious knuckles, this one will gladly attend your funeral rites," was the burden of his welcome.

"Is this a time for mere verbal pleasantries?" demanded the one who stood there in the harrying rain. "Behold, the master whom you serve, stricken with an unlooked-for hurt, turns back home from your gate."

"What is this that you say?" demanded the keeper sourly. "If there is a tale to be told, take hold at the beginning, friend, and not like the knife of some crafty juggler-haphazard as it comes."

"My tongue and your ear stand on a different footing," replied the other in a superior tone, "I being employed about the counting house and you a mere bolt-slider. Your offensively honourable name is Wang, doorkeeper?"

"That indeed is the mediocre style of my distinguished line."

"Let it suffice then, Wang, that the merchant has received various scars by the instability of one of his bearers on this misconstructed earth-road. He would have remained here through the night but for this affliction. As it is, he requires the delivery now of the one you guard. Here is the discharge of your answerableness for her."

The doglike Wang took the paper and held it to the light; then he compared the signature pressed on it with another that he had.

"This is well enough as far as the matter goes, but his memory is here at fault," was the reply. "Only a while ago he sent an urgent message, saying 'Accept no thumb-sign that is not made by me before your very eyes, for Dark Forces are about. This is my iron word.' Yet now you say he waits?"

"This is beyond my office," declared the stranger frankly, "and you had better make fast your bolts and then come to the gate. It may well be that this is a snare on Teen King's part to try your firmness in his service."

"If that is the case, he will find me grounded like a limpet," was Wang's crafty boast. "I make no pretence to any range of subtlety, but what is nailed into this head sticks there."

"Bring your lantern," said the messenger. "Things hereabout are none too bright."

When they reached the outer gate, two chairs were to be seen by the custodian's swinging candle. From the larger one a surfeit of groans and imprecations flowed, indicating, however crudely expressed, both pain and mental anguish. By the side of this a sombre-hearted carrier was still binding up his wounds.

"Commander," pleaded the supine Wang, thrusting his head through the curtains of the chair, "there has come to me one who bears a certain message, this requiring —"

The grossly outlined person dimly seen within did not cease to roll from side to side and to press a soothing cloth against his disfigured face. When he spoke, it was with difficulty, by reason of a swollen lip.

"Why then does not compliance hasten, thou contumacious keeper of my door?" he demanded with rancour. "Is it not enough that I am to broken bodily within sight of the lucky symbols hung above my gate, but that my authority should also be denied? Where is she whom I require of you?"

"Yet, master," entreated the abject Wang, "it may well be that this is but a snare to prove the tenacity of my allegiance. Was not your charge explicit: 'Accept no sign that is not pressed before your very eyes?' How then —"

"Enough," was the reply, and the one who spoke stretched out a requiring hand; "it is not ineptly claimed. After all, you have a sort of stultish justice to protect you, loyal Wang. Now submit the paper for the full requirement."

With this demand the keeper of the door at once complied, exultant that his stubbornness had been upheld before the others. The one whose authority he owned turned away for a moment as he searched about his sleeve for his pigment box. Then he pressed the paper and gave it back to Wang who saw against the former signature another, identical in every line and still moist from the attesting thumb.

"Nothing now remains but to execute your will," he freely admitted; "my own part in the matter being amply hedged. Say on, chieftain."

"In that I cannot stay, with my deep cuts unseen-to, Fragrant Petal must accompany me back, the affair having taken a prosperous turn," replied the other. "Bring her out now, not staying for adornment, for my condition does not brook delay, but at the same time hastily put together all that she may have so that her face is not clouded among women."

"It shall be done, O rewarder of great zeal," exclaimed Wang, preparing to comply. "How does this blossom among peach trees journey?"

"There is a chair at hand" —indicating the second that stood ready. "My underling, who rode thus far, must make his way as may be."

"Everything shall fall into place like a well-oiled mill at work," chanted the subservient Wang. "I hasten to merit your extremely liberal bounty, princelet."

"And this one," murmured the underling, he who had first summoned the custodian to the grille, as he prepared to follow, "will meet the Embodiment of Beauty on the way and break to her ear the signification of the issue."

"Unless," came a guarded voice from behind the curtains, "unless your father should have been an elderly baboon and your mother a standing reproach among she-asses, you will, on the contrary, withhold your egregious face until we are well clear of this stronghold of oppression."

"Your strategy has been consummate throughout, great excellence," replied the other, "and this one bends an acquiescent knee to whatever you direct." So that he faded into the imperceptible, nor was there anything to reassure the grief of Fragrant Petal when she was presently led forth.

"A thousand felicities, fountain of all largesse!" invoked the thirsty-handed Wang, as he stood at the opening of the first chair expectantly. "May the vigour of a leopard sustain your high endeavour."

"Ten thousand echoes to your gracefully phrased parting," was courteously wafted back from between the curtains, as the bearers raised their burden. "The moment is not propitious, but when next we meet do not fail to recall to me that the extent of my indebtedness cannot honourably be put to less than a full-weight piece of silver."

Nothing could have been more in keeping than the greetings of Wong Tsoi and the merchant Teen King when they again encountered beneath the burnished roof of the "Abode of Harmony." If the latter person had suffered a reverse in an unexpected quarter, he had the memorable satisfaction of having bent the mandarin to do his will in the matter of the unconscionable outlaw who had reproduced his thumb; if Wong Tsoi could not fail to recognize that in this affair the fullness of his countenance had suffered partial eclipse before the eyes of the superficial, he had the tangible offset that he had thereby been able to free his future of the Keu Chun obligation, and even yet he cherished an image that the one whose gravity would be the last to be removed might not prove to be Teen King.

Without waiting for any gracious intimation that his uninviting presence would be suffered, the mentally ill-nurtured huckster on this occasion thrust himself into the forefront of Wong Tsoi's notice by sinking incapably into a chair at that one's table. To cover his grotesque behavior, the deficient-minded pedlar at once plunged into the subject of their late contention with the absence of refinement that stamped his uncouth footsteps whenever he appeared.

"It nourished my heart to think that vice no longer triumphs about our city," he remarked with annoying freedom. "The two bodies now displayed in the Hoo-yang Public Relaxation Space prove that you have at length bowed your stubborn neck to the justice of this one's claim."

"It is recorded of the enlightened Emperor Yu that on one occasion he rose from his bath and bound up his hair thrice uncomplainingly to listen to the doubtless unreasonable demands of quite negligible persons," duly replied Wong Tsoi. "Why then should not I, who am in every way so inferior to the imperishable Yu, inconvenience myself to that slight extent to satisfy one in whom the parallelism is brought to an apt conclusion?"

At this well-guarded admission, the preposterous Teen King bowed several times, his wholly illiterate mind leading him to assume that he was being favorably compared to the great First Ruler.

"In one detail an element of ambiguity prevails," resumed the aggressive merchant, unable even at that moment to subdue his natural canker. "Admittedly, the real offender in this case has suffered, for the thumb of one of the two bandits corresponds to the most rigid test against my own. Yet that extremity bears every sign of having been cut away and subsequently restored. Why —"

"It is, as you, merchant, must surely be aware, an essential of our pure code of justice that the offending member of any convicted felon should be summarily struck off," replied Wong Tsoi dispassionately. "Later, to satisfy the ignoble curiosity of the vile-those who are notoriously drawn to gloat upon the accessories of low-class crimes-the parts were crudely united."

"Be that as it may," persisted Teen King stubbornly, as he began to regard the mandarin's well-rounded form with an awakening interest; "someone has in the meanwhile counterfeited this person's exact figure —"

"Forbear!" exclaimed Wong Tsoi, raising his face-cloth as though to shut out the vision of iniquity. "Such an atrocity is not possible among our chaste and grateful nation."

"Yet, nevertheless, the fact exists," continued the obtuse-witted condiment-blender, "and it is this one's intention now that you, mandarin, shall obtain a swift redress. Not only was that which has been stated done, but under the cloak of this deception the sanctity of an inner chamber has been usurped, a trusty henchman baffled, an unopened bud torn from the protecting branch —"

"Doubtless," interposed Wong Tsoi firmly, "but, as you would be the first to advance, merchant, in matters affecting purely domestic culture, it is hardly necessary for a really well-set and vigorous tree to disturb the soil that should conceal its roots."

"Public action need not inevitably ensue," maintained Teen King feebly, as he recognized the snare that he had contrived for his own misshapen feet. "You, as high official of the district, stand in the position of a salutary despot who can administer justice in discreet obscurity."

"Assuredly," agreed Wong Tsoi, "but the truly humane ruler turns a lethargic eye toward a great deal that might be actually pernicious in a cherished people's conduct. Should you be so ill-advised as to press your grievance further, it would be as well first to recall the special application of the proverb, 'It is better to lose nine changes of raiment than to win a lawsuit.'"

"Yet what remains?" pleaded the ineffectual merchant. "Shall these poverty-stricken hands be idly folded while an unending vista of spurious Teen Kings draws away my substance?"

"Suffer no apprehension on that score," replied Wong Tsoi with meaning. "Not again shall your notorious mould be counterparted in Hoo-yang."

"Can that be definitely assured?" asked Teen King cautiously.

"Subject to the usual clause against demoniac intervention, it can," replied the mandarin. "For the rest, remember, 'Even dragons know better than to appear too often.'"

"If this is actually the case, the prospect might have been worse," admitted Teen King. "Indeed," he added, with an unworthy impulse to ingratiate himself in the other's regard without incurring the customary outlay, "had it been allowable, a substantial token of esteem would have been forthcoming to mark appreciation of your prolific efforts."

"What is this barrier that stands in the way of so laudable a craving, amiable Teen King?" inquired Wong Tsoi in a very agreeable voice.

"Surely it is not unknown to your pure excellence that in order to discourage venality an official of your degree is strictly forbidden to receive any gift whatever, save only-not to exclude mere courtesy-an offering of fruit. But as an earnest of this one's thwarted yearning, a basked of the choicest Hoo-yang hedge-berries shall reach your hand tomorrow."

"Nothing could be more delicately flavoured than the compliment," murmured the engaging voice. "Yet had not a wise provision set a check upon your open-handed spirit, what form would the tribute to which an explicit reference has just been made, have taken?"

"In that case," replied Teen King, seeing no reason why he should restrict himself in a matter that could involve him in no outlay, "there would have been no limit to this one's profusion. Throwing open the door of his needy hovel, he would have bidden you enter and accept what pleased you most, saying, 'Put forth your hand on the right and on the left, and whatsoever it closes on is yours.'"

"It is no more than what would have been expected of your untarnishable father's nimble-minded son," replied Wong Tsoi, with a suitable display of appropriate emotion. "And now let your generous heart expand in gladness, Teen King. You would appear to have misread-though only slightly—a single character in the official prohibition. Not 'save fruit' but 'save in the shape of fruit' is the carefully thought-out exception."

"Yet wherein does the variation lie?" asked the merchant, in a deeply agitated voice.

"Embellishing your high-born serving board there stands a lordly silver dish, its cover in the likeness of a cluster of rich fruit, its base befittingly adorned with nuts," replied Wong Tsoi pleasantly. "Nothing could be more applicable or in severer keeping with the pronouncement of authority."

At this disclosure Teen King rose up from his chair and then illogically sank down again until he was no longer capable of the exertion. His unbecoming mouth opened and closed repeatedly, but it was not until Wong Tsoi had charitably begun to fan him that he disclosed his power of speech.

"What was spoken in the light of a graceful compliment is too delicate to be translated into the grosser terms of commercial equivalent," he stammered effetely. "The dish in question weighs not less than ten score standard taels, and its value in fine silver must be put at twice that indication. Why, then, should this almost bankrupt outcast tamely surrender it?"

"Nothing but the untrammelled purity of your upright nature could suggest so great a sacrifice," replied Wong Tsoi.

"If that were all," replied the other frankly, "I could sleep tonight in peace. But the extreme moderation of your manner prepares me for the worst. What remains behind, Wong Tsoi?"

"Alas, merchant," admitted the compassionate official, "I had hoped to shield this latest menace from you. Know then how it is whispered in the Ways that the irredeemable Thang-I spent the last hours of his solitude thumb-signing countless sheets of unwritten parchment, which the dissolute hope to use from time to time as the occasions offer."

"If," considered Teen King, after a length pause, "if one from my house should in due course appear about your door bearing a weighty gift and crave your acceptance of it, what would be the nature of his reception?"

"That one so charitably employed should return empty handed would put a barbarian of the Outer Lands to shame," replied Wong Tsoi. "The least that this person could do would be to send out into the Ways and beseech his many criminal friends, as a personal kindness to himself, to bring in all the offensive Thang-I's fabrications."

"Could a favorable response be relied on?" asked Teen King.

"It has already been successfully accomplished, and the package now merely awaits your accommodating slave's arrival."

"Would the third gong-stroke of the afternoon suit your distinguished leisure?" inquired Teen King, in very solicitous accents.

"Nothing could be more in harmony," was the genial reply.

"Thus and thus," remarked the merchant, rising. "The hour approaches when this one displays his shutters. Walk slowly."

"May your profitable commerce spread like a banyan tree and take root on every side," pronounced Wong Tsoi courteously.

"May swift promotion overtake your righteous footsteps and lead you to a more worthy sphere of usefulness," replied Teen King, in a voice equally devoid of added meaning.

At the Extremity of His Resource, the Continent Kai Lung Encounters One Who Leads the Unaffected Life

At a later period Kai Lung emerged safely from the waste marshes of Ying-tze and set his face hopefully toward the mountain range beyond, confident that somewhere about those barren heights he would overtake Ming-shu and (aided by the ever-protecting spirits of his approving ancestors) settle a final and exacting balance with that detested upstart.

But in the meanwhile an arid and unproductive tract of country lay between him and the valleys of Ki-che, and the cake of dried paste that had nourished him so far had shrunk to a state of no-existence. For a lengthy day he had sustained a precarious life on a scanty cup of disconcerting water extracted from a laboriously-dug hole, when, at evening, he espied one who wandered to and fro with a burden on his shoulders.

"This, doubtless," considered Kai Lung, "is the forerunner of others, who may, by an expedient, be assembled as a crowd, and surely to that, on one pretext or another, an applicable story should not prove fruitless."

He looked anxiously for the gathering signs of habitation that would indicate a village street (for a feeling of inadequacy in all his attributes was beginning to assail him), but finding none and fearing to miss the settlement on the one foot or to increase his weary march upon the other, he turned aside, meaning to greet the loiterer whom he had already noted. When he had approached sufficiently near to observe the detail, he saw that what the stranger carried was a coffin.

"Alas," exclaimed Kai Lung, "is this, then, so insalubrious a region that, when a man goes about his daily task, he takes with him the equipment for his obsequies? What scope is there for the storyteller's art in a spot so far removed from gravity-dispersal or the leisured amenities of life?" Yet, there being none else to question and no abode in sight, he continued on toward him. When the other perceived Kai Lung's approaching form, he laid down the burden off his shoulders and advanced to meet him.

"Welcome to this unattractive wilderness," he remarked hospitably. "Your becoming name and the number of your blameless years would be an agreeable subject for conversation."

"I am of the worthless house of Kai, my forbidding name being Lung," was the reply. "As regards my years-they have been few and quite devoid of interest, as this immature pigtail will readily disclose. Now, as regards your own distinguished self?"

"Thang am I, my father's name being presumably illustrious but unfortunately misplaced," replied the other. "My ill-spent age exceeds two-score by one. By ceaseless toil, I wrest a feeble livelihood from this tenacious soil."

"The occupation is a venerated one in our enlightened land, being only second, both as regards honour and inadequacy of reward, to the literary calling," replied Kai Lung. "And touching that same office-as between one necessitous person and another-is there within not too great a distance from this well-favoured spot a refined community who by some stratagem or other may be drawn together to listen to an epic from the masterpieces, with a reasonable outlook of the narrator being finally rewarded in one form or another?"

"A community!" exclaimed the stranger, enlarging both his eyes. "Know, traveler, that the one before you and those beneath his crumbling roof live so remote that they do not see an outside face from one moon to another. Whence, therefore, could even a sprinkling of bystanders be obtained to listen to your pleasing voice?"

"If this is so," observed Kai Lung dispassionately, "the voice to which you so flatteringly refer will very soon cease forever. Yet how comes it that you who are an alert and vigorous man have selected a region at once so desert and remote?"

"That," replied the peasant, "is to conform to the integral fitness of things. In his milk days, the one before you listened with becoming deference to the conversation of persons of every rank of life and studied what they said. From what he heard, when they were speaking freely, it was at once plain that he himself was so beneath all others both as regards the virtues and attainments that it was only seemly for him to withdraw and live apart. Accordingly, selecting a lesser one as unworthy as himself, he retired unpretentiously to this forgotten spot; for it is related of it that after the First Celestial Emperor had formed the earth, he wiped his toil-stained hands upon his heaven-born thighs, and this is what fell from him. Being neither earth, heaven, nor the region Down Below, it was ignored by the deities and protective Forces, so that here there are no winds, dews, spontaneous growth, nor variable seasons."

"Are there then no evilly disposed Beings either?" inquired Kai Lung with interest.

"For some reason or other, they abound," admitted Thang. "Thus, in spite of what a fostering care could do, our only he-child — one who seemed destined by his fearless and engaging nature to raise a squalid Line to something like an equality with others-came under the malign influence of a resentful Spectre that drew his breath away... . It is his coffined form that I am carrying from place to place to find, if possible, a spot immune from harmful spirits."

"May the Many-eyed One guide your footsteps!" voiced Kai Lung with a look of wide compassion. "Your condition is a hapless one. For how, being thus bereft, will your weak and trembling shade, when you shall have yourself Passed Beyond, obtain either food or raiment?"

"That is very true, but is it not tolerantly written, 'Even a mole can turn its eyes upward?' Within my stricken hut, two sadly deficient she-children still remain. If some lenient-minded youth can be persuaded to marry one of these, he may, when in a charitable vein, include my shivering ghost in the offerings he transmits. As I am well inured to privation here below, it is only reasonable to suppose that what is, after all, little more than an unsubstantial outline, will be satisfied with even less."

"It is aptly said, 'The strongest tower is built of single bricks,' and your steadfast attitude justifies the saying," remarked Kai Lung. "Did I possess anything beyond a general feeling of concavity I would pleasurably contribute to your store. As it is, I endow you with the confident prediction that your upright House will flourish. Farewell, esteemed." With these words and a deferential bow, in which he contrived to indicate his sympathetic outlook toward the other's unenviable lot and a regret that the circumstances had not conspired toward their more enduring friendship, the weary storyteller turned to resume the hopeless struggle of his onward march. An unpretentious voice recalled him.

"Hitherto, a sense of insufficiency restrained me," explained the lowly Thang; "for judging from the fullness of your garb and the freedom of your manner, I thought you to be a rich official, travelling at ease. If, however, as certainly your words may be taken to suggest, you are not really so well-equipped and can offer no reward for that which is really worthless, I am emboldened to beg your high-born acquaintance of the inadequate resources of my makeshift home. The more you can consume, the less will be this self-conscious person's shame at the insipidity of what he puts before you; the longer you can tolerate his worn-out roof, the greater will be the confidence with which he can henceforth continue to dwell beneath it."

"Yet your humane task?" urged Kai Lung, in spite of the despair of his position. "Should so slight a thing as the extremity of a passing stranger interrupt your rites?"

"About the city gate are many beggars, but on the plains all men meet as brothers," was Thang's reply. "Furthermore," he added prudently, "were you to die about this spot, the duty of providing you with a suitable bestowal would devolve upon me, and even then your annoyed and thirsty ghost might haunt my door."

"But you spoke of destitution. If less than a sufficiency for your own stock exists, how should another —"

"Where four can stand at all, five can just squeeze," replied the accommodating Thang. "Unless my repellent face displeases you beyond endurance, the last word of ceremonious denial has been uttered."

When they were come to the peasant's hut, Thang excused himself on a simple plea for passing in before his guest. From the approaching path Kai Lung soon overheard the reason.

"It had been our natural hope to spend the night in grief and lamentation, but chance has sent another-even more faint and needy than ourselves-to share our scanty hearth. Sorrow must therefore be banished to a more appropriate time, and in the meanwhile nothing should escape to dim the lustre of his welcome in this stranger's eyes."

A lesser voice replied, graceful yet docile:

"Where the ox clears a way, the sheep can surely follow... . There is a little cake which I had secretly prepared of fruit and sifted meal, put by against the joy-day of our two remaining dear ones. This will to some extent disguise the leanness of our ill-spread board, and toward it we can ourselves affect a cloyed repugnance."

"We," said a still smaller voice, "will cheerfully forego our separate share to relieve the stranger's need... . Have I not spoken with your polished tongue, Chalcedony?"

"Your fragrant words, O Musk, are my own feeble thoughts well set to music," was the equally melodious answer.

"Then we are all agreed" —it was now Thang again. "Conduct the politely awaiting stranger to a seat beneath our ragged thatch, ye two uncouth afflictions, while I go hence to gather such decaying herbs as our stubborn ground affords."

Kai Lung had moved to a more distant part-so that he should not seem to betray too gross an interest in the details of what was being prepared for his enjoyment-when the two sympathetic she-children approached together. Being dressed alike and so moulded that they varied in no single detail, it was beyond an ordinary person's skill to discriminate between them. Their years were somewhat short of half a score, and with a most engaging confidence each took the storyteller freely by the hand and drew him forward.

"She who leads you by the right hand is Musk," said the one who was thus positioned, "the other being Chalcedony. To me no special gift has ever come beyond a high discordant voice. Chalcedony can accompany this harmoniously with music blown on reeds. What is your attractive name, wayfarer, and are you as old as your meritorious aspect would lead one to suppose?"

When he had replied to these courteous inquiries in suitable terms, the one referred to added:

"Since it is inevitable that we should spend some hours together, how is it possible to know one from the other among you when both are perceptibly alike?"

"It is for that very reason that our sounds have been chosen so diversely," was the capable reply. "Being two alikes, born at a single birth, we have been named so that it is impossible to mistake one for the other, nor do either of our revereds ever now fall into so culpable an error... . That one, remember, is Chalcedony, your base slave here being Musk."

As Kai Lung reached the door, Thang's lesser one came forth and with a look of gladness made him welcome. When he had been protestingly composed into the one chair that the meagre hut contained, Musk and Chalcedony again approached, and standing one on either side before him sought to beguile his weariness by the artless means within their simple power, Musk lifting up her resolute voice in a set chant —"The She-child's Invocation" —and Chalcedony by no means lagging in the sounds that she extracted from an arrangement of pierced reeds. Nor did either desist until the rice appeared and was enticingly set out.

"It is less than would satisfy a family of midgets, and moderately self-respecting dogs would turn from it with loathing," remarked Thang, bowing before his guest. "It is quite possible, however, that your excessively politeness will compel you to make something of a meal. Approach, therefore."

"One hears of the lavishness of rich country nobles," aptly replied Kai Lung, standing before the board. "But this —"

Afterward a small pipe, charged with dried herbs, was passed from hand to hand, and tranquillity prevailed. When it was dark and a single paper lantern had been lit, they sat upon the floor, and the storyteller claimed that, as a circle had been formed, it was, by ancient privilege, incumbent on him to gratify their leisure.

"So that," he added, "the history of Tong So and the story of his ingenious rise to honours will linger pleasurably within your minds long after all thought of the large-mouthed Kai Lung shall have come to be forgotten."

The discriminating Thang, however, understood that the other wished to make some small return for the compassion shown to him, in the only way he had. He therefore indicated to Musk and Chalcedony (who were on the point of blending their energies in the exposition of a well-laboured ballad entitled "The More-desirable Locality") that they should restrain their acknowledged zeal, and admitted to Kai Lung that he has now favourable prepared for whatever might ensue.

The Story of Tong So, the Averter of Calamities

I. How There Fell to Him the Leadership of the Fraternity of Thieves Within I-Kang

When Tcheng the Earless, the accepted head and authority of the company of thieves that dwelt about I-kang, suddenly Passed Above, all of that calling came together to appoint another who should take his place. Finally, by an equal choice, the matter lay between Tong So, because he was able and discreet above the rest, and Pe-hung, who, though gross and boastful, possessed the claim that he was of the House of Tcheng. Those who favoured the cause of Tong So dwelt on the need of skill and resource in the one who should direct their strategy, while the voices raised on behalf of Pe-hung extolled authority and a dutiful submission to the fixed order of events.

"Illustrious brothers," exclaimed Tong So at length, for those who were to decide had by that time reached the pass of two wrestlers who are locked in an inextricable embrace where neither can prevail, "it is well said among us, 'Although the door is locked the shutter may be pliant.' The honey of smooth speech and the salutary vinegar of abuse having likewise failed to convince, it may be judged that the time is to explore another way."

"Say on," urged those around, for both sides were weary of the strife. "may the more integritous cause prevail."

"What a thousand eloquent words cannot achieve, a single timely action may accomplish," continued Tong So. "Let a facile test be set. In the innermost secrecy of the Temple of Autumnal Winds there reposes the Green Eye of Nong, surrounded by a never-sleeping guard. Whichever of the two shall bear it off, let him be acclaimed our head."

"It is well said," agreed the gathering. "He who performs that feat is worthy to be our leader. Furthermore, the value of the spoil will, when equally divided, add greatly to the dignity of all."

Standing somewhat apart, the contumacious Pe-hung would have declined the test had that been possible, but to do so then would have involved a greater loss of face than even he could stomach, for in the past he had never failed to speak of his own skill approvingly. He accordingly sought to attain his unworthy end by a more devious line, and while seeming to agree he contrived a hidden snare.

"The trial is a suitable one," he therefore said, " and its accomplishment is well within my own indifferent powers. For that reason, and also because the idea sprang from the enriched soil of his productive mind, the distinction of the first attempt lies clearly with Tong So. Thereafter I will speedily outshine whatever glory he may obtain."

Pe-hung's words, however, were but as the sheaf wherein one holds a keen-edged blade, for his inner thoughts ran thus: Tong So will make the attempt and be slain by those who guard the jewel. Obviously, it is unsuitable for a dead person to be a leader, so that the choice will automatically revert to me. Or Tong So will fail in the attempt but escape alive. In that case, his ineptitude clearly unfits him to be our chief and there will no longer be any opposition to this one's cause. If, however, by an unforeseen perversity Tong So should succeed, it will manifestly be impossible for another, no matter how competent, to carry away what is no longer there, and so the contest fails in its essential. To this end it is aptly written, 'he who would feast with vampires must expect to provide the meat.'"

In the darkness of a stormy night, the door-keepers of the Temple of Autumnal Winds were aroused by the clash of conflict beyond the outer gate. As the repeated cries for help indicated that violence of a very definite kind was in progress, they did not deem it courteous to interfere until the sound of retiring footsteps and a restored tranquillity announced that the virtuous might prudently emerge.

Outside, they found Tong So bearing all the signs of a speedy departure Upward. His robe was torn and earth-stained, his eyes devoid of light, while the ground around had been lavishly arranged with bloodshed. To the ordinary passerby, finding him thus, only one question would present itself: had those who had gone before efficiently performed their sordid task, or was there, perchance, something of value still concealed about the unconscious body?

"Danger lurks here, unless we move our feet with caution," observed the chief keeper of the door to the one who served his hand. "Should the inopportune wayfarer Pass Beyond in this distressing manner, his offended and vindictive ghost will continue to haunt the gate-house, regardless of our feelings and of the possible loss of custom to the temple itself which so forbidding a visitation may entail."

"Alas, master," exclaimed the other, "as it is, the gate-house has become overcrowded somewhat since the less successful deities have been thrust into our keeping. Would it not be well to take this distinguished personage, the one by the head and the other by the feet, and unostentatiously convey him to the doorway of another before it is too late?"

"If it could be prudently effected, such a safeguard would undoubtedly be wise; if, however, while in the act we encountered a company of his friends or the official watchers of the street, no excuse would serve us. Better endure the annoyance of another's ghost than incur the probability of yielding up our own."

"Nevertheless, there is the saying 'He who fails to become a giant need not remain content with being a dwarf,' and a middle way may yet be found. Beneath the innermost sacrary of the temple there is an empty vault. Should this ever-welcome stranger honour us by Passing while reposing in its commodious depth, his nobly born apparition will occasion no alarm, for by closing the upper and the lower doors we can confine its discreditable activities to that secluded region."

To this proposal the chief doorkeeper turned an assenting ear. Together they drew Tong So through the lower door and along a narrow passage, until they reached the cave hollowed beneath the walls. Here they left him, first securing his robe and whatever else of interest he possessed.

When Tong So had thus penetrated beyond the outer limits of the temple, he allowed a sufficient interval to elapse, and then raised himself out through the upper door, using for this purpose a cord that had been wound concealed among his hair.

In the sanctuary above, a band chosen for their vigilance kept guard by day and night. It was dark except for the pale lustre round about the jewel, for it would have been held disrespectful to the brilliance of the Sacred Eye to deem it necessary to require an added light. This favoured Tong So's strategy, but, as he crept forward, his benumbed foot struck against a column.

"One moves among us," exclaimed the readiest of the band. "Let each man touch his brother's hand, so that nothing may escape between us, and thus go forward."

Tong So pressed back into the wall, compelling his body to merge itself into the interstices of the sculptured surface. He closed his eyes, ceased to breathe, and composed his mind into an alert tranquility. A hand swept across his face as the line moved past, but the rigorous confinement of the cave had frozen his outer surface so that its touch in no way differed from that of the marble images on either side. The searchers passed on, and presently they stood before the farther wall.

"Nothing can have escaped our discovering hands," declared the leader. "He who was here has certainly crept out. Disperse yourselves around the inner courts, if haply we may yet take him."

When they were gone, Tong So came forth from his place of refuge and quickly forced the Green Eye from its setting. The jewel secured, he took his stand behind the open door and in a simulated voice raised a disturbing cry.

"Ho, keepers of the Sacred Nong, to your stations all! That which we guard is assailed by treachery!"

Like a wave of the flood-driven Whang Ho, back swept the band into the darkness of the sanctuary. When all had passed inside and were surging about the statue of the despoiled god, Tong So slipped out, drew close the door, and made fast the bolt. From that point the way of his escape was easy.

Memorable in the annals of the heroic brotherhood of thieves within I-kang was the night when Tong So returned among them and displayed the great green jewel called the Sacred Eye of Nong. A feast was called for the next day, all cheerfully contributing from their own store, and when they were assembled, Tong So was installed upon a dais with flattering acclamation. Pe-hung alone maintained a secluded air, although his gluttonous instincts impelled him to push forward at the feast, to which, however, he had contributed less than a righteous share. "The larger the shadow grows, the nearer is the sun to setting," was his invariable reply to those who taunted him with Tong So's success, moreover adding, "And the lizard that essayed to become a crocodile burst at the moment of attainment," until presently they ceased to molest him.

When the repast was over, the most elderly person among those present rose to express himself, at the same time pointing out the patriarchal length of his venerable pigtail in furtherance of his claim to lead their voices. As his remarks were chiefly concerned with the inscrutability of the gods, the uncertainty of the price and quality of rice-spirit, the insatiable depravity of the official watchers of the streets, and the unapproachable perfection of his own immediate ancestors, he was thrust somewhat impatiently aside and room made for another.

"The time approaches when the more industrious and less garrulous members of our praise-worthy craft would seek the Ways," he reasonably declared, "nor is it necessary to procure a sack wherein to bear away a single coin. A searching test has been made, and Tong So has conformed to its requirements. Is it agreed that he should be our leader?"

"Haply," interposed the foremost among those who had hitherto opposed Tong So's cause, "yet Pe-hung still remains."

"Inevitably-so long as any food likewise remains," capably replied the other. "Does Pe-hung then raise a claim?"

"The inference is inexact," retorted Pe-hung assertively, "nor is it necessary for this person to crave that which devolves by right. Out of a courteous regard for his youth and inexperience, Tong So was given the first essay, and by chance the jewel fell into his large open hand. Manifestly, it is contrary to our just rule that this person should now be set aside because through his benevolence the accomplishment of the test is no longer within man's power."

"It is but seemly," declared Tong So, checking with a persuasive glance those who would have answered Pe-hung's craft with ridicule. "Yet were the possibility still present would you now maintain your former boast that you likewise could bear off the jewel?"

"Assuredly," replied Pe-hung, his confidence enlarged by the impossibility of submitting him to the test, "and that by so daring and ingenious a scheme that the lustre of the deed would have brought undying honor to our fraternity within I-kang."

"Then let your unassuming heart rejoice at the prospect of our well-sustained felicity!" exclaimed Tong So. "Learn now, O fortunate Pe-hung, that the Green Eye of Nong again adorns his sacred face and awaits thy supple thumb!"

"It has been recovered?" cried those around. "You have suffered this ineptitude?"

"By no means," replied Tong So, "but, foreseeing this entanglement, I caused it to be restored to its socket after displaying it to you, so that no ground for dissension should exist among our harmonious band."

For a measurable space of time, all power of speech was denied even to the most fluent tongue. Then those who had favoured Pe-hung burst forth:

"But the loss to each one of us which this expedient entails-therein you have done evilly, Tong So. The value was that of a camel-load of jade."

"Loss!" exclaimed Tong So reprovingly. "Who speaks of loss while Pe-hung still remains? Not only will he duly fulfill his spoken word, but with the jewel he will bring back the lusty matter for an offensive song, which Chi-ching shall set to music for our winter fires."

"A full-throated verse shall therein be retained for your pestilential virtues, O ill-disposed Tong So!" replied Pe-hung with heavy-laden breath, as he made ready to depart. "Lo, I go to efface the memory of your puny efforts."

When he had gone and there remained only Tong So and those who were wholly favourable to his cause, that broad minded person further disclosed the reason of his course.

"It is one thing to cast a noose about a tiger's neck," he remarked, "but it involves another attitude to conduct it to an awaiting cage. Had we retained the sacred relic, the undying enmity of the priests of Nong would have sought us out. That, perchance, we might have evaded had it not been that those who traffic in such stones one and all refused to face the risk of its disposal. Another outlet could doubtless have been found were it not that our spoil consisted of a worthless counterfeit, the real gem having been abstracted by an earlier one in the distant past. Thus the path of Pe-hung's success is fringed by many doubts and harassments, against which it would have been well to warn him had he been a person of sympathetic outlook."

In such a manner Tong So became the chosen leader of the company of thieves about I-kang. In this he had their unanimous voice, for Pe-hung was never seen again among their haunts. The better-disposed toward him contended that he had fallen beneath the vengeance of the priests of Nong during a valiant attempt to repossess the jewel. Others, however, claimed that in a distant city there was one resembling him in the grossness of his outline who endeavoured to extort a meagre livelihood from the large-hearted by publicly beating his head and body with a brick. But this does not concern Tong So.

II. Showing How Slight a Matter Went Hand in Hand With Tong So's Destiny

At a convenient spot outside I-kang, where it was well protected from the attacks of passing demons by an intersecting gorge, stood the ornamental residence of Fan Chin, a retired ginseng merchant.

In spite of this, Fan Chin did not enjoy an immunity from every kind of evil, for, as the proverb says, "however deep you dig a well, it affords no refuge in the time of flood," and the distant and solitary position of the house encouraged those who were desirous of sharing in Fan Chin's prosperity. No matter the fierceness of the hounds he procured or the vigilance of the watchers he employed, few moons ever passed without some industrious person penetrating beyond his outer walls. Indeed, the hounds frequently attached themselves to those who thus intruded, for the training of all creatures of this kind lay in the hands of Tong So's associates, while the hired watchers were generally those of his company who had for the time found it desirable to seek a less violent manner of living owing to some injury received in the course of their ordinary occupation.

So convenient was it to despoil Fan Chin's possessions that Tong So himself charitably refrained, in order to encourage deserving but inexperienced members of his band or to leave a facile certainty for the aged and infirm. It was by such considerate acts that the affection of his followers was nourished, so that in time Tong came to be regarded as the Father and the Elder Brother of all good thieves.

One night, toward the middle part of the darkness, Tong So was walking with the hunchback Chu when by chance they found themselves outside the walls of Fan Chin's garden.

Up to that point, their discourse had been of a philosophical nature, concerned with the Essentials, the Ultimate Destinies, and the like, but discovering an iron implement within his sleeve Chu thereupon displayed it and began to speak to a more definite end.

"Ill fortune has of late attended all my efforts, while a misbegotten blow from a wooden staff, carried by an officious watcher of the street, has corroded my left thumb with acrimony. You also, Tong So, are but sparsely clad. Let us therefore accompany one another into the secluded part of this well-stocked mansion and there replenish our necessities."

"The project is a worthy one, and this person would gladly enter into it and perform an allotted part, were it not that for a specific reason he has hitherto refrained," replied Tong So candidly. "Nevertheless, without requiring any share of the expected profit, he will cheerfully remain here in an alert attitude and will at once fell to the ground any who should attempt to impede your intrepid progress."

Upon this understanding, Chu went forward and quickly forced his way into the remoter portions of the house. The watchers whom he encountered greeted him familiarly and courteously indicated in which direction the path of safety lay. Thus guided, Chu had no difficulty in filling his sack with suitable merchandise, and was on the point of withdrawing when the avaricious Fan Chin, whom an unworthy suspicion had kept awake, suddenly appeared at an angle of the wall. He was heavily armed at every point of his attitude, while the hunchback's movements were involved with the burden under which he staggered. In this extremity, it would have gone doubtfully with Chu had he not already resourcefully filled his mouth from a flask of Fan Chin's raisin wine against such an emergency. The stream of this he now vigorously propelled into the other person's menace-laden face, compelling him to drop the weapons in order to clear his eyes of liquid bitterness.

As Tong So and Chu again turned their steps toward I-kang, they resumed their former discourse, nor did either refer to the details of the undertaking until they reached the parting of their ways. There the latter person raised a detaining gesture.

"Although you have not actually shared in the full flavour of the adventure, yet by remaining aggressively outside and by sustaining me with your virtuous encouragement, you have undoubtedly played an effective part. Accompany me, therefore, to my criminally acquired hovel and there select from this much distended sack whatever is deemed worthy of your tolerant acceptance."

"The suggestion is a gracious one," replied Tong So, "and fittingly illustrates the high standard of benevolence which marks those of our band. Observe how the sordid-stomached Fan had been in possession of these goods for a score of years or more, but never during that period had he once invited this necessitous person to share the most attenuated fraction of his store; yet no sooner do they pass into your hands than you freely bestow on me the fullness of my choice."

"Your indulgent words cover me with honourable confusion," stammered the gratified Chu. "How should I divide an egg with you, who are my father and my elder brother too?"

Conversing in this mutually helpful manner, they reached the hunchback's home. Here they quickly made themselves secure and then proceeded to display the rewards of their industry. These included wares and utensils of many kinds, silks and fabrics from the walls and seats, suitable apparel as well as coverings for the head, the ears and feet, food of the richer sorts, and here and there a silver-mounted carving.

"Beneath my decayed but hospitable roof all things are yours," declared Chu, indicating by a gesture that he pushed the entire contents of the sack away from him.

"That which grows on the tree of enterprise should be eaten off the bough," replied Tong So no less generously, and he was indicating by means of a like gesture that he renounced all claim to any part thereof when the vigour of his action laid bare an object which an inadvertent movement on Chu's part had hitherto successfully concealed beneath the sack.

" —Nevertheless," continued Tong So as he took it up and regarded it with deepening interest, "a solitary fruit may sometimes legitimately fall into the basket of another. Whence blows this fragrant peach?" and he held out the depicted image of a maiden of surpassing charm, traced with inspired skill upon a plate of ivory set in a golden frame.

"Doubtless it was hidden away among the folds of a piece of silk and thus escaped our scrutiny," replied Chu freely. "Humiliating as the admission is, this person will not deny that he had until now no inkling of this distinguished prize."

"There will then be no sense of loss in its withdrawal," observed Tong pleasantly. "Out of the bountiful flood of your opulent profusion, O worthy Chu, this one object alone will I accept. From this resolve do not attempt to move me."

For an appreciable moment it seemed doubtful whether the hunchback would tamely submit to this decision, so deep and wide was the stream of his devotion, but at the sight of Tong So's impassive face he bent an acquiescent neck.

"Truly it is written, 'It is better to keep silence than yield wisdom,' " was his discreet reply. "I bow, chieftain."

III. His Meeting With Fan Chin and the Manner of His Many-Sided Qualities

On the following day, Tong So again turned his footsteps in the direction of Fan Chin's mansion, but this time he went alone. At the outer gate he spoke little, but that to a pointed edge, and the one who held the bolt admitted him, so that very soon he stood face to face with Fan Chin himself.

"Greeting," remarked Tong So affably. "Have you eaten your meritorious rice?"

"So much of it as an ill-nurtured outcast has generously left behind him," replied Fan Chin, indicating the despoiled confusion of the room. "Nevertheless, you are cheerfully welcome if you have anything to reveal." He was a man of middle height, dispassionate in manner and evenly balanced in his speech. From time to time he caressed an eye with a cloth of some soft fabric.

"Your moments are as pearls, while my worthless hours are only comparable with lumps of earth; therefore I will trim short my all-too-wordy tongue," was the reply. "In the deeper solitude of the night, this person chanced upon two who strove over the division of their spoil. By a subtlety he possessed himself of that which they most esteemed. This he would now justly return to the one who can prove his undisputed right."

"What you say is very surprising, especially as you yourself have all the outward attributes of a hired assassin," replied Fan Chin, after a moment's thought. "Can reliance be placed upon your mere assertion?"

"There are four witnesses here to all that I declare; how then can anything but the truth be spoken?"

"Four witnesses?" repeated Fan Chin, to whom this form of testimony was evidently unknown. "Disclose yourself."

"The heavens above, the earth beneath, and the two who here converse together," explained Tong So.

"That is undeniable," admitted Fan. "On the whole I am inclined to credit what you say."

"Furthermore," continued Tong, "here is the painted plate of ivory held in a band of gold," and he displayed the painting that had been the mainspring of his actions. "Is not this a valued part of your possessions?"

"There can no longer be any reasonable scruple as to your integrity," exclaimed Fan Chin. "You have restored that which alone occasioned an emotion of regret."

"Doubtless," assented Tong So; "yet there is an up and a down to every hill, and having convinced you of my virtuous sincerity it now devolves on you to satisfy me of yours."

"The angle of your misgiving remains somewhat obtuse to my deficient mind," admitted Fan Chin. "Fill in the outline of your distrust."

"On the back of the plate of ivory there are traced these words in characters of gold, 'Tsing Yung, of the righteous House of Fan.' Produce, therefore, the one thus described so that the similitude may stand revealed, and the essence of your claim is undisputable."

At this bold challenge, the nature of Fan Chin's breathing changed and he walked round the room several times before he could frame his lips to a sufficiently discreet reply.

"The requirement is unusual," he replied at length, "though the circumstances are admittedly out of the common. But, in any case, that which you ask is unattainable. The one depicted is the least of those of my inner chamber, and to add to the burden of this person's harassment she now lies suspended in the vapours of a malign distemper."

"Then it is not unlikely that my intervention has been brought about by the protecting powers, desirous of our mutual happiness," declared Tong So with confidence. "In the past I rendered a certain service to a learned anchorite who in return disclosed to me many healing virtues of the hidden kind. What is the nature of the stricken one's malady?"

"It takes the form of a dark stupor, whereby the natural forces of the mind and body are repressed. To counteract this, an expert healer from the Capital counselled a decoction prepared from tiger's bones."

"The remedy is well enough, but there are subtler and more potent drugs than tigers' bones," said Tong with some impatience. "Moreover, you who have been a ginseng merchant doubtless know that every bin has two components. Were the bones submitted to a searching test?"

"A lavish price was paid and a thumb-signed assurance of integrity was given. What added precaution could have been taken?"

"Do any still remain?" demanded Tong.

Fan Chin summoned an attendant and issued a command. This one quickly returned with some broken fragments, which at a sign he placed before Tong So. The latter blew shrilly from between his teeth, and the next moment the largest and fiercest of Fan Chin's watchdogs leaped among them in answer to the call and fawned upon Tong So.

"Oiya!" cried the one in question and threw toward it the weightiest of the pieces; without a moment's hesitation the hound caught it between expectant jaws and fled in the direction of its lair, closely followed by the bewailing Fan, striving to recover his possession.

"Restrain your ineffective zeal," exclaimed Tong So. "You are pursuing the wrong dog if you look for restitution."

"Which dog is that?" asked Fan Chin, gazing round expectantly. "I see no other than the hound escaping."

"The one from whom these goat ribs were procured. Where does the usurious mongrel dwell?"

"He is Sheng, the son of Ho, carrying on his necessary traffic beneath the Sign of the Magnanimous Pestle, and spoken of as both upright and exact."

Tong So drew a figured ring from off his thumb and gave it to the awaiting slave.

"Hitherto," he remarked in an unsympathetic voice, "traffic with Ho Sheng has doubtless been on a somewhat mutual basis, thou equivocal bondman. Enlighten that obscene refuse chafferer as to what has taken place and displaying this very ordinary ring before his shortsighted eyes require of him a double measure in place of what he has fraudulently withheld. To this add that he who sends requires no thumb-signed bond, but should the fiercest hound not tremble and retreat before the bones he now provides, on the morrow the emblem of his sign will be changed from the Magnanimous Pestle to the Disconnected Hand. To this obsequious message append the name of Tong So, and let your sandals be in shreds on your return."

"I listen and obey, high chieftain," replied the submissive slave.

When they were alone again, Fan Chin turned toward his visitor and spoke with some reserve.

"Your name and your general line of conduct remind me of what I have heard concerning one who haunts the secluded Ways. Is it unreasonable to conjecture that you cast the same shadow as that of So, of the line of Tong, who is the admitted leader to the thieves about I-kang?"

"To deny it would be superfluous," replied Tong So. "My revered father was of that craft before me, and his venerated sire likewise in turn. How then should I, without being unfilial to a criminal degree, seem to disparage their hallowed memories by rejecting what was good enough for them?"

"That certainly is a point of view which cannot lightly be dismissed," confessed Fan Chin, who was a staunch upholder of tradition. "In the past this person himself had leanings toward the insidious craving of a literary career, until he saw, as in a vision, seven generations of ginseng-providing ancestors beckoning him to follow. Recognizing the brink on which he stood, the one who is now speaking immediately burned all that he had written, together with the varied utensils of the art, with the happy result that today he is able to command a congratulatory ode of any length whenever he feels the need of one, instead of merely having to compose them for the delectation of another."

"It is well said that there are three of every man: that which he is, that which he only thinks he is, and that which he really had intended to become," agreed Tong So. "In the meanwhile, this person would seek, by tracing the origin of the adorable Tsing Yun's disorder to its hidden source and there controlling its malignity, to establish a claim on your approval."

"It would be inept to spread a fabric of evasion between our mutually straightforward minds," replied Fan Chin, as one who strives to be urbane and at the same time to disclose an unpalatable truth. "Already you have appreciably risen in my esteem since the first moment of our meeting, but your inopportune profession stands as an ever-present barrier against an alliance of a really definite kind. In any other direction, doubtless our congenial feet may continue side by side."

"Yet," pleaded Tong, "by the exercise of a frugal industry I should soon be in a position to lay before you an adequate proposal. Hitherto I have regarded the pecuniary side of our venture with a perhaps undeserved contempt, but the business is one that is admittedly capable of a wide development under more vigorous methods, and if only inspired by a well-founded hope of the one whom I have named, very soon the puny records of the past will be obliterated —"

"Forbear!" exclaimed Fan Chin in an access of dismay. "Already the insatiable rapacity of your never-tiring band is such that this careworn person would gladly submit to a yearly tribute of a hundred taels of silver to be preserved from their assault. If these activities should be increased, a flood deeper than the Yangtse will sweep over the awakening growth of our mutual esteem."

"Yet if, on the other hand, you should be wholly freed from the exaction, would you then be impelled to regard this person in the light of a favoured suppliant for the lady Tsing Yun's lotus hand?"

"That is a longer stride than one of my age can take forward at a single step," said Fan Chin guardedly. "The tree of reciprocal goodwill would certainly be cherished by such an act, but the obstacle of the means whereby your rice is earned remains."

"To change that, even were it possible in this strenuously competitive era, would risk alienating the protective spirits of my ancestors," remarked Tong So. "Unless," he mused thoughtfully, "unless, indeed, by some adroit syncretism the conflicting elements could be harmoniously reconciled so as to appeal to all."

"My moss-grown ears —?" interposed Fan Chin politely.

"A passing invocation to the deities," apologized Tong So. "But touching a possible arrangement of our various interests. May the suggestion of five-score taels of silver be regarded as a concrete proposition?"

"The remark was more in the nature of a flower of conversation than a specific offer," replied Fan Chin, somewhat annoyed that he had thus incautiously named so formidable an amount. "Even allowing for the most ruthless energy of your painstaking crew, the full annual tale of their depredation would not approach that sum."

"Yet there are incidental contingencies from which an assured immunity cannot be weighed in a money-changer's scale even against fine gold," suggested Tong, meeting Fan Chin's drooping eye sympathetically. "But among obliging friends a tael more or a tael less does not lead to strife. Assuming that five-score could be laid before my trustworthy gang as a basis for discussion —?"

"You have spoken of your knowledge of the hidden qualities of healing things," remarked Fan Chin, turning abruptly from both the subject and the path that they had been treading; "let us approach the one who stands in need of such an art and put your subtlety to a deciding test. Afterward, perchance, a jar of almond wine may be unsealed and matters of a varied kind discussed."

IV. In Which He Becomes Both Virtuous and Esteemed

When it was passed from mouth to mouth among the thieves throughout I-kang that an assembly had been called of the full Brotherhood, to which all were summoned on pain of ejectment from the Order's protection and estate, it was understood that affairs of distinguished moment were involved. In the face of so emphatic a command none ventured to abstain, so that when Tong So entered he saw before him all who recognized his leadership, whatever their degree. His first act, after the ceremonious rite of greeting, was to require a written tablet of their names and attributes, and this being taken, it was thereupon declared to form a full and authentic record of the Guild, with all other thieves outside.

"Let each one present now declare against his name the yearly sum of taels that his industry procures, judging it as he reasonably thinks fit, but with the full assurance that the sum once set down stands for good or ill unchangeable."

"Imperishable chief," ventured one, whose calling it was to steal tribute rice on its passage to the north (voicing the dilemma of many of his fellows), "we be mostly men of stunted minds and alien to the subtleties that lurk in the casting of accounts. Could but an indication of the outcome of this affair be given, it would greatly assist our stolid wits."

"One with enough wit to draw out an axle-pin while walking on his hands beside a cart, need not tremble at the task," replied Tong So, amid a general melting of their gravity. "Whether it be to reward you according to your proficiency or to tax you in the light of your success will presently appear."

"Doubtless you, as our ever-cherished leader, will be the first one to attest?" suggested another hopefully.

"Not first but last, according to my unconquerable regard for your superior virtues," politely declared Tong.

Thus baffled, as it were, each one considered well and in the declared himself according to his exact knowledge, lest haply he might fall upon the wrong extreme. When this was done, Tong so stood up again.

"In the past, we of this Brotherhood have laboured strenuously for an inadequate reward and have had, moreover, to endure the maledictory word of every rival. The powerful mandarin, holding toward each suppliant three expectant hands, the lesser official, pursuing the tribute-payer with three unrelenting feet, the merchant blending among that which is costly that which is similar but cheap, the stall-keeper propelling a secret jet of wind against the trembling balance of his scale, even the beggar in the Way, displaying that upon his body which is not really there-all these do not hesitate to extend toward us the venomed tongue of calumny. Who considers the perilous nature of our enterprise, its hidden dangers, its sudden alarms, its frequent disappointments where in much that appears solid and of good repute by the feeble rays of the great sky lantern proves to be hollow or of fictitious lustre when submitted to a corrosive test by the one to whom we offer it? Does any man ask us as we enter to remove our sandals and recline at ease, any maiden greet us with tea and a song of welcome? Plainly we are no longer wanted in I-kang. Thus positioned, we will toil no more. It is better to live in luxurious idleness than to labour for a meagre wage and salt our rice with broadcast words of scorn."

"Assuredly," interposed one of some authority, as Tong So paused to take up a cup. "Your lips drop rubies, chieftain, but when picked up they transmute to points of fire. For if we toil not at our craft, whence comes the means to live in any state?"

"You are plainly behind your era, worthy Li, and your deliberative type of mind is fast becoming obsolete," replied Tong So. "Henceforth, instead of being compelled to take what we desire by stealth or force, men will freely press it into our awaiting hands and greet us with regard and courtesy. The distinction hangs upon a subtle word: instead of working, we will covenant to abstain, and thus by our unanimity protect from loss those whom hitherto we have endeavoured to despoil."

"The outlook is so attractive that it must inevitably conceal some hidden spring to take us unaware," said one. "Men will not consent thus to reward us to remain in idleness."

"Bend then your ears," replied Tong So, "and listen to the scroll of those who are already pledged: Fan Chin, a retired ginseng merchant, in consideration of a hundred taels less five; Ling-hi, who keeps a den, for twenty-eight; Hi-eng, the dog-butcher, at two-score and a half; Tang-tso, of late reputed to possess a million taels, who offers twice what any other pays; Fung-san, at the Sign of the Upright Tooth Remover-but why drive home a wooden skewer with an iron mace? Be assured that already to each man will fall more than he earned by toil, and before a final count is made his portion will be double."

"How then shall we contrive to pass our time?" inquired another rapturously. "We who shall henceforth be as mandarins walking the earth!"

"Thus and thus," replied Tong, as this became a general cry. "In the morning you will doubtless remain undisturbed or smoke a fragrant pipe among your kind. After the middle-rice, attired in seemly robes and moving leisurely beneath a shading umbrella, you will approach those on our scroll whose dues have run their course, be graciously received, and give an official seal (the only form of evidence we shall recognize) for that which you receive. To each one will be apportioned a certain limit of the city, and as you make this dignified and pleasurable round, you will look from side to side and observe such houses as do not display our Company's protective sign. At each of these you will present yourself in turn, pointing out to the one whose ear you gain the peril of his case, warningly-but at the same time enlivening the argument by appropriate jests and instances. Of all the profits due to your persuasive threats, an added share falls to your sleeve, beyond your general portion."

"This is the Golden Age of the Han dynasty returned," murmured one whose method was to enter into conversation with whom he could entice by confidence. "But assuredly we shall very soon awaken."

"In the evening," continued Tong alluringly, "you will perhaps give yourself to homely mirth among those of your choice, to witnessing a play of a kind according to your mood, or, in season, to planting the earth around your flower-clad bower. Soon, in the fullness of your leisure and content, some may even become immersed in the art of attempting to ensnare fish upon a cord, in propelling a resilient core from point to point across a given space by means of weighted clubs, or in regulating the various necessary details of the city's management. And when, in the course of time, you Pass Beyond, you will lie in well-appointed tombs and your Tablets will be kept. If any should dissent from the prospect thus held out let him now speak freely."

"Your vision is that of an above-man, chieftain, and a monument of many heights will certainly be erected to your immortal name," a voice at length declared. "Yet this one pitfall still remains. Men of dissolute and improvident habit from other cities will from time to time pass through I-kang, and by unscrupulously robbing those whom we are pledged to guard will bring us to disrepute."

Tong So looked round on the company that wrought his will and raised his hand with a gesture of all-confidence.

"It is foreseen," he replied in a level voice, "and the hazard will be met. We know the Ways by day and night; we know each other and those who are not of our confederacy; and we know the Means. Those who come will not return, and that which is had away will be restored in full, to the vindication of our unbending name. Aught else?"

They made way for the next with laughter and applause: an aged man named Jin, who was proficient in only the simplest forms of crime.

"Gracious commander," said the ancient diffidently, "I who speak am beyond the years of pliant change, having been a robber of the commoner sort outside the memory of most. Now touching this new-garbled plan whereby we are to lift fish on a noose, or armed with a heavy club to go openly by light of day into the houses of those who display a certain sign—"

"Set your mind at rest, honest Jin," declared Tong reassuringly. "None shall depossess you from your timeworn way." He came down and took the venerable affectionately by the shoulder, adding in his ear, "There will always be those who would obstinately withstand our proffered help, to whom persuasion-in its various forms-must be administered. Do not despair."

Thus in the eleventh of the Heaven-sent Emperor Yung, Tong So became the first who undertook to insure to those who bargained with him protection against loss. Being now rich and well-esteemed, Fan Chin no longer maintained a barrier before his hopes, nor, it is to be assumed, did the spirits of his discriminating ancestors regard him as having transgressed their honourable traditions in any essential detail, for they continued to uphold him in his virtuous career. So zealously inclined and sought-after did he soon become that on the occasion of his marriage with the enchanting Tsing Yun he caused to be erected a many-tiered place of commerce at the meeting of the four busiest streets within I-kang, and outside this he hung a sign of polished brass, embellished with these words:

Tong So
Averter of Calamities

In time he added to the nature of his commerce protection from the peril of fire, of being drawn under the wheels of passing chariots, and the like. Yet in spite of his benevolent concern for the misfortunes of others, he was not wholly devoid of enemies, and these did not hesitate to declare that while Tong So could-and admittedly did-restrain his outrageous band from despoiling those who bought exemption, he was no demon to grant immunity from fire and the contingencies of life. To this narrow-minded taunt the really impartial would reply that if some among those who sought Tong's aid might occasionally experience fire or fatal injury, all those who stubbornly refused to do so inevitably did.

The Meeting by the Way With the Warrior of Chi-U and What Emerged Therefrom

At daybreak Kai Lung left the scanty hut of the hospitable Thang, and that obliging person accompanied him to the boundary of his knowledge.

"Before you now," he declared significantly, as they passed at the point of his return, "there lies an unknown and therefore, presumably, a barbarous and immoral country, doubtless peopled by wild and unintellectual tribes. Few travellers have reached our clay-souled plain from the quagmires of Ying-tze, but out of these misty slopes that lead through interminable valleys to the very peaks of Teen no message has ever come. It would be well for you, Kai Lung, to consider again before you tempt the doubtful Forces lying in wait for you ahead. The demons here are bad enough, but those elsewhere may prove much worse."

"That is a necessary evil to be faced," was the frank admission. "But I place very great reliance on the energetic influence of my ancestors Above. I do not despair of their invoking an even more potent band of worthy Powers to lend their aid, and my lucky ascendant has certainly so far triumphed."

"The connection between your auspicious number and this one's misguided age is both conclusive and exact," acknowledged Thang, to whom the storyteller had disclosed the obliging soothsayer's prediction. "Still, it is as well not to push these auguries too far: there is generally a concealed spring in them that releases itself when least expected. May your virtuous Line prosper in the end, however. Keen eyes and quick-moving feet in the face of danger is the last wish of the abject Thang."

"May all the felicities ultimately be yours," was Kai Lung's no less staunch rejoinder. "Were there no darkness, we should never see the stars, but by the light of your compassion the planets cease to be. Much happiness, esteemed."

At a distance they raised their hands again, Thang waving a short woollen cap that he wore about his ears, and Kai Lung lifting his almost deficient scrip high upon his staff. Beyond, an intervening barrier of rock hid them from one another.

As Kai Lung approached the border town of Chi-U, he could not fail to notice that a feeling of anticipation was in the air. Kites in the form of aggressive dragons floated above every point likely to incur assault, and other protective measures were not lacking, while the almost continuous discharge of propitiatory crackers could be heard even before the mud walls appeared in sight.

"All this," argued Kai Lung, "may not unreasonably concern Ming-shu and his invading host. Thus ambiguously positioned, it would be well to enter into affable conversation with one of leisured habit before disclosing myself too fully."

With this inoffensive object, the storyteller looked for some wayfarer whom he might casually approach with an unstudied request about the gong-stroke of the day, or to whom he might haply predict a continuance of heat. But all those whom he observed were at a distance and moving with extreme rapidity in one director or another-those from the east flying to the west as though in no other way could they preserve their lives, and those from the west pressing on to the east as if pursued by demons.

"It is well said, 'Men fear the noise more than they dread the missile,' " considered Kai Lung. "Rumour is here at work."

At length one who neither hastened nor glanced back approached, but so assured was the dignity of his bearing, and his attire so rich, that had the circumstances been less urgent than they were, Kai Lung would not have ventured to address him. The stranger had something of a martial poise, although he bore no weapon; instead, he carried in one hand a polished cane from which an eager bird, attached by a silken cord, sprang divertingly into the air from time to time and caught a fleeting seed cast in its direction; from about the other arm a substantial rope, with one end fashioned as a noose, depended. His nails were long and delicately sheathed, his skin like the outer surface of a well-grown peach, and as he moved his person diffused an attractive perfume even when several paces distant.

"Greetings, high eminence," was Kai Lung's obsequious salutation. "Has your rice settled?"

Without exactly replying in terms that would infer acceptance of this courtesy, the other made an indifferent gesture of assent and then began to regard Kai Lung more closely.

"You have not the appearance of being a Chi-U man," he remarked with some display of interest. "Are you from the waste lands of the south?"

"For such and such a length of days I have journeyed on a northward track, seeking a certain end," was the reply. "Say on, magnificence."

"I am in this difficulty: If I am to Pass Upward and rejoin my celestial ancestors under the most propitious sign it is very necessary that I should find a suitable banyan tree, growing in a valley that affords protection against spirits drifting from the east and west," explained the stranger; "my lucky direction being north and south, and the banyan my adopted tree. Have you, in your passage, marked such a spot?"

"Yet how comes it," ventured Kai Lung, "that you, who appear to possess all that an ordinary person could desire, should wish to self-end your being so unpleasantly?" and he indicated the cord that the other carried.

"It is better to miss a few superfluous years here below than to go through all eternity in the form of a headless trunk," replied the one who thus forecast his own misshapen future. "Being over-captain of the Ever-Valiant Camp of Tiger-Eating Braves stationed about Chi-U this one is bidden to attack the impure Ming-shu's rebellious lair without delay and to send that corrupt leper's obscene head to the Capital as a badge of his submission. This being clearly impossible, my own head will be held forfeit and it is to avoid this distressing humiliation that it becomes necessary to act thus and thus."

"Yet why, with so valorous a troop of death-deriders, headed by one whose mere appearance is calculated to strike despair into the hearts of the prudent and diffuse, should it be possible for the effete Ming-shu to defy your band?"

"That," was the reply, "arises from the complexity of our military system. Three hundred braves are the avowed total of this one's company, but in order to foster a becoming spirit of thrift the monthly inadequacy of taels is computed for half that number."

Kai Lung experienced a moment of regret that so many of those whom he had hoped to join in an attack on Ming-shu's fastness should be, as it were, struck down at the very outset. The emotion passed.

"There is a saying in the books, 'Two willing men can cleave a passage through the rock while four pressed slaves are moistening their hands,' " he remarked. "Seven or eight score valiants would set Ming-shu at naught and so uphold your face."

"Perchance," agreed the other, "but the path from the office of the Board of Warlike Deeds and Achievements, in the Capital, to the door of the military stronghold here in Chi-U, is both long and tortuous, and whoever travels it must receive the protection of many important officials on the way. There is the immaculate President of the Board itself, who checks the silver out on leaving, and the incorruptible civil overling here, who counts it on arriving, while between lurk the administrators of three districts, the chief mandarins of eight townships, and the head-men of seventeen villages. All these integritous persons are alert to see that the consignment has not suffered attrition in its passage through the previous zone, and each has a large and instinctively prehensile hand. Thus and thus —"

"Excellence," besought Kai Lung, not without misgivings, "how many warriors, each having some actual existence, are there in your never-failing band?"

"For all purposes save those of attack and defence, there are fifteen score of the best and bravest, as their pay-sheets well attest," was the confident response. "In a strictly literal sense, however, there are no more than can be seen on a mist-enshrouded day with a resolutely closed eye."

"None, illustriousness! Not one with which to bring the unanswerable Ming-shu to justice?"

307

In the ensuing pause the over-captain threw a dexterous succession of choice seeds to the expectant bird and applauded its unfailing effort.

"Despite all that a sordid economy can accomplish, there remains only so much-after allowing barely enough to maintain the one essential officer in a state befitting his position-as will keep the three hundred uniforms and the flags and banners of the imperishable company in a seemly condition of repair," replied the other. "That, and something inevitable in the way of joy-making and esteem-promoting when the appointed red-knob journeys hither to survey the band."

"Yet if the band is in a state of no-existence, does not disgrace ensue from that same one's report?"

"Wherefore, if the necessary formalities have been becomingly observed and mutual politeness reigns? Fifteen-score hard-striving and necessitous persons are never lacking in Chi-U, who for the honourable distinction and a few assorted cash are willing through a passing hour or two to obey the simpler signals of command and to answer to a name."

The sugared seed being no longer offered, the brilliant captive poised on the apex of the upraised rod and folded its tranquil wings. The stilling point of yellow took Kai Lung's eye with a deeper meaning. " 'A golden bud set on a leafless stem,' " leaped his immediate thought. "There is more than the outer husk herein."

"In this affair of Ming-shu, however," he prompted, speaking at a hazard and merely to detain the stranger, "does not your meritorious service in the past call for official mildness?"

"That which is only painted should not be washed too often," replied the over-captain with broad-minded resignation. "Therefore, if you can aid this person's search to what he now requires, do not refrain, and the obliged shade of Hai Shin will speak a good word for you in season."

"Truly, importance," agreed Kai Lung, "yet this matter is not one that can be settled as between the drinking of a cup of tea and the filling of another. In your illustrious proximity this one now recognizes the fulfillment of an inspired portent. Have you, on your side, no indication of his menial presence?"

"There certainly was a remark made by a priestly mendicant, to whom I threw a doubtful coin at the Camel Gate," replied Hai Shin. "This was to the effect that 'Even a paper leopard can put a hornless sheep to flight,' but the analogy is admittedly abstruse."

"High prominence!" exclaimed Kai Lung joyfully. "Surely nothing could be more pellucid in its crystal depth. As a leopard is the symbol of indomitable valour, what could so explicitly proclaim your own consternating image? And inasmuch as this one is a minstrel and reciter of written tales, the reference to paper is exact. How apter could the invincible alliance of the two persons standing here be classically portrayed? The paper leopard: device and intrepidity."

"The simile might strike the undiscerning as coming somewhat from a distance," conceded Hai Shin, not altogether unimpressed. "But who is to be sought in the allusion to a hornless sheep?"

"Who, high commander? Who but the promiscuous Ming-shu, for what could be more truly said to counterfeit the goat than to forego an assured life for the uncertain fruit of insurrection? —but a goat whose horns are predestined to be very closely shorn by your all-conquering sword."

"The prospect is not wholly devoid of glamour," the over-captain agreed, "but how are we, the one being an unspecified retailer of delusive fables and the other a fugitive devoid of followers, to overthrow Ming-shu — camped in a mountain stronghold and surrounded by armed men?"

"Is it not written, 'Every hedge has a rotten stake somewhere?' Ming-shu's defence will prove no exception to the rule. What cannot be pushed in by force may yet be drawn out by guile. This involves a stratagem."

"If you have any definite plan, it might be worth considering," admitted the other, "but the prospect of a speedy and not inglorious end-especially at an hour when the very cracks of hell are voiding their vapour upward to consume us — compares favourably with a long-drawn-out and speculative existence," and he continued to fan himself at leisure. "Disclose your artifice more fully."

"That is best explained by a recital of the story of Lin Ho and the Treasure of Fang-tso," replied Kai Lung resourcefully. "If, therefore, you will but inconvenience your refined and well-trained ears to the extent of admitting such harsh and ill-chosen phrases as I have at my illiterate command, I will endeavour to impart the necessary moral as painlessly as possible."

With this auspicious foreboding, Kai Lung arranged his mat so that it might offer an agreeable shade to both, and then, without permitting the more leisurely minded Hai Shin any real opportunity for dissent, he at once raised up his voice.

The Story of Lin Ho and the Treasure of Fang-tso

In the days before the usurper Yung-che arose to destroy the land (may the daughters of his outcast Line slant their eyes in vain along the byways of our desecrated city!) a conscientious lacquerer, Li Chu by name, plied his inoffensive craft in the township of Kiting. He had an only son, Lin Ho, whom it was care to instruct on all occasions in the pursuit of excellence.

"Yet how comes it, revered," inquired Lin Ho, when he was of an age to discriminate these things, "that I who am the outcome of your virtuous life should go in homely cloth and ofttimes gnaw the unappetizing husk while the sons of other lacquerers wear silk array and speak familiarly of meat?"

"It is even as it is," replied Li Chu, applying a pigment of a special brilliance to the work beneath his hand. "Doubtless if this person hung out a flagrant sign, hired one to chant his praises in the marketplace, and used a base alloy to simulate pure gold, you also might wear rich attire and eat your fill."

"Why, then, since others of your guild do this to their advancement, should you not act thus as well?"

"It is not the Way," answered Li Chu simply. "Have you already forgotten the words of the upright official Thang to those who inquired of him an easy road to wealth: 'All roads are easy if you do not disdain the mud'?"

"Nay," assented his son, "I had not forgotten. But to what does this Way you speak of ultimately lead?"

"To this end: that among future races, even in far distant lands, men searching for that which is precious will take up perchance this very casket and, examining it, will say, 'Here is the thumb-mark and the sign of Li Chu, the obscure craftsman of Kiting in the ancient days-lo, we require no further guarantee.' "

Thus inspired, it will occasion no surprise that Li Chu himself soon after Passed Beyond, stricken by a low distemper against which the natural forces of his ill-nourished frame could not contend. Lin Ho, still many years short of manhood, was left destitute and would doubtless have perished had not the fear of barbed whispers impelled his wealthy uncle Le-ung to succour him.

When Le-ung took Lin Ho into his household, he did so reluctantly, partly forecasting his meagre wife's displeasure but no less by reason of his own prevailing greed. Although full brother to Li Chu, they resembled each other only to this degree: that where the one succeeded the other failed, and likewise in converse, so that he who amassed five cart-loads of taels as the fruit of a sordid usury was at once forgotten, while he who was buried in a hired coffin is extolled by a thousand lips today when they declare: "Behold, the colours are as bright as those of the unapproachable Li Chu."

The smaller ones of Le-ung's house were not slow to bend toward this unworthy attitude, for, as the Verse proclaims, "When the dragon breathes out fire, the dragonets begin to blow forth smoke," and very soon Lin Ho found that extended hands were not to welcome him and that the feet turned in his direction, so far from accompanying him in friendship, propelled him forward with undisguised hostility. The most degrading and obscure of the household tasks were thrust upon him, so that ere long his state in no way differed from that of a purchased slave. Nevertheless, Lin Ho remained sincere and obsequious, and whatever he was bidden to do he did in a superior manner.

"Even if it is but the scouring of a cracked utensil, my aim shall be to scour it so that anyone taking it up will say, 'This is the work of Lin Ho and none other,' " he was wont to remark, with well-sustained humility. This, indeed, actually occurred on several occasions, but it did not enlarge Lin Ho in the eyes of those around.

When the years of Le-ung's hospitality had reached about a single hand-count that person was the victim of a severe and ill-arranged misfortune. An obsolete and heavily burdened junk-the outcome of his enterprise-in making a hazardous passage along an uncharted course, was not wrecked, and in spite of the distinguished efforts of the one in command-an adherent to Le-ung's cause-the undisciplined crew succeeded in bringing the superfluous vessel to its inopportune anchorage. Le-ung was obliged to take up his share of the merchandise (which he had already disposed of at an advantageous loss) and to extricate himself as best he could. The blow was an unbecoming one.

"Henceforth," remarked the pioneer of commerce to the discreet beneath his roof, "henceforth, the rigid line of economy must be strenuously maintained until this person's credit is sufficiently robust again. Restrain the generous impulse to out-vie all others in the cost and dimensions of everything procurable. Cultivate originality of taste in the direction of the inexpensively severe. Forbear to provide your table with lotus shoots when it is difficult to walk without treading on rice worms, but when there are no lotus shoots within ten thousand li; and with rice worms when lotus shoots abound around your door but when rice worms have to be brought in tanks from distant provinces at vast expense. In the matter of fans and general attire, that which was entrancing when the moon was crescent need not inevitably be regarded as unendurably grotesque by the time it is at the full —"

"Haply," interposed the leader of those chiefly concerned; "but he who is clumsy with his feet will be weak in his reasoning also. Turn your eyes inward, O thou financially concave Le-ung, and, as the adage counsels, eat what you have roasted. Henceforth, in place of the exclusive brands you habitually affect, learn to inhale the frugal 'Tame Chrysanthemum,' of which two brass cash procure five. For peach wine of the choicest sources substitute Ah-kong's Stimulating Orange-Joy at seven taels the gross. Avoid the robe marts of the Western Quarter, and about your lavishly proportioned form wrap the already-prepared garments —"

"Desist," exclaimed Le-ung ungracefully; "you cannot mend things with a broken needle, and your words are quite destitute of point. These are but trifles, and, in any case, they constitute this person's commercial frontage. Meet his wishes in a thoroughly large-hearted manner, and he, for his part, will give up something really substantial."

"In what direction will the promised economy tend?" inquired the speaker of the band, in a spirit of well-grounded mistrust.

"For upward of four years, Lin Ho has consumed our rice, and beyond a little manual labour of the unskilled type, he has done nothing in return. Admittedly, the one who is speaking has carried family affection too far, and he must now deny himself in this respect. Lin Ho shall go."

"That loss were an undivided gain," agreed the other. "But will not the ever-ready voice of censure assail our trembling prestige if we thrust him forth?"

"Refrain from instructing your venerated ancestress in the art of extracting nutrition from a coconut," replied Le-ung concisely. "One whose ships are incapable of foundering on the perfidious Che-hai coast is scarcely likely to lose bearings in so simple a matter as the marooning of Lin Ho."

It will thus be seen that already this mentally bankrupt speculator was deceiving himself by an illogical grasp of the ordained sequences. Can we deny the aptness of the saying, "He who has failed three times sets up as an instructor?"

Early the following day, Le-ung took Lin Ho aside and proceeded to unfold his ignoble plan. He was (to set forth his misleading words, though the discriminating, who will by this time have taken his repulsive measure, should need no warning cough) on the eve of initiating a costly venture and would enlist the special protection of certain powerful spirits. To this end it was necessary to sacrifice and observe the ceremonies at a notorious shrine on an indicated mountain. For this service, Le-ung had chosen Lin Ho, and having provided him with all things necessary, he bade him set out at once.

With no suspicion of treachery, the painstaking Lin Ho proceeded on his way, determined to conduct the enterprise in such a manner as would redound to the credit of his name. It was noon when he reached the foot of the mountain, the spot being a wild one and austere. Before ascending to the shrine, Lin Ho sat down upon a rock to partake of food and gather strength for the lengthy rite. He opened his wallet and found therein an adequacy of mien paste, a flask of water, and an onion. There was also a little spice to sprinkle on the food, and a few score melon seeds.

"If he whom I serve is not so light as day, neither is he quite so black as night," observed Lin Ho, for the nature of the fare surpassed what he had expected.

"To speak one's thoughts aloud, even in a desert, betrays a pure and dispassionate mind," exclaimed an appreciative voice from behind a crag. "I need have no hesitation in affecting the society of such a person."

With this auspicious presage the one who spoke came into view and stood before Lin Ho. He was above the common height and wore a martial air, to which his fiercely bristling whiskers gave a sombre increase. His robe was faded by the long exposure of a rigorous life; where the colours could be seen, they were both harmonious and rich. Whatever arms he bore he had laid aside in deference to the reputation of those heights whose shadows lay upon them, but he retained his iron sandals and a metal covering for the head. His manner had in it both something of the menace of the mountain brigand and the subtlety of the wayside mendicant, so that Lin Ho was not wholly reassured. Nevertheless, he waved his hand in greeting and indicated a smooth rock at no great distance from the one he sat on.

"You are two thousand times welcome," he declared hospitably. "If you are about to refresh yourself before you perform your rites there is no occasion why we should not eat together."

"It would be churlish to refuse an invitation so delicately advanced," replied the stranger. "Foreseeing the necessity of this halt, the one before you carried with him baked and steamed meats of various kinds, condiments of the rare flavours, rice and sweet herbs, fruit, wine, and a sufficiency of snuff. All of these —"

"Beside your rich abundance, my own scanty fare is a shrivelled weed beneath a towering palm," confessed Lin Ho in deep humility. "Nevertheless, if you will but condescend to share —"

"All of these were swept away at a perfidious and ill-conditioned ford a short li distant to the north," continued the other. "Of what does your welcome and appetizing store consist, O brother?"

"Very little, and that quite unattractively prepared," replied Lin Ho, his face by no means gladdened at the direction in which the episode was tending. "Accept this cake of paste and a cup of water to refresh your weary throat when it is finished. More I cannot allot, for I have an exacting service to perform and shall need all the sustaining vigour that food bestows."

"What is offered in friendship should not be weighed upon a balance," assented the stranger pleasantly, but at the same time so arranging himself that he could closely overlook all Lin Ho's movements. "With what is your own meritorious meal supplied, in addition to this wholesome though undoubtedly prosaic foundation, comrade?"

"The staple of it is a large but unsightly onion," replied Lin Ho, as he began to peel it. "Had there been two, I might have prevailed on you to overcome your high-born repugnance to such crude fare."

"An onion!" exclaimed the one beside him, stretching out his hand to take it, so incredulous were his eyes of their service. "An onion at this momentous hour! Would you affront the deities on whom you call by carrying so impolite a taint into their sacred presence?"

"That is very far from being my purpose," replied Lin Ho, colouring at the unbecoming imputation. "Not shall so gross a misdeed ever be set to my account."

"Yet you do not hold that the breath of your petition will rise before the faces of the gods you supplicate?"

"Such is the essence of the rite," Lin Ho admitted. "How else should they hear and concede my prayer?"

"Then how can your breath ascend on high without conveying in its wake the pestilential reek of onion if you permit yourself this rash indulgence? It is well for you that we encountered, friend!"

"That certainly presents the matter in a disconcerting light and one that I had never up to now been warned of," said Lin Ho in a very downcast spirit. "Must the better part of my sustenance then be wasted?"

"By no means," replied his companion, beginning to eat; "it shall not be lost. My own business with the Venerable Ones is the mere formality of rendering thanks for an enterprise achieved, and at the moment I have nothing to solicit. It therefore matters very little whether they maintain a sympathetic front or turn their backs on me disdainfully. In this matter of the onion, neighbour, be content: Lam-kwong will requite you to the full at some appropriate time."

"That may be," agreed Lin Ho, "but 'today is a blistered foot; tomorrow but an itching hand.' It is no easy thing to prostrate one's self continuously on a stomach sustained by mien paste alone."

"You have suffered no great loss," said Lam-kwong in a voice that began to lose its truculent assurance. "Already I am experiencing certain grievous inward qualms. Whence came this dubious root that you have so noticeably pressed upon me?"

"'Wan Tae, falling into the river while catching fish, accuses them of his misfortune,'" quoted Lin Ho, stung by the injustice of the taunt. "Touching the thing that you have eaten, I know no more than this: that it is from the hand of one who is not prone to bounty."

"Is his enmity so great that he would conspire to your destruction if it could be prudently achieved?" inquired Lam-kwong faintly.

"He is capable of any crime, from reviling the Classics to diverting water-courses," freely declared Lin Ho. "If you desire to speak openly of Le-ung, do not let the fact that he is closely related to the one before you impede the zealous fountain of your doubtless fluent tongue. Without question, he laid a dark spell upon the onion for it to contort your limbs so unnaturally."

"It is a spell that writes Lam-kwong's untimely end," exclaimed the one who thus alluded to his own up-passing. "The device is an ancient one, the pungent juices of the herb cloaking the natural flavour of the poison until it is too late. Between you you have outdone me who have outdone all others-may the two of you grill at a never-slackening fire throughout eternity! Him, neither my resentful hand can reach nor my avenging ghost discover, but you at least shall suffer for your inept share in this one's humiliation. Take Lam-kwong's last message!" A weighty stone, propelled with all that one's expiring vigour, accompanied this shortsighted curse, and chancing to inflict itself upon Lin Ho at a vulnerable point of his outline, the well-meaning and really inoffensive person groaned twice and sank to the ground devoid of life.

Lin Ho being dead, his spirit at once sped to the Upper World and passed the barriers successfully. An inferior Being received and questioned him and, setting a certain mark against his name, led him into the assembly of those who sat in judgment.

"Lin Ho," said the presiding chief in some embarrassment, "the circumstances of your abrupt arrival here are rather out of the formal order of things, and the necessary records are not as yet available. For this irregularity, Lam-kwong shall answer sharply. As for you, in view of your frugal and abstemious life, and taking into consideration the mission on which you are now engaged, it has been decided to send you back again to earth. Regard the Virtues, sacrifice freely, and provide an adequate posterity."

Lin Ho then had the sensation of being violently projected downward. When he recovered sufficiently from the exertion to be able to observe coherently, he found that he was floating in spirit above the spot on earth where he had lately been. Beneath him lay two lifeless bodies-those of Lam-kwong and of himself. For the first time he was inspired by an emotion of contempt toward his own placid and unassuming features.

"It is one thing to lead a frugal and abstemious life," Lin Ho reflected; "it is another to partake of meat whenever the desire arises. Hitherto this person has accepted servitude and followed the integritous path because with so narrow-minded a face as that any other line of conduct was not practicable. Had he possessed fiercely bristling whiskers and a capricious eye, he would not have meekly accepted the outer husk of things, nor would the maidens of Kiting have greeted him with derisive cries, that he should not respond to them when they encountered about dusk in the waste spaces of the city."

For a few short beats of time, the spirit of Lin Ho considered further. Then he looked this way and that and saw that there was none to observe him there, nor had any attending Being accompanied him to earth. He took a sudden resolution, and before a movement could be made to intercept him, he slipped into the body of Lam-kwong and animated it.

When Lin Ho, wearing the body of Lam-kwong, rose up, he was conscious of possessing an entirely new arrangement of the senses. The thought of Le-ung no longer filled him with submission, and he laughed sonorously at a recollection of the labours he had lately been engaged in, though hitherto he had regarded all forms of gravity-removal as unworthy of his strenuous purpose. The sound of his iron shoes grinding the rocks he walked on raised his spirits, and he opened and closed his great hands to feel their horny strength. From time to time, he leaped into the air to test his powers, and he shouted a defiance to any unseen demons who might happen to be lurking in the caves around.

So careless had Lin Ho grown that he had walked and leaped at least a li before he recalled his new position. To return to the house of Le-ung was now useless, for however passively disposed that one had formerly been toward a kinsman of his Line, it would be vain for a stranger of formidable hirsute guise and martial mien to appear and claim his bounty. In search of a deciding omen, Lin Ho turned to the inner sleeves of the one whom he now was, and he did not turn in vain. Among a varied profusion that he left for future use, he found a written message. It bore the name of Ku-ei and conveyed an affectionate greeting from one who dwelt beneath the sign of Righteousness Long Established, in the Street of the South Wind, within the city of Tsing-te. Toward Tsing-te Lin Ho now turned his adventuring feet.

It was not until three days later that Lin Ho reached the gate of Tsing-te called the Leper's Gate and entered by it. He had not hastened, for the encounters of the way were not distasteful to his newly acquired temper. Those whom he had greeted with a single upraised finger and an unbending neck acknowledge him obsequiously in turn, and when he spoke to of the appetizing air, food was at once forthcoming. Some made a claim to know him and talked familiarly of things, but though Lin Ho would have welcomed whatever led him to a fuller understanding of himself, he could not pursue the arising conversation to any lucid end. From one it would appear as though he controlled a Hall of Melody; from another that he dealt extensively in yellow fat. A third spoke as if the public lotteries lay beneath his guiding thumb, and yet a fourth cautiously disclosed a secret sign which Lin Ho had some difficulty in ignoring.

"The wealth of analogy possessed by our inimitable tongue admittedly lends itself to a classical purity of style, but it certainly tends toward a baffling ambiguity in the commonplace needs of life," reflected the one involved, and with a gesture of qualified agreement he passed on.

Once in the city he had come to, Lin Ho recognized that his course would be no less devious there. He forebore to ask the way lest it should be of any who might know him, so that it was the time of between-light before he chanced upon the street he needed. It was a deserted part and sombre, and the house that showed the symbol of a golden bar disclosed no window to the passerby. Lin Ho struck the well-protected door, and as no answer came, at once he beat upon it with an iron shoe.

"What errant lord stands there to wake the Seven Echoes with his unbecoming clamour?" growled a contentious voice within, and there came the creak of a shutter being more firmly wedged.

"One who is not wont to be questioned either before or after," replied Lin Ho, stamping with his massive heel upon the door-sill. "Let that suffice."

An iron plate slid open and an eye appeared. Then the defences of the door were drawn.

"Why was the usual sign withheld, chiefling?" protested the one within. "Had I not identified that richly mellowed voice, you might have stamped in vain."

"It was but to try thy wariness, reliant Ying," answered Lin Ho, with a confidence engendered by success. "I am newly returned from a lengthy journey and thought to test the watch you keep here."

"Your mood was ever light and whimsical," retorted the keeper of the door tolerantly, as Lin Ho entered. " 'Ying' indeed! For threescore years plain Wong has served, but 'Ying' is well enough."

"Do any await me now?" ventured Lin Ho, putting this lightness from him with an indulgent nod.

"She of the inner chamber broods expectantly," replied the docile Wong, bending a meaning look. "Furthermore, she laid a charge on me to bid you hasten to her presence."

"Then lead me there," Lin Ho commanded. "Her engaging interest fills me with a pleasurable confusion."

"Lead, forsooth! Surely by this time you must know the way," began the one who sought thus to excuse himself, but:

"I would have it so," replied Lin Ho, touching his efficacious whiskers significantly, and Wong obeyed.

From the nature of her written greeting, Lin Ho did not doubt the depth and weight of Ku-ei's devotion, and he was reconciled to the necessity of reciprocating it to the full when he should have been discovered in what direction the requirement lay. In a chamber hung with bright silks of eight appropriate blends, she was seated on a dais covered with a leopard skin when he entered, and the colours and arrangements of her robes exceeded anything that he had yet encountered. At the same time he could not fail to recognize that her years somewhat overlapped those of the one whose obligations he had assumed, and as regards his natural self, the comparison was even more remote.

"Ten thousand jewelled greetings!" she exclaimed with a dignified absence of restraint that convinced Lin Ho of their mutual affection. "Have you indeed returned?"

"Admittedly," and to impart a fuller flavour to the assurance he added, "What could detain this person's hurrying footsteps from your virtuous and attractive side?"

The one addressed rewarded him with a well-considered glance of approval from her expressive eyes and then indicated by a refined gesture that he should seat himself where they could converse without exertion.

"Tell me, then, of the various adventures of your quest," she commanded graciously, "for these bankrupt ears droop to learn your tidings."

"There is neither length nor width to the limits of that story," replied Lin Ho cautiously. "In which particular direction does your gratifying curiosity extend?"

"That needs no trumpet to proclaim it," was the ready answer. "Have you accomplished this one's freedom?"

"He who would deny it is malformed from birth, nor is father's Line unsullied," exclaimed Lin Ho, deeming his strategy to lie in a judicious evasion until he could satisfy himself more fully; and he would have raised a menacing hand to touch his responsive cheek, had he not doubted whether the gesture would be correct in Ku-ei's presence.

"Your sublime assurance is a never-failing support to the weak-kneed scruples of my own embarassment," confessed the lady Ku-ei gracefully. "There is, however, a time to speak in the flowery terms of poetical allusion and a time to be distressingly explicit. Descending to the latter plane for one concise moment, O my dragon-hearted, state definitely whether you have or have not succeeded in slaying this long-enduring one's offensive and superfluous lord, and in attaching to yourself his personal belongings?"

Alas, it has been truly said, "He who flies on an eagle's back must sooner or later drop off," and Lin Ho was experiencing the justice of the verse. But when it seemed as though he could no longer maintain an equivocal poise, an inspired recollection of Lam-kwong's boast-that he had achieved his enterprise-came back and decided him to accept the hazard.

"With these unworthy hands have your unmentionable sufferings been ended," he accordingly declared, "and here"—at this point he poured out before her feet the varied contents of Lam-kwong's inner sleeve—"here is the evidence that I do not lean on words."

"Truly your little finger is more achieving than the whole of Fang-tso's two-faced body," exclaimed the one beside him exultantly. "Here are his keys and signet and his personal authority as well! Who can any longer doubt that the band will acclaim you its chief and ruler in Fang-tso's stead-and this person has ever gone with the band!"

"It is more than enough to hear such gratuitously expressed words," said Lin Ho courteously; whereupon Ku-ei sang to him a melody expressing her deep emotions.

The next morning, after they had refreshed themselves with food brought in on silver plates by richly attired slaves and had smoked from a single pipe, Ku-ei took up the ring of keys that Lin Ho had brought, and indicating by a suitable movement of her swanlike hand that two bearers should attend with lights, she called that one to accompany her.

"Come," she remarked pleasantly, "it is fitting that you, who are shortly to be the chieftain of the place, should now learn the extent of the treasure that its vaults contain."

"It is an agreeable mark of confidence on your part," replied Lin Ho with polished unconcern, but he followed her down the ladder closely, for there was his own strategy to consider, and he had a far from tranquil stomach about the one called Fang-tso, whom, in an outside manner, he had heard spoken of as comparable with gods in strength and with demons in resentment.

"Doubtless in these remote beneath-parts there will be a store of gold and silver and precious stones which will smooth this person's path very appreciably should it become necessary for him to withdraw in unobtrusive haste," thought Lin Ho as he descended, full of hope and resolution.

The first cave, from its earthen floor up to its arching roof, was filled with rags. There were shreds of every colour, variety, and usage, from the wrappings which the afflicted cast off in obscure byways to the unused scraps such as the charitable bestow on persistent mendicants about their door.

"Nothing is too insignificant to have some use; nothing too ample to be beyond our power of assimilation," remarked the broad-minded Ku-ei with farseeing pride as she contemplated the mass, but Lin Ho was not disposed to linger.

The next cave was filled in a like manner with bones, and it was no less spacious than the first. Again the one who led him spoke encouragingly of the profits of this obscure traffic, but here also Lin Ho pressed forward dumbly, so involved were his feelings.

Jars, cruses, and receptacles in their several grades were the staple of the third enclosure; fragments of torn and rejected paper of the fourth. In immediate succession there were vaults of broken and abandoned umbrellas, of worn-out and cast-off sandals, of unserviceable fans and fabricated flowers.

"This is the very dustbin and the ash-heap of the city's voidance," reflected Lin Ho, as he passed a cave pressed to the full with driftwood, bungs, and halfburned joss-sticks. "What scope is there for one of my distinguished personality in this harbourage of refuse?" Twice or thrice he would have turned had not Ku-ei urged him on, and presently the nature of the commerce changed, and more in keeping with Lin Ho's mood, for here were cloaks and coverings for the head and face, the better sort of garments, and such things as could be worn with fitness. Weapons of all kinds there were and armour both for men and horses, ceremonial flags and wands of office, tablets, and even chairs.

"Yet how comes it," he remarked, "that these things are comparatively few and sparse, while of the cruder stock an interminable line of caves extends?"

"The answer to that requires no lantern to discover, seeing that the brigands of our band scarce number now a dozen, and they old and infirm in service, while of the mendicants a stalwart and increasing tribe responds daily to the roll," explained Ku-ei readily. "But, speaking as one in authority to another, there is no great matter for regret in that. The rewards of mendicancy, if severally minute, are sure, and the market is a never-failing one. The fruits of brigandage are uncertain and difficult to garner; indeed, several of the band are scarcely worth their rice, and had it not been for the local distinction that the gang confers, even the vainglorious Fang-tso would ere this have dispersed them to their homes. But in the end he was always wont to say, 'What we scatter on the brigands we gather up by the mendicants,' and thus and thus it remains."

"Her thoughts are forever set on gain and truckage, and her mind is ordinary in the extreme," reflected Lin Ho. "This one can have no lasting permanence for me."

"And now," continued she whom he thus inwardly denounced, "I have freely shown you all. Will you not, in return, disclose to me the one thing that is lacking?"

"When you open your golden lips, nothing is wanting to complete the circle of felicity," politely replied Lin Ho, his experience not being sufficient to enable him to detect the peril underlying Ku-ei's speech and judiciously to avert the impending sequence. "What pearl is missing from the rope of your desire?"

"Somewhere about these caves is hidden Fang-tso's private store of gold and jewels. That secret you would have extorted from him before you suffered him to Pass Beyond. Let us together now draw them forth and put them to a more appropriate use."

This request threw Lin Ho into a very complicated meditation. It disclosed that such a store did undoubtedly exist, but it led no further on a beneficial line. In the vastness of these caves, to dig at a hazard would be as profitable as to scoop for a grain of salt in a cask of water. And a moment might arise when Lin Ho would not be given the leisure to dig at all. Despite much that had cast a favourable shadow, the Destinies were not really well-arranged, so far.

"Can it be that one on whom this person has lavished so much disinterested affection maintains an ambiguous pose toward her only expressed wish!" exclaimed the lady Ku-ei reproachfully as Lin Ho remained aloof, and despite the restriction of the spot she prepared to indulge in a very extensive display of many-sided agitation.

"Defer your refined exhibition of virtuous annoyance to a more convenient gong-stroke," cautioned Lin Ho. "One in no way concerned approaches," and as he spoke, the sympathetic Wong discovered them.

"Well chanced upon, O chieftain," exclaimed Wong, with obtuse self-satisfaction. "The company of beggars are about to take their stations in the Ways. Would you exchange the usual greeting with them in the courtyard?"

"Let them disperse with an entire absence of ceremonial rite," replied Lin ho, in a tone of no-encouragement. "Dismiss them at their ease."

"Things were very different in the upright days before the coming of the Competitions," muttered Wong supinely. "What next, perchance? Indeed," he added at the recollection, "there is a case in point. One stands about the outer door, protesting to all who pass that he, in spite of every outward sign, is no other than the bountiful Lam-kwong."

"What is this one like?" demanded Lin Ho sharply. "Seeing that you have listened to his feeble pretensions."

"Nay, but I did no more than question him, by warrant of my office," replied Wong stubbornly. "If you indeed are our noble chief Lam-kwong,' I said, be it understood, 'there is a ready test,' and I held out my hand, palm uppermost, toward him. 'For,' I continued, this being the snare, 'that compassion and high-stepping leader suffers no single day to go without a piece of silver passing to my sleeve-and so far today the custom has escaped him.' To this the uncogenial dog made no adequate response and thereby stood exposed. 'Begone, witless,' I cried, justly annoyed, and I beat him about the head and shoulders with my staff. Then, as he put up no defence, I added, 'Wert thou his very likeness and the wearer of his embossed ring, still, after this, thou couldst not be Lam-kwong.' "

"There is more herein than hangs upon a wooden nail, as the saying is," pondered Lin Ho. "Describe him whom you beat," he commanded aloud. "Haply he is some obscure member of my clan who bears a portion of the name."

"He is small and undersized and his expression vile," declared the ready Wong. "His eyes are badly placed and have a complex bend, his forehead insincere, and the sound of his breathing unpleasant to the good-class ear. His dress is meagre and ill-fitting, his —"

"Enough," interrupted the one who recognized himself, although he was little disposed to hear from another what he had spontaneously avowed; "I would sift the essence of this mixture to the dregs. Remove the impostor to a cell apart, and there I will confront him."

"It is as good as done, commander," replied Wong with easy assurance; and he went.

When Lin Ho and Lam-kwong, each in the semblance of the other, encountered, the moment was a concentrated one. The former person had required that all should withdraw to a distance from the cell so that there was none to overhear their words. Lam-kwong was the first actually to speak.

"It is useless to curl your whiskers and blow out your cheeks in this one's direction," he remarked, and he spat familiarly and sat upon the ground.

"Yet how comes it," demanded Lin Ho, "that you, who could not oppose the feeble-minded Wong, should remain unmoved by a display at which the boldest tremble?"

"It is in the nature of things," replied Lam-kwong. "It must be already be known to you that, with so ineffectual a face as this, and all that it implies, subservience and a meek demeanour are foregone. Only one aspect fails to impress me, and that is the one you wear, for it having been my own so long, I cannot but know the hollowness behind. The contentious Wong may indeed be effete, but I am less familiar with his weakness."

"What you say is very reasonable," admitted Lin Ho, "for, from my own angle of observation, I have already experienced something of the kind. Since there is nothing to be gained by acrimony, let us disclose our minds," and he related to the other what-up to a certain point-had taken place.

"It is difficult to see that you are much to blame," admitted Lam-kwong courteously, "and in any case the involvement sprang from this one's shortsighted gluttony. Had he not coveted the onion that you would have eaten, everything might still be going on satisfactorily. were it not for the thought of you and the now unobtainable Ku-ei —" and he fell to pulling out much of his carefully arranged pigtail by the roots.

"Beware of jealousy," advised Lin Ho. "Remember it is written, 'Not everyone who comes down your street enters by your door.' Rather, occupy your mind by disclosing in turn how the High Ones arraigned you before them."

"That is easily explained," replied Lam-kwong, "and they doubtless acted for the best. I must have Passed Upward at a slightly later period than your own distinguished flight, for as I went up I encountered your high-born Shade descending. After having very properly been kept waiting for a lengthy interval, this one was at last called in for sentence. 'Lam-kwong,' pronounced an authoritative voice, 'you have over-ridden the Edict and set the Principles at naught. Your instincts are largely criminal and your tastes obscene. By this last act of violence you have seriously inconvenienced those who keep the books, for it was not intended that Lin Ho should close his record yet. To reward him for the wrong that has been accomplished, he has been returned to an ordinary state of life and given the opportunity to inhabit your body; to punish you in the most offensive way that can be thought of, you also will be sent back to earth, and in place of your own attractive and courageous frame you will be condemned to take up his. In this manner your defiant and salacious nature will be quelled, whether you like it or not.' 'Omnipotence,' I craved, 'before the word goes forth, hear an inserted plea; let the judgment be extinction, the sulphur pit, or being transformed into the likeness of one of the lower insects, but not —' 'Enough; it is too late,' interposed the voice. 'The sentence has been written and the ink is dry.' I then found myself lying among the rocks and suffering excruciating pain from the wound that I had inflicted upon you."

"That is no doubt your angle of regarding what took place, but there is certainly another, more acute," said Lin Ho coldly. "However, being in that barren place alone and with nothing in your sleeve, by what means did you extricate yourself?"

"Throughout the night I lay there and nourished my hurt on the dew that fell. Toward the dawn came one seeking, and presently, from his rancour and the familiar knowledge of his greeting, I recognized in him that ill-conditioned Le-ung of whom you spoke, come to see that his vengeance was complete. 'Much gladness!' exclaimed the misshapen outcast when he discovered me. 'Have you eaten your rice?' 'What little of it there was,' this one replied. 'Is it your humane purpose to supplement it with a further portion?' 'Will another onion serve?' he inquired smoothly, thus to test the limits of what I knew, and to this, seeing no profit in concealment, I replied, 'Assuredly. Being under the direct protection of the gods, its venom will pass from me.' At that, recognizing the frustration of his crafty plan, he disclosed himself without reserve. 'If you lie beneath the bosom of the gods, let them suckle you,' he scoffed. 'See to it that you cross my path no more,' and he drove me on with blows. Feeling incapable of raising a defence, this person fled as best he could, and thenceforward, begging diffidently from door to door, he made his laborious way."

"Yet what can you hope to achieve by coming here?" demanded the one who had usurped him. "Nothing awaits you but a place among the band of mendicants."

"A beggar in these Ways!" exclaimed Lam-kwong, changing colour. "Not even Lin Ho's face would countenance that. This one, before whom all others quailed, save Fang-tso only!"

"Doubtless," was the reply, "but no one fears the bull when he has lost his horns. As regards the one who you have named, I would speak further, for I have cherished an uneasy feeling from the outset that Fang-tso was somewhat beyond our common measure. What passed between you at the last encounter?"

"We two, being on a journey alone and in a desert place, I overcame him by a stratagem, and having securely bound his hands and feet, I sold him into slavery among a passing tribe of barbarian Khins."

"That was shortsighted to the last degree," declared Lin Ho. "Why, he being in your power, did you not then destroy him?"

Lam-kwong hesitated and would have turned the subject aside by a timely stress of coughing, but Lin Ho took him by the ears so that he could not avert his face and thus compelled the truth.

"I would have done so for several reasons," admitted Lam-kwong, seeing evasion useless, "but necessity ordained it otherwise. Fang-tso possessed a certain secret-not of any outside moment, but essential to my plans-and this he would not disclose. In the end I bargained with him on a mutually inviolate oath, covenanting his life in exchange for what he told me."

"This concerns the hidden wealth," thought Lin Ho instantly, "but Lam-kwong has now so little left in life that he will inevitably submit to death rather than disclose the spot. Adroitness alone will serve."

"The private affairs of Fang-tso and of yourself do not engage my mind," he accordingly remarked, with well-sustained no-interest — for he had also acquired Lam-kwong's duplicity as well as that one's valour —"but I would gladly learn what form the wealth took that he must undoubtedly have gathered."

"He has heard nothing so far of Fang-tso's buried hoard," considered Lam-kwong, more easily deceived than he was wont to be. "If I can but secure even a short time alone in the beneath-parts, all may yet be well." Aloud he said:

"He spoke more than once in the past of conveying it for safety to the stronghold of Hsin Foo, a well-walled city in the tranquil south, of which his brother, Ho-ang, is the governor. If there is no evidence of luxury about, this has assuredly been done."

"Assuredly," agreed Lin Ho; "for all this place holds would appear to be the wind-sweepings of the city byways."

"Naturally, to a being of your superior tastes, such commerce would seem gross," ventured Lam-kwong. "Very soon, however, the one before you must turn his reluctant feet upon an outward path, nor has he any trade whereby to earn his rice. If out of the large-stomached forbearance that you must feel for his in every way secondhand condition you would suffer him to carry off in his pack a few poor remnants of unserviceable traffic, he would secure the nucleus of a sordid livelihood, the store would not appreciably be lessened, and your imperishable name would be written in letters of pure gold above the Temple of Munificence."

"What was begun in friendship should not be wound up in malice," assented Lin Ho, taking out the keys that he had retained. "So much as you can bear away upon your shoulder shall be yours."

"I must contrive to divert Lin Ho from accompanying me," argued Lam-kwong; "but to suggest it too abruptly were to raise suspicion." So he remained silent.

"It is necessary to allow Lam-kwong to work in secret, so that he shall find the treasure," reasoned Lin Ho, "though to leave him for no good cause might defeat its end." And he also held his peace.

Together, therefore, they reached the opening to the vaults, and Lin Ho having unlocked the strong door they would have entered, but at that moment the supple Wong appeared.

"Fearless chieftain," exclaimed that officious person, "Tse, of the intrepid mountain band, has ridden in on an urgent rein and seeks your pressing ear."

"It distresses me beyond measure to leave you so inhospitably at the very outset of your laborious undertaking," declared Lin Ho; "but —"

"It grieves me inexpressibly to be deprived of your entertaining society just when I was looking forward to enjoying that felicity for a further period," retorted Lam-kwong; "however —" And with a mutually appropriate gesture of regret they parted, the latter person descending to his task, and Lin Ho unobtrusively locking the door upon him.

The one described as Tse stood at the outer gate and caressed his weary horse. He was of repulsive outline, having one eye only and an ill-cast face, but he seemed upright, and he accorded the sign of deference as Lin Ho approached.

"High commander," was his greeting, "when they should have buried alive this person's mother, in that she was an admitted witch, and your benevolence intervened and spared her, the one who speaks took an oath to discharge the obligation and bound himself thereby."

"Proceed," encouraged Lin Ho, "the occasion may fulfil your pledge."

"We have a saying, 'A word whispered in the ear can carry a thousand li,' and it would doubtless surprise you to know what details of the private doings of you upper ones reach us. Howbeit, that is neither caught on a hook nor shot by an arrow, as the motto goes, but herein lies the gist of it: As this one kept his station by the Gridiron Pass at daybreak, there came a wayfarer who pushed on his falling horse, and every time it stumbled he raised a curse of vengeance against one whom he did not name outright. Hearing this and seeing him, although no name was spoken, your menial hid among the rocks, and when that other one had gone he came past him by a secret way and has conveyed the warning."

"Wisdom has guided your feet so far," acquiesced Lin Ho, well knowing by the indications that the one anathematized was that Lam-kwong whose form he himself wore. "Did the horsemen bear no sign by which he might be known?"

"He showed such marks as disclosed that he was escaping out of bondage," replied the other. "But to the robbers of our tribe his upraised whip-armed hand was a not-forgotten symbol."

"Fang-tso returned!" uttered Lin Ho beneath his breath, and Tse bent his head in token, well content that he had done what he had and that no incriminating name had passed his lips.

"This embodies something of a paradox, for it both complicates and simplifies the matter," remarked Lin Ho, after he had stood awhile in thought. "You spoke of encountering him at dawn and avoiding his passage by a hidden track. Thus and thus at what hour may we expect to greet him with our loyal devotion?"

"According to the various influences, his ever-welcome feet should reach this gate at a gong-stroke before noon," replied the brigand.

"You have done well throughout and have all but repaid your oath. One thing alone remains. Achieve that, and not only what you set out to effect will have been accomplished, but five ingots of the purest will reward your zeal."

"Though one eye is useless, both ears are copiously alert," responded Tse. "Say on, most opportune."

"In the first place, it is necessary that your accomplished and bewitching mother should be here, for my business lies with her."

"That is easily done," was Tse's reply, and from a hidden fold of his ample garment he produced a lean gray rat and sat it upon his hand. "Since the incident referred to, she has generally accompanied me in one shape or another, to be out of harm's way."

"Filial piety carried to such a length deserves to be set to music," declared Lin Ho. "Nothing could be more propitious. Perhaps, in the circumstances, as we are unobserved, she would graciously revert to a condition in which mutual conversation will be on a more normal level."

"That also presents no obstacle." Tse shook off the docile creature down on to the ground, sprinkled a little salt upon it as he pronounced a magic word, and instead of a rat an aged and unsightly hag appeared before them.

"I have heard all that has been said, high excellence," remarked the ancient. "So that it only remains for you to disclose your need."

"To one of your venerable charm it should not be a weighty matter," suggested Lin Ho. "For a certain reason it is necessary that I should leave my ordinary body for a trifling moment and float in the Middle Air at will. Can you ensure me this?"

"If that is all you require," declared the witch, "it will involve no eclipse to contrive it. You have seen that this one is in the habit of changing herself into the similitude of various creatures of the lower part as the necessity arises, and for this one way is as well as another. Drink but a single drop of the liquid in this phial and presently a languor will assail you. Under this influence your unfettered spirit will float away at its own volition, free to enter any untenanted shape that it encounters or to return to its own body as it may desire."

"You have earned a full requital," admitted Lin Ho, counting the silver to the one who stood by expectant. "Yet what period spans the pause between the drinking of the potion and the lethargy descending?"

"It can be rated as the time in which an agile man might walk a li," was the reply. "May a coronal of shining lights illuminate your hazardous path, esteemed."

"May the immortal principles of equipoise be maintained within your venerable body," rejoined Lin Ho, no less agreeably, and they parted.

Had his position been a less ambiguous one, Lin Ho would certainly have called upon the shadows of his immediate ancestors to rally to his aid in their strength at this crisis of his fate. In view of the two-sided nature of his being, however, he deemed this to be inexpedient, so that, instead, he devoted the time that he could spare to perfecting his arrangements. It then wanting about two gong-strokes to the hour of noon, he unlocked the strong door of the caves and found Lam-kwong below.

"A few jars of one kind and another, an assortment of rusty iron, and a sundry profusion of rags wherewith to pack the whole," remarked the one in question, indicating the bale that he had bound with leather. "A scanty cash or two in the marketplace at most, but the limit for these degenerate shoulders."

"The rewards of industry were ever ill-allotted," sympathized Lin Ho. "When you have refreshed yourself at my poverty-stricken board, perchance you will be able to sustain more."

"Alas," replied Lam-kwong evasively, "the honour of sitting at the same table with your distinguished self would be so excessive that I should certainly sink under its weight alone. A crust as I go my uphill way —"

"Should it become known that I allowed so illustrious a guest to depart fasting, the stones of Tsing-te would leap into indignant hands when next I passed," Lin Ho insisted firmly; and because he was unable to withstand, Lam-kwong yielded.

When they were come to a suitable room, set at a distance from the rest, Lin Ho called for a repast of a generous sort, and he also indicated wine. At this Lam-kwong raised a protesting hand.

"For," he said, "we have no certainty of what shall thence arise. Should you in consequence become too self-centered to accompany me, the acrimonious Wong may resist my going with this bale of stuff and delay me at the gate."

"That is a point to be considered," admitted Lin Ho; "but because leprosy exists there is no reason why one should not enjoy the shelter of a tree. Let Wong attend."

"I heard and obey, magnificence," said the voice of the one indicated, as he appeared from around the open door. "Understanding that a feast was being prepared —"

"In due course a portion shall be assigned," interposed Lin Ho. "Meanwhile, feast your ears upon my words. This inoffensive youth will shortly be proceeding on his journey hence. See to it that nothing untoward occurs about our gate. Let neither hand nor foot be stretched in his direction, or I who speak will prune their overgrowth. Furthermore, all that he takes is his by special grace and free of any mulct or usage."

"A line of bowmen shall be drawn up to do him honour," replied the outrageous Wong, unsettled by the thought of the approaching meat; "and muted trumpets sound an appropriate march."

"Take heed lest their office is to play one who shall be nameless toward a hole made in the ground," remarked Lin Ho with sombre freedom. "An added duty, keeper of the latch: when our guest shall have departed, your charge is that none approaches or disturbs me here on any pretext, for I have deep matters to consider. Now let all withdraw so that we may eat negligently."

Lam-kwong being eager to get away, and Lin Ho no less anxious not to delay the parting, their etiquette was neither ceremonious nor involved. The former person, indeed, did not scruple to convey the choicer morsels of each dish to his inner sleeve, and Lin ho, though he must have observed the movement, forebore to challenge him. Presently, turning aside, he filled two cups with a special wine.

"Let us, as the custom is, pledge our mutual enterprises," and he pressed one of the cups upon Lam-kwong.

"There is no reason why we should not do so," replied the other. "Nor would I stand churlishly aloof were it not that I observed your surreptitious hand to linger somewhat about the cup that you have passed to me."

"That is a very one-sided view to take," exclaimed Lin Ho in some annoyance. "If I wished to effect your end, there hangs a trusty sword upon the wall and none to question how or why I use it; though where you unsophisticated death would profit me, the Great Serpent alone knows."

"Be that as it may," argued Lam-kwong, " 'It is too late to learn to swim as the vessel sinks.' "

"However," continued Lin Ho resourcefully, "in order to convince you of your error, I will drink the wine myself," and recovering the cup he did so.

"In that case, there can be no harm in accepting yours," declared Lam-kwong, who was feeling thirsty, and taking Lin Ho's cup he drained it.

"This only goes to show how our natures have become blended, neither maintaining a full share of any quality," remarked Lin Ho. "Thus, although I possess your strength I wholly lack your deftness. The skill with which you bound Fang-tso —"

"That is a very simple matter," contended Lam-kwong, who plainly had not entirely lost his former self-assurance among the milder nature of Lin Ho; "nor, despite your theory, has this hand grown less proficient."

"Such a boast is easily maintained across a peaceful table, and the method even traced in spilled wine on the board, but here are ropes and one who will submit his body to the trial. Bind this person so that his strength cannot surmount the bondage and he will forfeit a resolute-minded mule to bear your load, so that you yourself may walk in comfort."

"There is nothing to be lost in this encounter," reflected Lam-kwong, "since — like the fig tree at Ka-pi's boundary-the fruit is wholly on one side. It would be gratifying to humiliate the egregious Lin Ho, and the mule that he holds out is certainly worth having." He therefore took up the challenge with alacrity, and, Lin Ho submitting, he bound him hand and foot.

"Now, braggart," he announced, "the test is in the balance. Do what Fang-tso failed to achieve and you will deserve a peacock feather in your hat."

Lin Ho strained at the knows but failed to move them. He rolled his great form from side to side and threw his body into sudden jerks, but nothing would avail. Lam-kwong could not withhold derision.

"Already I seem to hear the hoof-beats of the mule upon the outward earth-road," was his taunt. "But give one heave more, princely warrior, and the toils may fly asunder."

"I must not be pressed for time," panted Lin Ho, "for that was not provided. Admittedly the bonds are capably arranged, but, more than that, a strange and sudden lethargy assails me."

"There is certainly a deficient look about your eyes, and your face has gone a very inferior colour," declared Lam-kwong. "Perhaps some inward cord at least has yielded. Would it not be prudent to summon an attendant?"

"Should you do so and I am found thus bound and helpless, your priceless body would be piecemeal-sliced before a word is spoken."

"It is well to bear that in mind," Lam-kwong confessed. "However, I can release you," and he made a movement of advance.

"In that case," came from Lin Ho very faintly, "the mule necessarily fades from the engagement."

"The path of compassion," remarked Lam-kwong, "seems beset with sharp-edged borders." Even as he spoke the magic began to involve him also, and he abruptly lay down on the floor. "This is highly distressing," he contrived to say. "The languor of which you spoke is now sapping my forces. What is this spell that has descended suddenly upon us both?"

Lin Ho made no reply. He was already in the Middle Air, watching his opportunity, and before the limit predicted by the witch had passed, the spirit of Lam-kwong had likewise left his body.

When Lin Ho contrived, through the other person's incapable suspicion, that he should drink the potion first, he recognized that this would give him a sufficient pause of time in which to outwit Lam-kwong. But in this he judged the ill-developed outlaw by a larger helmet than he could ever fill. No sooner did the spirit of Lam-kwong see its own discarded body lying there than it uttered a shriek of triumph and, projecting itself through space, occupied the empty tenement without a thought beyond the present. At the same moment the spirit of Lin Ho came down and resumed its rightful cover.

"Hai!" exclaimed Lam-kwong, displaying his teeth with all his former arrogance. "At last the day of vengeance dawns, and your downfall is achieved, O most treacherous Lin Ho!"

"Doubtless," replied Lin Ho deferentially, as he tore a shred from the bundle by his side and then approached Lam-kwong. "How is it your enlightened purpose to set about it, omnipotence?"

"When I have enjoyed your terrors to repletion, I shall raise my voice, and the guard, finding me thus bound and helpless, your offensive body will be piecemeal-sliced before a word is spoken."

"Perchance," agreed Lin Ho, and with every indication of humility he pressed the pad of cloth into Lam-kwong's slow-witted mouth. "Do not distress your already overtaxed throat, unnecessarily, chieftain. Presently one will enter and release you. Though," he added thoughtfully, "who that one will be and the manner of the release which he effects, it would be hazardous to forecast."

There being nothing now of a helpful nature to detain him, Lin Ho took up the bundle on his shoulder and turned to go, but in response to the message of Lam-kwong's outspoken eye he paused to add farewell.

"Prosperity, mightiest," was his unpretentious message. "Here at last our ways diverge. You remain stretched out in luxury, with a stalwart band of trusty followers responsive to your call. This one sets forth on an unknown path, with nothing between him and penury but the traffic of these simple wares which your forethought has provided. May you live a hundred years and beget a thousand sons!"

Lam-kwong would certainly have said something equally appropriate in reply, but he was unable to release the words that filled his throat, and the occasion faded.

At the gate the covetous Wong eyed Lin Ho's load aslant, but the warning laid on him had been too explicit to be disregarded, and with a cheerful saying the well-intentioned guest passed out and on his way.

At a crossing of the road he paused to listen. In the direction of the house of Righteousness Long Established silence hung like the untroubled surface of a tranquil dream, but from the opposite direction there was a sound that caused Lin Ho to press back into a secluded angle of the wall. Presently one came into sight riding upon a careworn horse which he beat with a naked sword. He was of the height and width of two ordinary persons, his teeth jutting forward, and his face like the rising sun when the day portends a storm. As he passed Lin Ho, he cleared his throat of a curse against one whom he would very soon encounter. It was Fang-tso returning.

The Ambiguous Face Upon the One Found in a Wood and the Effete Ming-Shu's Dilemma

As Kai Lung told the story of the treasure of Fang-tso, the overpowering heat and stupor slowly faded from the day, and when he had made an end of Lin Ho's trials, Hai Shin looked up with a much more alertly sustained air than he had before disclosed.

"Certainly the ingenuity of the diffident Lin Ho enabled him to triumph where less crafty means would have left him in subjection," he remarked. "Yet, this being a relation of the strategy by which you hope to outwit Ming-shu, explain to my deficient mind how the devices that were appropriate here can be shaped to that contumacious rebel's downfall."

"Omniscience," replied Kai Lung frankly, "it would be bootless to interpose a verbal screen between my very threadbare wit and the piercing rays of your all-revealing vision. The strategy involved in the story of Lin Ho was not that by which Ming-shu may be circumvented but the more pressing detail of how to retain you alive to effect our common purpose."

"Have you then," demanded Hai Shin, in a not wholly sympathetic voice, "no plan whereby to reduce Ming-shu, and is the plea on which you held this one from his pious errand merely and empty boast?"

"Exalted," was Kai Lung's just reply, "let your agile mind become an upright balance and weigh this person's claim. The story of Lin Ho was told to a specific end. Up to the moment when he began it, the notoriously incompetent Kai Lung had not so much as heard of that obscure one's being, and each of his successive involvements with its appropriate extrication was contrived from word to word. If, therefore, the one before you can so easily direct the fortunes of a person in whom he has no real concern, is it to be thought that he will fail to involve in destruction the opprobrious Ming-shu against whom he has a very deepset grievance?"

"There is certainly something to be said for that," admitted the over captain, in a more conciliatory manner. "How then will you set about beginning?"

"That will doubtless be revealed to me at the proper moment by the powerful spirits that are interesting themselves on my behalf," replied Kai Lung, assured that he had gained his point. "Even a weed requires congenial soil if it is to fructify, and the one discoursing with you is noticeably short of moisture."

"In any case it is now too late in the day for me to think about self-ending, my lucky hour being past," assented Hai Shin; "so we may as well return to Chi-U together."

"Your favour will protect me as a mantle, and on the strength of our being seen together I shall doubtless be able to arrange for shelter through the night and an occasional bowl of rice without an actual payment in advance," was the storyteller's hopeful forecast. "Tomorrow, at an early gong-stroke of the day, I will present myself before your charitable door with a scheme devised to meet the situation."

"When he specified 'together,' this custom-regarding person did not presume to imply the honour of going hand in hand," remarked the other, with an unworthy note of coldness in his tone. "Here, however, is a piece of money that will support you no less capably," and at the same time he indicated that Kai Lung should follow at a more respectful distance. "Let your leisurely footsteps keep time with a well-digesting mind, Kai Lung."

"Would that your ever-protecting shadow might cover a whole province," was the response, as Kai Lung shouldered his penurious burden.

It was characteristic of Ming-shu's low-minded taste that he had chosen as his stronghold a mountain pass that was inaccessible to force. Although the sides of this retreat were high and precipitous, the gorge in which the repulsive outlaw had pitched his camp was too wide for rocks or offensive messages to be hurled upon him from above, while the only portals that the fastness offered-one to the north and the other to the south-were so narrow that two defenders standing there abreast could resist an army.

"This calls for a more than special effort on the part of my sympathetic ancestors if they are not to see their menaced Line dwindle incapably away," ran the burden of Kai Lung's thoughts when he grasped the position as it then existed, though to Hai Shin, who fanned himself leisurely near at hand, he maintained an unbending face. "Even if no official band exists, pre-eminence," he remarked to the one who stood beside him, "there are doubtless many resolute-minded persons in Chi-U who would not scruple to lend their aid on the side of loyalty and justice once they were assured that it could be prudently achieved?"

"Suffer no derangement of your confidence on that account," replied the over-captain definitely. "In this matter of the extermination of Ming-shu's discordant horde we stand on a common footing and each will play an effective part. If you will but involve these chicken-stomached rebels in headlong flight, I will lead out a sufficiency of trusty henchmen to desecrate their shrines, pillage their abandoned tents, and stab fatally between the shoulders any who tarry too long about the scene of their undoing."

"A concrete plan is in the process of being revealed to me by inner sources, but I must have a substantial force behind, even though their tactics are a purely spectacular function," bargained Kai Lung. "That much is assured?"

"Short of taking part in actual warfare, blood-thirst in its most intensive guise may be safely looked for," was the agreeable reply. "There are not a few among the habitually disinclined of Chi-U who have grown respected and obese in this form of belligerency, they being, indeed, the mainstay of this person and his forerunners in office on those occasions alluded to, when from time to time it has been desirable to anoint the eyes of those higher in authority. Say on, O fount of ingenuity."

"It is no longer possible to doubt that inspiration decides my path," exclaimed Kai Lung as his mind sought backward. "In Ming-shu and the treacherous Shan Tien, opposed as they are by the empty arraignment of authority, it would be inept not to recognize the two hyenas and an effete tiger so presciently foreshadowed by the soothsayer of Ching; while the hollow sovereignty of a devastated province may be fitly likened to a sick cow's bones. This is the very quintessence of prognostication, and all uncertainty must fade and hesitation vanish."

"So long as you are fore-ordained to sweep the despicable rabble from our path, none will gainsay that inspiration gilds your palate," assented Hai Shin freely. "Indicate where we can the fittest lie concealed while you clear out this nest of pirates."

"Thus and thus shall you act," began Kai Lung; and he then proceeded to unfold his plan. "Anything that is still elusive in the way of detail will certainly be communicated by the attendant spirits of my ancestors as the occasion rises."

"It shall be as you ordain; for, 'Tranquillity will roof a house but discord can wear away the foundations of a city,'" was Hai Shin's notable admission. "Lo, minstrel, I go to instruct the apter of the hirelings in the simple parts they have to play."

When, on the morning of the day that next ensued, certain of the rebels were searching the ground that lay between Chi-U and their own ill-conditioned lair, to see if perchance an ambush lurked there (or haply a misdirected duck had opportunely strayed in that direction), the upraised voice of one in torment drew them to a grove of cedars. There, nailed by the ears to a tree of suitable girth and standing, was he who claimed their pity. He had the appearance of being a stranger from one of the Outer-Lands near beyond, for his skin was darker than the wont, his hair unplaited but trimmed in a fantastic spread, and his speech mild though laboured. For covering he wore crude cloth of an unusual pattern, and his manner was sincere and profuse.

"Here is a fitting target for our barbs," cried some of the more illiterate of the band, and they would have shot their arrows forth, but one who wore a mark of stentority upon his sleeve spoke out.

"It is not thus that refined warfare should be waged among polite and civilized communities," he cried, "nor could such an action be logically upheld. Inasmuch as the one before us has been harassed by the foe, it is only reasonable to sustain him. If on inquiry we are dissatisfied with what ensues, he will still be available for the more gravity-removing spectacle of goading blindfold among pits of boiling water, or being pegged down naked on a stirred-up ant hill. In the meanwhile, to have taken him alive increases our repute for zeal."

Accordingly they drew out the spikes that held the stranger to the tree and led him back in triumph to the camp where presently Ming-shu impeached him in his tent.

"Every detail of your two-faced past and discreditable present is recorded on our unfailing systematic tablets," asserted the pock-browed outcast, displaying his aggressive teeth in his usual manner, "so that no defence is lawful," and he continued to throw about the various weapons that were hung around him so as to confuse the other. "Now confess your various crimes unflinchingly."

"Magnificence," replied the supine captive, "your lowly thrall —"

"Slave!" interposed the insatiable Ming-shu.

"Your excrescence," amended he who stood there docilely, "Mang-hi my illsounding name is and I am of the Outer-Land of Kham."

"When I have consumed Chi-U, it is my fixed purpose to reduce Kham to an evil-smelling cinder," vaunted Ming-shu.

"It is as good as done-at the mere opening of your lordly fiery mouth," was the confident admission. "Howbeit, hearing in Kham that the Banners of the Knife had been raised in this our OverState, we held a muster, and the lot fell upon me that I should secretly encroach and extricate the truth."

"Ha!" exclaimed Ming-shu. "Then are you now an admitted spy. Yet herein lies the obvious falsity of what you say, for if they of Chi-U had caught you thus, not your ears but your narrow-minded life would have been forfeit."

"Such was their warmhearted purpose, highest, and without doubt it would so have been done, but as they led my too unworthy steps toward the roasting vat, an eagle, a mole, and a tortoise crossed our path. At this manifestation the augurs dare not proceed until the Books had been opened and the Omens searched, whereupon it appeared that the cause of those who destroyed me would be fated from that moment to be ruined."

"If this is as you say, how comes it, then, that the elders of Chi-U did not set you free, but, rather, insured that you should pass as a captive into our requiting hands?" demanded Ming-shu in slow-witted uncertainty.

"Omnipotence," replied Mang-hi, not without an element of reprehension in his voice, "wherefore? Why, but in the hope that you would fall into the snare and yourself incur the doom?"

At the disclosure of this pitfall, much of the assurance faded from Ming-shu's doglike features, and he caught several flies to gain time before he spoke again, but when he did so it is doubtful if his heart was single.

"A person of your stunted outlook need not be expected to know the Classics," he remarked, "but it is no less truly written, 'One cannot live forever by ignoring the price of coffins,' and your case, Mang-hi, is clearly analogous. Sooner or later in the day that powerful thinker, the Mandarin Shan Tien, will wake from his virtuous slumber, and then your fate will be decided. Meanwhile" —here the insufferable rebel beat upon an iron gong to summon an attendant — "you are, except for the formality of being tried, provisionally sentenced to one of the more distressing forms of ending. You, Li-loe, take charge of the condemned, and your head shall answer for his keeping."

"That, chieftain," grumbled the mulish Li-loe as he led the captive forth, "is the only part of me that can ever answer for the others."

The Concave-Witted Li-Loe's Insatiable Craving Serves a Meritorious End and Two (Who Shall Be Nameless) Are Led Toward a Snare

When they were come to a convenient distance from Ming-shu's tent, Li-loe indicated to Mang-hi that they should sit down upon the ground and converse more at their leisure.

"For," he explained, "it seldom occurs that nothing may be gained by the interchange of mutual ideas. Thus, for instance, it lies with me, as the one who holds the rope about your neck, to lead you along comparatively smooth paths, for the short time that you are destined to be here among us, or to bring you up sharply against the rock-strewn traverses of my disfavour, and this almost entirely depends upon how you treat me from the outset."

"Yet, if I am to be confined meanwhile, awaiting this high lord's pleasure, how shall the merit of ways or rock-strewn barriers affect our intercourse?" inquired Mang-hi simply.

"It is very evident that you are certainly a barbarian from an outer-land," replied Li-loe, with an air of superior culture. "The reference to the prudence of arranging for my priceless friendship was in the nature of a primitive analogy that would have been very well understood by a person having the least experience of refinement. As it is, the only path you seem likely to discover is that leading by very short stages to the public execution ground."

"But surely it ought not to be beyond our united effort to discover a path leading to a discreet seclusion where for a suitable consideration a jar of wine might shortly be obtained to quench our common thirst."

"It is scarcely credible," exclaimed Li-loe, pausing as he scrambled to his feet to regard Mang-hi with a look of wonder, "that one who is so obtuse at grasping a well-meant suggestion should be so alert in going to the very essence of the matter, as it were unaided.... What is the full extent of your negotiable worth, O brother?"

"Those who so charitably released me from the tree have already roughly computed that," explained the prisoner, "but we of the outer-lands are not prone to wear our taels about our sleeves," and by a movement which the covetous Li-loe could not satisfactorily follow, he produced a piece of money from a hidden spot among his garments. "Lead on, thou lodestone of moisture."

When the piece of money had been spent and Li-loe had consumed the greater part of what it purchased, that shameless bandit sought by dropping his voice to a sympathetic cadence to penetrate still further into Mang-hi's bounty.

"Behold," he urged, "between now and the moment of your extinction a variety of things may happen for which you are unprepared but wherein a trusty friend standing by your elbow and furnished with a few negligible coins to expend on your behalf would be worth his weight in jasper. Reflect well that you cannot carry money with you to the Above, no matter how ingeniously it is concealed about your person, and if you delay too long you will certainly incur the fate that overtook the procrastinating minstrel."

"It is good to profit by the afflictions of another," agreed Mang-hi. "Who was he to whom you so dubiously refer, and what was the nature of his failing?"

"Kai Lung the dog's name was, and this person succoured him as though we had been brothers. Yet in the event he played a double part, for having found a cask of wine concealed among some rocks he shunned this one ever after, so that at the last he came to a friendless and a very thirsty end, and his secret perished with him."

To this recital Mang-hi made no response at first, and his head was sunk in thought. Then he looked round with a slowly gathering sense of recognition.

"What you tell me is very unaccountable," he remarked at length, "for in some ambiguous way it is woven into the fabric of a dream that has accompanied me about the Middle Air for three nights past. This concerned a barrel of the rarest grape-juice spirit, as large around as three men's arms could span and very old and fragrant. Furthermore, one whom I now recognize as you accompanied me."

"Proceed, O eloquence, proceed," encouraged the dissolute Li-loe. "Even to talk about a dream like that is better than to exist in a state of ordinary repletion."

"Together we searched for this keg of potent liquid which, be it understood, was hidden from our knowledge...until we at last came to a rocky valley which I now recognize as this."

"This!" exclaimed Li-loe, leaping to his feet to regard the gorge with acquisitive eyes. "And you dreamed the dream three times? Come, O sharer of everything I have, let us explore its length and breadth until you recognize the very rock that guards this treasure. Employ bamboo upon your sluggish mind, O would-be grateful friend; quicken as with a mental goad each fleeting image, and by means of an intellectual crowbar raise the barrier that separates the dimly grasped from the half-forgotten."

"None of these will, alas, avail—" demurred Mang-hi.

"We will, if necessary, regard each point of the landscape from every variety of angle," pleaded Li-loe. "In a dream, remember, you would inevitably be observing what is below from above, whereas now you are regarding what is above from below. Adapt your supple neck to this requisite inversion, comrade. Are we to be duped in the matter of this cask of wine of ours—"

"It fades," rejoined Mang-hi definitely, "in that the keystone of the arch is missing."

"Disclose yourself more fully."

"When, in the progress of the dream, we reached this valley, we were met here by a being of the inner room whose face was like the petal of a perfumed flower. 'Inasmuch as she before you is a mouse,' she said with some significance, 'she creeps through narrow ways and she alone can lead you to the threshold of what you seek.' The vision faded then, but in a camp of warlike men it ensues that no such being—"

"Manlet!" exclaimed Li-loe, casting himself bodily upon Mang-hi's neck and embracing him moistly and repeatedly in the excess of his gladness, "your lips are honey and the ripple of your voice is like the music made by pouring nectar from a narrow-throated bottle. Such a being as the one you designate is here in our midst and this cask of wine of mine is as good as on the spigot."

"Here in this martial valley!" doubted Mang-hi. "Who then is the one whose furtherance we need, and how may we approach her?"

Before committing himself to speech, Li-loe looked round several times and made a displeasing sound among his teeth to imply the need of caution.

"It is necessary to have a thin voice now to escape the risk of a thick ear in these questionable times," was his modulated warning. "She whom you describe fills an anomalous position among us, for though a prisoner here, by balancing Shan Tien's rashness against Ming-shu's caution and setting the infatuation of the one against the disinclination of the other, she not only contrives to sway more authority than the leader of five companies of archers but walks along a muddy road dryshod."

"If she exercises so much rule among the high ones, how can we, being both men of the common sort, hope to engage her ear?"

"Leave that to me," replied Li-loe vaingloriously. "Although I have said nothing so far about it-for, after all, what is it to me who has occasionally held an umbrella above the heads of nobles? —when she was known as the Golden Mouse (whence the analogy of her saying to you) this Hwa-mei relied very greatly on my counsel in all affairs and though she has deteriorated overmuch in the ensuing years she seldom fails, even now, to return my greeting when we encounter.... I will contrive to cross her path when no one else is by, but it may be another matter to persuade her to give ear to an Outland man."

"As to that," replied Mang-hi, "I have thought out something of a plan. I will gather for this purpose a red flower growing on a thorny stem (as she was wearing in the Middle Air), and this you shall give to her saying that the one of whom she has dreamed of late has made his way here to rejoin her. Thus she will be somewhat prepared for what may follow."

"It may serve," admitted the shortsighted Li-loe. "The one thing needful is that you and she should have an opportunity to put your wits together to determine where this cask of mine is hidden."

"Under the fostering eye of your benevolent authority, that should not be beyond our united skill," was Mang-hi's pronouncement.

As Hwa-mei, warned by the sign that Li-loe had been enticed into conveying to her, did not fail to recognize Kai Lung through his disguise it would be obtuse to maintain the figment of Mang-hi's existence any longer. Let it be understood, therefore, that when, later in the day, the summon came and the feeble Li-loe led his prisoner to the tent where Ming-shu and Shan Tien sat in judgment, a movement of the curtain disclosed to Kai Lung that one who was not unmindful of his welfare was there to play a part.

"Before you, high Excellence," deposed the calumnious Ming-shu, "is the ferocious brigand chief, Mang-hi, whom a mere handful of our intrepid guard, while peacefully engaged in gathering wild flowers outside the camp, surprised in the act of lurking in a wood, and made captive."

"They would appear to have picked a very untamed blossom," remarked the gifted Mandarin pleasantly. "Why does his misfitting head still disfigure his unbecoming body?"

"Doubtless to afford your all-discerning brilliance the high-minded amusement of deriding the obscene thing," replied Ming-shu, with his usual lack of refinement. "To a less degree, it has been judged more profitable to hold the dissipated thug as hostage, rather than dispose of him offhand. Subject to that, he is at the will of your unquenchable sense of justice."

"Let the perjured transgressor give his own fictitious account of himself then," commanded Shan Tien, closing his eyes judicially.

"Greatness," replied Kai Lung with a submissive gesture, "my unassuming name and the pacific nature of my journey have already been declared. What more remains?"

"Clearly something, or the contumacious rebel would not be so desirous to conceal it," interposed a melodious whisper from behind the hangings.

"The difficulty obviously arises, criminal, that being a prisoner here before us it is essential that you should have committed something by which you become imprisonable or the whole of our well-thought-out judicatory system falls to pieces." Here the inspired lawgiver placed the ends of his fingers together in an attitude that never failed to convince even the most hardened of his rigorous impartiality. "If your naturally retiring mind is not equal to the strain of disclosing what the offence may be, it will automatically devolve upon this unworthy but incorruptible upholder of the peace to supply it."

"Wellspring of authority," prompted the hidden voice, "in that the recalcitrant clown has no obvious business here, is not the inference that he is an unusually determined spy reasonable?"

"The imputation that you are an alien intruder seeking to acquire military information occurs to us," continued the enlightened official tentatively, "and the crime, punishable as it is with every form of correction from ridiculing your immediate ancestry to extirpating your entire posterity, would serve as well as any. But —"

"As the insensate buffoon has been moving about the district freely, does not the opportunity present itself of enticing him into revealing something of the intentions of our adversary, high intelligence?" came the low-voiced suggestion.

"But in order to incriminate you on this head, felon, it is necessary that something of a definite nature should be allegeable against you. The details of our own impregnable position offer no scope for your admitted talent, but doubtless some interesting points in connection with the obvious weakness of the defences of Chi-U have come under your many-sided notice?"

"All-grasping," was the meet reply, "the one before you is a man of Kham, and Chi-U is of our Over-State. Is it becoming that a vassal should disclose particular information to those in arms against his suzerain?"

"There is marrow in this bone, sublime, if you will but probe it," was the sage monition. "The backward oaf has knowledge that he will not readily disclose."

"That remains to be tested," muttered the credulous Shan Tien, while Ming-shu, ever insistive, cried aloud:

"Who is this scrofulous Mang-hi that he should speak before a provincial governor and one who is destined to lead the all-conquering Knife to victory of what is or is not seemly? Words fade at nightfall, but a branded sign of guilt upon the forehead endures while life remains. Let the irons be made ready."

"Benevolence," entreated the one thus threatened, holding out his hands suppliantly toward Shan Tien, "is it your august will also that the unwitting should endure so oppressive a correction?"

"Maintain your autocratic upper lip, exalted, and you will yet wrest information of great value from the misgiving knave," was the whispered counsel.

"The mortar must harden if the wall is to hold good," replied Shan Tien inexorably. "Look for no flaccidity in this direction, culprit," and from outside there came the sound of dry wood being kindled.

In the ensuing pause the captive raised a fold of the garb he wore and drew it across his face, and for a space of time wherein a man might count a hundred nothing could be heard but the sound of preparation taking place beyond and the offensive beat of Ming-shu's low-class breathing. Then the one arraigned before them bared his face.

"It is contrary to the rites and strict observance of our high rule that the son of a chief's son should submit to this misusage. In our remote upland we have an adage designed to meet most of the contingencies of an ordinary person's everyday experience, and among us it is said, 'If when escaping from a dragon you should meet an advancing demon, turn back again.' " He lowered his hands submissively and bent an appropriate neck. "On this understanding, high puissance, ask what you will."

Shan Tien and Ming-shu exchanged glances of ill-hedged satisfaction and the latter person cleared his self-willed throat.

"In what way is it possible for us to inflict a calamity upon those of Chi-U without incurring any danger to ourselves?" he asked.

Kai Lung thought for a moment, while the others watched him narrowly to see by the changing phases of his emotion whether his disclosure would be sincere.

"The weakness of Chi-U lies in the leanness of its stores, not in any effeteness of its walls or vacillation among its intrepid guard —"

"There is no official band," interposed the stiff-necked Ming-shu.

"Your knowledge is exact," replied Kai Lung, "but each man of the city is trained to bear a part, while at no far-off date a strong company of the Tiger-clad is promised in relief."

"It would be well to make our presence felt before those weak-kneed miscreants impede our footsteps," remarked Shan Tien with well-arranged anxiety.

"Thus and thus," explained Kai Lung. "Tomorrow, about noon, a convoy designed to replenish Chi-U's need will slip through the western gorge. Without knowledge, the chance that you would be there to intercept them is remoter than the clashing of two stars. For this reason there will be no armed guard-for the cities of the route have none to spare. None will be there but the bearers of the loads and drivers, and this you will verify from a distance off before you swoop upon them. Baffled in the hope of this relief, Chi-U will succumb and its gates will open to the summons of your lifted hand. Lo, I have spoken and a noose is round my neck."

"It is well-or it may be," was Shan Tien's pronouncement. "Yet of what does this train consist that it should be worth our while to seize it?"

Ming-shu could not forbear a gesture of despair at the ineptitude revealed by this disclosure, for even to his unbalanced mind it was plain that the essence of the strategy lay in the deprivation of their foe rather than in the replenishing of their own store. He was recalled from this funereal mood by the gross elation of Shan Tien, rejoicing at what Kai Lung unfolded.

"Nothing could be more auspicious, for it is by the lack of these very things that we most suffer: had Chi-U sent a messenger to ask what we would have it could scarcely have been bettered." (From behind the screen a thread of silver laughter gladdened Shan Tien's fatuous heart.) "This project carries."

"How many of our company will the enterprise require?" demanded the more practical Ming-shu.

"Ten or fifteen score of your indomitable horde will baffle every chance of failure."

"That is as the destinies ordain," was Ming-shu's guarded answer; "for although we may protect the fruit we cannot see the roots. But" —here he bent on Kai Lung a sudden look of menace —"they will go armed and alert for guile, and you, Mang-hi, will travel in their midst with a gag closing your mouth and your throat chafed by a rope."

"Yet even then, esteemed, my unfettered mind will be free to dwell on the bright vision of your rising fortune," replied Kai Lung discreetly.

"Ming-shu and Shan Tien were ever of a cast," pondered the Golden Mouse, "and, as with a crystal jar, whatever is poured in at the neck can be seen filling the body. Had one come to them, freely offering knowledge, they would have derided his pretension, but now that they have had the appearance of exacting it by force, demons could not dissuade them. Truly it is written, 'It is easier to put an ox into an egg-cup than for a man full of conceit to receive wisdom.'"

In Which the Position of the Estimable Kai Lung Is Such That He Must Either Go Up or Down

At an arranged gong-stroke after daybreak, three hundred men-one half of Ming-shu's ill-clad force-marched from the rebel stronghold with Kai Lung in their midst, a gag filling his mouth, his arms bound, and a degrading cord (the noisome Li-loe controlling it) hung about his neck. From the opening of a spacious tent, Shan Tien and Ming-shu stood forth to see them pass.

"At the first sign of treachery, pull the noose tight and drive a heavily projected knife well between the uncouth shoulders of the repellent outcast," was Ming-shu's offensive order, and the supine Shan Tien concurred.

"Is it not due to the dignity of your button to be informed how the affair proceeds, mightiness?" enjoined an insidiously alluring voice from the shadow of the tent, and the obtuse Shan Tien coughed several times and arranged his girdle clasp to indicate high-minded unconcern. "Li-loe would prove a speedy runner in any case, so that his absence would entail no loss if there should be a fray. Would it not be in keeping with your special office that he should hasten back, either with or without the repulsive-featured hostage as the outcome may require, when the issue has been cast? This one, at any rate, will know no rest until the success of your strategic-minded foray gladdens her yearning ears."

"It was balanced on my finger-tips to make some such command," replied the egregious Shan Tien, and he beckoned to a lesser chief and spoke as had been said.

When the band had proceeded a short march to the west, Li-loe, under a pretext, dropped behind the rest, and as soon as they were unobserved he removed the gag from the storyteller's mouth.

"It is well enough to talk to you about this wine of mine that we are on the point of recovering," he said, "but it would be even more attractive to hear your assurance in reply. Now, as regards the exact size of the cask, whereof you spoke of three men's encircling arms? In this respect men vary, yet it would be manifestly unjust to take three of only meagre stature. Last night, on the feigning of a jest, I induced three sturdy fellows to join hands, and the full measure...."

In this strain the niggardly Li-loe filled himself with his own imagination until, about noon, the company reached the border of the rocky terraces that overlooked the plains. Here they lurked in hiding, not daring to emerge until the defenceless nature of the convoy was disclosed, and on this hung Kai Lung's fate. When, soon after the appointed time, a column of unarmed men was seen winding along the track that led toward Chi-U, the rebel host raised a loud cry of triumph and launched headlong forward in pursuit. At this display the assemblage of bearers cast down their loads in terror and, without staying to make any retort whatever, fled back to the safety of the intricate passes they had come by. At the same time the horsemen cut loose their charges and urged them incessantly on toward the safety of Chi-U. The effect of the surprise was immediate and complete, and Ming-shu's unbridled horde at once began to take possession of the spoil, for many of the bales had burst open in their fall, and the contents lay scattered.

"There is no longer any doubt as to the success of the foray," declared the under-chief to whom Shan Tien had spoken. "Ordinary warriors Li-loe and Kong are instructed to return without delay and relate to the High One in Command the outcome of the venture. And should the name of the reticent Chan be favourably garnished in the telling," added the one who thus described himself, veiling his voice discreetly, "it will be mutually creative of profitable esteem."

To this the sombre-mannered Kong made no reply beyond a servile flourish of his open hand, but Li-loe (distrustful for his share of what was taken) would have raised a dejected plea had not Kai Lung contrived to pluck him by the sleeve and whisper in his ear.

"It is better to have the chance of netting a turbot than to have already caught a shrimp," was his admonition. "Now, with the camp more or less denuded, is our chance to search unseen." And the ever-craving Li-loe assented.

With about half the distance still untravelled, they came to a cleft cut sharply through the rock, where each must pass alone. It was toward this spot that Kai Lung had shaped his preparation when he had stood in the open space within Chi-U and called for six intrepid men who should be the standard bearers of a righteous cause. "If there be any who have suffered the unforgettable offence at the unclean rebels' hands, now is the opportunity to exact a strict account," he cried, and twelve had answered to the call. "Your names will be extolled in characters of gold," had been his forecast as he made a choice, and to the remnant, "and yours no less than these, for to all a part will in due course be given." These chosen six now crouched beyond the rock and, as Kong and Li-loe passed through, their arms were seized and they were held securely.

"The time for dissimulation has gone by," pronounced Kai Lung in his natural voice, "and this business will shortly assume another colour. Which rogue of the two has the more supple tongue?"

The only reply Kong deigned was to spit in that direction, but the pusillanimous Li-loe fell upon his knees and beat the unyielding earth beneath his two-faced forehead.

"All-conquering," he exclaimed, to the steady clash of his abasement, "there is no evasion to which I would not bend my pliant throat to retain my worthless life. Lay the weight of your authority upon my allegiant shoulders to practically any extent, for I am not yet fit to face the Records."

"Not only will your life be spared, but enough wine will be allotted to float you in a state of bliss through three quarters of each moon-if you but play your part."

"Omnipotence," declared the other freely, "on those terms I am with you in this world and the next."

"Take heed lest you precede me very substantially in both," was Kai Lung's stern menace. "It is not befitting that the more abject is the one who must be spared, but yonder dog would maintain a stubborn end at any hazard. Howbeit, he has had the chance and made a becoming choice.... Now take the uncompromising outlaw to a little space apart, and there, with as slight an inconvenience to his distinguished self as possible, remove his attractive head."

"May your perjured-hearted father grill in Hades to the end of all time and apes void upon the fallen Tablets of your race," was Kong's farewell parting, and he was led away by those who held him.

"It is enough to recall the worthy Yen-tsu in a similar position —'Blessings will cause a strong town to flourish, but the curses of the vicious cannot destroy even a mud-built wall.' " Thus Kai Lung reassured his fellows, and he added, "Let each now move to his appointed task, and aptly."

Leaving one of the band to guard Li-loe, the rest fell to their different parts, and very soon a transformation had been wrought. One brought Kai Lung a special kind of lye in which he washed off his stain, while another combed and drew out his matted hair and trimmed it as a tail. In place of his Outland garb and barbarian trappings, they robed him in everything that Kong had worn and in various ways changed him to that one's likeness. Without much hurt, an appearance of wounds was given to his face and body, and blood was splashed both on him and on Li-loe, though it was not deemed necessary to indicate actual violence toward the latter beyond a spear-thrust through the rear part of his trousers. In the meanwhile, Kong's severed head had been transformed no less completely, a stain deepening its tone, the hair spread out as Kai Lung's hair had been, and the gag forced between his rebellious teeth; nor was the knife withheld to disguise wherein they differed. Thus prepared, the two resumed their journey, Li-loe, at a command, bearing the burden.

"Mightiness," ventured that feeble person when they were alone again, "so far a feeling of unworthiness has sealed these slow-witted lips. Yet have we not been as the two sons of one father, with all things shared in common? Now touching this ambiguous head I bear —"

"Peace, dullard," replied Kai Lung with some dignity; "for you are as you are and it is very necessary that I should now instruct you. Dwell well on this: that when we approach the camp my wounded face will be all but concealed within this bandage, and, for support, my clinging arm will be about your shoulder."

"So long as I am by your side, esteemed, you need fear no stumble."

"So long as you are, I shall not," was the admission. "But should you attempt to disengage yourself or to vary what you are to say, I may, perchance, and in slipping this small but extremely pointed knife that I shall hold beneath my cloak and against your middle ribs will inevitably be thrust forward...."

"Revered," protested Li-loe very earnestly, "I clearly begin to foresee that in whatever tale we are to tell our words will blend together as harmoniously as the two parts of a preconcerted ballad-though between the madness that has assailed you on the one hand and the madness that will certainly assail the bloodthirsty Ming-shu shortly on the other, I see very little likelihood of our song reaching a happy ending."

"That is because you have a weak, deficient mind, or you would have begun to deduce an ordered scheme emerging," explained Kai Lung more kindly. "What was in progress when we left the captured spoil, O witless?"

"That is easily expressed," was the overcast reply. "The sordid-hearted crowd were seizing what they could. The greater part of this by some mischance consisted of the dress and insignia of a strong company of the Imperial guard, and the ragged barefoot crew were triumphantly re-fitting."

"Thus," agreed Kai Lung. "And by a benevolent conjunction of the time and place they will return at nightfall waving the captured banners of authority and wearing the Tiger-garb. How regrettable will be the outcome if Ming-shu, having heard our tale of treachery and rout, should mistake them for the foe and fall upon them in the darkness unaware!"

"Stripling," declared Li-loe with a gathering look of insight, "what I hitherto took to be an empty shell would seem to enshrine a solid kernel. Yet this scheme of yours must proceed along the razor edge of chance so that a single false step will undo it."

"The same path confronts those who oppose us also," replied Kai Lung, "and Ming-shu and Shan Tien are notoriously uncertain on their feet. For the emergencies that may arise, remember that it is better to have an ingenious mind than a belt adorned with weapons."

"In the circumstances, there is nothing unreasonable in disclosing that I too have long nourished a secret ill-bred grudge against the obtuse Ming-shu," declared Li-loe profusely. "We go therefore hand in hand."

"Truly," agreed Kai Lung. "Yet it would be as well not to forget meanwhile that the unusually sharp-tempered knife to which this person has already reluctantly referred will still be grasped in the other.'

When Ming-shu and Shan Tien learned of the crafty snare in which one half of their followers had perished, and had seen the offensive head of the profane Mang-hi, it is questionable which of the two expressed himself with less regard for the pellucid style of the Higher Classics. The former person indeed had become so involved in a complicated analogy based on Mang-hi's remoter ancestors, that Li-loe, urged on by something that he felt rather than saw, did not deem it unwise to interrupt him.

"Thereafter, High Excellences," he continued, "lurking together in a cave we overheard their truculent war lords conferring. 'Let us,' proclaimed the highest in command, 'seek out this misbegotten nest of lepers, led by a weak-kneed upstart, and put them to the sword. The feeble-witted earthworm thus described' (so ran his veracious words, nobilities) 'can no longer have anything beyond a cringing remnant answering to his call. Added to this, we will so contrive that dusk shall mask our coming and the surprise will be complete.' To this they all agreed, rejoicing, and seeing that the assembly had begun, we crept away unseen."

"Wisdom guided your feet," murmured the recreant Shan Tien, after he and his Chief of Military Arrangements had engaged each other in a somewhat lengthy silence. "To retire unobtrusively is often the most unspeakably galling form of contempt with which it is possible to treat a despised antagonist... . The Way is still open to the north, and clad as two wandering pilgrims —"

"Mandarin," interposed Ming-shu, in a not entirely graceful voice, "when the path is slippery, it is safer to go two paces forward than one pace back. In the words of the not wholly felicitous apophthegm, we who stand here banded together are wedged in between the Head Evil Spirit and the illimitable Whang Hai... . Not even a sightless mendicant would take either of us for anything but a steady eater."

"High presence," came a meek but very attractive voice from somewhere unseen, "is it permissible for so small and abject a person as myself to whisper in your weighty ears?"

"Speak," was the grudging assent. "Even a gnat may disclose a hidden point somewhere."

"What is this sudden misgiving that has for the moment eroded your usually large-hearted stomachs?" exclaimed Hwa-mei reliantly. "The valiant Ming-shu was undoubtedly correct when he spoke of the danger of going back, and the ever-prescient Shan Tien was no less inspired when he shrank from the repugnant thought of pressing forward."

"Thus and thus," rose from Ming-shu's acrimonious throat. "That leaves us where we are."

The Golden Mouse struck her symmetrically formed hands together with a refined gesture of well-expressed relief.

"Ming-shu has gone to the very nucleus of the matter and plucked the ill-set words from my all-too-loquacious mouth," she exclaimed. "As he so epigramatically insists, this is the spot on which to meet the uninventive foeman and overreach him."

"Haply," conceded Shan Tien, with a hasty assumption of one of his most telling magisterial bearings, "but the versatile Arranger of Martial Exploits did not carry the analogy to the extent of revealing how the suggested snare is to be effected."

"Truly," agreed Hwa-mei; "your mind is like a crowded storehouse, and unheard-of wisdom drops from your ripe lips in masses... . As the Inscrutable was on the point of saying, the obvious way to baffle the frozen-witted interloper is to turn the looked-for surprise on his part into an even greater astonishment on ours."

"Doubtless," was Ming-shu's sombre comment; "and having thus exposed the farseeing Mandarin's inner thoughts, would it be too excessive a labour to penetrate a little into the rich mine of strategy and disclose a specific detail?"

"The deduction is inexorable," replied Hwa-mei, with a delicately balanced look of gratitude at both together. "When the loathsome marauders seek to creep up at the dusk of evening, they will find nothing interposed between them and success. The paths will be unwatched and the sentry of the gate engaged in the insidious charms of fan-tan elsewhere. Half, perchance, of the offensive crowd will have passed in and be assembled when our one heavily loaded but never so far discharged weapons of assault will be exploded in their direction. At the same preconcerted moment, a chosen band concealed in the heights outside will loosen an avalanche of rock down upon the throng lurking beyond the gate. When the confusion is at its zenith our intrepid host will launch itself against the unsightly rabble, and the distressing affair will be all but over. Was not that, Highest, the trend of your enlightened meaning?"

"Crudely expressed, you have indeed struck the skewer on its business end," admitted Shan Tien, rising. "Where is this person's most terror-inspiring suit of armour laid?"

Ming-shu made no remark, but he left the tent with a settled look, and presently his two-edged voice could be heard emitting orders.

Kai Lung was meanwhile seated on a high place apart, with his arm still cherishing Li-loe's support. Hwa-mei went from point to point, speaking hopefully to the various defenders of the camp and inspiring them to put up a stubborn resistance to the end. Thus the afternoon was worn away and the time of middle light arrived.

The battle of Running Mandarin Valley (as, for some reason, those who were there have designated it) has been so often described in terms of literary perfection that it would be almost profane for this attenuated brush to attempt its details. It is generally admitted that the mutual surprise of all concerned might have been less effective had not certain of Kai Lung's most intrepid followers imperceptibly joined the return throng under cover of the withdrawing light and at the first shock of attack raised the enlightened cry, "Treachery is here at work, and the camp has, in our absence, been carried by assault. Let us retake it at any hazard!" From that stage onward, every man on both sides fought with the tenacity of vampires, so that when Hai Shin, somewhat later, ventured to lead in a hastily collected bodyguard by the neglected northern gate, with the avowed intention of "obliterating as with a sponge the embers of rebellion," he found none to bar his passage. So evenly matched had been the two divisions of the force-the opening assault on the part of the defenders being exactly balanced by the superiority of the weapons with which the others had been refurnished-that from the outset a common extinction was the only logical and possible solution. So harmoniously was this accomplished that in practice every ordinary warrior slew every other ordinary warrior, every stripe-man every other stripe-man, every under-chief every other under-chief, and thus and thus, up to the two overlings of the two contesting sides whose bodies were found locked together in a tiger-like embrace. Ming-shu and Shan Tien alone survived (owing to both remaining), together with Kai Lung, Li-loe, and the Golden Mouse-these latter not being officially "in the vigour" as the melodious phrase of military usage has it. It is owing to this unshrinking demonstration of the Essential Principles of Poise and Equipoise, leading up by an inexorable chain of uncontroversial subordinates to the only rational and conceivable termination, that this otherwise commonplace encounter is so often given as a subject for antithetical treatment in the triennial competitions.

When the last person had been killed on either side, Kai Lung made his way to Ming-shu's tent, confident of coming face to face with that opaque-eyed usurper and of wringing from him an admission of his ill-spent life before he Passed him Upward. For this purpose, the storyteller, who still wore the habiliments of Kong, had removed the covering from his face, and he had rearranged his hair as Mang-hi's had wont to be and resumed some of that warrior's trappings, so that he might the more readily convince Ming-shu of his knowledge of these matters. In this the Destinies intermingled to an unexpected close, for no sooner had the conscience-haunted rebel discovered the one who sought him, standing in the admittedly deceptive light of the great sky lantern outside the open door, than he threw up his abandoned hands effetely and sank down to the floor.

"Behold," he exclaimed in an uncertain voice, "when an event of this sort happens, it is no longer profitable to deny that the one subsiding here has spent a thoroughly abandoned life and practised every sort of infamy. Kai Lung has been pursued relentlessly in the past, and is now doubtless Beyond; Kong has been struck down in this one's service, maintaining a disloyal cause, and he has obviously Gone Up, while Mang-hi's picturesque head is at this moment somewhere about the tent. That these three industriously disposed persons should spare their priceless time to appear in a composite Shape before me pithily indicates that I have nothing more to hope for." Ming-shu accordingly loosened the hold by which he maintained his Constituent Elements together, and his liberated Shadow at once set off toward the Upper Air.

The agreeable-minded Mandarin Shan Tien was never exactly seen again by any actual person. On this account it has sometimes been claimed that he must have thrust himself into the most fiercely contested quarter of the battle and there been cut to pieces. Others, however, contend that, rather than suffer the indignity of so important an official being touched by the profane hands of those inferior to his button, the High Powers had invited him to Pass Above without going through the ordinary formalities of defunction. At a later period, an unworthy rumor was wafted about the province that an impressive personage, who was liable in any emergency to assume a richly magisterial manner, was in the habit of making a desultory livelihood in a distant city by picking up articles of apparent value before the eyes of wealthy strangers. But this can only be regarded as being in the nature of a craftily barbed shaft from the invidious lips of malice.

Wherein the Footsteps of the Two Who Have Induced These Printed Leaves Assume a Homeward Bend

Nothing could exceed the honourable distinction with which Kai Lung was greeted by all classes of those dwelling about Chi-U after the destruction of the rebel host. The lean and expectatious were never weary of professing their readiness to consume an unspecified abundance of rice spirit to the accompaniment of a hope that the storyteller's sinews would be thereby strengthened, and no matter how urgent might be the business on which he was engaged rich merchants did not disdain to stop him repeatedly as he went about the Ways to enjoy the gladness of shaking hands with themselves before him. Some of the actually charitable expressed a willingness, in view of the obviously threadbare state of the one with whom they conversed, to supply him with the needs of life at an appreciably lower rate than was usually imposed on strangers, and on Kai Lung displaying the empty folds of his deficient sleeve, a special edict of the Chi-U Confraternity of Impost Adjusters was issued, permitting him to pass round his collecting bowl at any time without being liable to any humiliating regulations.

But among the marks of approval showered upon Kai Lung, that devised by Hai Shin was perhaps the most delicately arranged of all. In some obscure way unknown to the artless over-captain himself, the valour displayed by Hai Shin, so soon after the taking of the camp that it imperceptibly merged into the forefront of the battle, had reached the ears of his higher-lords in office, and to mark appreciation of the economical way in which he had conducted the affair throughout he had been raised to the position of under-overling, with authority to command six hundred warriors and permission to carry a green silk umbrella when on duty. Not to be outclassed, disinterested persons in Chi-U had suggested to others that to entice the unsuspecting Hai Shin into an assembly and there to weight his sleeve with a bag of silver would be a suitable return for their deliverance.

"So that," explained Hai Shin, on the morning of the day in question, "after this person has recovered from his bereft-of-words surprise, and has suffered the one seated upon a chair to compel acceptance of the tribute, there will ensue a more or less unpleasant gap before dispersing, to be filled up as inoffensively as can be. If, therefore, you could be induced to lift up your always harmonious voice, it would relieve the admitted tension, and at the same time, without any actual outlay to yourself, you would be privileged to witness the interesting ceremony from one of the foremost benches. Nor should it be ignored that early rice, enhanced by a reasonable allowance of health-giving raisin wine, will be provided."

"It suffices," replied Kai Lung gracefully; "and since a virtuous outcome could never have been reached without the miraculous protection of the watchful spirits of my ancestors, the mediocre story chosen for this seasonable occasion will be that which concerns Kin Weng."

The Story of Kin Weng and the Miraculous Tusk

In the golden days of the enlightened dynasty of Ming, a company of artificers who have remained illustrious throughout all later time dwelt about the Porcelain Tower in the city of Tai-chow. Their crafts were many and diverse, there being workers in gold and silver, in jade and precious stones, in wood, in lacquer and the various lustres, even in brass, leather, horn, and material of the cruder sorts on which the resource of their inspired art conferred an enchanting grace, but most highly esteemed among them all were those who carved ivory with patient skill and cunning lore, and of this favoured band Chan Chun was the admitted head.

For many years Chan Chun had dwelt beneath the gilt sign of the Conscientious Elephant, gathering in honours with his right hand and more substantial profits with his left, until nothing that an ordinary person could desire lay outside his grasp; but whether this unvarying prosperity was due to the directing efforts of good Beings, or whether Chan Chun was in reality the sport and laughing stock of malignant Forces, who, after the too-frequent manner of their kind, were merely luring him on through a fancied security to an end which should be both sudden and inept, cannot yet be suitably revealed. Nevertheless, it is aptly written, "The reputation through a thousand years may depend on the conduct of a single moment," and Chan Chun was no magician to avoid the Destinies.

As befitted his position, Chan Chun had an underling whose part it was to do the more menial service of his task. This youth, who bore the unassuming name of Kin and the added one of Weng, had thus long been accustomed to shape the blocks of ivory in their rougher state, to impart an attractive polish to the finished work, and to apply appropriate pigments in cases where the exact representation might otherwise have been in doubt. He also removed the evidence of toil and restored the work-room to a seemly state of order at the earliest beam of light on each succeeding day, sharpened the tools that had been in use and reassembled them on an appointed plan, bargained with tribes of beggars (when they were too numerous to be expelled by force) as to the price of an agreed immunity, intervened with reasonable excuses of Chan Chun's absence, infirmity, or, if necessary, death, before those who presented themselves inopportunely, and the like. Yet, in spite of the admittedly low-conditioned nature of his duties, Kin was of a sincere mind and a virtuous heart. Next to his own immediate ancestors he venerated the majestic carvers of the past, while to Chan Chun he gave an unstinted admiration, hoping that one day he might follow unostentatiously and at a sufficiently respectful distance in his master's well-established footsteps. Every moment that could be snatched from the rigorous execution of his unremunerative task he spent toward the attainment of this end, either in a contemplation of the Symmetrical or by making himself more proficient in the practice of the art, using for this purpose Chan Chun's discarded tools and such scraps of ivory as he himself might legitimately throw away and then pick up again. Thus the seasons passed, but Chan Chun saw in Kin only the one who served his hand.

To the south of Tai-chow lay a dense and pathless forest wherein might be found every kind of wild growth which the soil of that province could sustain. Recognizing in the harmonious contrasts afforded by this profusion all the essentials to a style of classical purity, Kin was in the habit of resorting to these glades in order to imbibe the spirit of their influence. Too often the few hours which the parsimonious usage of the exacting Chan Chun allowed were only sufficient for a meagre contemplation of the outer fringe, but sometimes, on a sufficiently convincing plea or during that one's absence, he was able to secure a longer respite.

It was on one of these occasions, when he had penetrated more deeply into the funereal recesses of the wood, that Kin (guided admittedly by the protecting shadows of his grateful ancestors) reached a grassy place, sufficient in extent to tax the skill of an expert bowman to shoot across. In the opening thus provided stood an ancient pagoda, its pinnacle merged among the branches of a spreading cypress tree, within whose shade a maiden of engaging personality sat in an attitude of graceful unconcern as she arranged her abundant tresses.

"Plainly there are things of which I am yet ignorant, in spite of a lifelong contemplation of the Symmetrical," remarked the youth aloud. "Here are three objects as widely differing in their forms as a maiden, a venerable pagoda and an overhanging cypress tree, yet each fully conforms to the most rigid standard of a classical perfection, nor is any one less harmonious than another. In view of the frequently expressed apophthegm that all Art is a matter of selection, to find these three, among which it is impossible to distinguish any one as pre-eminent, within so narrow a limit as a woodland glade, introduces an element of doubt."

"Such words would seem to indicate a student of the Higher Excellencies," remarked a sympathetic voice, and turning, Kin perceived, close at hand, one who had all the appearance of an elderly philosopher. "Doubtless you are a person of some literary attainment, qualifying for the Competitions?"

"Far from that being the case, my occupation is wholly menial in its ignoble outlook, nor does the future stretch beyond tomorrow's toil," replied Kin freely. "If, therefore, your agreeable condescension sprang from a mistaken cause, do not hesitate to continue our discourse in your ordinary voice."

"On the contrary," replied the other affably. "I would willingly learn somewhat more of your condition. As you unsuspectingly approached this spot, I cast the outline of your destiny according to the various signs you bear. Although I possess certain supernatural powers, I am not really proficient in this branch of geomancy, and my only thought was to obtain a trifling practice, but to my surprise I found that in some unaccountable way the lines of our future destinies converge."

"Even a snail can fly through space if it attaches itself to a dragon's tail," replied the unpretentious Kin, and thus encouraged he willingly laid bare the mediocre details of his threadbare life. When he had finished, the stranger continued to regard him narrowly.

"A noticeable career of one kind or another certainly awaits you, although my meretricious skill is unfortunately not profound enough to indicate its nature," he remarked benignantly. "Rest satisfied, however, that henceforth I shall certainly be exerting my unnatural powers in your direction."

"If the destiny is already assured, might it not more prudently be left wholly to the more experienced Forces?" suggested Kin cautiously. "You have spoken of your efforts in terms which indicate that the outcome of their use may prove somewhat disconcerting to the one on whose behalf they are invoked."

"Do not nourish any misgiving on that account," replied the philosopher with a reassuring smile. "Certain things lie beyond my admitted power, it is true, but I could, without inconvenience, change you into an edible toad or cause a thick growth of fur to cover you from head to food by the exercise of a single magic word. If you doubt this—"

"By no means!" exclaimed Kin hastily. "Your authoritative word puts me entirely at my ease. Yet, as the acrimonious Chan Chun will by this time have discovered an empty stool, I will, without further attrition of your precious moments, walk backward from your lordly presence."

"You have been honourably welcome to my feeble entertainment, which henceforth you can associate with the obscure name of Che-ung," courteously replied the one who thus described himself. "In the meanwhile, frequent indications of my protecting hand will disclose themselves from time to time to preserve intact the silken thread of your remembrance."

"If the suggestion should not be deemed too concise, a favourable occasion will present itself when the one upon whose bounty I depend stands at the gate to welcome my return."

"The occasion is befitting," replied Che-ung graciously, "and a timely intervention shall arise. Furthermore, in order to guide you through the forest by an unknown path-one more suited to your present haste-Fa Ming, the sole remaining blossom of my attenuated tree, shall, in a suitable guise, precede you on your way."

With these auspicious words, the venerable personage raised his necromantic staff and waved it toward the maiden who was still engrossed in the arrangement of her glossy hair before a shield of burnished copper. Immediately she disappeared, and in her place there stood a sleek white bird intent on preening its resplendent plumage. When Che-ung again made a magic sign, however, no further manifestation took place, the shapely creature remaining immersed in a gratified contemplation of its own attractions. A faint line of annoyance corroded the austere smoothness of the philosopher's brow.

"It is one thing to turn ordinary persons into the semblance of apparitions of a different part, but it is quite another to induce them to preserve the unities in their new habit," he remarked, with engaging frankness, toward Kin's ear. Indeed, the graceful being continued to regard itself approvingly from one angle after another, despite the formidable magic projected against it by the persistent waving of Che-ung's all-powerful staff, nor was it until, in an access of engendered bitterness, the painstaking wizard cast the wand violently in its direction that the one whom he had referred to as both the Hand and the Foot of his declining years began to bend her acquiescence toward his wishes. Thenceforward, however, her amiable compliance did not falter, and she hovered continuously before the grateful Kin, guiding him along a secret track so that presently he came clear of the forest at a point much nearer to Tai-chow than the most skillful wood-farer might have found possible.

It was not long before Kin encountered what might reasonably be accepted as a token of Che-ung's sustaining care. In the few hours that spanned his absence from its walls a great caravan of merchants had reached the city from the Outer Lands and filling the narrow Ways with laden beasts and hurrying slaves were even then vying with each other to extol the richness of their wares and to announce at what resort their commerce should be sought. Some, more zealous than their fellows, did not halt to shake out their sandals and partake of tea, but pressed forward without pause to offer the enticement of an early choice to those whose custom they esteemed. Thus it befell that, at the gate before the Conscientious Elephant, a laden camel stood while a sombre attendant, who restrained its impatience by means of a cord passed through its nose, from time to time spoke of his master in terms of unfavourable comparison with the Keeper of the Pit.

"Prosperity attend your gracious footsteps," remarked Kin in polite greeting (and also because he wished to learn their purpose there) as he raised the latch. "The Street called Fragrant is honoured by your restful shadow."

"It would not be, had not a misbegotten planet of the unluckier sort been in the ascendant at the moment of this person's ill-timed birth," replied the attendant darkly. "Is it not enough to have toiled across a self-opinionated desert, leading this perverse and retaliatory daughter of two she-devils by an utterly deficient cord, without being compelled to wait interminable gong-strokes in a parched and plague-infected byway of Tai-chow while the rest-house of the Garden of Musical Virtues spreads its moist allurement but a short span farther to the east?"

"Your well-expressed offence causes the strings of my compassion to vibrate in harmony," replied Kin with genial sympathy. "Who is he who has thus misused your forbearance, and what is the nature of his errand here?"

"Pun Kwan is his repulsive name-may the stomach of a Mongolian crow prove to be his tomb! From the Outer Land of Zam are we come with a varied commerce of the finer sort, so that, forestalling the less grasping of our band, he now seeks to make a traffic of six horns of ivory to the one within."

"My ineffectual voice shall be raised on your behalf," said Kin, as he passed on. "Do not despair; the fiercest thunderstorm is composed of single drops." With this amiable pledge, however, he merely sought to end the conversation in a manner congenial to the other's feelings, for his own hopes did not extend beyond entering unperceived. In this (aided, doubtless, by the exercise of Che-ung's secret magic) he was successful; the upraised voices of two, each striving to outlast the other, revealed that the hazard of the bargain was still in progress in a farther room, and Kin reached his bench unchallenged. Then, as if a controlling influence had been lifted when this effect was gained, Pun Kwan and Chan Chun began slowly to approach, the former person endeavouring to create the illusion that he was hastening away, without in reality increasing his distance from the other, while the latter one was concerned in an attempt to present an attitude of unbending no-concern, while actuated by a fixed determination not to allow Pun Kwan to pass beyond recall. Thus they reached Kin's presence, where they paused, the sight of the outer door filling them both with apprehension.

"It were better to have remained throughout eternity in the remote desert of Eta, leaving these six majestic tusks to form an imperishable monument above our bones, rather than suffer the corroding shame of agreeing to accept the obscene inadequacy of taels which you hold out," declared Pun Kwan with passionate sincerity. "Soften the rebellious wax within your ears, O obstinate Chan Chun! and listen to the insistent cries of those who call me hence with offers of a sack of rubies for six much matchless towers of ivory."

"If," replied Chan Chun, with equal stubbornness, "I should indeed, in a moment of acute derangement, assent to your rapacious demand of a mountain of pure silver for each of these decaying fangs, the humiliated ghosts of an unbroken line of carving ancestors would descend to earth to paralyze their degenerate son's ignoble hand. Furthermore, the time for bargaining has passed, thou mercenary Pun Kwan! For pressing forward in the Ways behold a company of righteous merchants, each proferring a more attractive choice for less than half the price."

Before Pun Kwan could make a suitable reply, there came from beyond the walls the sound of one who raised his voice at dusk. It was the evening chant of the cameleer, who, after the manner of his tribe, had begun to recite his innermost thoughts, in order to purify his mind before he slept. After listening to the various analogies in which his name was blended, Pun Kwan's expression gradually took upon itself a less austere cast.

"It is not unaptly written, 'When the shield is bent the sword is also blunted,' and neither person can reproach the other with a lack of resolution," he remarked pacifically. "Added to this, we are but men of natural instincts and must shortly seek repose."

"Say on," replied Chan Chun, as the other waited for his acquiescence. "Provided that a mutual tolerance is involved, this one will not oppose you with a brazen throat."

"Let the price be thus and thus, so that my unattractive face shall suffer no compression, while your enlarged munificence will be extolled. Then, to the balance of my offer will I yet add another tusk, freely and devoid of charge. By this, each shall seem to have profited at the other's expense though neither is the loser."

"Perchance," assented Chan Chun doubtfully. "But touching that same added tusk —?"

"Admittedly the six cannot be matched, did one comb the forests of the land of Zam and pass all matter through a potter's sieve. Seen side by side with these, any other tusk deceives the eye and takes upon itself an unmerited imperfection. Is it not truly said that what is gold by night —?"

"That which needs so much warming up may as well be eaten cold," observed Chan Chun in a flat-edged voice. "Behold the scales and an amplitude of silver bar. Let the promised tusk appear."

Thus challenged, Pun Kwan withdrew and presently returned with an object which he bore and set before Chan Chun. For an elaborate moment, the ivory carver was too astonished even to become outwardly amused (a poise it had been his previous intention to assume) for the tusk was of an ill-shapen kind never before seen by him or any other of the craft. It was of stunted form, gnarly and unattractive to the eye, and riven by some mishap while yet in growth, so that it branched to half its length.

"What infirmity contorts your worthy sight and deflects your natural vision from its normal line, O scrupulous Pun Kwan?" said Chan Chun indulgently. "This is not a tusk of ivory at all, but doubtless the horn of some unseemly buffalo, or of one of the fabled monsters of the barbarian Outer-World. This should be offered to those who fashion drinking cups from commonplace bone, who dwell about the Leafy Path, beyond the Water Gate."

"Peace, brother," said Pun Kwan approvingly. "To revile my wares is in the legitimate way of fruitful bargaining, but to treat them as a jest assails the inner fibre of one's self-esteem. Is there not justice in the adage, 'Eat in the dark the bargain that you purchased in the dusk?' The tusk is as it is."

Alas, it is truly said, "If two agree not to strive about the price, before the parcel is made up they will fall out upon the colour of the string," and assuredly Pun Kwan and Chan Chun would very soon have been involved as keenly as before had it not been for an unexpected happening. Ever concerned about the smallest details of his art, Kin had drawn near to mark the progress of the conflict and to lend a stalwart voice to his master's cause if Chan Chun's own throat should fail him. Judge, then, the measure of his wonder when in the seventh tusk he at once recognized the essential outline of the fair white bird as it hung poised above the path before him! Misshapen as the ivory seemed for the general purpose of the carver's art, it was as though it had been roughly cast for this one service, and Kin could no longer doubt the versatile grasp of Che-ung's fostering hand.

"A word in your farseeing ear, instructor," he said, drawing Chan Chun aside. "If the six are worthy of your inspired use, do not maintain an upper lip rigid beyond release. This person has long sought to acquire a block sufficiently ill-formed to conceal his presumptuous lack of skill. This now offers, and in return for a tusk of admittedly uncouth proportions he will bind himself to serve your commanding voice for four hand-counts of further moons and ask no settled wage."

"It suffices," replied Chan Chun readily, seeing a clear advantage to himself. "Yet," he continued, with a breath of slow-witted doubt, "wherein, at so formidable an obligation, can this profit you whose reputation does not reach any higher than the knee of a sitting duck?"

"The loftiest mountain rises gradually at first," replied Kin evasively. Then, on the excuse that the auspices of Chan Chun's purchase required the propitiatory discharge of a string of crackers, he withdrew, to venerate his ancestors anew.

As the days went on, it grew increasingly plain to Kin that he was indeed under the care of very potent Forces while the likelihood of Che-ung's benevolent interference from time to time could not be ignored. Despite the unworthy nature of the scanty tools he used and the meagre insufficiency of light remaining when Chan Chun's inexorable commands had been obeyed, the formless block of ivory gradually took upon itself the shining presentiment of a living bird. When any doubt assailed Kin's mind as to the correct portrayal of a detail, an unseen power would respectfully but firmly direct his hand, and on one occasion when, with somewhat narrow-minded obstinacy, he had sought to assert himself by making in inaccurate stroke too suddenly to be restrained, the detached fragment was imperceptibly restored while he slept.

It was at this period of its history that Tai-chow reached the cloudy eminence which marked the pinnacle of attainment among the illustrious arts. The provincial governor, an official of such exalted rank that it entitled him to wear a hat with a yellow feather even when asleep, returned after a long absence to gladden the city with his presence. To indicate the general satisfaction and at the same time allow the prevailing excess of joy to evaporate in a natural and, if it might be, painless manner, mutual feasts were given at which those most proficient in the sonorous use of words were encouraged to express themselves at various lengths upon whatever subject most concerned their minds. When by these humane means the city had been reduced to a normal state of lethargy, the Mandarin Tseng Hung (the one referred to) testified his enduring interest in the welfare of the company of craftsmen by a proclamation and a printed sheet displayed on every wall.

"He is a peacock among partridges, the one who rules our laws, and will doubtless become the founder of a promiscuous line of kings," exclaimed Chan Chun vaingloriously, on his return from the marketplace, where he had listened to the reading of the edict. "Has any rumour of the honour now foreshadowed to the tree of Chan already reached my usually deficient home?"

"None save a resolute collector of the bygone water dues has crossed your polished step," replied the chief one of his inner room. "Is then your fame proclaimed again, thrice fortunate Chan Chun?"

"Not in so many explicit words," admitted the unbecoming Chun, "but the intention cannot be obscured. Thus is the matter set forth at ample length: On a certain agreed day, any craftsman who dwells about Tai-chow, or even within the shadow of its outer wall, be he worker

343

in the finer of the cruder sorts of merchandise, may send the most engaging product of his hand to the Palace of the Lustres, to be there beheld of all. Chief among these will come the enlightened Mandarin Tseng Hung himself, wearing his fullest robe of ceremonial state. After glancing perfunctorily at the less attractive objects ranged about the Hall he will stop with an expression of gratified admiration before the one bearing the sign of Chan Chun and the seal of the Reverential Company of Carvers in the Hard. Then, to an accompaniment of laudatory trumpets, he will announce this to be worthy of the chief reward-and doubtless soon after that retire, leaving the disposal of inferior honours to integritous but needy Younger Brethren of his suite."

"Haply," remarked a shrewd maiden who was present, one who did not venerate Chan Chun, "yet the Wisdom has declared: 'It is easier to amass a fortune in a dream than to secure ten cash by the light of day.' By what inducement do you hope to sway the strict Tseng Hung, thou Conscientious Elephant?"

"The necessity does not arise," coldly replied Chan Chun. "The craft of carving ivory being the most esteemed of all, and this superlative person the acclaimed leader of that band, it inevitably results that whatever he puts forth must be judged to transcend the rest. To decide otherwise would be to challenge the Essential Principles of stability and order."

In an obscure corner of the room, Kin bent his energies upon a menial task.

"You have spoken without limit of those who may compete, esteemed," he said diffidently. "Is it then permitted even to the unassuming and ill-clad to incur this presumption?"

"Save only malefactors, slaves, barbers, official guardians of the streets, and play-actors — who by an all-wise justice are debarred from holding any form of honour-even the outcast leper in the Way may urge his claim." Chan Chun restrained his voice to an unusual mildness, in order thereby to reprove the maiden who had challenged his pretension. "If," he continued benevolently, "it is your not unworthy purpose to strive for some slight distinction within the bounds set apart for the youthful and inept, any discarded trifle from my own misguided hand is freely at your call."

"The compass points the way, but one's own laborious feet must make the journey," replied Kin tactfully. Then, to deflect the edge of his evasion and to recall Chan Chun's mind to a brighter image, he adroitly added: "What is the nature of the chief reward, so that we may prepare a worthy place, revered?"

"That," replied Chan Chun, "is as the one who achieves it may himself decide. The large-hearted Mandarin binds himself by his father's sacred pigtail that on this unique occasion whatsoever shall be asked will be freely given."

"That may aptly be related to the Ever-Victorious!" exclaimed the contumacious maiden with the conciseness of contempt. "Think you, O credulous bone-chipper, that if the one thus singled out should demand the life, the wealth, or even the favoured wife of the Mandarin himself—"

"To do anything so outrageous would clearly proclaim a subverter of authority, and thereby a traitor to the State. A traitor is essentially a malefactor, and as all criminals are definitely excluded from competing it automatically follows that the triumph of this particular one is necessarily null and void and another-more prudent-must be chosen in his stead. Thus justice moves ever in a virtuous cycle, and the eternal proprieties are fittingly upheld. For myself," added the not undiscriminating Chan Chun reflectively, "I shall gladden the face of this remunerative patron by the suggestion of a striking but more or less honorary distinction."

"To surmount above our sign the likeness of an official umbrella would cast a gratifying shadow of authority upon the Conscientious Elephant," remarked the keeper of his hearth.

"Accompanied by the legend: 'Under the magnanimous thumb of the auspicious Tseng Hung,' " amplified Chan Chun. "The hint is by no means concave."

As the day of the great event drew near, the air above Tai-chow grew dark with the multitude of rumours that went up on every side. While many of these were of a gratuitous and inoffensive nature, it cannot be denied that others were deliberately cast abroad by thrifty persons whose business it was to make a profit from the fluctuating hopes and fears of those who staked upon the chances of competing craftsmen. Few were so lacking in respect toward the Omens as not to venture a string of cash in favour of the one who appeared before them in a lucky dream. Even the blind, the deaf and the dumb, and the mentally deficient, lying about the city gates, forecast portents at their leisure in the dust and esteemed from the passerby a predictive word whispered behind a screening hand more than they did the bestowal of a coin in silence.

In the meanwhile, Chan Chun and Kin laboured at their respective tasks secretly and alone—Kin because the only leisure he obtained was in his own penurious room, the former person owing to his cold and suspicious nature. The task upon which he engaged was one wherein ingenuity combined with art to a very high degree. Selecting his purest and most massive block of ivory, he skillfully fashioned it into a measured counterpart of the great Palace of the Lustres as it stood. Then, to continue the similitude, within this outer shell he carved the core into a smaller likeness of the same, perfect in every detail, and thus and thus, down to the seventeenth image —a pygmy Palace no larger than the capacity of a cherry stone but equipped to the slenderest point. Yet despite the complex nature of the task, none of the sixteen smaller Palaces could be removed away from its encircling walls, all the cutting being achieved by Chan Chun through succeeding openings as he worked inward. When this truly elaborate piece should be placed within the walls of the Palace itself, the analogy would be complete, and the craftsman did not doubt that a universal shout of accord would greet his triumph.

On the eve of the day of trial, Chan Chun crept out secretly at dusk and distrusting all hired assistance carried his work by unfrequented ways to the Palace of the Lustres and there deposited it. As he reached his own door again he encountered Kin, who would have avoided him, but Chan Chun was feeling very pleasantly arranged within himself at the thought of his success and would not be disclaimed.

"Within the four walls of the arts, all men are brothers," he speciously declared. "Remove the cloth that covers your achievement, worthy Kin, and permit my failing eyes to be rewarded by a blaze of glory."

"Even a sightless bat would recognize its grotesque imperfections," deferentially replied Kin, and he disclosed what he had done.

For a measured beat of time, Chan Chun continued to observe the ivory bird with outstretched wings that Kin had fashioned, and although the expression of his face slowly changed from one extreme to another he was incapable of speech, until the youth, deeming the matter sufficiently displayed, passed along and into the outer way. Then the master sought a solitary chamber, and having barred the door he sank upon a couch as he exclaimed:

"Assuredly it breathes! I have carved with a chisel but Kin Weng has endowed with life itself."

That same night, at the middle hour of the darkness, the keeper of the door of the Palace of the Lustres was roused from his sleep by a discreet but well-sustained knocking on the outer wall. For some time he did not attach any importance to the incident, but presently the unmistakable sound of a piece of silver being tested against another caused him to regard the matter as one which he should in duty probe. On the threshold he found Chan Chun, who greeted him with marked consideration.

"You alone stand between me and humiliation on the morrow," said the craftsman with engaging freedom. "When the painstaking Mandarin who is to judge our efforts selects as the worthiest that which I have brought, how will his inspired decision be announced?"

"Should your hopes be fruitful, a full-throated herald of the court will cry aloud your name, the sign beneath which you dwell, and the nature of your handicraft. On hearing these, a chosen band outside will repeat the details to the four corners of the earth, to symbolize the far-extending limit of your fame, their voices being assisted when necessary by a company of lusty horners... . And thereupon this necessitous person will seek out one with whom he has wagered on the strength of your renown and claim from him an indicated stake. May your valiant cause succeed!"

"Doubtless it may in its essence, yet none of these things you speak of will ensue-particularly the last," replied Chan Chun. "By an incredible perversity, the written tablet of my name and the like required details has been omitted, so that when the choice is reached no announcement can be made. The vanquished, not slow to use this sordid weapon put within their reach, will claim the forfeit of my chance, urging that by this oversight I have not fulfilled the declared terms, nor can those who hold the balance resist the formal challenge. Not to further this act of iniquity, permit me to pass inside, gracious Pang, so that I may complete what is now lacking."

"This is a somewhat knotty tangle, chieftain," said the keeper of the door uncertainly, "and one not over clear as to which end leads to wisdom. Thus it was laid upon me as a solemn charge, that at the sounding of the eighth gong all further traffic in this matter ceased-that which is within remaining so and all beyond excluded from the Hall. Should it come to the ears of high ones that in this I have failed incapably—"

"It is foreseen," interposed Chan Chun; "nor is your complicity involved. As I awaited you, a piece of silver slipped down from my grasp and rolled some way apart. Should you seek this, your eyes will be upon the ground, and nothing else will come within their sight, while being at a little distance from the open door you will have no knowledge that anyone goes in or out. Thus, with well-chosen words, you can safely take the most convincing oath, nor will your phantom's future state be thereby held to bondage."

"That which has an inlet has an outlet also," assented Pang, now fully reassured, "and your mind is stored with profitable wisdom. Yet," he added thoughtfully, "it is no less truly said, 'As the glove smells, so the hand.' Is the piece of silver which is the basis of this person's attitude lawful in weight and of the stipulated purity?"

"If anything, it exceeds in both respects," affirmed Chan Chun. "Preserve a virtuous front in all contingencies and none can implicate you."

It has already been discreetly indicated that, in a moment of emergency, Chan Chun's character might undergo a downward bend. So far he had been able to withstand all the ordinary allurements placed about his path by evil Forces, none of these being on a sufficiently large scale to make the hazard profitable. But in Kin's great achievement he plainly recognized the extinction of his own pre-eminence among the craftsmen of Tai-chow, for none could miss its matchless qualities nor fail to accord to it an excellence above his own. To this contemplation was added the acuter barb that the one who should supplant him thus publicly was the disregarded underling who served his bench. In this extremity Chan Chun sent forth a message of despair to any passing demon who would succour him and even yet assure his triumph. To his weak and superficial mind, the solution at once offered by one seemed both adequate and just, and he accordingly proceeded to that end. Having gained admission to the unguarded Hall by the stratagem set forth, he treacherously removed the tablet of Kin's name from off its owner's work and placed it on his own, and in like manner transferred his own name and description to the creation of his servant's hand, well knowing that Kin had none to support his claim, and that, if dissent arose, the word of an obscure hireling would not emerge above Chan Chun's outstanding voice. Then, after again exhorting Pang to maintain an unswerving denial in the face of any question, he returned to his own abode, quite satisfied that, in a very difficult manner, he had acted up to the requirements.

On the following day, Chan Chun would have denied to Kin any respite from his task, the better to effect his crafty scheme, but as soon as it was light, a herald passed along the Ways announcing in the Mandarin's name that to mark so special an occasion no one should engage in any work that day, but should, instead, receive a double wage, and so great was the respect now paid to Tseng Hung's slightest wish that, among all those who laboured in or about Tai-chow, there was not one who did not instantly comply.

At the appointed hour every person in the city and the boundaries round who was capable of movement was clustered about the Palace of the Lustres, Chan Chun and Kin among them. The former of the two had purchased a position upon an erected structure draped with red, which enabled him to maintain an attitude of ease and arrogance toward those who stood below, while Kin had been content to arrange himself among the feet of the foremost line. When the Mandarin Tseng Hung appeared, surrounded by his guard, so loud and continuous was the thunder of his welcome that several flashes of lightning are credibly asserted to have followed, owing to an excess of zeal on the part of the conscientious but inexperienced Being who had charge of it. Yet it is to be doubted if Kin heard a sound or saw any of the moving crowd, for at a single glance he plainly recognized in Tseng Hung the agreeable philosopher who had assured him of protection when they encountered in the wood.

In order to avoid the possibly profanity of the Mandarin being actually touched by a person of no distinction the Hall of the competition had not been opened since the preceding night, nor were any allowed to pass within when Tseng Hung entered it, save only his chosen band. To those among the throng outside who were competing craftsmen the moments were as leisurely as the shadow of a branchless pine tree moving across a level sward.

At length one in authority came forth, and at the sight of him, expecting this to be the herald who should proclaim the victor, speech and movement died away, so that the only sounds heard throughout the vast multitude were the indignant cries of those who enjoined silence on each other.

"Let two approach and with downcast eyes prepare to be received into the very presence of the august Tseng Hung himself," announced the messenger, in an all-powerful voice. "These be Chan Chun, who carves ivory beneath the sign of a golden elephant, and Kin, the attendant of his hand. Hear and obey."

"Your wholly abject servant hastens to comply," cried Chan Chun, almost casting himself bodily from the height of the barrier in a passion of servility, and still more in a praiseworthy determination to be there before the inopportune Kin should gain the Mandarin's ear. Kin, however, was no less speedy, although the obstruction of his passage was equally involved, so that, as a result, they reached Tseng Hung and prostrated themselves, each with his face pressed submissively into the dust, side by side."

"Rise, unassuming ones," said the Mandarin, with a consideration almost unparalleled in an official of his illustrious button. "Your attitude, though complimentary in itself and eminently suited to a merely formal greeting, is frankly embarrassing to all in the light of well-extended conversation."

"Your gracious words sink through the back of my threadbare head and reached even this ill-nurtured brain, so clear-cut is the penetration of their brilliance," replied Chan Chun, scarcely daring to obey so indulgent a command.

"Doubtless," assented the Mandarin, with high-born tact, "But owing to the necessary inversion of our respective postures yours unfortunately do not possess a reciprocal capacity. Furthermore," he continued, in a voice from which the sympathetic modulation began imperceptibly to fade, "in order to avoid a very regrettable strain upon your neck, it will be necessary for you to use your eyes adroitly. Raise yourself to a position in keeping with your wide repute, upright Chan, and state deliberately wherein lies the pith of associating your ornate name with a merely shapeless block."

The matter having thus become too intricately arranged to be parried by evasive flattery, Chan Chun raised so much of himself as was permissible and looked toward the indicated point, but at the benumbing sight he dropped back into his original abandonment, partly because his two-faced joints betrayed his flaccid limbs, but also to gain a precious moment in which to rearrange his mind. What he had seen was the foundation of Kin's work indeed, still bearing the tablet of his own name and sign, as he had unostentatiously contrived, but the bird itself was no longer there. So lifelike had been Kin's inspired touch that the sound of one of its own kind calling from outside had enticed the creature into flight.

"In order to give your inventive mind an unfettered range we will pass for the moment from the question of punishing contumely to that of rewarding merit," continued the justice-loving Tseng Hung impartially. "This ingenious but by no means heroic device of concentric palaces, bearing the name and symbol of Kin Weng, the underling of the momentarily indisposed Chan

Chun, must be selected to receive our highest commendation. Let the herald therefore proclaim —"

"Imperishable!" exclaimed Chan Chun, unable any longer to retain between his teeth the bitterness of seeing his achievement surrendered to another, "before the decisive word is spoken, hear the ungilded truth of my misshapen lips. In the darkness of the night, having discovered an essential detail to be lacking from my task, I sought to remedy this. Deluded by the misguiding beams of the great sky lantern, my inept hand must have stumbled in the direction of its quest, and thus the tablet that I would have placed about my work found a resting place upon the immature effort of this inoffensive youth."

"His in like manner?" inquired the painstaking Mandarin.

"Possibly unseen Influences have therein been at work," Chan Chun ventured to suggest. "Or, perchance, one of those concerned about the Hall, seeing a deficiency, removed a tablet from the space where two appeared, and thus and thus—"

"What fits the right foot does not necessarily fit the left," remarked the judicial-minded administrator, keeping a firm grasp upon the intricacies of the case. "Is there present anyone who can bear witness to your cause, Chan Chun?"

"Pang, who guards the outer door of the Palace, will uphold what I have said," replied Chan Chun, endeavouring to convey by a veiled glance toward the one in question a knowledge of the changed necessity pursuing him. "He it was who, measuring the extremity of my need with a forbearing rod, admitted me by night."

"High excellence," declared the inauspicious Pang, thrusting himself forward from among those who were stationed round, "may my lot through all futurity be a rigid arm and an itching sore if my discovering eye beheld the sight or if this forbidding hand was raised to suffer any man to pass," and the slow-witted person who had spoken closed one eye in the direction of Chan Chun in order to reassure him that he would, despite all enticement to the contrary, tenaciously follow his instruction.

"We have heard it said, 'One may ride upon a tiger's back but it is fatal to dismount,' and you, Chan Chun, are experiencing the wisdom of the verse," declared Tseng Hung. "Pang having bent within your hand, it behoves your expectant eyes to seek another prop. Is there, by chance, none who has seen you busied at your task?"

"Alas, omnipotence, I wrought in secret lest another should forestall my plan."

"Can you then implicate Kin Weng with this emblem of contempt and save your own repute by calling to your aid those who have marked it beneath his fashioning hand?"

"I also strove unnoticed at my toil, benevolence, nor has any ever deigned to tarry as he passed my despised bench by," interposed Kin, not thinking it necessary to declare himself more fully until it became apparent on which side justice lay.

"He whose sandals are in holes is seldom asked to ride," quoted Chan Chun, plainly recognizing that disgrace would attract few toward his need. "Having reached the end of my evasion, mightiness, I bend an acquiescent neck."

"In that case your suspense should not be long," was the humane assurance, but before Chan Chun could frame a submissive line a disturbing tumult reached their ears.

"Great Head," cried a captain of the guard which stood outside, entering with an absence of all seemly form, "there is an omen in the sky to justify my uncouth haste. A strange white bird has three times circled round the tower above and now remains suspended in an unnatural poise, high in the middle air."

"All this is according to a definite line of augury and moves toward an end," remarked the Mandarin, leaving his ceremonial chair and indicating that those concerned should follow him. "If this celestial creature can be brought to earth and is found to fit a place upon the sculptured block, Chan Chun's contention need not be gainsaid, while distinction of a very special kind will appertain to Kin. Let the most skillful with his bow stand forth."

"Wang, of the Crouching Leopard Band, display the opening attitude!" commanded an under-captain of the guard.

"A weighty bar of silver for thy needy sleeve if the first shaft shall reach its destined mark," promised Chan Chun in a beseeching voice.

"Begin to prepare to affix a trusty arrow to thy bow in accordance with the prescribed requirements of the distance to be attained," continued the one who led the movements. "Extending a propitious hand in the direction of the upper —"

"All-powerful chief!" exclaimed Kin suddenly, casting himself before the Mandarin's feet. "Suffer the inoffensive bird to live in safety, and the penalty that Chan Chun has merited I will myself incur."

"Rise, estimable Kin," replied Tseng Hung, raising a jewelled hand with a gesture indicating that if his position had been slightly less exalted he might even have extended it; "your orthodox way of behaving in this emergency, together with the low-class efforts of the usurpatory Chan Chun, make any display of judicial alertness on this one's part superfluous. Your humane wish is granted."

"In any case," remarked the morose Wang, as one who forebodes oppression, "the discriminating bird has by this time passed out of the range of a merely human skill. Yet as a certain sum was specified —"

"Revert to your original attitude of unalertness!" interposed the under-captain definitely.

"There is still another page to be unrolled if the Destinies are to be fulfilled as the Omens would direct," declared Tseng Hung expectantly. "Turn your capable eyes toward the west, Kin Weng, and search the path that gives access to our weed-grown park."

"None approaches from your well-kept grounds, esteemed," replied Kin, after a penetrating scrutiny.

Tseng Hung leaned upon his staff and his lips moved, but so discreetly that none save Kin (who saw in this an added likeness to the one called Che-ung) detected the enchantment.

"A vision of the inner chamber lifts your latch and makes as though an unseen power directs her steps this way," reported Kin.

"Is she known to your remembrance?" asked the other, with a warning glance.

"He who dreams by night may also dream by day, but who shall recall the colours of a rainbow that is past?" was the guarded answer.

Tseng Hung signified his approval of this speech and moved his staff again.

"Should any further auspice seem worthy of remark, do not hesitate to free your mind," he said protectingly.

"She holds a white bird in her arms, which nestles there; but to presume a mutual bond from that would not be opportune," replied Kin with ingrained diffidence.

"Do not hesitate; remember that it is better to be the forefront of a rabbit than the hind quarters of an ox; and should the portents be maintained, your pre "But the moment for the final test is now at hand.

eminence is well assured. Come." With this condescending familiarity of speech, the unworldly Mandarin led Kin aside and brought him back into the Hall where they had lately been. Here, without actually concealing themselves, they stooped behind an upright beam of sufficient size, and thus screened they watched the maiden enter. Straight to the spot where Kin's work had stood she bent her feet, then stopped, and there from her releasing hands the bird flew lightly down and, taking up again its exact place upon the sculptured block, passed at once into its former state of lifelike poise.

"Fa Ming, daughter of my all-but-extinct Line, what aim has brought you to this spot?" mildly inquired Tseng Hung, discovering himself to her.

"That is a matter which lies beyond my feeble lore, revered," was the suitable reply. "As I sat in my leafy bower, sewing pearls upon a golden ground, a white bird entered by an open lattice and flew into my heart, filling its empty void. Then with a message that I may not speak, it drew me on and on until, about this place, its purpose being fulfilled, it passed into another state, leaving me tranquil."

"This is the end to which I have striven through many gloomy years, and it was with this in view that I finally applied myself, with varying results, to the questionable arts," remarked the gratified father, beckoning Kin Weng forward and addressing himself chiefly to that one's ear. "At an early age the last enduring offspring of my decrepit trunk came under the perfidious influence of the spirit of an uprooted banyan tree, who, to revenge itself for an imaginary slight in the choosing of her name, deprived her of the gentle and confiding habit which up to that time she had invariably displayed and in its stead imposed its own unbalanced and vainglorious nature. To neutralize this powerful influence was by no means so simple as an ordinary person might at first imagine, as it necessitated gaining a profound knowledge into the customs and circumstances of every kind of Being, Force, Spirit, Demon, Vampire, Shadow, Ghost, and other supernatural creature inhabiting earth, air, water, fire, and wood. The possible intervention of dragons, phoenixes, tortoises, and unicorns, both ill and well disposed, had also to be delicately balanced, and the contending influences of tides, planets, winds, inundations, eclipses, and dynastic changes accurately divined. In addition to these, no single omen, portent, augury, prediction, conjecture, foreboding, dream, or imprecation could safely be ignored. In the end, the movements of practically every living person in Tai-chow and its surroundings were more or less drawn into the scheme, so involved had the counter-charm become, while the discovery that only one short measure of time during the next ten thousand years was really auspicious for the test necessitated an immediate effort."

"Your labours have been both wide and profound, esteemed," remarked Kin deferentially. "Yet," he added, with an admiring glance in the direction of Fa Ming, "were they multiplied by ten their troubles are repaid a hundredfold."

"It will be gratifying if all concerned, Chan Chun specifically, prove as outspoken in their loyalty," replied Tseng Hung.

"Omniscience," reported a privileged slave, entering hurriedly, "the populace has begun to assail the keepers of the routes with missiles of the riper sort, and the official few, fearing a popular rising, await your gracious word to announce that the promised entertainment is not yet commenced or has already reached its determined end."

"Let all be freely admitted whatever their degree, and bid the several troupes of music-players to engage at once in harmony to the full extent of their capacity," commanded the Mandarin resourcefully. "We ourselves will display our interest in the animated scene from the seclusion of this conveniently arranged cupola."

Yet, despite the attraction of his urbane presence, Kin Weng and Fa Ming neglected to accompany him, and when the Hall became thronged with persons of the usual kind, it was noticed by the more observant that the two referred to stood side by side apart, and that, although without having anything in the nature of spoken language to exchange, they did not appear to realize a deficiency.

When Kai Lung had related the story of Kin Weng, there was no longer any reason for his presence, nor, with sincere courtesy, did the hospitable band around make an actual effort to detain him. For a moment he had the low-minded impulse to pass round his penurious bowl, but seeing that those about had become inextricably absorbed in conversing with each other, he judged that the movement would be deemed inept.

Outside the door, Hwa-mei was waiting, an inconspicuous bundle at her feet and a trimmed lantern placed beside it.

"The oppressive closeness of the day has gone, and presently the great sky light will rise to guide our footsteps," she remarked agreeably, after they had exchanged words of an appropriate nature. "Is there any reason why we should not at length return to the scene of our disturbed felicity?"

"It had been somewhat to my purpose that the trivial Li-loe might journey by our side, he having in a measure contributed to our cause," was the rejoinder. "But the witling was ever of a stunted warp, and now he steadily declines to forsake the valley. He is even now there, digging-doubtless for the cask of wine, of which he cannot recognize the no-existence."

"Doubtless," assented Hwa-mei abstractedly, and they set forth together, she still maintaining a grasp upon the slight burden she had brought while sustained the lantern. The lights of Chi-U grew fewer, less, and vanished, and soon even the melodious clamour of hollow wooden drums, resonant stones, bells, gongs, and cymbals that marked Hai Shin's exultant homeward progress sank to a faint tremor on the unruffled air...then, when sought for again, had faded.

"Though it was but a small cottage it was seemly," remarked Kai Lung, with the first trace of sadness. "Alas, this time, cherished, there is nothing but a ruin."

"He who can command four hands shall never lack a shelter," replied Hwa-mei, undaunted; "and that which is built on mutual affection has a very sure foundation. Furthermore, if the roof is low it will be the nearer to our thoughts. Is it not, O storyteller, written, 'When the wine is rich we overlook the gilding in the cup?' "

"Yet the peach tree at the gate has been destroyed, the sown field wasted, and the scanty store put by against the day of drought has melted."

"As to that," said Hwa-mei, with a certain gaiety in her manner, "an adequacy of, as it may be expressed, seed, has by the forethought of the Sustaining Ones been provided for the renewal of our harvest." Thus speaking she untied the knots that bound the cords and then disclosed her burden. It consisted chiefly of a nest of pearls, but there were also eleven other varieties of precious stones and a reasonable amount of both gold and silver. "Ming-shu and Shan Tien would each seem to have provided for the morrow, and since neither of them will have occasion to pass that way again, it would have been inopportune not to search beneath the ground whereon their tents had stood."

"As you must clearly have been led by the guiding spirits of your-no less than my own-ever-to-be-reverenced ancestors, it would, perhaps, be impious not to accept their gift in the way it was intended, and to make use of the various possessions here, in a good sense, gradually," declared Kai Lung, after he had tested a chance selection of the gems and metals. "Inexorable is the saying, 'However much the river winds it finds the sea at last.' "

**Part II
The Great Sky Lantern**

How Kai Lung Sought to Discourage One Who Did Not Gain His Approbation

To Kai Lung, reclining at ease within the lengthening shadow of his own mulberry tree, there came the sound of contest, as of one strong in his assurance, and the melodious laughter of another who derided what he claimed. Recognizing therein the voices of Chi Lin, the son of a rich neighbour, and Precious Jade, the matchless blossom of his own matured years, the discriminating relater of imagined tales slowly closed the scroll upon which he had been absorbed and imperceptibly composed himself into an attitude of wary unconcern-not with the ignoble purpose of listening to their words, but so that he might haply correct any inelegance of style in such stray phrases as should reach his ear.

"Thus and thus, perchance, it has been in the past," came the boast of the vainglorious youth, "but this person will yet pluck a whisker from the tree of Fame, and even hang the silver buckle of his shoe upon the crescent of the great sky light itself."

"Thus and thus indeed!" mocked the answering voice, and a laugh, musical as a stream of pearls falling into a crystal lake, stirred the perfumed air. "Beware of arousing the envy of the sleeping shades of Yao-u and Shun, O thrice-valiant one!"

At the mention of these unapproachable heroes of the past, Chi Lin plainly realized the unseemly loudness of his challenge, for he moved yet closer to the maiden's side and began to express himself very ardently into her well-placed ear. Kai Lung, therefore, had no alternative but to leave the shelter of his arbour and to display himself openly before them.

"Noble youth," he remarked with becoming mildness, "consider, if but for a breathing-space of time, the harmonious balance of the unisons. Trees put forth leaves, flowers, and fruit, each in due season; men-those who attain the honourable appendages of virtuous old age-wear whiskers or moustaches and the like. The analogy was ill-contrived."

"Venerated master," replied the self-confident one whom he had thus arraigned, "in the unsophisticated days of your distinguished minstrelsy, it was doubtless well enough to speak of things as they really were. In our own more exacting times, however, in order to entice the approbation of the throng it is necessary to cultivate a studied obliquity of style. To pluck the natural verdure of a tree foreshadows no romance, but what imagination is not stirred by the bold conception of a doubtless retaliatory arboreal whisker being torn from its parent stock?"

"Alas," admitted Kai Lung sadly, "it is well written, 'The shell must crumble when the young emerge,' and this obsolete person's literary manner is both thin and very fragile."

"Yet," protested Precious Jade, rearranging his pigtail affectionately, "it has been freely said that no arising emergency has ever found you unprovided with an appropriate theme."

"Who stoops to gather fallen leaves when the full fruit bends to meet his hand?" replied the one concerned. "Since your curiosity clearly tends that way, however, doubtless this opportune and intellectually replete young man will relate by what means the great sky lantern came to have that crescent point toward which the latter part of his painstaking ambition is directed."

"The requirement finds me unprepared," stammered Chi Lin, by no means grasping how the exigency had arisen. "It is one thing to speak in terms of classical allusion, as of a 'peach'; it is quite another to have to declare who grafted the stem that bore the analogous fruit and where he performed his Rites. The words were but in the nature of an imagined feat."

Kai Lung shook his head as one not wholly satisfied.

"Before setting out for a distant and barbarian land, it is prudent to learn all that is available of the difficulties to be encountered by the way," he stubbornly contested. "Turn, accordingly, your highly connected footsteps in the direction of my very incommodious summer-house, O Chi Lin, and then, after this deformed and altogether unattractive she-thing of my decaying Line has brought fruit and wine wherewith to sustain you through the ordeal, I will endeavour to remove your lamentable want of historical polish as agreeably as possible."

Chi Lin would have refrained, it having been his intention to pass the time pleasurably in Precious Jade's society without any reference to Kai Lung himself, but this no longer seemed feasible, and he began to recognize that he had conducted the enterprise in a manner unworthy of his all-embracing reputation. Nor did the engaging maiden return with the promised viands, her place being taken by a one-eyed hag of forbidding outline, but the self-opinionated story-teller behaved with all the narrow-minded obstinacy of his unsympathetic tribe, for ignoring his reluctant guest's well-displayed air of no-enthusiasm, he seated himself upon the floor and proceeded leisurely to unfold the story of the alluring Chou.

The Story of the Philosopher Kuo Tsun and of His Daughter, Peerless Chou

In the reign of the patriarchal Chun-kuh a venerable philosopher occupied a position of some distinction outside a small village in what is now the province of Shan Si. This versatile person, Kuo Tsun by name, had an only she-child, Chou, in whose welfare he was sincerely concerned. In view of what happens even within the limits of this badly told and ill-constructed story, it is hardly necessary to describe Chou's outward semblance, beyond stating generally that, for some time afterward, it was not unusual to meet quite elderly ascetics whose necks had become permanently bent from an inability to remove their eyes from her perfection after they had passed.

At that remote cycle of time, matters had not become organized on stable and harmonious bases. A thick mist still obscured the land (for the canals were not yet dug), and under the cover of its malignant shade Forces of various kinds, both Good and Bad, were accustomed to frequent the earth and to reveal their conflicting energies more openly than they are prone to do today. Dragons of all the eleven sorts might be encountered anywhere. Winged snakes and phoenixes disturbed the air. Unicorns and celestial tortoises wrought the omens of their presence, and from numerous water-courses the voices of singing serpents-whose song is like the clashing of melodious rocks-tempted the passerby. The more ordinary manifestations of spectres, ghouls, vampires, demons, voices, presages, and homeless shadows excited no comment. For lengthy periods, sometimes exceeding years, the rain never ceased to fall, the lightning to be displayed, and the thunder to announce the labour of the High Ones, as the Immortal Principle strove to adjust the Eternal Equipoise. Owing to the absence of fixed barriers between the Upper and the Lower Airs many of the deities strayed down upon the earth and formed connections of the more intimate kind with ordinary beings. From this cause it came about that not a few people found themselves to possess qualities for which it was difficult to account, and it was widely admitted that, sooner or later, anything might be expected to come to pass.

Besides being a discriminating sage, Kuo Tsun was also a powerful magician, and it was, indeed, chiefly due to his attainments in the latter capacity that he was able to procure the means of sustenance. While not failing to profit by the circumstance, the contrast was one that did not gladden his understanding.

"It cannot cease to be an element of bitterness in this one's stomach," he was wont to remark, "that while he has no difficulty, as a mediocre wizard, in converting the baser metals into gold, as a farsighted philosopher the full extent of his laborious system has been to reduce Everything to Nothing."

Chou, also, was not entirely devoid of unnatural gifts. She could, she had learned by chance, transform herself into the appearance of certain of the lower creatures, and in moments of concentrated emotion, when words became inadequate, she had the power of breathing out fire. But with a seemly regard for the proprieties she gradually relinquished both these practices, although a few sparks occasionally betrayed the sincerity of her feelings even in later years. Her own she-children enjoyed the same corrosive attribute to a less visible degree, while her he-children walked in the integritous footsteps of their accomplished grandsire. One became a high official, the second a fearless warrior, and yet a third a person of commercial eminence. All possessed the serviceable capacity of transmutation, but the process was rather more protracted and involved than it had been with the inspired founder of their Line, and it was not infrequently discovered that what looked like gold in its creator's hands had in some obscure way assumed another and inferior guise after it had been successfully disposed of.

In the interval of his meditations, Kuo Tsun did not disdain to take Chou indulgently by the hand and to point out to her the properties of things and the inferences that his well-trained mind evolved.

"We perceive," he thus explained, "that by a beneficent scheme of spells and counter-charms when the light goes darkness gradually appears, and when darkness has run its appointed span the light is ready again to take its place. What, however, would occur if by some celestial oversight this had not been foreseen, and both light and dark had been withdrawn together?

The logical mind bends almost double beneath the weight of so dire a catastrophe, but it is inevitable that in place of creatures of the day and creatures of the night the Empire would have become the haunting-place of a race of pale and uncertain ghosts."

"You are all-knowing," replied Chou with ingratiating candour, though it did not escape the philosopher's notice that she was gazing in several other directions as she spoke. "Your eyes see round the corners of the earth, and wisdom distends your waistband."

"Say on," remarked Kuo Tsun dispassionately. "Yet should this appreciation forecast another robe of netted gold, or a greater sufficiency of honeyed figs, let it be cheerfully understood among us that this afflicted person's eyes are practically opaque and his outline concave."

"Your large-handed bounty satisfies in every way," declared Chou openly. "The reference to your admitted powers was concrete and sincere. Something in the nature of an emergency confronts the one before you, and she would lean heavily upon your sympathetic lore."

"In that case," said the magician, "it might be well to have all the support available," and he would have proceeded to trace the Symbols on the ground with his bamboo wand had not Chou's lotus hand restrained him.

"It is by raising your eyes, rather, than bending them upon the earth, that enlightenment will come," she urged. "Behold, before us stretch the disputatious waters of the Ch'hang Ho."

"Truly so," agreed Kuo Tsun; "yet by pronouncing a single word of magic I can, should you desire to cross, cause a solid shaft of malachite to span the torrent."

"The difficulty is not so easily bridged as that," replied Chou, directing an evenly balanced glance of some significance. "What detail on the west bank of the river most attracts your never-failing gaze?"

"Upon a convenient crag there rises the strong tower of Ah-mong, the robber chief," pronounced Kuo Tsun. "At the moment it is rendered doubly conspicuous by the fact that the revolting outlaw himself stands upon the highest pinnacle and waves a two-edged sword in this direction."

"Such is his daily threat," declared Chou with a refined shudder of well-arranged despair, "it being his avowed intention to destroy all people by that means unless this one will consent to grace his inner chamber."

Although Kuo Tsun could not repress an element of surprise that the matter had progressed to so definite a complication without a hint even of its inception warning him, he did not suffer the emergency to impair the broad-minded tolerance of his vision.

"Thus positioned," he judicially remarked, "it might become more prudent to recall the far-reaching length of Ah-mong's sword rather than the distressing shortness of his finger nails, and to dwell on the well-lined depth of his treasure-store to the exclusion of his obvious shallowness of mind."

"Perchance," assented Chou; "yet now direct your all-discerning glance to the east bank of the river and indicate what feature of the landscape most forcibly asserts itself."

"The meagre hut of the insolvent scholar Yan is in itself a noticeable landmark," was the reply. "As the versatile student of the Classics is even now-by a process quite outside this inefficient person's antiquated wizardry-projecting a display of lightning flashes from a revolving wheel, the spot assumes an added prominence."

"The perfection of that device is the assiduous Yan's continual aim," expounded Chou. "This effected, it is his lamentable design to require the diffident one now conversing with you to share his penurious cell, and should this be withheld, to consume the world with fire."

At this further disclosure of the well-spread range of Chou's allurement, Kuo Tsun did not deem it inept to clear his throat of acrimony.

"Doubtless it is as it was designed from the beginning of time," he took occasion to remark, "for had the deities intended that men should control the movements of their lesser ones, instead of two eyes in front, they would have endowed us with sixteen, arranged all round."

"Doubtless," assented Chou with commendable docility, "but pending the arrival of that Golden Age, by what agile display of deep-witted philosophy is it your humane purpose to avert these several ills?"

"The province of philosophy," replied the one who thus described his office, "is not so much to prevent calamities befalling as to demonstrate that they are blessings when they have taken place. The only detail that need concern us here is to determine whether it is more unpleasant to be burned to death or to perish by the sword."

"That is less than my conception of the issue," declared Chou with an indomitable air. "Is then mankind to become extinguished and the earth remain a void by reason of this one's inopportune perfection? Rather than suffer that extremity, she will resolutely set out to conform to the requirements of both positions."

"Restrain your admitted reluctance to jeopardize the race for at least a few beats of time," counselled Kuo Tsun, withdrawing his mind from a deep inward contemplation. "There is an apt saying, 'What appear to be the horns of a bull by night stand revealed as the ears of a mule at daybreak,' and something in the nature of a verbal artifice occurs to me. Exactly what form this should take eludes the second-rate functioning of my misshapen brain at the moment but light will doubtless be vouchsafed... . Had the ill-dispositioned chieftain of an unsightly band of low-caste footpads possessed even the rudiments of a literary style, an eliminating test in the guise of an essay in antitheses might have been arranged between them."

"With so unexacting a trial, the contingency of both succeeding should not be overlooked," interposed Chou decisively.

"Leave that to one who in his youth composed an ode containing seven thousand conflicting parallels, so deftly interwoven that even at the end the meaning had to be sought in what was unexpressed," replied Kuo Tsun with inoffensive confidence. "Putting the same glove on the other hand, if the effete seeker after knowledge known to us as Yan had any acquaintance with the martial arts, a well-contested combat would seem to be the obvious solution."

"Yet, with so formidable an encounter, the possibility of both succumbing must not be ignored," urged Chou with humane solicitude; but Kuo Tsun did not applaud her bias.

"It is easier to get honey from the gullet of a she-bear than sincerity from between the lips of an upright woman," he declared with some annoyance. "If it is neither your will that both should fail nor yet that both should triumph, indicate plainly which of the two permeates your eye with the light of gladness?"

"That," replied Chou modestly, "is as it will of itself appear hereafter; for if it is no part of the philosopher to avert misfortune, neither is it within the province of a maiden to hasten it."

As she made this unpretentious reference to the one who should in the fullness of time possess her, the radiant being took from her sleeve a disc of polished brass to reassure herself that her pearl-like face would be worthy of the high occasion, and she also touched her lips with a pigment of a special tincture and enhanced the slanting attraction of her accomplished eyes. But when she would have fixed at a more becoming angle the jewelled comb of scented wood that restrained the abundance of her floating hair, it slipped from her graceful hand and was lost in the darkness of a crevice.

"Alas," she exclaimed, in an access of magnanimous despair, "that is by no means the first which has escaped my unworthy grasp among these ill-constructed rocks. Would that I might have a comb fashioned of the substance of the great sky lantern hanging there, for then its shining lustre would always reveal its presence."

"Even that shall be accorded if in return you will but share this degraded outcast's sordid lot," cried a harsh and forbidding voice from near at hand, and at the same moment the double-faced Ah-mong disclosed himself from behind a convenient boulder. At the first distant glimpse of Chou he had crept up unheard to gloat his repulsive eyes on her complicated beauty as his obscene habit was. "Entitle me to the low-minded felicitations of my questionable friends, and all the resources of a nimble-fingered band of many-footed mercenaries shall be pressed into your cause."

At this proposal, an appropriate saying, in which a bullfrog sought to pursue an eagle, rose to Chou's lips, but before she had made the unflattering reference Kuo Tsun contrived a sign enjoining caution.

"All this shapes itself to some appointed goal," he whispered sagely. "The actual end of Ah-mong will certainly be painful and obscure, but in the meanwhile it is as well to play an ambiguous role."

"Disclose your mind," continued the obtuse chief robber (the philosopher having, by witchcraft, propelled his speech toward Chou's ear alone); "for the time has arrived when it is necessary to be explicit. On the one hand is raised this person's protective arm; on the other, his avenging sword. Partake of either freely."

"Your amiable condescension retards for the moment the flow of my never really quick-witted offspring's gratitude," interposed Kuo Tsun tactfully. "I will therefore lift my discordant voice on her behalf. Your princely dignity requires that your lightest word be unbending as a wedge of iron, and in this matter my verbal feet are hastening to meet your more than halfway spoken gesture. Procure the slice of heavenly luminary to which allusion has been made, and the ceremonial interchange of binding rites will no longer be delayed."

"The task is so purely a formality that, among broad-minded friends, the suggestion of delay would imply a distorting reflection," remarked Ah-mong, hoping to outwit Kuo Tsun among the higher obscurities. "Let mutual pledge be made on this auspicious spot."

"Friendship," replied the philosopher no less ably, "has been aptly likened to two hands of equal size dipping into one bowl at the selfsame moment. How well-balanced must be the shadow cast by so harmonious a group!"

"May two insatiable demons dip their rapacious claws into your misbegotten vitals!" exclaimed Ah-mong, throwing off all restraint as he recognized his impotence; and with ill-advised precipitancy he seized the alluring form of Chou in his unseemly arms, intending to possess her. In this, however, his feet moved beyond his mental balance, for as his offensive touch closed tenaciously upon her, Chou merged her volition inward and with maidenly reserve changed herself into the form and condition of a hedge-pig. With a full-throated roar of concentrated anguish, Ah-mong leaped back at any hazard, and escaping thus she found safety in a deep fissure of the earth. Not to be wholly deterred in his profane endeavour, Ah-mong then turned upon Kuo Tsun and advanced, waving his voracious sword and uttering cries of menace; but as soon as he was assured of Chou's security, the farseeing sage passed upward in the form of a thin wraith of smoke. Brought up against a stubborn wall, Ah-mong threw a little earth into the air and tried several of the simpler forms of magic, but so illiterate was his breeding that in no single instance could he pronounce the essential word aright, and the extent of his achievement was to call down a cloud of stinging scorpions through which he struggled back to his tower morosely, arraigning the deities and cherishing his scars.

On the day following that of this encounter, Chou walked alone along the east bank of the river. Owing, doubtless, to the involved nature of her meditation, she was within sight of Yan's obscure abode before she realized the circumstance; nor did she at once turn back, partly because so abrupt a movement might have seemed discourteous if he had observed it, but also because she knew at that hour Kuo Tsun would be safely asleep within his inner chamber. As she advanced, slowly yet with graceful ease, the following inoffensive words, sung by one to the accompaniment of vibrating strings, indicated the nature of her welcome.

> "Seated on the east bank of the Ch'hang River,
> I tuned my lute into accord with its dark and sombre waters;
> But presently the sun appearing every ripple sparkled like a flashing jewel,
> And my glad fingers swept the cords in unison.
> So when this heaven-sent one approaches all sad and funeral thoughts are banished,
> And my transported heart emits a song of gladness."

"The time for such palatable expressions of opinion is, alas, withheld," remarked Chou, as Yan stood hopefully before her. "The calamitous Ah-mong has brought things to a sharply pointed edge among our several destinies, and the future is obscure."

"So long as our mutual affection thrives, no time can be otherwise than bright," replied the scholar.

"From a poetical angle that cannot be gainsaid," admitted Chou. "None the less truly is it written, 'Even flowers turn their faces from the sun that sets', and my revered father is, after all, semi-human."

"Are then the feet of the profound Kuo Tsun's regard still reversed in my direction?"

"Detestable as the admission is, your imperishable Treatise on the Constituents of Voidness is his daily execration," acknowledged Chou. "From this cause a line of dissimulation has necessarily arisen, and the one whom we are now discussing regards you merely as a studious anchoret, instead of a rival philosopher of dangerously advanced views."

"How then —?" began Yan, but Chou interposed her efficient voice.

"The situation has slipped somewhat from its appointed base," she explained, "and the commonplace strategy by which I sought to entice his esteem in your direction has taken a devious bend." In a few well-arranged words, the versatile maiden disclosed the unrolling of events, adding, "Foiled in his besotted might, the intolerant Ah-mong now kow-tows to the requirement of a no-less-grasping strategy. He has sent a written message of contrition to the all-wise of my noble Line, admitting that his punishment was just, but holding him to the promise by which he may yet acquire me."

At the mention of his low-conditioned rivals' name, Yan could not restrain a gesture of dignified contempt.

"Admittedly Ah-mong's mouth is large," he declared, "but the seat of his intellect, if indeed it has not completely shrivelled up, must be stunted in the extreme and of less than average quality. Furthermore, so corrupt is his daily life that, even on the most lenient scale, it can have very little longer now to run, while the greater likelihood is that a large adverse balance will have to be expiated by his weak-kneed descendants and all those connected with his effete stock."

"In what way is this-this doubtless just punishment incurred, and how will it affect the lesser persons of his household?" demanded Chou, with a manifest solicitude that Yan was too high-minded to impugn.

"Besides his ordinary crimes," he replied, "Ah-mong is known to do things of which a strict account is kept. These are punished by shortening his span of life here on earth before he goes to the Upper Air, where he will atone for the more serious offences. Thus he has been seen to point repeatedly at rainbows, to tread on grain destined for food, to annoy working bees, and to cook his rice, when pressed for time, over unclean sticks. In the extremity of danger, he hisses noisily between his teeth and he has an offensive habit of spitting up at shooting stars. Taking one thing with another, his end may come at any moment."

"Yet if in the meanwhile he conforms to the imposed condition and procures the comb of silver light, how regrettable would be this one's plight!" exclaimed Chou, restraining with some difficulty an impulse to breathe out her sentiments more forcibly.

"Set your mind at rest on that score," replied Yan with ready confidence. "An obvious solution presents itself to one of philosophical detachment. This obscure person will himself bear off the stipulated spoil, anticipate the sluggish-hearted Ah-mong, and then, despite the shadow of his inimitable theme, hold your honourable unnamed to the performance of his iron word."

"That would certainly smooth out the situation appreciably," agreed Chou with more composure. "But how shall you" —thus corroding doubts again assailed her— "being small and badly nurtured, as well as unskilled in the proficiency of arms, succeed where the redoubtable Ah-mong falters?"

"It is a mistake to judge the contents from the size and fabric of the vessel," declared the one who made reply; "nor is the assurance of the branded label always above corruption."

"Your whisper," admitted Chou with inoffensive tact, "is more far-reaching than the vindictive outlaw's loudest summons. Yet has it not been written, 'Beggars point the way to fortune'?"

"Not less aptly does the saying run, 'No stream is mighty at its source,' " Yan made rejoinder. "Let mere misgivings fade. One who has brought down to you a diadem of stars to set upon your brow" —in this expressive way he indicated the string of poems extolling Chou's perfection that hung about his stinted cell —"is scarcely prone to tremble at the thought of ravishing the moon to deck your floating hair."

"It is enough to have reached this apex," confessed Chou as she listened to Yan's discriminating tribute; "for my unworthy name will shine by the pure light of your renown forever. I am a queen upon a golden throne, and the people of the earth will bow down before my glory."

At an early gong-stroke of the following day, after performing his simple rites, Yan took up his staff and set forth on a journey. Distantly related to him by an obscure tie, there lived in a cave among the higher Quang-ling Mountains an elderly astronomer, Cheng his name and his house the reputable one of Chang, who had chosen that barren and austere retreat out of a painstaking resolve to miss no portent in the starry sphere. To consult this profound recluse was now Yan's object, for who could advise him better than one who had spent the fullness of his life in watching the movements of the Inner and the Outer Upper Paths and the ever-shifting flux of the Beyond? As he passed Ah-mong's stronghold that truculent leper himself appeared upon his rugged tower and began to whet his great two-handed sword meaningly upon a marble hone, purposely throwing the drip in Yan's direction. To this insult the scholar replied with a suitably barbed apophthegm, but beyond this they ignored each other's presence.

Chang Cheng received his kinsman gladly and set out a choicer sufficiency of food and wine than was his own abstemious custom. For some time their conversation was restricted to a well-kept-up exchange of compliments, but gradually the visitor introduced the subject of his ambition. When he fully understood what was required of him, Cheng's face altered somewhat, but he betrayed no resentment.

"In temporal matters involving force or strategy, it is this one's habit to be guided almost wholly by the wisdom of misshapen Mow, the dwarf who waits upon his person," he remarked. "Retire now to your inner recess of the cave, and when the pygmy alluded to returns from gathering herbs, some scheme advancing your felicity may be propounded. In the meanwhile prosperity and an absence of dragon dreams from about your couch attend you!"

"May the planets weave the lucky sign above your virtuous head!" replied Yan with equal aptness, as he lay down upon the floor. Weary as he was with the long exertion of the day, thoughts of Chou and of the great enterprise upon which his feet had entered kept him for many gong-strokes from floating off into the Middle Air, but as long as he remained awake, whenever he raised his head he could hear the distant murmur of thoughtful voices as Chang Cheng and the gnomish Mow discussed the means of his advancement.

The next morning Yan would have questioned Chang Cheng as to the outcome of the discourse, but the astronomer parried the inquiry with a ready saying.

" 'He who can predict winning numbers has no need to let off crackers,' " he made reply. "What we shall offer for your enlargement will be displayed at the proper moment."

"If it is not inopportune, I should like to exchange greetings with one whose cunning stands so high in your esteem," said Yan. "Will the dwarf Mow presently appear?"

"He has set out upon a distant journey," replied the other evasively. "Now that the light is here, let us go forth."

He led the way across the mountains, avoiding the path by which Yan had come, and soon they were in a hidden valley, between two projecting crags.

"These two rocks have been called Jin and Ne-u for a certain reason," remarked the astronomer, stopping midway through the ravine and searching the stunted growth around his feet. "Formerly a learned sorcerer lived about this spot, but he was changed into a rivulet by an even stronger power whom he had rashly challenged."

"Doubtless, in a modified way, he can still disclose his wisdom?" suggested Yan.

"For a time he did so, and the spot had some renown, but during an excessive drought the wellspring of his being dried up and nothing now remains of him. He left a pair of magic iron sandals, however, with the message that whoever could wear them would get his heart's desire."

"Was the accommodating prediction verified?" inquired Yan with heightened interest.

"It has never yet been put to the corroding test. Of those who tried to profit by the charm, many were unable to don the gear at all, and of those who could, none were successful in moving from the spot. Therein the requirement failed."

"If it is not taking up too much of your meritorious time, I would gladly make the essay," declared the student. "Priceless as your help will be, it is as well to remember the saying, 'Do not carry all your meat held on one skewer.' "

"It is for that very reason that I have brought you to this forgotten place," replied Chang Cheng. "Here are the sandals lying among the brake; it only remains for you to justify your boldness."

Yan knelt beside the iron shoes and, with some exertion, adapted his feet to their proportions. The astronomer meanwhile lent his aid, and at a certain point he bent down and pressed the fastenings of the sandals in a special manner. This done, he stood aside.

"The omens of success are not wanting," exclaimed Yan, standing upright but remaining on the spot. "Yet so far my self-willed limbs betray my exalted spirit."

"That is not to be wondered at, seeing that the iron rings, now inextricably fixed about your feet, are chained to the rocks Jin and Ne-u, on on either side," replied Chang Cheng, speaking in an altered voice. "The time has now arrived when sincerity may prevail and subterfuge be banished. This design to bind the planets to your purpose, O shortsighted Yan, is a menace to the orderly precision of the Paths and it cannot be endured. Desist you shall, either by force or by entering into a bond pledging your repose, and the repose of the one whom you most covet, throughout futurity."

"That oath will never be exacted, thou detestable Chang Cheng!" cried Yan, straining at his chains. "Is this then the hospitality of the house of Chang, that was a kennel in the courtyard of my forbears' palace? Or do malignant changelings haunt the Quang-ling heights?"

"It is better to destroy a shrub than to mutilate a tree," stubbornly maintained Chang Cheng, but he kept his face averted from that time onward. "However, as it is truly said, 'If there is meat at one end of a boar, there are sharp tusks at the other,' and so long as you reject the pacific course there still remains the coercive." With these insatiable words the perfidious astronomer took from beneath his cloak a cake of paste and a jar of water and placed them on an adjacent rock. "From time to time further sustenance will be provided, and when you are ready to bring your weak-eyed period of restraint to an accommodating close, a pacific sign will not find me hard stomached. May the All-knowing lead your feet to wisdom."

"May the Destinies guide you even on the edge of a yawning chasm," responded Yan with absentminded courtesy, though on recalling what had passed he added, "and also over."

In such a manner, the inoffensive student Yan came to be abandoned in a narrow pass among the desolate Quang-ling Mountains, with the noontide sun sapping the inner source of his nutrition. Resolved never to relinquish the hope of procuring that which alone would enable him to claim Chou's fulfillment, the likelihood of remaining chained to two massive rocks to the end of all time did not seem to be a far-distant one. Presently, his thirst having become intolerable, he began to drag his reluctant fetters toward the place on which his food was spread when, for the first time, the deep-laid malice of the offensive plot revealed itself. Thrust how he would, the rock was a full half score of paces still beyond his reach.

In setting forth the exploits of Yan toward the attainment of peerless Chou, later historians have relied on a variety of excuses, some even describing the exact Forces that lent him their aid. Yet this should be deemed superfluous, for putting aside the protecting spirits of his devoted ancestors (who would naturally assist in a matter affecting the continuance of their Line), the outcome was one of logical conclusion. Yan's determination to avail himself of the challenge ruling Chou's disposal was unbending and sincere; to do so it was necessary that he should remain in a condition of ordinary existence; and in order to sustain life, food and drink were essential to his being... . Toward sunset, Yan stretched out his hand and drank, and ate, for by the tenacity of his purpose he had plucked up Jin and Ne-u from their rooted fastness and drawn them at his need.

The next morning he awoke, encouraged and sustained. A renewed adequacy of food and water had been placed there in the night but at a yet greater distance from him than the other. By the time that the heat of the day was at its full Yan had reached this also, nor was the exertion so strenuous as before.

For a period of which no exact record has come down, Yan continued chained within the valley of the rocks, and during the whole of that time of inauspicious trial the false-hearted Cheng did not disclose his two-headed face. Yet no day passed without bringing its sufficiency of food, but each time with the labour of obtaining it increased, until Yan had to traverse the entire space of the ravine. This he could at length achieve with contemptuous ease.

When there was no greater test of endurance to which Yan could be there submitted, Chang Cheng one day appeared suddenly before him. Already Yan had striven to escape out of the valley, to confront that most perfidious kinsman eye to eye, but the ill-arranged protrusion of his prison walls had thrown back his most stubborn efforts. Now, with the thwarter of his ambitions and the holder of the key of his release almost within his grasp, a more concentrated range of the emotions lent a goad to his already superhuman power and with a benumbing cry of triumph Yan gathered together his strength and launched himself in Chang Cheng's direction. But in this he was, as the proverb has it, dining off fish for which he had yet to dig the bait, for with a vigour astonishing in one of his patriarchal cast the astronomer easily out-distanced him and, by his knowledge of the passes, gained the upper peaks. Howbeit, Yan had thus reached a higher point along the outward path than he had ever before come to, and the noise of his progress, as he dragged Jin and Ne-u crashing from side to side and destroying in his wake, spread the rumor far and wide across the Province that the Ho-ang Ho had again burst through its banks in flood.

After that, Chang Cheng frequently appeared at this or that spot of the valley, and Yan never failed to extend himself in further pursuit. Each he attained a higher level on the barren slopes enclosing him, but the last peak ever defied his power. Observing this, the astronomer one day cast back an unbecoming word. Under the lash of this contumely, Yan put forth a special effort and surmounted the final barrier. Outside he found Chang Cheng waiting for him no diminution of his former friendship.

"The moment has arrived when it is possible to throw aside the mask forever," remarked the astronomer benignly. "The course of your preparation, Yan, has been intensive and compact, for in no other way was it possible for you to gain the necessary aptitude within a given time."

"Revered!" exclaimed the student, recalling the many occasions on which the venerable must have suffered extremely in his dignity at the hands of the pursuit. "Can it be—?"

" 'Our troubles are shallow; our felicities deepset,' " replied the other, tactfully reversing the adage for Yan's assurance, "and in contemplating your spreading band of sons I shall have my full reward. When I have removed your shackles, be guarded in what you do, for the least upward movement will certainly carry you out of sight into the above."

"Has not the hour arrived when I may put my presumptuous boldness to the test?" inquired Yan.

"It will do so at a certain instant of the night, for then only, out of the millenaries of time, all the conjunctions will be propitious. Should you fail then through instability of mind or tenuity of will, demons could not preserve you."

"Should I fall short in so unflattering a manner," replied Yan capably, "I would not preserve myself, for all hope of possessing Chou would thereby have faded. Yet out of your complicated familiarity with the heavens would it not be possible to indicate some, as it were, sharp-pointed ends for guidance?"

"There are no abbreviated ways across in the infinite," replied the profound, pointing. "There wheels the shifting target of your adventurous flight, and should you miss the mark your fall into the Lower Void will be definite and headlong. Now wrap your inner fibre round my words, for when you wing your upward track through space, the rush of wind and the shrieks of adverse Forces will be so marrow-freezing that all thoughts which are not being resolutely held will be blown out of your mind."

"Proceed, esteemed," encouraged Yan. "My ears stand widely open."

"When you take your skyward leap from off this plateau, my staff will guide your initial course. If your heart is sincere and your endurance fixed, the momentum will carry you into the Seventh Zonal Path, whence your drift will be ever upward. Speak to none whom you encounter there."

"Yet should I be questioned by one who seems to have authority?"

"In that case your reply will be, 'I bear the sword of Fung,' as you press on."

"The reference to a sword being doubtless an allusive one," suggested Yan, with a diffident glance at his shortcoming side.

Chang Cheng moved his shoulder somewhat, thought the gesture was too slight to convey actual impatience, and he raised a beckoning hand.

"At a convenient break in the instruction, it was this ill-balanced one's purpose to disclose the point," he remarked concisely. "However, for strictly literary exigencies, yours is doubtless the better moment. Let the dwarf Mow appear."

"I obey, high excellence," was the response. "Here is the sword, indomitable Yan."

Yan took the weapon that the gnome had brought and balanced it upon his hand before he slung it. Of imperishable metal, it was three-and-thirty li in length and three across and had both an upper and an under edge for thrusting. The handle was of brass.

"I have somewhere seen the dual of this before," thought Yan aloud. "Yet few warriors have come my way."

"It was formerly the sword of that Ah-mong who lived in a strong tower above the Ch'hang River, being both the secret of his power and the reason of his confidence that he should achieve the test," explained Chang Cheng.

"That accounts for much that was hitherto obscure," admitted Yan, and he would have inquired further, but the astronomer's poise did not entice discussion.

"The instant presses on when you must make the cast," declared the latter person, closely watching the movements of the Paths through the medium of a hollow tube. "The Ram's Horn has now risen and lying off its sharper end there winks a yellow star. Mark that star well."

"I have so observed it," declared the student.

"That is the Eye of Hwang, the Evening Star, and on it your right foot must come to rest. For the grounding of your left you must take Pih, the Morning Star, for that conjunction alone will form the precise equilibrium on which success will hang. Now gird yourself well and free your mind of all retarding passions."

"I call upon the revered shades of my imperishable ancestors to rally to my cause," exclaimed Yan boldly. "Let none refrain."

Chang Cheng indicated that the moment had arrived and held his staff at the directing angle. Mow, who knew the secret of the clasp, cast off the shackles. Then Yan, gathering together the limits of his power, struck the ground a few essaying beats and fearlessly cleft upward. Freed of the clog of Jin and Ne-u there was no boundary to his aspiration, and he sang a defiant song as he spied the converging lines of spirits string out to meet his coming. When he looked back, the earth was a small pale star between his ankles.

The details of Yan's passage through the Middle Space would fill seven unassuming books, written in the most laborious style, but wherein would Chou reside? One only spoke of her-Ning, who with a flaming faggot at his tail, as the Supreme had ordered, was threading his tormented path among the Outer Limits. Ning had the memory still of when he dropped to earth to become enamoured of the slave girl Hi-a, and as he shot past Yan he threw back a word of greeting and would have liked to have Chou's allurement described in each particular.

Let it suffice that "Between He and Ho," as the proverb goes, Yan gained his celestial foothold and bending forward cut with the sword of Fung what he deemed a sufficiency out of the roundness of the moon. As he withdrew, a shutter was thrown open and a creature of that part looked forth.

"What next!" exclaimed the Being rancorously when he saw what Yan had taken. "Truly does this transcend the outside confine! Is it not enough that for a wholly illusory crime this hard-striving demon is condemned to live upon an already inadequate sphere and burnish its unappetizing face for the guidance of a purblind race of misbegotten earthlings?"

"There will be so much the less for you to keep polished, then," replied Yan competently. "Farewell, moon-calf. I bear the sword of Fung."

"May it corrode the substance of the hand that holds it!" retorted the other with an extreme absence of the respectful awe which Yan had relied upon the charm producing. "Hear a last word, thou beetle-thing: that once in each period of measured time I will so turn this lantern which I serve that all may see the havoc you have wrought, and suffering the loss of light thereby will execrate your name forever."

Yan would have framed an equally contumacious parting had the time at his disposal been sufficient, but remembering Chang Cheng's warning, and his design being now accomplished, he turned and set a downward course back again to earth.

His purpose would have been to embrace the astronomer affectionately, but, owing to some deflection which lay outside his sphere of control, he found himself transported to the region of his own penurious dwelling. As he neared it, he saw Kuo Tsun, who led Chou by the hand, approaching.

"To confess a former error is but a way of saying that exactness now prevails beneath one's housetop," remarked the philosopher auspiciously. "Owing to the misreading of an obscure symbol, this deficient person had hastily assumed that matter originally began as Everything and would ultimately resolve into Nothing. He now perceives, on a closer perusal of your inspired thesis, that its first principle was Voidity and that the determinate consummation will be a state of Allness. In addition to being a profound thinker, you have competently performed an exacting test." Here Kuo Tsun pushed Chou slightly forward. "Take, therefore, the agreed but wholly inadequate reward."

"Yet, munificence," urged Yan diffidently, "this meagre hut —"

"All that has been suitably provided for by the justice-loving System under which we live," replied Kuo Tsun. "During your absence the decayed Ah-mong has Passed Beyond, and as he was a person of notoriously corrupt views, I invoked my own authority as District Censor to depossess his band and to transfer your Ancestral Tablets to his tower."

"It is well said,'The Destinies arrange, but under our benevolent government all must help themselves,' " commented Yan, after he had suitably referred to Kuo Tsun's undoubted service. "Yet what was the nature of Ah-mong's Out-passing?"

"An element of vagueness shrouds the incident," confessed Kuo Tsun. "It is whispered that a mysterious Being appeared among the gang and, proving his authority by the precision of his knowledge, enticed Ah-mong with the promise of a certain way to gain his end. This consisted of a stupendous javelin, having bamboo cords attached, with which it was proposed to transfix the great sky light and draw it down to earth. In the end the contrivance proved so unwieldy that the cloven-footed outlaw fell upon its point from off his lofty tower, when there was none but the Being near. Thus and thus —"

"This concerns Mow, the subtle dwarf," though Yan, but he said nothing then, being desirous of keeping the full recital until he could compose it as a song, to give Chou gladness at some winter fire. He had, indeed, arranged an opening antithesis when Kuo Tsun's voice recalled him.

"By a complexity of circumstances, rare in this belated person's experience of the Province, very little appears to be wanting to create a scene of ideal felicity," the venerable sage was remarking. "The Ch'hang River, for probably the first time in history, is neither in flood nor completely evaporated; an almost poetical verdure has suddenly appeared where no vegetation was ever known before; several of the rare kinds of feathered creatures have raised their harmonious voices, and now and then it is quite possible to see the great-grandfather of the sky above the mists. If only a company of musicians could be inspired..."

Even as he spoke, a band of village dwellers of the younger sort began to pass that way. The maidens carried ropes of flowers which they had gathered at some toil, but many of the most powerful of the other kind had iron gongs and hollow metal tubes, sonorous ducks and fish of wood or stone, and a variety of implements capable of producing sound, with which they beguiled the time. Chou's many-sided interest in the welfare of all had raised her in their esteem and Yan's unassuming virtuous life was a byword far and wide. When the leaders of the band grasped how the position stood, they covered the two with whose involvements this threadbare narrative has largely been concerned with sprays and garlands and set out with them upon a joyful path, the minstrels, urged to a more tenacious vigour, leading the way. Thus, at the conclusion of their exacting trial, Yan and peerless Chou were brought in some triumph to the strong tower of the turbulent Ah-mong that was henceforth to be their home.

For several æons after these commonplace events, the comb was a venerated relic among the descendants of Yan and Chou, but during the insurrections of a later age it passed into undiscriminating hands, and being then much worn and broken, it was thrown aside as useless. It fell in the Province of Kan Su and became the Yue-kwang range. It is for this reason that the upper peaks and passes of those sacred heights are always clothed with brightness, while at certain periods of the year the lustre they reflect equals the splendour of the great sky light itself.

Part III
The Bringer of Good News

Whereby the Angle at Which Events Present Themselves May Be Varied

It was still the habit of Kai Lung to walk daily in his garden and to meditate among the shady walks of the orchard grove beyond; but in this exertion he was prone to rely increasingly on the support of a well-tried staff, and even with this assistance Hwa-mei was disinclined to encourage him to go unless Valiant Strength, Worthy Phoenix, or some other supple branch of his now spreading tree was at hand to sustain his elbow.

"Revered," exclaimed Hoo Tee, who thus attended on the occasion with which this pointless relation is concerned; "behold, there approach along the stone path nine persons of distinction and with them one of official rank. Would it not be fitting that I, on whom their high-minded conversation would certainly be lost, should serve a useful end by bringing forth an assortment of choice food to refresh their weary throats?"

"Restrain your admitted zeal in that direction," replied Kai Lung, "until they have declared themselves. Should they come with expectation in their step, whatever you could offer might fall short of their desire; should they have no such purpose it would equally prove too much. Your pigtail has still some length to grow, Hoo Tee."

When the nine wayfarers drew near they disclosed themselves as three philosophers of the district round, three young men of literary tastes, and three who without any particular qualification or degree were in the habit of attaching themselves to whatever seemed to offer a prospect of reward. In their midst was the stranger who displayed a badge.

"Greeting, venerable Kai Lung," remarked the leader of the band. "May your meritorious Line increase like the sprouting of a vigorous ear of corn in the season of Much Rain."

"May all your virtuous tribe be no less favoured," replied Kai Lung, with a desire to be courteous but not yet convinced of the necessity for any special effort. "Are your constituents well balanced?"

As they slowly passed along the conveniently arranged ways of Kai Lung's flower-strewn garden, with a due regard to the ceremonial precedence accorded to their age, the nature of the occasion was presently made clear.

"He whom we have guided was in the out-paths seeking the house that bears your worthy sign," explained the chief of the philosophers. "Plainly the occasion would seem to merit our felicitations."

"My superfluous task," enlarged the one thus pointed out, "is to be a Bringer of Good News, and in this pursuit I take my daily stand before the Official List-board of our provincial city. There your pleasant-sounding name is honourably displayed, Kai Lung, and in accordance with the immemorial right of our exclusive guild I have hastened hither to be the first to reach your grateful ear."

At this agreeable announcement, the nine neighbours of Kai Lung shook hands with themselves effusively, and several admitted that it was what they had long foreseen, but the storyteller himself did not at once step into the full lustre of the moment.

"What," he inquired, with a rather narrow-minded precision, "is the nature of the title, and are the initiatory expenses set forth in detail?"

"The latter part of the subject would appear to have been overlooked," replied the other, after glancing at his tablets. "The distinction carries with it the privilege of unrolling your mat and relating one of your inimitable tales before any member of the Imperial House who strays within three-and-thirty li of your Domestic Altar — provided that you are able to reach his exalted presence and that he is not at the time engaged on serious public business. It also entitles the holder to style himself 'Literary Instructor to the Shades of Female Ancestors' in all official pleas."

"It is doubtful if so exceptional an honour was ever bestowed before," passed from lip to lip among them, though one of the less worthy added beneath his voice, "It is more profitable to step upon an orange skin before a cloyed official than to offer pearls of wisdom to a company of sages."

The venerable storyteller, however, continued to shake his head with supine misgivings, nor did the added prospect of having two compose a deferential ode in answer tend to restore his spirits.

"Tou-fou and Li-tai-pe were not distinguished in their lifetimes, nor was a crown of leaves ever offered to Han Yu," he demurred. "Why then should I, who only stumble in their well-made footsteps, be thus acclaimed? The ungainly name of 'Kai' is easily mistaken and 'Lungs' greet one on every side: the brush of some underling has, perchance, blundered to this arisement... . Yet, which of my negligible productions was singled out for mention?"

"Munificence," replied the expectant messenger, "the quality to which you owe your distinctive popularity would not appear to have been specifically of a literary trend —"

"The frustration of Ming-shu's detestable rebellion might certainly have been deemed a notorious public service, by a too-indulgent eye," continued Kai Lung more cheerfully. "The delay of some two-score years in extending recognition is not unusual in a State Department connected with —"

"Truth adorns each word," interposed the Bringer of Good News, not in any way desirous of becoming involved in a speculative discourse, "but your flattering reputation does not stand on that foot either. Rest assured, benignity, that it is wiser not to test a coin found by the roadside but to spend it."

"Speak frankly," urged the invidious voice that had already murmured. "We being all friends here, one among another," and he looked pleasurably forward to hearing something of an offensive nature.

"A wet robe is more becoming than a borrowed umbrella," was Kai Lung's tolerant pronouncement as he signified assent that the stranger should proceed. "Withhold nothing."

"However dubious the soil, the rice conveys no taint," aptly replied the other. "But, since you persist, the unexpressed part of the occasion is as follows. A rumour has of late sprung up, esteemed, that you have been miraculously endowed with the unusual gift of being able to walk on the side of a house, or in any other upright place, with the superior agility over our own race possessed by all winged insects. 'If,' the analogy has thence continued, 'the one in question (of whom we have never previously heard) is so remarkably conformed, it necessarily follows that his inspired productions must possess a very unusual blend.' Within a moon, benevolence, you have thus become what among those who put forth the printed leaves is termed a 'leading cash-enticer.' Seeing this, it behooved authority to move, 'For,' flowed the rhythm of their thoughts, 'inasmuch as flowers turn their faces to the sun and all men, when untrammelled, seek the highest, he who can claim the greatest number of adherents in any walk of life is necessarily the worthiest of his kind, and for our own repute we must profess acquaintance with his works and do him honour.' "

"Alas," exclaimed Kai Lung, when he understood that he was thus indebted to a fallacious comparison with an illiterate insect, "how shall I meet the shades of Tou-fou and Han Yu hereafter? In our highly favoured land of unparalleled refinement is it essential to a just appreciation of his literary style that an unassuming relater of imagined tales must stand upon one foot for a record span of time, or be secretly conveyed to an unknown spot by a providential dragon, or consort with apes upon a trackless desert, or by some other barbarian wile appeal to the trite and superficial?"

"Who shall ordain in what form the deities bestow their gifts or question the wording of the inscription upon the outer wrapper?" asked the philosopher Wan Fo-he who in earlier life had provided for a virtuous old age by arranging competitions. "The husk which in the case of the salubrious nut protects the desired food is, when we turn to the equally nutritious date, itself similarly surrounded-clearly with the humane intention both of warning mankind against hasty generalities and of exercising the teeth diversely. That which-as may demonstrated with a coin-is round when looked at from above, is flat when seen edgewise —"

"Besides, O instructor," interposed one of the studious youths (less, perchance, with the desire of assuaging Kai Lung's umbrage than of deflecting the profuse Wan Fo), "have you ever yet attempted to progress upon an upright wall in the manner indicated?"

"This one has never bent his commonplace feet to so grotesque an essay," replied Kai Lung, with an appreciable distance in his manner.

"Then for all that an ordinary person can declare you may be gifted to that extent, and as you are certainly now too patriarchal to put the contention to a test, it will never be possible to gainsay the achievement. How then," concluded the disciple, "can you logically reject a distinction which in addition to being founded on an admitted merit may even in its circuitous process be exact?"

To this plea the others joined their voices, especially the Bringer of Good News, who foresaw no certain gain if the one whom he had come to apprise maintained a stubborn outline. Therefore, as they slowly trod the walks and admired the ingenious vistas-being prompted thereto by a whisper in his ear that he might thus induce Kai Lung to forget resentment-he approached the storyteller more directly.

"Beguiler of men's leisure," he remarked astutely, "it is asserted out among the more trodden Ways that in your time you have framed stratagems, led armies, and fought battles. How is it possible for one who has thus controlled events to have passed his later life in a state of unbroken ease, plying his simple calling?"

Before replying, Kai Lung led his guests among the remoter outskirts of his orchard where, on a few neglected trees, a shrivelled after-growth of fruit still lingered. These he laboriously sought out and pressed on each in turn, with hospitable insistence.

"Had we been earlier here, the fare might have been more full-flavoured," was his mild extenuation. "But who shall blame the tree that has already of its nature yielded crops when autumn finds it wanting?" Then turning to the Bringer of Good News he added, "Since you put it in that way, it will be necessary for me to explain matters by relating for you, to the best of my decayed proficiency, the Story of Ching-kwei."

The Story of Ching-kwei and the Destinies

I. The Manner of His Setting Forth, His Encounter by the Way, and the Nature of His Reception at Wang Tae's Hostile Door

Not idly is the warning given, "Destiny writes with an iron spear upon a marble stele; how then shall a merely human hand presume to guide her pen?"

This concerns Ching-kwei of the dwindling Line of Ying, Wang Tae the dauntless warrior, and the philosopher Ah-Yew no less also Shen Che, known later as the Poising Butterfly from the graceful lightness of her movements, and her sister Mei to whom no other name was ever given. It involves likewise the aged grandmother of Ching-kwei, the sorcerer who dwelt beneath the rugged tower of Ya, Shang king of the upstart power of Tsun, certain friends, associates and relatives of those chiefly engaged, warriors and captains of the various armies raised, usurpers and upholders of the dynasty, sages and historians, merchants and artificers, holy men, outlaws, and peasants, and a great variety of persons of the ordinary sort for whom no particular description here is necessary.

Ching-kwei was of the age of manhood when he first beheld Shen Che. Thereafter he marked the day with a special sign (binding a knotted cord about his wrist), so that on it he might initiate any great enterprise on which his mind was fixed. It was the thirteenth of the Month of Peach Blossom, and on that day he united with Wang Tae in the Compact of the Cedar Grove, led the assault on the walled city of Hing-foo, and, last of all, turned home again.

"Truly art thou thy father's very son!" exclaimed his grandmother one day, at a period before any of these things had come to pass. "Are we to starve by slow degrees? Here are but nineteen goats where yesterday a score responded to my call. Pursue the misshapen recreant with all speed before another shall have killed and eaten it. Take with you rice sufficient for a lengthy search, and if, in the course of your wanderings, you should fall in with a reputable magician sitting by the wayside, do not neglect to traffic a portion of it with him for a written charm against this person's pestilential cramps."

"Venerable one," replied Ching-kwei dutifully, "your spoken word is my unwritten law. Yet how, encountering a recluse of this description, may it be assumed with confidence that he is all you would desire and not an unscrupulous imposter?"

"Commiserate with him upon the malignity of his own afflictions. If he enlarges on the subject, pass him by."

"Your words enshrine the essential germ of wisdom," agreed Ching-kwei. "Although," he added sombrely, "to one whose forefathers bore banners in the van of many famous wars, the pursuit of an erratic four-legged creature across a precipitous land is an enterprise neither dignified nor heroic."

"Those who cover themselves with martial glory frequently go in need of any other garment," replied the ancient capably. "Be content that by peaceful industry you have goats to pursue."

Being of a docile and obedient nature-and also because no adequate retort occurred to him- Ching-kwei respectfully withdrew and at once made his simple preparations for the search. In this he was assisted by the praiseworthy honesty of that region, for so humiliating was it felt to be that the animals of one family should ingratiate themselves into the herds and flocks of an unsuspecting neighbour and enjoy his confidence that to render this contingency as remote as possible it had become the time-honoured custom for each household to stain all its removable possessions with a distinctive dye. Thus Ching-kwei's inquiries tended to a definite end.

"Has there by any chance a base-born interloper lately appeared among your lordly herd of distinguished-looking goats?" he might have vainly asked at every farmstead.

"Is the one whom you address a hungry dog that the odour of one goat differs from that of another across his path?" would have been the discouraging reply. "Or have you counted the hairs of that which you claim to have lost, so that you shall describe it? Behold, within

371

my flock are goats of every shape and kind, and by a meritorious fruitfulness their numbers increase from day to day. Begone then with this quail-and-dragon story of a wandering goat, the counterpart of one of mine, and seek a less wary victim."

Truly; but what words of evasive contumely could be directed against one who should draw near remarking:

"Greeting, opportune possessor of this majestic flock of vermilion goats which so decoratively sets off the fertile hillside."

"Greeting," courtesy would demand in answer. "Yet the creatures are themselves evil in every bone, and the pasturage is meagre and full of bitterness."

"On the contrary, only one blemish mars the harmonious unity of the engaging scene. Have I your genial permission to disclose it?"

"Say on-if you must," would be the morose reply, the one addressed seeing no other course before him. "But a virtuous life speaks louder than a brazen trumpet."

"Your gracious encouragement moistens my laborious tongue. Among such perfection even these afflicted eyes at once recognize yonder ungainly outcast, whose ineradicable coat of blue is very thinly disguised beneath a recent dressing of red earth. Permit me, therefore, to attach this commonplace thing to its rebellious horns and to free your nobly descended herd of its distasteful presence."

In this mutually inoffensive way, Ching-kwei had already on several occasions recovered defiant members of his flock, and had himself not infrequently suffered a similar loss at the hands of equally determined neighbours. But this time an unstinted measure of no-success marked all his efforts, and his persistent endeavour to implicate one after another of those whom he distrusted led to nothing but a spot ever increasingly distant from his own domestic hearth.

It was toward evening on the second day of his quest that Ching-kwei encountered a brighter omen. He had then reached a barren and forbidding waste and was contemplating turning back from so cheerless a prospect when he noticed a little wizened mendicant seated upon a rock a few paces farther on. As even the rock had not been there the previous moment, Ching-kwei at once doubted the ordinariness of the occasion, and this emotion was added to when he perceived that the Being's teeth were composed each of a separate jewel of unusual size and brilliance, and that he had four eyes and held four books in either hand. A golden centipede was coiled about his feet, and from his escaping breath there was formed a river of clear water. Ching-kwei's first impulse was to render obeisance of the lowliest kind, but as he would have done so, it was put into his mind that the one before him, by invoking the threadbare garment of an aged beggar, wished to assume a part. He therefore approached the venerable one in an upright position, but saluted him obsequiously.

"Ching-kwei," remarked the vision in some embarrassment, "the fact that you see me half as I really am, and half in the appearance that I have assumed, plainly shows that you yourself are not entirely normal. This foreshadows a life of chequered fortune, nor would it seem to be wholly settled yet to what end your destiny will tend. All this, however, is for your inner ear alone, for it would certainly involve me in humiliating censure if it became known in the Upper World that I had, in a moment of indiscretion, exceeded my imposed task. This is simply, in the guise of an aged native of these parts, to influence you from turning your dejected feet on a homeward bend by observing in your hearing,'Many hoof marks point inward at Wang Tae's gate but few lead out again,' adding,'To the deaf ox a meaning word is as efficacious as a detailed statement.' "

"Your timely warning falls upon a nutritious soil," replied Ching-kwei gratefully, but without any especial reverence for one who was so inadvertent. "On your return, you can safely claim that your message has not failed."

The venerable made a gesture of familiar understanding.

"Anything that I have said beyond, regard strictly as between one semi-supernatural Being and another," he remarked diffidently. "At some future period in The After, doubtless an opportunity of doing no less for your accommodating Shadow will occur."

Having thus discharged his mission, the one in question sought to vanish, but being still confused by the mischance of their meeting he failed to pronounce the charm efficiently, so that, while he and the rock disappeared entirely, the robes of the patriarchal mendicant remained in a seated attitude upon a void.

"Clearly it would seem that you do not necessarily act like a deity merely by being one," thought Ching-kwei as he resumed his forward path. The intimation that he was himself of remote kinship with the Immortals did not gild his imagination, for he had often recognized that he was in some undetermined way superior to those around him, although the circumstance did not appear to have any direct pecuniary advantage.

He had soon other things to engage his mind upon, for, as he advanced, he heard from the scanty peasants of that inhospitable tract that Wang Tae's dwelling was near at hand. It was spoken of as being strongly staked about, but when Ching-kwei would have learned something of the nature and attitudes of the one whom he was seeking, those he questioned ceased to speak and replied only by signs of such profound significance as to be wholly unintelligible.

"It is truly said, 'A fly on the window may be taken for an eagle in the sky,' and Wang Tae is doubtless no more formidable than any other man upon two feet," reasoned Ching-kwei aloud, as he approached a stronghold of the kind described to him, and he would have continued in the strain when a defiant voice caused him to turn. One whom he had not observed in his eagerness to press on had stepped forward and now stood barring the path of his retreat.

"Perchance," retorted this inopportune stranger, "but Wang Tae does not go upon two feet, and as he therein differs from the generality of men, so are the depth and lustre of his power not to be measured by a wooden rule," and the one who spoke indicated with a gesture of contempt the staff that Ching-kwei carried. "If our agreeable conversation is to continue in the same harmonious vein, let your persuasive tongue acquire a more businesslike point," and he struck the handle of the sword he wore.

"It is certainly my intention to speak a few pacific words at Wang Tae's door, touching the movements of an erring goat I seek," replied Ching-kwei mildly. "Should his reception of what I have to say not be entirely thus and thus, however, it will then be time to shape my tongue to a more incisive edge."

"Your well-chosen language fills me with the most joyous anticipation," said Wang Tae, moistening his hands with gross elaboration. "Here is the gate of my neglected hovel. When you have seen all you want of the outside world, pass within."

It is in this not entirely sympathetic manner that Wang Tae now comes into the narrative, and it is chiefly owing to that voracious person's large military appetite that the onward history of Ching-kwei moves to the measured clash of arms. At the time of this encounter, Wang Tae was of a middle age and very lusty in his strength. His hair was long and matted, his eyes open and sincere, and the expression of his face both bold and menacing. So bushy were his eyebrows as to give rise to the saying that phoenixes might build there, and with the closing of his hands he could crush a rock. In height he would have been above the ordinary had not both his feet been lacking; for having at an earlier period displeased the ruling lord of Tsun, that prince had caused them to be sawn off, to correct, he said, Wang Tae's rising ambition.

"Henceforth," declared the conscientious ruler, when this act of justice was accomplished, "it can no longer be hinted that your aspiring footprints point toward a throne, Wang Tae."

"Benevolence," replied Wang Tae unmoved, "by cutting back the branches of a tree, you do but increase the vigour of its fruit, and I will yet leave the impress of my thumb upon the age."

Carrying with him the echo of this vainglorious boast, Wang Tae retired to a desert place apart and there built himself a strong retreat, guarding it with a trench and a palisade of teak. He lived by establishing a system of taxation for the benefit of travellers of the richer kind who passed that way, and gradually he found around him a company of necessitous persons who were of his own way of thinking. From time to time secret messengers went to and fro throughout the province, and as the land continued to grow more troubled, men's thoughts began to turn toward Wang Tae as to a leafy banyan tree when the rain threatens to fall.

II. The Influence of the Wise Philosopher Ah-Yew and the Inspired Assurance of His Parting Forecast

When Wang Tae with a ceremonious welcome threw wide the gate of his outer yard, Ching-kwei did not hesitate, nor did the sound of the bolt being wedged against his escape cause him to stop. He found himself overlooking a considerable enclosure wherein every sort of beast displayed every variety of colour; a goat stained with his own distinctive shade of blue sported among its kind.

"In the matter of the colour of my herd I am content to preserve the harmonious blend of nature," remarked Wang Tae, reaching his side again and speaking with polished insincerity. "What is good enough to arch the heavens is good enough to adorn my pastures."

"It is well said," agreed Ching-kwei. "Furthermore, by the same analogy, both manifestations would appear to be of spontaneous origin."

"The honey of your continual approbation is too rich for my weak mental appetite," said Wang Tae, by no means pleased at the insidious courtesy of Ching-kwei's replies. "Is there haply nothing here to displease your fastidious eye?"

"On the contrary, there is that which amply rewards my inefficient sight, for at no great distance this person perceives the object of his footweary search. Permit him, therefore, to lead the truant home in triumph and your virtuous name shall ever remain a synonym for uprightness."

"Put forth your self-reliant hand and take it, then," replied Wang Tae, leaping down into the yard to draw his impatient sword. "There is but one slender bar between."

"No obstacle is both too high to get over and too low to get under," retorted Ching-kwei no less resolutely, and he suddenly thrust his staff forward in a way that Wang Tae was not prepared for.

In considering the various facets of the not altogether dignified encounter that ensued, it is necessary to hold an impartial balance. Admittedly Wang Tae was by repute one of the most skillful sword users of his day, while Ching-kwei was then wholly deficient in the simplest passes of that weapon. The latter person, however, was wont to rely in every emergency on the dexterous manipulation of his herdsman's pole, while Wang Tae in all his numerous encounters had never yet gained experience of so contemptible an arm. The inevitable outcome was that neither could subdue the other, for while the length of Ching-kwei's weapon kept Wang Tae at a humiliating distance, the thickness of the outlaw's leather armor saved him from the full impact of the blows propelled against him. Yet it is not to be denied that Ching-kwei, by concentrating his efforts upon a spot somewhat lower than his adversary's waistband, found a means to corrode the tempered surface of Wang Tae's self-confidence and the loud cries of defiance which that person had at first raised in the hope of sapping the other's valour began imperceptibly to assume a more personal tone. It was at this point, while they thus strove, that one of benign aspect and patriarchal cast drew near and held up a restraining hand before them.

"It has been wisely said, 'If he is a stranger, do not give offence; if he is a friend, do not accept it,' " remarked the auspicious person judicially. "How then does strife arise between you?"

At this interruption both lowered their weapons, Wang Tae because he was not desirous of adding to the pain he already felt, while Ching-kwei had not sought the encounter.

"I have no wish to conceal my part in the arisement," replied the latter person unassumingly. "I am of the forgotten Line of Ying and the separate names conferred on me are Ching and Kwei. Touching the cause of this, I did but claim my due."

"That is the essence of all dissension," remarked the philosopher, but he averted his face at the mention of the stranger's name lest the conflict of his thoughts should mirror there. Then he took Wang Tae aside.

"Say what you will," declared the outlaw, forecasting the reproach awaiting him, "but suffer me at the same time to continue rubbing the seat of my affliction."

"If Ching-kwei's blows remind you of the teeth of vampires, my words will associate themselves in your mind with the tails of dragons," continued the sage, who may now be disclosed as Ah-Yew, the crafty counsellor. "You have done ill, Wang Tae, and by the anger of a moment imperilled what the patience of a year may not restore."

"Continue in the same entrancing strain, excellence," interrupted Wang Tae bitterly. "Already this person's bodily pangs begin to fade."

"When the time is ripe for action, who is there that is most essential to our common hope?" continued the wise adviser with measured sternness. "Not you, Wang Tae of the lion heart, nor I, venerable Yew of the serpent tongue, nor yet any of the ten thousand nameless ones who, responding to our call, will sweep on like driven leaves in autumn and with as little compunction be crushed down into the earth. But with us we must have, at every hazard, one of the banished Line of Ying to give a semblance to our unstable cause and to proclaim a mission accepted of the gods. Such a one, inspired by his destinies and suitable in every attribute, came to your gate today with a supplication in his hand and you, with contumely, have flung him back again. Could demons do more to bring about your fall, Wang Tae, than you have done yourself? Let me hence, that I may cleanse my throat of the memory of this ineptitude!"

"Press your correcting heel on my submissive neck, instructor," murmured Wang Tae penitently, "for my all-too-ready sword admittedly outruns your more effective tongue. But in this matter surely it is not yet too late to walk backward in our footsteps. Ching-kwei, despite his royal line, is but an inexperienced villager, and a few words of well-directed flattery—"

"Mayhap," replied the prescient one, "but even the guileless turtle does not put his head out twice. However, proceed to unfold your verbal strategy."

On this understanding they returned to where Ching-kwei was endeavouring to entice the goat into a noose, and at that moment, by a device, he succeeded in doing so. To Wang Tae this seemed a fitting opportunity.

"Nimbly cast!" he cried effusively. "Never has this one seen it better done."

Ching-kwei wound the loose excess of rope about his arm, and still grasping the staff he turned to go.

"Your experience is both far-flung and all-embracing," he made reply; "nor would the confines of your landmark seem to be any barrier to your exploiting loop. Henceforth our goats must learn to become more nimble."

"You have come on a bleak and irksome march," continued Wang Tae, ignoring the venom of the thrust. "At least honour my deficient hut by entering to recline at ease and to partake of tea. To do less is to brand this person far and near as a bankrupt outcast."

"I have already tasted of the hospitality of Wang Tae's stockyard; that of his house will certainly be still more overwhelming. As it is, I have so far preserved my life. I go."

In this extremity Ah-Yew came dispassionately forward and stood between the two.

"May the Threefold Happiness be yours, Ching-kwei," he said benevolently, "but for a single pause of time listen to my voice, for I am old and very fragile and doubtless we shall never meet again."

"The venerable length of your blameless pigtail compels my profound respect," replied Ching-kwei deferentially. "Proceed."

"There is a ready saying of these parts, 'The Northern men ride horses, but the Southern men sail boats,' thereby indicating the various paths assigned to us by nature. Similarly, Wang Tae is rude and strenuous from the shock of continual warfare, while you, Ching-kwei, living in a sequestered valley, have a bland and pacific guise. Yet when you go into the street of potters, there to bargain for a jar, how do you proceed to make a choice?"

"Selecting one that seemed to meet my need, I would strike it sharply, thus to detect its secret flaws," was the reply. "Should it fail beneath the test, I would pass it by."

"Therein lies Wang Tae's policy and the enigma of your welcome," declared the subtle Yew. "From afar, Ching-kwei, you have been marked out for great honour of a very special kind and to that end were your steps attracted to this place. Should you prove diligent and apt, there is no ambition to which you may not rise. But first it was necessary to submit your valour, enterprise, and temper to the test of sudden action; had you in this disclosed some hidden flaw, the call would have passed you by."

"What you say is certainly plausible," admitted Ching-kwei, "but the industrious bee is not attracted by the brightest flower," and remembering his grandmother's rebuke he added, "Those who cover themselves with martial glory frequently go in need of any other garment."

This reply was far from meeting Ah-Yew's expectation, for he had hoped that so definite a prospect would not fail to entice one of a simple mind, and the refusal found him unprepared. Seeing this, Wang Tae interposed his voice.

"Those who cover themselves with martial glory do not stand in need of any other garment," was his arrogant retort. "It is both food and raiment and an elder brother too, so that he who wears it feels neither heat nor cold, neither does he sleep alone by night."

Whatever might have been the outcome under other auspices, this speech finally decided Ching-kwei's course. "Wang Tae is admittedly my superior with the sword," ran the current of his inner thoughts, "and when she who has authority over me put forth that argument, I was unable to disclose its weakness. Herein Wang Tae has also proved his mastery, and it is not agreeable to a person of even remotely divine origin to be both physically and mentally inferior to the one whose rice he eats." From this resolve, nothing occurred to move him, so that, now leading the recovered goat upon a cord, he presently set out again along a homeward course. The last words between them were those spoken by the age Yew as the closing of the gate marked their diverging ways.

"Ching-kwei," he observed on parting, "it is well always to remember that men are not conquered by their enemies but by the decree of fate. This enables the wise to bear an unruffled front in all extremities. Sooner or later, ambition will lead your footsteps here again to seek Wang Tae's assistance, but who shall compel the flower to fruit out of its season by plucking off the petals?" To this, Ching-kwei would have waved an appropriate farewell had not the goat leaped forward and thus foiled his purpose. When he looked back again, later, the patriarch had withdrawn.

III. His Visit to the Soothsayer Who Dwelt Beneath the Tower of Ya, and the Incoming of the Two Maidens Whereby the Destinies Become Involved

It was not until Ching-kwei had reached an intermediate village on the following day that a chance allusion to a holy man recalled the second detail of his journey. The gifted hermit referred to lived beneath a ruined tower on the wildness of a certain hill, at a convenient distance from the village. He was spoken of as being reliable and not exacting in his demands. To keep his mind from dwelling on merely worldly details, he unceasingly counted from one up to four when not engaged upon matters of divination and the like, and in this scrupulous manner he had succeeded in regaining a state of natural purity. At one time a rival soothsayer, encouraged by the repute of Ng-tung's sanctity and by the stream of pilgrims attracted to his shrine, sought to establish himself upon another hill, but presently it was discovered that this later one, in order to endure the monotony of his life, found it necessary to count up to ten, and the craving for variety in his mind thus being revealed, he became discredited in consequence.

Bearing a gift of rice, Ching-kwei accordingly turned aside and sought out Ng-tung. The way led through an avenue of flowering trees where the sunlight came in shafts, it then being past the middle hour. As he proceeded, a distant sound of melody came down the aisle, and on its near approach Ching-kwei stood aside to watch. Soon two maidens came in sight, one dancing as she sang, the other more restrained but equally attractive. There being a sward about that place, they loitered there, the one displaying a variety of very graceful attitudes to the rhythm of her words while the other moved apart and sought for certain chosen flowers which she broke off between her shining teeth and held there. This one wore a cloak of plaited straw dyed an engaging shade, and having once seen her face, Ching-kwei watched her unceasingly, scarcely sparing a glance to regard the other.

"She is certainly a high official's daughter," was his thought. "Were it otherwise, I might offer her the gift of rice, but it is extremely unlikely that she eats anything beyond the scent of flowers and possibly an occasional fruit of the more sumptuous kind." While he was debating with himself how he should inoffensively attract her notice an incautious sound betrayed him, and seeing one of another kind so near at hand, the maidens fled, the cloak wearer dropping the flowers she had gathered in her becoming haste but the other still continuing to sing and to dance along her path.

"Plainly my fitness for the society of goats and outlaws is self-evident," thought Ching-kwei in an access of despair. Nevertheless, he recovered what the one had dropped and secured them in an inner sleeve, remarking:

"Today I have only occasioned her this loss; doubtless in future years I shall find an opportunity to restore them."

It was but a short li farther on to Ng-tung's retreat, and the anchorite welcomed Ching-kwei affably when he understood what was required of him and had received the rice. The nature of the task occasioned him no concern, as with unfailing accuracy he at once detected, by a few well-chosen diagrams, the personality of the malign influence at work.

"Should any of the indicated substances be difficult to procure, do not let that disturb the confidence of your venerable progenitor," he remarked considerately, as he inscribed certain words and symbols on a shred of parchment. "If she will inconvenience herself to the extent of swallowing the written directions in the suitable form of a pill, the result will be equally beneficent."

"Your mere words carry conviction," replied Ching-kwei. "No wonder your harmonious name is sown broadcast through this land."

"Agreeably so," admitted Ng-tung diffidently. "Yet there is necessarily a period between seed time and harvest. Thus today, until your noteworthy shadow obscured my prosaic meditations, I had only been called upon to forecast the destinies of two adventuring maidens at the recompense of an inadequately made pair of unfitting sandals," and the versatile recluse displayed his brightly adorned feet disparagingly.

"Did they whom you mention proceed from your hospitable door toward the west, and was the more symmetrical of the two covered by a plaited cloak of straw dyed an attractive shade? If so, I would willingly devote two or three brass cash to learn toward what end your divinations led."

"It is never my aim to frustrate a natural thirst for knowledge," agreed Ng-tung, passing across his wooden bowl. "The one cloaked as you specifically describe, Shen Che by name, is fore-ordained to become a queen and in the end to jeopardize the throne. In the case of the other, her sister Mei, nothing particular is indicated."

"This is sufficiently surprising, although her mien admittedly suggests a royal destiny," said Ching-kwei, endeavouring to subdue his strong emotion. "Perhaps, though, their distinguished father is some high noble of the court?"

"By no means," replied Ng-tung. "He is an indifferent maker of the least reliable variety of threadbare sandals, his name being Kang, and his dwelling place about the cattle pools, beyond the marsh expanse. So humble is his craft that in times of rigour he is glad to make straw coverings for the feet of swine."

"While you are in the mood, perhaps you would be so obliging as to become inspired as to this one's ultimate future also," suggested the other. "There must surely be occasions in after life when such knowledge could be of practical value even to an ordinary person."

"Undoubtedly," replied Ng-tung. "Thus, if one's prescribed end is to be drowned at sea, it is possible to ensure a favourable extent of life by never venturing away from land until the natural end approaches."

"Yet in such a case," reflected Ching-kwei, "would it not be possible to remain here on earth forever by not venturing away from land at all?"

"It is never well to carry such matters beyond a reasonable length," explained the soothsayer with an experienced smile. "Without actually eating their words, the Destinies generally contrive some hidden outlet, by which, if unduly pressed, they are able to give an unexpected meaning to a stated fact. However, in your straightforward case, at an added expenditure of eight brass cash, I will prognosticate to the outside limit of my power."

To this Ching-kwei assented and Ng-tung at once engaged himself upon the task, skillfully contriving a fabric of deduction upon the stable foundation of the inquirer's nativity and the outstanding features of his life. Yet from time to time he seemed to have occasion to begin anew, and even when he had sufficiently tested the precision of his chart, he had resource to the manipulation of the sacred sticks. Finally, he prepared a little tea and poured its leaves upon the ground.

"There is no getting away from the fact," he at length admitted. "Long-armed as the coincidence will doubtless seem to later and less romantic generations, all the tests confirm that the drama of your life also will reach its zenith within the shadow of a royal palace. The indicated outcome of your destiny, Ching-kwei, is this: that at the call of some great passion you will end a sovereign's life and by the same act terminate a dynasty."

This intimation threw Ching-kwei into a profound abstraction. If the beautiful Shen Che, who in so short a time had grown inseparable from his thoughts, was destined to become a queen, while his own fate was to destroy the existence of a king, it was difficult not to attribute some link of connection between their lives, and in any case a not unnatural desire to trace the progress of the involvement to a slightly later period arose within his mind. To this inquiry Ng-tung turned a not wholly warmhearted face.

"It is one thing to forecast destinies," he said, "that being an integral part of this person's occupation. But it is quite another branch of the art to explain how these things arise and what occurs thereafter. Furthermore, Ching-kwei, in the matter of the eight brass cash agreed upon, it has not escaped my inauspicious eye that an unworthy deficiency still lurks within this unpretentious bowl."

"The oversight might have been more tactfully referred to in the circumstances," declared Ching-kwei with dignity as he made up the full amount. "Between one who is the mouthpiece of the Destinies and another who is fore-ordained to overthrow a dynasty should two brass cash this way or that lead to discord?"

"The amount may not in itself be formidable, but an essence is involved," maintained the seer. "Even the gods must live."

"It is equally true that no dust rises from an unstirred soil," replied Ching-kwei. "Clear your mind of acrimonious currents, O Ng-tung, and integrity will no longer be obscured."

Upon this slight derangement of the harmonies, the visit ended, and although they exchanged appropriate quotations from the poets at their parting, Ching-kwei did not ever again contrive to pass that way, nor did Ng-tung allude to a hope that he would do so.

In the days that followed, Ching-kwei found a new distaste toward his former occupations, and he who in the past had been content to lead a company of goats from one place to another, to open water-courses, and to secure the harvest as the seasons came, now took little pleasure save in listening to the recital of tales of bygone valour from the lips of passing minstrels or in strengthening himself by contests with the most expert whom he could meet. Under the plea of an advantageous bargain to be pursued, he made an early journey to seek the house of Kang, near the cattle pools beyond the marsh expanse, but he found it deserted. The sandal-maker, replied an argol-gatherer about the pools, had fled to avoid being seized to satisfy a debt, and his household was now scattered. Shen Che and Mei were spoken of as going north to crave a refuge at the hands of one who professed a kinship with their Line, but the seasons were lean and bitter and who should say? Fine argols, in particular, were hard to come by.... Ching-kwei returned in a headlong mood, and for a while he would contend with any but hold intercourse with none. Later, he sought out his grandmother and reproached her.

"Where is the sword of finely tempered make that our devastating ancestors were wont to bear? In former times it had its place above the Tablets of our race, but now that honourable space is empty."

"It now has its place above the board on which the goats' food is chopped, out in the farther shed," replied the one addressed. "Thus for the first time in the history of our race it serves a useful purpose. Should you need it elsewhere, see to its safe return."

"Its only becoming use is to add further lustre to our diminished name," declared Ching-kwei with feeling. Then, remembering Wang Tae's retort and being desirous that his grandmother should recognize the falsity of her argument, he added, "Those who cover themselves with martial glory do not stand in need of any other garments."

"It is well that you should have reminded me of the gemlike truth in time," replied the other. "I was on the point of contriving for your use another pair of lower garments to hide the open deficiencies of those you wear. Henceforth, cover the outstanding portions of your lower limbs with martial glory and I will save my cloth."

"Probably Wang Tae could have matched this saying with another still more pungent," thought Ching-kwei, "but I have yet something to learn from him in most respects," and having no seemly retort in view he silently withdrew.

Nevertheless, he took down his father's sword, and, as the days went by, he began to bend his powers to its use. At first, among the peace-loving dwellers of that untroubled part, he could find none able to instruct him or even willing to stand up against assault, but eventually he discovered an aged gatherer of water weed, Hoo by name, who in more prosperous times had been a pirate. Inspired by the promise of an occasional horn of rice spirit, this accommodating person strove to recall the knowledge of his youth, and in the end he did indeed impart to Ching-kwei the outline of most of the positions both of defence and of attack. Let it, however, be confessed that, owing to his instructor's style having been formed at the capricious angle of a junk's unstable deck, where he was either being cast bodily upon his adversary or receiving that one's full weight upon himself, Ching-kwei's swordsmanship to the last conformed to the rigid canons of no existing school but disclosed surprises and benumbing subterfuges against which a classical perfection could accomplish little. To this day the saying lives, "Like Ching-kwei's swordplay-up, down, and sideways all in one," to testify to the baffling versatility of his thrust.

When Ching-kwei had learned all that the well-intentioned Hoo was competent to teach him, and could parry each of that hard-striving person's fiercest blows and beat down his defence, he cast about again for a means whereby to extend his knowledge further. In this extremity he was visited one night by the shadow of a remote and warlike ancestor and a means disclosed to him under the figment of a dream. Profiting by this timely intervention, on the following day Ching-kwei made a shield of toughened hide and took it to the forest. There he bound it in an appropriate position on the sweeping branch of a giant cypress tree. To the relentless force and gyrating onslaught of this indomitable foe, Ching-kwei now fearlessly opposed himself. Whenever a storm of exceptional violence shook the earth, he hastened to take up the challenge, nor was the blackness of the wildest night any bar to his insatiable zeal. Often he was hurled reeling a full score of paces back, frequently struck, stunned and bleeding, to the ground. More than once, being missed, the one who sought him found him lying there insensible; but he carried at his heart the flowers dropped from the lips of the maiden in the glade, and after every overthrow he returned again with an unconquered look of cheerful acquiescence. It is even claimed by poets and history makers of a later time that in those dark encounters Beings, and those concerned with the outcome of the age, gathered about the spot and strove to various ends-some entering into the fibre of the tree and endowing with special qualities while others protected its antagonist through all and sustained his arm. In this painstaking way, Ching-kwei rose to a great mastery with the sword.

IV. The Offensive Behaviour of Shang, Usurpatory King of Tsun, and the Various Influences Under Which Ching-Kwei Resolved to Menace Him

In the seventh year of his reign the usurper Shang exceeded all restraint, and by offering sacrifice in a forbidden place he alienated the goodwill of his own protecting gods. What was even more important at that moment, by this act of defiance he roused the just suspicion of the neighbouring power of Chung, and the potent ruler of that State withdrew the shelter of his indulgent face. From that inauspicious day, Shang's strength might be likened to a river on the summit of a hill.

Nearly twelve moons had come and gone since the recovery of the wandering goat. Ching-kwei was drawing water from a pool when he looked up and saw a solitary wayfarer who leaned upon his staff as though the burden of the heat and dust were too great for him to carry. Remembering the many occasions when he himself had experienced a similar distress, the sympathetic one hastened forward with his jar and offered it, remarking:

"It is too trivial an act to merit even thanks, to pass on to one that which heaven freely sends for the use of all. Drink to repletion, therefore, and what you do not need pour out upon your weary feet so as to strengthen you in each extremity."

"May the All-providing reward you with a hundred sons and a thousand grandsons, to sustain your age," exclaimed the grateful stranger as he thirstily complied. Then he returned the vessel to Ching-kwei's hands, but as he moved away his rod touched it, seemingly by chance, so that it gave out a ringing note. This incident, and the exchange of looks accompanying it, at once recalled to Ching-kwei his encounter with the broad-minded Yew, and suspecting something deeper he would have questioned the wayfarer, but before he could frame the substance of his speech it was too late.

"Had there been a spoken sign, I would willingly have met that upright man again," thought Ching-kwei, and he was stooping to refill the jar when a gleam within its depths arrested him. He turned it over, and there fell out a golden fruit growing on a silver stem. He could no longer doubt the message of the sage's beckoning hand.

As Ching-kwei returned, he met his grandmother at some little distance from the door, for the passage with the stranger had delayed him beyond what he was wont, and she had grown to misgive his absence. Seeing him, she would have turned back, but he called to her to stay, and when they were come together he delivered the jar of water into her hands.

"My sword is by my side," he said; "the only wear that I possess upon my back. In the first wood I can cut a staff; in the last village, earn a bowl of rice. Henceforth, I must follow the pursuit of my destiny."

"If you will but tread this path far enough, it will bring you to what you seek at last," was her reply.

"Were we on the great earth-road, a few li farther to the north, that might well be," assented Ching-kwei; "but you forget that this unfrequented track leads only to our door. Furthermore, there is a certain peerless maiden, now wholly necessary to my very life, whom I must find."

"In that case you had better stay at home; for if you are equally necessary to hers, be well assured that she will infallibly find you."

"Customs have perhaps changed since the days of your own venerable youth, esteemed," replied Ching-kwei tactfully. "Nor is the one whom I indicate to be computed by our earthen measure, inasmuch as she exists on the smell of flowers, wears a robe formed of floating light, and is fated to become a queen-whose king it is my destiny to slay. Her imposing father, being a merchant of the princely sort, has gone hence on business of the state and I would follow. Nothing delays my journey now but your ceremonial blessing."

"May the concentrated blight of eighteen generations of concave-witted ancestors ride on your back!" exclaimed the one invoked. "Is she who cherished you in infancy to perish in her own old age like a toothless dog whose master's house is closed? Where is this person's future recompense for twenty years of disinterested care and self-denial if contending camps are now to swallow you?"

"What you have done is assuredly recorded in a golden book," declared Ching-kwei with flattering conviction; "and for this the High Ones will one day reward you."

"Doubtless," replied the other adequately, "but not in the exact way that I should myself select. However, as was truly said when this person left her father's palace, 'Pity leads to love; love leads to madness.' If it is to be, it will be, but first return with me for a purpose that I will inform you of."

On this persuasion Ching-kwei accompanied her, and being now free of her dissuasion, stayed to partake of food. When this was finished, she led him to an inner room and there unlocked a box that had lain concealed beneath the floor. From this she took a complete suit of the finer sort together with a cloak richly trimmed with costly fur, a shield of polished steel inlaid with gold, and a lavishly embossed scabbard fitting to his sword. When these were arranged about his person, she drew five bars of silver from a secret place and, leading him to the door, put them into his hand.

"Go, son of my own son, and fittingly uphold the imperishable glory of our noble race!" was her parting word, and behind him Ching-kwei heard the thrusting of the bolt.

That night Ching-kwei slept in a ruined temple, and at a little after noon on the following day, he stood once more before the strong stockade of Wang Tae's fortress. He measured the width and depth of the ditch with an appraising eye and judged the stoutness of the palisade, deeming each one sufficient for its purpose. Then he examined the resources of the massive door and the tower protecting it and could find no weakness there. Afterward he beat upon the metal of the outer gate with a heavy stone and continue until a watchman appeared at the grille.

"Greeting to the valiant Wang Tae," he called across the space. "Bear word to him that there stands one without who would disclose toward his private ear a weakness in the chain of his defence."

"He sleeps upon that side; begone, O clown," scoffed the keeper of the gate, seeing no profit to his own sleeve from the encounter (for Ching-kwei now carried what he had received wrapped in a skin and stood there as a meagre goatherd), and he turned away.

"Perchance a familiar sign may awaken him," came back Ching-kwei's retort, and with it his trustworthy staff winged past the menial's head, carrying with it the lattice from the door. "Give him that message, brother."

With gratifying promptitude, the door swung open, an ample beam was thrust over the gulf, and Wang Tae passed across. When that large-stomached person recognized Ching-kwei, most of the fury with which he had set out upon the enterprise melted from his expression, and finally he shook hands with himself cordially.

"Ching-kwei," was his open-hearted welcome, "whether you are now come to claim tithe of the ill-assorted offsprings of that prince of profligacy you sought, or whether you have come to hazard for a throne, my roof is equally above you."

"These things must take their proper turn," was the discreet reply. "But first of all, Wang Tae, I would disclose to you a serious error in the scheme of your protection."

"Some word of this affair has already reached my backward ears," said the warrior. "Bring me to the point at which the danger lies."

"Willingly," replied Ching-kwei, and taking from the pack his sword he unsheathed it. "So long as there is a mightier one outside your walls than there is within, your security is menaced."

"That is a matter which is very easily put right," said Wang Tae, suffering his gravity to become very grossly removed at the well-planned jest. "Join the felicity of our commonplace circle, and the inference will manifestly be reversed."

"Before I can do that it is necessary to see what sort of entertainment your hand provides," declared Ching-kwei, fastening on his shield. "When last we met, you were somewhat lavish of receiving and sparse to give-perchance being a stranger then I kept you too much at a distance. Now we can mingle freely."

"It is impossible to misunderstand the challenge of your two-edged meaning any longer," said Wang Tae, taking up an appropriate poise and unsheathing also. "Your genial invitation warms me like the glow of very old wine. If only you are able to speak at all when I have done, nothing will be wanting to complete my happiness."

The nature of Wang Tae's appearance has already been described, so that it is only necessary to declare wherein he differed from it. His armour was more massive than before, being embossed on every plate with studs of shining brass, and in place of one sword of awe-inspiring size he now wore two. But his great height obscured all else, for having lately found his shortened limbs to thwart his reaching stroke he had contrived wooden pegs to replace the missing feet and these his domineering nature led him continually to lengthen until he towered above a world of dwarfs. When he spoke, his voice resembled a multitude of corncrakes, calling at variance.

"Should you have any preference for retaining a right or a left ear, speak before it is too late," said Wang Tae as they engaged. "But do not plead for more than one."

"Take both freely," replied Ching-kwei, offering them in turn, "for so far nothing favourable to Wang Tae has come near either. First, however, let me correct your ill-balanced outlook," and by a movement which the other person could never clearly understand he cut off at a single blow the lower part of one of Wang Tae's props.

It has already been admitted that Wang Tae was an expert swordsman, and in an ordinary sense he was able to maintain his supremacy in a variety of attitudes, but the necessity of bending his mind to carry on the conflict with one side so materially lower than the other soon began to disturb the high level of his skill. Seeing this, Ching-kwei assumed a sympathetic voice.

"What ails the great Wang Tae that his blade no longer slices where his hand directs?" he said. "Take out your other sword, chieftain, and see if haply you can accomplish something more with two. Or beg a moment's rest whereby to find your scanty breath. Or call one from your inner room to wipe the drip out of your smarting eyes. Or suck the juice up from a bitter fruit to ease your gasping throat. Or —"

"May the nine bronze tripods of Yu fall upon your pest-infected tongue!" exclaimed Wang Tae with concentrated feeling, and he made an incautious stroke that laid his defences bare.

"Plainly I took too much before and I must restore the balance," remarked Ching-kwei and with a blow similar to the former one he cut through the other of Wang Tae's supports. "Now that you are somewhat come down in the world, eminence, we can associate more on a level."

At this fresh indignity Wang Tae cast away his sword and bent his neck in shame. Finding that it was not Ching-kwei's intention to triumph over him, he recognized the justice of that one's victory, and after embracing him affectionately he led him into the stronghold of his walls with every mark of ceremonious deference.

V. Wang Tae's Just Tribute to the Prescience of Ah-Yew, and the Conference of the Cedar Grove, Wherein Ching-Kwei Learned How Shen Che Was Scheming Toward a Throne

That night there was a feast given in Ching-kwei's honour, and at it he was the recipient of many flattering compliments, although it was not considered prudent by the more discreet to refer to the recent encounter within Wang Tae's hearing. When they were all come together, Ching-kwei looked round.

"There are assembled here a hundred swords capable of putting me on a throne," he remarked, "but I have yet to hear one voice able to keep me there. Where is the farseeing Ah-Yew, whose counsel is a better safeguard than a towered wall of seven heights?"

At this there was a sudden and profound silence, each man looking toward another who should speak. At last Wang Tae was forced to make reply.

"He had finished his ordinary work among us here and he has now Passed Above," he said.

"When did this take place?" inquired Ching-kwei sadly.

"Yesterday, at such and such an hour," they told him.

"If that is indeed the case, how can we gather here to feast together?" he demanded. "It would be more seemly to be eating dust rather than drinking wine. I, at any rate, will have no part in it," and he began to rise.

"It is easier to judge than to administer justice," replied Wang Tae, "and in this matter your exactitude is much at fault, Ching-kwei. Learn now how this has come about. Foreseeing your return and being desirous that no untimely omen should arise to mar its complete success, the one whom we all venerate laid a most strict injunction on our band that not even his own up-passing should be allowed to interfere with the rites of hospitality whenever you arrived. Thus, in feasting we are really exalting his decree above mere custom, and by rejoicing we mourn an irreparable loss."

"This admittedly puts another face on the affair," confessed Ching-kwei, permitting his cup to be refilled. "Yet it is aptly said, 'When the tree has gone only then do we appreciate its shade,' and before long the fierce rays of a retaliatory sun will certainly attempt to reach us."

By most of those assembled, this speech was well received, but there was one present who in the past had been rebuked by Yew for the ordinariness of his character, and seeing now an opportunity to barb an insidious dart, he looked ingratiatingly toward their chief and spoke.

"So long as we have in Wang Tae a well-lined silk umbrella, the fiercest sun will shoot its beams in vain, nor is the reference to a defensive wall wholly to be praised. Ah-Yew was well enough in his proper sphere, but the present need requires a warrior's voice, and this one has yet to learn that he who has been so servilely extolled had ever drawn a sword."

Almost before he had finished speaking, a score were on their feet to express their indebtedness to Yew, but Wang Tae himself waved them all aside.

"When we who are here shall all have passed away and our swords be corroded into rust, our names will then be utterly forgotten," he declared in a loud and compelling voice. "But to the end of time men will come together in moments of great stress and being perplexed will say, 'In such a case thus and thus enjoined the clear-sighted Yew, the wily counsellor of the ancient days in the State of Tsun, and his advice was good.' In that lies immortality."

This testimony so pleased Ching-kwei that he rose up from his place, and taking Wang Tae by the elbow he exclaimed:

"It is one thing to reach behind your sword, Wang Tae, but I can never hope to get level with your supple tongue. Yet I would rather have said that about Ah-Yew than have found a ballast-load of topaz."

"If you have felt it, what need of further speech, and why then should there be a rivalry between us?" replied Wang Tae, and from that time they were close in friendship.

When the repast was over, Ching-kwei and Wang Tae walked together in the cool fragrance of a cedar grove, beneath the full radiance of the great white daughter of the sky, and the warrior freely then disclosed his plans.

"As yet," he said, "it would be unwise for us to aim at the throne direct, for by doing so we should alienate the weak and doubtful without attracting to our incipient cause those who have wealth or authority to lose. Nor have we a walled city on our side in which to raise our banner and to give protection to a sufficient host. For this reason, it will not be prudent to declare you publicly just now, but before those whom we trust your sovereignty shall be maintained."

"I regard you as the living symbol of the profound Ah-Yew," replied Ching-kwei. "For that reason, I am wholly in your guiding hand."

"I am not without hope that he will occasionally find time among his important duties elsewhere to return to counsel us. In the meanwhile, he left an explicit chart of how to act in every arising circumstance. For the next year, our course is one of wariness, sowing ferment like a flung mesh across the land and enrolling the dissentious to our cause, but moving ever with our faces to the ground. At the end of that period of repression, we must, by a single well-planned blow, seize and contain an influential town."

"Where the Shay River bends far to the north and then bends south again, there lies the great walled city of Hing-foo, which once this person beheld," remarked Ching-kwei.

"Hing-foo is the target to which our arrow wings its devious flight. Thrust like the menace of a hostile elbow out into the plains, Hing-foo holds all the land south of the Shay and at the same time threatens irruption to the north. Already there are many worthy officials of the town who acknowledge our sign and give the countersign and when the time arrives the more intelligent of the defenders — after a few examples have been made-should have no difficulty in recognizing on which side virtue lies."

"What follows next?"

"Turning over on his perfumed couch, the usurping Shang will languidly exclaim, 'Two armies to the south and stamp these contumacious beetles down into their native mire.' Yung and Wen-yi will rally to the call and begin to enrol their forces to that end. Wen-yi is incompetent and old, Yung vigorous and a commander by no means to be despised."

"If that is the case," suggested Ching-kwei, "would it not be prudent, at the essential moment, to ignore the menace of Wen-yi's advance, but, concentrating all our resources upon Yung, to offer him a sufficient price to turn the scale of his allegiance?"

"The arrangement has already reached completion, and the amount is fixed," replied Wang Tae. "Yung will be delayed outside the Capital and suffer Wen-yi to proceed alone. This chance to achieve the greater glory to his single arm, and so discredit Yung, Wen-yi will greedily accept, and, regarding prudence less than speed, he will urge on his weary force beyond a judicious limit. At a convenient obstruction in his path, our troops will bar the way, and, checking his advance, without permitting him to hazard a decision, will crush him between that agile wall and Yung's arriving hosts... . It is almost inevitable that Wen-yi will also discover the justice of our cause when he realizes his position, but it is difficult to see in what capacity we could make use of one so senile and inept."

"Yet Tsun must have other leaders besides these and other armies ready to be led, nor can Shang dare to remain acquiescent in the face of defeat."

"There are other leaders without stint and doubtless other armies can be raised, but to keep them from falling down again their sustenance must be assured, and here another force among the intersecting lines of destiny appears to play a tortuous part... . In the seclusion of your native valley, has the rumour penetrated yet of the wonder of Shen Che-why do you pause?"

"I heard something that held me," apologized Ching-kwei. "Pray continue."

"A shout doubtless from the banquet hall; some still linger there. In any case, a reliant watch is kept."

"It was nothing but a distant echo. You spoke of one —?"

"Shen Che, to whom the fashion of the day has given the name of Poising Butterfly, from the winged balance of her grace. Her life recalls a passage from the missing epics of T'ai Chang, traced on bamboo slips and strung on cords of silk. A year ago she cooked her father rice in a meagre hut set in a barren place — if haply there was any rice to cook, he being but an indifferent worker in some cruder staple. The household scattered by misfortune, Shen Che, together with her sister Mei, went forth into a larger sphere, and being seen dancing by an affluent merchant, she cast her spell so that he lavished the surplus of his gold upon her capriciousness. From the feet of the merchant Shen Che stepped into the ya-men of a powerful mandarin, from the knees of the mandarin into the inner chamber of a high official, and from the shoulders of the functionary into the palace of the king. Now the whisper grows that Shang's royal wife will shortly fall into an obscure decline and, being thus removed, that Shen Che will take her place."

"She will then become a queen!" murmured Ching-kwei.

"She will become a queen, but in the end her influence will jeopardize the throne," replied Wang Tae. "In her, all the attributes grow to a large excess, her matchless beauty being rivalled only by the resistless witching of her charm, and the sum of both equalled by the splendour of her wanton prodigality. Shang is besotted with desire, and beneath her scattering hand the hoarded wealth of Tsun is already gnawed by dogs. To chase a dark look from her face, a loyal counsellor will be disgraced today; to win a passing smile, ten thousand footsore men pressed to a futile task tomorrow. When that time of which we speak arrives, there will be nothing left to support another army on. Men may be procured by force, but the bare earth cannot be compelled to fructify by blows."

VI. The Standard of the "restoring Ying" Being Raised, Ching-Kwei Is Hailed as Rightful Lord of Tsun, the Capital Is Besieged and an Unworthy Dissension Thereat Engendered

The history of Ching-kwei and the nature of his deeper thoughts, his spoken words, the omens cast about his path and the genealogy of each of those who rallied to his cause-these might perchance be fittingly set forth in nine-and-forty meritorious books, but though the finest paper and the smoothest ink were used, who should remain to read? Rather, in these later times of groundless stress, men would reach for their street attire, the one exclaiming as he went, "What befell this long-throated goatherd, storyteller?" and, "Impart a movement to thy tardy brush," another.

Let it suffice, therefore, that for the space of moons Wang Tae had spoken of, the confederacy persisted in its righteous task, linking the members of its scattered force into a living bond, and sapping the power of Shang's detested rule by various means. Then, when the fruit was ripe, the gatherers appeared, for in a single night they fell upon Hing-foo from every side and carried all its gates. Ching-kwei, seeing in the significance of the day a portent of success, led the assault and acquired much renown. All the more worthy of the citizens at once recognized in him the fulfilling of an ancient prophecy, and the city keys were laid before his feet.

"Not that their necessity exists in the case of one who wears a master key about his waist," declared the spokesman of the band, "but Hing-foo has been taken and restored threescore and eighteen times in the history of its walls, and the polite formality has ever been observed."

After the lukewarm and contentious had been humanely dealt with, the remainder of the populace settled down to existence as before, the unchanging motto of their city being: "Above Hing-foo are the heavens, on three sides of it the Shay, and on the fourth a ruler."

At a later period, Ching-kwei was publicly enthroned in the Temple of the King and greeted with the royal salutation of, "Ten thousand years!" The execrated name of Shang was removed from every seal and record amid an outburst of tumultuous joy, it being proclaimed that all documents and obligations in which it had appeared should thenceforth be held as void. Having by these acts definitely cut off the path of their retreat, every person in the city was set to the task of repairing the shattered walls and mounting a sufficient guard.

Events in the meanwhile followed on Yew's prescient course. Yung and Wen-yi converged as specified, and the former person brought a pacific face into Hing-foo and with him the stores and furnishing of all his force together with the staunchest of his men. On this foundation Wang Tae and Ching-kwei began to build the wedge that should drive the usurper ignominiously from his throne, for until he lost that last vestige of authority Ching-kwei might hold the handle of the sceptre but Shang still grasped the head. Across the intervening land, trustworthy spies were ever on the watch in suitable disguise, and no day passed without a message of encouragement being brought. Sunk into a deeper lethargy, the effete Shang scarcely deigned to turn upon his marble couch to listen to each succeeding recital of disaster; by his side Shen Che rose to more unbridled heights of recklessness until, in despair at the inadequacy of her own desires, she caused slaves to shoot priceless jewels from hollow tubes against the stars; while at the palace gates men and women fought for the sweepings from the kennels, and in the Ways the changing prices of a he-child and of a she-child went from mouth to mouth. It was at this pass that Ching-kwei and Wang Tae launched their force against the Capital.

At the northern water-gate of Hing-foo, flat-boats were drawn across by bamboo ropes, and in this way the army of the "Restoring Ying" moved out. As the different companies with their appointed chiefs passed across the river, a notched record of their strength was kept so that Wang Tae should have an exact knowledge of the various kinds of warriors under his control.

Of iron-caps, armed with spears, there were as many thousand as could be counted upon the fingers of one hand; of bowmen, each with threescore crimson arrows in a sheath, the same; almost as many slingers with their gear; five chosen groups of fierce-voiced leapers clad in striped and spotted cloth to represent bloodthirsty creatures of the wild, and a suitable proportion of stalwart men equipped with horns and gongs. In addition, there were banner-men who waved insulting messages of scorn; firework throwers, of the kinds both loud and offensive to the smell; several stuffed animals propelled on wheels, and a full camp of diagram-men, whose secret craft it was to spread confusion by their mysterious artifice. Every warrior possessed a wooden bowl, a fan, and an umbrella, and many had also brought iron swords and leather shields. Stores and utensils of the necessary sort followed the army on two thousand wheel-barrows in charge of the elderly and weak. Many of the chief leaders rode small horses of a hardy build, and in front of all went a cloud of war-chariots filled with picked fighters of established valour. The omens had been duly sought, and nothing was wanting to assure success.

When this great army-which despite its vast extent moved with such precision that no part of it at any time completely lost sight of all the other-arrived before the Capital, the craven defenders at once retired behind its gates, nor could the most offensive taunts or gestures of the keenest provocation induce them to emerge. On the other hand, with weak-kneed lack of originality they stood upon the well-protected walls and by remarks of an objectionable personal nature endeavoured to luring passing members of the "Restoring Ying" to come within their reach, but all Wang Tae's troops were too highly disciplined to fall into the snare. Finding the defences stronger than it was prudent to assail, and despairing of the garrison ever having the refinement to come out and face a decision on equal terms, Wang Tae disposed his forces round the city and proclaimed a siege.

Had the matter simply been left to its proper and foreshadowed course, the speedy subjection of the enemy could never have been in doubt. But it is truly said, "Even black may become unclean," and the immediate conduct of the corrupt Wen-yi imparts a double-edge of penetration to the adage. This squalid-souled person has already been fittingly referred to, so that it is unnecessary to do more than record the actual happenings. Not being deemed worthy of the honour of pursuit, after his troops were scattered in dismay, it was assumed that he would be driven to the necessity of sustaining life by begging from door to door-an occupation logically suited to his low standard of attainment. It must be inferred that Wen-yi had always played an insidious part, for, instead of acquiescing to a defeat that was final and complete, he treacherously began to get together his ignoble followers again, and even to induce other credulous and slow-witted outcasts to rally to his offensive cause. Working with the most unbecoming secrecy, and assembling in distant and misleading spots, he brought on his illiterate and deluded rabble by a serious of one-sided marches until he was able suddenly to insert his contaminating presence between the army of the "Restoring Ying" and their essential city of Hing-foo.

Owing to this degraded act of perfidy, after several months of conscientious effort on everybody's part, the position may thus be outlined: the defenders of the Capital were capable of resisting any onslaught but were powerless to emerge and free themselves from the encircling foe; the army of the "Restoring Ying" was safe within its camp but was not adequate to the task of entering the Capital or of reversing a position on which all its system had been based and turning round to engage the despised Wen-yi; the garrison of Hing-foo was sufficiently protected by the river from the menace of Wen-yi's invasion but was itself too weak to march out and assist Wang Tae; and, finally, the decayed Wen-yi, having now exposed his feeble effort, was unable to move in any direction whatever.

But however badly arranged this unmentionable person's despicable strategy had been toward a martial end, it had an outcome which that superficial one had never even though of, and very few more days had passed before Wang Tae called an assembly of the inner chiefs together at the council tent.

"When Yu, the pike, lay upon the river floor waiting for a bird to fall into the stream, and Yen, the kestrel, sat up in a tree waiting for a fish to leap on to the bank, both went supperless to bed," he began. "Hing-foo, from which we draw our daily sustenance, is now a thousand li beyond our reaching hand, and the case is thus and thus. Let any speak his mind."

"Your words are ruled with accuracy," agreed Ching-kwei, "but let there be no fear on that account. It is decreed that I shall most certainly destroy the usurping Shang and by the same act end the sway of his ignoble Line."

"The fear to which reference has been made, imperishable," interposed a discordant voice, "is not so much whether you kill the vindictive Shang but whether in the meanwhile hunger will not kill us. What store of food is there yet remaining, chief?"

"Some threescore sacks of rice-sufficient beneath a frugal eye for three days more."

"Here again destiny sets whatever qualms one has at rest, for the third day hence is the thirteenth of the month of Peach Blossom, and that is your imperishable's lucky day," declared Ching-kwei with confidence.

"Yet between now and the digging of our graves, what miracle will come to pass, omnipotence, unless we lay our elbow to the pole forthwith?" inquired another murmurer.

"What exact form our deliverance shall take will in due time appear, being doubtless revealed in the shape of a nocturnal vision," replied Ching-kwei. "To pray for rain and then give water to the drooping vine is to deride the faces of the willing gods."

"The celestial air you breathe, supremest, is too refined for the gross nourishment of those whom I command," declared a third. "An empty bowl will come within their scope, but not the sustaining approbation of the unseen powers."

"Peace-enough!" exclaimed Wang Tae, being in a double mind himself but fearing an open rift. "Words make a deeper scar than silence can always heal. Let all consider well our present state until we meet again at a like hour tomorrow. Then when each one has contributed the weight of his deliberate word unto the common cause, we will blend the accumulated wisdom into the weapon best suited to our need. In the interval, let mutual harmony prevail, for, remember: 'Fire spreads of its own accord, but every jar of water must be carried.'"

VII. The Nature of the Stratagem Discovered to Ching-Kwei, and the Measure of Its Success. His Meeting With One Whom He Had Thought to Be Queen of Tsun and the Rearrangement of the Destinies That Then Ensued. His Return and the Greetings Passed

That night Ching-kwei fasted and made sacrifice to the full extent of all he had, and having thereby purified his mind into harmony with the protecting influences around, he composed himself into a tranquil state to await their guidance. At dawn he sought out Wang Tae before that quick-moving person left his tent.

"In the past, Wang Tae," he said, when they had greeted formally, "we have reposed an unshaken trust in one another, and in the clash of battle my defending sword has struck out from underneath your weary arm, and your protecting shield has been held before my bleeding face."

"It is true," replied Wang Tae with dignified emotion, "and the confidence that I still maintain in you is that of two men who walk along a narrow plank together at some great and rocky height. With me, at least, speak the first words as they rise upon your lips."

"You are the front and authority of all our force, while in me resides the Immortal Principle. What, therefore, we two cannot do, shall the discording voices of a score attain?"

"I am with you in this also," replied Wang Tae. "Should you demand an attack upon the Capital, I will myself drive the first wedge into its gate."

"Our united mind could split a granite rock!" cried Ching-kwei joyfully. "But a less hazardous way has been revealed to me, as I indeed proclaimed. Is the extremity of our strait known beyond the camp?"

"Spies from both sides pass in and out as usual on one plea or another, nor, hitherto, has it been well to conceal our obvious strength. Now, this weakness also has inevitably been carried to the councils of both Wen-yi and Shang."

"Let there be no uncertainty upon that head. Instruct a judicious captain of your own to conduct the spies all round our bankrupt store. At the same time, let every warrior in the camp begin openly to furbish up his arms, to sing of victory, and to create a general stir. This, to the spies, the various chiefs shall briefly indicate, with 'Thus,' and 'Haply,' or, 'I might, if yet I would —,' but nothing more."

"It shall be done," replied Wang Tae. "Before another gong-stroke sounds, a tincture such as you desire shall colour their reports."

"Once they have left the camp, there must be no return. Appoint a double line of sentinels and instruct them to use even force if necessary."

"That, any rate, will convince the spies that something unusual in progress."

"All shapes round that end. Tonight a letter must be sent toward Hing-foo.

This is its purport:

"Illustrious Wang Tae to the Ever-alert Martial Governor of Loyal Hing-foo, Greeting:

Our need is great, our stock being now but two-score bags of mouldy rice. In the mists of tomorrow's dawn we attack the Capital, having learned of vast hoards of grain and richer food of every kind secretly stored within the palace there. If at the same time we can tempt out the ill-made Wen-yi, assail his rear with all your force. He is very credulous and may enter the snare."

"The scheme might be well enough," remarked Wang Tae, "but it is doubtful if our messenger can pass through Wen-yi's line and reach Hing-foo."

"To make sure of that miscarriage, send the worst we have-in fact, two had better go on separate ways: even the obese Wen-yi can scarcely miss both. How next shall a similar implication be contrived to fall into Shang's unruly hand?"

"I begin to smell the gravy of your pig," exclaimed Wang Tae with deepening interest. "There was a discontented eunuch of the palace guard who at first conspired with us, and messages have passed, but now the rumour goes that, one being dropped incautiously out of his sleeve, he has been charged and strongly pressed to tell everything he knows."

"His name will serve. In this case it will run:

" 'To —?' "

"Tsan, of the Third Green Banner displaying Righteous Truth," contributed Wang Tae.

" —From one whom he has knowledge of, greeting," went on Ching-kwei, continuing to write:

"Our need is great, our stock being now but two-score bags of mouldy rice. In the mists of tomorrow's dawn we attack Wen-yi, having learned that his camp contains vast stores of grain. Hing-foo will sally and assail his rear so that we shall have no lack of men. A snare has been contrived to take the ill-made Shang and all his force, if he can but be tempted out at the sound of conflict. Urge him to this, and you and your well-born descendants in perpetuity shall be entitled —"

"Eminence!" interposed Wang Tae hastily, "the one in question is —"

"True.

" —you and your illustrious ancestors in retrogression shall be entitled to an open green silk umbrella with yellow tassels on all state occasions. He is very credulous and may enter the snare."

"Seal it with your special sign, Wang Tae, and dispatch it by a thoroughly unworthy hand."

"Whom, further, I will omit to recompense. It shall reach Shang's council without fail. This scheme of yours, Ching-kwei, whatever the final shape, has a meatiness about its bones that stirs my appetite."

"When the camp is free of all whom we distrust, about the hour of dusk, about the hour of dusk, let two-score chariots be emptied of their gear and drawn in secret to a hidden dell. To each pair appoint a tent of trusty men, some carrying digging tools, the others bearing for each car a sack of rice. The rest will soon unfold itself before your eyes, Wang Tae, but of this be well assured: the grain that we throw upon the earth tonight will bear a speedy crop and that a hundredfold."

Is there a single one, aspiring to a polished style today, who has not heard or even used the phrase: "Like Wang Tae's rice —a little on the top?" Yet he who has followed these commonplace words so far and put up with their painful lack of finish need not be told that the whole scheme and strategy devolved upon Ching-kwei. Who should then erect a public arch, or compose a written book, or even found a dynasty, if in a few thousand years his labour is thus to be accorded to another? Certainly it was not so in the glorious days of Yao-u and Shun.

But in order to bring this badly told narration even to an unpretentious close it is necessary to uphold the sequence of events and to state what followed after. That is the present way, and, as the saying goes, "If you would dine with dragons you must not stay to chew the meat."

On the succeeding day, before the hour of dawn, both the hosts of Shang and Wen-yi became aware of something very violent taking place elsewhere. In the obscure distance a noise composed of every variety of martial strain, shout, roar, boom, blast, shriek, firework, rattle, imprecation, thud, musical instrument, and explosion grew and died down as it came across the intervening space at intervals, while fires at different points began to show and a great cloak of pungent smoke darkened the rising sun and shut out all the further details of the inauspicious scene. It was plain to each that the other was being vigorously attacked, while a demonstration in the nature of a feint was carried out against himself, but having been warned by intercepted messages, neither fell into the snare but lay behind his own defensive walls and watched.

When the battle had been in progress for a sufficiently convincing time, a combined shout of victory rent the air, and soon everywhere signs of rejoicing could be seen and heard. Shang and Wen-yi strove to pierce the veil of uncertainty surrounding them, to learn if haply any remnant of their ally stood, but the distance and the glow of fire and the drifting smoke conspired to baffle the most discerning eye, and presently each had a more convincing sign of the other's overthrow than all that went before. Winding through Wang Tae's camp, on its way to some secure place of storage, came a long and noble train of chariots, each one full and well heaped up with shining rice. Four well-trained horses went to the ropes of every car, with two henchmen at either wheel and four to follow after, so weighty was the load, and as they moved at certain parts more at their ease, the men laughed and frolicked and threw rice by the handful at each other in wanton joy to see so much. Forty such chariots there were in sight at once, and then, after a pause, a score more, and then another score, and a little later a second forty as before. Wen-yi first saw the offensive sight and knew the worst, and after him in turn the abject Shang and all his court, for Ching-kwei's rice-train wound in and out among the camp for half a day.

"They have penetrated to the very heart and treasure of the citadel and taken what they would. Without doubt the garrison is all put to the sword and the ineffectual Shang now cast in chains or slain," exclaimed Wen-yi. "Get me four bearers and an emblem of surrender so that I may hasten to eat dust and make what terms I can with this new line of kings."

"The flat-stomached Wen-yi has failed again–as usual," remarked the ill-starred Shang in an accent of refined despair, at about the same time and inspired by a like sequence of events; "and without doubt he has been taken in the snare. As our last hope is thereby brought to voidance, the hostile camp re-stocked, and their road to Hing-foo clear again, nothing remains for this much-depreciated sovereign but to put on an appropriate robe of sack-cloth and to suffer himself to be deposed without further ceremony by the morally deformed Wang Tae."

"Chieftain," reported a lesser captain to Wang Tae, as Wen-yi and Shang set out, "two separate groups approach the camp, one from the north, the other from the south, with banners of submission. What is your iron word concerning them?"

"At the peril of incurring each one of the seventy-five recognized ways of inflicting pain, let them be kept apart," replied Wang Tae.

Thus it came about, Shang's band by this time being brought into camp, that a message reached Ching-kwei, who had stayed within his tent alone, of one who sought his ear.

"Suffer the messenger to pass the guard," pronounced Ching-kwei, for the word brought in had seemed to speak, though darkly, of the time which he knew must now approach, and they led one in whose face was masked by a visor of worked steel.

"Omnipotence," pronounced a low but very golden voice, "I have a name to speak that merits your private ear. Furthermore, I bear no weapon anywhere while you have a notorious sword beneath your ready hand."

"If I disclose my ear to you," replied Ching-kwei, motioning to the attendants so that they withdrew, "it is no less fitting that you should reveal your face to me," and he indicated the covering which the other wore.

"Your magnanimity is itself a better shield than any I could wear," was the gracious reply, and what he asked for being done, they stood there for a poise of time, facing each other.

"Shen Che!" whispered Ching-kwei, falling back a step in wonder. "You who are now a queen!"

"I recognize in you the one who loitered in the glade, that day the holy anchorite warned me that we should meet. But wherefore do you call me by my sister's name, and why greet me a queen?"

"Your sister's name?" replied Ching-kwei, with a great and sudden happiness singing like a nest of radiant birds about his head. "Are you not then that Shen Che who should become a queen?"

"I am Mei of the lowly house of Kang, and to me no other name was ever given. For her of whom you speak I come to plead, that being my errand here. Of your illusion that I was other than I am-doubtless it grew from this: that we encountered only once and that but for a single passing glance. Let it not weigh against my cause, high excellence."

"Not once but many hundred times, O dazzling one, have we two met, for every day that meeting is renewed within my heart; and though it was a single glance, so deep the image cut that the stone of life itself must be destroyed to wear away a line."

"Benevolence!" pleaded the maiden, who had not expected to be involved in so abrupt and emotional an arisement. "The one for whom I crave your countenance —"

"The fault lay with that hoary soothsayer," continued Ching-kwei, who was by no means concerned about Shen Che now that he had learned that this one was no longer she. "I described you beyond the possibility of doubt, and he then played me false."

"Great majesty," murmured the bright vision, advancing more than the single step that the other had gone back, and gazing into Ching-kwei's eyes beseechingly, "by what feeble attributes did you chance to depict this in-no-way-striking one?"

"How else than by the glory of your matchless presence, by the pearly splendour of your lustrous being, which at every point outshines that of all other dwellers upon earth, by the constant wonder of your deigning to remain among mere mortal things at all-there could be no mistake. Further, as the venerable necromancer's polite attention seemed to begin to wander at this point, I added that you wore a high-born cloak, your sister having none."

"In this then, not the hermit but the very fates themselves have conspired toward a surreptitious end," exclaimed the one henceforth to be described as Mei. "Know now, all-powerful chief, that until we left the pious Ng-tung's cell, it was the more-admired Shen Che who wore that distressing cloak of plaited straw, which presently, to dance for joy at what the seer foretold, she cast about my form."

"Then you indeed are not a queen, nor married to a king?"

"I am married to none," replied Mei, indicating by a refined gesture that a contingency had been reached when it would be more suitable if she replaced the concealing mask, but to this Ching-kwei did not accede. "Nor am I likely now to encounter so forlorn an end, for the divination ran that my destiny lay with a guileless one who herded goats and led a tranquil life. Thus I stand secure, for such a man could not be found in camps or capitals."

"Yet I have herded goats and led a tranquil life," maintained Ching-kwei. "So that in me the prophecy takes root."

"But can never come to fruit, esteemed, for from that life you have cut yourself irrevocably away, while to it I must straight return, like a homing swallow to its ingrained thatch."

"Would you not instead become a queen, fair Mei, and found with me an undying line of kings?"

"Against that I am sworn. One queen from the inglorious house of Kang exceeds the moral limit, and having marked that same one's upward flight, I trim my own wings now into a lowlier atmosphere."

"Why, then, I also would not be a king," declared Ching-kwei, approaching her. "And yet," he added gloomily, "the iron line remains-to 'end a sovereign's life and by the same act terminate a dynasty,' was the unbending fate. How else than by setting up my own?"

"Ching-kwei," exclaimed a stern voice from the door, as Wang Tae threw back the fold, "what note of doubt is this? The day is ours, gained by your stratagem. Shang and Wen-yi have both made full submission and recognized your claim. The army of the 'Restoring Ying' only awaits the sight of you to raise an overwhelming shout of triumph and to carry you upon the impulse of its valour to any misty height. This is the very apex of your destiny, but though the point is here for you to grasp, the sides are smooth and steep. Fail to assert your right at once and all may yet be lost. Miscarry now, and you end your sovereign life and by that act now and for all time terminate the dynasty of your imperishable Line."

For such a space of time as wherein one might count a score the three chiefly concerned stood in their different moods. Then Ching-kwei answered back, and his voice rolled like a ceremonial drum.

"There spoke the several voices that conjoin in me to piece my destiny and to reconcile all things! This is the kingship that I put an end to now and ours the dynasty which I thereby terminate. Wang Tae, your words have been inspired and you at last have cut the knot of all my difficulty."

"Yet what remains?" demanded Wang Tae darkly. "Can the people be left to revert to savagery, and Tsun, deprived of every royal hand, become a vassal state?"

"Still less so than before. Tomorrow, in the Temple of the King within the Capital, Ching-kwei will voluntarily abdicate, and turning to his right will crown Wang Tae first of a martial Line. That is what Tsun requires today — a strong and vigorous ruler of natural force, not one whose kingdom is a dream and his chosen throne a chimney-seat."

"This is what generally happens sooner or later when a capable general and a weak-minded sovereign are concerned," declared Wang Tae, not wholly reconciled, "but in our exceptional case I certainly did not expect it yet." Then, as he turned to leave the tent, Ching-kwei unsheathed his sword, and raising it before his face he very gladly cried: "Ten thousand years!"

"Yet what remains?" repeated Mei, as they again stood there alone. "You have lost all, nobility, and for-for a vagarious thought renounced a jewelled crown."

"Not all," replied Ching-kwei; "I still have what I value most," and from an inner sleeve he took some faded flowers. "These I have kept unharmed through the dust of weary marches and the shock of furious battle, hoping perchance that if I bore them worthily, when we should meet, you of your own free will might requite me for everything with one."

"One is a very little to expect, high prince," said Mei, turning away her face as she received the flowers, "though certainly more might seem to be too much. Therefore the two I offer you are now but one, and the one that you receive has hitherto been two," and in a tumult Ching-kwei perceived that in the hand held out to him were two stems tightly bound together by the crimson thread of mutual betrothement. "What more," she continued with a still averted face, "what more can one to whom all initiative is rigidly denied say-or even do-Ching-kwei?"

As Ching-kwei, leading Mei by the hand and at the same time controlling a wandering goat of his own flock that he had recovered by the way, neared his door, his grandmother came out to gather wood and, seeing them, awaited their approach.

"What is the latest apophthegm from the front just now, Ching-kwei?" she asked. "And how does this new gear of martial glory fit about your limbs?"

"Those who cover themselves with martial glory appreciate a homespun robe at last," was his reply; yet even as he spoke the thought went up: "Wang Tae would certainly have produced something more keen-edged than that."

"At all events, the maiden whom you sought has found you, it appears," remarked the ancient, nodding sagely. "Perhaps it was as well that you should have returned-another goat has cast off his allegiance and gone hence upon us."

When Kai Lung, having thus successfully disposed of Ching-kwei, looked up, he discovered he was there alone, not even one of three whom he daily instructed in his art having lingered.

"It is doubtful if circles were quite so destitute of true refinement in the golden days of Tou-fou and Li-tai-pe," he murmured; "though the comparison is admittedly vainglorious. What call is that?"

It was the voice of Hwa-mei, seeking him in the darkness of the garden, and as Kai Lung went at once toward her, they very soon encountered.

"There were nine of our neighbours here with me but now, to whom I owe some reparation," he explained. "In the nature of analogy I pressed sour fruit upon them, so that now I would offer them both food and wine. Are they, perchance, awaiting me within?"

"There are none within, neither have there been any with thee here in the garden, save only Hoo Tee, who has already tasted bamboo for leaving thee alone, musing by the arbour. Hast thou slept again, O dragon-hearted one, and dreamed a dream of ancient valour?"

"I may have mused somewhat," confessed Kai Lung, "as I sat there by the arbour. But I can hardly, as you say, have slept, for a Bringer of Good News has sought me with a message."

"Truly so," replied Hwa-mei, with a ripple in her voice of both laughter and affection. "Your evening rice awaits you."

The End